Catherine cupped the woman's chin in her hand.

"Can you not say hello to me?"

"She does not speak," Ann said.

Catherine stroked Martha's cheeks. "Do you not want to talk with your old gossip?" For a moment it looked as though Martha might respond. Her eyes seemed to focus on Catherine, but then they resumed their blank stare. The girl took a slow step backward, and then another, her eyes on her mother. When she reached the doorway, she spun around and dashed out. Catherine now put her mouth close to Martha's ear. "Talk to me now," she said, "for we only have a moment."

Martha moved her lips, but the only sound that came out was a grunt, or a moan, like pain that could not be formed into words . . .

Praise for *The Dumb Shall Sing*:

"Seventeenth-century flavor and a strong, independent, original character make this an interesting read. Steve Lewis has done his research, and it obviously pays off."—Robert Randisi, author of *Murder Is the Deal of the Day*

"Lewis ably captures both the atmosphere and the language of seventeeth-century New England . . . This is an absorbing and historically accurate read."—Mary Beth Norton, Mary Donlon Alger Professor of American History, Cornell University

THE DUMB
SHALL SING

STEPHEN LEWIS

BERKLEY PRIME CRIME, NEW YORK

For Carolyn

THE DUMB SHALL SING

A Berkley Prime Crime Book / published by arrangement with
the author

PRINTING HISTORY
Berkley Prime Crime edition / August 1999

The Penguin Putnam Inc. World Wide Web site address is
http://www.penguinputnam.com

ISBN: 0-425-16997-9

Berkley Prime Crime Books are published
by The Berkley Publishing Group,
a division of Penguin Putnam Inc.,
375 Hudson Street, New York, New York 10014.
The name BERKLEY PRIME CRIME and the BERKLEY PRIME
CRIME design are trademarks belonging to Penguin Putnam Inc.

PRINTED IN THE UNITED STATES OF AMERICA

10 9 8 7 6 5 4 3 2 1

Explanatory Note

Newbury is a fictional town intended to represent a typical seventeenth-century New England Puritan settlement. I have imagined it to be on the coast where a river valley meets the sea. It is populated by people who would have lived in such a place. It has nothing more than its name in common with the actual town of Newbury, Massachusetts, which was, in fact, settled in the seventeenth century. I chose the name simply to suggest its newness.

The story begins after an historical event: the Pequot War of 1637, which climaxed with a massacre by the English and their Indian allies of the Pequot fortified village near the Mystic River in Connecticut. My character Massaquoit is, of course, fictional, although I invest him with memories of the historical event. Catherine Williams, our rich, widowed midwife shares some qualities with the historical Anne Hutchinson, who, along with her followers, opposed the war.

Throughout the book, every effort has been expended toward historical accuracy. In this regard, I would like to thank the scholars of the Omohundro Institute of Early American History and Culture, a number of whom answered my specific queries on matters of seventeenth-century detail. Professors Mary Beth Norton and Merril D. Smith have been particularly helpful.

S.L.
Long Island, New York
March 1999

Say to them that are of a fearful heart, Be strong, fear not: behold, your God will come with vengeance, even God with a recompence; he will come and save you. Then the eyes of the blind shall be opened, and the ears of the deaf shall be unstopped. Then shall the lame man leap as an hart, *and the tongue of the dumb sing*: for in the wilderness shall waters break out, and streams in the desert.

Isaiah 35:4–6

ONE

❧❧

T HE SLOOP *Good Hope*, its crowned lion figurehead
pointing to the sea, rode the outgoing tide past the
mouth of Newbury Bay toward deeper waters whose
color changed from light blue near shore to an almost
midnight black. The late-afternoon sun was hidden by
thick clouds that threatened a summer storm. The air was
hot, moist, and still. A lone seagull circled the vessel, and
seeing nothing of interest, rose into the clouds.

The year was 1638, and the English settlers' army had
just routed the Pequot Indians in an uneven war that dec-
imated the tribe. A half-dozen soldiers stood on the deck
in a loose line in front of the captives. The soldiers wore
steel corselets and morion helmets. Some carried swords,
others pikes, and two held muskets. The ones with muskets had leather bandoliers draped over their shoulders,
containing pouches for powder and shot. Sweat gathered
in the corners of their eyes and dripped down their necks
and back, chafing the skin. They would have loved to remove their armor, but one look at their lieutenant convinced them that he would not be sympathetic to this

request. It was not as though they needed to prepare for battle, or to defend themselves against the enemy, for the enemy was clearly vanquished and unable to offer any threat. But this was an occasion rich in ceremonial and symbolic significance, and the lieutenant, as well as the dignitaries who stood not far away, would not tolerate any laxity in military decorum.

The Pequots were tied with heavy ropes, hands and feet. Until the ship left land a safe distance behind, they had also worn a long chain wrapped around their necks, one after the other, and then attached to rings on the deck. It would not do to have them ruin the solemnity of the occasion by a premature leap into the waves. But with land now out of sight, Governor Samuel Peters had extended his long arm in a gesture to Lieutenant Waters to loose them so they could be dealt with, as planned, one at a time.

Once the chains were removed, none of them so much as brought a hand to the deep welts on their necks left by the heavy weight of the chain. They wore nothing but a strip of leather cloth around their loins. Their skin was streaked with dirt and blood. The miasmic stench of the swamp where they had hoped to avoid the pursuing English lifted ripe off their skin and into the heavy air. They had sustained themselves on roots and berries for three weeks until they could no longer tolerate watching the women and children sicken from hunger, and so they had come out under a truce whose terms they had no power to soften. They stood now, their eyes vacant. Their slow breaths pressed their ribs against their skin. Only Massaquoit seemed to be taking an interest in the proceedings.

He stood away from the others. He alone still had the long chain wrapped around his neck and body, but no longer attached to the rings on the deck. A soldier menaced him with the blade of his long pike. The ship rolled on a wave and the motion caused Massaquoit to lean into the pike. The soldier did not move the weapon away, and Massaquoit stared down with contempt as the blade pierced his chest just enough to draw a little blood. The ship righted itself and Massaquoit swayed away from the pike. The soldier remained holding his weapon so close to the captive's chest that any movement of Massaquoit toward him would impale him on the blade.

The dignitaries, aboard to witness the activities about to occur, stood on a raised portion of the deck aft. Behind them were the captain and a sailor at the helm. In the center of this group of men stood Catherine, a woman in her fifties, short, and a little plump. Her red and rounded cheeks gave her face a gentle, nurturing look, but her eyes were dark and bright as they darted from one man to the other.

"Sirs," she said. "We did have an arrangement. Did we not?"

"That was with your husband, as you well know," replied one of the men, short and round, whose white hair protruded from beneath the dark maroon skullcap perched on his head, giving him the look of a medieval Talmudist as much as the seventeenth-century Puritan minister he was.

"Well, then, Master Davis, as his widow I act in his place."

"The arrangement is now unsuitable," the minister replied. Governor Peters, a head taller than anybody else on the ship, held a rolled document in front of her. He waved his large-brimmed hat in front of his face. Perspiration glistened on his forehead and on the triangle of a beard beneath his chin.

"The Court has decreed their fate," he said. "I am here to see that the order is carried out as written."

"We are only thinking of you, Catherine," another said. The fine blue linen of his shirt, along with its fully expressed white ruff, implied the prosperous merchant he was. "As much as I would like to respect the word we gave to John, you are not he and it would not be a proper living arrangement."

Catherine shifted her gaze over to the line of listless captives, who were now watching without much visible interest as two sailors contrived to secure one end of a split log, which still had bark on the underside, so that the other could extend over the railing.

Catherine stared hard at the merchant. Not only had he been her husband's partner, but she had known him as a child back in Alford, in old England, where he had been a regular visitor in her father's house. Since his own children had not survived into adulthood, and he had not remarried after his wife died, he had treated her as though she were his own daughter. She understood that he was trying to negotiate on her behalf with the governor and the minister, but still she could not entirely restrain her anger.

"Joseph Woolsey, do you think I want to take one of them to my bed?"

Minister Davis frowned, but a smile fought to establish itself on Joseph's face. The other men remained silent, their faces expressionless. They were younger and deferred to the two older men.

"Look at them," Minister Davis said.

"I am," Catherine replied.

"Savages," the minister snapped.

"Men," Catherine said, "no more nor less, only without the benefit of your condition." She turned to the captain. "Sir, are you ready to bring her about and head back to port?"

"Aye, mistress, if you say so."

"You cannot do that," Master Davis said.

"Joseph, is this not now my vessel, as it was my husband's?"

"To be sure," he replied, "But the Court has decided, and your ship is only the means to serve its purpose."

"It is, nonetheless, my ship, and Captain Gregory here knows that if he wants to sail it again as master, he will do as I say."

The captain nodded.

"I would not want to be the one to tell Mistress Williams that she cannot have what she has a mind to have."

"It is not my temper you need to fear," Catherine said, "but the money my husband, in good faith, loaned out to the town to finance the late war, and which I have chosen to have repaid in flesh rather than coin. I have more need for muscle and sinew than money. And gentlemen, by relieving you of your debt so cheaply, I am giving you a bargain you can hardly refuse, for as you yourself have observed, these poor wretches are not worth much, nor would they bring you much return on the market were you to ship them down to Barbados."

Master Peters drew back a step or two and the others followed. The men spoke together in hushed voices for a few moments, and then Peters approached Catherine.

"Pick, then," he said. "But remember the terms of the treaty. They apply to him you choose. And you, as his mistress."

She did not hesitate.

"That one." She pointed to Massaquoit. Blood still

oozed from the fresh wound on his chest, but he seemed not to notice.

"Surely not him," Joseph said.

"Captain," Catherine said.

"As you wish," the governor said. "One devil will serve as another."

"Business," Catherine replied, "only business. It is a pity your obligations to my poor dead husband were not greater, for then I would have purchased the lives of more than one of these."

Master Peters whispered something to Lieutenant Waters, who was sweating in his armor and impatient to be finished with his task. He nodded, and spoke to the soldier whose pike still rested against the chest of Massaquoit.

"I wouldn't loose this one, just yet," the soldier said.

"Nor would I," the lieutenant said. "Just push him further back, away from the others."

The soldier pressed his blade against Massaquoit's chest, but he did not move. The soldier pressed harder, and turned the blade so that its point pierced the skin next to the recent wound. Still, Massaquoit did not move.

"What do you say, Lieutenant?" the soldier asked. "I can stick him like a hog for the fire."

The lieutenant looked at Catherine and then back to the soldier.

"Push him back. We've seen enough of his blood for now."

The soldier turned his pike so that he could shove the shaft up under Massaquoit's jaw. He pushed hard, and Massaquoit stumbled back.

"Right," the soldier said. "You could have done that before, and given me a break in this blasted heat."

Governor Peters walked to the log, which was now securely fastened. He unrolled a document he had been holding.

"The General Court, in concluding the treaty with the Pequot nation, has made specific mention of these eight sachems here assembled, who did lead their people into the swamp known as Cuppacommock, or the Hiding Place, and there did stubbornly continue their unlawful war against us, and as a consequence to punish their perverse refusal to surrender and to have them stand as a warning to others who might rise up against the lawful English settlements here and elsewhere in New England, have sentenced these eight, now standing here, to death."

Magistrate Woolsey strode toward Massaquoit, stopping an arm's length from him.

"You, Massaquoit, are to be spared. Mistress Williams has interceded on your behalf, according to terms previously agreed to by the Court, and you are to be handed over to her care, and under her instruction you are to abandon your savage ways and accept Our Lord."

"When we surrendered," Massaquoit said, "we understood all our lives would be spared."

"Perhaps you misunderstood the terms," the lieutenant said.

"My English is too good for that," Massaquoit replied. "Many years I have traded with the English. I was never confused before."

The lieutenant shrugged.

"I wouldn't worry about all that if I was you, as you are to live."

"I have no wish to be this woman's slave."

"Enough!" Minister Davis said, his voice a deep rumble over the quiet waters. "Let us proceed."

The soldiers shifted about. Two went to the first Indian in the line, each taking an arm. The Indian remained listless. Two other soldiers attended to their matchlock muskets, adjusting the smoldering matches so that only the ends protruded from the serpentine clamps. They blew the ash off the end of the matches so they glowed red.

Catherine stepped a little closer to Master Davis.

"Are you going to offer a word for them?"

"I will do my best to find a way to pray for their heathen souls, though I know them to be butchering savages."

"God has already spoken," Governor Peters snapped. "Our good minister need add nothing further. That they are here, and about to die under our orders, vouchsafes their utter damnation." He turned to Lieutenant Waters. "You can begin."

"Hoist him up," the lieutenant said.

The two soldiers holding the first Indian lifted him onto the log. He did not resist, and when they stepped back, he stood. His expression now was one of stubborn contempt for his captors.

"Move, then," one of the soldiers said. When the Indian did not stir, he drew his sword and pressed it against his stomach. Still the Indian remained motionless. The soldier pressed harder and the blade pierced the skin. The Indian had steeled himself against the thrust, but still the pain caused him to shift his weight, and as he did, he lost his footing and he began to fall off the plank. The soldier withdrew his sword and used the flat of its blade to push the Indian off.

He fell into the water with a splash that seemed louder than it was. He disappeared beneath the surface for a few moments, but then his body reappeared. Although his hands and feet were bound, and he bled from his wound, he managed to float on his back. The rain that had been threatening all afternoon now began to fall. The musketeers bent over their weapons to shield them from the rain.

"We can't have him making shore," the lieutenant said, and he then nodded at the two soldiers holding the muskets. One of them now sighted down the long barrel of his weapon. The soldier opened the pan, pressed the lever-like trigger, bringing the end of the match down into the pan, which was now being wetted by the rain. There was a loud pop and a flash, but that was all. The soldier pulled down his musket in disgust.

The Indian was managing a little kicking motion, which propelled him over the waves. The second soldier now aimed.

"He is floating out to sea," Massaquoit said. "Do you expect him to make land in Southampton?"

Minister Davis pulled off his skullcap, strode over to the soldier, and held the cap over the sputtering match.

"Fire," he said.

This time the flash was followed by an explosive sound. The body of the Indian in the water spasmed against the impact of the ball that ripped through his gut. His legs stopped kicking, and he sank. All eyes remained on the spot, now red with his blood, where he had disappeared, but he did not again break the surface of the water. From someplace in the distance, a gull swooped down and landed. It was soon joined by half a dozen of his fellows. One paddled through the spot where the Indian sank, and when it rose, its feathers were stained red.

Minister Davis turned his head to the skies and received the pouring rain on his face. He replaced his skullcap and joined the others, who were now huddled against the pelting drops.

Catherine stepped in front of him. His eyes seemed not to focus.

"Master Davis," she said.

He did not respond.

"Master Davis," she said again, in a louder voice. He turned his glance toward her. She looked up at the pouring rain and then at the soldier who had shot the Indian.

"Do you think it providential?" she said.

"What is that?"

"The rain that doused the powder until you saw fit to intervene."

"I was only helping to do God's work," he said.

"I see," she said. "I had thought that maybe the rain meant that God did not approve. If He did, perhaps He would have kept the powder dry Himself."

He stared coldly at her.

"Mistress, you overstep yourself."

Catherine knew she had gone as far as she could, and maybe a step farther. Even as the widow of one of the wealthiest men in the colony, even while standing on the deck of the trading sloop she owned, and even though she had just relieved these gentlemen of a debt the Colony owed her, still she should not spar with the likes of Minister Davis, a man who served God and his own ambitions in equal measure. Still, Catherine thought, she had seen the flint of his heart chip, if not soften, from time to time. This, however, was clearly not one of those occasions.

"As you say," she said, and stepped back.

The lieutenant walked over to the soldier who was bending over his musket.

"Well done, Henry," the lieutenant said.

The soldier shoved the ramrod down the muzzle. He looked up, but did not smile. Instead his eyes seemed both intent on the task at hand and at the same time a thousand miles away.

"Yes," he muttered, and yanked the ramrod out of the barrel. He pulled open the drawstring on his pouch and poured powder into the pan. He hunched over more as the rain began to pelt down more heavily.

"You won't need any more of that," Catherine said. "This is not a turkey hunt."

The other Indians stared silently into the water where their comrade had disappeared. The gulls, not finding anything to eat, had deserted their vigil. The soldiers guarding the remaining captives shifted from leg to leg, waiting for the next command. Magistrate Woolsey held his hands before his eyes. The lieutenant looked at Governor Peters and Minister Davis.

"Continue," Peters said, but his voice was barely audible. He took a deep breath. "Get on with it," he said so that he could be heard.

"It is the Lord's work we do here," Minister Davis said.

Lieutenant Waters barked a command and the soldiers lifted the next Indian onto the log. While he stood there, the lieutenant checked the ropes binding his hands and his feet.

"He will sink before long, I warrant," he said.

"Let us see, then," Governor Peters replied. "Do not fire on him unless he stays afloat."

The rain had slicked the log so that all the soldiers had to do was push against the Indian's shoulders until he lost his balance and rolled off. He hit the water with a splash, managed to float for a minute, and then sank beneath the surface. The next Indian was placed on the plank, and he did not wait to be pushed, but managed to jump off and go straight under. Each of the others followed in kind. After each splash the gulls swooped down, circled, and left.

Only Massaquoit remained. He tried to climb onto the log.

"That is where I belong," he said.

"Agreed," Governor Peters replied. "But you are bought and paid for. And if we were to let you join your companions, we would again be in debt to Mistress Williams here, and that is a circumstance none of us would enter into lightly. So I am afraid that you must live."

Catherine was left alone with Massaquoit and the one soldier who had been his guard throughout the proceedings. The others had gone below. Governor Peters said he felt the need for rest after the strain of the day. Minister Davis said that he wanted to find a quiet place in the hold of the ship where he could meditate on God's wondrous providence in sending the savage enemy into the hands of the English, and from which he could offer up his thanks to the Lord.

The sloop held a course back to the harbor. As they approached their anchorage, the sailors prepared the shallop that would carry the visitors to shore.

"You might as well take the chains and ropes off of him," Catherine said to the soldier.

"I cannot until the lieutenant so orders me, and I don't think you should want me to."

"If I am not safe with him here, how am I going to be safe with him ashore? Untie him."

"Ashore he'll knock you over your head when you sleep."

"Then you are talking to a ghost. Let him go."

"Do as Mistress Williams says," the lieutenant commanded as he emerged from below. "This savage is no longer our responsibility, and now as passengers on Mistress Williams's ship, we need to act the guest."

The soldier unsheathed a short sword from its scabbard. He held the blade in front of him, and then pressed it against the wound on Massaquoit's chest. The Indian did not respond, nor did he take his eyes off the blade. The soldier then lowered the blade to the rope binding Massaquoit's hands, and with one sharp movement he sliced it apart. He knelt and cut the ropes around Massaquoit's feet.

"Into the boat, then, if you don't mind," the lieutenant said. "You first, Mistress Williams."

The lieutenant helped her onto the rope ladder that hung over the rail and down to the shallop. The soldier nudged Massaquoit forward with the flat edge of his sword's blade. They clambered down the ladder and into the shallop. Catherine sat on the long bench that ran on one side of the vessel. Massaquoit stood at the stern.

"Do not worry," he said. "I have lost my taste for a swim in these waters."

"I never feared it," she replied. "I hope you do not think that I enjoyed the spectacle we just witnessed."

"You did not stop it."

She stared at this proud man, who stood with his back to her, glancing over his shoulder as he spoke.

"You think I should thank you," he said, "but I should have died with the others. I fear their spirits will haunt me."

He turned back to face the waters that were now the graves of his companions. She turned her attention to the two sailors, one on each side, who plied the heavy oars. One was an older man, his face badly scarred from smallpox, whom she did not recognize. The other was young Ned Jameson. Her late husband had hired Ned to learn how to be a sailor on the sloop after extensive conversations with Henry Jameson, Ned's uncle, who was the boy's guardian since both his parents had been killed by Indians at the beginning of the war. Henry Jameson had five daughters and was happy to take in the young man as his son. When Henry's wife, Martha, now in her late thirties, became pregnant again, the house seemed to become too small for Ned, and so Henry convinced Catherine's husband to have him train as a sailor on the *Good Hope*. Two weeks earlier, Catherine had helped Martha deliver a son. Just before he boarded the sloop as it carried the captives to Newbury, Ned learned that his uncle now had the son he so earnestly desired.

The craft slid over the waves into the breakers. Ned hopped over the bow and his companion threw him a line with which he could haul the shallop onto the sand. When the boat was beached, the older sailor offered his arm to Catherine, but she scrambled over the bow unassisted. The sailor shrugged and looked back at Massaquoit, whose eyes had not left the point in the now distant waters where the others had disappeared.

"What about him?" the sailor asked. Without waiting for an answer, he clambered out of the boat and onto the sand. "He makes me nervous, he does, that one."

Ned, who was still holding the bow rope, now handed it to his companion.

"Have you decided what you are going to call him?" he asked Catherine. "The lieutenant told us we were not to use his heathen name, nor was you."

"Matthew," Catherine said simply, "only he does not yet know it."

Massaquoit gave up his vigil and made his way to the front of the shallop. His intense eyes held each of the English in turn, starting with Catherine and then resting on first one sailor and then the next. The sailors took a half step back, their hands reaching for the knives they had in their belts. Catherine smiled.

"Are you ready to see your new home?" she asked.

Massaquoit lowered his eyes and nodded.

"I will do what I must."

"What you must do, then," said Ned, "is get off our boat so we can head back to the ship, where we belong, and leave you here, where you ought to be, but as far as that goes, I don't know why we didn't send you after your friends."

"Enough," Catherine said. "He is now a member of my household, and you will treat him with the same respect you would me."

"As you wish, mistress," Ned said. "Begging your pardon, but I won't be bowing my head before no savage."

"Then when you reach your vessel, be so kind as to tell the captain that he, your uncle, and I will discuss your continued employment on my vessel. If you do not know how to heed me as your mistress, perhaps you need to feel your uncle's hand."

"I am a grown man, mistress," Ned said. The color had risen to his cheeks, and he pulled the knife out of his belt. Massaquoit's eyes fastened on the blade while the other sailor stepped several paces back.

"Maybe I should just finish what we started there," Ned said.

"I don't think so," Catherine said. She held out her hand. "Give it here."

"Stand aside, mistress," Ned said.

"I cannot do that."

"At your peril, then," and he lunged at Massaquoit. The Indian brought his forearm up hard against the sailor's arm, and the knife went spinning into the sand.

They grappled and rolled after it. Massaquoit's hand recovered the weapon first, and he held it to the sailor's throat.

"Go ahead, then," Ned said. "You might as well, just like you did my family."

Massaquoit stared hard at the boy, and then stood up.

"You are still a child," he said. He handed the knife to Catherine. "He needs a spanking."

Ned leaped to his feet and lunged at Massaquoit, but the Indian sidestepped him and tripped him down into the sand. Ned got up spitting sand out of his mouth. The pox-marked sailor grabbed him by the shoulders and led him back to the shallop, which was now being lifted by the incoming tide.

"Get in," the sailor said. "I'll push us out."

Catherine and Massaquoit watched as the sailor put his shoulder to the boat and shoved it out into the water. Then he hopped in and grabbed an oar to pole them out to deeper water. In the meantime Ned sat sullenly in the stern. Finally, he took his place on the bench and picked up his oar. The shallop made slow but steady progress against the tide. They stood watching in silence until they saw the rope thrown up from the shallop and caught by a sailor on deck of the sloop.

Catherine put her hand on Massaquoit's arm and turned him toward her. He did not resist.

"That lad," she said. "His mother and father were killed at Wethersfield, and his sister, a girl of twelve, was carried away. He was working in the field with his father when the village was attacked. His father told him to hide in the corn, which he did. When he came out he found his father dead, with an arrow in his chest, and then at his house he saw his mother, who had been knocked on the

head. He did not speak for two weeks after he came to
live with his uncle."

She still had her hand on his arm, and he lifted it off,
gently, but irresistibly.

"Yes," he said. "He is angry at all Indians for what
those did. But what do you think he should say to me?
My wife and son were at the fort in Mystic when the English came."

"I cannot talk for him, but I can say that I am sorry. For
both of you."

She began the walk up from the beach and toward the
town of Newbury. Massaquoit waited a moment or two,
and then he followed. Neither of them found use for further words until they reached Catherine's large house, set
on a hill. She went inside, and he sat down in the shade
of a maple.

Massaquoit remained sitting under the tree long after the
activity in the house had stopped and the last candle had
been extinguished. Catherine had come out once to invite
him in to supper, but he had refused.

"You know, I don't consider you a servant," she had
said. "Calling you that, and agreeing to take you into my
household as such, is the only way I could secure your
freedom."

At the word "freedom," Massaquoit raised his eyebrows, if barely, as though wondering how the word applied to him. Then he resumed staring in the direction of
the harbor.

"You are more than welcome to join me at the table.
It's a big house, bigger still now that my children have
moved on and my John is dead." When Massaquoit still
did not respond, she turned back into her house.

He looked up through the branches of the maple to the

sky, which glowed softly from a full moon. The air was warm and humid. He recalled how on nights such as this he would press against the sweat-damp flesh of his wife while their son slept soundly a few feet away. But now he remembered how he had last seen them. She was lying on top of the boy. The broken blade of a sword protruded from her ribs, and her blood pooled an inch deep over her punctured heart, and then it spilled over onto the face of the boy, or what was left of his face, as fire lit by the soldiers had reduced his skin to little more than ash. It looked as though she had tried to smother the flames when she was stabbed, for her flesh was scarcely singed. He squeezed that memory from his mind, and instead recalled the pressure of his wife's thighs, and he heard again his son's sleep-laden words in the morning, even as he sat outside the white woman's house, and he felt his heart harden into a clenched fist of hatred.

He thought about killing the woman who had saved his life. It would be very easy to do, even though he had no weapons. There were only two servants in the house. He had watched and counted as he sat. He had seen the man going out to the garden. He was stooped, and his step was slow. Later the girl had walked toward him a few tentative paces, and then she had placed something on the ground, covered in a cloth, and beckoned him to take it. Neither the old man nor the girl would put up much resistance if he sneaked into the house and found the woman in her bed.

For a moment his heart rose at the thought. His hands felt her neck in his tightening fingers, and that feeling drove away the memory of his wife's body as this woman's dying gasps would erase his son's words. And then he could flee into the woods.

There his thoughts stopped. He had nobody to seek in

those woods. Who would take him in? Uncas and the Mo-
hegans, or Miantonomi and the Narragansetts? Hadn't
they both fought for the English? Hadn't they proved
they were happy to cut off the head of a Pequot and carry
it on a stake to their English masters? He knew that some
of his companions had been given to Uncas and
Miantonomi as slaves in payment for their service to the
English. Any others of his people, such as his wife's
mother, who had survived the slaughter at the fort or the
flight into the swamp, must now be in hiding, perhaps
across the water on the island called Munnawtawkit, or
even farther on Paumonok. He would have to bide his
time.

And yet none of these reasons by themselves stopped
him from climbing in through a window and putting his
hands around the white woman's neck. He had seen the
others drop into the water. The first, the one who had
been shot, was his cousin. Massaquoit had grown up with
the others, fought and hunted with them. Their blood
called to him. The problem was he could not make himself believe that the woman whose life he contemplated
taking was responsible for their deaths, nor would killing
her ease the pain in his heart. There was something about
her that impressed him; perhaps it was her courage in
speaking her mind to the Englishmen who would have
been just as happy to see him drown.

He stretched out beneath the tree with his eyes fixed on
the moon and watched it as it sank toward the horizon.
He slept, briefly, between the moon's setting and the
sun's rising.

In a window on the second floor of her house, Catherine
sat in her rocking chair and stared at the unmoving shape
of her new servant. She wondered just how she was going

to deal with him. She had told Phyllis, her servant girl, to leave a plate of food on the ground where he could see it, even though she knew he would not accept the offering, not tonight, and maybe not for days, if ever. Still, she knew she had to try. Now she saw the white cloth that Phyllis had set over the plate lift in a sudden breeze and fall half off. It did not matter, for Massaquoit had glanced once when the plate was set down, and had not looked at it again.

She did not fear him, although others did. In her own way, which was not always consistent with the Word as preached by Minister Davis, she relied on her understanding of her God's will. She depended on her intuitive understanding of the deity's intentions in a particular circumstance rather than the applications of the minister's sermons, in which, she felt, mere language was squeezed into dogma that suited the convenience of both ministers and magistrates and had very little to do with God as she liked to think she experienced Him. And so now, without being able to put into words her own thoughts, she somehow still knew that Massaquoit was not going to knock her over the head, whatever his hatred of the English might be, and she did not doubt that he had cause for his rage.

She was not so presumptuous to think that in saving Massaquoit from the watery grave to which his comrades had been sent that she was serving God's will, that she had become, in a phrase she detested hearing from the pulpit, "an instrument of His will." No, she did not feel that way at all. She had merely done what she thought was the right thing to do, and something she was sure her late husband would have agreed to, once she had taken the time to explain why he should.

This thought took her mind away from the Indian sitting beneath her tree and to her husband, dead these three months, a man with whom she had lived for twenty-five years, and with whom she had borne six children, all of whom had survived into adulthood and now lived scattered in different towns up and down the river valley that cut a long line from the north through the hills down to Newbury Harbor where it emptied into the sea. None of her children, two daughters and four sons, and their families were now close enough to see more than occasionally. She reasoned that the next time they would be together would be to bury her. That thought gave her ironic comfort.

John had been a kind and gentle husband, conscientious, even aggressive, in business but neglectful at home, so that he had given the management of the household over to his wife to an extent that caused tongues to wag behind their backs. She sensed these criticisms; if John did, however, he did not seem to pay any attention. When he died suddenly of a fever, which took him from active middle age to the grave in two days, she had been shocked into numbness, from which she recovered into a thankfulness that their lives had been so accommodating to each other, even though their relationship had never burned with much passion.

She turned her attention back to the crouched figure, now just visible in the shadows beneath the tree. There was so much she would have to teach him, and she knew how recalcitrant a student he would surely be.

She must start on the morrow by telling him that his name was now Matthew. If he did not approve, he could choose another Christian name, for the "treaty" imposed on the surviving Pequots that after their disastrous war forbade their language, including names, from being spoken. If she succeeded in convincing him to accept a

Christian name, at least for the benefit of their neighbors in the tight, gossipy community that was Newbury, she could then begin the much more arduous process of making him a Christian not just in name, but in some semblance of practice, or appearance, if not belief. She found it almost amusing that she, whose love of her church was far less than her love of her God, was now forced to proselytize, to make a convert of one whose stubborn heart would make him an implacable enemy of that very church.

Massaquoit awoke, still sitting squat-legged beneath the tree, his back pressed against its rough bark, when a twig brushed against his cheek on its way to the ground. He looked up through the branches to find the bird whose housekeeping had dislodged the twig. Halfway up the trunk, he saw the flutter of wings as the brown-feathered female robin flew off. He stood up slowly against the ache in his legs and back. The bird circled overhead, but did not leave the area. After a few moments it landed on the ground near the plate of food. He heard the door of the house open and saw the same servant girl who had left the food looking at him. Although he was too far to see her eyes, he knew they were fearful by the timid movements of her head as she glanced in his direction. He wondered why she was so afraid of him, but then he realized they all were. He found it strange that the defeated captive should excite such terror among those who had defeated him. He watched as she walked ever so slowly toward the plate of food. Her eyes remained on him, and so she did not notice the bird, which had lifted the cloth entirely off the plate and was now pecking at a crust of bread. The bird, testing the limits of its courage, stayed with its task as the girl approached, until it suc-

ceeded in ripping off a piece of the bread. Then, the crust
protruding from both sides of its beak, it launched itself
with a flutter of wings that brought it dangerously close
to the girl's head. She raised her hands to her mouth as
though to shriek, but no sound came out. In a quick motion, her eyes still on Massaquoit, she stooped down and
lifted the plate, and then hastened back into the house.

He felt the smile form on his lips, and realized that he
had not smiled in many weeks. Still, the ache in his muscles and the emptiness in his belly told him that he must
do something to find a way to survive in this strange and
hostile environment of the English. He would begin by
providing himself with a place to sleep.

Of course he realized that he was not absolutely free to
go. He was not restrained by ropes or chains, as he had
been, but he was the white woman's property. If he just
left, she could order the soldiers to come after him. He
had no stomach to become the hunted animal again, as he
had been when he led his people into the swamp. He
would wait for the white woman to come out of her
house, and then he would tell her what he intended to do.
He did not mean to seek her permission, but to inform her
of what he needed so she would let him go in peace into
the woods.

He did not have long to wait, for Catherine, who had
been watching him and Phyllis again from her window,
now stepped out of her house, and with her bold stride,
which belied her plump body, strode toward him.

"If you do not want to eat my food, I will not bother
leaving it out to feed the birds," she said. "They eat well
enough in my garden."

"I was not hungry," he said.

She looked at the way his ribs pressed against his flesh
and shook her head.

"Were you cold, then? If you want to sleep outside, I can give you a blanket."

"The air is still warm," he replied. "But it will not continue so, and I need to build a shelter for myself."

"So you think you might stay?" she asked.

"If I left you would send the soldiers after me, would you not?"

She shook her head.

"It wouldn't matter what I did, they would go after you like a pack of wolves hungry for fresh meat."

"Would you try to stop them, again, as you did on the ship?"

She considered for a moment, and then shook her head.

"I do not think so."

"Good," he said. "I will stay. I will cause you no trouble." He took a breath. "I will try to do what tasks you give me."

"Your labor will be light, but as you stay with us, you must contribute your strength. It is the one thing, as I am sure you have noticed, that we lack."

Massaquoit remembered how he had contemplated making his way into the house, encountering no more resistance than water to a rock, and he nodded.

"I need a knife, or hatchet, if you are bold enough to give me one."

"Follow me," she said, and then she turned on her heel and followed a path that led around to the garden at the back of her house. The old man was stooped among the beans, a basket on the ground next to his feet.

"Edward," Catherine called to him. The old man looked up. "Be so kind as to bring us a knife and a hatchet."

The old man did not move.

"Edward," Catherine said, in a louder voice. "Do not

pretend that you have not heard me. And I know perfectly well what I am doing."

Edward slowly stood up to stretch the stiffness out of his limbs, and then he shuffled off toward the house. He went in a door, and when he emerged a couple of minutes later, the sun glinted off the blades of the knife and the hatchet. He walked toward Catherine and Massaquoit until he was a half-dozen paces from them, and then he laid the implements down. Without a word, he returned to his basket and his beans.

Massaquoit glanced at Catherine. She nodded, and he walked over to the tools and picked them up. He ran his thumb over their blades. Both were sharp enough to slice his flesh with just a little pressure.

"I will be back before dark," he said.

"Tonight is lecture night," she said. "I may not be home when you return." She searched his eyes to see if he understood, but his expression remained blank. "We go for instruction in God's words."

"Your English God must be very hard to understand."

"Some think so," Catherine replied.

"Your minister, on board the boat, offered thanks to your God for defeating us."

"He did."

"Do you then blame Him when you lose?"

She knew how she would like to answer that question, that she would not invoke the Prince of Peace to make war, but she did not think the time right to offer such a radical thought to this heathen.

Massaquoit waited a moment for further explanation, but when it became clear that this strange white woman was not going to offer any more, he trotted off into the woods behind the maple tree beneath which he had spent the night.

• • •

He wanted to make his way to the shore to gather reeds for a sleeping mat. He knew that the water lay to the south on the other side of the English village. He had no intention of testing the attitudes of the other white people he might encounter, so he circled the village, staying in the woods.

Once he was halfway around the cluster of English houses, he spied a stand of young birch and it did not take him long to hack down enough saplings for his purpose. These he stacked, and then he searched for older, larger trees whose roots would run along the surface of the ground. Not far from the birch, he located two tall pines. He scraped away the dirt from one until he could feel a long taproot, and then he tracked it as it moved away from the tree. Five or six feet from the trunk the root had thinned sufficiently, and he hacked it off with the hatchet. He did this again with one more root from the first tree, and then cut two strips from the other tree, until he had eight or ten feet of ropelike roots to bind the saplings into a frame. He used one long piece of root to tie together the stack of saplings, along with the other, shorter roots. A short distance away a mature beech tree, felled by a recent storm, lay on the ground. With the hatchet he skinned as much bark as he could carry.

He was anxious to move on, in part to complete the gathering of his materials, and in part because he felt that the English soldiers might come upon him at any moment. He was not sure that he could trust the woman to keep them from following him. But he also could not much longer ignore the ache in his stomach. Not far from where he sat, he saw the dark blue berries on vines growing in the sun between the trees. The berries were bitter, but he knew they were safe.

If he ate too much, he would become sick, so he stopped as soon as the ache in his stomach lessened. He felt some strength returning, and for a moment his eyes turned to the shadows in the darkening woods, and he thought he might go in that direction. But then he turned his back on the woods and headed for the shore. The sun had long since passed its zenith and was sliding down toward the west. He did not have much time.

When he reached the southern edge of the village again, he saw a crowd gathering on the main road. The English, men, women, and children, were coming out of their houses to join the crowd as it marched past them. As the crowd swelled, so did the angry noises emanating from it. The men were gesticulating to each other. Some carried what seemed to be clubs. Others lit torches against the deepening darkness. He came as close to the edge of the crowd as he dared while still keeping the last trees of the forest between him and the English. He strained his ears to hear their words. He could not be sure, but he thought he heard his name muttered.

Their eyes, though, remained staring ahead. Nobody looked into the woods where he hid. He noted the direction of their movement toward the white woman's house. He did not know why the women and children were walking along with the men, but he was sure that they were all coming to find him. He considered running back into the safety of the woods, where they would not follow in the dark, but then he would not be sure of their intentions. Instead, he stayed among the trees at the edge of the forest and followed the crowd as it approached Catherine's house.

TWO

❧❦

CATHERINE HAD JUST come out into the garden with Phyllis to see what vegetables might be gathered for supper when she heard a confused cacophony of voices rise from the road that skirted the hill on which her house sat. She and Phyllis hurried around to the front, and there she saw a crowd heading toward the northern edge of Newbury, where the town ran abruptly into the untamed woods. The voices seemed to carry an angry tone. She turned to Phyllis.

"Catch up with them, if you can, and see where they are going, and to what purpose."

She watched as the girl hurried down the hill and trotted toward the people, whose voices were becoming less distinct as they moved farther away. Catherine strained her eyes, keeping them focused on the white cap Phyllis wore, and she saw it bobbing up and down behind the crowd. The cap stopped moving next to a man's dark brown hat. After a few moments she could see the cap turn back toward her while the hat moved away, and shortly Phyllis stood before her, catching her breath.

"They are going to the Jameson house. They say the babe is dead. And they want you to come to say whether it was alive when it was born."

She recalled holding the babe in her arms and seeing that he was having trouble breathing. She had seen that his nose was clogged with mucus and fluids, and she had cleared it with a bit of rag she carried in her midwife's basket for that purpose. The babe had snorted in the air as soon as she removed the cloth and then he had bellowed a very strong and healthy cry. The only thing out of the ordinary during the birth that she could now remember was how the Jamesons' Irish maidservant eyed the babe as though she wanted to do something with it. Catherine had seen dozens of births, and usually she could tell when a babe was in trouble. This one had given no indication of frailty.

"Come along with me, then," she said to Phyllis. "Just stop to tell Edward to watch for Matthew."

Phyllis did not respond, and Catherine motioned to the tree under which Massaquoit had slept.

"You know," Catherine repeated, "Matthew."

"I see, yes, he should wait for Matthew," Phyllis said.

"Edward need not think about going to lecture."

"He does not think about that anyway," Phyllis replied.

"Be that as it may, I do not think there will be lecture tonight," Catherine said. "Now go along with you."

The Jameson house was a humble structure of two sections, the older little more than a hut with walls of daub-and-wattle construction, a plaster of mud and manure layered over a substructure of crisscrossing poles. Henry Jameson had recently built a wing onto the back of the house to accommodate his growing family, and this new room was covered in wooden shingles outside and was generally more luxurious inside, having a wood-plank floor and whitewashed plaster walls.

It was in this room that Martha had delivered her babe. Catherine remembered that the Irish servant girl had a little space, not much more than a closet, for a bed so that she could be near the infant's cradle, and that the parents' bedroom was in the original portion of the house. She also remembered how the girl had fashioned a crude cross out of two twigs, tied together with thread, and then hung it over her bed until Henry had found it there and pulled it off. He had taken the cross outside and ground it into the mud with the heavy heel of his shoe. There was a separate entrance to this side of the house, which gave onto a patch of wild strawberries, and it was before that door that the crowd had gathered.

As Catherine shouldered her way through the crowd, she felt hands grabbing at her sleeve. She was spun around, and for a moment she lost sight of Phyllis. Someone said, "I've got her," but Catherine pulled away. Phyllis emerged from behind the man who was holding Catherine's arm. A woman placed her face right in front of Catherine. She was missing her front teeth, and her breath was sour. She held a smoldering torch in one hand, and she brought it down near Catherine's face.

"Here, mistress," the woman said, "we've been waiting for you, we have."

Phyllis forced herself next to Catherine, shielding her from the woman.

"Go," Catherine said to Phyllis, "to Master Woolsey, and tell him to come here right away."

Phyllis pushed her way back through the crowd, which was advancing with a deliberate inevitability toward the house. Catherine moved with the energy of the crowd, but at a faster pace, so that soon she reached its leading edge, some ten or so feet away from Henry and Ned Jameson, who stood with their backs to their house. Ned had his arm around the Irish servant girl, flattening her breasts and squeezing her hard against his side. She held a pitcher in her hand. It was tilted toward the ground and water dripped from it. The girl's eyes were wide and starting as they found Catherine.

"Please," she said, but then Ned pulled her even harder toward him, and whatever else the girl was trying to say was lost in the breath exploding from her mouth.

The Jameson girls, ranging from a toddler to the oldest, a twelve-year-old, were gathered around their mother, who stood off to one side. Martha's gown was unlaced and one heavy breast hung free as though she were about to give her babe suck. Her eyes moved back and forth between her husband and the crowd, seemingly unable or unwilling to focus. The toddler amused itself by walking around and around through her mother's legs. The oldest girl seemed to be whispering comfort to her younger siblings. Then the girl turned to her mother and laced up her gown. Martha looked at her daughter's hand as though it were a fly buzzing about her, but she did not swipe it away.

Henry was holding the babe, wrapped in swaddling, and unmoving. It was quite clearly dead. He took a step toward Catherine and held out the babe toward her. His face glowed red in the glare of a torch.

"Here she is," he shouted. He lowered his voice a little. "Tell us, then, if you please, Mistress Williams, was this babe born alive?"

"Who says nay?" Catherine asked. She looked at Martha, who stood mute, and then at the Irish servant girl, who did not seem to understand what was happening. Always the finger of blame, she thought, lands on

some poor woman while the men stand around pointing
that finger with self-righteous and hypocritical arrogance.
She recalled how Henry had asked first what sex the babe
was before he inquired as to his wife's health. "Henry
will be glad," Martha had said as Catherine had held the
babe in front of her so that she could see its genitalia. And
then Martha had collapsed onto the bed, a woman exhausted by fifteen years of being pregnant, giving birth,
suffering miscarriages, and nursing the babes that were
born, and always there had been the poverty. She had not
wanted to take Ned in, for there was never enough food.

"Just answer the question," Henry insisted. "We have
heard how soft your heart is for a savage. How is it with
this babe? Here, look at it, which is not breathing now
who was when it was born. Was it not very much alive
when you pulled it out of my wife's belly not three days
ago?"

A voice came from the back of the crowd, strong,
male, and insistent.

"An answer, mistress, we need to know the truth."

Catherine turned toward the voice, but she could not
identify the speaker. It came from a knot of people that
had gathered just beyond Ned in the shadow of a tall tree.

"The truth," the voice said again, and then was joined
by other voices, male and female, rising from the group
beneath the tree, and then spreading across the surface of
the crowd like whitecaps in a storm-tossed sea. "The
truth," they clamored, "tell us the truth."

"What says the mother, then?" Catherine demanded.
"What says Goody Jameson?"

"Nothing," came the response from the group.

Catherine turned back to Henry.

"Your wife, Henry, what does she say?"

"Nothing," Henry repeated. "She no longer speaks.

She came to me not an hour ago, holding the babe in her arms, and handed it to me, and she does not speak."

Catherine studied Martha's face. Its expression did not change as her children moved about her. She did not seem to see that her husband was holding her dead infant in his arms, and she did not hear the insistent cries for the truth. It was as though she were standing in a meadow daydreaming while butterflies circled her head. Every moment or two she extended her hand toward the toddler that clung to her knees, but the gesture was vague and inconsequential, and her hand never found her child's head.

Catherine stepped close to Martha, close enough to feel the woman's breath on her face.

"Martha, you must speak," Catherine said, and Martha's eyes now focused on her, as though she had just returned from that distant meadow. She shook her head, slowly at first, and then with increasing agitation. Catherine took Martha's shoulders in both hands and squeezed and then the nodding motion stopped. Still Martha did not speak.

"My poor wife is distracted by the death of our babe," Henry declared. "Can you not see that? Mistress Williams, you must answer for her."

"Well, then," Catherine said, "if Martha Jameson will not attest to the truth, I needs must say that this babe was born alive, and alive it was when I left it. Truth you want, and there it is."

A murmur arose from the crowd. It pushed toward Catherine.

"It is surely dead now," somebody said.

"If Goody Jameson won't speak, we have ways," said another.

"Yes, press her, stone by stone. She will talk, then, I warrant."

"You will leave her alone," Henry said, and the crowd, which had come within several feet of the clustered Jameson family, stopped. Henry held out the babe toward his wife.

"Tell them, Martha," he said. He thrust the babe toward her, but she did not hold out her arms to take it. He shook his head. "She brought the babe to me. It was dead. She said she had been asleep, and when she woke she saw the servant girl leaning over the babe. When she picked it up, it was not breathing. Then she brought it to me. That girl, she did something while my wife was asleep."

Catherine felt the anger rise in the crowd toward the servant. She remembered once, when she was a girl in Alford, how a crowd just like this one had fallen upon a little boy whose family was Catholic, and how they had beaten him with sticks until he lay senseless in the road. She strode to Ned and grabbed his arm.

"Let her go," she said.

"You are now interfering in my household, mistress. Leave be."

"Step away, mistress," a woman in the crowd said. "You have told us what we needed to know."

"She," Henry shouted, "standing there with the pitcher, ask her what she was doing with our babe."

The servant girl turned her terrified and starting eyes toward her master. Their whites loomed preternaturally large in the failing light of the early evening.

"A priest, it was, I was after," she said.

Ned pushed the girl forward so she stood quivering in front of the crowd.

"That is it," he said, "that is how we found her, practicing her papist ritual on our babe, pouring water on its innocent face, and mumbling some words, a curse they must have been."

"Its poor soul," the girl muttered. "There was no priest. I asked for one. So I tried myself to save its precious soul."

Henry looked at his wife, whose eyes were now studying the ground at her feet. Then he stared hard at the girl, his face brightening as with a new understanding.

"You drowned it, for certain," he said. "Or you cast a spell on it so it could not breathe. What, a papist priest? In Newbury? You have killed our babe and driven my poor wife mad."

"Try her, then," came the voice from the knot of people, still grouped by the tree. "Have her touch the babe. Then we will know."

The crowd surged forward and Catherine found herself staggering toward Henry, who dropped to one knee against her weight. Henry threw one hand behind him to brace himself, and Catherine reached for the babe so as to stop it from falling. As she grabbed for it, its swaddling blanket fell. The babe's skin was cold. Henry regained his balance and wrapped the babe tightly in the blanket.

"Try her," again came the cry from the crowd.

"Surely not," Catherine said. "Magistrate Woolsey is coming. This is a matter for him."

"We need not wait for the magistrate. We will have our answer now," shouted one.

"Now," said another.

"Right," said Ned. "We will try her now."

Catherine turned to face the crowd and to peer over it to the road, where day was giving way to dusk. She thought she saw two figures approaching.

"The magistrate is coming even now," she said.

Henry looked at Ned, and the boy pushed the servant girl toward him.

"Touch the babe," Ned demanded.

"Yes, touch it," Henry said. "If it bleed, it cries out against you."

"There is no need for that," Catherine said. "Talk of the dead bleeding. It is surely blasphemy."

"The blood will talk," came a voice from a crowd.

"Yes," others confirmed, "let the poor dead babe's blood cry out against its murderer."

The girl clasped her arms in front of her chest, but Ned pulled her hands out. She struggled, but he was too strong, and he was able to bring one hand to the exposed skin of the babe's chest. He pressed the hand onto the skin, and then let her pull her hand back. Henry peered at the spot she had touched, and then lifted the babe over his head in a triumphant gesture.

"It bleeds," he said. "It bleeds."

He held the babe out for the crowd to see. Catherine strained her eyes as Henry and the babe were now in shadows. Henry turned so that all could view. Catherine was not sure she saw blood on the babe's chest, but something on its back caught her eye, and then she could no longer see.

"Blood," cried voices in the crowd. "The babe bleeds! Seize her!"

There was a violent surge forward, and Catherine felt herself being thrown to the ground. She got to her feet just in time to see rough hands grabbing the servant girl and pulling her away. Catherine hurled herself to the girl and threw her arms around her. For a few moments there was a tense tug-of-war, all the more startling for the silence in which it occurred. Then a resonant, commanding voice rose above the struggle.

"I am here now," Magistrate Woolsey said.

All eyes turned to him as he made his way through the crowd. He was accompanied by the constable, whose sword was drawn. The crowd parted, permitting them to reach the girl. The grasping hands dropped from her, and she pushed herself against the constable.

"The babe," Magistrate Woolsey demanded, but Henry clutched it to his chest.

"I need to bury it."

"There will be time enough," Magistrate Woolsey said. "You have tried the girl by having her touch it, and now you must hand it to me so that we can examine it."

Henry held out the babe, and the constable sheathed his sword and then took the babe into his arms. The blanket fell to the ground, and Ned picked it up.

A high-pitched cry rose above the crowd.

"No! You cannot take him!"

All eyes turned toward Martha.

"Give him to me!" she said. "You do not know. He is mine."

She reached for the babe in the constable's arms, stretching out her strong hands, reddened and callused by hours of rough labor at the laundry tub and in the garden, but Catherine stepped between them.

"Let me," Catherine said, and the constable handed her the babe with its back toward her. She saw a bruise there, and when she turned it she noted its perfectly formed nose. Martha held out her hands and stroked the babe's face. Then she dropped her hands and Catherine handed the babe back to the constable.

"Martha," she said quietly. "We will bring him back to you as soon as we can."

"It does not matter," she said. Her eyes were again vacant. She stepped toward the house, but then seemed to forget where she wanted to go. Her daughter came to her side. The constable looked at Woolsey, and the magistrate nodded. Then he beckoned to the servant girl.

"Come with me, child." The girl clung to Catherine, and so together they followed the magistrate and the constable through the crowd. People hissed at them as they passed, but nobody dared to challenge the magistrate's authority. As they passed the knot of people by the tree, the same male voice that had been shouting throughout could be heard.

"The babe bled, sir," it said. "We know you will come to see that the girl killed it." The speaker was the pox-marked sailor Catherine had seen in the shallop.

Woolsey stared in the direction of the voice, but did not respond. The rest of the crowd moved toward Henry and Ned to see what they would do. Nobody paid any attention to Martha, who remained where she was, rocking on her heels, moving her tongue to form soundless words. Her oldest daughter picked up the toddler and steered her mother into the house.

In the darkness, Catherine did not see Minister Davis in the shadows in the rear of the crowd. He stepped forward, and she recognized the resonance of his voice.

"A terrible, old superstition," the minister said.

"Why say you that to me now?" Catherine asked.

Minister Davis shrugged.

"I arrived too late. The people's anger seemed stronger than I could quell."

"So I see," Catherine replied.

"What think you?"

"Yes, a terrible thing, superstition."

"About the babe," Minister Davis said.

"I know not. I, too, was too late," she replied.

"I see," he said, and walked away.

She watched his shape disappear. A man carrying a torch walked up to the minister to say something to him. As they stood, heads close together, the glare of the torch illuminated a figure darting behind a tree. Catherine continued to walk with her arm around the servant girl. It is good, she thought, for him to keep out of sight, for the anger of this crowd would be looking for a new target to spend itself on, and Massaquoit would do very nicely. Of course he hadn't killed this babe, any more than the poor, shivering girl in her arms, but Magistrate Woolsey's influence had been just strong enough to shield the girl from the mob; it would doubtless be too weak to protect an Indian.

From behind a tree, Massaquoit watched. He saw the white woman leave with the man who was on the boat when his comrades were killed. Then the other English in twos and threes walked off into the night until only a handful remained in front of the house. They must be the ones who live here, he thought. Then all but two of them went into the house. The two left were men. He could tell that by their height, although it was getting too dark to see anything clearly. One of the English was taller than the other, and he leaned down as though to speak to the shorter one. The shorter one nodded and then trotted back into the house. Massaquoit waited for the larger one to follow, but he did not. A few moments later the shorter one came out. He was carrying something under his arm. The taller one motioned to the woods behind the house and the other carried his bundle in that direction and disappeared into the shadows. Then the taller man made his way into the house. Massaquoit peered at the place where the shorter one had vanished. He thought he saw movement, another figure, much smaller, going off in the same direction. He stared harder but it was gone.

The house was quiet and the yard in front of it where the mob had gathered was deserted. He was relieved to think that the English seemed to have forgotten him in the excitement provoked at this house. He looked down the road the Englishwoman had taken with the old man from the ship, but he did not follow them. Instead, carrying his saplings, roots, and the reeds he had gathered among the marshes at the shore, he returned to his tree on the white woman's land. The sun had set. He laid the makings of his wigwam down near the maple tree and stared at the small pile that awaited him there. First he picked up the white linen shirt, then the leather doublet, and finally the buff-colored breeches of a heavy cloth lined with leather. He was familiar with the way the English dressed, although he had never worn their clothes. He held the shirt up to his shoulders and saw that the size was about right. He was not quite sure how the doublet should be worn, so he contented himself with pressing it against his chest. The breeches barely reached his knees, and he recalled seeing Englishmen wear another item that stretched from the knees to the feet. He looked on the ground, and found a pair of shoes, and beneath them two pieces of cloth, bright blue, with feet on their ends. He dropped the breeches next to the shoes and hose and stretched out in his weariness onto the cool ground. He looked toward the house from which came no sign of activity.

He did not know if the white woman would return. But still, in the morning, whether she did or did not, he would begin constructing his wigwam.

He had no other place to go.

THREE

CATHERINE WAS UP before dawn, rising from a sleep troubled by the images of the night before—the dead baby limp in Henry's large, rough hands, Martha's lips tightly pressed together while her eyes stared off into someplace nobody else could follow, and most of all the terror in the servant girl's eyes as the crowd called for her blood. Catherine sat staring into the morning darkness, hearing the voices from the night before. A half hour later she was startled to discover that the sun was now up and that she was sitting, fully dressed on her bed, though she did not remember putting on a single item of clothing.

She walked through the kitchen toward the door at the rear of her house. She heard a snore and then she smelled the bread baking. Phyllis sat with her head on the table fast asleep. Catherine opened the door to the oven, which was built into the wall of the fireplace. The bread's crust was just starting to turn brown. She walked quietly past the sleeping servant.

She pushed against the heavy door. The air was humid and the wood of the door had swollen so that she had to lower her shoulder and force it free from the embrace of the frame. She gave a hard shove and the door opened into the half-light of the rising sun. A moment later she heard steps and turned to see Phyllis stumbling up from the table, her eyes still filled with sleep.

"What's the matter?" the girl asked.

"Never you mind," Catherine replied. "Tend to your bread, and then put another one in to bake."

"Another?"

"That is what I said. I have use for the one that is baking now."

She walked out into the yard. The grass was wet beneath her feet. She made her way through the vegetable garden, passing by a row of pole beans on one side and Indian corn on the other. The bean plants were heavy with blossoms, but the cornstalks came only to her knees. Her eyes stayed focused straight ahead to the very rear of the garden. When she arrived at the patch, she knelt down and sought ripe fruit. Most of the strawberries were still green, but she found one that was red and soft. She squeezed it between her thumb and forefinger, and the juice left a faint, but discernible red stain. She ran her fingers over the stain, and then wiped her hand on her apron and stood up. Her knees and back complained and she stretched until they quieted.

She returned to the kitchen to find Phyllis taking the loaf of bread out of the oven.

"Let it cool and then wrap it in a napkin," Catherine said. She stirred the pot of powdered corn, called samp, that was simmering in milk in the large pot in the fireplace. Then she ladled a generous portion of the mixture into a wooden trencher and carried it over to the table board.

"I could have done that," Phyllis said.

"Of course, but I did."

"You needn't be so sharp with me this morning."

"Well, then," Catherine said, aware that her tongue had more of an edge than usual, "just bring over the molasses and we'll sweeten this samp, and maybe my nature along with it."

"It's all the trouble," Phyllis said as she spooned generous amounts of the sweet, thick liquid into Catherine's trencher.

"Yes, it is," Catherine replied. She smiled as her tongue tasted the molasses and then grimaced in pain.

"That tooth, is it?" Phyllis asked.

"Yes."

"I saw Goody Hawkins passing by this morning. I think we should nail a horseshoe over the door. Just to be certain."

"It is the molasses," Catherine replied. "My tooth only pains me when I eat the molasses. Not when Goody Hawkins visits."

"Well, for that, you know she does not have to be here to afflict you. People say she is not to be trusted, ever since her husband and her two sons drowned."

"It's the molasses," Catherine said. "Now hush about Goody Hawkins and wrap that bread for me so I can take it to the jail."

Catherine took a few more spoonfuls of the samp. With each swallow her tooth ached, and each stab of pain running down her jaw and into her shoulder made her think of Goody Hawkins and wonder if Phyllis might be correct. Goody Hawkins was a woman of near seventy whose tongue was sharp and temper short. Few townsfolk visited her, and only those people who wanted to draw on her expertise in curing intractable illnesses. Because of her nasty disposition and her occasional success in helping those who came to her, gossips in the town made it known that her cures resulted from her witchery, and that she had made those whom she helped sick in the first place. Catherine, though, saw in her only a sad old woman who had outlived husband and children and now faced life wearing a stubborn frown. Still, Catherine was not willing to discount all the talk, and so as she stood up, her tooth aching, she tried to recall the last time she had seen Goody Hawkins. As though she could read her mistress's mind, Phyllis provided the answer.

"Don't you recall," she said. "Goody Hawkins grabbed hold of your arm as we walked to the Jameson house, and when you would not talk to her, she growled at you like an angry dog."

"Her voice bears the weight of her years, as her hair is as hoary as the snow in January. It is no more than that."

"Like a dog," Phyllis insisted.

"Never you mind," Catherine replied. She had not decided about Goody Hawkins. She might be a witch after all, or she might just be the poor old woman Catherine sometimes thought she herself might become. Still, she could not chase the thought that Goody Hawkins had been at the Jameson house when the babe was born. In fact, she had extended her arms to hold it while Catherine fumbled for a knife to cut the cord. It was when Goody Hawkins had handed the babe back that Catherine saw that its nose needed to be cleared. And Goody Hawkins's face had worn a twisted frown, rather than a smile, when Catherine had cleared the babe's nostrils and it had cried its relief.

Catherine picked up the wrapped bread and put it into her pocket.

"I'll be gone some time," she said.

"You're not going to leave me here alone with that savage lurking about."

"Edward will be here shortly."

"Cannot I go with you?" Phyllis insisted.

"You are not truly afraid of Matthew, are you?"

Phyllis nodded.

"Surely, I am."

"You want to see that man's punishment."

Phyllis reddened.

"I had most forgotten."

"I do not think so. You can follow after me once Edward is here. Maybe Matthew will want to come with you."

Phyllis brought her hand to her mouth and then expelled her breath loudly. Catherine took the opportunity to wave good-bye. Catherine knew she permitted Phyllis too many liberties, but she liked the girl, and the house was too quiet when the girl was gone on an errand. So before Phyllis could catch her breath and continue to plead, Catherine walked out of the door.

She looked northward, up the road the crowd had marched along with glaring torches the night before toward the Jameson house. A stray hog was rooting in the dust and weeds at the edge of the dirt road. She turned toward the south and the center of Newbury Town, which consisted of three large houses in two of which lived the minister and Joseph Woolsey. The third sat vacant after the governor had moved from it to his new mansion overlooking the harbor. Across from them was the meetinghouse, where workmen were removing a damaged section of the roof. The road widened there into a square and then it gave way to a meadow on which the militia drilled. Past the meadow, the road narrowed again on its way to the harbor. Although it was early in the morning, a number of people seemed to share Catherine's destination, if not her purpose. She nodded to each in turn as she bustled past them, first a young servant boy, and then an elderly man stooped over a cane, and then two middle-aged women walking side by side, their heads close in conversation. All were heading to the jail that stood just where the road turned down a hill in sight of the water.

In its outward appearances, the jail looked like an ordinary house, and a very modest one at that. It was a simple square building, its walls sheathed in clapboard, and a heavy oaken door, studded with square nail heads, at its front entrance. One fair-sized glass window flanked the door on its right. But the other windows, one on each side of the building, announced its function. They were little more than slits, with an iron bar running across their openings.

A knot of people was gathered next to the pillory in front of the jail. Catherine made her way through them and was about to knock on the door when it swung open and she found herself staring into the unshaven face of Matthew Drake, the jailer, a man in his fifties with yellow teeth and a bulbous red nose, on the tip of which sat a tuft of coarse black hair. He glanced at the small crowd and then leaned toward Catherine in an obsequious manner.

"I suppose you have come to see about the girl," he said.

"That I have." Catherine reached into her pocket and pulled out the shilling. "Here," she said, extending her hand palm up so that the sun could catch the bright coin, "make sure that she has enough to eat and whatever else she might need."

His dirt-encrusted hand closed over hers. The skin felt like coarse leather. His mouth opened into a crooked smile.

"Of course, but I don't think she will be enjoying my hospitality very long." He nodded to the open space in front of the building. "I saw Fred Hainesworth looking for a nice level place out there this morning."

"He'd be better off building a six-plank chest than planning a gallows."

"Somebody has to do it, what with the town's master carpenter so involved in the proceedings."

"Just let me in so I can see the poor girl."

He leaned his back against the door to open it fully, and with a sweeping gesture of his right hand, he beckoned her in.

The doorway let immediately into the small room in which the jailer lived. Drake was now unmarried, and perhaps had never been. He had come to Newbury just as the jail was being completed, looking for employment and a place to stay. The town's selectmen sought a jailer, but they were not having much success in filling a position that offered no material advantages in land or salary. They were about to set up a rotating system of enforced volunteers, much as they used to provide Newbury with its constables, ward and watch, fence viewers, and so forth, when Drake offered to take the job if he could live in the jail. He would be paid a small stipend, which he could supplement any way he chose as long as what he did was discreet and did not infringe on the rights or property of the good citizens of the town. What was understood, but not spoken, was that he would add to his meager wages by skimming a few pennies out of every shilling that the town paid him toward the room and board of his prisoners. Thus he found himself again in a minority position. Not only was he alone among the men in the town in not having had a wife, or showing much interest in a woman companion, and not only did he fill a position nobody else wanted, that position made him peculiarly interested in a regular breakdown in law and order, which would provide him a constant supply of prisoners. When his jail was occupied, in short, he prospered.

Catherine stepped into his living quarters and waited for her eyes to adjust to the semidarkness as he shut the door behind them. Two doors had been cut into the crudely plastered wall that separated Drake's living area from the prisoners' rooms. She saw his rope bed, on which his bedclothes lay in a heap, and next to it the small, roughly hewn plank table and bench. A wooden trencher containing the scraps of some indeterminate food sat on the table.

"I was just finishing my breakfast," Drake said.

Catherine pulled the loaf of bread out of her pocket and broke it in half.

"Here, then," she said. "Take this."

He bowed, and swiped the bread out of Catherine's hand with the practiced ease of a bear sweeping a fish out of a stream.

"As you like, mistress, this way."

He took a step toward the door on the left of the wall that separated his living area from the prisoners' rooms. It was secured by a heavy board that sat in iron brackets. A confused murmuring of voices, one male and the other female, reached them through the shut door. Catherine strained to make out the woman's words, but they were too entangled in the deeper tones of the man.

"Quickly, then," she said.

"It is nothing," Drake insisted, but he hurried to the door and, lifting the board, opened it. Catherine saw two bodies moving together, side by side, on the floor. The one on the right was the man, and his hand was reaching under the skirts of the Irish servant girl, whose face was bright red. The man turned his head toward the opening door. One side of his nose was collapsed into his face, and as he moved his lips to speak, he revealed yellowed, uneven teeth.

"What's this?" Drake shouted. He crossed the room in two giant strides and thrust himself between the two bodies, and shoved them apart. The man rolled away from the girl and very slowly removed his hand from between her legs. The girl turned her face to the wall. The man squinted in Catherine's direction.

"Begging your pardon, mistress," he said. "I didn't see you."

"This one, he's Simon Oldcastle," Drake said. "The thief," he added.

"Yes, I recognized his nose," Catherine said.

Simon smiled, and placed his forefinger against the collapsed nostril.

"They're going to slit the other one, this time," he said. He motioned toward the girl, and then he brought the palm of the hand that had been between her legs up to the good side of his nose. "I was just getting a smell of her while I still could."

"I'd like to speak to the girl alone," Catherine said to the jailer.

"I have to take him outside shortly, if you know what I mean," Drake said.

Catherine looked at Simon. He shrugged and then opened his mouth in a crooked grin. Saliva dribbled down his chin.

"I could have used another minute or two with her," he said.

"Take him, then," Catherine said.

Drake grabbed Simon by the shoulders and hauled him to his feet.

"I'm coming," Simon said. "You don't have to pull me about like I was a sick cow, or some other silly animal."

The jailer steered Simon toward the door.

"I don't suppose I have to lock you in," he said to Catherine.

"What do you think?" Catherine demanded. "We'll be right here when you are through with that one." Drake pushed Simon through the door. The jailer pushed the door back so that it was halfway closed. Catherine waited until the jailer and Oldcastle were gone, and then she knelt down next to the girl.

"I have come to help you, if I can," she said.

The girl turned toward Catherine. Her cheek bore the impression of the uneven plaster of the wall.

"You were there last night," she said.

"That I was," Catherine replied. "And I am here again this morning. What is your name, child?"

"Margaret Mary Donovan."

"Well, Margaret Mary Donovan," Catherine said, "was that man forcing himself on you?"

Margaret began to shake her head and then nodded.

"I was afraid and lonely. I couldn't stop my shivering, and he said he could take care of me."

"Did you invite him to come by you?"

"No. I didn't say anything."

"Did you want him to continue what he was doing when we came in?"

She shook her head.

"I didn't care one way or t'other. It's just what men do, I'm thinking."

"Had you before, then?" Catherine asked.

Margaret nodded. Her eyes remained expressionless,

as though she had just been asked if she had eaten breakfast.

"Back home, in Ireland, I was in service, don't you know, and the master took me to his room, the first day. He said it was his right to be the first, seeing as how he was an English lord, and me the daughter of a papist pig who didn't own the land he worked." She looked down at her hands for a moment. "They took my babe from me and put me on the ship to come here. The master said I was too stupid and too ugly to keep, so he was giving me to somebody else."

Catherine looked at the girl's bright blue eyes set a bit too high and unevenly above her small nose, at her thin lips and pointed chin. She could be no older than sixteen. Catherine put her arm around the girl, but she did not respond. She sat stiffly, her eyes staring straight ahead. She placed the half loaf of bread into the girl's hand, but she did not close her fingers about it, and let it slide onto the floor, filthy with mouse droppings.

"What were you doing with the Jameson babe?" Catherine asked.

"Saving its poor, immortal soul."

"Did you know it was already dead?"

Margaret shook her head.

"It wasn't moving. There was no priest, so I did what I could."

"Is that all you can tell me?" Catherine asked.

"I only did what I thought I should," the girl repeated. "I didn't intend to do it any harm." She seemed suddenly to remember the bread, and she picked it up. She stared at it for a moment as though trying to remember what it was. Then she scraped off a pellet of mouse dropping with her fingernail and bit into the freshly baked bread. A rich aroma escaped through the broken crust and lifted into the close air of the room.

"I am hungry," she said.

Massaquoit watched Catherine's plump body hurry down the road in her rolling gait. She barely looked at him as she passed, offering a quick wave of her hand. He surprised himself by realizing that he was disappointed in her lack of attention to him, and he even caught himself as he took a step toward her as though to ask where she was going.

He turned back to what he now called his tree. He had been at work since sunup and he had already formed his saplings into a skeletal dome a little more than six feet on the ground and decreasing to the top, which he would leave open to provide egress for the smoke of his fire. The wigwam, when completed, would be just large enough for him to lie down in. He would not be able to stand upright. He did not care. He was not expecting to entertain company, nor did he plan on spending more time than necessary in his shelter.

He tied another sapling horizontally to one of his uprights, using the roots as rope. He would weave two rows of these, working them in and out of the vertical supports, tying them well at the junctures. When completed, the structure would be stronger than a first glance would suggest. Then he would work the bark into overlapping strips to form a covering that would serve as his walls. He would first cover the side of his wigwam opposite the house. He would build his doorway so that he could sit in it facing the harbor. He would be able to feel the breeze lifted from the waters where his comrades had drowned, and thereby keep their memories fresh in his mind.

He heard the door of the house open slowly, and he

knew before he looked that the young white woman was trying to make her way out quietly enough so that he would not see her. He felt her eyes on his back as clearly as if they were her hands, cold with fear. He turned, and as he did, the sounds of her movement ceased. He fixed his glance on her, and she took a step back toward the door, which she had just shut.

"Your mistress has already gone," Massaquoit said. To his ear his voice sounded kind, but she started as though he had hurled a bloodcurdling scream at her. He took a step toward her, and he could see her chest expanding and contracting as she fought to calm herself. "If you hurry," he said, "maybe you can catch up with her."

"I left you some breakfast, on the table inside. Mistress Williams told me to tell you that you should eat it."

Even though his stomach was empty, he said, "Maybe later."

"Edward will be here any moment," she said.

"That is good," Massaquoit replied. "Are you waiting for him to go with you after your mistress?"

"No, he does not like to see what I am going to see."

"And what is that?"

"Mistress said you could come along. If you want to see how we punish one of our own."

"I think I would like that."

"You will have to let me call you 'Matthew,' then."

"It does not matter what you call me. My name is Massaquoit."

Phyllis walked onto the road.

"Come along, then, Matthew. I suppose if you are going to knock me on the head, there is nothing I can do about it."

"If I was going to do that, you would already be dead."

Phyllis shuddered.

"And Mistress wonders why you scare me so."

"It is your thoughts only that scare you," Massaquoit said.

"No," Phyllis insisted. "I believe it is you. But come along if you are coming."

Margaret wiped the crumbs from her lips with the tips of her fingers, a delicate gesture that belied the vehemence with which she had attacked the half loaf of bread.

"When did you last eat, child?" Catherine asked.

Margaret shrugged.

"I cannot remember. Master Jameson told me I could always have what was left after his family had theirs, and lately there has not been but a few crumbs of bread or a couple of bites of rotten meat that they were too good to eat, but what was good enough for me."

"I have given Jailer Drake some money to see that you are fed while you are in here."

"It seems I hunger all the time," Margaret said, and then clasped her hand over her mouth as though she had permitted a secret to escape.

"Are you indeed?" Catherine asked, and her glance shifted down to Margaret's belly. The girl drew her knees up.

"It's just, with all the trouble. I forget myself."

"Did he force you?" Catherine asked in her gentlest voice.

"Oh, what does it matter now?" Margaret said. "They mean to hang me. Or send me back to Ireland on a boat. If they are going to do that, I think I would rather they hang me now so I can go up to heaven and find my mother, who has been there waiting for me ever since I was a little girl, so my Da used to tell me."

Catherine swept the girl into her arms as though she were still that child she remembered being.

"Hush," she said. "You will not hang. And you will not be sent back to Ireland."

Margaret rested her face on Catherine's breast, but still moved her lips to form the same words.

"It does not matter," she said.

Phyllis and Massaquoit arrived in front of the jail just as Drake finished fastening the pillory over Simon Oldcastle. The device was a hinged board with circles cut to accommodate the victim's neck and wrists. Drake lifted up the top section of the board and shoved Oldcastle forward so that the thief stumbled into the pillory's embrace. Drake then brought the movable board down hard and secured it with a leather thong that passed through iron rings mounted in each section of the board. The townspeople gathered in front of the pillory cheered as Drake finished tying his knot with one last sweeping pull on the thong. As he stepped back, something flew past and crashed into Oldcastle's face. Drake jumped back, and the thief blinked his eyes and spat in an effort to rid himself of the mud that now caked his face.

The dignitaries, including Minister Davis and Magistrate Woolsey, had recoiled as the mud splattered at their feet. They now both strove to recover their composure by straightening their bodies and taking a step toward the pillory.

"Have you come to join me, then?" Oldcastle asked.

Minister Davis turned to the crowd.

"The mud that oozes now on this man's face is but the visible sign of his sin, showing the blackness of his heart, and as it hardens, it typifies the hardening of his heart away from our Savior."

He turned back toward Oldcastle. "Do you now repent of your ways?"

"That I do, but I regret chiefly that I got caught, I do."

From the back of the crowd, Massaquoit observed this English form of punishment. Phyllis motioned him to come forward.

"I will watch from here," he said.

"Suit yourself," she replied, "but I want to see."

"What is going to happen to that man in the wooden collar?"

She leaned toward him.

"Look, there, off to the side. Do you see that little fellow?"

Massaquoit looked in the direction she indicated, and then nodded.

"The one holding the blade."

"Yes. George Firkin. He can cut your hair, shave your beard, or bleed you."

"Which is he going to do to that fellow?"

"You'll see. Just keep your eye on him while the minister is talking away up there. When he's through, George will do his job."

Phyllis pushed her way through the crowd, smiling at each person she had to shoulder out of her way, but permitting no impediment to block her progress until she stood with an unobstructed view of Oldcastle.

Catherine still sat with her arms cradling Margaret. The girl's breathing became so regular that Catherine thought she had fallen asleep. However, when she tried to remove her arm from around the girl's shoulders, she shook her head. So Catherine held her, and as she did she listened to Minister Davis's mellifluous voice reach its full stride just as though he were in the meetinghouse delivering a sermon. That's what he does, wherever he is, Catherine thought, spreads the word of God as he understands it. Pity his understanding was so dim. She smiled at a thought she would never utter out loud.

"This building behind me," Minister Davis said, "was built from the scraps of lumber that we did not use for our meetinghouse." He paused, and Catherine imagined that he must be gesturing across the square to the meeting-house, and she recalled how Henry Jameson, using the full extent of his carpenter's skills, had managed to con-struct the jail from a pile of oddly assorted boards. Only one looking carefully would see the occasional odd seam where two boards of different widths joined, or how the floorboards contained so many small lengths of wood.

"The solid lumber formed the walls, and the floors, and the ceilings of our meetinghouse, lumber as solid as the members of the congregation sitting on its benches. But some lumber was rotten, or warped, and these boards could not serve to build God's house, and just as they were thought unfit to stand in God's sight, just so thieves like Simon Oldcastle, behind me in the pillory, is no bet-ter than a pile of dung in the shape of a man, but a man whose heart is so hardened that he cannot fail to sin, and, having sinned, is not capable of begging forgiveness. If he will not offer a confession or statement of contrition, let us show him how we deal with sinners."

Minister Davis's voice paused, and Catherine knew what was going to happen next.

Massaquoit, too, noted the pause. His eyes shifted to the man Phyllis had pointed out. George Firkin stepped forward. He was a little man, with one shoulder raised a little higher than the other. In his right hand, he held his razor. Its bright blade glinted in the sun. Simon Oldcastle also stared at the shining implement coming toward him.

He started to sneer, but then closed his eyes. George looked first at Minister Davis and then at Magistrate Woolsey. Each man nodded in turn.

"Proceed," Woolsey said. "He has broken our law."

"Mark the sinner," Davis added, signifying that God's law and man's law, in this case, were the very same.

The crowd now stirred. A man in front of Massaquoit raised his son onto his shoulders so that the boy, who was no more than three or four years old, could witness.

"Mark you," the father said, and the boy obediently craned his neck forward.

Massaquoit stepped back, and his motion was detected by the man who turned to stare hard at him.

"You, too," the man said. "I know who you are."

Massaquoit did not reply. He watched as George Firkin lifted his bright blade to the face of the man in the wooden collar, and with one swift movement brought it down across the man's nostril. Blood spurted, and Old-castle opened his eyes. The blood dripped down onto his lips, and he stuck out his tongue to catch it. The people watching let out a communal gasp, a sound that seemed to express joy, relief, perhaps admixed with just a little terror, as the criminal stood bleeding his red blood in front of them.

"Let him stand here until noon," Minister Davis said, "so that he will long remember this day."

"And at noon," Magistrate Woolsey added, "the con-stable will release him, and he will leave this village of Newbury before the sun sets, for we will not have the sun shine on him again while he is among us."

Margaret had finally fallen asleep. She snored gently as the crowd gasped in response to Oldcastle's blood. Catherine sat for a long while in the silence of the jail.

She heard Drake's footsteps and then the scraping of his chair. Apparently he had forgotten that she was still there, or he did not care to remember. When she managed to stand up without awakening Margaret, the jailer's deep and rasping snore was offering a counterpoint to the girl's more delicate sounds. Catherine walked quietly past Drake, whose head was cradled in his arms on his table.

She made her way outside, where Oldcastle stood in his lonely ignominy. Only a few children remained staring at him in intervals of play, which had nothing to do with the man or his crime. Catherine reached into her pocket and removed the small jar containing the paste formed from comfrey leaves. She strode directly to the pillory. Oldcastle's eyes had been closed, but he opened them as she approached.

"This will help," she said. And without further explanation she applied the paste to his wound, which was now crusted in dried, brown blood. Oldcastle tried to jerk his head away, but he was restrained by the pillory. Catherine studied his face, with both nostrils now collapsed.

"Do you have something in that jar," Oldcastle asked, "that can give me a new nose?"

"I am afraid I cannot offer you that."

"A pity," he said, "but I must learn to suffer with what I have left."

"That you will," Catherine said, "whether you want to or not."

FOUR

❧❧

MASSAQUOIT HEARD THE footsteps, and without opening his eyes, he reached across the reeds he slept on, which still smelled pungently of the brackish waters from which they had been removed, until his hand found one of the stones that formed his fire circle. The steps were coming from the west, from the direction of the house. He had managed to shingle this side to shield him from the eyes of the English. He knew by the slight warmth on his cheek that the sun had just risen and that its rays were finding their way through the open eastern wall of his wigwam. The steps came steadily but without stealth. Apparently his attacker was careless or so confident as to ignore the advantage of surprise. Massaquoit pulled the stone toward him, feeling its roundness against the palm of his hand, and breathed the ash from last night's cooking fire. He tensed as the steps stopped a few feet from where he lay. He extended his arm so that he could bring the stone crashing down on his adversary's head.

"Matthew, are you awake?"

For a moment he did not respond to the strange name, but he did recognize the voice, and then the name made sense and he let his arm drop. He replaced the stone on the circumference of his fire circle. He crawled through the frame of his doorway, smelled the brine of the harbor, a half mile away, and inhaled deeply. Phyllis stood before him. She was wearing a crisp white cap.

"I did not mean to startle you," she said. "But it is the Sabbath."

"And you want to tell me that I should not offend your English God by working."

"More than that. Mistress wants me to tell you that we are all going to meeting together, you, me, her, and even Edward. And she wants us to arrive early. Before the others. So that we can watch them come in, instead of them watching us."

Massaquoit stiffened, but he controlled his face so as not to show his anger. He had known this day would come, and he recognized that his immediate safety depended on showing the English that he could learn their ways so as to prove to them that it was not a mistake to spare his life, but still, he despised being made a fool of, of providing the English a spectacle they could gawk at. And he had little intention of becoming a Christian. All this flashed through his mind, but he simply nodded to the girl.

"I am ready to go to meeting."

She did not turn back to the house as he expected. Instead, she stared at him.

"Is something the matter?" he asked.

Her eyes moved from him to the clothes Catherine had left for him, which were lying next to the tree.

"You should put those on, you know. You don't want to be going to meeting looking like a savage."

For a moment he thought she was mocking him, and the anger rose like a hard fist in his belly. But her face wore an expression of such honest concern that he had to conclude that she was unaware of the insult she had just offered.

"But is that not what I am?" he asked.

"Surely," she replied with a smile, as though happy that he understood his position, "but that is why we are taking you to meeting. So you can unlearn your savage ways."

"Ah, now I do understand," he replied. "That is why I was spared. So I could learn these things. And will you teach me how to obey your God?"

At this, she blushed.

"Go on, now. You know I am not fit to instruct you. It is the mistress and the minister that will do that." She looked again at the clothes.

"I will put them on," he said.

"See that you do. I will leave you now." And to show that she respected his need for privacy, she turned on her heel so hard that she almost lost her balance. She righted herself and hurried back to the house.

Massaquoit knelt beside the clothes. He chose the shirt and pulled it over his head. It stretched tight across his shoulders, and when he breathed he felt it press against his chest. He managed to pull on the breeches over his loin covering, but he decided not to wrestle with the hose. He attempted the shoes, but he could not make his heels fit inside of them. He tossed the shoes aside. Lastly, he put on the sleeveless doublet.

The shirt and the doublet felt like a coil of rope wrapped around his chest. He took a few steps, but he could not swing his legs in his natural gait. They felt heavy even though the breeches were of no greater weight than the deerskin leg coverings he wore in the winter. He squatted beneath the tree to wait. After a few moments, though, he felt the muscles in his thighs and calves tighten, so he stood up. He paced around the tree until he heard the white woman's voice calling to him. She was standing midway between the house and his wigwam. Edward and Phyllis were already on the road. Catherine, too, had on her Sunday gown, of rich, dark blue material, with a cap of the same color.

"Matthew," she called.

He looked at her, but he did not respond.

"Matthew," she tried again.

He squatted.

"Massaquoit," she offered.

He stood up and walked toward her. When he reached her side, she started toward Phyllis and Edward. He followed.

"Magistrate Woolsey is meeting us," she said. "He has brought someone to sit with you." They came abreast of Phyllis and Edward, who was wearing the same clothes he wore to work in the garden. "When we get there," Catherine said, "and I have to address you, I will call you 'Matthew.' You shall respond."

Woolsey was standing in front of the meetinghouse. Next to him was an elderly Indian. The sun was already beating down, but the man was wearing a full beaver hat. A fringe of white hair protruded from beneath the hat and circled his head. He was dressed in a doublet, breeches, and hose, all of which he seemed to wear comfortably. Woolsey stepped between them.

"Matthew, this is Wequashcook. But we call him William, as we are pleased to call you by your new Christian name."

The two Indians nodded at each other.

"William has accepted Our Lord," the magistrate continued. "It is our hope that he can help you do the same. He will sit next to you inside."

Wequashcook motioned for Massaquoit to follow him, and the two walked into the meetinghouse.

"Did you notice anything?" Catherine asked Woolsey, once the Indians were out of hearing.

"Why, no more than that your idea to have William tutor Matthew seems to be off to a very hopeful start."

"They know each other."

"I can't believe," Woolsey replied. "Else would they not have greeted each other before I introduced them?"

"That is exactly the point."

"What is?"

"Their manner of greeting."

"But they did not."

"It is in the way that they did not that I am talking about."

"You have left me far behind, I am afraid. As usual." The magistrate smiled, and then he offered his arm. Catherine took it and they walked into the meetinghouse. She looked to the rear of the building and saw the two Indians sitting together, but there was space for another to fit between them. She wondered, for a moment, what would happen if that rear bench filled, and they were forced to close the distance that they had quite obviously decided to keep between them. Woolsey took his seat on the bench closest to the pulpit, on the side of the meetinghouse where men of his social position sat. Catherine cast one more glance at Matthew and William, who sat like stone, their eyes fixed straight ahead, and then she took her seat, also on the foremost bench, but opposite Woolsey's, on the side where the women of her caste sat.

Massaquoit had nothing to say right now to Wequash-cook. He would have liked to open up even more space between them, but he knew this would be insulting to Wequashcook, who probably was just as uncomfortable with this seating arrangement, and it would also reveal more to the English than he cared to do. Yet he could not compel his body to sit any closer. He occupied himself watching the English fill the meetinghouse.

They came in mostly as families. The better-dressed ones took seats on the benches near the front, the men on Woolsey's side, and the women and children on Catherine's side. Those whose clothes were coarser, or whose hands and features betokened a greater acquaintance with physical labor, sat farther back. The benches immediately in front of Massaquoit were occupied by the few young adults who seemed to be servants. Among these was Phyllis, who sat down directly in front of him. She turned her head and nodded. The expression on her face indicated that she felt it right that he was now in the meetinghouse where he could begin to turn his soul white even if his skin must remain red, and further that she was delighted to have been, in some little way, responsible for his presence. Finally, several Indian women sat on one side of Wequashcook, and an old black man took his place on Massaquoit's side, although he was careful not to sit too close. The Indian women and the black man wore English clothing, but only Wequashcook sported a hat, which he did not remove.

When the congregation was seated, Minister Davis strode in carrying an immense book, which he placed on the finely carved pulpit, its richly polished oak contrasting sharply with the simple, unfinished pine benches. Massaquoit recognized the minister as the one who had held his skullcap over the sputtering matchlock so that the soldier could fire again. Now he saw that same skull-cap sitting arrogantly on the minister's head, and he noted the sharp nose and the closely set eyes, promising himself that he would never forget that face, no matter how many years might pass.

Minister Davis opened his huge Bible and then looked up. He wore spectacles and his eyes struggled to find those sitting on the back bench, and when his glance settled on Massaquoit, he nodded.

"Sitting among us today," he intoned, "is a savage, late a participant in the war recently concluded. We have taken it upon ourselves, to serve God and to offer Him thanks for our victory, to bring this savage to Our Lord. May God speed our efforts and soften his hard heart so that he might receive His word."

Massaquoit felt the eyes of the congregation stare at him, and he set his face into a blank mask. He would not give them the satisfaction of any response. Out of the corner of his eye, he saw Wequashcook looking at him, with just the trace of a smile playing on his thin lips.

He sat through the service as Minister Davis led prayers of thankfulness for the victory in the war, and sought guidance from the English God so that His servants would learn from the recent crisis that their help was only with the Lord, and that they needed to strive to so live according to His teachings that they would not again provoke His anger, for it was their waywardness, no doubt, that had brought the wrath of God down upon them in the form of those hellhounds, the Indians, whose attacks were countenanced by God as fitting retribution for their sins.

Massaquoit sat stunned behind his blank mask, listening to the English wise man offer this explanation for the war, which Massaquoit had seen quite simply as his people's attempt to secure their ancient lands against the encroachment of the English, who seemed determined to spread like the water covering the sands of a beach until his people would be drowned beneath the flood. He found it quite strange, and not a little amusing, that the English now said that because they were bad people, their God had sent him, Massaquoit, and the other Pequot warriors, to remind them of their need to reform their ways.

The English wise man had been speaking directly to the congregation in a voice that rose in volume in proportion to the blackness of the sin he was describing. As far as Massaquoit could tell, this black sin was part of every person's nature. It was an illness for which there was no cure, for the illness was so deeply rooted that it could not be pulled out like a weed can be removed from a garden. He found this concept foreign to his understanding of people, his own, other Indians, or the English themselves.

Minister Davis now paused to look down at the open page of his Bible. His voice affected a sweetness that Massaquoit found disingenuous. He waited for the barb on the smooth shaft.

"Our text today," Davis said, "is from the Acts of the Apostles, where it is written that Our Lord appoints a minister 'to open their eyes, and to turn them from darkness to light, and from the power of Satan unto God, that they may receive forgiveness of sins, and inheritance among them which are sanctified by faith that is in me.'

"Now, then, let us consider the mission of God's ministers, according to His holy Word, for He says that we must 'turn them from darkness to light.' Consider first that those being spoken of are those lost in the hardness of their hearts and in their refusal to accept the grace that is proffered to them. We must turn them so that they may receive their inheritance, turn them from sin to a Christian life.

"And what is this Christian life but one that is sanctified, that is, one that is made holy, by God's free grace that lifts us out of the clutches of Satan, frees us from our love of sin, turns that love of sin into a detestation of its loathsome nature, and trades it for a love of Our Lord and His selfless sacrifice on our behalf.

"Those who are not sanctified, who are not made new creatures, will fall into hell, where they will burn in the fiery furnace for all eternity. There will be no redemption for them, no hope of relief from the flames. They will look back on their lives as the briefest flicker of a candle, which, when it had burned itself out, dropped them into Satan's claws, which even now are clasping and unclasping themselves waiting to rip apart the souls of the reprobates, and for these there is no longer any hope of succor from God, for they have not been sanctified, they have not heeded God's ministers, nor have they listened to God's word, and therefore they are forever doomed to the terrible torments of hell."

Massaquoit listened hard, although his expression did not change. The words again rose and fell as though they themselves were either falling into sin or rising into grace. He was familiar with benign and malevolent spirits. He conceived of Manitou, the spirit of spirits in the skies. And he knew of dozens of individual spirits that informed every aspect of the physical world. He tried to reconcile his Manitou with the English God, and here he found common ground. He attempted to find an analogy for Satin and hell. In these, he failed. He knew that when he died, as all people under the sun and moon, he would travel to the land to the southwest where his spirit would live, as it had in his life, among the spirits of his departed family and friends. There would be no fire, any more than there was in his life now in his fire circle. And as for a tormentor like Satan, the concept simply made no sense to him.

He listened, and he strained to find in the minister's words something that would clarify these foreign concepts. When it became clear that he would hear no such thing, he fixed his eyes steadily on the minister while he permitted his mind to wander where it chose. Seemingly a moment or two later, but in truth closer to an hour after he decided that Master Davis was not going to say anything of interest to him, he felt a sharp nudge in his side. He looked down to see Wequashcook's elbow jabbing him. He stayed the other Indian's arm with his hand. He looked up to see that the English wise man had shut the covers of his great book, and he had his hands clasped in front of him and his eyes closed while his lips moved in silent prayer. After a few moments he snapped his eyes open, smiled at his congregation, and turned on his heel to leave the meetinghouse. He took up a position by the door, and the congregants filed out from their benches in the order of their rank, with those such as Catherine and Woolsey sitting closest to the pulpit leaving first, and then followed by those sitting behind them in a very orderly procession. Massaquoit noted that each English stopped to say a few words to the minister.

He followed Wequashcook down the center aisle and joined the moving queue passing in front of the English wise man. Wequashcook bowed when he stood before the minister.

"A most instructive sermon," he said.

"Thank you," Minister Davis replied, and Wequashcook bowed again before exiting. "And what did you think of your first Sabbath-day service, Matthew?" The minister's voice strove for genuine concern, and he offered a full smile of his yellowed teeth.

"I found it wondrous strange," Massaquoit said.

"And are there points you need explained? I would be happy to offer to do so at a time meet for both of us."

"You are too kind, sir," Massaquoit replied.

"Not at all."

"I will take your words home with me, where I will study them over in my memory."

"I am sure Mistress Williams will also be very willing to explain things to you."

"Then she, too, is too kind," Massaquoit said, and walked out of the meetinghouse.

He found Wequashcook standing by himself outside of the meetinghouse as the English drifted by in family units, exchanging greetings to each other before strolling toward their homes. Catherine and Woolsey stood to one side, far enough away to be out of earshot. Massaquoit concluded that he was supposed to have a private conversation with Wequashcook, Indian to Indian. He decided that he would humor the English. He walked to Wequashcook and put his head close enough so that he could smell the other man's breath. It reeked.

"That is a nice hat you have on," he said in a whisper. He glanced at Catherine and Woolsey. The magistrate smiled at him so as to offer encouragement. But the Englishwoman was not so easily fooled. Her eyes were hard as she stared at him, and he knew that he would have to explain himself to her before very long.

"It is nothing special," Wequashcook replied, also in a low voice.

"It is a hat warm enough for the coldest snows of winter," Massaquoit said. He looked up at the sun now overhead and beating down on them. He wiped a drop of perspiration from his forehead.

"You know very well why I wear it even now."

"Yes," Massaquoit said, "I do. And I hope you remember that I know why."

"Do you think I would forget the man who took half my scalp off?"

"The important thing," Massaquoit replied, "is that it was only half, and that you are here to complain about having to hide your humiliation under a ridiculous hat in the middle of the summer." He nodded and smiled at Woolsey. The magistrate grinned back at him. Catherine shook her head slowly from side to side. Wequashcook put his hand on Massaquoit's shoulders, as though offering a benediction, and he, too, smiled at Woolsey.

"I remember that you did not kill me when you had the chance," Wequashcook frowned, so that the wrinkles on his aged face met to form double and triple lines of tightened flesh. "We are in the English world now. My debt to you for leaving me my life must be settled in our world. And you will not live to see me there unless you do a better job of living in this one."

"We may be in the English world, but we have not changed into English."

Wequashcook smiled, and he lifted his beaver hat just enough to reveal the patch of raw scar tissue on the top of his head.

"I hear," he said, "that there is now a business in scalps. The English will pay, and the French, and maybe even the Dutch. They will all be in the market for Indian scalps." He put his hat back down and placed his palm on Massaquoit's scalp. "And you know, they can't tell the difference between a Pequot, or a Wampanoag, or a Massachusetts, so how will they know whose hair they are buying?"

Massaquoit seized Wequashcook's wrist and held it.

"And how many beads of wampum do you think somebody will pay for mine?"

Wequashcook freed his wrist with a sudden, strong gesture that demonstrated he retained some of the strength that had made him a formidable warrior in his youth. He uttered a quick laugh.

"You. Somebody will feed you to the dogs. Maybe they will want your hair."

Catherine and Woolsey strolled over to the two Indians before Massaquoit had a chance to reply. Wequashcook set his face in an obsequious expression as he addressed the magistrate directly, ignoring Catherine.

"I was just saying to Matthew that he will learn, as I did, how much greater the English God is than our puny spirits."

"Spirits, pshaw!" Woolsey exclaimed. "Devils and incubi, you mean, looking for a teat to suck."

"Yes. I was about to tell him that as well," Wequashcook said.

Woolsey put his hand on Massaquoit's shoulder.

"I trust you will prove to be a good scholar, for I cannot think of a better tutor than one of your own kind, such as William here, who has already profited in great measure from accepting Our Lord."

Massaquoit wanted to slap the magistrate's hand away, and he pressed his lips together to prevent the escape of the words he wished to say. Instead, he simply nodded. He was beginning to understand that the less he said to the English the better off he was. After all, except for the woman, they didn't expect him to have anything to say anyway.

"I am sure William will teach me well," he said.

"Good, good." Woolsey smiled broadly at Catherine. "Things are going just as we had planned," he said.

Phyllis joined Catherine and offered a quick half bow in the direction of the magistrate.

"Come then," Catherine said. "We can talk about how well things have gone on the way home."

"Tell me what you were talking about with William."

They were two-thirds of the way home, and had left the other villagers behind them.

Massaquoit shrugged.

"Wequashcook was telling me about your English God. He was advising me to learn to accept Him, as he had done."

Catherine felt her temper rise at his stubborn insistence on using the forbidden names, but she had a more important concern.

"And what else?"

"We also talked about his hat."

"His hat?"

"Yes."

"It is a marvelous hat."

"That is what I told him. You know, we Indians like to compliment such things."

"And we English are not such fools as you make us out to be," she replied.

"It was a lovely hat," Phyllis said. "But I cannot understand why he wears it in the summer."

Catherine eyed her servant. Sometimes she marveled at her innocence, seeing in her a type of Eve before the fall, totally without guile in herself and unable to see it in others. At other times she simply wondered how she managed to get by from day to day in a world so much more complicated than her own simple nature. She shifted her gaze to Massaquoit, and she could see by the set of his chin that he would offer no more information today.

Waiting on the path to her house, eyes staring anxiously in the direction Catherine would be coming from the meetinghouse, was Sarah Plover. Catherine hastened her steps. She recalled looking in vain for Mercy Plover in her usual place on a bench three rows behind her own, but neither she nor any other member of her family had been there.

"Is it time, then?" she asked.

The girl nodded.

"Mother did not feel well this morning, and then the pains started. Father sent me to fetch you."

"You go back home, then," Catherine said. "I will be right behind you."

FIVE

❧❧❧

MERCY PLOVER WAS a strong woman whose previous three births had presented no particular problem. Catherine, therefore, did not anticipate any difficulty with this delivery, although her years of practice had taught her that one pregnancy was often not a very useful predictor of the next one. Childbirth was part the Lord's mystery and part a natural bodily function. She could only accept God's will, but she could certainly exercise her God-given skill.

"Go into the house," she said to Phyllis, "and gather up the birthing stool, and see if we have any fresh butter, and if we do, bring a goodly slab. I will be in the garden."

"I do know what you need," Phyllis said.

"Then get it," Catherine replied.

She walked quickly through the garden to its farthest edge, where she found the red raspberry bush, burdened now with clusters of small white flowers in anticipation of the fruit soon to emerge. She knelt down in front of the bush and examined the heart-shaped leaves, which grew in groups of three off the main stem of the plant. She turned the leaves over, studying the green top and the whitish, fuzzy underside for pests. She decided on a dozen pest-free leaves, snapped them off, and put them in her pocket.

"You'll be making some tea, then," Phyllis said as Catherine found her standing in front of the garden.

"That I will, if you will be so kind as to boil some water as soon as we arrive. Mercy will want a drink of this to ease her pains."

Phyllis held out a greasy napkin. Catherine opened it and put her nose down to smell the butter.

"It will do," she said. "It is not for the table."

Phyllis lifted the stool and tucked it under her arm. She held out her hand, and Catherine gave her the napkin.

Without waiting for Phyllis, Catherine strode onto the road leading to the Plover house at a pace that belied her plump body and short legs. Phyllis staggered after her, as the weight of the stool in one hand, and the napkin now beginning to ooze butter in the hot sun in the other, made walking at any decent speed difficult.

"Come along now," Catherine called back over her shoulder. "The Lord has decided that Mercy shall deliver today, and His call to her is also His call to us to do what we can to ease her travail."

Phyllis caught up with Catherine, her chest heaving from the effort. Catherine seemed not to notice.

"Do you think Mercy will have a beer for us?" Phyllis managed to say between pants.

"Surely, for herself and for the neighbor women," Catherine replied. "And as we have a drink with those goodwives, I will want to talk with them about Goody Jameson."

*   *   *

Goodman Plover was standing outside his house with his arm around Sarah. The girl's eyes were wide with excitement. Catherine nodded at father and daughter and walked into the house, through the front room that served as kitchen and common area to the room in the back, where she found Mercy sitting on the edge of her bed, her face contorted in pain. Catherine turned to Phyllis, who followed behind. She pointed at a spot on the floor beside the bed, and Phyllis deposited the birthing stool there with a loud sigh.

"Go and send the child for the other goodwives," she said. "But first see to the water for the tea." She put one hand on Mercy's cheek and the other on her belly. She waited until she felt the hard muscle of the uterus contract beneath her palm, and then she stroked Mercy's face from forehead to chin with the other. Mercy bit down hard on her lip and held her teeth there until the pain stopped. When she relaxed her mouth, a drop of blood formed on her lower lip where her front teeth had broken the skin. She ran her tongue over the blood to clean her lip, and then she swallowed.

"I think I'd rather have some groaning beer," Mercy said. "There's some on the table in the kitchen."

"I'll get you some, soon enough," Catherine replied. "But I will also brew you some tea with raspberry leaves, and that will ease your pain considerably more than the beer."

"Ah, but I don't think it will taste so fine," Mercy said.

Catherine smiled, but her eyes remained fixed on Mercy's face, waiting for the change of expression she knew would come before long.

"I've got the terrible toothache," she said.

Mercy nodded. "Do you not have a remedy, then, for yourself?"

"I can make a poultice of hops."

"You could drink the hops as well," Mercy said.

"That I can."

They sat in silence for a few moments, awaiting the next pain. When it came, Mercy stiffened and threw her head back. Catherine leaned over to cradle her until the contraction subsided. Phyllis came in with an earthenware mug, steaming with raspberry tea. Catherine beckoned for her to wait. The contraction stopped and Mercy relaxed. Sweat beaded her forehead. Phyllis handed the mug to Catherine, who pressed it to Mercy's lips. She took a deep swallow.

"It's not the beer," she said.

"You are past wanting that. This will give you greater ease."

Mercy took another swallow, and then she lay back on the bed. She began to breathe more slowly and easily. Catherine stroked her forehead, and Mercy closed her eyes. When the next few contractions came, she tensed for only a moment before relaxing again.

"That's the way," murmured Catherine. "The tea is doing its work, and you can get some rest for the ending when it comes."

Mercy nodded, and her breathing turned to a raspy snore. Catherine waited until she was sure that she was dozing, and then she stood up and stretched. Her body had tensed with each of Mercy's contractions. She had sometimes joked about this phenomenon that her body was as ancient as though it had given birth a hundred times, for all of the labors it had experienced, spasming in sympathetic pains with those of the birthing mothers. She stretched and walked into the kitchen. There she found Phyllis, sitting at one side of the plank table, pouring beer into mugs for Goody Samuels and Goody Richards, who sat on the other side.

Lucinda Samuels was about forty-five, short, plump, and with a large mole on her chin. She lived in the next house. Addy Richards, who had had her first child only two months before, was in her early twenties, tall and slender with a very pretty, triangular face that narrowed to a delicate chin. She lived across the way, a little closer to the Jamesons than the Plovers. Catherine sat down next to Phyllis.

"Are there no more mugs, then?" she asked.

For answer, Phyllis shoved hers toward her.

Catherine lifted the mug to her lips and let the beer flow into her mouth, where she held it before swallowing, tilting her head so that the liquid sat for a while on the troublesome tooth that throbbed in her lower jaw on the left side. She swallowed the beer and ran her finger over her jaw, which felt swollen.

"Have you got the toothache, then?" Lucinda asked.

"A wicked one," Catherine said.

"I try to tell her that she should be aware of Goody Hawkins," Phyllis said. "Her tooth rages whenever that woman is about."

"Then where is she now, I'd like to know?" Catherine replied.

"Hereabouts," Phyllis said.

"Pshaw. Finish your beer and go sit with Mercy."

Phyllis drained her mug and stood up.

"Hereabouts," she repeated.

"There may be something in what that girl says," Lucinda said. "Why, just the other day, I woke up feeling unwell, and when I went out of doors, there she was. She mumbled something in my direction that I could not hear, and I swear I did feel so faint I had to go back to bed."

"And wasn't that where you wanted to be anyway?" Catherine said.

"To be sure," Lucinda replied, "as my husband, John, was out looking for our hog that had strayed away, and there was nobody else in the house to disturb my rest." She offered a cackling laugh that caused a blush to work its way up Addy's face from the tip of her chin to her high cheekbones and then past her forehead until it disappeared under her cap.

"Goody Hawkins was about the night the Jameson babe died," Catherine said.

"I did not see her," Addy said.

"Aye, but I did," Lucinda said. "Didn't she pull at you as you walked by?"

"Maybe she did," Catherine replied.

Lucinda nodded her head.

"Trouble does follow her." She leaned closer so that Catherine could smell the beer on her breath. "But I don't think she had anything to do with that babe dying like it did."

Catherine forced her eyebrows up in surprise.

"What do you mean?"

Lucinda leaned even closer, so that she was in danger of falling into Catherine's lap. Catherine steadied her with her hands on her shoulders.

"And it wasn't that Irish girl, I'll warrant, whatever Henry Jameson said, though that girl was a problem in that household."

"My William worked sometimes helping Henry," Addy said.

"And?" Lucinda demanded.

"William says that Henry worried he had made a mistake in hiring that girl."

Lucinda brought her hand down hard enough to shake the table. Her mug tottered at the edge. Catherine reached across her and righted the mug before it fell.

"That is the very thing I was going to say. That girl with her cross and her prayers mumbled in some strange tongue."

"It wasn't that at all," Addy said. "It was the money he put out for her when he didn't have it to spend, and with business so slow, he was in a terrible way."

"If you ask me," Lucinda said after another deep swallow of her beer, "that lad Ned was part of the girl's problem. I was walking by one day when I happened to look in through the window, and what I saw I should not have seen." She slid her mug toward Catherine. "Have a sip." Catherine shook her head. "As you like," Lucinda said, and downed what was left in her mug. "There is something else about Martha Jameson I must tell you." She stared into her mug, as if just realizing it was empty. She filled it from the pitcher and began to drink.

"You were about to say something about Martha Jameson," Catherine reminded her.

"That I was. What I want you to know, as you were the midwife at the birth and suspicion might alight on your head before long, if it has not already done so, is that I was speaking to Martha Jameson just last month when we were out together gathering strawberries in her garden. I was helping her, you know, because of her belly, she was having trouble bending down to see the red ripe ones."

"Forget the strawberries and get on with it," Catherine said.

"Right. Well, there we were in the strawberries and

Martha puts her hand to her forehead like she was feeling faint, and I get set to try to catch her, but then she just sits down right on a bunch of ripe berries. When she stood up, it looked like she had been bleeding."

"Yes," Catherine said.

"Well, while she was there sitting in the berries, wiping her hand across her brow, she said something I remember. What she said is she could not know how she was going to take care of another child, where she would get the strength, and where they would get the money. She said she was just too tired."

"I sometimes feel that way," Addy said.

"So do we all," Lucinda agreed, "and more and more with each new babe. But there was something more. Martha said it was all very well for Henry to send Ned to sea, but where was she going to send Henry?" She settled back then, looking pleased with herself.

Catherine nodded, careful to appear as if she were considering the other woman's information while concealing her surprise. Just then a groan came from the back room, and Catherine stood up.

"I will be needing you both before long," she said.

"We will wait here as long as we need to and as long as the beer holds out," Lucinda said.

Catherine found Mercy lying tensed on her bed, her head resting on Phyllis's lap, the perspiration beading her forehead and her hands clenched. Phyllis stroked her cheek with one hand and gently squeezed her shoulder with the other.

"Now, now," Phyllis said. "You have done this afore and you will do it now."

Catherine motioned for Phyllis to get up.

"Go get the butter now," she said.

She sat on the edge of the bed. She reached under

Mercy's shift and ran her knowing fingers over her belly. She waited for the contraction, and when it came she pressed her palm down against it to measure its intensity. Her nose told her when Phyllis returned.

"Where did you leave that butter?" she asked.

"On the table."

"In the heat of the sun, no doubt," she said. "Give it here."

Phyllis handed the napkin to Catherine. The grease had oozed completely through the cloth, and the rancid smell caused Catherine to jerk her nose away. Still, she opened the napkin and dipped the fingers of her right hand into the butter, which was near liquid.

"At least I won't have a problem getting it on my hands," she said. With her left hand, she raised Mercy's shift over her knees and bunched it around her hips. Mercy opened her thighs, and Catherine probed with the grease-covered fingers of her right hand into the opening. She felt the babe's head, and she smiled. It was positioned correctly for a smooth descent. Catherine ran her fingers over Mercy's perineum, coating it thickly with the butter. Another contraction elicited a moan from Mercy.

"Are you comfortable?" Catherine asked.

Mercy shook her head, and looked toward the birthing stool that sat next to the bed.

"Call the others in," Catherine said to Phyllis.

"I fear it has stopped moving," Mercy said. "I no longer feel it moving."

"That is natural," Catherine said, although she did not think it so. "Take my arm." She helped Mercy roll onto the floor so that she was kneeling in front of the stool. Lucinda and Addy came into the room. Lucinda took Mercy beneath her right arm, and Addy took the other.

Catherine held Mercy's hands, and then all three lifted. Mercy groaned but settled into a squatting position with her buttocks on the U-shaped seat of the birthing stool. Lucinda and Addy remained at her side, and as the contractions came, now closer and closer together, they squeezed the laboring woman, as though the pressure and the warmth of their bodies could lessen the pain.

Catherine felt for the top of the head until her fingers found it about to push through. She rubbed the stretched skin of Mercy's perineum. A contraction came and Catherine felt the skin tear, just a little, beneath her fingers. She looked down to see if there was much blood, but saw only a couple of drops. Then a tuft of curly black hair appeared.

"Almost there, love," Catherine said. "I can see a little hair."

"Well, that's a relief," Mercy said between clenched teeth. "I was afeard it might be bald, and you know that is bad luck."

"It is indeed," a voice said from the doorway.

Catherine turned to stare at Goody Hawkins, who, unannounced and unbidden, had come to the birthing. Mercy's eyes were closed against the pain of yet another contraction, and Catherine placed her body in front of her to shield her from the visitor. Phyllis was standing next to Goody Hawkins by the doorway, her eyes large with fear. She seemed both eager to throw the old woman out and at the same time anxious to flee her presence. Catherine motioned with her head for Phyllis to remove Goody Hawkins. Phyllis began to shake her head, and then she nodded.

"This way," Phyllis said to Goody Hawkins.

But instead of leaving, Goody Hawkins approached the bed and looked over Catherine's shoulder.

"Aye, a tuft of hair it is, just like the bristles in a hog's nose," she said, her voice breaking into a cackle. "A hog's nose on a babe," she said again. And then she turned sharply to leave the room. She paused beside Phyllis and jabbed her forefingers at her.

"Just like a hog, didn't I say so?" she demanded. And then she was gone.

"Who was that?" Mercy asked, her eyes now open and looking toward the door.

"It was just me," Phyllis said. "I thought I saw a hog rooting about your garden."

"Silly girl," Mercy said, "at a time like this." Her mouth tightened again.

"Push now," Catherine said.

For answer, Mercy groaned and leaned forward so hard that both Lucinda and Addy staggered. They regained their balance and held Mercy as she strained. Her thighs tensed and she leaned forward until her knees touched the floor. The head of the babe crowned.

"Again," Catherine said.

Mercy's face was red. She breathed deep and pushed. The babe dropped into Catherine's hands, but it did not come all the way out. Instead, it stopped halfway, with both its shoulders out, but it would come no farther. Its umbilical cord was wrapped around its neck. It was blue, and it was not breathing.

Catherine cupped the babe's head with her palms and pulled gently. It dropped another couple of inches but stopped. She tried to force her hand between the cord and the neck to relieve the pressure, but the cord was wrapped too tightly. Mercy rolled her eyes back into her head and gasped.

"Oh, sweet Lord, it hurts," she said. "Pull it out. Any way you can, or I will die."

Catherine slid her hand over the babe's shoulder and into the birth canal. Her fingers found the cord inside Mercy and pulled. The babe inched out, but it turned as the cord acted as a tether on which the body rotated. One shoulder now presented itself in the front while the other caught in the back. Another contraction came, and as Mercy pushed and Catherine tugged, the rear shoulder tore the flesh and blood spouted. Catherine reached to that rear shoulder and tried to turn it. But as she turned, the umbilical cord tightened more around the babe's neck, so she had to let it revert to its previous position. She took a deep breath.

"Close your eyes and open your mouth in prayer," she said to Mercy. "I am going to take the babe."

Mercy nodded.

"Please. Do it now, or I die."

"When I pull," Catherine said to Lucinda and Addy, "you hold her tight." She wiped the butter on her hand off on her gown, and then steadied both hands on the babe's shoulders and started to pull. The babe slid five or six inches farther out and no more. Catherine knew that if she forced the issue, she might rip the placenta and cause a massive hemorrhage.

Mercy bit down hard on her lip until the blood flowed freely down her chin, and then, unable to keep the howl building within her contained, she opened her mouth and screamed her agony.

"Hold on," Catherine said. "Just a little longer."

She reached again for the rear shoulder that blocked the babe's movement.

"I must needs do this," she said, and the women nodded.

She pulled hard on the tiny shoulder until the scapula cracked with a discernible snap. Catherine placed her hands on either side of the babe's head and forced it back into Mercy's womb. It slid up, its passage now cleared by the collapsed shoulder. Sweat beaded on Catherine's forehead, and Phyllis leaned over with a rag to wipe it away.

"Never mind that," Catherine said. Mercy's moans had settled into a continuous, low wail. Catherine, her hands around the babe's head and in Mercy's womb, rotated the head. She felt an ear now parallel to each of Mercy's legs.

"Now push," she said. "For your life."

Addy and Lucinda braced themselves and Mercy pushed until she seemed about to rise off the stool. Catherine felt the babe's head start downward and she guided it gently. She pulled her hands out and the head followed. The babe now slid out, and as it did, Catherine unwrapped the cord from about its neck. Catherine kept her eyes on the babe, searching for breath, which she did not see. Mercy collapsed into Lucinda's arms.

Catherine squeezed the babe's nostrils and opened its mouth with two fingers. She slapped its back softly, once, and nothing happened, slapped again, and then the babe's mouth snapped open and it howled.

"It breathes," Catherine said.

Mercy looked up from Lucinda's embrace and opened her blood-streaked lips in a grin.

"That is good," she said.

Catherine sensed somebody looking in, and she turned about to command Goody Hawkins, again, to be gone. But at the door was little Sarah, who stood with her hand in front of her mouth, staring at her mother. Catherine followed the child's eyes to where her glance rested on the puddle of blood on the floor in front of the birth stool.

"She needs to rest," Catherine said. "That is all."

• • •

Mercy lay asleep. She had lost more blood expelling the afterbirth. Her breathing was labored, and Catherine feared for her. She took the swaddled babe to Addy.

"It will be some time before she wakes, poor thing. The babe will be hungry before then. Can you give it suck for a bit?"

Addy nodded and unbuttoned her gown. The babe opened its eyes and cried. Addy held it to her breast, and the babe fastened on her nipple. Addy let it drink for five minutes, and then switched it to the other breast. When she pulled the babe away, it cried for a moment and then shut its eyes in sleep.

"Mine own is very hungry," Addy said.

Catherine took the babe from her.

"You have done enough. Mercy has never had trouble with her milk."

Catherine walked into the front room of the little house. Josiah Plover and Sarah sat at the table. Two smaller children, a boy and a girl, played beneath the table.

"Well, then?" Josiah said.

"Mercy sleeps. It was not easy, but your baby girl is alive."

Catherine saw the quick expression of disappointment on Josiah's face, but he said nothing. He extended his arms and took the babe from Catherine. He lifted the swaddling to examine his child. Beneath the swaddling, the babe was wrapped in a cloth that held its left arm tight to its side. Josiah placed his large, callused forefinger on the bound arm and lifted his eyes to Catherine.

"I said it was not easy. The shoulder will heal."

Josiah nodded.

"I saw that evil woman here where she was not wanted."

Catherine shook her head.

"Goody Hawkins is what she is, but she had nothing to do with this babe, or its difficulties in being born."

Josiah shrugged.

"That be what you say," he said.

"It is," Catherine replied.

Josiah handed the babe back to Catherine.

"I'll be getting back to work, then," he said, and stood up. Without another glance at his child, he walked to the door. There he paused long enough to motion to Sarah. "Come along," he said to his oldest daughter.

"Shouldn't I stay to help mother?" Sarah asked.

He motioned more emphatically with his arm.

"There's other grown women here to do that," he said. "And I have need of you."

Sarah looked at Catherine.

"Go with your father," she said. "We will tend to your mother."

"There was so much of her blood on the floor," the girl said.

"Yes. But that is what happens sometimes. Now go along with you."

The girl left with her father, and Catherine sat down for a moment alone at the table. She had done all that she could, and now the matter was in God's hands. Addy sat down next to her.

"What do you think?" she asked.

Catherine shrugged.

"I am hopeful," she said.

Lucinda came in.

"They are asleep, mother and babe. Phyllis said she would sit by them."

Addy brought her hands up to her breasts.

"The babe is strong. I can vouch for that."

"Strong, do you say?" Lucinda said. She reached for the pitcher of beer and shook it. "Still a little left." She poured herself a mug and took a drink. "Strong. And so was the Jameson babe, I warrant."

"It was," Catherine said.

Lucinda's face turned red and she brought her hand to her mouth just as her breath exploded in a beer-laden belch.

"Look to that lad Ned, I say. And remember what Martha said about her husband. There you will find something, I daresay."

Addy put her arm around Lucinda.

"Come, then," she said, "it is time to go home." She looked at Catherine.

"That it is, for you two," Catherine said. "I will bide here."

Mercy stirred and Catherine roused herself from the stool where she had been sitting for the past several hours after Lucinda and Addy had gone home. Phyllis was sitting on the edge of the bed, her eyes closed.

"She wakes," Catherine said, and Phyllis opened her eyes.

"Why, her face is as white as her bedclothes," she said.

"Lift her shift," Catherine said.

The cloth between Mercy's legs was dark red, with only a couple of splotches of bright, fresh blood. Catherine removed it, and replaced it with another cloth soaked in comfrey that she had prepared. Mercy's eyes opened for a moment and then shut again.

"I've sent for Master Davis," Josiah said from the

doorway. "You can go home now, as soon as I pay you. You have done what you can." He spoke in a tired monotone, but Catherine heard the suspicion that edged his tone.

"I can stay," she said. "She may start to bleed again."

"Master Davis is coming. We will pray." He handed her a couple of coins, which Catherine put into her pocket without looking. "Thank you," he said.

SIX

❧❧❧

CATHERINE COULD NOT permit herself to sleep that
night. She had convinced herself that as long as she
could hear herself breathing, Mercy Plover would also be
drawing breath. She reviewed the birth again and again
but could not think of anything she might have done otherwise. So she lay still in bed watching the sunrise. Not
long after, she saw Magistrate Woolsey walking up the
path toward the house. She roused herself and pulled on
her gown, expecting any minute to hear a knock on the
door, but the only sound that came to her window was the
piercing, high call of a cedar waxwing, reaching her from
the wild cherry tree just beyond her garden where the bird
was breakfasting on overripe fruit. She looked out and
saw that the magistrate had stopped abreast of Massaquoit's wigwam, and stood standing there as if trying to
come to some conclusion about the structure. Then he resumed his measured pace toward the house.

She knew that Woolsey would announce his presence
as he usually did, with three sharp raps, evenly spaced,
with pauses of a second between each, of the knob of his

cane on the door. By the time the first knock came, she was already on the stairs. She had her hand on the latch as the door shook for the third time. She swung the door open and there was the magistrate standing with his cane still raised and his eyes full of surprise.

"I saw you coming up the walk," Catherine said.

"But—" he began.

"I could not sleep," she said.

Understanding registered slowly on his face, first smoothing the furrows in his brow and then sliding down to widen his lips into a knowing smile.

"I hear Goody Plover was delivered of a girl child yesterday, with your usual excellent assistance," he said.

"Yes, but Mercy is in my prayers. I am about to go back there to see how she is."

"I need to talk with you, then, for just a moment. I can walk with you, if you like."

"Yes. I must go to her right away."

"Is Mercy not well, then?" he asked as he struggled to accelerate from his accustomed, stately gait to match Catherine's hurried stride.

"I know not if she survived the night. Perhaps I should have stayed by her, but Josiah insisted I go home. He said he and his children could tend to his wife."

"And the babe?"

"Fine. Now, what is it that brought you so early to my house?"

"Something concerning the Jamesons."

"Yes?"

"They have charged the servant girl with killing their babe. There is to be a hearing tomorrow. Before me and Governor Peters."

"I must be there, then," Catherine said.

"But Mercy?"

"If she lives, I must be with her as well."

"But you cannot be there and here at the same time."

Catherine stopped and looked hard at the magistrate.

"You should know, Joseph, that I can always do what must be done."

Minister Davis was standing in front of the Plovers' house as they arrived, and Catherine felt her heart tighten. Woolsey took her arm.

"Wait here," he said. "I will just go ahead and inquire."

Catherine pulled her arm free from the magistrate's weak grasp.

"I can do that as well as you, and it is my place, more than yours."

Master Davis turned toward them. He was standing in the morning sun, and sweat had plastered the wisps of white hair protruding from beneath his skullcap against his cheeks. Catherine tried to read his face, but it wore, as it always did, no matter if the occasion be birth, death, wedding, or funeral, its ministerial mask, its grave expression, stating to the community that God was represented in his person. It was the look he had had on his face when he sheltered the soldier's musket from the rain, and it had softened only for a moment then when he had let the rain splash against his flesh, and for that brief second, Catherine recalled now, he had almost seemed like an ordinary man. His customary expression, though, announced that human grief or joy were both but misunderstandings of God's purpose, which was to be accepted on faith as right, no matter what the circumstance. The minister nodded at Catherine and then turned back to Josiah.

"Remember," he said, " 'for whom the Lord loveth he chasteneth, and scourgeth every son whom he receiveth.' Hebrews, 12:6. He shows His love most when he afflicts us most harshly."

Woolsey caught up to Catherine.

"How goes it with your wife, Josiah?" he asked.

Catherine steeled herself for the answer.

"As Master Davis says, the Lord's will be done."

"We have prayed over her all night," Master Davis said. "And we will continue so."

Catherine let her breath out and sighed.

"I must go in to her," she said.

"Do you intend to help us pray, mistress?" Master Davis asked. He placed himself between Catherine and the door.

"Did not Our Lord send his disciples to heal the sick?"

"Are you then a disciple?" the minister asked.

Catherine pressed close to him, so that their bodies almost touched. She stared hard into his eyes until he turned away and withdrew just enough to let her pass into the house.

She stopped in the doorway and turned back to him.

"You do remember what happened when Pharaoh ordered Shiprah and Puah, the Hebrew midwives, to kill the sons of the Hebrew women?"

Minister Davis did not respond. Some expression behind his mask struggled to emerge, but Catherine was not sure whether it was one of anger or embarrassment.

"The midwives feared God more than the pharaoh, and so they did not do as they had been commanded. 'Therefore God dealt well with the midwives.' Genesis 1:20. I do God's work," she said, and walked into the house.

"You will not find a baby Moses inside, I warrant," Minister Davis called after her.

Catherine did find the infant girl sleeping in the cradle at the foot of Mercy's bed. Sarah rocked the cradle with the toe of her foot while her eyes remained fixed on the uneven movements of her mother's chest. Catherine squeezed the child's arm and then sat down on the bed. Mercy's complexion was still frighteningly pale, but her breathing was easy. Catherine ran her hands over Mercy's forehead, which felt cool, and then under her shift over her belly and onto the comfrey poultice, which was still in place from last night.

"Will my mother live?" Sarah asked.

"She is a strong woman," Catherine replied. "I have every hope for her."

"Master Davis prayed all night," Sarah said, "and I have been praying, too, except for the few minutes that I fell asleep. I tried so hard to stay awake so I could keep praying."

"I am sure God hears you," Catherine replied. She took a small vial out of her pocket. "Give your mother as much of this as she can swallow at once," she said.

"What is that?" Minister Davis's deep voice filled the room.

"Just a syrup of licorice root."

The minister opened the large Bible he had been carrying and leafed through the pages until he found the psalm he wanted.

" 'God is our refuge and our strength,' " he intoned, and Catherine found her lips shaping the words along with him. Sarah repeated, too, but a half beat behind, her face contorted in concentration. Minister Davis looked up at her, and then slowed down so she would be able to follow more easily.

Catherine bowed her head, eyes closed, until she could no longer hear his mellifluous tones. She held Mercy's hand and let her thoughts find their own path to her God, to thank Him for Mercy's life. After a while she heard the covers of the great Bible shut, but she continued her private meditation while the minister walked out of the room.

Massaquoit had sensed the presence of somebody outside of his wigwam, and so he had sat still. He felt vulnerable without a weapon, and he tensed for a charge against the intruder. Then the stale smell of an old man's perspiration wafted to his nostrils, and he relaxed a little. Even unarmed, he was not afraid of an ancient white man. The smell weakened after a few moments, and then he heard the slow dragging of the man's shoes in the dirt as he walked, without completely lifting his feet off the ground, toward the house. He heard the knock of the cane against the door, and then Catherine's voice followed by one he recognized as belonging to the white man who had been on the ship, the same man who had also introduced him to Wequashcook. Although he believed the man meant him no harm, he kept himself hidden until they left.

When he was sure they were gone, he crawled out of his wigwam. The house was quiet, but a rhythmic thudding came from the garden, where he saw Edward bringing a hoe down between the young stalks of corn. He walked over and watched. Edward glanced up when he felt Massaquoit's eyes, and his fingers tightened around the shaft of the hoe, but he said nothing.

"Your mistress says that I should help you," he said.

"I did not hear her say such a thing," Edward replied, and then he brought the hoe down with unexpected vigor. He grunted as the hoe dug into dirt mere inches from Massaquoit's feet. Massaquoit understood the gesture and stepped back.

"Yet that is what she says."

"I need no help."

Massaquoit knelt down next to a cornstalk. Its green

color was tinged with yellow, and he judged that by this time of the summer it should have been both more vibrant and maybe twice as high.

"Next time you plant, you should bury dead fish in the hole with the seed."

Edward now looked up and stared at Massaquoit, his face beaded with sweat. He swiped at the perspiration gathered in the corner of his eye.

"And then I suppose I should drop a fishing line in the ocean and catch a loaf of corn bread." He did not wait for Massaquoit to answer. Instead, he swung around, the hoe on his shoulder, and walked to the far end of the row of corn, muttering and snickering beneath his breath. Once he was as distant from Massaquoit as he could be, while yet remaining in the garden, he resumed his attack on the weeds, bringing his hoe down with renewed energy, as if to forestall any possibility of continuing the unwanted conversation.

Massaquoit returned to his wigwam and squatted in the entranceway. He peered in and saw the pile of English clothes lying where he had discarded them in the far corner. The sun beat down on his back and felt good. The English clothes made him sweat without exposing his flesh to the sun. And then the sweat pooled where his flesh creased beneath the heavy cloth. He had decided that he would wear these clothes only when he had to, and today was not one of those times. He knew Edward did not care, and he was going into the woods where he did not expect to meet any other English, for he had a very different kind of appointment to keep.

Half an hour later he sat on an overturned log in a clump of birch and pine trees on the edge of the beach where he had landed in Catherine's custody a few days before. He had taken note of this clump of trees at that time, as a place where he might be able to have a private conversation with his comrades' spirits, which still hovered above the waters where they had drowned. He wanted them to know that he had not forgotten them, and that he would figure out a way to take vengeance. He listened to the waves roil and swirl against the rocks that lined the shore, and he felt the breeze lift the perspiration from his flesh. He knew that the man he had come to meet was watching him from behind a pine tree not twenty feet away. He nodded in that direction.

Wequashcook emerged from behind the tree and sat down on the far end of the log. He was dressed in doublet, breeches, and hose, as he had been the day of the service. His forehead glistened beneath the heavy beaver hat. He removed the hat and placed it on the ground between his feet. He ran his hand over the crown of his head, where the flesh was still raw from its imperfect healing.

"Not so long ago," he said, "when I put my fingers to this place on my head, they touched bone."

"Yes, and that is because my tomahawk lifted the skin off there. And that you are sitting here today, feeling your wound, is only because my hand respected your kinship with my wife, even though that reason alone should have driven my blade down through your head without stopping until it cut out your heart."

"I did not know the English would do what they did."

"Even if I believe that, you should not have trusted them when your brother's daughter and her son were sleeping in that fort."

"I did not know they were there."

"For a man who prides himself on his wisdom, you seem to know very little."

Wequashcook shrugged, the color full in his cheeks, either from the sun or the memory of his betrayal.

"But I speak the truth."

Massaquoit permitted himself a bitter little chortle.

"It does not matter now. I am glad that I did not kill you. You can be of some use to me."

"Do you want me to explain the English God to you?" Wequashcook asked, with just the trace of a smile on his thin lips.

"I want you to get me a boat, one sturdy enough to sail across the waters to the land they call the fish island."

"And where am I supposed to find this canoe?"

Massaquoit stood up. He towered over the older man.

"I will want it hidden here, in these trees. Do not take long. No more than—what do the English say? A fortnight at most."

Wequashcook reached down and picked up his beaver hat. He balanced it on his knee.

"You are right to use the English words, because I am now English."

Massaquoit seized Wequashcook's wrist and held his hand up next to his own.

"You do not have English skin any more than I do."

Wequashcook pointed to his forehead with his free hand.

"No, but I am English here. And if you will be wise, you will learn to be English in your head as I have."

"The English have killed my wife, and my son, and my comrades."

"That is why you must become English."

Massaquoit threw the other's hand down.

"They do not think of you as one of their own. There will come a time when they will remember that you are

an Indian, and they will do with you what they have done
with all Indians."

Wequashcook shrugged.

"I do not say you are wrong. Only that I do not see a
better path." He stood up, and with a sudden motion, he
drew a knife from a sheath hidden beneath his doublet.
He pressed the blade against Massaquoit's neck, and then
he moved it up to his scalp.

"The English like to trade. Sometimes they trade trin-
kets for furs, and sometimes they trade pots and pans,
which we cannot make, for our money, our wampum, and
then they trade the wampum for furs. And sometimes
they are not so interested in animal hair, but the hair that
grows on the head of those they think are their enemies."
He pushed the blade of the knife against Massaquoit's
flesh with one hand while with the other he grabbed a
handful of hair. "Someday, and I don't think it will be
very long now, the English will pay me for your head."

Massaquoit had stood silently, knowing that these
words were merely taunts and not preludes to action.
Now he took Wequashcook's wrist again in his hand and
squeezed hard enough to convince the other to drop the
knife. He picked it up, tested the blade with his thumb,
and then handed it back to Wequashcook.

"I do not think you would dare betray me a second
time."

"No," Wequashcook agreed, "I would not, at least not
until you had so betrayed yourself that I would have no
choice. I will get you your boat. That, and the wound on
my head, will be payment for guiding the English to the
fort where your wife and child were killed by them. I
freely admit my guilt in that. But it is also true that they
lied to me. They said they would surround the fort and request a surrender. I had gone along to negotiate that sur-

render. I was trying to prevent exactly what happened there."

"That is a fine story," Massaquoit said, but then he remembered how he and his comrades had surrendered on a promise of their lives being spared, and how they had been tossed into the sea one by one. "It may be the English lied to you, as it may be you are lying to me now."

Wequashcook shrugged.

"You must choose who you will believe."

"I choose," Massaquoit said, "to believe nobody."

SEVEN

❧❧❧

T HE MEETINGHOUSE WAS crowded. The building held, it seemed, every man, woman, and child from New-bury, and possibly a number from the neighboring vil-lages. All were there to hear the Irish servant girl accused of murdering the newborn infant of Martha and Henry Jameson.

A table had been dragged in front of the pulpit, and be-hind it sat Governor Peters and Magistrate Woolsey. Both of them wore their full dress ruffs, as if to assert their privilege under the sumptuary laws to wear elaborate clothes forbidden to the lesser citizens. The air hung hot, and both men sweated heavily. Woolsey fanned himself with his fine leather gloves while the governor just glared through the beads of perspiration that dripped into his eyes. In front of each on the table were paper, ink, and quill to take notes of the testimony presented to them.

As if by habit, the people of Newbury had seated them-selves on the benches in the same order required for Sunday church service. Catherine, therefore, found her accustomed seat in the front row. Woolsey nodded at her, but his brows were furrowed with worry. Catherine had already confided in him her firm belief the girl might be guilty of a number of indiscretions and acts stemming from naïveté, but she was not a murderer. Woolsey's worried expression told Catherine that he had reason to believe that her guilt had already been established in the mind of his colleague the governor, a man known for his stern temperament and quick, if not always sound, judgment.

Seated on a bench that had been pulled up close to the magistrates' table were the Jamesons, Henry, Martha, Ned, and Ann, the oldest daughter, who seemed always to be at her mother's side. Catherine was not surprised to see the adult Jamesons, since they were going to accuse Margaret. But sitting next to them was Matthew Drake, and Catherine could only wonder what he might have to say in these proceedings. There was always something in his manner that told Catherine that he could not be trusted, that he could be bought. She could only guess at the nature of the bargain he had made.

Margaret sat alone on a stool directly in front of the magistrates. She looked steadfastly down at her feet. Catherine heard a barely audible clacking sound. She leaned forward and saw that the girl's lips were moving in silent prayer as her fingers counted the wooden beads of her rosary. She wanted to tell the girl that this act of Catholic devotion would not sit well with her Puritan accusers, but there was no way to communicate with her just now, and in any case, the girl looked as if she needed the comfort provided by the beads.

Governor Davis cleared his throat until Margaret looked up. When she did, he motioned her to stand. Then he looked toward the Jamesons, and Henry Jameson also got to his feet.

"Margaret Mary Donovan," he said, pausing between her first and second names, a combination common enough to her native Ireland, but quite exotic in Newbury, where single given names, usually biblical, were much more common, and where "Mary" still recalled "Bloody" Queen Mary, the bitter persecutor of the Puritans in old England before the more tolerant Elizabeth, and thus was not a name often bestowed on the grandchildren of those Puritans who had suffered under the Catholic queen. "You stand accused of infanticide, of willfully killing the babe, recently born to Henry and Martha Jameson, left in your charge. This proceeding is a hearing to determine whether sufficient evidence can be offered to justify trying you on this charge." He motioned for her to sit down. "We will first hear the statements of those who accuse you. Then you can answer as you like."

Henry offered a quick bow of his head toward the magistrates, and then he raised his arm to point at Margaret.

"That one was a maidservant in my house these past six months. I bought her time from a settler since gone back to England, who did not find our climate hospitable, and as my Martha was pregnant and I thought to provide her some help, I took the chance to take this girl into my house and to trust her with my family. If I had known the blackness of her heart, I would never have done so."

"Yes," the governor interrupted, "but we need to hear the specific act you accuse her of."

"Why," Henry said, "she murdered our babe. That is what I accuse her of doing. And I can tell you all you need to know about that."

"Then please do," Governor Peters said, and he settled back to listen.

"Why, then, as Your Honor pleases," Henry said. "The

girl using the black arts of her papist religion killed our babe."

The governor's face tightened in frustration.

"What *exactly* did she do?"

"My wife, newly delivered of the babe, was too exhausted to tend to it, and so she left it in the care of the girl, which was right and proper of her to do. And the girl mumbled strange words over the babe."

"Do you mean to say," Governor Peters said, "that the girl's words killed your child?"

"I can only tell you what I did see. My wife had fallen asleep after she gave the babe to the girl, and when I came into the room from outside, where I had set my nephew to work sharpening our ax to chop wood with less effort, I see the girl kneeling over the babe, and she has a pitcher of water in one hand that is dripping onto the babe, and she is saying these words, Latin words from the papist mass or something akin to that, calling Satan, I wouldn't doubt she was, and when I took the babe from her, she looked at me with eyes that was rolling back into her head, and the words kept coming out of her even though her lips did not move anymore. And my babe was not breathing. I put my ear to its little chest, and I could not hear its heart, which had been beating strong as you please that very morning." He paused for breath, and then he pointed at the girl. "That is what I saw."

Catherine listened to Henry's accusation, wishing that she could question his odd story. As she could not, she hoped Woolsey would. She fixed her eyes on him, intending to will that placid man into action. He had listened to Henry without any visible change of expression. As Henry finished his statement, punctuated with the flourish of his gesturing at Margaret, an audible gasp rose from the audience, and Catherine reminded herself that many of these people had been in attendance in front of the Jameson house when Margaret was put to trial by touch. As if reminding himself of that moment at the same time that Catherine thought of it, Henry now shook his outstretched hand at Margaret.

"Yes, you saw the proof, many of you did. We put her to the test. And where her fingers touched our poor babe's body, still warm it was, it bled. You who were there saw the babe bleed under her hands!"

The gasp rising to the rafters of the meetinghouse now seemed to gather itself into an angry swell as it swirled around the heavy air and focused on Margaret's bowed head. The sound intensified until Margaret stood up and turned to face her accusers. Her face pale, and her chest heaving, she brought her hand down from her forehead and then from shoulder to shoulder in the sign of the cross.

"By the blessed Virgin, I swear I did not harm that babe," she said.

But the gesture and her words only inflamed the people, and instead of a hostile murmuring, there were now words of hate hurled in her direction.

"Listen to her," one said. "She convicts herself with her own words."

"She makes the sign of the papist," said another, "and it is a call to the wicked one, well we know."

"We have heard enough," cried out a third.

Woolsey's face reddened as the voices in the meetinghouse rose to a chaotic crescendo, and he cleared his throat repeatedly, intending to quell the boisterous crowd. Finally, he rose to his feet and pounded on the table with his fist. When even that noise failed to quiet the audience, he walked over to Henry, who still stood pointing at Margaret. Woolsey seized the accusing arm and lowered it to

Henry's side. This gesture silenced the crowd. Woolsey then returned to his place behind the table.

"Now, Jameson," he said, "let me understand what you are saying."

"Let us hear how the girl answers the charge," came a voice from the middle of the crowd. Catherine saw that it came from the pox-marked sailor, the one who had cried out several times in front of the Jameson house that night when Henry stood there holding his dead child in his arms.

Woolsey glanced in the direction from which the voice came, but ignored the request. Instead, he turned back to Henry. "Are you saying that the girl drowned your babe, or that she caused it to stop breathing by uttering a malediction?"

Henry nodded.

"Which did she do?" Woolsey demanded.

Henry shrugged.

"She did both, and the babe died. Maybe something else while I was out chopping wood. That is all I can tell you."

Governor Peters nudged Woolsey and whispered something in his ear. Woolsey nodded.

"Now, Goody Jameson," Woolsey said, "can you add anything to what your husband has just told us?"

Martha did not respond. She looked at the magistrates as though she did not understand the question. Her eyes appeared glazed. She rubbed the back of her hand across them, and they focused, narrowing into a bright accusatory stare as though she now saw her enemies.

"My babe is dead," she said.

"Yes," Woolsey encouraged in gentle tones, "but how came him to be dead?"

Martha nodded her head vigorously.

"We buried him, we did, as soon as you gave him back to us."

"Can you not tell us anything further about your servant girl?"

Martha turned sharply for a moment toward Margaret and then snapped her head back as though unable to look at her servant.

"No," she said. "I cannot."

Ann took her hand, and Martha sat back down. Henry took his seat next to her, stroking her arm. She did not seem to notice him.

The building was silent. Nobody seemed to be sure what to do or say next. In the lull, Catherine gathered herself, rose, and went forward to stand next to Margaret. She had considered the significance of this gesture, knew that it would bring the opprobrium of her neighbors down on her head, and still felt she must do it.

"I would like to tell the court what I know."

"Mistress Williams," Governor Peters said, "we know you were there when the babe was born, but not when it died. Is that not right?"

"Yes," Catherine replied. "But how the babe was at birth is important."

"In due time," the governor said, "we will hear what you wish to tell us."

"Do you only want to hear from the Jamesons, then?" Catherine demanded.

"Catherine," Woolsey soothed, "we will hear you out fully."

Catherine squeezed Margaret's arm, and the girl looked up. Her eyes were full of an unspeakable fear.

"Take your seat, Mistress Williams, if you please," Governor Peters said.

Catherine released Margaret's arm and sat down.

Ned now rose to speak. Catherine recalled how strangely he had been acting since the babe was born, picking a fight with the much-stronger Massaquoit and then turning savagely on Margaret when Catherine now had reason to believe that two young people had either been lovers or that Ned had forced his attentions on the girl. In either case, Catherine now feared that what Ned would say might provoke another outburst from Margaret. If she held up her beads or made the sign of the cross one more time, this pious congregation would condemn her without the need for further testimony.

Ned glanced at Henry, who nodded, and then he began.

"I cannot say I saw her harm the babe. I was not in my uncle's house at that precise moment, as I had just finished sharpening the ax and chopping wood when I entered the house and saw her sitting in a corner mumbling her curses and making those strange signs across her body as just she did when she forgot herself and where she was. For most of the time she did these things when she thought she would not be observed, but I have a keen eye, I do, and a keener nose to smell out Satan-serving papists wherever they may be, and one of them she is as surely as I am standing here before you."

"Do you not pray yourself?" The question came from Margaret, who had finally roused herself, realizing that nobody else in that building would, or could, help her. Her eyes had lost their panicked look as they focused on Ned, and now held the expression of a soul fighting for its survival against terrible odds. "Do you not pray, both in private, as I have seen many of you do, or in public, as I have seen you all do, in those meetings you force me to attend even against my conscience and the religion I was raised in?"

"Aye," Ned answered, something approaching a smirk

on his face, "but we pray to Our Lord in a proper way, and not the way such as you do. I have seen you. I have seen you with your beads, counting them like they were the very thirty pieces of silver that is mentioned in the Bible."

"Your tongue is running away from your thought," Governor Peters interrupted in a dry tone.

"Yes, that it is," Ned said, but still he smiled.

Woolsey raised his hand, palm out toward Ned, as a way of announcing the significance of his next questions, as though Ned's words would float to his outstretched hand, where he could weigh their credibility and relevance.

"Now, Ned, tell us this. Did you see Margaret Mary Donovan harm the babe?"

Ned's face reddened, and it looked as though he was about to offer an inappropriate rejoinder, such as he might give a slow-witted companion. But the magistrate was not his companion, and he restrained the impulse.

"No."

"Because you were not in your house at the time, isn't that so?" Woolsey continued.

"Yes."

"What you did see was that she was praying, in her fashion, after the babe was dead?"

"Yes," Ned said, "after her heathenish fashion."

"You are merely establishing a pattern of popish prayers, using dumb pieces of wood, as though they could carry the words to God's ear. Is that not so?" Governor Peters asked, and Ned's face again relaxed into a grin.

"I don't know what she hoped to do with those beads, but she did speak to them."

"That is not it at all," Margaret said. "It's the counting

of my prayers I do with my beads, my paternosters and
aves."

"Why, if it is counting you are after, you have ten fingers and ten toes," Ned replied.

A ripple of laughter began in the front rows, closest to
Ned, and as Margaret's face darkened, in shame and
anger, the ripple grew until it rolled to the very back rows
and then filled the hot, moist air of the building with an
explosion of derisive mirth, which hung suspended for a
moment and then dissolved into the ongoing murmur of
hostility. Margaret, however, had now so lost her original
trepidation that the waves of derision seemed only to
strengthen her courage. She waved her rosary above her
head, holding it by a small cross on one end. The wooden
beads clicked in the suddenly silent building.

"Since I've come to this forsaken land, you have not
permitted me Holy Communion, keeping the wafer and
the wine only for yourselves while I sit on the back bench
compelled to listen to your blasphemy, nor has there been
a priest to hear my confession, so if I was to die I would
die heavy with my sin, and you call yourselves good
Christians after all!" She clasped the rosary over her head
in both hands. "With this, I can still offer my devotions to
my God as I was taught to do as a little girl."

The murmur again intensified, now into a roar, until
both Governor Peters and Magistrate Woolsey struggled
to their feet in haste to quell the angry energy of the
townspeople of Newbury, whose patience with this igno-
rant immigrant girl from that benighted country of Ireland had now reached its limit.

"I say quiet," Governor Peters said, and Woolsey
added his voice, but to no effect. Then Master Davis, who
all this time had sat with his head in his hands in the first
row of benches, arose and walked past the table to his

usual place at the pulpit, and as he ascended the three steps that led to the small platform that elevated him above the stanchion supporting the great Bible, the crowd's noise subsided. He waited until everyone's eyes were on him before he said a word.

"We are to hear evidence of a crime committed by this girl, and not to argue theology with such as her. She is in error in these matters, of course, and she will be corrected, whether she is allowed to continue peacefully among us, or whether she awaits the gallows. And it will be my office to offer that correction for the better hope of her immortal soul." He turned to Margaret. "As a first step in your education into becoming a proper Christian, I will need to have your beads."

"No," Margaret shrieked, and she clutched her rosary to her breast.

"Constable," Governor Peters said, and a sturdy young man of about twenty-five approached Margaret. "Take them from her."

Margaret turned as though to run, her eyes now white and starting. Catherine hurried to the girl's side. She hugged her to her chest.

"You must give them to me," she whispered. "I will hold them safely for you and get them back to you."

Margaret nodded dumbly.

"Will it suffice if I take the beads from her?" Catherine asked.

"Yes," Woolsey said before Peters could deny such a reasonable request.

Margaret handed the rosary to Catherine. The beads were coated with her perspiration.

"I would like to have those," Minister Davis said.

"I have given my word to the girl," Catherine said, "that I would hold them for her."

Minister Davis considered for a moment.

"I am content," he said, "so long as she has been stripped of that superstitious nonsense, which encourages her to mumble prayers over and over, so that the very words are reduced to little better than a mindless incantation."

The crowd murmured its assent. Catherine remained standing next to Margaret with the rosary in her hand. Governor Peters turned back to Ned.

"Do you have anything else to add?"

"No."

Peters looked at Margaret.

"And you will please to answer questions relevant to our investigation, and not give voice to your heathenish views."

In response, Margaret stared at the magistrate and then sat down.

Jailer Drake now rose to speak.

"While that girl was in my jail, she played the whore with Simon Oldcastle. I found them together and had to pull them apart."

Catherine felt the blood rush to her head, and then it seemed to settle in her troublesome tooth, which commenced a terrible throbbing.

"That is not so. I was there," she said.

Drake bowed in her direction.

"It is true Mistress Williams was there. She held me in conversation while the girl and Oldcastle were alone. When I then opened the door, they were lying together. Is that not how it was, Mistress Williams?"

"Yes," Catherine agreed. "We stopped Oldcastle from forcing himself upon the poor girl."

"No," Drake said with a malicious smile, "we stopped her from lying with him for the coins he had in his pocket. He told me as much when I took him out for his punishment." Drake reached into his pocket. He held up two bright silver coins. "These are the very coins he gave me for saving him from himself and the girl, those being his very words."

"The girl tells a different story," Catherine insisted. She glanced over her shoulder at the people on their benches, and she could see that they believed Drake and would not be budged from a conviction that conformed to their view of Margaret. So she simply said, "God, at least, cannot be fooled by lies."

"That will be enough," Minister Davis's voice rolled down from the pulpit.

"Yes," Woolsey said. "We have heard what you said and what the jailer said." He looked at Margaret, but she only sat, her eyes again vacant and defeated.

"Fornication, at least it was that," Drake said, "even if there was no exchange of money."

"Do you have anything to tell us about the death of the Jameson babe?" Peters asked.

"Why that, too," Drake said. "Oldcastle told me the girl said something about that matter to him."

"Why would she do that?" Woolsey asked.

"What did he say?" Peters asked.

"Why, he said that she said that she only wanted to stop it from crying, and that is how it happened."

Catherine squeezed Margaret's shoulder and leaned down to talk into her ear.

"Tell them, child," she said, "tell them what you did."

"The babe was not crying," Margaret said in a voice barely above a whisper.

"What is that?" Woolsey asked, cupping his hand to his ear.

"Louder," Catherine encouraged.

"The babe never cried," Margaret said in a fully audible voice. "It was a good babe. I only wanted to baptize it when I found that it would not wake up. There was no priest."

"And what else did you do?" Catherine asked.

"I said my beads, again and again, but it did not stir."

"She's leaving out the important part, what she did before all that." Henry's voice carried like the slap of his hand to where Margaret sat. "I tell you I saw her kneeling over my babe, and when I pulled her away, the babe was dead."

"I think we have heard enough," Governor Peters declared.

"The babe bled when she touched it," Henry insisted.

"We have heard you so say," Woolsey said.

"We will make our recommendation to the grand jury," Peters said.

Woolsey nudged his colleague.

"Sir Edward Coke, you know, two witnesses in a hanging crime," he said.

"Yes," Peters said dryly. "We will confer and we will make our recommendation, remembering the wisdom of Sir Edward, who I do not need to remind you died in old England these several years past, while we are here on New England marrying English law to the law of Scripture."

The governor stacked the papers on which he had been recording his notes so that their edges were even. He replaced the cap on his inkwell. Then he drew on his gloves. Woolsey looked toward Catherine.

"Ah yes, Mistress Williams," Peters said. "I remember me now that you wanted to tell us something of the babe's birth."

"Yes," Catherine replied, although she realized that

there was not now anything very useful she could say. What purpose would be served by declaring that the babe was healthy when it was born, since they had already concluded that the girl had killed it? And nothing she could say about the birth itself would exculpate the girl. She could not swear she did not see red spots on its flesh when Margaret touched it, and what could she tell them about the mark on its back? She was not sure even now if it had been there, and if it had been, she was sure she did not know what to make of it.

"Only this. After the babe was born, I handed it to the girl and watched how tender she was of it, so careful the way she swaddled it. I do not believe she would harm it."

"Yet that is what she did," Henry's voice boomed.

Catherine did not respond. She had one more point to make for the governor's benefit.

"You may well be marrying English law to Scripture, and that is a good thing, for we are told in Deuteronomy, 'At the mouth of two witnesses, or three witnesses, shall he that is worthy of death be put to death; but at the mouth of one witness he shall not be put to death.' As you worthy gentlemen consider your recommendation, consider that you did not hear two witnesses say they saw Margaret harm the babe."

Minister Davis paused on his way down from the pulpit.

"Am I not right?" Catherine asked him.

"You say the words as they are in the Book," the minister said. "It does say so in that place."

Governor Peters rolled his papers and brought them down on the table.

"Quoting Scripture with our learned friend is one matter, mistress, but advising your magistrates how to apply the law is quite another. Is that not so, Woolsey?" He did not wait for a response but stood up and strode out of the meetinghouse.

Minister Davis followed the governor. Woolsey nodded to the constable, who took Margaret by the arm and encouraged her to stand. He led her out and the crowd sat silent as though disappointed that the entertainment was over. The Jamesons left next, although Ned seemed to hang back. Catherine watched as he motioned to the pox-marked sailor. As they began to follow the crowd to the door, she placed herself in their path.

"A word with your friend," Catherine said.

"I do not think he has anything to say to you, mistress," Ned said.

"Has he a tongue?"

For answer, the sailor thrust his tongue out until he drooled. A rivulet of spit gathered in a crater left by the disease on his chin.

"Aye, but cannot it talk?" Catherine asked.

They were now alone in the meetinghouse. Ned pulled on his companion's arm and they made their way past Catherine. At the door stood Massaquoit. They stopped. He remained before them, arms crossed in front of his chest. Ned made a jaunty show of stepping toward Massaquoit, but his companion made no move to follow. Ned looked back over his shoulder and waved him on.

"Come on, mate, you are safe here in the Lord's house. The savage will do you no harm."

"I want no part of him," the sailor said.

Ned shrugged.

"As you like."

He walked straight at Massaquoit. Catherine gestured for the Indian to step aside, and he did.

"See, mate," Ned called, but then Massaquoit took his place again in the doorway.

"What would you know?" the sailor asked Catherine.

"You seem to be an especial friend of young Ned."

"Aye, ever since he came aboard the *Good Hope*. I took him under my wing, like him being just a lad with his shoes still covered with the dust of the road, if you take my meaning." He looked past Catherine to Massaquoit.

"Soon," she said. "What can you tell me of why he came aboard."

"Why, only that he needed to get out of his uncle's house, seeing as there was a problem touching that Irish girl who killed the babe and was just sitting in this very place."

"What kind of problem?"

The sailor smirked.

"That kind of problem." And then, as though he had regained his courage, he strode at Massaquoit, who stepped aside.

After he left, Catherine walked up to Massaquoit.

"I was returning from the woods," he said, "when I saw the people leave. I waited. I looked through the door when everyone had left and saw you talking to those two. I remember them well."

"I am sure you do. You did me a service."

"This is what I am to do, is it not?"

"Yes," she said. She paused for a moment. "Perhaps I shall ask you for another."

Catherine sat on the edge of her bed listening to the chirping of the crickets outside of her bedroom window. It was pointless to try to sleep. Her mind was still back in the meetinghouse replaying the words she had heard, and seeing again the hatred in the eyes of Margaret's accusers, not just the Jamesons but the good people of

Newbury as well. And in the governor's actions and words she read his determination to play the politician rather than the judge. Whatever he might feel privately, he had apparently decided it was very much in his interest to ride the wave of the people's anger. And the girl, the poor thing, clutching her cross, saying her beads, swearing by the Virgin. If she were as innocent as a lamb, these acts in the eyes of these people would redden her fleece to crimson.

Yes, Catherine concluded, she was headed for the gallows, and in a hurry at that. If they were back in old England, where the law was just as brutal but moved more slowly, maybe the girl could plead her belly to save her life, but here she might well be at the end of a rope before the new life in her swelled enough to satisfy a man such as Governor Peters, who would use an amalgam of scriptural and secular law to his own purpose.

She knew she must listen to her heart, and believe that it was beating in consonance with God's purpose for her. And as she listened to it, she knew what she must do, a deed that would require her to enlist the aid of Massaquoit. She smiled grimly to herself at that idea. At least he was a long way from becoming a Christian, so he would not scruple to violate the Christians' law. She might have to barter something with him, but that did not concern her at the moment. All she thought about was keeping the rope from around the neck of Margaret Mary Donovan, late of County Cork in Ireland, and now, sadly, with child and lying on the floor of the Newbury jail.

EIGHT

MASSAQUOIT STARED INTO the eyes of the English-woman who stood before him, blinking in the dawn sun in front of his wigwam. He had heard her steps, which he now recognized by their rolling movement over the grass, so he had been more surprised than alarmed by such an early visit. He had poked his head through the opening to his wigwam, and there she stood, her mouth already framing her question, while he groped for something to cover his nakedness.

It had been an extremely hot night, and he had slept in the nude. His hand found the breeches that he so disdained, and he thought for a moment of putting them on, but rejected that notion. He searched in the half-light for his usual loincloth, but he had tossed it into some corner where it now was out of sight. He settled on pulling up the blanket, which the white woman had given him in anticipation of cooler nights to come, and which he now used as a sleeping mat.

"And why should I do this thing?" he asked.

"Because if you do not, an innocent girl will die. And

innocent as she is, even more innocent is the child she now carries."

Massaquoit hardened his heart.

"You English seem to kill the innocent regularly."

"You know I would have stopped what happened to your people on board that ship if I could have."

Massaquoit shrugged.

"Yes, I know that, but I do not know why you should care."

"For the same reason, I suppose, that I care about this girl."

"Why should I risk my life? How do I know that she is innocent, any more than you do?"

"I know she did not," Catherine said.

"Your God has told you?"

"I would not say that."

"You would not say so, but you think so."

"Just tell me if you will do what I ask."

"What do you propose to trade?"

"Your freedom."

Massaquoit had not expected such a bold and frank offer. He pulled the blanket about him more tightly, even though he was beginning to sweat.

"You cannot guarantee that."

"No, but I can give you an opportunity to seize it."

"If I succeed . . ." he began.

Catherine nodded. "You need not come back. I will find some way to prevent the militia from chasing after you. I do not think they will have much stomach for such a pursuit anyway."

He did not respond right away.

"I would give you time to consider, but I do not have it to give," she said. "If I am not very much mistaken, you were planning to make away before I spoke with you today. Maybe you can take her with you."

He was not surprised that she had guessed his intentions, but he did wonder why she would seek his help. He had traded many years with the English, and he had learned to read their intentions behind the mask of their expressions and through the mist of their words. Apparently something had gone very wrong at the meeting she had attended with the other English.

"She is in your jail."

"Yes. That is why I need your help."

"I will need certain things."

Catherine relaxed.

"You shall have them."

Wequashcook was waiting openly for him this time, sitting on the pine log where last they had talked. Massaquoit sat down on the far edge of the log. Pitch, warmed by the hot sun, ran through the cracks of the dry wood. Massaquoit felt the warm, sticky substance cling to the back of his thighs, but he did not move from the spot he had chosen.

He held out his hand, palm up, so that Wequashcook could see the coins Catherine had given him glinting in the sun.

"These are yours when you have the boat for me that you promised."

"You are in a great hurry," Wequashcook said.

"I do not intend to become an English, as you have done."

"Then you are the greater fool."

Massaquoit smiled.

"You try to anger me, but all I want is the boat you promised."

Wequashcook took the coins from Massaquoit's hand and weighed them in his own.

"For one so anxious, you come ill prepared to do business," he said.

Massaquoit extended his other hand, which contained an equal number of coins, and dropped them on top of the others in Wequashcook's palm.

"That is much better," Wequashcook said. "I might now be able to speed you on your way to folly, whatever folly that is."

"Yes," Massaquoit responded, "you can, and it is mine."

Phyllis acted as though she could not trust her ears.

"Give it to him," Catherine insisted. "It is necessary, I tell you."

"But we are not supposed to, Mistress Williams, and you know that better than I do."

"Just do as I say," Catherine replied.

Phyllis shrugged and handed the mug to Massaquoit. He sipped the beer and frowned against its bitter taste.

"I never did enjoy your English beer," he said.

He emptied the mug in two or three deep gulps. Then he walked over to Catherine and breathed directly into her face.

"What do you think?" he asked.

"That you reek of beer as though you had been drinking a good deal of it."

Massaquoit held out his mug to Phyllis, who was holding the pitcher. She looked at Catherine with disbelief still full in her eyes.

"Fill it for him," Catherine said.

Phyllis poured the beer into the mug until some ran over and spilled onto his hand. He rubbed his hand over his cheek. Then he poured the cup over the doublet he had put on for just this purpose.

"I need more," he said, and he took the pitcher from Phyllis and poured its contents over his doublet and let it dribble down his breeches. He took a deep breath.

"I think that I have enough now," he said, and handed the pitcher back to Phyllis.

"It is for drinking and not bathing," she said.

"It now suits my purpose," he replied.

Phyllis just shook her head and glanced at Catherine.

"Go back into the shed and refill the pitcher," she said. "Go on now."

Phyllis took a deep breath as she walked by Massaquoit and drew her head back as the pungent odor of beer reached her nose.

"So this is your plan?" Catherine asked when Phyllis was gone.

"Do you not think it a good one?" Massaquoit asked. "A drunken Indian will arouse no unusual suspicion. I will be acting as you English expect me to act. The rest should not be so difficult." He walked toward the door, stepping with an exaggerated motion as he lifted his feet against the unwonted weight of the clumsy English shoes he had put on. He muttered under his breath and looked down at his feet. "I must dress the part," he said, "from my shoes to my head."

Catherine took his arms in her hands. She expected him to recoil from the gesture, but he did not.

"My word is good, you know."

"I must hope so."

"It is. If you succeed, you need not come back."

"And the girl?"

Catherine sighed. She had not thought that far ahead herself, other than a plan to seek out Woolsey and advise him that Massaquoit was acting under her orders. She would need her old friend to shield her from the very dangerous repercussions of the act she was now putting into motion.

"We will figure out something to do once she is safe," she said.

"I will send word," he said. He took a step toward the door, but Catherine stayed him with her hand gently on his arm.

"One more thing," she said. She took down a pouch that was hanging on a peg next to the door. "Take this," she said. "It may be of use to you, if things go awry."

He opened the pouch and took out a paper, folded in half. He uncreased the paper and stared at the unfamiliar markings. He raised his eyes to her.

"I am not English enough yet to read," he said.

"Of course. It says that you are in my employ, on an errand of mercy for me."

He cast his eyes back down at the paper.

"You English and your words on paper, in your books. You swear by them." He placed his hand on his breast. "But you do not live by them."

"Some of us do," she replied, aware that no words of hers would ever soften his anger. He permitted his face to relax for a moment, and then he folded the paper and returned it to the pouch. His fingers felt coins.

"Money is always useful," she said. "There is one more item in the pouch."

He felt around in the pouch and pulled out Margaret's beads.

"Give them to her when you have succeeded."

He held them to his neck as though they were a necklace. She shook her head.

"They are not an ornament. Perhaps Margaret can explain them to you herself."

He nodded. He put the beads back into the pouch and then ran his fingers over its rich leather before slinging it over his shoulder.

"This looks like something carried by an Englishman, not a woman such as yourself."

"It belonged to my husband."

He tossed the pouch to the floor.

"I cannot carry it. His spirit will come to me. You should have buried it with him."

She picked up the pouch and extended it toward him.

"Do not worry," she said. "I know that his spirit would approve its use by you."

"You mock me," he said.

"Surely not."

He did not believe that she had spoken with her husband's dead spirit, but he knew that the contents of that pouch might save his life. He took it from her hand and put it lightly on his shoulder, waiting for it to indicate the presence of its owner's spirit. When nothing happened, he let it sit more fully near his neck, and then he left.

As he headed toward town, he practiced his walk. He took a step and staggered to his right. Then he took another and let his body shift its weight hard to the left so that he almost had to trot to stay upright. He struggled to control his motions in the English shoes, which blunted his contact with the ground. He wondered why the English would wear such thick footgear when there was no snow on the ground, as though they feared the very grass beneath their feet.

Low clouds scudded in front of a full moon. Not until he was halfway to the town center did he meet another traveler, a large man who approached him from the opposite direction. The man walked unsteadily, and he was carrying a thick staff, which he leaned on from time to time to steady himself. Massaquoit imitated the man's stagger and fell to one knee as they came abreast of each other. The man reached over to clasp Massaquoit on the shoulder. Massaquoit started to parry the motion, but then realized that it was being offered in camaraderie.

"And a good night to you," the man said, before stumbling to rest on all fours in the road, and dragging Massaquoit down with him. Massaquoit could smell the beer on his breath. He struggled to his feet and offered the man his hand. As the man gained his feet, the moon emerged from behind a cloud and the man blinked as he saw Massaquoit's face. He stepped closer and drew his nose as Massaquoit expelled his breath.

"Why, what is this? Who are you? Why Mistress Williams's savage. And you be drinking, I will swear by Our Lord. Get you home before I get the constable after you."

The man lunged at Massaquoit. He sidestepped him easily, and the man fell heavily to the side of the road. Massaquoit leaned over him and saw that he was unconscious. He resumed his walk, with a broad smile on his face. He had passed his first test.

Most of Newbury was already in bed as he stood before the public house. He peered through a window into shadows cast by the candles on the tables. He pressed his face against the glass, straining to see better. He was startled to find another set of eyes staring back at him. The eyes, however, did not seem to focus on him, and after a few moments they turned away, and he could just make out the back of a head moving unsteadily through the shadows and then dipping as the person sat down at a table.

Having satisfied himself that there were only a few patrons in the public house, he took a breath to steady himself and then he pushed open the door. He scanned the people sitting at the table. A young man was sitting at a table with an older woman. The man looked up from the mug of beer in his hands and smiled at Massaquoit. It was Ned Jameson.

"Well, Matthew, isn't it?" Ned said.

Massaquoit did not respond.

"You needn't worry," Ned said. "Even though you and me has unfinished business, that is not what I am about tonight." He looked at the woman, who smiled nervously, never taking her eyes off Massaquoit. Ned grinned at the Indian.

"She is afraid of you like you was the very savage, but look at you in your new clothes, why now, sit down and have a drink." He swung his arm in the air, and a small man with a large belly appeared with a pitcher in his hand. "Pour Matthew here one, if it please you," he said.

The tavern keeper looked at Massaquoit, but made no move to serve him. Instead, he leaned toward him and took a deep, noisy breath.

"Now, Ned," the man said, "think you it is a good idea to serve this savage more beer to further inflame his blood?"

Ned brought his own mug down hard, causing the beer in it to slosh over the top and spill onto his companion, who now looked at him with barely concealed distaste.

"I think I will be going home now," she said.

Ned shrugged.

"And why not? My friend Matthew here is better company."

The woman's face turned ugly in anger for a moment and then she laughed.

"Young Ned, come back and see me when you are old Ned, when you have hair on your face more than these poor things." She yanked a couple of scraggly hairs on his chin and rose unsteadily to her feet. She balanced for a moment, and then sat back down. "Do you think you might grow if I sit here and wait?" she asked, her hand seeking him between his thighs.

Ned bent over and whispered something in her ear. She threw her head back as though to reject the idea, but he put his arm around her shoulder and breathed heavily on her neck before again whispering. This time she nodded.

The little man watched this dumb show, and when he turned back, Massaquoit was holding out one of the bright coins Catherine had left for him in his pouch. The man pressed the coin into his palm without saying a word, and then he poured a mugful of beer and placed it in front of Massaquoit. Massaquoit raised the mug to his lips and took a deep swallow. He slammed the mug down, as Ned had done, and again beer spilled onto and then off the table, this time onto him. He rose with a yelp as though he had been shot. Ned looked up at him.

"Easy now, Matthew," he soothed, but Massaquoit only howled the louder.

"Englishman's poison," he said, and tossed the remainder of his beer at Ned. Ned jumped up and out of the way, and then reached across the table to seize Massaquoit's arm.

"Ayee," screamed Massaquoit. "Away, white devil," he yelled.

Another man now approached. He was middle-aged and carried himself as though he were used to exercising authority. He had been sitting in the corner, drinking alone and observing the scene.

"Now calm yourself," he said. "What is the matter, Ned?"

"Why, this savage, the one we should have thrown over the side with his friends. He came in here and he demanded a drink, and then he said some things to Edwina here, things of a very personal nature about a certain part of her body that he was interested in. When I told him to behave himself, why, he jumped up and made those devilish noises you just heard. And so, Constable, if I was you, I would do something with him right now before he comes to harm or harms some other person."

The constable looked at the woman.

"Is this so?"

She belched, hiccuped, and then nodded.

"He did say some things he should not have, the filthy animal," she said, and she leaned against Ned, as though for the protection of his arm.

"Will you come along easy, then?" the constable said to Massaquoit.

Massaquoit had listened to Ned's invention with a growing mixture of anger and amusement. He gave vent now to his anger at the insulting story, even though it suited his purpose absolutely, for he had come into this tavern with every intention of being arrested, and he had not known that Ned would be there to assist him, nor that the constable would be close at hand to effect the business. Still, he had to continue his playacting.

"Lies," he yelled. "White man, white woman, all lies!"

The constable was a sturdy man, and he reached a strong hand to Massaquoit's shoulders and pressed him down into the chair. Massaquoit felt the pressure, respected the strength, and wished, for a moment, for the opportunity to test himself against it. That would have to wait, however, for another time. For now, he permitted himself to be pushed down, and he slumped his head on his chest as though in a drunken stupor.

Jailer Drake opened the door after the constable pounded on it for several minutes. He was holding a candle, and his eyes were heavy with his disturbed sleep. He extended his candle until its light flickered on Massaquoit's face.

"What have we here?" he asked.

"Just a drunken Indian," the constable said. He placed both hands on Massaquoit's back and shoved. Massaquoit felt the pressure and took the opportunity to hurl his body in a drunken stagger against Drake and into the front room of the jail. He made sure that his arm knocked against the candle and sent it sputtering to the floor. He sat down next to it. Drake picked up the candle and held it in front of Massaquoit's face. He blinked his eyes away from the light and then buried his face in his arms.

"He belongs to Mistress Williams," the constable said. "It is late. I would prefer not to disturb her sleep."

"He can stay here, right enough," Drake replied.

"Do you need help with him?" the constable asked.

Drake nudged Massaquoit's knee with his foot. Massaquoit rolled into a fetal position on the floor.

"No, I think not," the jailer said. "I will just roll him into his room."

"His name is Matthew," the constable said. "In case you have occasion to address him when he wakes up."

"I will call him 'Devil,' I will, and that will do, for that is what he is," Drake said. "But who is going to pay me for his keep?"

"Mistress Williams. She has the money."

"To feed savages," Drake said.

"Aye, to feed savages, just as Scripture commands us: 'If your enemy is hungry, feed him; if he is thirsty, give him drink; for by so doing you will heap burning coals upon his head.'"

"Can you open that passage for me?" Drake asked.

"If I could do that, I would be preaching on Sunday," he said. "But I will tell you this. There is something strange about this one here. I was aboard the *Good Hope,* you know."

"So why do you tell me that?"

"Only this. I saw this savage here never lose his composure while his comrades were sent into the ocean, and whilst he was sore tried by one of our soldiers thrusting a blade against his chest, and he never blinked an eye. So I wonder how he comes to be like this so sudden."

"Why, man, there is a simple enough answer. He was not drinking spirits when he was on board that ship."

"Aye, that be true. Still I wonder."

"Wonder is for Sunday meeting," Drake said.

"That it is, but still I do it betimes."

"Take it with you, then, and good night to you."

Drake waited for the door to shut behind the constable, and then he placed his shoe on Massaquoit's cheek. "Burning coals on his head," he muttered.

Massaquoit slid away from Drake's foot, but he did not get up. The jailer leaned over him and felt the pouch. He lifted the flap and slid his fingers in until they could gather the coins. Massaquoit rolled over so that his weight trapped the hand in the pouch. Drake struggled to free his hand, but to no avail until he let go of the coins, flattened his fingers, and then slid his hand out of the pouch.

"Well, keep your money, then," he said. "I am sure

Mistress Williams will reward me well enough." He nudged him hard in the ribs with the toe of his shoe. "Get up now. I will not be lifting you."

Massaquoit placed his palms flat on the floor and pushed himself up to a sitting position. Drake unlatched the door to the inner room and pointed to it.

"In you go," he said.

Massaquoit made as though to get up, but collapsed onto his knees.

"Come on, then," Drake insisted. "You will have a tender head in the morning." Massaquoit crawled toward the open door. Drake started to step out of his way, when Massaquoit wrapped his arms around the jailer's legs and with a sudden motion rose to his feet while upending him. The jailer crashed against the door.

"Well, you *are* the devil, then, aren't you?" he muttered, and started to rise to his feet. As he did, however, Massaquoit grabbed him by the ears and pulled his head down while bringing his knee up against his jaw. Drake's head snapped up, and his eyes lost focus for a moment. When they cleared, he launched a wild swing, which Massaquoit avoided. His momentum spun him around. Massaquoit grabbed his hair and drove his head hard against the wall three times, until he collapsed to the floor. Massaquoit waited, but the jailer did not stir. All was quiet. Massaquoit peered into the dark room, but he could not see the girl.

A moment later, though, he sensed something hurtling toward him, and before he could move out of the way, a hard object crashed into his stomach, and he bent over, unable for a moment to catch his breath. He managed, however, to grab the object that had buried itself into his belly. It was Margaret's head. He pushed the girl back and held her at arm's length. Her white bonnet had been pushed back, so that it hung over her right ear.

"I have come to take you away," he said. "You could have given me a friendlier greeting."

She tried to pull herself free for a moment or two, and when she could not, she stared hard at him, her eyes glinting. She opened her mouth as though to spit at him, and he turned his face.

"I know what you want from me."

"And what might that be?" Massaquoit asked, although he knew what she feared.

"Why, to take your liberties with me," she said. "I have heard what people say about you savages."

"I had a wife," Massaquoit said slowly, "that I would not have traded for a hundred of you Englishwomen, and then your English soldiers killed her."

"Well, there you are mistaken," Margaret said. "I am not English, any more than you are, and as for that, I hate them as much as you do."

Drake stirred on the floor. "I do not have time to argue with you," Massaquoit said. He reached into the pouch and pulled out the beads. "Mistress Williams wants you to have these."

She grabbed the beads and held them to her breast. She looked down at the jailer and then back into the darkness of the room where she had been lying awake, as she had done every night.

"You could run this one through," she said. "Do you have a knife about you?"

"No," Massaquoit said, "and I came here to take you out, not to kill this poor fool." He took her arm and pushed her toward the outside door. She stumbled but she did not resist. When she was outside, he remained in the doorway. He pointed toward the road leading to the shore.

"You start walking that way," he whispered.

"Not likely," she said. "I will get lost, I will."

"Just stay on the road, follow where your feet take you. I will be with you before you have a chance to stray too far."

She started to walk on the road, and Massaquoit stood still in the doorway. After no more than five minutes he heard the footsteps he had anticipated. As the constable hurried by, Massaquoit stepped out of the doorway and grabbed him by the shoulders. He spun him around and pushed him toward the door. They struggled for a moment, but Massaquoit proved too strong for him, and he shoved him into the room.

"I had my suspicions," he said.

"Yes, you did," Massaquoit replied, and then he closed the door. He had noted the pile of firewood stacked against the jail when he arrived, and now he took two of the sturdiest logs he could find from the pile and jammed them against the door. Then he trotted down the road after Margaret.

After a few minutes, when he had not yet overtaken her, he stopped running so that he could peer into the half darkness. A breeze had risen and it shook the trees lining the road, causing their shadows to dance to the rhythm of the wind, pushing long, black fingers across the yellow moonglow that gilded the road.

He waited until his eyes adjusted to the latticework of light and shadow. He satisfied himself that all he saw were shadows. There was no sign of Margaret. He considered how much time had elapsed since he sent her down the road, and he calculated the speed at which he had traveled. He was sure that he should have caught up to her by now.

If he retraced his steps, he might lose any chance of overtaking her. If he hurried on, he might miss her in the dark. She could have run off into the woods on either side of the road. He entertained the thought of just forgetting about her, and making good his escape to the shore. But he rejected the idea. He had to find her before she decided to take her chances with the English rather than with him, for if she did that, the English would redouble their efforts to capture him, and he did not want to play the hunted deer being pursued by the clumsy but admittedly persistent and numerous English hunters.

He walked slowly up the road. He paused after every third step to study the underbrush. It did not take long for his patience to be rewarded. Several feet past an obvious break in the line of low-growing vegetation, he saw the white of her bonnet emphasized by the black shadow of the huge pine next to which she had sought to hide.

He saw her lying next to the knee-high plant, covered in thick red leaves. She did not respond to his presence, even when he brought his foot down hard enough to make a discernible thud not six inches from her ear. He knelt down next to her. She was breathing, but her eyes remained closed. He touched her cheek, and she rolled her head toward him. Saliva dribbled out of the corners of her mouth. She snapped her eyes open and parted her lips, but said nothing.

Her left fist was still clenched. He knew what he would find when he pried her fingers open, and there they were, two of the poisonous white baneberries. He did not have much time if he was to keep her alive, and, in preserving her life, protect his own, for if she were found dead, the English would not rest until they had his head on a pike while his body was fed to the dogs that roamed the town looking for scraps.

He forced her mouth open and rammed two fingers down her throat. Her teeth clamped down on his forefinger, but he grimaced the pain away. He held his fingers against the back of her throat until he felt it begin to spasm. Then he removed his fingers just as she started to retch. She turned her head to the side and vomited. He waited for her to finish, and when she had, he cradled her head in his lap. She opened her eyes now, and he thought he saw gratitude in them. That expression turned to terror when he again pried her jaws open.

"You must. Again," he said.

She shook her head, but he wrapped his arm around it to stop the motion while his fingers sought the inside of her throat. She retched again, her chest heaving, her bile spilling onto his thigh. She lay back exhausted and did not protest when he had her vomit a third time. She heaved but could bring up no more from her stomach.

He left her lying where she was, too weak, he knew, to move. He crawled back to the edge of the road. Nobody was coming yet, but it would not be long before the English figured out which way to hunt for them.

"We must move from here," he said, when he returned to where she lay, but she did not respond. He squatted next to her and put one arm under her knees and the other behind her shoulders. He started to lift, grunted, and then straightened up. She rolled her head against his chest. After it bumped against him a couple of times, her body stiffened and then struggled to free itself.

"Where? What?" she said.

"We have to leave this place," he said again. "Or the English will capture us."

"Oh," she replied, and he saw her make that strange

gesture that only she did, and not the other English. She touched her forehead, and then brought her hand down to her midsection, and then up to her left shoulder and then across to her right, a series of rapid motions, on which she apparently placed great significance. Her body relaxed, and he was able to shift her over his shoulder, the same way he would carry a deer, only she was much heavier.

He made his way down the road for a quarter of a mile, looking to right and left for a natural break in the woods. He did not think the English could track very well, but they would surely convince some other Indians to help them, just as they had employed Wequashcook to lead them to Mystic, where his wife and son lay sleeping their last sleep. He tensed his shoulders at that memory, and Margaret's weight shifted, so that he had to stagger to keep her from falling.

He righted himself and saw what he was looking for, a narrow break in the undergrowth, already beaten down, leading between two young pines whose needles had been nibbled to just about the height of a deer's mouth. He sidled through the opening, being careful not to disturb the branches of the trees or to trample the underbrush where it was not already lying flat. After a few steps he found a clearing behind the trees, screened from the road, and he eased Margaret off his back. She looked up as she hit the ground, but then closed her eyes again. He did not know if she was sleeping or preparing herself to die. After a few moments he heard her breath become regular, and he squatted beside her.

The sun was just rising when she stirred. She opened her eyes, let them close, and then opened them again. She stared hard at him as though trying to remember. Then she looked down at her palm, which was still stained by the berry juice.

"I was hungry," she said.

"It was almost your last meal," he replied.

"It will be that soon enough," she said.

"Are you strong enough to walk?"

She rose unsteadily to her feet and nodded.

"Good," he said, and guided her back to the road. She looked down the road toward town.

"They will be coming soon," he said.

She took a wobbly step in the other direction, toward the shore, and looked at him over her shoulder. He strode next to her and then a half step ahead.

"Stay with me," he said, "for your life."

They hurried along, and she managed to match his pace. Soon he could smell the salt air, and he scanned the right side of the road for the marker Wequashcook had promised to leave. He stopped in front of an overturned log that was mostly hidden by the underbrush. He knelt next to it and ran his hand down its length until it stopped at a branch rising from its center.

"Are you mad, then?" Margaret asked. "This is no time to rest."

"This log has been dead a long time," he said, and pointed to the places where the bark had been peeled off and the wood was rotted.

"We must be off," she said. "I'll go me own way, then."

He took her arm as she started to leave.

"Do you see this branch?"

She nodded.

"Do you see its leaves?"

"Yes."

"A branch newly lopped from a different tree, still

holding its leaves, growing out of a dead log. Very strange, do you not agree?"

She shuddered and made that strange movement with her hand, which she let stay clutching her right shoulder.

"The devil is hereabouts," she said.

"No," Massaquoit replied, "only an Indian friend of mine. Step this way."

He took her arm again and pulled her toward the log.

"Step over," he said.

The branch was angled toward the woods, as though to point a direction. He sighted along the line suggested by the angle of the branch, and then he lifted it out of its hole in the log and tossed it into the underbrush.

"This way," he said, and she followed. After a few steps they found themselves on a narrow path that led them deeper into the woods.

NINE

❧❧❧

T HE MAIDSERVANT, A young girl whom Catherine recognized as a member of a recently arrived family, opened the door at Catherine's knock and turned her head to the bed at the rear of the front room where Magistrate Woolsey lay.

"He says he cannot rise," the girl said.

"Not at all," Woolsey said, but he made no effort to get up. The girl shrugged and disappeared into the rear of the house.

Catherine sat on a stool next to the bed. Woolsey tried to lift himself, but his face contorted in pain, and he clutched at his right arm before collapsing back onto the mattress, which shuddered under his considerable weight for a moment but held.

"I tell you, Catherine, that woman walked by the front of my house yester evening, and I have lost the use of my arm, it pains me so."

"Pshaw," she replied. "Do you think you are bewitched, then?"

He started to nod, and then he shrugged.

"I know not. But people say Goody Hawkins is to be feared."

"What people say is not always to be believed. That poor girl in the prison, convicted before her trial."

Woolsey frowned.

"Some people also say that Goody Hawkins bewitched that baby and caused it to die out of spite, as she was not invited to attend the birth." His expression turned darkly serious, and he reached a hand to touch Catherine's arm. "And let us not forget who *was* at that birth. Some say you have something to hide."

"I trust you know better than that, Joseph Woolsey."

"I do, but I must ask you what you know of what happened last night. The constable was here at dawn to tell me that your Indian, Matthew, was drunk last night, and when he was quite rightly put in the jail, he attacked the jailer and made good his escape. And, it seems, the girl took advantage of his action and fled into the night."

"That is right, in part."

He looked hard at her.

"This is a serious matter, Catherine. Do not speak idly to me."

"I do not. The girl did not flee when the opportunity arose. She fled with Matthew, because I sent him there to free her."

Woolsey shook his head slowly from side to side.

"Catherine," he said, and then again, "Catherine. Why? You were an impetuous child, but you are a woman of years now."

"I needed the time," she said.

"But to disobey the magistrates of this town. Not that *I* take offense. I have known you too long. But as your magistrate, I must be offended. Do you not see? As the

Lord, Jesus, is the father of the church, and the husband
the father of the household, so is the magistrate . . ."

Catherine had heard her mother say that she must obey
her father, as head of the household. She had heard her
father say she must obey the minister, because as head of
the religious community he was another father. She had
heard the minister say she should obey the magistrate, because as head of the political community, he was yet another father. And the magistrate had talked of the king as
the father of the nation. But only the first of these held a
place in her heart, while she was not at all sure how she
should consider the surrogates.

"Joseph, you are not my father, nor is the governor, or
any other official of the colony. As you well know, as you
were at his grave with me when I was a little girl, the
man, my father, to whom I might have shown disobedi-
ence, is in the ground these forty-five years."

"It was," he stuttered, "just a manner of speaking."

"Well, then, a very poor manner, I should say," she said
with a stern voice, although a smile played at the corners
of her mouth as she saw Woolsey's discomfort. She
reached across to touch his arm. "Let us not lose the point
in these words," she said gently. "The girl was going to
hang, and you know as well as I that she is innocent."

He shook his head.

"I do not know that. I do doubt, to be sure, but I do not
know."

"Well, then, is not that enough for you, to doubt?
Would you see her on the gallows while your heart
doubts? And she with child?"

"Why," he sputtered, "she did not appear so. Who is
the father?"

"Joseph. Does that matter? But as for that, I do not
know."

"Why, of course it does. I heard what Jailer Drake said."

Catherine felt her anger rise, and she fought to quell it.

"His words are bought, one by one."

"Can you prove that?"

She shook her head violently.

"No, not that or the other, for that matter. You must take my word."

He took her hand.

"I can do nothing else, and you well know it."

"I know your heart opens easily," Catherine said, "but that I have to knock that much harder at the door to your reason."

"It is not just me, you know," Woolsey said. "For I am in no hurry. But the governor hears the clamor of the people who desire vengeance."

"Can you not hold him off, then?"

He nodded.

"If I put my whole weight against his motion I can, for a little while."

"Then I will have to be prompt."

He settled himself back against his pillows, his face wrinkled with exhaustion.

"Did you not sleep?" she asked.

"No," he replied. "I could not find a place for my arm where it did not plague me."

"Let me have a look, then," she said, and without waiting for his reply, she leaned toward him and ran her hand from his wrist to his elbow. He winced. She pulled his arm out, but it would not straighten. She pushed it back to a forty-five-degree angle.

"Is that comfortable?" she asked.

"Tolerable," he replied.

"Your arm is like a dry old branch on an old tree. It no longer bends."

"Pshaw." He swung his good arm. "Do you not think I should find a way to bring Goody Hawkins here?"

"To lift her charm from you?"

"Yes."

"And then what? Hang her for a witch?"

"I do not know."

"Think you on it. But if you did, that poor arm would still ache."

Martha's oldest daughter, Ann, was waiting in the shadow of an ancient oak tree several hundred yards up the path from the magistrate's house. Catherine recognized her at once, even before she stepped fully into the sunlight. The girl's face had been imprinted in her memory from the night she stood by her mother, buttoning her gown, and then leading her back into the house, as though their roles, mother and daughter, had been reversed.

"May I speak with you, Mistress Williams?" she said as she joined Catherine on the road, and measured her stride to keep up.

"Yes, certainly, Ann."

She looked up the road for a moment, and then she raised herself on her toes so that she could whisper into Catherine's ear.

Catherine felt her breath against her ear, but heard only a faint buzzing.

"Why, child," she said. "Speak up."

"I am afraid," Ann said, but in an audible voice. "My father sent me to talk to you."

"What does Henry Jameson want from me?" Catherine said, unable to soften the edge in her voice as she remembered Henry's testimony at the hearing.

Ann raised herself again and spoke into Catherine's ear again but this time more loudly.

"It's about my cousin."

"Ned?"

"Yes."

"Why, what does your father want to tell me about Ned?"

Ann shook her head, and again stared up the road.

"Nothing," she said. "He wants you to tend to my mother. It is myself that wants to tell you about Ned. And my father as well."

Catherine stopped walking and took Ann by the child's thin shoulders.

"Make sense, child," she said.

Ann wiggled to get free from Catherine's grasp so she could keep her eye on the road.

"Who are you looking for?" Catherine asked.

"He will be along soon."

"Your father? Perhaps we should wait right here for him, if you cannot remember what you are supposed to tell me."

The girl's face reddened and her eyes flashed.

"I am not a silly girl. I know very well what I am supposed to say to you."

"Well, then."

"Well, then, it is this I must say to you. My father wants you to see if you can make my mother speak again. And to eat again."

"She does neither?"

"Her tongue remains fixed between her teeth. She sits by the cradle all the day long. She moans sometimes, and my father has made her to drink some water, but that is all."

"I will do what I can," Catherine said as she felt herself responding to the poor woman's misery. Why, Catherine thought, she must be blaming herself for the babe's death. But her sentiment argued against her sure sense that she would be wise not to let herself become any further involved in the Jameson family than she already was.

The girl seemed to relax now that she had delivered her father's message, and could tell him that help was on its way. They walked together in silence for a few moments, and then Ann stopped.

"He will be here around the next bend in the road. I am sure of it."

Catherine pointed toward an overturned log on the side of the road.

"I am feeling a little tired," she said. "Let us sit down so I can recover my breath."

Ann permitted herself a quick smile that vanished the moment she sat on the log.

"It is about that girl and my cousin Ned. I saw them once. At night. We were all sleeping in the same room. They thought I was asleep, and would not hear them. But I did."

"What did you hear?"

"Why, them talking in her bed. He was next to her. Then there was a thud as one fell to the floor."

"Which?"

"I do not know. I was afraid to open my eyes. I only heard what I heard."

"And what was that?" Catherine was trying not to become impatient with the child's halting story. She was clearly very afraid of something, or somebody.

"I heard her say, 'First your uncle, and now you.' That is what she said. I am sure of it."

"Do you know what she meant by that?"

Ann looked at Catherine in disbelief.

"Do you not?"

A loud step surprised them coming around the bend, and there, as Ann had predicted, was Henry Jameson.

Catherine looked up and smiled, as though she were ashamed.

"I was feeling tired," she said, "and your daughter kindly said she would bide by me until I recovered myself."

Henry looked hard first at Catherine and then at his daughter.

"Did she tell you about my poor wife?" he asked.

Catherine nodded, while weighing his words for sincerity and finding them a little light. It might be that Henry was surprised to come upon them sitting there, and had surmised that they were talking about something other than his wife, or it might be that he did not worry as much about his wife as he would like her to believe.

"Are you coming, then?" Henry asked. He reached down and took his daughter by the arm and yanked her off the log so hard that the child's feet left the ground. Without waiting for Catherine to reply, he started back down the road. He did not let go of Ann's arm, so that she had to trot to keep up with her father's longer stride. Catherine watched them until they turned the bend, and she could no longer see them. Then she rose to her feet and walked after them. She was in no hurry to catch up, or to arrive at the Jameson house, where she knew that she would encounter something bizarre, something she might well not be able to remedy.

Ann was sitting on the ground in front of the door. Catherine heard the sound of an ax, and followed it to see

Henry at work at the woodpile on the side of the house. He did not look up from his labor, although she was quite sure that he was aware of her presence.

"He said for you to go right in," Ann said, "for there is nothing he can tell you more than your own eyes shall see." The girl stood up and opened the door. Catherine followed her into the house. She waited for her eyes to adjust to the dimness inside, for the one window in the front room was covered with a heavy piece of black cloth, and the only light came through the opened door. Before she saw Martha clearly, she heard her labored breathing. Ann scurried by and pulled back the cloth to reveal her mother sitting on a stool in the corner of the room. Martha blinked as the unexpected light hit her eyes. She turned toward Catherine, but she did not say anything. It was apparent that she could not have spoken had she wanted to. Her tongue, swollen and dark red, was thrust between her teeth.

Catherine walked over to Martha and cupped the woman's chin in her hand so she could examine her more closely. Martha's mouth was so firmly shut that, Catherine surmised, her teeth must be pressing painfully against her tongue.

"Can you not say hello to me?" Catherine asked.

"She does not speak," Ann said.

"You say she does not eat either?"

The girl shook her head.

"Father has tried forcing her. He has been able only to get her to drink some water, which she then spat out right away."

Catherine stroked Martha's cheeks.

"Do you not want to talk with your old gossip?" she asked.

For a moment it looked as though Martha might respond. Her eyes seemed to focus on Catherine, but then they resumed their blank stare. She rocked back and forth on the stool, tipping first its front legs and then its rear off the floor. Catherine found the place behind her cheeks where she knew the jaw hinge to be. Martha's mouth opened a crack, and then clamped shut. She rocked more vigorously until it looked as though the stool was about to fall over. Catherine stepped back.

"Can you leave us?" she said to Ann.

The girl shook her head.

"My father said I must stay with you while you are here."

"I see," Catherine replied. "But I must talk with him, and he will not hear me if I call him. Go ask him to come in so I can talk to him."

Still, the girl hesitated.

"Go, child," Catherine said. "I will tell your father that you are doing my bidding, as you ought."

The girl took a slow step backward, and then another, her eyes on her mother. When she reached the doorway, she spun around and dashed out.

Catherine now put her mouth close to Martha's ear.

"Talk to me now," she said, "for we only have a moment."

Martha opened her mouth and Catherine could see flecks of fresh blood on her tongue. Martha moved her lips, but the only sound that came out was a grunt, or a moan, like pain that could not be formed into words.

"Here, now," Henry's voice boomed. "Has she spoken to you?" He strode through the door and placed himself next to his wife, on the side opposite of Catherine. He was still holding his ax, and he let its head drop to the floor. Its edge bit into the plank.

"Not a sound that I can understand," Catherine replied. "But I think she wants to say something concerning you."

"She can have nothing to say about me. I didn't call you here so you could listen to idle tales from my wife's poor tongue. Why, look at it. It cannot stay in her mouth, and yet she says no word from day to day."

"Perhaps if you withdraw again, I can coax a word or two from her."

"No, that I will not. If you can have her speak, she can do so in my hearing."

"As you like." Catherine shrugged. She took Martha's hand. It was clammy with sweat.

"Can you tell me what ails you?" Catherine asked. Martha's fingers squeezed hers, but she shook her head. Catherine returned the pressure and stood up.

"I will be back with something for her."

"Will it loose her tongue?" Henry asked.

"It might."

He took a step and towered over her.

"It would be well for you if it did."

Catherine held his gaze until he turned away.

"And for you as well, I warrant," she said.

Henry picked up his ax and swung it onto his shoulder.

"I have work to do," he said, "and no time to be trading barbs."

After he strode through the door, Ann, who had been crouching in the far corner of the room, where the light did not reach, emerged and hurried to Catherine.

"I did not finish telling you what I wanted to tell you."

"Go on, then," Catherine said, "and be quick about it."

"Before, when I told you what I heard that girl say, I did not tell you what Ned replied."

"What did he say?"

"He said that if my father knew what they were about,

he would have them both whipped out of town at the end of a cart, he would. My cousin is very wayward. Mother used to say that, and father, too."

"But your father . . ."

"He was never so happy as when my little brother was born. But as for Ned, as soon as he came home and saw the babe, and heard how my father talked about at last having a son, his face turned black, and black it stayed. That is why I think he did it."

"Did what, child?"

"Why, persuade that girl to kill my little brother."

Henry stood in the doorway and beckoned for the girl to join him.

"There's wood to be stacked," he said, and then walked away, not pausing to confirm his daughter's obedience. Ann watched him go, before turning again to Catherine.

Henry's statement reminded Catherine of a question.

"Ann, doesn't Ned usually stack the wood?" she asked.

"Yes."

"Did he do so when the babe died?"

"No. He was inside the house talking to that girl, like I said."

"Convincing her?"

"Yes."

Catherine sensed Henry before she saw his figure again block the light in the doorway.

"I was just on my way," Catherine said. "Ann was asking me if I thought I could help her mother."

"There is wood to be stacked," he said, and Ann followed him into the yard. Catherine waited a moment, and then she followed them out of the house. She saw Henry point to the fire wood that he had split. Ann nodded but then turned back toward Catherine. She said something to her father while pointing at Catherine. Henry shook his head and pushed her in the direction of the wood. Ann stepped slowly toward the stump on which the wood had been split. She bent down and picked up the first log, and then another, laying them carefully on the ground to provide a basis for the stack she would construct.

Catherine ambled on the path leading away from the house. It passed within ten feet of the area where Ann worked. She hoped for an opportunity to hear what else the child might say, now that her father had gone off to attend to some other chores out in the field behind the house. But as Catherine approached, and slowed even more to provide the girl a chance to step forward, a figure emerged from beneath a huge maple tree that towered over the yard. The man looked at Ann, and then at Catherine, and walked so as to place himself between them. He stood looking at Catherine as she passed.

"And a good day to you Mistress Williams," Ned said.

"Aye, it is that," Catherine said, "and better still it will be when I come back with something to help your poor mother."

"My mother is in the grave, as you know very well, Mistress," he replied.

"And you know just as well that I refer to that poor woman in the house who is now your mother."

Ned glanced back at Ann and then toward Catherine.

"Well, then, Mistress," he said, "as you say, so must it be."

TEN

❧❧

THE SUN HAD been up for two hours now, and Massaquoit was worried. He and Margaret had traveled the path, whose entrance had been announced by the branch in the dead log, and they had followed it to its end in a small clearing a safe distance from the road, and yet close enough to the shore so that they could hear the surf crashing against the beach. The clearing was screened from the water by a thin row of scraggly pines and one massive boulder that had been deposited on this spot eons ago by a receding glacier.

Massaquoit has risked exposure by climbing to the top of the boulder so that he could search the horizon. From time to time he thought he saw a black speck riding the blue waves, but then it would disappear in the shadow of the low-lying black clouds darkening the eastern sky, only to reappear in a different place. He shifted his gaze away from the shadows and stared until his eyes ached and began to blur against the glare of the sun reflected off the water. He clambered down from the boulder and made his way through the pines to the perimeter of the clearing. He did not immediately enter the clearing but continued past it onto the path, which he followed all the way back almost to the road. This took some time, but he would rather be forewarned if the English were anywhere near. He stood still and listened. At first he heard nothing, and then the scurrying of small animals fleeing his arrival in their territory. From above, birds twittered and took flight. An acorn dropped at his feet, and he looked up to see a red squirrel on a branch of an oak tree. A chipmunk darted out from the underbrush and seized the acorn, and though it was almost too large for its mouth, it managed to carry it off back into the low-lying vegetation. Still, Massaquoit stood, and when he heard nothing else, he was sure that the English were not approaching, for he knew that in their clumsy shoes and their careless ways they would make enough noise for him to hear them from a considerable distance and thus be able to retreat long before they came upon him.

When he returned to the clearing, he did not see Margaret, and he cursed himself for trusting that she would wait patiently for him to return. She had been jumpy all night as they waited for the dawn, and he should have realized that her nerves were stretched too tight to tolerate sitting alone in a forest clearing. The clearing was covered by a thin layer of pine needles and dead leaves over soft earth still moist from a recent rain. A moment's inspection revealed the direction she had taken.

He found her on the boulder where he had been not half an hour before.

"It is not wise for you to be sitting up there," he said.

"Were you not here yourself not so long ago? Don't deny it, for I saw you from behind those trees." She pointed at the pines, and he was struck by the stark recognition that he had been so careless as not to have felt her presence staring at him, or to have heard her step following him. "I was very quiet," she said, as though reading his thought.

"Not so quiet, as I was not heeding," he said.

She pointed to a place up the shoreline several hundred yards where the road from town reached the beach.

"Would not those following us come from over there?" she asked.

"Yes," he replied, "unless they found our path."

"Well, I have been studying that place, and have seen nobody." She turned toward the water and pointed to a spot about a quarter of mile offshore. "But I have been watching that."

Massaquoit shielded his eyes and looked to where she was pointing. He saw the same black shape that had been appearing and disappearing before. Only now its form was clearly recognizable. It was a canoe bobbing on the waves, climbing a crest and then sliding down into the trough, and with each second showing itself larger until he could see the lone figure in the rear switching his paddle from one side to the other.

"Is that your friend, then?" she asked.

"It is."

"It's a good thing that the English are tardier than he is," she said.

"Yes, that it is. But they may not be so tardy as you think, so you had better come on down in case they show up before Wequashcook reaches us."

She sat down on the boulder and let herself slide. She landed in a heap at Massaquoit's feet and held her hand up. He helped her to her feet.

"You heathen and your names," she said. "How is a body supposed to remember such as that?"

"The same way I can remember that you are Margaret Mary Donovan," he replied.

She permitted a small smile to curl her lips and she blushed slightly.

"It is not at all the same thing," she said.

He did not respond. He did not have the time or the patience to begin to teach her that strangeness was only a matter of perspective. It was a lesson he himself had only begun to learn, and that imperfectly. Instead, he looked again to the eastern skies, where the black clouds were accelerating toward them.

"If the English do not catch us, we may get caught in that," he said, pointing to the approaching storm.

"And how far do you intend to take us?" she asked.

"Not very far. To that island. It is called Munnaw-tawkit."

She strained to see what he was looking at.

"Is that far enough away?" she asked.

"I know a place on it where we will not be found, and where we can wait until it is safe for you to come back. And I have hunted and fished from there, and I know where food is hidden."

She nodded, apparently satisfied, and having no better alternative to offer, sat down at the base of the boulder. He remained standing, looking first at the approaching canoe, and then at the clouds, and every once in a while glancing at the place where the town road reached the beach. It seemed clear to him that the English army coming down that road would arrive at about the same time as the storm and Wequashcook in his canoe.

The canoe arrived first, but just barely. Massaquoit waded out into the surf that now roiled in the winds spinning out from the storm. Wequashcook had navigated these waters for many years, trading with both English and Indians, and sometimes even venturing far enough to the west to deal with the Dutch, but he still struggled to keep his canoe from tipping. At the same time Massaquoit, waist-high in the waters, sought to keep his balance while steadying the craft and nudging it toward the shore. Within a few minutes they were able to ride one last wave into the white waters near the beach. Massaquoit shoved from his position on the side of the canoe while Wequashcook paddled furiously on the other side, until the canoe bounced through the surf and grounded itself upon the sand as the water receded. Wequashcook leaped out and they pulled the canoe onto the sand.

"You are late," Massaquoit said.

"And you have no time," Wequashcook replied. "I have seen the English coming down the road. They will be here in minutes."

"You are late," Massaquoit said again.

"And you are too stubborn to stay alive long. I was going to get a shallop for you, but the man had a change of heart, and I had to find this."

Massaquoit ran his fingers over the side of the canoe. It was a small dugout, a log that had been hollowed by weeks of controlled burning.

"It still feels a little warm," he said.

"It is seaworthy," Wequashcook said, "or I would not be here. Are you going far?"

Massaquoit did not hesitate. He nodded and pointed to the distant horizon.

"To the island they call Paumonok, the fish."

Wequashcook looked at the advancing storm clouds and then the horizon and shook his head.

"That is a long way to go in a storm."

"Not so long with the English snapping at our heels."

Margaret emerged from behind the boulder and stared at the crude craft.

"I hope you don't think I am getting into that, do you?"

"Only if you don't want to hang," Massaquoit said, and he pushed the canoe a few feet back into the surf so that he could float it out onto the receding waves. Wequashcook offered his arm, and Margaret allowed herself to be guided to the seaward side of the canoe. She clambered in and knelt down.

"You will find another paddle there," Massaquoit said. He glanced back toward the road, and he saw the sun reflect off metal. "They are almost here," he said.

"When you are safely on Paumonok, I will come find you," Wequashcook said, and then he trotted with surprising speed for a man his age into the woods that bordered the shore and disappeared.

Massaquoit shoved the canoe out and slid into it. He picked up the paddle. Just then the first musket shot rang out. He looked back to see the sand at water's edge being lifted by the musket ball at the end of its trajectory. An English soldier bent over his piece, beginning the cumbersome process of reloading. He was well out of range, but his comrades were charging past him to get close enough for a meaningful shot.

Massaquoit leaned his weight against the stern of the canoe, but the waves beat it back almost as fast as he could push it out. He could hear the confused and excited voices of the English soldiers as they gathered on the beach. Their muskets started to fire one after the other, explosive pops followed by the dull plunk of the balls hitting the water. The soldiers had not yet gotten the range, but they were getting closer. The waves flattened for a moment, and Massaquoit raised himself into the canoe. He could now make out individual voices coming from the soldiers. "Get the Indian first," one said. "Be careful not to hit the girl," another said. Massaquoit understood their intent. A musket ball thudded next to his arm.

"Paddle for your life," he said to her.

Margaret picked up the paddle and slapped it down into the water in a motion that provided more splash than propulsion. Massaquoit leaned into his paddle, but the canoe made slow progress against the wind-driven tide, and the soldiers were getting dangerously close. Musket fire exploded from the shore now, in an increasing crescendo rolling over the water like muffled thunder. Massaquoit looked behind him, and he saw the thin wakes left in the water by the spent musket balls. The soldiers were now directly in line with the canoe and they were wading into the water, well within range. He could hear the English yelling to each other.

"Paddle," he yelled to Margaret.

She dug her paddle into the water, to better effect now, but he feared they were out of time. A musket ball thudded against the side of the canoe, lifting a sliver of bark. He looked again at the pursuing soldiers. He saw that they were wearing, as usual, their steel corselets and were having some difficulty wielding their clumsy matchlocks as the waves, increasing in strength as the winds picked up, broke against their thighs. They would not be able to advance too much farther into the water. He needed to find a way to put some more distance between them before one of them got lucky with a shot. He could think of only one way to buy a little time. He leaned toward Margaret to make sure she understood what he said.

"Do not be alarmed. I am about to fall into the water, but I will be right next to the canoe."

"Why, that's a fine thing," she said. "And what am I

supposed to do while you take yourself such an untoward swim?"

"Keep paddling. That is all. They will not shoot you. They want to hang you, not shoot you. They will happily shoot me as to capture you. I will be only one more dead Indian. You will be an entertainment and a lesson for them as you swing at the end of a rope. Now paddle!"

She did, digging her paddle furiously into the water. Another musket ball thudded against the side of the canoe. The soldiers were at the extreme range of their weapons now, and they were having difficulty raising their shot the last couple of feet into the canoe. Massaquoit waited until he heard several musket explosions in succession, and then he stood up. He heard a lone shot and then he felt the ball graze his right arm with enough force to spin him around. He tottered and slid into the water. As he fell, he heard the cheer go up from the English soldiers. He let himself sink into the water, but he kept his left hand on the side of the canoe. He worked himself behind the canoe. The water was just deep enough so that when his feet touched bottom his head was several inches below the surface. He planted his feet and shoved. He felt the canoe move and he pushed again. He floated up just far enough to lift his nose out of the water for a breath, and then he sank again, dug his feet into the rocky bottom, and threw his weight against the canoe. He lost his grip. He swam underwater until his lungs ached, and then he sought the surface. He gasped for breath and blinked the salt water out of his eyes. His vision was blurred, and all he could see were the waves, and the lowering black clouds. He spun around, and he could make out the figures of the soldiers still leveling their weapons, and he could even see the flash from the exploding powder. He floated to the top of a cresting wave, and then he saw the canoe, eight or ten feet ahead of him. He swam toward it. Margaret was still paddling. He reached for her paddle and stopped its motion. She looked down, startled.

"Why, I thought to have seen your dead body floating," she said.

"Not just yet," he replied.

"Well, then, you might want to get back on board. My arms are about to fall off. I don't think I can stroke one more time."

The soldiers had stopped firing, having finally understood that the canoe was now out of range.

"Lie down in the canoe," Massaquoit said. "Carefully."

She did not move.

"Do it," he said, "or you will join me in the water."

She let herself slide down onto the bottom of the canoe. He swam to the back and grabbed the sides as far toward the front as he could. The canoe rose and fell with each wave, and he used this motion to help him pull himself slowly forward. The canoe rocked from side to side and he stayed still until it settled. He waited for the lift of another wave, and he pulled himself over the aft of the canoe as smoothly as possible. Again it rolled, and almost tipped, but righted itself. His stomach was now resting on Margaret's face, and he could hear her sputtering beneath his weight.

"Do not move yet," he said.

He managed to gather his legs into a kneeling position and lifted his torso up.

"Now," he said. "Get up, slowly."

She did. He picked up his paddle and saw that it had a piece gouged out of it by a musket ball whose impact he had not felt. He dug it into the water and leaned into a powerful stroke.

"Your paddle," he said. "Do not think I am going to do this by myself."

Margaret, however, was staring at her hand, which was covered in blood. Then she lifted her hand to her face. Some of the blood transferred from her hand to her cheek. She felt her cheek with the fingers of her other hand, and then gazed in horror at the blood on her flesh.

"I will die," she said.

"It is my blood," Massaquoit said. He pointed to his arm. She stared dumbly for a moment, and then she nodded.

"It's a good thing, then," she said, and picked up her paddle.

The rain now began to pelt down with a fury, and the wind blew toward shore. The waves, driven by the wind, rose and threatened every moment to drive them toward the English. The little craft dipped into each trough of each wave and then seemed to soar toward the crest of the next. Massaquoit paddled like one possessed, and Margaret plied her paddle to the limit of her strength and then continued past exhaustion. The canoe made torturous progress away from the shore, and then as both tired, their efforts did not more than keep it from being driven in. Massaquoit laid his paddle down and reached forward to touch Margaret's shoulder. She shrugged him off and kept paddling until he squeezed harder. She turned to him.

"Stop for now, and rest. The English must have gone home. They will think we are drowned."

She pulled her paddle into the canoe and slumped forward. He did not think the English would give up so easily, but he saw no reason to alarm her any more than she already was. They both needed to regain their strength. And he had felt the wind shift slightly, so that now it blew at an angle to the shore. It would drive them in, yes, but at such an angle that if they did nothing, they would land a mile or two away from the English. He sat still and watched the waves as they floated before the wind.

The rain was now only a drizzle and the black clouds had started to break apart. They were a quarter of a mile off-shore, but hidden from the place from which they had launched the canoe by a small headland around which the wind and current had taken them. Margaret picked up her paddle.

"You told your friend that we were going to Pau-monok. That is not the name of the island you told me."

"You need not concern yourself," he said. "We are going where I said. But Wequashcook has lived long among the English, so that maybe he has forgotten the color of his skin."

"You think he will tell them where we are headed?"

"He might."

"He will take them to Paumonok."

"Yes."

She smiled, and began to paddle.

The island, at first no more than a black protuberance on the horizon, now loomed larger, showing the green of its vegetation. Directly ahead of them, the golden yellow of a beach emerged from between the blue of the water and the green of the trees. Gulls swooped overhead and called to each other. Margaret began to paddle with more enthusiasm.

"I will never be so happy to have my feet touch the good earth," she said.

Massaquoit dug his paddle into the water and held it on the right side of the canoe as Margaret continued to propel the craft. His paddle acted as a rudder and the canoe's head turned to the right. When the canoe was headed parallel to the shore, he resumed paddling. She turned to him, dismay darkening her features.

"We were headed toward a beach," she said. "I'm tired and hungry, and I want to lift my poor body out of this boat."

"As we could see that beach so easily, so could the English."

"But you said they would not follow us," she said.

He shrugged.

"Maybe not, maybe later. Why take the chance?"

They continued in silence on a course that kept them a hundred or so yards offshore. Massaquoit steered them in a little closer, and they could see a great blue heron standing motionless in the shallow water. From time to time it jabbed its beak into the water, but apparently was not having any luck catching the fish it was after. Massaquoit pointed at the heron.

"We will steer toward him," he said.

"I have eaten the turkey that the English have become so fond of. Do you eat that bird as well?" she asked.

"Would you believe me if I said the bird, because its blue color is the color of Father Sky, is sacred to my people?"

"Surely I would. I know you savages worship all sorts of creatures, because you are not better instructed in the true faith. If you were, you would know there is only one Father, the Father of Our Lord, who died for our sins."

She scowled, and lifted her hand, around which her beads were wrapped.

"Is your god in those beads?" he asked.

"No," she said.

"And mine is not in that bird. The truth is I would eat

that great blue bird if I was hungry. It is not the bird I am interested in, but what is behind him."

They were now closing in on the heron, which seemed not to notice their presence. But then, when they were still fifty or so yards from it, it stretched its huge wings and beat them laboriously against the storm-bruised air. The bird rose, slowly, and gained altitude with difficulty. When it was fifteen or so feet off the ground, it turned toward the island and disappeared behind a hillock covered in straggly pine. They continued toward where the heron had been standing and then paddled past the spot, directly toward the shore. The water was no more than a foot deep here, and the canoe began to scrape the bottom. Margaret lifted her paddle out of the water and turned to Massaquoit.

"Are we going to stop now?" she asked, and turned back to the shore. "There is no beach here."

Massaquoit stroked the water gently with his paddle, his eyes studying the foliage along the shore.

"Those great blue birds hunt for their dinner near hidden little inlets. I know there is one near here. That bird served as a marker for me."

He guided the canoe a few feet to the right and toward a narrow arch formed by overhanging branches of two cypress trees. The arch was only three or four feet above the surface of the water, and just wide enough to accommodate a heron, or a canoe. Margaret ducked as they slid beneath the branches. Massaquoit leaned forward until his body was parallel with the water, and he continued to paddle. The depth of the water had decreased to only a few inches, so he wound up poling them through the opening. The canoe bounced along the rocky bottom, but on the other side of the arch, the water deepened into a shallow pond bordered by cedar trees.

"We need to push," he said.

He clambered over the side of the canoe and reached his hand up for Margaret. She grasped his wrist and started over the side. The canoe tipped and she slid into the water. She stood up with march grass hanging from her cap. She spit out a mouthful of water.

"You could have held it steady," she said.

He indicated an opening in the cedar.

"Over there."

He stood at the rear of the canoe and waited until Margaret shook the water out of her eyes and then grabbed the bow. They slid the canoe onto a little incline of mud and sand. He pointed to an opening in the trees through which the thin strand of beach could be seen.

"We may have to leave in a hurry," he said, "without being seen."

She sat down on the side of the canoe and wiped the sweat from her forehead.

"I am very hungry," she said.

"Do you know how to cook with cornmeal?" he asked.

"Yes," she said. "I have learned since I have been in this wild country."

"Good," he replied. "Then we will be able to eat if we do not find Minneseewa."

ELEVEN

❧❧❧

PHYLLIS PACED IN front of the table at which Catherine sat.

"Do you think you could stand or sit still?" Catherine asked.

"I think better when I walk about."

"Well, then, walk as far as you need to, and when you have thought of something we can give to that poor woman, come back and tell me."

Phyllis paced for a few moments more and stopped.

"Beer," she said. "To loose her tongue."

Catherine began to chortle in dismissal of such an outrageous idea, but then she stopped herself. She stood up and walked to the shelf where she kept her remedies in jars, boxes, and cloth bags.

"Well, thank you very much," she said to Phyllis. "You have been an inspiration. The wonder is why I couldn't think of it myself."

Phyllis began to smile, and then her expression turned to confusion as she watched Catherine touch each container in turn, as though to confirm its contents.

"Excuse me," Phyllis said, "but I thought you said that giving Martha Jameson beer to loose her tongue was an excellent idea."

Catherine looked up but did not immediately respond.

"There is no beer among those things you are looking at," Phyllis said.

"Why, of course not," Catherine replied. She picked up a cloth package and laid it on the table. "But there is this." She opened the cloth to display a desiccated and brown mushroom. She shook her head. "This will not do. We will need to gather some fresh. Cook them into a stew. That might be just the thing. It had better be, for if it fails, I know not what else to try."

"But the beer," Phyllis said. "An excellent idea."

Catherine clapped her on the shoulder.

"And indeed it is, for it made me think of this remedy, which otherwise I would never have recollected."

Phyllis stood next to the table, her shoulders drooped in defeat. Just then a soft knock came at the door. When Phyllis did not rise to answer it, Catherine opened the door, and there stood Ann Jameson, her face puffy and bruised. Catherine pressed her fingers gently against the girl's cheek. She winced and stepped back.

"Why, child, what has happened to you?"

"My father sends me to ask when you are to return with a remedy for my mother. He says he fears you are the cause of her illness, and he wants you to fix it."

Catherine cupped the girl's chin.

"Did he beat you, then?" she asked.

"No, he did not."

"Somebody did."

The girl looked over her shoulder as though she feared that she had been followed.

"You are safe here," Catherine said.

"After you left, Ned sat under that tree and watched me as I stacked the wood. He was supposed to help me, as he is a big strapping lad, and I am only a girl, but he did not. And so I just worked, stacking the logs, and he watched, and then when I put the last log on the very top of the stack, he walked toward me. The pile was quite high by then, and I found it difficult to lift that last log as high as my head, and I thought he was coming at last to help me. But he just placed his hand on the log and pushed down until I was on my knees. I said I would tell my father, and then he hit me, hard, with the back of his hand across my face."

"And then?"

"Why, he said he was sorry. He said all he wanted to do was to go back to sea. Then my father came out. He told me to hurry on my way here. He was very wroth when he saw me talking to Ned. He don't like anyone talking to Cousin Ned these days."

Ann stopped, and her shoulders sagged. Catherine could see that she was staggering under the weight of a truth she did not understand. It would be pointless to question her further. The child was confused and terrified. Catherine could not expect this little girl to separate out the kernels of truth from this matrix of fear and suspicion. She put her arms around the child. Ann struggled to free herself for a moment, and then permitted Catherine to embrace her. The girl sobbed, and when finally she looked up, she swiped a tear from her eye.

"You will help my mother, won't you?" she asked.

Ah yes, Catherine thought, and at the bottom of it all was that, the daughter desperate for the love and support of a mother no longer capable of giving anything like that to her child. "Yes. And you can run off to your home, and tell your father I will be there this afternoon with something I think will be of use."

"I will not hide this time. I will sit there right next to her so I can see how you are helping her."

"Yes, child, you do that."

Ann began to smile, but stopped herself. It was as though, Catherine thought, the child was afraid to express any joy. The girl turned on her heel and trotted down the road. She stopped abruptly.

"You are coming, aren't you?" she called back over her shoulder.

Phyllis, who had been standing a deferential distance away so as not to appear to be overhearing the conversation, could now no longer contain herself and she bustled by Catherine.

"But of course she will," she called out. "Mistress Williams's word is not to be taken lightly, you know."

Ann blushed, nodded, and ran on.

"You needn't have scared the child so," Catherine said. "She is already in fear of breathing too deep without offending her father, or her cousin."

"I wouldn't know anything about that," Phyllis said.

"You wouldn't, would you? But I thought sure you heard every word we said."

"No," Phyllis replied, "not every word."

"Never mind that now. We need that certain mushroom. You know the one."

Phyllis started.

"Why, Mistress Williams. Did you not warn me against that very plant, saying its powers were strong enough to think you was in the hand of the devil himself if you so much as took a bite of it?"

"Yes, I did. But maybe it is time for the devil to help us out."

"Mistress Williams, that ever you would call on him."

"Hush, you know better. It is just a matter of speaking. The mushroom is not of the devil or of God, it is of the earth. We need you to fetch a number of good-sized ones."

Phyllis shriveled her nose as if against an offensive odor.

"As you say. But cannot Edward fetch them."

"It is better he not know what we do. He would not understand."

"I warrant not. But you know well where they grow."

"I do indeed. And I will come along with you."

Phyllis nodded, but she made no effort to move.

"Now," Catherine said. "The poor woman can brook no further delay. Fetch your basket and come along."

She started to walk on the path that led to the rear of the house. Phyllis snatched her woven basket from the hook by the door and trotted after her. She caught up and passed her, leading the way into the garden. Edward was hoeing between rows of squash that had just begun to flower. He put his hoe on his shoulder and walked toward them. As was his wont, he did not speak to Catherine. Instead, he stood like a soldier waiting orders. He would stand that way a long time, Catherine knew, and she had sometimes thought she would try him to see just how long he would stand mute, but today was not an occasion for such games.

"We do not need you now," Catherine said.

He looked at her without comprehension.

"Back to your hoeing," she said.

Without a word, he returned to the exact place he had been when their arrival had interrupted him. He raised the hoe slowly and brought it down. Catherine watched until he had developed a rhythm she knew would absorb

his attention, and then she took Phyllis by the arm and
led her past Edward, through the garden, and to the pasture out back where two milk cows knelt in the shade of
a maple tree, their jaws working their cud. The rich, or-
ganic smell of manure filled the air. Phyllis knelt beside
a dried-up lump and shook her head.

"Hot and steaming," Catherine said. "Else all you will
find is cow dung and the dust it is becoming."

Phyllis rose to her feet, mumbling.

"What's that?" Catherine asked. "Are you still wondering why I didn't send Edward?"

"He is the one for mucking around dung heaps, you
know," Phyllis replied.

"That he might be. But he is not the one to gather what
we seek." She pointed to a small, fresh ball of dung.
"There," she said. "Have your basket ready."

Catherine led the way and started to crouch down, but
her knees betrayed her. She stood with her hands on her
thighs, bent over from the waist, looking at the mushroom growing from the lump of cow manure. The plant
was four inches high, with a white cap sitting atop its
frail stem, looking as though it was about to topple from
the weight. Phyllis got on her knees carefully so as to
leave space between her and the dung. She put one hand
to her nose, and with the other she pincered the plant between her thumb and forefinger and lifted it up.

"Check to be sure," Catherine said.

Phyllis stood up and stepped away from the manure.
She held the mushroom up to eye level and turned it so
she could see the underside of the cap. It was ruffled and
brown.

"That is one," Catherine said. "We will need four or
five more."

Phyllis dropped the mushroom into her basket and

stalked off, her eyes resolutely on the ground. Ten yards away she knelt down next to another turd and lifted up the mushroom growing from its center. She inspected the underside of its cap and turned to Catherine.

"Good," Catherine said. "And I have one here." She managed to stoop far enough down to grab a mushroom. She walked over to Phyllis and dropped it in her basket.

"One more," she said. "And let us see if we can find a bigger one. These are all a little small, and they will lose some of their potency when I cook them."

Phyllis scanned the pasture and shrugged.

"Maybe we had better have a talk with those cows, then, and tell them to get busy, for I do not see any more."

"I will start preparing the stew," Catherine replied, "while you look, just to be sure that we have not missed one."

"Do you not think three is enough?"

"Just look as I bid you," Catherine said, and walked back to her house.

By the time Phyllis came into the kitchen with her basket displaying one six-inch mushroom sitting atop the smaller ones that they had already gathered, Catherine had the other ingredients for a stew ready. Phyllis dumped the mushrooms from her basket on the table next to the chopped carrots, onions, beans, and cubes of salted beef. She held out her hand for the knife Catherine had been using.

"I will finish," Phyllis said.

Catherine shook her head.

"No. I must do this myself, and just right. Now don't pout about it."

Phyllis sat down at the table, resting her head in her

hands. Catherine dipped the mushrooms into a basin of water, chopped them, and put them into a small iron pot along with the other ingredients.

"We need something to sweeten this with," she said, "so she will eat some."

Phyllis did not seem to hear, but a moment later she lifted her head from her hands.

"Honey," she said.

"Right," Catherine replied. She poured a generous amount of honey into the pot and put it to simmer in the fireplace. She tasted it with a large wooden spoon. Her tongue enjoyed the sweetness, but her tooth rebelled. She dropped the spoon back into the pot and clutched her jaw.

"That tooth," Phyllis said. "I thought I saw Goody Hawkins on the road as I came back from the pasture."

"It is the honey," Catherine said. "But I do believe this is sweet enough to entice Martha to eat."

When Catherine and Phyllis arrived at the Jameson house, Ann was crouched on the floor next to her mother, who sat with spine erect in her chair this time, her tongue, as it had been, thrust between her clenched teeth. There was no sign of Henry. Catherine placed the pot on the floor next to Martha's chair, and then she motioned for Phyllis to stand by the door.

"You can look out for Goodman Jameson," she said.

"I can go seek my father," Ann said.

"No," Catherine replied, "it will be better if you stay here with your mother while I tend to her. Phyllis will let us know when he comes."

"I can tell her where to seek him."

"That is not necessary, child."

Ann looked warily from Phyllis to Catherine and then squeezed her mother's hand. Martha did not respond.

"Mistress Williams is here now," she said, "with something for you to eat."

Martha looked at Catherine for a moment, and then shook her head.

"Yes, Mother, you must," Ann said. "Please, Mistress Williams, you see how it is with her."

"I do, child." Catherine pulled over a chair and sat down next to Martha. She uncovered the pot and dipped a long-handled wooden spoon into it. She lifted the spoon toward Martha's mouth. Martha turned her head away with such violence that the tendons on her neck bulged. She kept her head turned as far as it would go while she stared back at the approaching spoon as though it were an instrument of evil. Her pupils were turned tight into the corners of her eyes, leaving the whites to catch the glare of the smoldering coals in the fireplace. Catherine guided the spoon slowly toward the protruding tongue. Just as it neared her mouth, Martha swiped it away with her hand. Catherine put the spoon back into the pot and caressed the back of Martha's neck with her free hand.

"There is no hurry, no hurry at all," she said. She continued stroking for several minutes, and the tendons disappeared beneath the skin of Martha's neck. Martha turned her head toward Catherine. "That's the way," Catherine said. She lifted the spoon from the pot. "Now, you don't have to swallow this. I am just going to place a drop or two on that poor tongue of yours, that looks so dry that it is like to fall out of your mouth if you were to open it." She raised the spoon, and Martha started to turn away again. Ann threw her arms around her mother.

"Please, Mother, for me."

Martha's eyes glistened, and she lifted her head up and down in a barely discernible gesture of concession. Catherine tilted the spoon so that a drop of the stew, more honey than anything else, fell onto Martha's tongue. The woman's jaws opened against her conscious will, and her tongue retracted into her mouth. Immediately, she thrust it out and set her upper teeth on it so as to prevent it from again disobeying her intention to starve herself. But Catherine tilted the spoon again, and this time a larger globule fell onto the tongue. Martha seemed to set her jaw muscles against opening. Catherine stroked the jaw where it hinged, and again Martha's mouth opened enough to accommodate the tongue as it retracted. She swallowed and her throat muscles, as though unused to working, tightened and she gasped.

"Why, I do believe you have forgotten how to eat," Catherine said. "But if you practice, you will remember."

Catherine gave the spoon to Ann.

"Be ready, child," she said. Then she ran her thumbs over Martha's lips and then back to the corners of her mouth. She massaged this place with growing pressure until Martha's mouth opened. The woman's eyes opened wider and darted about the room as though looking for a presence that only she could see. Her glance came to rest on the cradle in the corner of the room. She began to shake, but her mouth remained open. Ann looked in the direction her mother was staring, and then placed herself between her mother's eyes and the cradle. Martha stopped shuddering, and Catherine took the spoon from Ann, lifted it to her mother's mouth, and tilted it, dropping in a full measure of the stew. Martha started to swallow, and then her throat convulsed. Catherine stroked her throat muscles until they stopped spasming and began a more normal swallowing motion.

"How does it feel to have something in your belly again?" Catherine asked. She brought another spoonful to Martha's lips, and this time the woman accepted the food without resistance and swallowed it easily.

"One more, for now," Catherine said. "We do not want to feed you more than you can take comfortable, after not eating for so long."

Martha swallowed the last spoonful, and then kept her mouth open, like a baby bird waiting to be fed another worm. Catherine pressed her jaws shut, and Martha let herself collapse against the back of her chair. After a few moments she started to rock back and forth. A little while later her face reddened, and the pupil of her eyes expanded. Flecks of saliva dribbled out of the corner of her mouth. She started to mumble inaudible sounds. Catherine leaned closer and cupped her ear. Ann, too, came forward to hear what her mother might be saying to break her silence, but Catherine motioned her back.

"No, child," she said. "It is better that I first hear what your mother has to say." Ann stopped where she was, but still leaned forward. Catherine positioned her ear close enough to Martha's mouth to feel the woman's breath.

"Try," Catherine urged.

Martha moved her lips again, and a hissing sound came out.

"Henry?" Catherine tried. "Me?"

Martha nodded her head.

"Henry," Martha said, and then her voice sank to a whisper Catherine could not hear.

"He's coming up the path," Phyllis said, and a moment later Henry was at the door. Catherine remained bending toward Martha. She looked past Catherine's shoulder to see her husband. Again she said her husband's name, but this time she continued in words Catherine could hear. Then she stopped.

"What says she?" Henry demanded.

"Your name," Catherine said, "as you came to the door."

"Is that all?"

"All that I understood," Catherine replied.

Henry scowled.

"You would be telling me all of it, wouldn't you?"

"Certainly."

He stepped closer and placed his fingers on his wife's face. They looked huge and coarse against Martha's pale skin. He pressed his forefinger against her lips. It seemed to have a piece of dirt or perhaps manure wedged under the nail.

"You must have gotten some food into her, haven't you?"

"Yes."

"And she said my name?"

"Yes."

"And no more?"

"No more."

"You can leave now, then, mistress. And I thank you."

"I will be back in the morning, to see how she does," Catherine said.

"I'll send the girl again," Henry replied, "if there is need for you."

Massaquoit steered Margaret along the path that led deeper into the island. His feet knew the ground as well as his eyes, for this is where he used to come in the summers with his wife and son. At the end of the path he would see the wigwam he had built right before the war.

In it now, instead of his wife and son, he hoped to find his wife's mother. She had been on the island when the fort on the mainland had been overrun and burned by the English. He did not know if she would have been able to see smoke and flames or to hear the screams of those whose flesh was being roasted by the fires started by the English, or whose bellies were being ripped open by the swords of the English, but he knew that she would have learned of the disaster before the ashes were cold and the echo of the last scream had died over the waters that separated her from massacred friends and relatives. She would have realized that this island was the safest place for her to remain.

Margaret stumbled over a root that grew across the path and fell down to one knee. He offered his hand, and she allowed him to assist her back to her feet. She reached her hand into her pocket and removed her rosary beads.

"When we get where we are going, do you think I could pray?"

He held out his hand for the beads. She hesitated and dropped one end into his palm, while holding on to the end that had the wooden cross.

"You pray with these?"

"Yes," she said. "But they have not let me since I have come here."

He let his end drop and she gathered the beads into her hands.

"Maybe you will teach me how to use them sometime."

"Do you mock me?"

"No," he said, "for I would be happy to teach you how to pray to my gods."

They had come to the end of the path where it opened

into a small clearing that was filled mostly by the wigwam at its center. The wigwam was clearly intended for warm weather, as its exterior was covered only in thin strips of woven reeds that now swung softly in a light breeze. In front of the wigwam, an old woman crouched over a fire. She poked a long, forked stick into the embers and lifted the coiled body of a snake. Its eyes stared out of its charred head. On the edge of the fire sat a flat stone, which was serving to heat two round loaves of bread. The woman placed the snake back into the embers and covered it with ashes. She looked up and nodded at Massaquoit. He gestured to Margaret, who stood behind him as though seeking shelter behind his broad back.

"I have this Englishwoman with me. Please speak in her language."

"Are you hungry, my son?" the old woman asked.

"Yes," he replied, "but it is this white woman who must be fed first."

The old woman's face, already deeply lined, wrinkled even more profoundly as she contracted her brows. The gesture of bemused confusion was one Massaquoit realized, with a start, he was used to seeing in another face. He studied her eyes, and then he understood. In their unusual roundness and brilliant black color, they were the eyes of his dead wife in the face of her mother.

"Did you capture her?" the old woman asked.

"I will explain to you later," Massaquoit said. "She is in my care."

The woman motioned Margaret forward. Margaret stepped out from behind Massaquoit and approached the fire. The woman lifted the snake back out of the embers and held it out for Margaret to see.

"This is almost cooked," she said. "Then you can eat."

Margaret let out an audible gasp and crossed herself.

"Hungry as I am, I will not touch that creature, in the very form of the devil himself."

The woman looked at Massaquoit, and pointed at her own forehead.

"Is she all right?"

"Just give her some of the bread when it is ready." He motioned for Margaret to squat next to the woman. "This is Minneseewa. She is my wife's mother, and mine."

"Can you eat bread?" the woman asked.

Margaret smoothed her skirt over her belly. "That I can," she said, "and gladly."

Minneseewa kept her eyes on Margaret's hands, which had remained on her stomach as though holding it up. Margaret removed her hands under the old woman's glance, and then thrust out her chin.

"I will not hide the fact. I am with child."

Minneseewa nodded, and the lines of her wrinkled face relaxed into a smile.

"Mistress Williams did not tell me this," Massaquoit said.

"I am happy that she did not."

"You do not have a man?" Minneseewa asked.

Margaret blushed and shook her head.

"My son is a good man," Minneseewa said, and her voice broke into a cackle.

"Why, the idea!" Margaret said.

"Let us eat," Massaquoit replied. He squatted next to the fire. Minneseewa handed him the forked stick, and he used it to lift up the snake. He picked up a knife lying next to the fire and cut the snake's head off with one quick stroke, and tossed it into the embers. Then he sliced off a piece of meat and ate it. As he chewed, he saw Margaret, white-faced, staring at the head. With the blade of the knife, he covered it with ashes. A little color returned to her cheeks. She stared at the bread.

"Is it done?"

He stabbed the bread with the knife and held it out toward her. She blew on it, and then removed it from the blade. She nibbled a piece off with just her front teeth, and chewed it slowly. Then she took a fuller bite, and did not stop until the round loaf was gone. The old woman smiled a toothless smile. Massaquoit, meanwhile, had finished the first hunk of snake meat, and then another. He rose. The woman got up and walked to his side.

"Wequashcook," she said. "He was here a few days ago."

"I am not surprised," Massaquoit replied. "In the morning, I will go back to the water to see if we are safe. If I do not come back, take the Englishwoman deeper into the woods and wait for me."

She looked up at the full moon, barely visible in the thinning blue of the late-afternoon sky. "In a day, or two," she said, "the moon will be asleep. It will be a good time to hide from the English."

He walked into the wigwam. Margaret followed, the last piece of bread in her hand.

"Do you mind?" she asked. "I am afraid."

He pointed to a woven mat on one side of the wigwam, and he lay down on another on the other side.

"Go to sleep. The old woman will stay up and watch."

The sun had just risen and he was still some distance from the beach when Massaquoit knew that the English had arrived. He heard their voices before he could make out even the sound of the waves slapping against the shore. Apparently, stealth was not part of their plan when stalking their prey. He left the path and made his way through the woods. The birds stopped their chirping at his approach, and he wondered if the English would notice that sudden silence. He did not think so. When he reached the edge of the woods, he crawled forward through the underbrush on his belly. He lifted his eyes just high enough to see the beach. Two English soldiers were no more than twenty feet away, starting a fire for their breakfast. Another group of a dozen or so were sitting on the rocks at water's edge, near where they had beached their shallop. One man sat in the rear of the shallop. He was wearing a large beaver hat.

Massaquoit noted the hat and shrugged. He had expected as much. He realized he could wait for the English to eat and then make their clumsy way inland, probably along the path. If he sat still, he was sure they would not see him. Then he could get the canoe and make good his escape. At worst, he might have to contend with one or two English left behind to guard the campsite on the beach. He could overpower them, or outrun them.

But then he thought of the Englishwoman waiting for him with his wife's mother. He realized that she had changed in his mind from a necessary burden imposed upon him as a condition of his freedom to a person whose fate he cared about. He did not want to see her hanging at the end of an English rope.

He crept backward on his belly to a safe distance, and then he stood up. He made his way back onto the path, and followed it to the beach as though he were unaware of the English there. He froze, as though in shock, as he stepped onto the sand. He waited for a soldier to notice him. After a while one looked up from hanging a pot over the fire and saw him. He nudged his companion, and they both grabbed their weapons, one a pike and the other a musket, and approached him. He knew that the musket being lowered at him had not been made ready to fire. The pike, on the other hand, did pose a threat. The one carrying the pike called loudly enough for his mates on the rocks to hear.

"Here now, what is this?"

The other soldiers turned and stared at Massaquoit. He bowed toward them.

"Good morning, English," he said. "Am I in time for breakfast?"

The one holding the pike stepped forward and pressed it against his belly. Massaquoit recognized him at once as the same one who had cut him with that weapon on the ship. However, it was clear from the soldier's expression, mostly blank but colored in part by fear, and in part by hostility, that he did not recognize Massaquoit.

"What do you here?" the soldier demanded.

"Why, I live here."

The soldier advanced closer and lifted the blade of his pike up beneath Massaquoit's chin, forcing his face first one direction and then another.

"Don't I know you?" he asked.

Massaquoit shrugged.

"I live here," he repeated. "I always live here. Sometimes I trade furs with the English. Maybe I trade with you?"

"No, I never traded furs with no savage," the soldier said.

"Maybe with somebody who looks like me?"

"No, not that neither," the soldier insisted. He jabbed the blade of his pike against Massaquoit's arm where the musket ball had opened the skin. "I know how you came to get that, I do. You just stay where you are."

Out of the corner of his eye, Massaquoit saw the lieu-

tenant who had been on the boat striding toward them.
The officer unsheathed his sword as he approached. The
soldiers who had been on the rocks gathered behind the
officer, so Massaquoit now faced the whole company.
Lieutenant Waters put his hand on the soldier's pike and
pushed it away from Massaquoit's arm.

"So, then," he said, "what is Mistress Williams's savage doing here on this island where we just happen to be
looking for the woman that escaped from jail, helped by
a savage that probably looks very much like this one
standing right in front of us?"

Massaquoit moved his head in rhythm to the lieutenant's words and forced an uncomprehending smile
onto his face.

"I live here," he said.

"Maybe you do, and maybe you don't," the lieutenant
said, "but I think where you was last living was that very
same jail."

"Is he the one from the boat?" asked the soldier holding the pike.

"Yes," said the lieutenant, "didn't I just get through
saying that?"

"I wasn't sure at all what you were saying."

The soldier lifted his pike and poked at the pouch that
Massaquoit still wore around his neck.

"Who'd you steal that from?" he asked.

"Never mind that," the officer said. "What we want to
know is where the girl is. Maybe if you tell us that, we
can forget that we found you on this island. I didn't have
much stomach feeding your friends to the fish."

"I do not know anything about a girl," Massaquoit
said. "It is true I belong to the Englishwoman. She gave
me the pouch." He slid his hand beneath the flap and
pulled out the paper. "And she gave me this to show any-

body who might question what I am doing." He extended the paper to the soldier with the pike. He took the paper and held it in front of him.

"I thought he said he lived here," the soldier said.

"What does the paper say?" the officer demanded.

"By Jesus, I don't know. I can't read, you know. Here, you have a look, then."

The lieutenant took the paper from the soldier and squinted against the sun at Catherine's gracefully formed letter.

"It says here that the bearer of this paper, one Matthew, an Indian, is doing her bidding and should be permitted to finish the errand on which he is engaged." He handed the paper back to Massaquoit.

"Are you this Matthew, then?"

Massaquoit shook his head yes, and then looked past the lieutenant toward the water and the mainland in the distance. Out of the corner of his eye, he saw the soldier with the musket lighting the match on his weapon with a smoldering stick from the campfire.

"Maybe I am." He pointed to the mainland. "Over there."

"I see. Stubborn as ever," Lieutenant Waters said, not without a trace of respect in his voice. "And just what is that business you are on for Mistress Williams?"

"I say he stole that pouch," the soldier with the musket now offered. He grabbed the pouch and shook it so that the coins in it clanged together. "Why, you hear that? There's the king's good coin in that pouch. Ask him where he got that money, who he stole it from."

"Give him his pouch back," the lieutenant said. The soldier released it, and as Massaquoit took it, he leveled his musket at him. The match now glowed red, and the soldier opened the pan, exposing the powder. Lieutenant

Waters closed the pan and then pushed the weapon down.

"None of that," he said. He turned to Massaquoit. "You see how it is," he said. "It would be better if you told us where the girl was, and then maybe I can manage to get you out of here alive."

"I do now know," Massaquoit said.

The color rose in Waters's face.

"I am not that patient a man, Matthew," he said.

"And I am not Matthew," Massaquoit replied. "Matthew is somebody in the mind of the English."

"I am going to walk over there a bit," the lieutenant said, motioning vaguely down the beach away from the campfire and the beached shallop, "and when I come back, you will tell me what I want to know, or I'll turn my back on these two." He pointed to the two soldiers, and then he walked ten or fifteen paces away.

Massaquoit knew he had stalled and prevaricated as much as he could. He needed now to get them to chase him without being caught. He lifted the pouch and shook it so the coins jangled.

"You can have the coins," he said, "if you let me go."

The eyes of the soldiers widened, and the one with the pike put down his weapon to extend his hand for the pouch. As he did, Massaquoit lifted it off his shoulder and then swung it as hard as he could into the side of the soldier's head, slamming it into its target with enough force to drive the man into his companion. As they struggled to untangle themselves, Massaquoit grabbed the musket and then in two strides he was racing at full speed toward the spot where his canoe was hidden. Something whizzed by his feet and the pike skidded past him on the sand. He strained to increase his pace. He heard the confused shouting of the English soldiers on the rocks as they became aware of his flight. Lieutenant Waters's voice rose above the others until they quieted.

"Shoot him," the lieutenant screamed.

Massaquoit heard the familiar explosions as the muskets ignited powder and then the sand rose in fury around his knees. He stretched his legs even farther and gasped for breath. He would soon be out of range as the soldiers reloaded their clumsy weapons. For the moment he was very glad that they did not have bows and arrows, which could be shot with much greater speed to much greater effect in a situation such as this.

"If you can't hit him, then run him down," Lieutenant Waters shouted.

Massaquoit glanced over his shoulder and saw three soldiers ahead of the rest throw down their muskets and begin to run after him in earnest. They labored to keep up with him in their heavy armor and clumsy footwear that seemed to find difficulty in obtaining purchase on the sand. One soldier slipped to a knee and another was falling farther and farther behind. Only one, and he the smallest of the three, seemed able to keep up. Massaquoit looked past the three and saw that two soldiers had stopped running, and the others were doing no more than a halfhearted trot. He did not want them to get too discouraged too soon, so he slowed his pace as though he were breathless. He leaned over, his hands on his knees, and made a visible show of gasping for air. The small soldier now closed to within twenty feet or so, and Massaquoit started to run again, but slower than before. The soldier kept pace but did not gain. Suddenly Massaquoit spun around and lifted the heavy musket to his shoulder. The soldier froze and then fell to the ground. Massaquoit raised the barrel to the sky and pulled the trigger. The match came down into the firing pan and ignited the powder in a loud puff. All the soldiers in pursuit stopped in their tracks at the sound. Massaquoit staggered against the heavy recoil that pounded into his shoulder. The weapon had not been loaded with a ball, and the shot would have been harmless, even had he not taken the precaution of making sure that the only thing he could hit would be a seagull. He threw the musket down and started off again, this time at a trot. He looked back, and saw that the soldier had gotten to his feet and was after him again. More importantly, the shot seemed to have angered his comrades, so that they, too, took up the chase with renewed vigor. He needed one more ploy to lure them on.

He stumbled and rolled onto the sand. He started to get up, but collapsed back to one knee. The soldier now quickened his pace. He was brandishing his sword, swinging it in wide arcs as he ran. The others were still a distance behind. Massaquoit figured he would have just enough time if this little man with the sword did not prove to be more difficult than he looked. The soldier was now upon him, thrusting his sword toward him. The soldier's eyes were wide and sweat glistened on his face. His chest heaved beneath his corselet and his helmet slid down over his forehead, almost blocking his vision. He swung his sword with the energy of a man possessed either of tremendous anger or fear.

Massaquoit kept himself just out of range of the sword thrusts. The soldier was clearly not very expert with his weapon, as he took no measures to mask his motions with feints, so that Massaquoit had only to wait for the sword to start toward him and then rock back on the balls of his feet to avoid being struck. The soldier's face reddened, and this time he took a long step toward Massaquoit before jabbing his weapon at him. Massaquoit

dodged the blade as it rushed by his side. The soldier's
momentum pushed him off balance and Massaquoit
drove his fist into the nape of the man's neck between his
helmet and corselet. The force of the blow drove the soldier face forward into the sand, where he lay still,
stunned and exhausted. His arm holding the sword
stretched away from his body. Massaquoit stepped hard
on his wrist and the hand opened. He picked up the
sword. The others were within twenty-five yards and
they were calling to their fallen comrade and cursing
Massaquoit. He started to run again, and by the time he
reached the stand of cedar behind which his canoe was
hidden, he was fifty yards ahead of them and still pulling
away.

He trotted into the trees and reached his canoe. He
placed his shoulder against it and dug his feet into the
muddy sand. The canoe was sitting on the incline pointing down toward the narrow beach over which the surf,
now at high tide, was swirling. With two shoves, he
moved the canoe into the surf. One more push and it was
in water deep enough to float and he was sitting in it,
paddle in hand. Two of the English soldiers were close
enough to kneel and fire their weapons. The musket balls
fell well short of him. He saw them gesture to the others,
who reversed themselves and started running back, just
as he had hoped.

He paddled slowly out into the water and watched the
English soldiers as they traveled over the ground they
had just crossed in their pursuit of him. They arrived at
their shallop and he paddled a little faster. He saw the
man in the beaver hat gesticulating and pointing toward
the mainland. The soldiers buzzed around the shallop in
confusion for a few moments and then they organized
themselves into two parties, one on each side of the craft.

By the time they had their clumsy boat in the water, Massaquoit was paddling in earnest, heading for the mainland and the beach from which he had left.

He could only hope that Minneseewa had heard the musket shot and so was warned that the English had arrived.

TWELVE

❧❧

CATHERINE HEARD THE knock at her door although it was well past sundown. She was not expecting ordinary visitors, but she was not surprised to see Massaquoit standing in front of her. She knew that Lieutenant Waters had been sent after him and Margaret.

"You had better let me in right away," he said. "The English soldiers will be here before long looking for me."

As he walked through the door, he clutched the pouch she had given him to his side and, in so doing, brushed against the frame. He winced and brought his hand up to cover the wound.

"Come here into the light, then," she said, pointing toward a candle on the table in the front room where she had been sitting.

"Do not concern yourself," he said, but he let himself be led into the room. She ran her fingers over the raw scab.

"I have something for that."

"Do not bother." He pointed to his head. "I am more concerned about keeping this attached to my neck."

"You should not have come back here," she said. "I thought you would have fled to your people."

He handed her the pouch.

"You didn't come back to give me this, did you?" she asked.

"No. I came here because I was playing the hare to the English dogs."

"This is not the time for riddles. Come with me while I attend to your arm. You can explain yourself later."

Her tone, which he had come to understand, did not permit refusal, and so he followed behind her as she led the way holding the candle through the darkened hallway of her house and into the kitchen. There she lit another candle on the shelf where she stored her medicines and placed the candle she had carried onto the table. She motioned for Massaquoit to sit at the table while she ran her hands over her jars until her fingers found the one containing the paste made from comfrey leaves. She dipped her fingers into the jar and found the paste had dried. She gathered saliva in her mouth and wet her fingers before putting them back into the jar.

"Is that what you used on the man whose nose was cut?" Massaquoit asked.

"It is," she replied, and pressed a generous daub to his wound. Her fingers traced the outlines of the scab and then worked to the center. "He will never breathe the same way again, but you should be fine ere long."

"My mother on the island would have tended to me, but I had to leave before she could gather what she needed." He noted the confusion cross her face. "My wife's mother. She is skilled as you are in these things." He paused as though reminding himself of something. "I left the girl with her while I tried to lead the English away."

"Playing the hare?"

He nodded. "Sometimes when I walk in the forest I will see a hare jump into my path as though he wants me to see him, and I understand what he is about. He thinks he can outrun me, and he wants me to chase him."

"To lure you away from his burrow?"

"Exactly. He cannot fight me, for I am too strong for him, but he can try to trick me, to save his young. That is what I did. And some of the English followed me, and they will seek me here."

"And the others?"

"I fear they stayed on the island and will find my mother and the girl. After I arrived here, I hid my canoe and waited for some time, and then the English who had followed me in their boat came. They talked together on the beach. Then some of them got back into their boat. They looked to be going back to the island. The others will be here before long."

"They cannot just come into my house. They will go to a magistrate to get permission to approach me here."

"Are you that powerful, then?" he asked.

"My husband was, and I, although in his shadow, retain some of his light."

He slid the pouch across the table to her.

"You should have this back. It was his."

She opened it up and pulled out the paper.

"Did you show them this?"

"They did not care what it said."

"And the money?"

"They were more interested in that than me, for a moment or two."

"You are a clever man, Massaquoit." She lingered over his name. "I will use that name in this house."

"I am sorry I could not do better for the girl."

"You have done more than I could have expected. I will wake Phyllis. You can sleep in her room tonight."

"By tomorrow, the English will surely be here."

"By then we will have decided how to prove the girl innocent, and in so doing, we will lend the color of justice to your actions, which now seem black with rebellion."

"I think I might be able to help you. There is something I saw the night they took the girl away. Something that was hidden."

"Can you find this something again, do you think?"

"If I am safe here tonight, I will leave in the morning before the sun rises. I will be back if I am successful."

"And if you are not, you will not, is that so?"

"There will be no further reason for me to stay."

"Then for the girl's sake, if not your own, I hope to see you."

"I will send word, if I cannot come myself."

"I will pray for you."

"To your English God?"

"Of course."

"Your soldiers said that your God helped them to kill my people."

"They are mistaken. They did that by themselves."

"Giving my bed up to a savage," Phyllis complained in the morning. "And he did not even sleep in it. When I went back to my room, it was as though he had not been there, and would that he had not been."

"He needed it more than you."

The sound of drums rolled into the house.

"Wasn't yesterday the Sabbath?" Phyllis asked.

"It was."

"Then why are they drumming us to meeting when my poor head aches so."

"Come with me," Catherine replied. "It is not a meeting they are summoning us to."

They followed the sound of the drumming down the road and toward the village square. With each step, the drumming got louder, and Catherine's apprehension grew apace. The drummer was called out only for meeting or to summon the townspeople to witness some significant expression of communal action, such as bringing a condemned person to the gallows.

"I fear they have captured him," she said.

Phyllis only grunted in response, and they continued toward town in silence. The drumming was quite loud as they rounded the last curve before the road straightened on its way to the square. As they reached the square, they saw the source of the drumming arriving from the other side. A sizable crowd of fifty or sixty, drawn by the drumming, had already formed in front of the meetinghouse and stood watching the approaching column of soldiers. Catherine hastened into the crowd, and people, in deference to her position, grudgingly yielded space to her so she could pass through them to the front. The same people, however, closed ranks immediately after Catherine passed, so Phyllis had to force her way through amid a fair amount of grumbling. Catherine looked back.

"Let her pass," she said, and the people did. Phyllis arrived, red-faced, by her side.

"You would think they would know their betters," she said, and then her eyes followed Catherine's to the spectacle unfolding in front of them.

Lieutenant Waters, sword drawn, led two groups of soldiers as they marched onto the square and toward the jail. Their gait was measured by the slow thumping of the drummer at their front. In the first group, six soldiers walked in rows of two. In the middle of them, her steps hobbled by the heavy chains holding her ankles no more than a foot apart, and her hands behind her back in irons, was Margaret. The leg irons were also fastened to a heavy log that she had to drag behind her. Her cap was askew on her head, and her hair hung undone and matted down her back. Her face bore purple bruises on her cheeks, and one eye was swollen shut.

Behind this group came another eight soldiers in two columns. The first six held long poles that supported a wooden platform on which sat a makeshift cage formed out of freshly cut branches tied together with heavy rope. Inside the cage sat Minneseewa. Her face was covered with mud, and the dried blood of an English soldier crusted beneath her fingernails. That soldier was one of those supporting her cage, and his face bore the tracks of her nails from his forehead across his right eye and down to his neck. He wiped the sweat from his wounds from time to time and glanced at Minneseewa with murderous hatred. At the very rear of this second group, flanked by the last two soldiers, in slow dignity walked Wequash-cook. His head was bare, so that the jagged white scar was clearly visible in the bright sun. His beaver hat was held aloft on the end of a pike by one of the soldiers.

A small knot of citizens followed behind. Catherine noted Ned among them, along with his pox-faced companion. Ned was carrying a bucket filled with manure. He offered the bucket to his companion, whose ravaged face glistened with perspiration. The man dipped his hand into the bucket and heaved a lump of manure at the cage. It hit the top of the cage and splattered onto Minneseewa's face. She did not wipe it away. A constable stepped forward and took the bucket from Ned.

Hurrying as fast as he could to keep up with the slow-moving parade was Magistrate Woolsey. As he came abreast of Catherine, he stopped, his face red and his chest heaving from exertion.

"So you can see," he said, gesturing toward the soldiers and their prisoners as they passed.

"Indeed I can," Catherine said. She pointed to Margaret. "Was there any need for so much iron on the poor girl?"

"Why, look at her face," Woolsey replied.

"I am."

"She would not be taken easily," he said.

"Would you? With a rope awaiting your neck?" She turned toward the cage. "And that? I suppose she, too, fought for her liberty."

"She did. They both did, from accounts I have heard. They are to be held in the jail, under closer guard this time. And I must ask you, Catherine, since he is so firmly implicated in this matter, where is your savage?"

"He is no more mine than yours," she replied. "And as to where he is, I cannot say."

Woolsey pointed at Wequashcook.

"We have his comrade, as you can see for yourself. And it won't be long before we have him." He put his hand on Catherine's shoulder. "Understand me. I take no pleasure in these proceedings, and I will do what I can."

Catherine looked into the face of the man she had known so many years, and recognized his good intentions while also appreciating the limitations of his perceptions. Still, his temperament was gentle, so the anger he had flashed a little while before was unnatural to him. She removed his hand from her shoulder and nodded.

"We will talk later," she said. "I must see to the girl."

She walked out from the onlookers and placed herself

parallel to Margaret. The marchers halted in front of the jail. The drummer stopped beating his instrument. Jailor Drake, his eyes red, his face unshaved, and his shirt clumsily stuffed into his breeches, waited in front of the door. The lieutenant walked stiffly toward him.

"Are you ready to receive the prisoners?" he asked in a voice loud enough to be heard by the crowd. Drake looked bemused, but he nodded, turned around, and opened his door. Waters motioned to the drummer, who brought his sticks down in a staccato beat, a signal for the soldiers to pace toward the open door. When Margaret reached the doorway, she stumbled to her knees. Catherine helped her stand again. Margaret looked at Catherine as though she did not know who she was.

"If it please you, Mistress Williams," the lieutenant said, "step back and let us conduct our business."

"I will be watching," she said, as much for Margaret's benefit as for the lieutenant's, whose face reddened for a moment.

Margaret struggled into the doorway, but the log was too wide and she had to stop.

"Jailor," the lieutenant said, and Drake stepped forward. He grabbed the log and yanked it back out of the doorway, bringing Margaret back outside. Then Drake turned the log so it would go straight in and he shoved Margaret toward the door. She turned to him, her bruised face darkening with anger.

"I'm in no hurry to get back into your stinking hole, you know," she said.

Catherine reached out her hand to reassure her with a touch on her shoulder, but the lieutenant interposed himself.

"Please, Mistress Williams, let us be about what we have to do."

"Yes, Catherine," Woolsey said. The old man was breathing hard as he had had to force his way through the crowd that was now packed solidly in front of the jail. Catherine permitted him to lead her away. He took her a short distance from the doorway, but out of earshot of the lieutenant and the onlookers.

"You must tell me if you hear from him," he began.

"I do not know where he is," Catherine replied, "but I pray he is away free."

Massaquoit was not very far away at all. From his perch atop the meetinghouse roof, he watched. He, too, had heard the drums when they began to beat, and he had followed the sound to the beach where the shallop had just returned from Mummawtawkit to disgorge its cargo of English soldiers and their captives. He had seen the Englishwoman first, noted the bruises swelling dark purple on her face, saw the desperate anger in her eyes as she dragged the heavy log through the surf and onto the beach. And he had seen Minneseewa in her cage. He cursed himself for exposing them to the English instead of shielding them with his life. Rage rose in his chest until he shook like one whose fever was beyond medicine. It was a sickness that could be eased only with blood, yet he knew he could only watch as Minneseewa was carried clumsily out of the boat in the cage, as she was dropped once in the roiling surf, and as the English laughed while she was lifted up again, sputtering and spitting out the salt water she had swallowed.

And so, in his impotent fury, he had followed the procession from the shelter of the forest edge, not wanting to be captured, exactly, but not unhappy with the prospect of being seen and therefore provoked into a confrontation that would provide him the opportunity to close his hands around one English throat and squeeze until life fled with the man's last, pained breath.

It did not take him long to figure out that the procession would proceed to the square where the English worshiped their God on one side and sliced the nostrils of their criminals on the other. And so he had made his way ahead of them. When he arrived at the deserted square, for all the citizens of Newbury had rushed to follow the drum, he saw some thatch lying next to the meetinghouse, which was going to be used to replace a section of the roof that had been singed by a spark from the chimney. He took a bundle and climbed up a ladder that had been left leaning against the wall by the thatcher, who had also gone to see the excitement. Once on the roof, he covered himself with the thatch, and thus virtually invisible, watched the scene unfold beneath him.

He saw the same English boy he had fought with on the beach. He saw him dipping his hand into the bucket and hurling filthy handfuls of cow dung at Minneseewa, and he did nothing, but with each handful that splattered against the cage, he promised himself another act of vengeance, a finger snapped back, an eye gouged, a tongue pulled out, all performed without haste and with exquisite attention to the details of pain. He could only hope the boy would prove to be braver than he looked so that he would be justified in prolonging his agony.

Catherine stood by Woolsey's side as the door first closed behind Margaret and then after a few minutes opened again to receive Minneseewa. A soldier cut through the ropes securing the sides of the cage, for in their haste to construct it, the soldiers had not fashioned a door. When one side was cut free, the soldier pulled it back and motioned for the old woman to walk out. She sat motionless.

"Pull her out, then," Lieutenant Waters said.

The soldier reached to take her arm, but his hands closed around the cow dung that had dripped onto her there. He pulled his hand back in disgust, and then tried her other arm. He yanked until she half walked and half fell out of the cage. Two other soldiers pointed the sharp edges of their pikes at her and motioned toward the door. She rose unsteadily to her feet. A daub of manure was on her forehead and threatening to slide down her face, but she would not brush it off. One of the soldiers holding the pike scraped it off with the point of his weapon. Catherine could not be sure whether it was a gesture of generosity or contempt. Minneseewa seemed not to notice and she strode into the jail where Drake waited for her. The door shut behind her.

A few moments later two soldiers led Wequashcook into the jail.

"What is this?" the jailor said. "Another one? I've told the governor and anybody that would listen, I don't have food for the two inside."

"I wouldn't worry much," Lieutenant Waters said. "You won't have any of the three on your hands very long, if you get my meaning."

"Aye, I do, but still they will be moaning for a bit to eat before then," Drake grumbled, and pushed Wequashcook toward the open doorway.

"Keep a close watch on them," Waters said. "And we will have a guard outside as well. The governor was very particular in telling me that a jailor who cannot keep his prisoners won't be a jailor long in this town."

Drake shook his head and pointed at the wall, where obvious gaps permitted the sun to shine in.

"I am not saying anything, but the governor might want to consider making a better jail as well as replacing the jailor." He walked into his building and slammed the door hard enough behind to cause the frame to shake.

Catherine watched the door close and then waited. The crowd seemed reluctant to disperse, as though disappointed the spectacle was over, hoping perhaps to see it culminate in a hanging. But soon, in ones and twos, people began to walk away, talking in low voices that occasionally rose to a higher pitch as the excitement of watching the captives taken to the jail was told over, each time with a new embellishment. When all but a few stragglers remained, Catherine strode to the door where Magistrate Woolsey stood and Lieutenant Waters leaned at his ease between two soldiers, standing next to him at attention with their pikes' butt ends on the ground in front of them. Catherine pulled on Woolsey's arm.

"Come along, then, Joseph," she said. "I need you to get me inside the jail so I can attend to that girl. I do not think the Indian woman will let me help her, but perhaps I can try. As for the Indian man, I do not know why he is here."

"That is not a good idea," Woolsey said. "The people are inflamed against the girl. And the savages as well."

"I know. Come along now."

The magistrate did not move. Catherine leaned her face close to his.

"I now know the girl is innocent."

"Know?"

"Yes. I spoke with Martha Jameson just yesterday. She told me something that assured me I was right about the girl."

"What . . ." Woolsey began.

"Just trust me, Joseph. In good time I will tell you."

He nodded and then he freed his arm from Catherine's grasp and raised his hand to straighten his ruff, which was stained with perspiration and creeping up uncomfortably beneath his chin.

"Lieutenant," he said, "a word with you."

Catherine caught herself marveling at the sudden change of tone in her old friend's voice, which now assumed in this public setting an assertive air that was at odds with the perplexed and uncertain timbre she was accustomed to hearing in their private conversations.

"Would you be so kind," Woolsey said, "as to call the jailor so as to conduct Mistress Williams to his prisoners, where she can tend to their wounds?"

"Pardon me for asking, sir," Waters said, "but you can vouch for her, can you not, for we have reason to think that it was her savage what helped the girl escape."

"Lieutenant," Woolsey said, "remember who you are talking to and about."

"I was just doing my duty, as the governor has instructed me to take special pains, is all," Waters said. "On your word, then." He knocked on the door. Drake appeared.

"You don't have another one do you, Lieutenant?"

Waters did not respond, but motioned Catherine forward. He stepped several paces back as he did so, as if to distance himself from an act he clearly thought inappropriate. She passed him and approached Drake, close enough so that she could smell his fetid breath.

"You will not be playing the hangman," she said loudly enough for Waters to hear and to drive the jailor's head back. "You have my word on that. And as for food for those inside, I and Magistrate Woolsey will make sure there is enough. You just be certain that it does not get mislaid."

Drake stood silent and Catherine entered the jail. Once inside, she blinked in the half-light of the front room.

Drake shuffled by her and made his way to the door on the back wall of the room.

"She's in here," he said. "And this time in here she will stay." He lifted the latch. Catherine walked by him and into the room, which was even darker.

"Do you have a candle?"

"Yes, for me. She don't need one in there, mumbling her prayers she is."

"She might not, but I do."

Drake muttered something inaudible, but he picked up a candle from his table and lit it with a brand from the fireplace. He handed it to Catherine.

"I will be in the dark myself before long," he said.

"I will replace this one for you with three," Catherine replied.

Margaret sat huddled in the corner, her beads drawn tightly around her hands. She looked up when Catherine came in. Catherine knelt by her and ran her fingers over the bruises on her face. Margaret winced.

"I will be back with something for these hurts," she said.

"You are taking great pains for a dead woman," Margaret replied.

"No, Margaret, it is to make sure you stay alive that I take pains."

THIRTEEN

M ASSAQUOIT LAY on the roof of the meetinghouse
until the crowd was gone, Lieutenant Waters had
walked off, and only the two sentries, looking very bored,
remained in front of the jail. Then he crawled backward
to the rear of the building and climbed down the ladder
he had left there.

He had taken due note of the three prisoners, and now
he needed to sort out his impressions. Of course, he did
not have to analyze his response to seeing Minneseewa in
the cage being pelted with cow dung. That sight incited a
rage that was as understandable as it was necessary to
control so that he did not permit his anger to lead him
into a stupid or self-destructive act. He was, however,
strangely moved by viewing Margaret in chains, for as he
now understood, he saw in her another victim of the English. And then, and most troublesome for him, was the
spectacle of Wequashcook's scarred head and expressionless face as he, too, was led into the English prison
building. He did not know whether Wequashcook was
genuinely also a prisoner or was being shown as one to

mask his duplicity. For that reason, Massaquoit had stayed long on the roof, even as the sun began to bake him beneath his covering of thatch and as giant black flies seemed to find his face an inviting target. He waited to see if Wequashcook would emerge out of a back door after the other English went home. He did not, and Massaquoit was left to ponder how to fit that piece into the picture that was forming, however inchoately, in his mind.

He brushed off the thatch that clung to his chest and permitted himself the pleasure of scratching the swelling left on his cheek from a fly bite. He was standing at the rear of the meetinghouse, which was separated from the edge of the forest by only a narrow clearing of felled trees that had been planted into a garden for the benefit of Minister Davis. He was hungry. He had not eaten anything since the night before last on the island. He shook his head at the thought that it seemed as if he was always hungry, that as long as he lived near the English, he would have an ache in his empty belly. He examined the pole beans, and picked two handfuls. He started to lift the longest bean to his mouth, but then thought better. He would wait until he was in the shadow of the trees, where it was cool and he could eat in peace. Then he listened to the argument that was developing between his head and his heart.

Magistrate Woolsey was waiting with Phyllis in the front room of Catherine's house when she came back from the jail.

"I hope you forgive me," he said, "but I must talk with you. Phyllis has been so kind as to make me comfortable here."

"What is it, then, Joseph?"

"It is the governor. He has summoned a grand jury for tomorrow morning. He says the grand jury will find a true bill in the morning, that a petit jury will find the girl guilty in the afternoon, and that the hangman will have her by nightfall."

"Indeed, does he?" Catherine said, although her anger thickened her tongue so that she found it difficult to form the words.

"Indeed he does. He says the girl's escape from jail and her desperate fight to remain at liberty prove that she is guilty."

"I suppose he would have preferred confession, contrition, and repentance. I wonder what he would do in the same circumstance, unlikely as it is for a magistrate whose back is spared the whip to ever face the gallows."

"Catherine," Woolsey began, but he stopped himself.

"You would like to say that I go too far."

"Yes."

"Or maybe not far enough." She looked at Phyllis as though just remembering she was still there. "Do you not have vegetables to gather for dinner?"

"Edward will be bringing them in," Phyllis said.

"He needs help," Catherine replied, and Phyllis came slowly to her feet and turned reluctantly, as though she were being made to leave a party that she had been attending uninvited, for never before had she seen her mistress so combative, even with her old friend Joseph Woolsey.

After she left, the magistrate stood up, as though to leave.

"I must attend the governor," he said. "I was hoping you would tell me something I could carry back to him to dampen his enthusiasm for a hanging."

"And just why is he so anxious, do you think?"

Woolsey reddened.

"I think it has less to do with the girl than it does with you. He has said as much to me, that he does not value the Jamesons, that he feels that Henry has abandoned his stewardship of the family, and that his wife has now entirely lost her wits. He was angrier than ever I saw him when he learned that your Matthew helped the girl escape. When I told him the girl was with child, he said he would issue a writ *de ventre inspiciendo* to impanel a jury of matrons to make sure she was not lying to save her life, and if he cannot have Matthew, he will have the girl, although the truth is he would like to see them dance together at the end of a rope."

"He will not," Catherine said.

"But what can I say to him?"

"That the woman whose wits he thinks are gone has spoken to me."

"Yes?"

"And that in a day or two I will have proof of the girl's innocence."

"If not the girl, then who?"

"I cannot tell you that yet."

Woolsey shook his head slowly from side to side.

"Catherine, you give me a twig when I need a stout log to shut the door on the governor's rage."

"Clothe it in a Latin phrase, if you must, to stay him."

The magistrate furrowed his brows as the idea came to him.

"You await something from somebody," he said.

"Yes."

"Matthew? Is he not fled?"

"Go, Joseph, and see if you can be my shield awhile longer."

"The Psalmist says, 'The Lord shall cover thee with his

feathers, and under his wings shall thou trust; his truth shall be thy shield and buckler.' "

"I do trust the truth, Joseph," Catherine said as she led Woolsey to the door, "and I trust you as well."

Massaquoit concentrated on the pain. His calves had passed into numbed indifference an hour ago, and his back muscles had spasmed into tight pulsing knots, so he focused on his thighs, where the pain now radiated down toward his knees and up toward his hips. It was not quite symmetrical. The ache in his right leg was both more intense and moved quicker than that in his left.

He savored the pain. It seemed right that he should be feeling it. All else was confused. He did not know which way to direct his steps should he straighten his legs, so he remained squatting until muscles screamed in defiance and demanded a decision that would permit him to stand up and relieve them. All afternoon he had vacillated. A dozen times he had begun the search in the woods behind the Jameson house to put himself in the service of Catherine and her efforts to save Margaret, but after a few vague steps he had stopped. Then he had turned in the opposite direction toward the water and the implausible possibility of safety if he could recover his canoe and paddle it beyond Munnawtawkit to Paumonok, beyond the reach of the English and their muskets and pikes. But each step in that direction took him away from Margaret and, just as importantly, from Minneseewa. He had never been so paralyzed by indecision.

He pressed his fingers into his thigh muscles to increase the pain. His eyes closed against it. He saw the face of his wife, the little scar on her forehead from her childhood fall from a low-hanging branch of a young oak, her prominent cheekbones, her eyes as bright as the fire that danced in the night, and her lips curved into a smile of pleasure. He studied this image, drawn from his memory, and so he did not hear the soft footsteps in the underbrush until a twig snapped, and he was brought back to the present. He opened his eyes expecting to see the muzzle of a musket or the blade of a sword. He would rise and present his chest to the English weapons, and so wrench himself from his confusion.

What he saw was the face of an English girl staring curiously at him, without the fear he was used to seeing.

"Why are you here?" she asked.

He struggled to his feet, and she took a step back.

"Are you lost or hurt?" she asked.

"No."

"I have seen you with Mistress Williams going to meeting. They say you helped the papist girl escape."

"I am Massaquoit. I am looking for something that Mistress Williams needs to keep that girl from the gallows."

"Oh," she said, and her face brightened. "I know what you seek, and I know where it can be found."

Massaquoit remembered the small figure he had seen that night of the torches and angry voices. It had been just visible darting in the shadows. He now knew that it had been the girl standing in front of him.

"Will you show me?" he asked, for in the child's face he read something that blew his indecision away like a wind clearing a storm cloud from the horizon.

He waited until dark and then he approached Catherine's house. As the moon rose, he remembered what Minneseewa had told him that night he spent on Munnawtawkit. He did not know if the Englishwoman would find Minneseewa's prediction credible or interesting, but he would tell her anyway. The clouds were gathering in front of the moon, just as Minneseewa had said they would. The next night they would collect in even greater force.

He stayed in the shadows and worked his way to the rear of the house, where the kitchen door led out to the back garden. The window next to the door glowed a faint yellow from a candle inside. He strode to the window and peered in. He expected to see Phyllis or maybe even Edward, but he did not want to be surprised by finding some other English visiting Mistress Williams.

Edward was sitting at the table with a knife in one hand and a stick he was whittling in the other. The old man seemed to sense his presence at the window, for he looked up and stared in his direction. Massaquoit knocked loudly on the door and watched as Edward stood slowly to his feet. He put down the stick, but he held the knife in front of him as he walked toward the door. He disappeared out of Massaquoit's line of vision, and so the Indian waited, expecting the door to swing open. When it did not, he knocked again.

"Open up, old man," he called.

"Who is it?"

"Matthew," he replied. "I must talk to Mistress Williams."

Catherine was on her way from the front room, where she had been going over an account book, before Massaquoit had knocked a second time.

"Open the door, Edward," she said.

"He says he is Matthew, but I do not think so."

"Open the door, and we will see, won't we?"

Edward turned the door handle and pushed it open, stepping back as he did so.

"It's that savage," he said. "He wants to talk to you, he says."

"Come on in," Catherine said. "You can return to your carving, Edward."

"He can't have my knife," Edward mumbled, and walked back to the table.

Massaquoit followed Catherine past Edward and into the front room. She sat down at her desk and stared absently at the figures on the page. Then she closed the book. Something in her manner told Massaquoit that she was uncomfortable.

"Do those numbers have anything to do with the *Good Hope*?"

She nodded.

"I am afraid so. But I do not apologize for my business."

"I did not come here to talk to you about your ship, but to give you this." He held out his hands. In it was a small blanket. "The little girl led me to it. She followed her cousin that night."

Catherine shook the blanket open. It was woven of coarse wool that might once have been white but was now gray. She held it to the candle's flickering light and examined both sides. Then she folded it back into a small square.

"Henry will recognize this, and so will Martha. And most especially Ned."

"Are you going to return it to them?"

"Yes."

"And that will help the girl?"

"It will."

He took the blanket from her and held it to his cheek.

"I think I feel the coldness of a bad spirit living in this blanket."

"I truly hope so. But if it is not, I will help it seem as though there is."

"You might want to make haste to give it back to him, then, by tomorrow night. Minneseewa has told me the moon will hide then."

"Did she indeed?"

"Yes. And I do not think she is ever wrong about such things."

"Then tomorrow night it will be. Will you be there?"

He had prepared for this question.

"Yes, but not where you will see me."

"I have spoken with Magistrate Woolsey about Minneseewa. She will be released. The soldiers should not have taken her."

"I do not think she gave them a choice."

"I saw what young Ned did. But you must not take vengeance on him. He is a foolish boy."

"I cannot forgive him his insult."

She put her hand on his arm.

"Do not do his work for him, for that is what you will do if you strike out at him."

He handed the blanket back to her.

"I will sleep outside as I am used to. It is the safest place I can think of. The English soldiers will not look for me there."

She felt herself smile at his audacity.

"You are probably right."

"And I will be gone before the sun rises."

She conducted him to the back of the house. Edward still sat at the table working his piece of wood. She closed the door behind Massaquoit, and then she turned to Edward.

"The first thing in the morning," she said, "I want you to gather the ripest strawberries you can find."

He did not look up.

"Did you hear?" she said.

"It is early for strawberries," he said.

"Find some that are ripe. The girl's life depends on it."

"I thought you wanted some for breakfast," he replied, and dug his knife into the wood.

Catherine stood at the back door staring through the early-morning sun at Massaquoit's wigwam. She walked across the dew-laden grass and pulled back the woven reeds that formed a flap over the entrance. He was gone, as he said he would be. When she returned to the house, Phyllis was waiting for her.

"Magistrate Woolsey is in the front room," she said.

"Did you ask him to join us for breaking the fast?"

"He says he has already done so, and needs to speak a few words with you."

Woolsey was pacing back and forth between the fireplace and the doorway to the front room.

"I am on my way to the grand-jury inquest," he said.

"I have no doubt as to the outcome. It is foreordained."

Woolsey shook his head in disapproval.

"By the evidence, Catherine, by the evidence."

"Yes. The evidence."

"Do you have anything to present to the jury that might change their decision?"

"I will have, by tonight."

"That will be too late."

"You are not telling me that the girl will hang before tonight, are you?"

"Too late for the grand jury. You know there are steps between that and the gallows."

"Steps Governor Peters will happily abridge."

"I can make sure he pauses on each."

"At sunset tonight, I will be at the Jameson house. Let that be known after the jury does its business."

Woolsey turned his head vaguely toward the back of the house.

"Will Matthew be there?"

"I cannot say."

"I see," he replied. He picked up the wide-brimmed hat, which was on the table next to the door. "Will you walk with me?"

"No," she said. "I follow after."

"Here will be just fine," Catherine said, and Phyllis placed the two chairs she had been carrying down onto the grass in front of the meetinghouse, inside of which the grand jury was convening. Phyllis was breathing hard and she wiped the sweat from her brow.

"We could have waited at home, couldn't we have? Master Woolsey said he would come right by and tell us what happened."

"Yes, he did. But I know what they are going to do. They are going to find a good bill and indict that girl. I want to be here to look them in the face as they come out."

Phyllis opened her mouth as though to continue the conversation, but Catherine motioned for her to be quiet. Her mind was refining the scene she had been inventing since her conversation with Massaquoit the night before. She had gone to sleep and dreamed it, and now this morning she kept playing if over and over. It was not working. All she heard was laughter coming from Henry and Ned Jameson while Martha sat mute in the shadows with Ann at her side stroking her forehead and rubbing her shoulders. The laugh began as a snicker and built to a howl as it merged with the contemptuous roar of the townspeople who witnessed her failure. She moved her lips to explain, but the laughter swallowed her words. High above the pitch of the laughter, she heard a thin buzzing, insistent but distant. Then something tugged at her sleeve. She turned to see Phyllis's mouth moving and felt her hand tightening on her arm.

"Mistress Williams," Phyllis said, "do you not hear me?"

"Of course, I do."

Phyllis glanced up at the sun. Perspiration gathered on her upper lip, and she ran her tongue over it.

"Perhaps we should move over there," she said, and pointed to the shade cast by a huge maple.

"Go, if it suits you," Catherine replied.

"Are you sure?"

"Go."

Phyllis picked up her chair and carried it to the tree. She set it down near the trunk and leaned her head back. Catherine closed her eyes to try again. This time she added an element that had been missing before and there was no laughter, only stunned amazement on all those laughing faces. She knew what she had to do, and she could only hope this last element would appear tonight as clearly as it had just manifested itself in her thoughts.

The large oak door of the meetinghouse swung open and Woolsey emerged. He glanced once at Catherine, and then he looked down at his feet. Catherine strode over to where Phyllis still sat beneath the maple.

"We can go home now," she said.

Phyllis looked toward the magistrate, who was talking to a knot of people, including Governor Peters and Minister Davis. The crowd around him thickened as more people walked out of the meetinghouse.

"Do you not want to talk to Master Woolsey?" Phyllis asked.

Catherine shook her head.

"I know what the jury has said. I do not need to hear it spoken."

Phyllis's face registered her usual confusion.

"Is he telling them, then?" she asked, pointing to the small crowd that grew as people continued to emerge from the meetinghouse.

"No, I trust he is giving them an invitation from me."

"Indeed," Phyllis said as she struggled to her feet and picked up her chair. "I did not think you would be inviting people to our house at a time like this."

"Not our house," Catherine replied as they walked back to where she had been sitting. Phyllis shifted her chair to one arm and picked up Catherine's. "To the Jameson house, this evening," Catherine continued.

"I see," Phyllis replied, but it was clear that she did not.

"And as soon as we reach home, we must be sure that Edward has gathered the strawberries as I asked him to do."

"Yes, strawberries. I am hungry," Phyllis said.

Catherine began walking down the road, and Phyllis stumbled after her, trying to balance the chairs evenly on each side of her body as she hurried to catch up.

"The strawberries are not for you," Catherine said. "They are for the babe's blanket."

"I see," Phyllis said. "For the blanket. What else would we want strawberries for?"

"Exactly," Catherine said.

FOURTEEN

❧❧❧

THAT EVENING, BENEATH a bright full moon, Catherine and Phyllis made their way toward the Jameson house. When they arrived, they found Henry and Ned waiting for them some twenty yards from the house. A number of people were clustered about them, for the road was so narrow there that the two men, standing with their arms across their chests, blocked all passage. An expectant murmur arose from the crowd as Catherine and Phyllis approached.

"Here she is, as she said she would be," one said.

"And why does she come here, bothering the family in their grief, that is what I want to know. She plotted with that savage, you know she did," said another.

"Aye, so they say."

Catherine heard these murmurings, but walked through the crowd with her eyes fixed on Henry. She knew more people were following behind, and among these, according to rumor being bruited about, were Governor Peters and Minister Davis. A few steps behind her and in a hurry to keep up, as evidenced by his labored breathing, was

Woolsey. Phyllis remained a few feet to her side, standing with her arms clasped over something that she held to her chest.

"Henry, where is your wife?" Catherine asked.

Henry, his face dark with anger, turned his head back toward his house.

"Is she sick?" Catherine asked. "For I have come to talk with her, as well as you and young Ned here."

"If that is why you have come, you can turn around. We do not have nothing to say to you."

Catherine glanced up at the moon. A few moments before it had been perfectly round. Now one curve was flattened ever so slightly, as though a giant hand had just begun to slide a piece of black paper across its surface. She breathed a mental sigh of relief at the confirmation of Minneseewa's prediction. Still, she would have to be careful. The timing of what she was about to do would be delicate, and made much more difficult by the sullen intransigence already exhibited by Henry, and the insolent ill temper she could anticipate from Ned, whose color was heightened and who was finding it difficult to stand still.

"Will you not bring your wife out?" Catherine asked.

"No," Henry said. "She is in her bed, where your medicine put her." He turned his back to Catherine and took a step toward the house. "Come, lad," he said to Ned. "Magistrate Woolsey is here, and he can see that we are left in peace. We need not talk more."

Catherine felt a cool breeze float across her face, and she looked up to see that the black paper sliding over the moon had now quite definitely squared one side. Several people near her followed her eyes upward. There had been a constant murmur of conversation among the people watching the confrontation, but now that buzz ceased.

The silence fell over them hard, like the aftermath of a crack of thunder rattling down from the heavens, and Henry, as if he heard the hush, stopped. Ned kept walking for a step or two, and then he, too, paused as though caught by the grasp of an invisible hand. Catherine motioned Phyllis forward.

"Now," she said.

Phyllis unclasped her arms and extended them. In her hands she held the carefully folded blanket. Catherine took it from her. The night was becoming darker.

"Go inside the house and fetch a torch," Henry said, "so I can see what she is holding there that has struck everybody dumb."

Ned looked up.

"The moon," he said, "it was bright as day just now."

"What are you talking about, lad? A cloud, nothing more."

Ned continued looking up.

"I don't see any clouds. And the moon is disappearing."

"Get the torch."

Ned walked back toward the house. A few moments later he returned, carrying a blazing brand. Several paces behind him came Martha, followed by Ann.

"Now then, mistress," Henry said, taking the brand from Ned, "what do you have here?"

"Only the babe's blanket," Catherine said. "And it is right that your wife see it, too."

"Hmmph!" Henry said. He turned and held the torch toward the house. Its flame cast a weak and flickering light on the expressionless face of Martha, who stood looking without seeming to see. "Get you back into the house."

Martha did not respond. Ann tried to turn her, but Martha remained still.

"Well, then, I guess it don't matter," Henry said.

"Good," Catherine replied. She snapped open the blanket and held it high above her head. "Come and have a look. Bring the torch close and see how the babe's blanket calls out against its killer."

From where he stood in the shadows on the hill overlooking the Jameson house, not far from where Ann had led him to the blanket, which had been shoved beneath a pile of brush, as though in haste, by someone who intended to return to do a better job of concealment, Massaquoit stared at Ned. He noted, of course, how Catherine held up the blanket he had given her, and he knew that somehow that piece of cloth was going to declare Margaret innocent. He saw the old Englishman, Catherine's friend, and in the crowd behind them he could make out the round skullcap of the minister, and the towering figure of the governor beneath his wide-brimmed hat, but none of these held his interest to nearly the same degree as the boy who had fought with him on the beach, who had insulted him in the tavern, and who had hurled dung at Minneseewa as she rode in her crude cage. So absorbed was he in directing his silent rage at Ned that he almost did not hear the soft footsteps coming up behind him. He whirled about just as a firm hand grasped his arm.

Wequashcook took a step back and released his hold. His beaver cap slid down his forehead, and he pushed it back.

"They gave you your hat back," Massaquoit said.

"I bought it back, with more wampum than it is worth."

"You are fortunate to still have a head to put it on."

Wequashcook offered the trace of a smile.

"I am useful to them. When I came upon you, you were staring at that English boy, as though your eyes could send arrows through his heart."

"Yes," Massaquoit said. "Can you deliver him to me like you delivered Minneseewa to the English so that boy could amuse himself with her?"

Wequashcook recoiled as though he had been slapped, and then he shook his head with exaggerated slowness.

"You should believe what you see with your eyes."

"I saw you in chains. And now I see you here."

"And I am come to tell you that Minneseewa waits for you on the beach." He looked up. "She said to tell you that you must come to her before the moon goes to sleep." The moon was now more than half-covered by the creeping wall of blackness. The air, too, was cooling down, as though warmth were being lost with the light. "Do you not see?" he asked. "The English boy is like a fly nibbling on the flank of a horse. Come with me and Minneseewa back to Munnawtawkit. Let the English do what they want to each other. It is none of our business."

"The old Englishwoman saved my life."

Wequashcook spat on the ground.

"I know you too well, Massaquoit. It is the boy's blood you want." He reached beneath his coat into the waistband of his breeches and pulled out a knife. He handed it to Massaquoit, handle first. "If it is blood you want, here is a weapon for you. I got it in trade."

Massaquoit took the knife from him and tested its balance. Then he held it out for Wequashcook to take back.

"It is good. Do you not need it?"

Wequashcook shook his head.

"My warrior days are over. Fight the English if you

must." He looked up at the darkening moon. "But I am not so foolish." And he was gone into the shadows of the trees. Massaquoit listened, waiting for his footsteps to disappear. When they were gone, he placed the knife in the waistband of his loin covering, and then he turned his eyes back to the scene unfolding below. The English boy was holding his torch near the blanket. It almost looked as though he intended to set it afire.

Catherine took the torch from Ned and held it a safe distance from the blanket, which she had draped across her other arm. She turned to the crowd. Those closest leaned in to get a better look, and then those behind pushed forward as well so that the crowd of people around Catherine seemed to thicken. Phyllis placed herself between the crowd and her mistress, and Woolsey motioned for the people to retreat, but they did not.

"Minister Davis," Catherine said, "I know you are there. Can you step forward?"

The crowd murmured and the minister, as though pushed along by the energy of the people's voices, emerged and stepped toward Catherine.

"Mistress Williams," the minister said, "you have summoned the people, and they grow impatient."

"Do you not see the moon retreating?" Catherine asked.

"I do indeed," Minister Davis replied. "And what signifies it? What has it to do with this man, and this family?"

"Why, just what I hoped you would open for us." She turned to Henry. "Do you not have something to say to us?" she asked.

Henry shook his head.

"Do you not see this very blanket that swaddled your babe?" Catherine demanded.

"It is dark, in truth," Henry said.

"Why, then look closer," Catherine demanded. "Do you not see the spots of your babe's blood? Do they not call out to you, as they did on the night you brought us all here to see your dead babe bleed when Margaret touched it? Why, she is in the jail tonight, and you are here. Will you touch the blanket, Henry?"

"What means this, mistress?" Minister Davis asked.

"Why, no more than what is just," Catherine replied. "Henry knows what this signifies. Don't you, Henry? You know what your wife, Martha, whispered in my ear not two days ago when I came at your bidding to loose her tongue."

Henry let out a grunt as though he had been hit.

"Why, mistress, you know well that you would not repeat her words to me."

"That I would not until I had confirmation, and now I do. Come, Henry, touch the blanket, as you had your servant girl touch the babe. She is in jail facing the gallows. What fear you?"

"Why, I, nothing do I fear."

"Then touch!" The cry came from one voice in the front of the crowd, and then it carried like a wave rolling over a succession of rocks, pausing to gather at each one until the whole assembly of citizens demanded, "Touch the blanket, Henry Jameson."

Ned edged a step or two away from his uncle. His movement caught Catherine's eye and she pointed the torch in his direction.

"Where go you, Ned?"

"Why, nowhere."

"It was you that hid this blanket, was it not?"

"I never hid nothin', mistress," Ned replied, although

the tremor in his voice belied the confidence of his words.

"He did no wrong," Henry said. "If you spoke with my Martha, you know that."

"Tell us about it, then," Catherine demanded.

"Tell us," the crowd echoed.

It was now almost completely dark except for the uncertain glare of the torch. The breeze was now both cooler and stronger, and the flame bent before it.

"There is blood and there is dark," Catherine said. "Is that not providential, Master Davis?"

"Why, what blasphemy, woman?"

"None at all, for it is written, 'I will show wonders in heaven above, and signs in the earth beneath blood, and fire, and vapor of smoke. The sun shall be turned into darkness, and the moon into blood.' "

"Yes," Minister Davis said, " 'before the great and notable day of the Lord.' What has that to do with Henry and Martha Jameson and their dead babe?"

"A sign, Master Davis," Catherine said, and then she raised her voice to a shout, "a sign indeed that the Lord will have us see the truth amid this dark and fire and smoke and blood." She waved the blanket in front of Henry. "Touch it," she said, and the crowd echoed, "A sign, touch it."

Minister Davis shook his head, but it was clear he would not contest the mood of the people.

"Touch it, Henry," he said. "You have nothing to fear."

"What say you?" Henry replied, incredulous. "Why, listen to the people." He took a step toward Martha and embraced her. He leaned to whisper in her ear. She did not seem to respond. He pushed her toward the house. "Take her inside," he said to Ann. The girl took her mother's arm and would have walked with her the few steps toward the house, but Martha stopped and would not proceed. Henry shrugged and turned back to Catherine.

"She that killed our babe is in the jail." He looked up toward the moon, now invisible behind its black cloak.

"Put your hand on it, then, Henry Jameson, and let the truth be revealed," Catherine said.

Henry began to extend his hand and then put it down. Master Davis touched Catherine's arm.

"A word with you, mistress," he said in a voice just loud enough for her to hear above the expectant murmur of the crowd. Catherine took one step back, but she kept her eyes on Henry.

"What do you think you will show?" Davis said, his voice a nasty hiss between teeth open just enough to permit egress to the words he spat into the dark air.

"Why, no more than what was proved the night Margaret Mary Donovan was made to touch the skin of that dead babe."

"Pshaw. You know what I think of such superstitions."

"So you say to me in a voice only I can hear. None heard you say so that night."

"There was no point. The girl was to be tried."

"And so she was. And now if you will excuse me, I am trying to undo the damage done that night. That is what I intend to show." She stepped back toward Henry and waved the blanket before his face.

"I say again, you must touch it."

And he did. With a motion as tentative as though he were placing his hand into a pot of boiling water, which he knew would scald him through his skin to the bone, he reached forth his hand, and loath though he was to bring his flesh against the cloth that had swaddled his dead child, still he did, and then as though he actually felt the boiling heat, he yanked his offending fingers back. Catherine held the blanket in front of her for several moments, and then she pulled her face into an expression of astonishment.

"Blood appears, do you not see it, Henry Jameson?" she said, and she thrust the blanket at Henry.

"I see nothing but the same cloth I touched a moment ago."

Catherine brought the torch closer to the blanket.

"Master Woolsey, what do you see?"

Woolsey peered at the cloth, bringing his face to within several inches.

"I see several red spots," he said.

"Blood! There is blood!" came a voice from the darkness.

The crowd pressed closer. A young woman in front said, "Blood on the blanket." An older man, his eyes tearing from the strain of looking through the darkness toward the cloth he could barely make out, nodded his head. "Aye," he said. "To be sure, there are stains of newly risen blood on that blanket." There was a shuffling of feet, and a cry of "Make way, make way for the governor," and Master Peters made his way to stand next to Catherine.

"You, too, then, Governor," Catherine said. "Do you not see the red spots of the babe's blood on that blanket?"

Governor Peters bent his long frame into a stoop so that he could examine the cloth, and then he nodded very slowly.

"Yes, but I know not what it signifies."

Catherine looked past the governor to the crowd that seemed, in the darkness, to have formed itself into one common body with a hundred heads, with a hundred mouths speaking a constant hum that flowed past Governor Peters to Henry Jameson, and she understood that the governor, politic as ever, would not offer a significant impediment to the will of the crowd.

"You know well enough, I believe," she said.

Just then another voice rose, plaintive above the crowd's muttering.

"Mother," Ann said, "Mother, what ails you?"

Martha Jameson's face was contorted into a twisted grimace, and her mouth opened as though to emit a shout that wouldn't rise. Her mouth closed and then opened again, and her face contorted even more, so that it appeared that her left eye had risen an inch higher than her right. Her nostrils flared, and then the sound started. It began as a giggle, almost like the laugh of the little girl she had been thirty years before, and then it deepened into a genuine guffaw, and finally it metamorphosed into a moan of despair such as would more likely come from an animal whose legs felt the iron teeth of the hunter's trap than from the mouth of a woman. And as the moan grew into a howl, the murmurings of the crowd ceased as all stood with eyes fixed upon her. Henry's body shook with the tremor of muscles in spasm as he strove to control his anguish. Catherine lowered her torch and clutched the blanket to her chest. Ned slipped into the enveloping shadows. When Catherine thought to raise the torch again, he was gone. She handed the torch to Phyllis and embraced Martha. She held the woman until the howl lowered into a moan and then the moan softened into an almost gentle laughter, and then Martha allowed herself to be led back toward her house by her daughter. Catherine accompanied her for several steps and then she turned back to Henry.

"Tell us, then," Catherine demanded.

He reached out his hand and took the blanket from her.

He held it in his powerful workman's hand as gently as though it were woven of glass.

"We have no money. We never have enough to eat. My poor wife could not care for the babe. She has not been herself since the birth. She could not give it suck. We had no way to pay a nurse. We were all so tired. We just wanted to sleep. I picked up the child. Maybe I shook it. I do not recall. Then I put it down. Later I saw that girl hovering over it. I lifted my dead child up, and she was saying those strange prayers of hers, and then I sent Ned to get help. You know the rest. I have no more to say. I must tend to my wife."

He strode toward the house, and nobody thought to detain him.

Massaquoit, his eyes fully adjusted to the growing darkness, focused on Ned. He heard the clamor, and his stomach tightened against the howls rising from Martha, but his eyes stayed steady on the boy, as though he were a deer that would startle at the slightest disturbance. So he saw Ned as he slipped out of the crowd while everybody else watched Henry lead his wife back into the house. He saw him retreat into the tree line behind the house, and a moment's thought gave him the clue as to where the boy might head. He would seek the water. He would not venture too far into the woods. That is why the blanket had been stowed beneath the brush not twenty yards into the trees. The English thought that strange and marvelous creatures inhabited the woods, but they felt secure with sand beneath their feet and the smell of water on the breeze. Ned would have no other place to run, even if he did not know what he would do when he reached the beach. And Massaquoit would be there waiting for him.

•   •   •

Catherine and Phyllis walked behind the dispersing crowd.

"God does show us the way," Phyllis said, looking up at the moon, again fully visible.

Catherine brought her fingers to her mouth to lick off the strawberry juice.

"That He does," she said. "And He shows him to help Him."

FIFTEEN

❧❦❧

GOVERNOR SAMUEL PETERS'S new mansion stood on a low hill overlooking Newbury's town square. Until recently he had been living in a more modest house in the town center. In England he had been a lawyer living partly on fees, but primarily on income from his family's lands in Suffolk. The Peters' estate sat on property that the governor's grandfather had bought from the crown after King Henry VIII confiscated it from the Catholic Church, as part of England's reformation. In New England, however, having left his family fortune behind, he had abandoned his profession as lawyer to become a merchant, importing Englishmanufactured items and exporting the cod that swam in abundance off the coast of Newbury. He had, as it turned out, a better head for business than he did for the law, and had become, in a short time, very wealthy, and at the urging of his wife, who frequently reminded him of the manor house they had left behind, he contracted for the construction of the mansion where he now sat at his large desk as he talked with Minister Davis, Magistrate Woolsey, and Catherine.

From her place on one of the few upholstered chairs in Newbury, if not New England, Catherine was more aware than she had ever been before of the governor's transformation from a devout Puritan seeking a place where he could worship his God as he chose, to a businessman and, not incidentally, politician, who seemed to care at least as much for his purse as his soul. An oil painting of the governor's stern grandfather looked out from the wall behind the desk, and linen curtains of regal blue hung before the two windows on the east wall of the room, in bold contrast to the whitewashed walls. An oak chest with two large drawers and three smaller ones sitting on a frame of elaborately turned legs occupied the space between the windows. Two tall candles on the chest and another two on the desk flickered from silver holders, reminding Catherine that Governor Peters had introduced forks to Newbury, and had presented a silver one to her husband as a token of their friendship. Now, however, she was quite sure that the memory of that ancient friendship had been strained, if not eradicated, by the evening's spectacle in front of the Jameson house. He bent his long frame over the desktop and toward Catherine, giving to her mind the impression of a snake uncoiling at the mouth of its lair.

"Well, Catherine," the governor said, "you do surprise me, that you would so upset the community when the matter was under the watchful eye of the law."

"Do you refer to that poor girl in prison?"

"I do, of course, but more of the process which put her there."

"And which will release her as a consequence of Henry's confession?"

"That is what we are here to discuss," Peters said. "It is not so certain to my mind that releasing the girl after hearing the ravings of a man whose facilities were unsettled by the crowd and the strange occurrence of the moon, and not least, your dramaturgy, would be wise. I did not know you had acted on the stage."

"She has certainly not," Woolsey interjected, "and I think we should talk about our common interest in seeing that justice is served."

"Justice and the well-being of the community, to be sure," the governor replied with a smile so cold it all but frosted his lips. He nodded at Woolsey. "Is that not so, Joseph?"

"The interest of the community and justice for the girl," Woolsey said, "are they not the same?"

Peters straightened up and the smile disappeared from his face, replaced by an expression of studied seriousness. "Of course, they should be. But before we act, I think we must have an opportunity to talk to Henry Jameson, and perhaps Martha as well, if she can be encouraged to speak words we understand. I would not want to act in haste, nor would I want to be bullied by the emotions of a mob."

"Are you not going to arrest the man?" Catherine demanded. "He has confessed."

"I have sent the constable to watch over his house, but I intend to let him sleep in his own bed tonight. Tomorrow, we shall have him taken to the meetinghouse and we will interrogate him."

"And the girl?"

"She must be asleep already. I do not think the jailor spends overmuch on candles. If Henry Jameson repeats his story to us, in the calm of a magisterial inquiry, she can be let free soon enough. And then put her on the first boat back to Ireland, where she can have her bastard child."

Minister Davis had been sitting stonily in his chair, as though everything about this proceeding irritated him. He now stood up and adjusted his skullcap.

" 'Justice and judgment are the habitation of the Lord's throne.' Let us remember that tomorrow. Justice and judgment. Both are the Lord's."

"Of course," Peters said. "We labor only to do His will."

Catherine looked from one to the other, and then to Woolsey.

"Joseph, if you will be so kind as to walk with me?"

They walked away from the stately house. Catherine looked back at the windows of the governor's front room, still yellowed by the candlelight, and she imagined the governor and the minister, heads together, discussing how God's justice and judgment might be applied to Margaret Mary Donovan.

The moon, risen again from its sleep, had reasserted itself, bold, round, and golden in the night sky. Its light illuminated the shore where Massaquoit squatted behind the huge boulder on which Margaret had perched the night of their escape. It was twenty feet onto the sand that began where the forest gave way to the beach, and it was in a direct line with the road the English had built through the woods from the town center to the harbor.

He had been resting long enough for the night breeze to have carried away the perspiration that had coated his body during his run along an older and narrower trail that paralleled the road. He had exerted himself so that he would arrive well ahead of Ned, but now he wanted to be calm, and breathing easily when he put his hands on the boy, his cool purpose setting off in clear relief the boy's terror.

As he squatted beneath the bright moon, listening to the breeze slap the surf against the shore, waiting for the sounds of Ned's hurrying footsteps to break the even rhythms of the water, he suddenly realized that he had heaped upon Ned his pent-up anger at the English, at all of the English. He told himself that the boy deserved his hatred, but he could not deny to himself that Ned had become for him the reification of the evil spirit that had blown across the ocean with the winds that drove the English ships to these shores, bringing a decimation from disease and war from which his people would never recover, and that in this sad story the boy was no more than a twig on the great and oppressive English tree whose branches cast such a devastating shadow over his land. Perversely, the more he thought of the general ruin caused by the English, the harder it was for him to sustain the heat of his anger toward the particular English boy. As he waited, he stoked the fire of his hatred, and yet he felt that his passion might soon consume itself and let drift its ash onto a heap of exhausted despair. He did not know what he would do when Ned fell into his hands.

He did not have to wait long to find out. Just as he stood to stretch his legs, he heard branches snapping as something hurtled heedlessly through them, and beneath the sharp sound of the breaking wood was the uneven, stumbling thud of an exhausted runner who continued to drive his legs forward by a force of will that coerced yet one more stride, and then another, from fatigued muscles.

Massaquoit stepped from behind the boulder just as Ned staggered down to one knee on the sand where the road met the beach. Ned's sides heaved and his eyes were closed. Sweat soaked his shirt and his breeches, causing the sand to adhere to him as he lay down and rolled onto his back, his eyes still closed and his mouth opened wide

to gasp for breath. He opened his eyes just in time to see
Massaquoit's foot come down on his chest. He grabbed
Massaquoit's ankle and tried to wiggle free. Massaquoit
just stepped down harder. Ned's face flushed as he tried
to breathe against the increasing pressure. Massaquoit
dug his heel into Ned's sternum, and the boy's mouth
opened again and his eyes bulged. He tried even harder to
pry Massaquoit's foot off of him, but the effort rendered
him weak and breathless.

"Please," he managed to wheeze.

"Where is your bucket of dung now?" Massaquoit
asked. He eased the pressure just a little. He wanted to
hear what Ned might say.

"What?" the boy asked.

"You know. What you were throwing at my mother the
other day."

The blood drained from Ned's face.

"I didn't know."

"It wouldn't have mattered, would it have?" Massaquoit said, driving his heel down again. "Just some old
Indian woman in a cage. That is what you saw."

"The soldiers are following me," Ned said, without
conviction.

"I do not think so," Massaquoit replied. "And if they
are, they will not get here in time."

"Are you going to kill me, then?"

Massaquoit did not answer right away. He formed his
face into an expression of concentration as though the
thought had not occurred to him until that moment. He
eased the pressure again, enough for Ned to think he
might be allowed to rise, but the moment the boy started
to roll away, Massaquoit stepped down again, just hard
enough to keep him pinned. He took the knife out. It
glinted in the moonlight. Ned's eyes locked onto the

blade as Massaquoit ran his fingers up and down the edge.

"Good English steel," he said. "We Indians, not so long ago, used crude stones. You English have shown us how to use steel." He leaned down and held the blade against Ned's cheek. When the boy grabbed his wrist, Massaquoit drew the point slowly along Ned's cheek and watched as a thin line of blood followed the movement of the blade. "This cuts much better," he said.

Ned brushed the blood away with his fingers, licked them clean, and then spat into the sand.

"Do it, then," he said. "I do not care."

"Patience," Massaquoit said. He heard steps behind him, light steps, not the heavy tread of the English in their clumsy boots, and he knew before he turned who would be standing there.

"I thought you would have left with Wequashcook," he said.

Minneseewa took his arm.

"You do not want to kill this boy," she said.

"No, not yet," he said.

"Not now, or later," she said. "We do not need more trouble."

"You know who he is?"

She moved her hands over her face as though removing the encrusted dung.

"Yes," she said. "And still I say, let him go."

Her tone was calm but firm, and it touched something in Massaquoit, something that he felt had adhered to the hard bubble of his hatred for Ned. It was not mercy, certainly not for this arrogant English boy, nor was it fear of English retribution, as Minneseewa seemed to suggest. It was, instead, a weariness, as though he had suddenly had enough. He stepped back and Ned looked at Minneseewa and then back at Massaquoit. A smile began to curl his lips.

"Listen to the old woman, do you?" he said.

Massaquoit shook his head. The boy was incorrigible. He would not kill him, but he would give him a remembrance. Ned got up to his feet and brushed the sand from his clothes. Massaquoit took his time, and then he brought his foot up as hard as he could between Ned's legs. Ned gasped and crumbled to the ground. He broke out into a heavy sweat and then his sides started to shake and he put his hand to his mouth.

"You are right," Massaquoit said to Minneseewa. "He is not worth the killing."

Ned tried to get up and dropped down to one knee. He wiped vomit from his lips.

"Let the English take care of him," Minneseewa said. "He has to answer to them, not to us." She walked toward the water. "Wequashcook waits. He did not want to, but he does, for me." She did not look back. Massaquoit watched her depart, and then he turned to Ned, who had now managed to regain his feet and was backing away toward the road to town. In one direction was Minneseewa, who was too old to give up the old ways and would live out her days beyond the reach of the English. In the other was Newbury, where the English governed and from which their infection spread. He had no business where Minneseewa was going; the boy was part of unfinished business in Newbury. He waited for Ned to stumble into the woods, and then he followed.

Catherine lay in bed with her eyes wide open. She had been turning it over in her mind since coming home from the meeting at Governor Peters's mansion. She had wanted to talk the matter over with Woolsey, but it was clear by the time they had reached her house that her old friend was well past his day's store of energy. Phyllis, too, had gone straight to bed as soon as Catherine had her bring the blanket and then assured her that she did not need her for anything further this night. Catherine found herself wishing that Massaquoit were there. He was one, she thought, to talk to about this nagging doubt, that a few hours ago had been only the germ of an idea, but that had now raised itself in her mind as a proposition whose worth she might be forced to test.

Sometime before the morning, before they listened to Henry Jameson tell his story again, she would have to prepare. Was he telling the truth? For the more she thought about how he had reacted to the blanket as it was presented to him, the less sure she was. That reaction argued with her memory of the joy she had seen in his eyes when she told him that his new babe was a boy. She held the blanket, now, up to the light cast by the candle on the table next to her bed. She turned it to the side where the strawberry stains were. Could these have fooled him? she wondered. Maybe they could have, along with the fortuitous eclipse of the moon. But maybe he had just seized the moment, and it was that thought, she knew, that was going to keep her awake for the better part of the night. She stared out of the window at the full moon, willing herself to remember everything she could about Henry and Martha Jameson, and Ned Jameson as well, every word she had heard, every gesture, what the other women had said at Mercy Plover's birthing, yet none of it seemed to provide an answer. And then she sat upright in bed as though raised by the realization of how blind she had been in missing the most obvious answer of all.

It was not hidden in the vaults of her memory or carried out of reach by the passage of time. Rather, it was the prejudice of her own ears that kept her from hearing all that Martha had had to say when Catherine had finally loosed her tongue enough to utter a word. Henry. Her husband's name. No more, and no less. Catherine had thought, until this moment, that she had understood the simple significance of Martha whispering "Henry" into her ear. But now she understood that she had been very much mistaken. She let herself fall back onto her bed and she closed her eyes. All she could do now was wait until the morning to prove she was right. She was sure enough that within a few moments she was deep into a dreamless sleep.

Massaquoit sat down beneath a birch tree and leaned against its trunk. He rubbed his back against its bark to quiet his mosquito bites. He had been walking through the woods, directed by the sounds of Ned tearing his way through underbrush and crashing through low branches. Every once in a while, and with increasing frequency, Ned would raise his voice in a stream of profanity as yet again he stumbled and skinned his knee, or walked into a branch that snapped back across his face. The boy had been thoroughly lost for a couple of hours now, ever since he realized that Massaquoit was following him and had tried to lose his pursuer by turning off the road and into the woods. The moon was still bright, but in the shelter of the trees its lights dimmed among the shadows that lifted and swayed in a night wind.

Ned's curses and the sound of his clumsy steps were moving away now, and so Massaquoit got up to close the distance between them. He knew they were heading toward Newbury, but in a very circuitous and uncertain way. Still, it would not be long before they approached the town, and he wanted to make sure he had Ned in sight at that moment.

He walked in the direction from which he had last heard Ned's voice rising in anger and frustration. He knelt down and listened for footsteps, but he did not detect any. He started moving again, his ears and eyes straining for any sign of the boy. He knew he must be close. Then he heard the snapping of a large branch, followed by a thud. He trotted toward the noise, and before long he saw Ned lying on the ground. He moved quietly past him, and Ned did not even note his presence. Not ten feet from where Ned now lay was the edge of the woods, and beyond, clearly visible in the moonlight, was the town square. Massaquoit returned to Ned and nudged him with his foot.

"You are almost home," he said.

Ned looked up, and then just shook his head.

Massaquoit pointed.

"There," he said. "Just walk there."

Ned struggled to his feet, but did not move.

"I cannot go home."

"Why?"

"My uncle. I fear what he might say. If you have that knife about you, you can use it. It will do as well as the rope." He sat down. "I am too tired."

"You hid the blanket. Did you do more than that?" Massaquoit asked.

"As my uncle bid me. But he will not say so."

"Will he not?"

"I am tired," Ned said.

Massaquoit sat down next to him.

"We can wait until morning," he said.

In the light of the rising sun, Massaquoit led Ned to the Jameson house. They saw the constable nodding at the

front door, saw him rouse himself when another constable came to relieve him, and together they awakened the
Jameson family and led Henry, Martha, and Ann toward
the meetinghouse. As Massaquoit watched the Jamesons
walk toward the town center, with one constable in front
and the other behind, Ned darted off into the woods. With
an exclamation of disgust, Massaquoit took off after him
one more time.

Holding the folded blanket beneath her arm, Catherine
strode through the meetinghouse door, walked between
the rows of empty benches, and stopped before the table
that had again been placed in front of the altar, and behind which again sat Governor Peters and Magistrate
Woolsey. Minister Davis, too, had taken a place behind
the table instead of standing in his accustomed spot behind the pulpit. On the front bench sat Henry, Martha,
and Ann, flanked by the constables who had summoned
them. Ann held her mother's hand, looking up now and
then to examine Martha's uncomprehending stare.
Catherine shifted her gaze from face to face and then
glanced behind her to the empty building.

"We thought we should hear this evidence without the
clamor of the people," the governor said. "We will inform
them of our judgment." He paused. "You can sit you
down, Mistress Williams. We do know how to proceed."
He picked up a paper that was lying on the table in front
of him.

The front door swung open and Ned came hurtling in,
having been propelled by Massaquoit's hands on his
back. Ned stood blinking as though trying to adjust to a
bright light. His face was covered with scratches, and his
shirtsleeves were dirty and torn.

"Here is the boy," Massaquoit said. "He got lost in the

woods last night, and I retrieved him. When I guided him to his house, he saw the constables and he wanted to run again into the woods. I have convinced him that his place is here."

Governor Peters put down the paper.

"Ned?" he asked.

"It is as he says. He brought me here." He looked at Henry and then the paper in front of Peters.

"What has my uncle told you?" he asked.

"Nothing yet," Governor Peters said. "Sit you down." He looked at Massaquoit. "You are skilled, it seems, both in taking our people away and in bringing them back."

Massaquoit stood with his arms crossed.

"He is in my service," Catherine said, "as you remember you put him."

"Perhaps that was a mistake, mistress," Peters replied. "But it is good to have all the Jamesons here." He slid the paper to Woolsey.

The magistrate peered at the paper and his face reddened.

"Why, this is a deposition from Henry Jameson," he said.

"So it appears," Peters replied.

"But is that not why we are here, to hear what the man has to say?" Woolsey insisted. "Not to read his words, but to hear them?"

"What does he say?" Ned demanded, his face red with agitation.

"Silence!" Peters snapped. "You are here to listen." He turned back to Woolsey.

"Indeed, that is so," he said, his voice and face as blank as stone. "I wanted to dispose of this matter. I took this deposition myself, late last night. I saw no reason to disturb your sleep for so menial a chore as writing down Henry Jameson's words."

"Indeed," Woolsey said. "This is most irregular."

"As is the killing of a babe," Governor Peters said, "and as is a prisoner breaking out of our jail, and as is the dead babe's flesh being made to bleed at a touch, and then that magic repeated with a blanket bleeding, and the moon disappearing and reappearing, as though on command, all of it highly irregular."

"The moon," murmured Minister Davis, "obeys the Almighty."

"To be sure," Peters replied. "As do we, I trust." He took the paper back from Woolsey and held it up to Henry.

"Henry Jameson," he said. "We have summoned you before us to determine if you see fit to repeat your confession." He held up the paper. "You have stated it again in this deposition, taken by me last night at your house, have you not?"

Henry stood up. Catherine fixed her attention on his eyes. They shifted from his daughter to his wife. He seemed reluctant to take his glance away from Martha, but when he did, he looked straight at the governor.

"Yes," he said, and although his tone was firm and his body steady, Catherine knew that he was about to repeat a lie. She had thought this all through in the hour before dawn as she lay in bed in that state half between sleep and waking. She knew that she would have to let him tell his lie before she attempted force the truth out of its hiding place. And she had committed herself to letting that truth lead her where it may, although she recognized that if her suspicions were correct, she would shudder at its revelation.

"Then say so, out loud, so we may all hear, and so my

learned colleague can satisfy himself that I took your words down truly."

Henry shrugged.

"I killed the babe," he said. He pointed to Catherine. "With that very blanket Mistress Williams is now holding."

"Your reasons?" Governor Peters asked, his tone as dry as though he were taking inventory of some cargo in which he had no pecuniary interest.

"Poverty, as well you know," Henry said.

"Be plainer," the governor insisted, as though he were inquiring about the specific contents of a hogshead.

"We did not have enough to eat before the babe arrived. I hired that Irish girl to help my wife, but when the meetinghouse was to be repaired, as Your Honor knows, I did not get that job, as I had hoped—" Henry broke off. "It is all there in that paper. I do not want to recite it over again."

Peters nodded, and then looked down at the deposition. After a moment he slid the paper to Woolsey.

"I am satisfied," he said. "Woolsey?"

"What he says agrees, in the main, with what is written here," Woolsey said. "I take no position on its veracity or his."

"Do you not believe me?" Henry demanded.

"I do not know," Woolsey said. "It is not reasonable to have you first accuse that girl and then confess for the very same crime."

Henry ran his hands over his throat.

"I did not want to hang. The girl did do what I said she did, leaning over my babe, muttering those words, splashing water on it. My memory led me astray."

"And there was the question of the rope," Woolsey said

in a tone even drier than that used by Peters. "Let us not forget that."

"And the rope," Henry agreed.

"Do you not fear it now?" Woolsey asked.

Minister Davis cleared his throat and waited for eyes to turn in his direction.

"I trust that Henry values his immortal soul more than his neck."

"Yes," Henry said, "my soul."

Peters glanced from Henry to Woolsey to the minister.

"I repeat, I am satisfied that we now have the truth."

Catherine stepped forward.

"If it please you, Governor, I would like to ask Henry a question or two, as the matter touches me closely."

"Our business is concluded, mistress," Governor Peters said.

"Let her speak."

The words were slurred, as though from a tongue unused to speech, and delivered in a tone approaching a screech. They came from Martha, who had risen to her feet.

"Please," Martha said, in a softer, more articulate tone. Catherine looked at the woman, who stood with her arms out as though she would seize the moment, if she could, and shake the truth out of it. Her strong red hands waved in front of her, trying to find something solid to hold. Catherine looked at those hands, and with a shudder was reassured that she was right. Ann took her mother's arm and held it tight.

Peters shrugged.

"I do not see the purpose, nor the harm. Ask your questions, mistress, so we may finish this affair."

Catherine stared hard at Henry, until perspiration beaded the large man's forehead and he twisted his hands behind his back as though unable to control them. She held the blanket toward Henry.

"Is this what you used to kill the babe, Henry?" She waved the cloth slowly, almost enticingly, in front of his eyes. He pulled his head back.

"It is, as I said."

"And what exactly did you do? Did you wrap it around the babe's head?"

"Yes."

She handed the blanket to him.

"Can you show us?"

He shook his head.

"I will not. I do not remember."

"How long did you have to hold it over the babe's face?"

"I do not recall." Sweat now glistened on his whole face, and he looked at the governor in silent appeal, but Peters was now leaning forward, showing more interest than he had during the whole proceeding to this point.

"Did it kick, or struggle?" Catherine asked.

Henry now stood mute, shaking his head from side to side.

"Did you press this very blanket down on the babe's face until it stopped breathing?" She lifted the blanket again and pushed it hard against his nose. "Did you do that?" she asked.

Henry swiped the blanket aside.

"Yes."

Catherine snapped the blanket away and turned to the three dignitaries behind the table.

"Master Davis, you should have instructed Henry that a false confession is worse than no confession at all, is that not so?"

"It is, of course," Minister Davis said.

"Can you come to the point?" Peters now demanded.

"Just this. I delivered that babe. It was a perfect little babe, and the birth did it no harm. When I saw it the night it died, it was still perfect. Its nose was as it was when I cleared it to start drawing breath. If Henry had smothered it, as he said he did, there would have been some show of that on the babe's face."

Henry held out his powerful hands. He stared at them as though they belonged to somebody else, and then he let them drop to his sides.

Catherine took a deep breath and walked over to Ned. He shrank away from her, but the constable sitting at his side pushed him to sit upright.

"Tell us, lad, why you prevailed upon my husband to allow you to go to sea as apprentice sailor?"

Governor Peters half rose out of his chair, his face red.

"Mistress, where go you?"

"Why, to the truth, Governor."

Woolsey's face wore a perplexed expression. Catherine nodded at him, and he changed it to one of stern command.

"Answer, lad."

"Why, my uncle's house was getting small for a grown man such as myself."

"Was that the only reason?" Catherine demanded.

"It was as the lad says," Henry interrupted.

"Ned," Catherine said, "did not your uncle order you out of his house because you could not keep your hands off the servant girl."

He pointed at Henry. "Ask my uncle that question, if you dare."

"I never," Henry began to say.

"What we want to know," Peters said before Henry could finish, "is who killed the babe, not who the father of the Irish girl's bastard is. For that, I am content it is the thief whose nostrils we just slit."

"A marvelous conception that would be," Catherine said, "quickening faster than flies, as she was in his company but once not a week ago."

"He will do for me," Peters declared. "Do you have any place further to go, mistress?"

"Yes, and soon we will be there. We have just heard how Ned was forced out of his uncle's house after he had taken advantage of Margaret. And it is known that Ned was unhappy when his little nephew was born, the first male child to Henry and Martha."

"How is it known?" Peters asked.

"It is known," Catherine repeated.

"Women's gossip, no doubt," the governor snorted. "But proceed."

"And, from the same sources, as well as the girl herself, it can be learned that he had forced himself on Margaret Donovan, who now carries his child."

Ned took in his breath.

"Why, she never told me."

"Silly boy." Catherine drew close to Ned. "Do you think she would? After your uncle threatened to have you both whipped out of town for fornication, you turned against her, valuing the skin on your back more than the girl you had seduced. You conspired with your uncle to cast the blame for the babe's death on the girl."

"He said she would be banished, he did."

Catherine looked toward Massaquoit, who still stood by the door, and nodded.

"He is the one who hid that very blanket," Massaquoit said.

"Pshaw," Peters said in an explosion of breath. "Evidence from a cross-worshiping papist and a savage."

"Ned hid the blanket, but he did not kill the babe," Catherine said. She turned to Henry. "No, nor did Henry, for all that he has said."

Suddenly a wail began, starting as a whisper and growing to a howl, and Martha shrugged off Ann's restraining hand and walked to her husband.

"Henry," she said again, the one word she had whispered into Catherine's ear, and Catherine now understood that it was only the start of an unarticulated thought, a thought so disturbing that Martha could not form it in her mind, much less give it full voice. And it was not that her husband was a murderer, but that he wasn't, and that he would offer himself to protect herself. "Henry," she said again, and this time added, "don't."

She collapsed against Henry's chest and sobbed. He held her to him. Ann started to cry. Martha turned away from Henry. She walked back to her daughter. Catherine followed and waited until Martha stood in front of her child.

"I should not have told him," Ann said.

Catherine put her arm about the child. "You must tell it," she said. "You cannot let this child carry the burden alone." Martha's eyes brightened as though she now understood something that had eluded her.

"Me," she said.

"Yes," Catherine prompted.

"Me," Martha said.

"Me," Peters said. "What does that signify?"

Only he, Woolsey, Minister Davis, and Catherine remained in the meetinghouse. The Jamesons had gone home in the company of the constable.

"Why, that she is confessing," Catherine said.

"I heard no such thing," Peters declared.

"Nor I," Woolsey asserted.

"The man himself told me," Minister Davis added. "Told he did this terrible thing, with the full peril of his immortal soul in the balance."

"He was protecting his wife," Catherine said. "He felt he must."

"And why is that, mistress?" Peters asked.

"Because he was ashamed, because although Ned is the father of that girl's child, it is only because she rebuffed Henry, and Martha knew about that. That is why she almost let him hang for her, but in the end she could not."

Peters's face said he did not want to believe any of this. "You say the babe's nose was not crushed. Then how did it die?"

"In its mother's arms. That night, when Henry was holding the babe up for all to see that it had bled, I thought I saw something on the babe's back. Now I know what it was. It was the mark left on the babe by Martha's hands, which are near as strong as her husband's. What I do not know, nor she, I warrant, is whether she squeezed the breath out of that babe in love or anger, or perhaps a despair that was an equal admixture of both.

"Maybe she did not start out to do so, but the idea came upon her as she held the babe. And then she left the babe on the floor, not knowing whether it still breathed. Margaret found it and tried to save its soul. Henry saw Margaret and accused her. It was only later, his daughter told him what she had seen. Then he offered himself."

"She did not say any of that," Peters insisted.

"She now does not know more than that one word," Catherine replied.

"Her rational faculties," Woolsey said, "do not seem sound."

"They are not," Catherine replied. "And they were not."

"The learned doctors say that when a person falls into madness, it is the rational faculty that collapses," Minister Davis said. "Such a person has lost the power to understand."

Peters brightened, as Catherine had hoped he might.

"Then you agree that she is mad," he said to Davis.

"So it appears," the minister answered.

"Then, perhaps, we cannot . . ."

"Surely," Catherine finished the thought, "she did not know what she was doing."

The governor stretched his long frame and closed his eyes. When he opened them, his expression was clear and confident. "I do not want to hang the mother. I have no stomach for that. Nor the father. The boy can go back to sea. They will all be banished. It troubles me to set them at liberty, but it would trouble me more to see them on the gallows."

"They will be at liberty only in their bodies," Catherine said.

"Banishment," he repeated. "The Jamesons must not pollute us any further."

"Excommunication," Minister Davis offered. "The church must also be free of them."

"Margaret?" Catherine asked.

Woolsey looked over at Peters.

"She will be at liberty as soon as we can notify the jailor of our decision."

"As you wish," the governor said. "Yet she must be released to Mistress Williams, who has shown herself willing to take in unfortunate girls along with savages."

"She can abide with me as long as she likes," Catherine replied, "although she may want to leave Newbury."

"That would be most fortunate. Perhaps your savage can be persuaded to take her to wife." He stood up. Without another word, he strode to the door in long, efficient strides.

SIXTEEN

T HE CLANG OF iron against wood thudded into the morning air and startled two gulls who had been floating on the water.

Woolsey looked past the two men as they drove a substantial log into the soft sand at water's edge to where the sloop *Good Hope* lay at anchor in Newbury Harbor. The shallop sat on the beach. The two men stopped working and pointed at the sloop. Their voices suddenly rose and one lunged at the other. Captain Gregory stepped between them.

"What is the trouble, Captain?" Catherine asked.

"Just some nonsense about that," he said, pointing to the figurehead, a crowned lion, on the bow of his ship. "Nate here," he said, pointing to one of the sailors, "says we should strike that crown off the lion's head, since our King Charles is an enemy of the true religion. The other man says he cares not about the king, but only that the ship stay afloat. It is all nonsense."

"Indeed," Woolsey said. "But my correspondent in

London has written me to say that this king may lead the country into war."

Captain Gregory shrugged.

"As for that, I am glad that I am on this side of the ocean." He looked at the two men, who were now peacefully back at work. "It will be a pleasure to be able to walk up a gangplank from a dock," he said. "The governor does make some good decisions for our advantage."

"That he does," Catherine said, "as long as he is dealing with the price of a barrel of flour or a bolt of cloth, which he makes sure is to his advantage."

"Now, Catherine," Woolsey said.

"And now, Joseph," she replied. "Do not try to distract me from my worry."

A small smile curved the corners of his lips.

"Catherine, I know better than to try to distract you from any thought that has seized your attention."

The sound of a tuneful whistle announced the arrival of Ned, who came strolling onto the beach, carrying his duffel on his back. He strolled to where Catherine and Woolsey stood, and smiled.

"Good morrow, mistress." He offered a little bow to Catherine. "And to you, sir," and he extended the same mocking gesture to Woolsey. Captain Gregory trotted to them.

"Ned," he said. "What do you here?"

"Why, to come aboard your good ship," Ned said. "I've been banished, you know. It suits me to leave Newbury behind and to take me where you sail, as sailor or passenger, I care not, so long as I leave this place."

Gregory looked to Catherine. She shook her head.

"You are welcome to leave with Captain Gregory next

time he sails, after he returns from his present voyage."
The captain's eyes, used to scanning the distance, had
locked on two figures coming slowly toward them.
Catherine followed his gaze.

"My passengers arrive," he said.

"And why is that, mistress?" Ned asked.

"Look at who comes, and you will know that you are
not traveling with them."

Massaquoit and Margaret made their way across the
sand to them. He carried a small wooden chest, which he
placed down next to them. Massaquoit took Margaret's
arm and led her to the shallop.

"My uncle says I cannot stay longer with him."

"We have told Henry and Martha they can stay a fortnight to gather themselves," Woolsey declared.

"Aye, a fortnight. But they, too, want to put this town
at their backs. They leave for Dudley on foot tomorrow.
My aunt has a cousin there. I am not welcome. My uncle
says he will burn the house down before he leaves. I do
not fancy sleeping in the woods."

"There is the jail," Woolsey suggested. "Perhaps Jailor
Drake can accommodate you." The thudding of iron
against wood increased. Woolsey looked toward the
water, where two more workers had begun driving in another piling. "There, you can earn your keep in jail, by
lending a hand to those fellows."

"He was a good hand, before this trouble," Captain
Gregory offered. "I would not be displeased to try him
again when I return."

"You will find him working here, or in the jail,"
Woolsey said. "Is that agreeable to you, young man?"

"It is better than the woods." He looked toward Massaquoit. "I do not fancy meeting that savage in the dark
again." He looked at Margaret and then Catherine.

"You may have a moment," she said.

Ned took Margaret's arm. She shook it free, but walked a few paces away with him. He said a few words, and then trotted off to join the workers. In a moment he had relieved one of them and was leaning into his chore with enthusiasm. The girl watched Ned work for a few moments and then walked back.

"He asked where I go," she said. "He's sorry, he said. It was fear of his uncle, he says."

"Did you tell him where you would be?" Catherine asked.

"Yes, for he said he might want to come visit his child."

"Visit, indeed," Catherine said.

"It is time," Captain Gregory said. Margaret embraced Catherine and walked into the surf so that she could climb into the shallop, which now bobbed in the gentle waves. Catherine waded out with her and Massaquoit followed. He heaved her chest over the low side of the shallop to one of the sailors who was ready to ply the oars. Another sailor had his oar dug into the sand to steady the boat.

"Are you sure this is what you want?" Catherine asked. "You can stay here with me. You know that."

Margaret held her beads.

"As long as I have these, I will not rest easy in Newbury, and I am not going to forgo them. I have heard of a new plantation where Lord Baltimore has opened the doors for the likes of me."

Catherine clasped her hands around Margaret's.

"And when you enter Lord Baltimore's house, inquire if it is worthy; and if it is, abide there with the Lord's blessings. And if you find it not worthy"—she pressed her hands harder around Margaret's—"shake the dust from your feet and return to Newbury, where my house awaits you." She released her hold, and Margaret turned toward the shallop. Massaquoit positioned himself next to the boat, and Margaret used his shoulder to lift herself over the side.

"Thank you," she said to him.

Massaquoit stood with Catherine and Woolsey as the shallop made its way, riding the crest of the outgoing tide toward the *Good Hope*.

"And you, Matthew," Woolsey said, "do you stay with us in Newbury?"

"I do not know," Massaquoit replied. "The girl has her people to go to in Maryland. You are among your people here in Newbury. On Munnawtawkit is an old woman roasting a snake in the fire, and she is my people. When she dies, there will be nobody left to call me by my name of Massaquoit. And I do not know if I can ever become 'Matthew.'"

Catherine pointed to the boulder.

"The wind sometimes rushes against this rock with all its fury, and yet it remains unscathed, and so will you if you stay among us."

She took Woolsey's arms and they began to make their way across the beach and to the road that led to Newbury.

Massaquoit squatted for a moment in the sand, looking toward the water and Munnawtawkit. Beyond, he knew, lay Paumonok, but Wequashcook had told him that the English would soon be there. Wequashcook said he would go on ahead of the English so he could be there to greet them and help them to trade with the Montaukets. He had asked Massaquoit to join him there. Perhaps he would. But for now, he stood up, and walked slowly after

Catherine and Woolsey, who had not looked back for him.

He walked fast enough to keep them in sight, but not to overtake them. He was not in that much of a hurry to meet this fellow "Matthew."

Death arrived
just before quitting time.

The victim was the owner of a tobacco store on
G Street, found behind the counter. A homicide,
according to Patrol Division. Dowling knew
how that went. They were right a lot of the time
and wrong a lot of the time. Sometimes people
hit the floor fast when their coronary artery
called it quits. Sometimes they left a piece of
their head on an edge of the kitchen table. Head
wounds bled a lot, and young patrol officers
confronted with a lot of blood would call for
Homicide. But that was okay with Dowling.

"I'd rather roll on a natural than come in late on
a murder," he preached to his team. "Besides,
you learn by looking at dead bodies."

He had learned a lot in fifteen years of looking.

Other Avon Books by
Jack Mullen

IN THE LINE OF DUTY

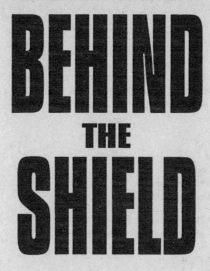

BEHIND
THE
SHIELD

JACK MULLEN

AVON BOOKS NEW YORK

BEHIND THE SHIELD is an original publication of Avon Books. This work has never before appeared in book form. This work is a novel. Any similarity to actual persons or events is purely coincidental.

AVON BOOKS
A division of
The Hearst Corporation
1350 Avenue of the Americas
New York, New York 10019

Copyright © 1996 by Jack Mullen
Published by arrangement with the author
Library of Congress Catalog Card Number: 96-96127
ISBN: 0-380-78236-7

First Avon Books Printing: September 1996

AVON TRADEMARK REG. U.S. PAT. OFF. AND IN OTHER COUNTRIES, MARCA REGISTRADA, HECHO EN U.S.A.

Printed in the U.S.A.

RA 10 9 8 7 6 5 4 3 2 1

Dedicated to the memory of
John J. Mullen and Mina L. Mullen,
Henry S. Wetmore and Lucille Wetmore

And to all of the Homicide Team 1
detectives who slugged it out

⚉ One

He was stimulated. Energized. The woman in the orange-and-white striped shorts emerged from the mom-and-pop market carrying only a carton of cigarettes and walked past the first street south of the store. Maybe, hopefully, home was several blocks away yet.

He looked at his wristwatch and calculated. Just past nine. If he connected within a few minutes, he wouldn't have to answer questions at home.

His night vision was keen. Even driving San Diego's streets at a snail's pace a half block behind, he could track her. She walked slowly, leisurely. All the better. If she didn't enter a house on this block, he would maneuver ahead of her.

When she crossed Monroe Avenue, he made a hurried U-turn, shot east a block, then drove the speed limit south on Thirtieth Street. He took his first right, and when six car lengths from her street, he made another U-turn and parked under a pear tree by the curb, where rays from the street lamp at midblock didn't reach. Now if he had to leave in a hurry, he wouldn't be giving her a look at the car.

Before he got out, he stuffed wallet and wristwatch in the glove compartment. Then he reached to the rear and transferred the package of diapers and the grocery bag from the seat to the floor behind him. He covered them with an old car blanket, grunting when he stretched to reach for it. The car keys still hung in the ignition. He felt satisfied. Some neighborhood-watch hero sticking their nose in his car wouldn't have much to report now. A person had to think things through. That was how you stayed out of jail. He'd said it over and over to himself. Control the things you can control, 'cause all the rest is a fuckin' crapshoot.

His dark-colored Nikes glided over old, cracked sidewalk with the contractor's name and 1933 branded upon it. He was graceful and agile and wore a T-shirt and Levi's, like thousands of other men wore on a warm Fourth of July evening. Night-blooming jasmine filled the air, but he barely noticed it. A few yards from her street, he realized he had almost a full erection and touched himself through his pants. Peeking around the corner, partially hidden by a six-foot Eugenia hedge, he saw nothing. He cursed, then spotted her half a football field away on the opposite sidewalk. Still walking casually. Still alone. He stepped off the sidewalk onto a front lawn and paused. A quick look around. Most of the houses had lights on and he worried. An eighty-year-old bitch in a rocker by a window, sipping tea. With eyes like a schoolgirl. Seeing everything that passed. Or a goddamn jogger or dog walker or a kid kissing his girlfriend in some car. Looking in all directions, he saw and heard nothing, save faint music from a house several doors away in the opposite direction.

He was hard. Sliding his fingers inside of his pants, he was gratified because he was not wet. Jesus, last time he had thought he was going to come as he reached for the Mexican. He sure didn't want to do that. Give up his control. Relinquish his power to the lousy bitch. If he could just hold off again.

As the man on Kansas Street lurked in the shadow of a tree, another man, sixty-one blocks to the east, was emotionally wasted. Vincent Dowling gripped the lower rung of the wooden chair he was sitting in and pulled upward. The rung snapped, but he didn't realize it. Tears streamed down both cheeks though his eyes were closed tight.

"Oh God, Helene. Why did you have to die?" He yelled as loud as he could. "Why did you have to die?"

The woman sitting in the chair facing him cried, too. Her knees brushed his because no space separated them. He focused on the woman and spoke to her, looking into her eyes.

"It was the murders," he pleaded. "The lousy murders. I couldn't let go of them." Dowling was afraid he might throw up. He released the chair and clutched his stomach with both hands.

The group leader hurried to Dowling's side. She wrapped her arms around him, pulling his head against her breast. Her eyes were moist.

"You did good," she said. "You did good."

She freed one arm and reached out to the woman sitting on the other chair. "Thank you, Carol," she said softly. "You can take your seat now." The woman rose, dabbing at her eyes with a Kleenex.

Dowling got up, wiped his face with his forearm and ran his fingers through his red hair. He looked around the room, making brief eye contact with some of the others, then started to cry again. The group leader ushered him to a vacant chair in the circle. She kissed him lightly on the cheek, then returned to her own seat.

"For those of you who are here for the first time, Carol was playing the role of Vincent's late wife. Her name was Helene. She committed suicide a year and a half ago. Vincent is working through a lot of things."

Next morning, Dowling sat at his desk in the homicide office, alternating his attention between the stack of Polaroid photographs and the yellow legal pad that contained his to-do list. It would be two days before the five-by-five-inch crime scene photos would be developed. He tuned out the voices and ringing telephones of the squad room, wiped his reading glasses, then picked up one of the prints and stared at it. The point of view was from the middle of the street, looking toward a 1930s-style bungalow. The patched roadway took up most of the foreground. An old-style narrow driveway ran perpendicular to the street, two strips of concrete with grass in the middle. A Volkswagen convertible sat in the driveway, its rear about even with the front of the small white stucco homes bordering each side of the driveway. A pair of orange-and-white striped shorts lay in the narrow flower bed between the driveway edge and the side of the house. That was where Holly Novikoff had been raped. Directly under the living room window of the house with the red tiled roof.

Dowling glanced at a sheaf of reports he had read twice, and let his pencil roam to one of the paragraphs. The shorts and panties were found draped around the victim's left foot when the discovery was made by a woman in a second-floor bedroom of the house next door pulling her shade down for the night. The woman said Holly had been lying on her back, head rolling slightly, with legs spread and arms in a crucifixion pose. Her brassiere and blouse had been pushed upward and ringed her neck.

Dowling picked up another photo and ran his fingers over the smooth surface. A closer view demonstrated how easy it would have been for a passerby to see it all. The rapist had choked Holly Novikoff, dragged her to the flower bed, choked her again and mounted her. Thirty feet from the public-fucking-sidewalk.

The kid had got only one break. She was alive. He hoped she wanted to be.

Vincent Dowling stood and stretched. He was just a shade under five eleven, with short red hair, one thatch hanging slightly over his forehead. The part in the hair was uneven, atop a lightly freckled face and brown eyes. His waistline measurement matched the caliber of gun he carried, a .38 Smith & Wesson revolver with a five-inch barrel. It had taken him fifty years to develop the paunch, though it was much less of one than he had carried two years ago.

When Dowling sat down again, the to-do list came easily as he penciled it out, first scribbling the date in an upper corner.

Tuesday, July 5

Check all outlying departments plus L.A. for M.O.
Check all traffic tickets written in area
Check all field interrogations made in area
Run recent sex crime parolees
INTERVIEW VICTIM
Do neighborhood check again
Live-in at 9 p.m. tonight

The last entry meant two of his detectives would loiter around the crime scene at the critical time. Stopping everything that moved, looking not so much for a suspect but for a witness who may have seen something and attached no significance to it at the time.

"You'll turn up zero most of the time," he preached to his team, "but when you score it makes all the goose eggs worthwhile."

Tossing the pencil aside, he leaned back in the swivel chair and looked at the gray ceiling. Last year at this time he had been having trouble putting one foot in front of the other. Uncanny, he thought. Sergeant Vincent Dowling, San Diego Police Department, homicide detail, attending weekly group therapy sessions. Not so long ago he would have preferred being horsewhipped.

Yeah, he was working through a lot of things all right. And he did feel better. A lot better. *Now you have the memory of the pain but not the pain itself* was a favorite saying around group. Before therapy, he likened his recovery efforts to cleaning his garage. Shuffling stuff from one side to the other, giving it a sweep, thinking you'd done a helluva job. Like shuffling emotions around in your gut and thinking the job was getting done. In group he'd learned to put his feelings on the floor, right out there in the light. Kicked them around, examined them, held them up for everyone to see and came to terms with them.

He'd felt good last night when they'd all hugged and sung their corny song before breaking the circle. He'd felt real good. Inspired. A cigarette would have gone well. It would now, too. How long had it been? Over two months. It occurred to him it was a good sign he could no longer break it down to days and hours.

Three phone calls in the next twenty minutes brought Dowling back to the job. He pulled the first case file from a corner of his desk. Annabelle Dominguez had been assaulted by the same suspect three weeks prior at the same time of night. Five blocks from last night's case. And he didn't need a crystal ball, thank you, to know it was the same suspect because the method of operation was the same, and Vincent Dowling, like most cops, was a great believer in the value of M.O.

Dowling had uncommon sympathy for both women, but it gnawed at him that his team had been assigned cases that were not homicides. Years of working for Captain of Homicide Tom Stacy had taught him how unpredictable Stacy could be. A give-and-take relationship had been born of the union, so he hadn't complained the day his team had been assigned the Dominguez case. But Holly Novikoff made it two in a row, so he decided to brace Stacy.

"How come I'm the only sergeant you give two non-murders to?" he asked.

"Because I got a gut feeling," Stacy said.

"The sign on the door says HOMICIDE, Tom. I've got three mysteries we're trying to make some sense of and—"

"Yep, a gut feeling," Stacy said. "This son of a bitch is gonna kill one of them, and I don't want us picking it up from sex crimes detail starting from scratch." Stacy ran his fingers through white wavy hair. "You always lose something in the transition. Course you know that.''

''How come my team?'' Dowling asked, sensing he was losing ground.

''Because I figure your team can solve the goddamn thing.''

Dowling flopped into a chair, grimacing.

''I got one more how come,'' he said. ''How come I come in here all fired up to win an argument, and you stroke my ass and I slink out of here with more work?''

Stacy hooked his thumbs behind his suspenders and leaned back. ''A character flaw, Dowling. You got a serious character flaw.''

''The most serious character flaw I got is working for you for fifteen years and not having the good sense to transfer out.'' Dowling looked at the empty styrofoam cup in his hand and added, ''That's another thing. Most bosses have a pot of coffee going so they can offer their troops something while they're being abused.''

''True,'' Stacy said, ''and most bosses today are breeding a bunch of coffee shop commandos whose idea of solving a caper is having the crook walk into the squad room and give himself up instead of being on the goddamn bricks wearing out shoe leather and—''

''Well, I'm history,'' Dowling said, getting up, seizing his chance to interrupt. He had the door open when he added, ''By the way, Tom, Speedy Montoya makes sergeant effective tomorrow and goes back to patrol. I want to replace him with Gus Denver from robbery. We can work with Gus. He'll make a helluva homicide cop.''

Stacy walked around his desk. ''Uh . . . that's another thing, Dowling. Sit down.''

''What's another thing? You're going to tell me a homicide sergeant can't handpick his troops anymore?''

''They still can, normally. But the chief is instituting an exchange program with a couple of police departments. Wants to take advantage of what cross-training may have to offer. You know, see what they're doing that we're not. That sort of stuff.''

Dowling draped both arms over the side of the chair and took a deep breath. "So I'm not getting Gus Denver? I'm getting some son of a bitch I don't even know who's living out of a suitcase."

"For about six months," Stacy said. He smiled. "It's a new world out there, Dowling. And you and I have to quit resisting it if we're gonna survive. We've got what . . . over sixty years between us on this job. Welcome to the nineties."

"Where's my guy from?" Dowling asked without looking up.

"The Republic of Ireland. Detective Sam Mulcahy. And you have to figure he'll be a good one because all the chiefs want to shine in a program like this."

"Yeah."

Stacy sat on the edge of his desk. "I suppose you're going to go across the street after work and get half-juiced because I wrecked your day."

It was Dowling's turn to smile. "I don't do that so much anymore, Tom." He got up. "I'm just slow to accept change is all."

"No." Stacy drew the word out. Dowling had the door open again when Stacy said, "It's been a hell of a long year for you, Vince. You've come a long way back."

Dowling nodded.

"How are the kids?"

"Making some progress. They go to group with me every third session. Matt starts his second year at the University of Redlands in September. Jenny will be a high school senior. Jeez, I can't believe that."

"Helene would be proud," Stacy said.

"Yeah, she would be." He put his hands in his pockets and looked away. "She was really something, wasn't she?" After a pause he said, "How did she ever let herself get hooked up with a cop?"

Stacy said nothing.

"But that's what life's about, isn't it, Tom? Nice women like Helene falling for ordinary guys like me."

He called over his shoulder when he was halfway out of the door, "I sure as hell wanted Gus Denver, though, not some traveling salesman."

At his desk the next day, Dowling retrieved his pencil, added "pester lab re semen?" to his to-do list, then sighed as a secretary dropped several telephone messages in front of him. One, from a deputy coroner inquiring about property from an old case, he put back on the desk; another, from the dentist verifying an appointment tomorrow he slid on top of his calendar. He probably wouldn't make that one unless they put some flesh-and-bones in jail, and nothing looked promising yet; a third message he put in his pocket, then smiled. From Jenny. "Can I sleep over with Maggie tonight—please. BATH." Their private acronym. When she was a tot she would squeeze him and say, I love you "bigger'n all the houses," which Dowling took to mean as much as you could possibly love someone. BATH was their code when the message was conveyed through strangers. The final one, from Stacy, was a one word-message: "Update?" He wadded it, aimed for the trash can and missed. He missed again from a bending position, then sunk a bank shot off the side of his desk. There was no use talking to Stacy until after the critique.

Frequent critiques were one of Vincent Dowling's trademarks. His team met in one location, going over events of the past several hours. Making sure everyone knew *exactly* what everyone else knew. No assumptions, no "I thought somebody already told you that," nobody branching out on some half-assed tangent wasting time and energy chasing down a dead end that another team member could have squelched with one tidbit of information.

Dowling tried to have a minimum of two critiques a day. They could be an inconvenience, sure, but good homicide work was always an inconvenience. The small room next to the homicide office was the ideal place for them because the blackboard and the flip chart gave him a sense of organization. And Vincent Dowling was nothing if not organized.

But any place the investigation took them would do, and there had been a lot of anyplaces over the years. Back alleys and railroad tracks and white sandy beaches under blistering suns. Vacant lots, huddled under an isolated tree providing a tad of shelter from San Diego's infrequent rains. Convenience store parking lots.

And once, in Thaddaeus McCastle's garage, with remains of Thaddaeus himself sprinkled here and there. After at least three unsuccessful attempts at ending it all, Thaddaeus had concocted a miniature death chamber. Perched near the top of a rickety stepladder, he fashioned a competent noose on the end of a rope secured to the overhead beams. The top shelf of the ladder held his vial of phenobarbs, a tumbler of gin and a butcher knife.

In one swoop, as Dowling reconstructed it, Thaddaeus McCastle put the rope around his neck, swallowed the pills, stabbed himself in the chest and, with his free hand, yanked on the wire that, pulleylike, fired the two twelve-gauge shotguns secured to custom-built shelves six feet in front of him. The Remington, carefully angled to blow his head to bits did just that, but the Winchester, intended for the stomach, blew his balls off. The twin claps of thunder knocked what was left of Thaddaeus from the ladder, and he was still dangling when a neighbor peeked in to investigate.

"You motherfuckers ain't got no respect for the dead, is what," the elderly neighbor said later, a tattered Bible sticking out of his pocket. He had heard Dowling ask the photographer for an extra set of prints for an investigations class he taught at the community college.

From that day on, for Dowling's team, the term "Thaddaeus" became a synonym for a sure thing. "Take the Chargers and the points next Sunday. It's a Thaddaeus." Or, "The ID techs just made our boy on prints, Sarge. Thaddaeus."

But on this day, the critique would be held in an air-conditioned room in the headquarters building of San Diego P.D., on the edge of downtown, a few blocks east of the glitzy center of commerce, and another few blocks from the crime-filled sectors of Logan Heights and Golden Hills.

Dowling watched his men file briskly into the room, the oddball-shaped solvers of his murder puzzles. Forty-year-old Bones Boswell, ten years younger than his sergeant, well over six feet tall, gaunt, with black hair graying at the temples. Tenacious and loyal, he had worked with Dowling for eight years. Larry Shea, the rotund one. Also forty. With a shiny pate roofing a cherubic face and twinkling eyes. Disarming eyes. Eyes that had coaxed a lot of confessions from assorted murderers who made the mistake of liking him. Shea had been with Dowling for five years, which translated to about one hundred thirty murders in squad room terms. The first one into the room—always the first one into the room—the youngest and newest member, Speedy Montoya. The only homeboy on the team, whose thirty-two summers had all been spent in San Diego. As an eighteen-month homicide veteran he was just beginning to feel a zone of comfort and accomplishment in the business of murder. His smooth olive face was still unlined.

"When you get haunted by enough failures, your face will look like ours," Dowling had told him.

They took their places at an oblong table while Dowling stood near the blackboard, his shoulder propped against a wall. He pointed to the Ace bandage on Shea's right wrist.

"That's all that's left of the accident, huh?" he asked.

"Yeah. Piss on this exercise stuff. Those streets are dangerous."

"What was left of your bicycle, Larry?" Speedy asked.

"Damn little. The old bag pulled out from the curb without a clue. I'm lucky I'm here to talk about it."

"You said there weren't any witnesses," Speedy said.

"There weren't," Shea answered. "I told you. She hit

me and never looked back. Probably hit three or four others on her way to the knit shop.''

Dowling loudly cleared his throat and fished paper
work from the inside pocket of his sport coat. A report
he had phonied up.

''Traffic sent this over a little while ago,'' he said.
''Let's see. Occurred midafternoon, medium traffic . . .
Here it is. *Witness statement.*'' He looked at Shea and
raised his eyebrow before reading on. ''Roscoe Jorgensen.
Age nine. Roscoe says, 'It was the hottest day yet, so I
got the stand set up, watered down the lemonade and
waited for customers. This fat guy came riding by huffing
and puffing. There were a couple of dogs screwing on the
lawn. The fat guy slowed down to watch them. He was
still looking at 'em when he ran into the rear of the parked
car. The fat guy fell off the bike and kept rolling and
rolling. It was kinda funny.' ''

Larry Shea shook his round head, trying not to laugh
with the others.

''Down to business,'' Dowling announced, grabbing a
piece of chalk and clacking data onto the blackboard.

> Wed. June 15, Arizona St. Annabelle
> Dominguez—24 years
> Mon. July 4 Kansas St. Holly Novikoff—19 years

They all stared at the board and said nothing. The
streets were five blocks apart, in a section of the city re-
ferred to as Normal Heights. Made up of older, middle-
class homes stuffed between new apartment complexes,
the area was three miles north of where the critique was
being held, six miles from the beach and a few blocks
from the lip of a parched hillside forming one edge of
Mission Valley, known to the locals as Hotel Circle.

On the flip chart Dowling used a marking pen to write:

| No <u>known</u> witnesses | Unconscious |
| plain view of sidewalk | weeknight |

9 PM to 10 PM   north-south streets
choke-out   "what time is it?"

Below that he added:

SUSPECT

White male	5'9" to 6',	dark short hair
	medium build	
Mid-20s	Nice-looking	T-shirt

"I don't want to leave until we get this guy," Speedy Montoya said.

"I wish we could take you out and have a few good-bye drinks tonight, Speedy," Dowling said, "but Bones and Shea are going to be hanging out on Kansas Street and I'm going to be door knocking. Maybe we'll get lucky."

"The Irish guy isn't due for another week. How about getting me an extension so you don't have to work short?"

"I tried, Speedy. At midnight you're a big-shot sergeant, and this time tomorrow you belong to patrol division."

Dowling folded his arms and faced the data. "The hospital says Holly Novikoff has enough of her voice back to talk. I'm going to see her when we break here. After I go to the lab."

The lab had been unable to help them on the Annabelle Dominguez case.

"No sperm detected on the vaginal swabs, Sergeant," the criminalist told him.

Without sperm, Dowling knew, there could be no DNA examination. No autoradiogram with a zillion lines and numbers from which a genetic fingerprint could be gleaned. A genetic fingerprint that could be matched to lines and numbers from a blood sampling on another autoradiogram when the correct suspect's finger had been pricked. Looking to Dowling like a blurry supermarket bar code, really. All the result had to do then, he thought, was stand up before a jury. After a couple of high-priced defense experts had whored themselves, spicing their testimony with a ton of "could be's," "possibly's" and "maybe's."

"Not only no sperm, Sergeant. No semen either. This guy didn't ejaculate."

That was different. Dowling was used to aspermic samples. Rapists who'd had vasectomies. Rapists who'd had the shit knocked out of their reproductive system by some debilitating venereal disease. But no ejaculation?

"Maybe he used a condom?" Dowling said.

"Maybe. But more likely it's retarded ejaculation."

"Retarded as in slow?"

"Retarded as in no ejaculation," the criminalist had answered.

They all stared at the bulletin board while Dowling fussed about the four things homicide detectives cared most about: physical evidence, circumstantial evidence, confessions and witnesses. In no particular order. Sometimes one was enough and sometimes all four were too few. As when physical evidence could be explained because a murdering handyman's fingerprints figured to be in the kitchen anyway, or a star witness got intimidated by friends of the killer or a confession got tossed for any number of reasons. But circumstantial evidence. That was what Dowling liked. A whole bunch of it. A little could rightfully be explained away, and a medium-size helping didn't mean the case was solid, but a whole bunch was gold.

The book defined circumstantial evidence as "evidence of fact or circumstances from which the existence or non-existence of a fact in issue may be inferred." Dowling had heard old Angus Crowe explain it to a jury once, in the days when prosecutors tried to get cases before him in the morning session. Afternoon sessions were chancy, because Angus Crowe, judge of Superior Court Dept. 14 was fond of five-martini lunches.

"You see, ladies and gentlemen. If you wake up in the morning and the streets are wet, and the newspaper is wet, and your car is wet, you can figure it rained during the night. Now, rain wasn't expected, and you didn't hear it rain. And you didn't see it rain. And nobody told you that it rained. But circumstantially, you can make an inference that it rained while you were nighty-night."

Dowling watched Larry Shea drum his thick fingers on the critique room table. "He was doing it to Holly Novikoff under the living room window while the family was sitting there watching TV," Shea said, mopping light perspiration from his brow.

"The sidewalk was only fourteen goddamn feet from where he had Annabelle Dominguez under the tree," Speedy added. "Fourteen goddamn feet."

"This guy's driven," Dowling said. "What do you make of all this, Bones?"

"Tough case." It was said absently.

"Yeah," Dowling replied, looking back at him. "Tough case."

"He asks them both what time it is. Did Annabelle see if he's wearing a wristwatch?" Speedy asked.

"She can't say. She did good to recall the clothing," Dowling said.

"Neither of 'em can describe the pants, huh?" Shea asked.

"Can't describe the pants or if anything was written on the T-shirt. Annabelle says he's in good physical condition. Patrol tried getting info from Holly by having her write things down. Not much luck," Dowling said.

Shea was still tapping on the tabletop. "He's walking toward them. Stops and asks them for the time. They tell him, he says 'thanks,' they start up again and the next thing they know the arm's around their neck from behind?"

"Exactly," Speedy said. "The way Annabelle lays it

out he couldn't have taken more than two steps past her before he wheeled around. She doesn't remember anything except being jerked up and backward on the sidewalk before she went out. When she woke up under the tree her pants were down, her top was up and she could hardly talk. He was gone. It took her a couple of minutes to realize she'd been raped.''

"He's got a reason for being in that neighborhood,'' Dowling said. "He works there, or lives there, or visits there.''

"I'll keep in touch,'' Speedy said as they filed out of the room. "You guys are gonna have to get that bastard without me.''

Dowling noticed Bones getting to his feet slowly. "What's the matter, Bones?'' Dowling asked when the others had gone on ahead.

"Nothing.''

"What's the matter, Bones?''

"I'm all right.''

"Remember who you're talking to.''

The slender detective with the lantern jaw took a deep breath. "My daughter turns eighteen today. She and my ex will be cutting birthday cake in Phoenix, and I'm five hundred miles away playing cops and robbers.''

Dowling put his arm around Bones. "You talk to her today?''

"Tried to this morning. Denise answered the phone, though, and it went to shit. I thought we could at least have a civil talk on the kid's birthday. I swore it wasn't going to happen this time and . . .''

"Bones, listen to me. I've seen this coming. Let's get you set up with the police psychologist.''

"That's not me, Sarge.''

"That's what all cops say. That's what *I* said. You need help, Bones.''

"Some other time maybe.''

"It's free and it's confidential. I wouldn't even know you're going.'' Dowling sighed. "Will you do this much for me? Keep your mind open to it. Think about what I said for a while. If it turns out you think I'm full of shit, tell me and I'll let it alone.''

Bones smiled. ''Like a good detective, I'll keep an open mind.''

''You're a helluva detective, Bones. A helluva detective.''

''I used to be. I'm not anymore, though. If I was holding up my end maybe we'd have this guy in jail.''

''That's crap and you know—''

Bones picked up his jacket and looked around the squad room. ''I've worked my whole life, and I've got nothing to show for it.''

Bones had started walking away when he stopped and returned to Dowling. He said softly, ''It's the memories, Sarge. I can't get unchained from the memories.''

Dowling watched Bones push the door open, vowed to monitor him closely, then hurried to the lab and received another disappointment.

''I examined Holly Novikoff's vaginal swabs twice, Sergeant. No sperm cells to separate from her epithelial cells because again, *no* semen.''

''You not only can't get a DNA, you can't get us his blood type either?''

''If we even had a little pre-ejaculate, a tiny amount of fluid, we *might* be able to do a PGM grouping for the blood type.''

Dowling stood by the window and watched traffic on Broadway. ''If he hits again and doesn't ejaculate but you get a little bit of fluid, can you DNA?''

''With pre-ejaculate, there's either no sperm or such a low count it makes it terribly doubtful.'' The criminalist moved to pick up a ringing telephone. ''Not ejaculating isn't all that rare with rapists, Sergeant.''

''What kind of a city do you have here?'' the woman yelled at Dowling. ''My God, we've been here less than two months and I've gotten a ticket, had my car stolen and now some animal has raped my daughter.''

They were standing in a hallway at the University of California at San Diego Medical Center.

"You haven't caught him, have you?'' The woman didn't wait for an answer. "Do you care? Does anybody in this town care about anything?''

"Please know that I am very—''

"We came here because I was making crap wages in Montana and . . .'' She clenched her fists and shook them at Dowling. "My God, she's nineteen years old.''

A few minutes later, he sat in a chair next to Holly Novikoff's bed. She pulled the covers up under her chin and looked at him through watery brown eyes. She looked at him for a long time, then turned away.

"I can't begin to know how you feel, Ms. Novikoff, but I'm very sorry this happened to you.''

"You can call me Holly and please, just ask me the questions.'' Her voice was raspy.

"Will you know him if you see him again?''

"I'll never forget him.'' She was still looking away.

"What was he wearing?''

"All I remember was the T-shirt. White, I think.''

"But definitely light colored?''

She nodded.

"Any writing on it, Holly?''

"I don't know.''

"How about his voice?''

She shrugged. "Average. Whatever that means.''

"Did he ever say anything except 'What time is it?' ''

She shook her head.

"Was he wearing a wristwatch?''

"Don't know.''

"This question may sound strange, but I need to get a feel of this guy. What do you—what kind of work do you see him doing? Where does he fit?''

For a long time she didn't say anything and seemed to be thinking. She was a good witness. Dowling pretended to scribble in his notebook while listening to doctors being paged.

"In a coat and tie," she said finally. "Like in an office or something." She rolled into the fetal position.

Fifteen minutes later he'd run out of questions and, after thanking her, headed for the door. Her tapping on the bed rail brought him back.

"He had a nice smile, if that helps."

"That helps a lot, Holly. A whole lot."

Ten minutes later he reached the emergency department, seeking the physician who had treated and admitted Holly Novikoff.

"You're lucky," a clerk told him. "Dr. Lord is on duty now. Getting ready to check a prisoner the Highway Patrol just brought in." The girl shook her head. "High-speed chase. The guy got dinged up a little when he spun out." She pointed to an empty examining room. "Wait in there and let me see what I can do."

Dowling sat on the edge of the hard table, letting his feet dangle, rubbing the stubble of beard that had accumulated since the early hours. He had loosened his tie in the men's room and forgotten to cinch it. The soft, clean pillow looked inviting and he fought the temptation to stretch out.

Twenty minutes later he looked up when a woman in a white smock started to enter, then stopped abruptly.

"Hey nurse. How long is it going to be before—"

"Where's the officer?" she said sternly.

"Huh?"

"Where's the Highway Patrol officer who's supposed to be guarding you?"

He slid off the table and she backed up a step. "I'm no prisoner, lady."

"I'm no nurse."

"Well I'm Vincent Dowling. *Sergeant* Vincent Dowling. San Diego P.D., Homicide."

"Angela Lord. *Doctor* Angela Lord. Chief of Emergency Medicine." Her hands were on her hips.

They stared at each other until Dowling said, "Holly Novikoff, admitted at 2145 hours last night. She's my victim."

"Your victim! Great phrase." She folded her arms. "Why Homicide? That girl didn't die."

"It's a long story but I'm in charge of the case. I'd like to know whether the suspect tried to kill her. Maybe left her for dead or—"

"No way of knowing. Pressure exerted on the sides of the larynx closed the opening of the glottis. Or the lumen closed, shortening its anteroposterior diameter."

"Kindly repeat everything after larynx?"

"The injury is consistent with the choke hold, as you cops so affectionately call it. Fingernail marks on the front of the neck suggest to me that after she was out, he kept choking her while he was on top of her."

"But you can't tell me whether he tried to kill her?"

"Asked and answered." She looked at her watch then turned to leave.

"Hey, Doc," he said loudly, "you must have snoozed through the bedside manner class in med school."

When she did turn she looked him over carefully. "Jesus, to think you're what's standing between me and Holly Novikoff and all of the scum committing crimes in this city." Then she was gone.

On the drive back to the station, through Hillcrest to avoid the freeways, Dowling concentrated on the things he had learned. His suspect was twenty to twenty-five years old. Definitely a white guy. Clean and neat. Short dark hair. No facial hair that Holly could recall. No recall of a man looking anything like him in or around the market.

Dowling drove around a blue-and-white city bus spitting exhaust fumes. If the guy didn't live or work in the area, he damn well drove through it regularly. That was what the history lessons taught. The trick was to work the case from the inside out. Start at the two scenes and draw a tight circle. What else *could* he do in a county with a geographic area the size of Connecticut and over two million people?

Stopping for a light one block from the entrance to Balboa Park, he couldn't remember getting this tired when he first came to homicide. Couldn't remember women yelling at him so much. Patting his paunch, he wondered how many cheeseburgers lined his coronary arteries after shoveling down so much junk food at fast-food joints, all the while scribbling notes and plotting strategy, thinking about the good adrenaline rush he was going to feel when they got close to somebody.

Being a cop was more than an occupation, and being a homicide detective was more than just another assignment. Dowling was convinced it was a calling, a passion, and the only people who really understood were his team and a few of the others. It was seductive. Almost divine. Helene had braced him once.

"You're not God, you know," she had said.

"You have to believe in yourself."

"Self-confidence is one thing, Vincent. But you—"

"Wait a minute, Helene. Who would you rather have out there chasing *your* killer around? Me, or some cop who'd rather be playing bridge?"

She had given him the look. Head tilted slightly. Long dark hair brushing her shoulder. The faintest of smiles. "You don't have to be everybody's savior."

"Oh yeah? Try telling that to some of these families. You take a hard look into their eyes and tell them that. Do you know what some of them say to me?" He took a deep breath. "They say that every night they pray for me to catch the guy. That's a lot of pressure."

But he'd thrived on it and never complained. Old bodies, young bodies, black bodies, white bodies, brown bodies, smelly bodies. Putrefied and decaying and maggot-ridden bodies.

The odor had sickened him when he worked a patrol car. Until an old sergeant took him aside at a particularly foul scene.

"Stick a dab or two of this in those red nostril hairs of yours, rookie," he said, holding out a pharmacy vial of oil of orange. "You won't smell nothing but orange blossoms for an hour or so."

It had worked, and worked well. But it didn't help the stench that clung to him when a body had lain undiscovered for days in the summer heat. He kept a plastic bag and a towel at home in the detached garage, and he would strip, stuff the outer clothing and underwear in it, then scurry into the house with a towel around him.

"Gross, Dad. Just gross," Jenny would yell if she encountered him between the back door and the shower.

Helene had badgered him from time to time about promotion, though he knew she didn't have a thing about "social" ranking. "Just think. If you made lieutenant, you'd work regular hours somewhere. Maybe Juvenile or Forgery. No call-outs. We could have a *life*."

But it took time to study for the lieutenant's examination, precious time that Dowling needed to chase down leads and devote to unsolved cases. Actually, he had passed the last three writtens, but something always went haywire when it was time for the orals, which weighed heavily as well.

Once he missed the oral because he was in the middle of an interrogation, trying to pry the truth from a teenager who'd conspired with his best friend to murder his father. Another oral took place a month after Helene had died, and he still couldn't remember anything about it. Except that he did poorly.

Then, years ago, the suspension had come the day before the oral. Ten days for conduct unbecoming. It had been a spontaneous thing. He and Bones were at a robbery scene where a black suspect had died on the floor. The guy had got the money from the liquor store clerk, all right. But the gun discharged when he stuffed it in his waistband and a bullet pierced the femoral artery.

Dowling thought the scene was cleared and never considered a TV crew with a telephoto lens on the far side of the parking lot. Even at that he would have been all right because the news director had no sound bite to work with. But the head of the local NAACP chapter, who'd stopped off for a six-pack of Dr Pepper, stood close enough to the door to overhear, and he filled it in nicely for the mayor and the chief and the media and anyone else who would listen.

"There he was, this red-haired fellow, looking down at the deceased and smiling. Then he pointed his finger at the cash register, pretending he was holding a gun, and then he said, 'This is a fuckup, mothersticker.' Then they all started laughing.''

The squad room wags called him Dan—as in Rather—Dowling for the next few weeks. But the truth was, he really hadn't wanted to be promoted anyway, and that was all there was to it.

Dowling shifted his thoughts back to Holly Novikoff and Annabelle Dominguez as he rolled into the police parking lot. There was a lot of work to do, but he knew they would make the case.

Tom Stacy intercepted him in the hallway and steered him toward his office.

"I've got things to do, Tom."

"This will just take a minute. What's the matter with you?"

"Oh, at the hospital I ran into a snotty doctor and an upset mother and—aww hell, it isn't even worth talking about."

They waved to two uniform officers before Dowling muttered, "Some of them think they run the whole world."

"Some of *who*?"

"I told you, Tom, it's not worth talking about."

When they opened Stacy's door, the captain of homicide pointed to someone seated by the desk.

"Meet Sam Mulcahy, Dowling. From Ireland."

Stacy turned. "This is your new boss, Sam. Sergeant

Vincent Dowling, the peerless leader of Homicide Team One.''

Dowling stared. First at Mulcahy, then at Stacy, then back to Mulcahy. She was pretty, and a redhead. Hair the same shade of red as his own.

Stacy stepped toward him, smiling. ''Are you all right, Dowling, or should I call nine-one-one?''

Two

Samantha Mulcahy, tall and athletically built, stood, extended her hand and firmly gripped Dowling's.

"Sam Mulcahy, and a pleasure it is to meet you, Sergeant."

Her voice was pleasant, clear and very Irish. Blue eyes met his without wavering. Dowling nodded, looked again at Stacy, then pulled his hand away quickly when he realized he was still holding hers. "Mulcahy," he said.

"Aye. Mull-kay-hee. Like the priest on *M.A.S.H.*"

She had a strong face. Not delicately boned but earnest. Her shoulders were square, and the only jewelry visible was a gold cross around her neck. Sam Mulcahy's red hair was not curly, but some natural wave turned under at the bottom. It was cut in a simple bob, straight across, midway down the neck, then tapered down to the front.

"I guess this is no joke," Dowling said, then felt awkward. "That is, Stacy and I, we, uh . . . anyway, here we are." Now he felt stupid.

"Officer Mulcahy hit town a week early," Stacy said, grinning a bit. "As a matter of fact, Sam, Dowling and I assumed we would get a man. Did something cops aren't supposed to do. Assume." Clearing his throat, he continued. "But I'll tell you, it's good to have you here. A woman will bring a fresh point of view to the team. And we can surely use that. Can't we, Dowling?" He handed him a folder. ''Here's the paper work on officer Mulcahy. After you've looked it over, I'm sure you'll want to sit down and brief her. Personnel needs her downstairs for a while first, though. Good luck, Sam.''

Dowling found an elevator, descended to ground level and made his way out to the Fifteenth Street side of the building. Two derelicts shared a green bottle in a paper bag on the east sidewalk. Black-and-white patrol cars, TO PROTECT AND SERVE painted on the doors in English and Spanish, honked at him as they hummed in and out of the E Street entrance to the lot. Dowling had constantly complained that the seven-story, concrete, steel and glass structure looked more like a hotel than a cop shop, but he didn't care today. When he reached Fourteenth Street, he paused on the corner and opened the folder.

Samantha Caitland MULCAHY
Born Sept 2, 1965 5-9 135 Red-Blue
Born Templeboy, County Sligo, Ireland
Sociology Degree: (T.C.D.)
Trinity College, Dublin
April 1989: Began two-year training at Garda
Training Center, Templemore, County Tipperary

Crissakes, a *social worker* living out of a suitcase. Going on twenty-nine years old. Born the year he became a cop. This was never going to work, and he would have a pointed talk with Stacy, who could then convince the chief's office that Juvenile or Forgery or Crime Suppression was the place for her.

If he was going to get a woman on the team, why not one from his own department? They started on the job like the men, working the streets in a tan uniform. Getting a handle on crime and getting to know what made people tick. By the time they graduated to detective they were ready. Hell, Myra Moore had walked into burglary detail recently and done some good police work. Solved a two-year-old rooftop series that detectives with moustaches had struggled with.

What good—what possible earthly good—was this Irish kid going to be to his homicide team? The answer was zero. Absolute fucking zero.

There'd been only a handful of policewomen when he'd come on the department, and they'd worked the detective division. Patrol work for them was unthinkable.

When had it all started? Twenty years ago? He'd been in Vice or Burglary when it happened. The women became police officers and walked around the patio with gun belts and nightsticks hanging from their tapered waists, and some cop wives called in raising hell because their husbands were spending more time every week working with female partners than home by the barbecue.

And jeez, the stories and rumors floating around, most of them started by salty patrol veterans. If a patrol sergeant *did* give a woman a good evaluation, they said he had to be screwing her. And if he didn't give her a good eval, the rest of the women cops said he was getting revenge because she told him to stick it when he made a move on her. And the macho officers, who couldn't believe *any* woman wouldn't want to lie down with a cop, said she had to be a damned lesbian.

Dowling sat on a bus bench, tugged at a loose lace and retied his shoe, the sun hot against his shoulders. Everything had changed so much. He smiled, remembering running into a half-drunk police chief off duty at Miyako's one night. "Dowling, I have a male patrol cop who wants to wear an earring, and I have a lady cop who says I can't make her wear a brassiere to work. Fuck this job."

And running into an academy classmate in the patio at the old Market Street station. The patrol sergeant, from Northern Division, always an upbeat guy, that day looked like his dog had died. He'd had a tale to tell.

"A month ago, Vince, they assigned me one right out of the academy. She came with a warning from Training Division, no evidence to go with it, that on grad night she

serviced six of her classmates in a phone booth. So who
am I going to team her with? I pick an old veteran, most
stable guy in Northern. Married nineteen years."

Dowling said, "Let me guess."

"You got it. Yesterday the guy ran away from home."

The light changed and Dowling retraced his route along
E Street, back to the corner of Fifteenth, across the street
from the boarded-up fight arena, where he'd seen Ken
Norton make his pro debut. If only he wasn't losing
Speedy Montoya. He didn't begrudge Speedy's promotion
to sergeant—he had helped him study and grilled him
with mock orals—but he was losing a talented homicide
detective and he wanted Gus Denver, not Samantha Mulcahy.

He would definitely talk to Stacy, but there was more
to read.

Appointed: April 11, 1989
Assigned: Killarney, County Kerry

Samantha Mulcahy had no sisters but five older brothers: Colum, Patrick, Seamus, John and Barry. The superintendent of her district had commended her for setting
up community policing and attending Neighborhood
Watch meetings. There was little, Dowling noted, about
her investigative experience, save a training stint in Dublin.

As he reentered the building, he didn't know which he
wanted more, Gus Denver or a cigarette.

"We're Team One of seven homicide teams," Dowling
told Sam as they sat at his desk. "Stacy has us on a
rotation for dead body call-outs. We roll on all murders,
plus any death where the cause is up for grabs. So we end
up looking at some suicides, some accidentals, even nat-
urals, then we make our call based on what we find and
what the coroner has to say." He saw her start to take

notes. "You don't need to write this stuff down. This is the easy part."

"I feel more comfortable recording it," she said.

"Well, you can feel more comfortable doing your recording if you go to a murder scene."

She pushed the notebook aside. "*If* I go?"

"As I was saying, we rotate. But all the teams work day shift. We take unmarked cars home with us when we're on call, then roll from there." He yawned. "In case you're wondering why we don't have a crew here around the clock, it's unproductive, sitting on your can at three in the morning waiting for the phone to ring. Most all of our follow-up work is done in day and evening hours. Then there's my dress code—"

"Excuse me, Sergeant. Just what did you mean by 'if I go' to a murder scene?"

Dowling looked at her and tried to buy a few seconds to think. Her jaw was set and she seemed to be staring him down. "It's just that nothing is definite," he said finally.

"Could it be you don't fancy working with women detectives?"

"I didn't say—"

"I suspect they work out keenly in the Juvenile Division. Or handling *sex* crimes." She brushed bangs off her forehead. "This assignment to America was one I wanted. I'm a damn good police officer, and I don't get weak in the knees when I see blood, Sergeant. True, we don't see many homicides in County Kerry. But I've worked some murders with Garda detectives from Division and with Technical Bureau specialists from Dublin handling forensics." She leaned toward him. "But I interrupted you. You were talking about a dress code."

Dowling cleared his throat and pretended to straighten his tie. "I was starting to say . . . *my* team always wears coats and ties . . . and dresses. A homicide detective should by God look like a homicide detective. When some son of a bitch detective approaches you sixty minutes after your only child has had his brains blown out and needs to question you about his personal life, you sure as hell don't want that detective looking like all the other bozos standing around gawking at the murder scene." He banged his fist on the desk. "You need some assurance, some validation that this by-God detective is going to do something about all of this and you sure as hell believe it more if he *looks* like a detective. Any questions, Mulcahy?"

"I'll certainly try to live up to *your* standards, Sergeant. So far none of the roadblocks you've thrown up have scared me off."

After a silence, he raised both hands. "Look, Samantha. Sam. Officer Mulcahy. My daughter, Jenny, bought me a little green rubber dinosaur and put it on my dresser. See, I'm kind of slow to . . . adjust to some things. We've got some really good women cops. But homicide has always been—Look, one of these days after work we'll go across the street and get a pint of Guinness and talk about it. Okay?"

"Okay."

"I don't mean a date or anything. Some of us, well we toss a few down once in a while. Do you drink?"

She smiled. "Am I Irish?"

Dowling shuffled some papers. "By the way, Team Six just rolled on a jumper, so we're it if something goes down."

"A jumper?"

"A suicide. She jumped from a building. And, because it was a city-owned building, homicide does the workup."

"How tall?"

"Probably about five four before she landed."

"I meant the building, Sergeant."

"Fourteen stories."

"Ugh."

Watching her walk across the room, he granted Samantha Caitland Mulcahy a wonderful smile and world-class legs.

*   *   *

Death arrived a few hours later, just before quitting time. The victim was the owner of a tobacco shop on G Street, found behind the counter, a homicide according to Patrol Division. Dowling knew how that went. They were right a lot of the time and wrong a lot of the time. Sometimes people hit the floor fast when their coronary artery called it quits. Sometimes they left a piece of their head on an edge of the kitchen table going down. Head wounds bled a lot, as the mother of any three-year-old knew, and young patrol officers confronted with a lot of blood would call for Homicide. But that was okay with Dowling.

"I'd rather roll on a natural then come in late on a murder," he preached to his team. "Besides, you learn by looking at dead bodies."

He had learned a lot in fifteen years of looking.

Dowling dispatched Bones and Shea in one car while he and Sam led the way in a late-model medium blue Ford Torino.

G Street was in a part of downtown that politicians and the chamber of commerce did their best to ignore. They seemed to think their job had been completed when they did a patch job on the Gaslamp District, a touristy haunt of twelve square blocks, just west of the porno flick, massage parlor, cokeheads-standing-on-the-corner area where Dowling pulled to the curb. He saw patrol officer Melancholy Johnson standing on the sidewalk.

"How come they call him Melancholy?" Sam asked as Dowling noted his time of arrival.

"Because he's paying alimony to four wives."

Taco sauce stains near the pocket marred the otherwise clean tan uniform of thirty-year veteran L. L. Johnson, who had managed to set up yellow police-line tape, corral the customer who discovered the body and notify the coroner's office. Johnson was tall, broad shouldered and square jawed. His hair, once gray but now colored brown edged out from under the old-style soft uniform cap with a polished black visor. He was the only cop in the entire Patrol Division who still possessed one.

"Joseph Schiller is your guy's name," he told Dowling. "Eighty-three years old. The fella who discovered him is in the back of my car. A regular. Went in to buy a pack of smokes—Lucky Strikes for Crissake—imagine that."

They stood on the sidewalk—the entire team plus a crime lab photographer—being briefed, always Dowling's first investigative step before going inside, speaking too softly for curious ears on the other side of the tape, everyone having an opportunity to pick the brain of the uniformed officer who responded, so that everybody knew what everybody else knew.

"What kind of scene, Melancholy?" Dowling finally asked.

"Jesus, the old guy's run this shop ever since I can remember, Sarge, and I grew up in this town." He blew black cigar smoke that Sam managed to duck. "Course, that last fuckin' lawyer said I never did grow up. Said it in open court, right in front of my kids. Should have sued him."

"Come on, Melancholy, my crime scene."

"Yeah. Well, looks like somebody painted the walls red. That's how much blood you're lookin' at. He's layin' on his back."

"Beaten bad, huh?" Shea asked.

"He looks like a hamburger pattie with arms and legs."

"Weapon?" Dowling asked.

"A Louisville Slugger, sawed in half. Fella next door says the old guy kept it for protection. Should of kept a goddamn three fifty-seven." He scanned his small pocket notebook. "No cash register. Made his change out of a cigar box according to the customer. Money's gone. That's about it. By the way, I walked around the edges best I could."

Dowling released the officer after his shoes were photographed. For comparison, in case they found shoe impressions, he explained to Sam. Melancholy Johnson was pulling away when he stopped, leaned out of the window and said, "Get the prick, will you, Sarge? That was a nice old man."

Dowling made assignments. Larry Shea would do the crime scene and Bones would make a witness search.

"Nail every person on the sidewalk, Bones. Every storekeeper. Our suspect has a lot of blood on him. Somebody saw *something*."

"Larry, take your time. This guy's going—"

"I know, Sarge," Shea interrupted. "This guy's going to be dead for a long time."

"Sam. Don't you do anything. Just stay next to me."

It disturbed Dowling that because of the extra Irish baggage, he would have to violate one of his cardinal rules of death investigation. Never did he allow more than two people in the scene at one time. It was difficult enough identifying and preserving and documenting evidence, and the more hands and feet trampling around the more chance for contamination. He enjoyed being able to surprise defense attorneys with that little tidbit during cross-examination. Jurors sometimes smiled when he pulled the documentation out of his jacket pocket.

"Not at all like on TV," one had told him after a guilty verdict came in.

"The photographer and I usually go in alone, Sam, while Shea waits outside. Then when the photographer backs out, Shea comes in to start the scene." Dowling waved off a television camera crew that was calling to him from behind the taped barricade. "But today, you come in with me. Walk in my footsteps. Ready?"

"Ready, Sergeant."

The three of them stood one step inside of the shop. Dowling and the photographer looked down, studying the old-fashioned black-and-white checkerboard tile. Whatever was left of Joseph Schiller was not visible, but blood splatters covered the far wall, and rivulets trickled in several directions from behind the counter. Acrid odors of blood and pipe tobacco filled the shop, and Dowling saw every magazine imaginable stacked on crowded racks along the perimeter. They stood in that spot for several minutes while distance shots were taken.

"Moving around is going to be tricky," Dowling said, looking at shoe impressions in the blood. "It wasn't a traveling scene. It all took place behind the counter. Let's go have a look."

Melancholy Johnson's description had been crude but accurate. Joseph Schiller lay on his back, one spindly leg tucked awkwardly under the other, his right fist clenched across his chest and the other arm alongside. No friend or relative could possibly identify him.

One eye was partially visible, the rest of the face a grotesque mask of flesh and tissue. Dowling glanced at Sam, who was kneeling near the feet.

"There's blood splattered under the countertop," she said. "Proves he was beaten where he lay."

"How can you see it from this far away?" Dowling said, squinting. "We'll need prints or dental for a positive on this poor old guy." He squatted again and squeezed the jaw. "No rigor." He looked at the pale underarm. "No postmortem lividity." The purplish discoloration caused by the settling of blood by gravity.

"Gross blood loss reduces the degree of postmortem lividity," Sam said. "Of course, you know that, Sergeant."

When Dowling stood, he looked at his victim for a long time. "What a hell of a way to go after you've fought everything else off for eighty-three years."

When the photographer left thirty minutes later, Dowling and Sam stood in a corner and listened to Larry Shea, speaking into a handheld microcassette recorder.

"The heel of the decedent's right shoe is twenty-two inches south of the north wall and eighty-four inches east of the west wall. A copy of the *St. Louis Post-Dispatch* newspaper is touching the decedent's left shoe which is . . ."

Dowling's hands had been in his pockets since he entered the shop. Taking out his notebook, he glanced at Sam, admonishing her. "Look, I know you don't have pockets in that dress, but stick your hands under your armpits or something. Get in that habit. Leave our prints at a scene and nobody takes us seriously."

An hour and a half later, Shea finished his preliminary recording and a deputy coroner removed identification from the pockets of the dead man.

"Protocol," Shea explained to Sam. "We have a good relationship with the coroner. They wait patiently outside while I do my act, and we let them fish through the pockets for ID."

The team was on the sidewalk when the body was loaded into the ambulance for its trip to the morgue on Overland Street. Sam said little, intently watching the methodical collection of hairs, fibers and other trace material.

"On TV they put plastic bags on the hands," Dowling said. "Know why we use paper bags?"

"On TV they don't show moisture collecting because of the plastic," Sam answered. "Moisture can foul up evidence."

It was just getting dark when Bones cornered them at the tobacco shop.

"The guy who runs the pawnshop two blocks over was out on the sidewalk earlier talking to a friend. Saw a guy come by all bloody. Figured he'd been in a fight. Time frame's about right."

"Tell me he knows the guy," Dowling said.

"He never saw him before, but the guy went into the James Madison. White dude. Late twenties, early thirties."

The James Madison was run-down, like most of the other pensioner's hotels south of Broadway. The old lobby carpeting was badly stained, and the clerk, thin-lipped and gaunt, barely looked up from his magazine. He peered over his glasses with little interest in the badge Bones showed him.

"I didn't see anyone."

"This guy was bloody," Bones said.

"Nope."

"Who was the last person you did see come in, sir?"

"I haven't seen anybody come in all day. I'm a busy man."

"Look, I appreciate that you're busy. But I told you we're from Homicide, so we're not talking stolen bicycle here. We need help."

"We all have our troubles," the clerk said, smiling.

"Don't we?" Bones answered, smiling back. "By the way, how long have you worked here?"

"Nine years, if that's any business of the police."

"I was just curious," Bones said. "We're playing big casino here. If I have to find that bloody guy on my own, we're gonna show up with the fire department where my brother works and close this shitbag down. Then you won't be working anywhere. Sorry we bothered you." He pivoted and headed toward the elevator. Sam hesitated, then scurried after him, looking back at the clerk.

"You might try three-oh-eight, Detectives."

They returned to the desk and spent another ten minutes with a talkative clerk. Robert Boyd was the name on the register, signed three weeks ago, address listed as a post office box in Sacramento.

"An unfriendly type," the clerk said. "Comes and goes at odd hours."

Bones and Sam took the elevator to the narrow corridor leading to room 308.

"This may be nothing, but be careful, Sam." Bones unsnapped his holster.

Sam gripped her gun, keeping it buried in her large purse. Bones made sure they were both standing to the side of the door before he knocked, his right hand inside his jacket on the butt of his weapon. The man who opened the door was bare-chested and husky, with a can of beer in his hand. A bloody T-shirt lay on the foot of the bed behind him.

"Police detectives," Bones said. He was starting to say more when the man tried to close the door. Bones blocked it with his foot and elbow. "Hey, we just want to talk to you. We need some help."

"You got a warrant?"

"Hey, man. I said, we just need some help."

"You got a warrant?" A demanding tone this time.

Bones allowed his eyes to shift quickly from the man's hands to blood-stained tennis shoes. "I got something as good. You probably heard of it, asshole. It's called probable cause." The heel of Bones's hand rested on his gun. "I'll have a search warrant in about an hour, but none of us are going anywhere in the meantime."

Dowling delivered the telephonic warrant in just under an hour. It bordered on the thin side, and Dowling, the deputy district attorney and the judge on the three-way phone conversation all knew it. But Dowling had been writing search warrants for a long time, and elderly Joseph Schiller, beaten to a sympathetic pulp, advanced the cause.

Blood was what they recovered. Blood on shoes, blood on socks, blood on clothing, and even blood in the suspect's hair. In a pocket of bloody pants they found sixty-five dollars in cash and an old railroad watch with "A.S. B&O 1945" engraved inside. In a drawer, on top of a Gideon Bible, were the parole papers of Robert Boyd, released from Folsom Prison twenty-two days before. Robert Boyd didn't want to talk with anyone except a lawyer.

"I like it," Dowling told the team in the critique room just after Boyd was processed and booked. "If we get a DNA match, he's bought and paid for."

An hour and a half later Bones and Sam drove to Lindbergh Field and picked up Joseph Schiller's daughter, a professor of history at Cal Berkeley.

"That was my grandfather's," she said, looking at the

watch in the evidence envelope. "He retired from the Baltimore and Ohio Railroad in 1945. Dad carried it everywhere." She started to cry. "That tobacco shop put me through college. He opened it at five in the morning and didn't shut down till eight at night. He'd even take a lunch to work so he could save money. Sometimes I'd catch the old trolley car and bring him sandwiches. Liverwurst and mustard and onions. God, he loved liverwurst. Isn't that a silly thing to think about at a time like this?" she said as Sam hugged her.

Team One headed for their cars. "Sometimes it all comes together," Dowling told Sam. "We caught a break tonight."

"Maybe we'll catch another one," Sam said. "Like a wee print of Mr. Schiller's on the railroad watch. In case our lad tries to claim he's had it forever. Tightens up the daughter's story."

"Yeah," Dowling answered, looking at her thoughtfully. "It would at that."

 # Three

Dowling's talk with his boss was pointed, and very short. Stacy didn't quite throw him out of his office, but it became clear Samantha Mulcahy would serve her entire six-month tour of duty under the care and guidance of Sergeant Vincent Dowling.

Dowling had shrugged. Worse things had happened to him in his twenty-nine years on the department. And she was pleasant enough. She'd filled a notebook at the murder scene, then fired off a slew of questions. There was nothing wrong with her cerebral process either. It occurred to him there were a few detectives who wouldn't have thought about checking the railroad watch for the prints of their dead man.

In a long talk about the post arrest process, Sam had been interested to learn that they could take blood, saliva, fingernail clippings, head, body and pubic hair from Robert Boyd without a court order.

"We get it for free until we book him. After that, we need paper work," Dowling explained. "How about in Killarney?"

"We get it for free, too, under Ireland's Forensic Evidence Act of 1990. But why pubic hair in a crime like ours?"

"Because you never quit getting surprised in this business. Better to get too much than too little."

When he told her the case might not go to trial, could well be plea-bargained, she made a nasty face.

"Come on," he said. "You're acting like a citizen. 'Plea bargain' isn't a dirty word. Hell, if it wasn't for plea bargains the whole system would grind to a halt. The trial calendars are jammed as it is."

"But justice doesn't get served."

"Yes it does. A good D.A.'s office won't take anything less than a first-degree on this case. His incentive will be life instead of a death penalty."

"But Robert Boyd should die, Sergeant. The bastard deserves to die."

"Juries are funny. Maybe they won't come in with a first. Maybe they'll come in with a second. Maybe they'll come in with a first and knock down the death penalty. Remember, in California the defense only needs one juror. We need all twelve."

He saw she wasn't satisfied. "On *L.A. Law* you never see plea bargains. You see some cop on the witness stand and the defense attorney is making the cop look like a dork. Naw, if they plea this one out, the judge will hammer him. He'll either die in the joint or be too old to swing a baseball bat when he comes out."

"I heard you talking baseball yesterday, Sergeant. Are you a fan?"

"Sure. Ever been to a game?"

"Now, where would I have seen one?"

"Then you and me and Shea and Bones will go see the Padres some night. What's your game?"

"Gaelic football, of course. Different from your Yank game. And rugby. I play them all."

"*You* play roog-be?" Mocking her brogue.

"Sergeant, I have five older brothers. I'm a tough lad."

Dowling made his decision the following day without consulting Stacy. For thirty days, Sam would roll every time a SDPD homicide team rolled. She wouldn't be able to work the entire case because a fresh body would pop up just about every day. A lot of sleep would be lost, but a lot of experience would be gained.

"You'll be able to check out how all seven teams work. How they do crime scenes. How they map out their work. How they talk to people. That kind of stuff."

"Don't you all work alike?" she asked.

"Nope. That's what learning police work is all about. Forget the book crapola. See how everybody does it. Then pluck out the things you like and shitcan—I mean, throw away the rest."

"So, I'll see a lot of dead bodies, won't I?"

"That's the idea, Sam. You're a tough lad, remember."

The next two weeks went quickly. Dowling's team, minus Sam, worked the rape series but remained in the call-out rotation. Dowling spent time looking out of the window but not seeing anything. It was how he did his best thinking.

Why *did* their suspect let his face be seen? Why didn't he approach his targets from the rear? Maybe walk up silently, or lie in wait behind a car or a hedge or a tree? Maybe it was simply because it worked for him that way. Crooks were like businesspeople. If a hardware-store owner tried a Saturday morning 15 percent off sale and the place filled up, he was sure as hell going to run another one in a couple of weeks. So why should a rapist or a burglar or a stickup man change his M.O. if the job was getting done?

Dowling pulled the M.O. folder from the file. Their query to other departments had yielded a few responses, but nothing turned out to be promising. They had been interested when the Pomona Police Department, about sixty miles east of Los Angeles, told them about an in-custody case where their suspect had put an "armlock" on his victim from the rear. The suspect was white and in his twenties and described as attractive. Larry Shea drove to Pomona for a follow-up but turned around a few minutes after he arrived. A Pomona detective determined the guy had been in jail in San Bernardino for disorderly conduct while Annabelle Dominguez was being attacked. And the armlock in the Pomona case turned out to be a two-handed choke hold.

Seeking a witness, Team One trampled through the neighborhood two more times, but it was not to be, and none of the sex offender parolees they looked at lived in the area of the crimes nor had a similar M.O.

Dowling picked up a report. "June 15, Annabelle Dominguez; July 4, Holly Novikoff."

His desk calendar read July 22. They would have to wait. He didn't think they'd wait long.

Sam was a novelty in the squad room, but the barrages directed toward Dowling from the other teams were beginning to ease up. A little.

"Here comes Dowling and his sister."

"Same color hair, but it can't be the same father."

"Not with a face like Dowling's."

"God made Sam to make up for Dowling."

"Stacy was smart. Assigned her to someone who can't get a hard-on."

Dowling kept track of the cases she rolled on and noted that the variety was about what he had anticipated. A drug deal gone sour left a young black man dead in a Southeast San Diego alley, shot twice in the chest. A murder-suicide in La Jolla. An apparent suicide leap from the San Diego side of the Coronado Bridge, but the case was clouded because the victim had received a threatening phone call at work a few days prior. A gang shooting in East San Diego left two dead and three wounded. "AVA-NHI," Sam was told by a uniformed officer.

"Asshole-Versus-Asshole-No-Humans-Involved."

"We don't see that kind of street-gang violence in Ireland," she told Dowling. "The two dead lads were raping a girl as part of their initiation. Their luck ran thin because the girl's brother happened upon it. Shot them first, then cut off their peckers."

It was why, she explained, San Diego gangs had been chosen as the subject of a graduate paper she was researching. The gang detail had proven happy to spend time with her, and she was filling notebooks about Asian gangs in East San Diego, Latino gangs in Logan Heights and Crips and Pirus in Southeast.

"Both Crips and Pirus originated in Los Angeles," she told Dowling, who feigned interest. "They came to San Diego in the seventies. Crips are stronger in L.A. Pirus stronger here."

There were other cases. A dead sixteen-year-old boy in a living room, shot through the neck when his best friend was showing him a new rifle.

"Team Four ruled it accidental," she told Dowling.

"Then it's an accident."

"But what if it was a murder? The perfect murder?"

"Then he beat us, Sam."

She was also perplexed over a case with Team Six, a barroom fight where a man shot in the chest with a .45 caliber bullet walked a block before dying in the gutter.

"That surprised me, Sergeant."

"People boozed up or fired up can do it."

"It was a forty-five."

"Doesn't matter. A good head shot's the only thing that has to put you down. Most people hit the ground because they think they're supposed to." He pointed to a folder on his desk. "Think about that when you roll on a case where a police officer kills somebody coming at him with a hatchet. And half the town bitches. Says, 'Why couldn't the cop just have shot to wound the poor fellow?' "

The case that disturbed Sam the most she had worked with Dowling's team. Belinda Anne Birney had been dead on arrival at Mercy Hospital, brought there because her breathing was irregular. On a routine autopsy, the forensic pathologist in the coroner's office determined the cause of death was a lacerated liver. Probable homicide. Trauma: death by blunt force, foreign object or person. Slight bruising was noted on the right side of the face.

Belinda Anne Birney was four months old.

It was the kind of case that most stressed Dowling. They were eight hours into the investigation. The mother's boyfriend waited patiently in the interview room. He had been left to watch the baby while Belinda's mother was cashing a welfare check. At the hospital, he told patrol nothing irregular had occurred, but when questioned the next day by a deputy coroner, he recalled Belinda had fallen out of bed.

Dowling had seen enough. He knew two things instinctively. The boyfriend had probably done it. And if he failed to get a confession, there *was* no case. No avenging Belinda Birney's short stay on earth. He had to be talented enough or lucky enough or devious enough to pull it off. And if he should fail . . . well, the guy would be back home in a couple of hours, sitting in Belinda Birney's living room. Pulling on a can of Budweiser. Watching *Inside Edition*. Telling Belinda's mother to rustle up a ham sandwich for him.

He wasn't worried about getting the guy past the Miranda warning. The guy knew he'd look bad if he didn't talk. The world would figure he was guilty. He'd waive his rights in a second; Dowling was pretty certain of that.

Sam sat to Dowling's right and they were twenty-five minutes into it, having danced around the get-acquainted how-are-you-doing, where-were-you-raised, how-long-have-you-been-seeing-Theresa stuff.

"All I know is I heard a thump and went in there and she was on the floor," he told Dowling. "I guess I shouldn't have put her on the bed. Should have used the crib like Theresa said to."

"How long had she been gone at that time?" Dowling asked.

"Theresa? I dunno. Maybe an hour."

"Then what?"

"I put her in the crib."

"And?"

"And what? She gets home, checks the kid and says,

'She's not breathing right.' So we put her in the car and take off for the hospital. Crissake, you guys think I'd do something to that baby?''

Dowling had seen him write with his left hand earlier, but he planned to ask the question later so the guy would hear his own answer. It was time to put it all out there and hope. It was the best and worst part of the job.

"Can I tell you what we think happened?"

The guy looked up quickly.

"Me and Sam here think you and Theresa got into an argument. Not a knockdown fight or anything, but women can get pretty unreasonable sometimes. They can get a guy right on the edge."

The guy didn't deny it. Good, thought Dowling, and he quickly went on. It was time to deliver the "out."

"Anyway, after she leaves you're still pretty steamed. Hell, she probably slammed the door on her way out. My wife does that, and it burns my ass. Theresa slams the door and it wakes the kid and the crying starts."

The guy was still listening.

"You go in there. Maybe pick her up. You're a caring type and you walk her around a little, try and talk to her."

He was still listening, leaning a little forward now.

"The kid keeps it up. Crying real loud now. Nonstop. Getting all red in the face. And now—here is where I can really identify with you. Mad as you are with Theresa and all, you kind of slap the kid. Not *hard*. Maybe open handed."

Dowling paused and nobody spoke.

"Are you right- or left-handed?" he asked.

"Left." It was said softly.

"See, the truth is real important to me and Sam. We have to make a report to the district attorney on our talk with you. When the lab guys, the men of science, when they get through, everyone is going to know the kid didn't just fall off the damn bed. See, the doctor told us it didn't happen falling off the bed. This is a coroner's doctor. A doctor who spent *ten* years studying this type of injury."

Dowling knew he had to press on. It was important he not give the guy a chance to deny. Denials, once made, were hard for people to call back.

"Donny." Dowling gently put both of his hands on the guy's forearm. "There's bruising on the right side of her face. Where a left-handed person would give a slap. Be truthful with us. Did you slap her hard, or did you slap her kind of lightly?"

That's how you asked it. Hard or light? Not "Did you slap her?" and invite a "no" answer. The guy put his head down.

"Real light. I slapped her real light. Just trying to get her to stop crying is all."

Dowling hoped the guy didn't hear him sigh, didn't sense Dowling's relief.

He patted him on the arm. "I've got a kid about your age. Kind of looks like you, too. If he was jammed up like this I'd want to know the whole truth from him." He paused. "Look at me, Donny."

When the guy looked up his eyes were watery. Dowling rubbed his chin. It was time to pull the trigger.

"You know what guys in your spot have told me and Sam before? They've told us they feel real good when they finally get it out, finally tell somebody about it. Get it cleaned up."

Dowling pretended to wipe a tear. "This is real hard for me, too."

The rest was easy, and in the hour that followed, Donny the boyfriend gave a tape-recorded statement, detailing without emotion how he had doubled up his fist and punched the infant in the stomach. One hard punch.

"Does he really look like your son?" Sam asked when they were making out the reports.

"Hell no. My son's good-looking. Like me."

A few days later, Sam heard Dowling's well-known "De-Miranda" spiel. It was a dope murder and the emaciated suspect with body odor had already acknowledged that he understood his rights.

"Course you got a right to *talk* to me, too," Dowling said.

"I do?"

"Sure. Your right to talk to me is guaranteed by the Constitution."

"Constitution?"

"Yep."

"How about that lawyer you told me I could have?"

"What about the lawyer?"

"Can I talk to you without the lawyer?"

"Sure. If you want to. That's your right."

"Well fuck it. I'll talk to you then. Ain't nobody going to tell me what I can and can't do."

"Okay then. Where's the gun Bad News saw you with Saturday night?"

Sam took no part in the hard squad room banter. Bones had become a favorite target since his divorce, and the day before had made the mistake of showing off a burn mark on his forearm.

"He didn't get it working on his car engine like he said. He got it from the oven, probably baking *cookies*."

"Nah, not cookies. He was using the oven to dry his one pair of shorts. Doesn't know how to work the clothes dryer."

"Yeah, he was trying to scorch them. Make them brown all over."

"Hey, Bones. You still buying your clothes from the same car?"

As Sam's month of corpse viewing drew to a close, Dowling decided she had earned a visit to the 153 Club. Across the street from the station, owned and operated by a retired policeman, named after the numbered incident form that all officers were required to complete when they were suspected of violating department policy, the bar and grill was the safest of havens. Cops constituted 95 percent of the clientele, and the remainder were young women who demonstrated a certain fondness for San Diego's finest. Off-duty uniformed officers lined the bar, and various detective teams hunched over the beer-stained tabletops. Dowling negotiated a small table where, with difficulty, they could hear each other. A large pitcher of beer and two bowls of tortilla chips separated them.

"So Stacy's an okay guy," Dowling said. "Just give him a chance."

"I already like Stacy."

"He can be tough. Close as we are, he transferred me out once." He threw down half a glass of beer. "Put me into a nothing job. Course I had it coming. I just couldn't see it then."

"What in heaven's name had you done?"

Dowling reeled a bit at the question, started to close down, then remembered the painful lessons he had learned in group therapy about the importance of honesty and feelings.

"My wife died." He hesitated. "Committed suicide actually. I wasn't doing well. Messing up murder cases."

"But surely—"

"Stacy tried to work with me. Tried to get me help. Tried to get me to take time off. He was being a friend."

Dowling reached for the pitcher. "I had a lot of guilt. Well-earned guilt. And I wasn't hearing anything."

A table of robbery detectives sent over another pitcher and Dowling blew them a kiss. "Those guys never sprang for a pitcher when I was sitting here with Bones or Shea. Where was I? Oh, yeah, Larry Shea. Shea's one of the best I've ever had. Never quits. He'll keep you sharp and he'll keep you laughing." Dowling dipped chips in the hot red sauce. "Now, Speedy, he'll make a run on you, even though he's in Patrol now. So I wanted you to be ready for that."

"What's a run?"

"Not a 'roon,' Sam, a 'run,' " he said, teasing again.

"A move. A hustle. He's going to ask you out. Say no. Speedy has a harem."

"I hear you, Sergeant. *Gradh gach cailin i mbrollach a leine.*"

"This Yank beer must be getting to you."

"That's Gaelic. It means, 'the love of every girl in the breast of his shirt.' "

Dowling laughed and she added, "I'm sure Sergeant Montoya has ruined the character of many a lass in the neighborhood."

"And Bones. A detective's detective. Quiet as cops go. *Never* lets go of a whodunit. Loyal to a fault. Saved my bacon a couple of times when I was struggling."

"He has a brother in the fire department as well."

"Not Bones." Dowling leaned forward to hear, battling an old-fashioned jukebox against the far wall.

"It's so. I heard him tell the desk clerk at the James Madison." She told him the story.

It was Dowling's turn to laugh. He told her stories about the need for ploys and intimidation to get lying or reluctant witnesses to turn things around for them. "Check with some old detective Garda when you get home, Sam. He'll lay some tales on you."

"Maybe the Garda will be a 'she,' Sergeant."

"You got me. But back to Old Bones. He's the one having a rough time right now. His wife ran off with a CPA. To Arizona yet. Took his daughters and a year-old grandson that Bones was daffy about." He poured for Sam. "Guess his wife needed a guy with a boring job who came home to dinner every night."

"He hasn't let on to me. Not a wee bit."

"That's Bones. Cops can't let anybody know they're hurting." When Dowling paused, Sam excused herself and headed toward the ladies' room.

"Funny thing, too," he said when she returned and their glasses were full. "Bones came to San Diego in the navy, then joined the department. Always talks about going home—he's from some little burg in Virginia—but police work got in his blood." He called for more chips and salsa. "Hell, I'd only been on for about three months or so when some old patrol sergeant says to me, 'Well, rookie. You're ruined for life. Cause once you've been a cop there ain't nothing else worth being.' Naw, Bones isn't going anywhere.

"I want to hear about Ireland," Dowling said as they ordered another round. Then he listened as Sam told him about her family. Her mother and father had a farm in County Sligo, on the coast. They had enough milk cows to scratch out a living. She asked about Dowling's Irish name.

"I don't know much about my heritage. My mother died when I was a kid, and my father passed away three months ago. He never talked much about private stuff, family stuff. In fact, we never talked much about anything until a year or so before he died. We were just getting to know one another." He blotted puddles on the table with a napkin. "But we were talking about you. Did you join the force right out of college?"

"I wanted to. But they had a two-year hiring freeze while the government commissioned an investigation into the justice system. Then the Walsh Report recommended that Garda training be two years. It had been much less."

"Two years?" Dowling whistled.

"Broken into five parts with a lot of on-the-job time mixed in. But the first five months we were lodged at the Garda college."

"Competitive?"

"Eleven thousand applicants for one thousand vacancies," she answered.

"And your time so far has all been spent in uniform?"

"Except for my detective training."

Dowling decided it was time to brief her about the series. "He's hit twice. Three weeks apart. It's been four weeks now. Maybe he quit," Dowling said, saying it but not believing it. "The one victim says she'll know him if she sees him again."

He filled her in on the investigative steps they had taken, detailing their frustrations and impressed with her attentiveness.

"What else do you do?" Sam asked after Dowling told her he didn't want to talk shop any longer.

"Do? Murders is what I do," Dowling answered.

"No hobbies?"

"Well, I bake once in a while." He looked a little sheepish.

"How interesting. A murder cop who knows his way around the kitchen."

Dowling changed the subject. "We left something dangling a few weeks ago when you braced me about not wanting you on my team."

"We did at that. You were being a shit."

"Look, Sam, we've got some terrific women cops in this department. But there's something I want to tell you. I teach criminal investigation at the community college one night a week. Back when women were just starting to work patrol, I had a student who wanted to join the P.D. She was an ice skater. Marie Fielding. Tall and pretty and leggy. About twenty-two years old." He leaned back in his chair. "I remember thinking at the time, I wouldn't want Helene—that was my wife—or my daughter to be cops. One month out of the academy Marie stopped a car and two guys beat her unconscious with her flashlight. She lost an eye. Retired on a disability."

"It could have happened to a man officer," Sam said gently.

"Could have. But it didn't. It happened to her. Sometimes that old tape keeps playing." He looked at his empty glass. "These bitters are pretty good. Let's have one more, Irish."

 **Four**

He was the only person in line not smiling or saying cute things to the little girl. She tugged at her mother's skirt with one hand while the other clutched a runny chocolate ice-cream cone. When they did make eye contact he looked at her sternly and she quickly turned away.

When the clerk handed over his cleaning, he shifted the twelve-pack of diet soda to his other arm, slipped a finger through the ring on his car keys and held the plastic-wrapped hangers well above the ground on his way to the car. Odors from the Baltimore Bagel shop drifted over the parking lot, and he carefully avoided stepping where oil had dripped in vacant parking slots. It was a mild August eighth, in the low seventies maybe, an agreeable relief from the hot Santa Ana winds of the previous three days.

He wore well-fitted shorts, a bright red tank top with "BUGLE BOY" printed in white across the front and floppy shower shoes.

When he reached the car, his keys fell to the ground as he groped for them. Rather than reshifting the box of soda, he hurled it to the ground, hard enough that the cardboard on one end split and three cans rolled away. He cursed, kicked one, kicked and missed another, then threw the dry cleaning in the car and slammed the door getting in.

Sitting behind the wheel, he scanned the lot before starting up. One woman, climbing out of a Jeep, had long tan legs. Long tan legs like bitch number three's long tan legs, and he pictured how white the leg had become when he got the shorts down. She had almost regained consciousness while he was fumbling with the string on the end of the goddamn Tampax, and he'd had to stop and choke her again.

He raced into traffic, cutting off two cars and made the decision on something he had been wrestling with. Tomorrow, tomorrow for sure, he would ask for a transfer to another division. A transfer that would mean a step up, away from his bitch boss. God knows he'd earned it.

Sam had worked a hitchhiking I'll-kill-you-if-you-don't-put-out-for-me murder in the first week of her thirty-day internship. The seventeen-year-old victim had chosen to shove open the passenger's door and roll out—at fifty-five miles per hour on Interstate 8. She might have survived the fall, the coroner said, but got run over by a truck as she careened from lane to lane. She lived long enough to say that a blond-haired man had menaced her with a gun. Another motorist took care of the rest, noting the license number, which led Sam Mulcahy and Homicide Team Five to the last known address of Plato Smith. Plato was gone, but the car and gun were recovered near the Santa Fe train station at Kettner and Broadway later in the day.

A murder warrant was obtained, and Plato was connected to the mugging of an elderly traveler in the station men's room. Purchases on the old man's credit cards started turning up in Texas, and Sam tenaciously tracked the path.

"Forget him, Sam," the team sergeant told her. "He'll drop somewhere. He's in the NCIC computer. We've got open cases to work on."

"He was in El Paso, Big Springs, San Angelo and a wee town called Columbus." A map was in front of her.

"It looks like Houston will be next. Then a place called Galveston if he goes south."

"With a name like his, Sam, he's probably too smart for us."

A few days later, the sergeant called Dowling aside.

"Cassidy addressed a bogus letter to Sam, put it in a bigger envelope and sent it to a friend in Dallas. Asked him to postmark Sam's letter from Texas."

On the thirtieth day, two things happened. The letter arrived, and later in the day, Sam rolled on a suicide.

"I don't know anybody in Texas," she said, holding the envelope to the light. "There's no return address, is there?" Most of the office found a reason to be in the vicinity of Team Five's desk at the critical moment. It was a two-sentence letter.

> You redheaded Irish mick. You couldn't track a bleeding elephant in a snowstorm, much less a clever murderer like me.
>
>   Erin Go Braugh,
>   Plato Smith

Hours later, when she returned from the suicide case, one look told Dowling she had been crying, and he hurried her into an interrogation room. The blue eyes were watery and her lips trembled.

"It was a teenager, she was. A lovely girl. Christine Muir."

"I'm sorry, Sam. Those are rough. We've been seeing more teen suicides."

"She and her boyfriend. A lad of just nineteen." Sam wiped tears. "They'd been sweethearts since the seventh year of primary school, but they couldn't get on without quarreling of late." She lowered her head. "They didn't want each other and they didn't want anybody else. They made a suicide pact."

"Jesus," Dowling said.

"Christine backed out. Couldn't go through with it. She thought he'd backed out, too. Then, yesterday, he ran his car off Sunset Cliffs, right through the barricade." She pulled Kleenex from her bag. "They wouldn't let Christine see him, so she parked in the lot right next to the coroner's building and took pills with a bottle of champagne. She died in the car."

"That's a rough scene to do," Dowling said.

She shook her head. "It wasn't the scene. 'Twas the note she left."

A few minutes later, she had steadied herself. "It's piling up on me emotionally. I'd done okay until this one. I'd done okay with poor Mr. Schiller. Even with the wee baby, which was horrible. I'd done okay with the lads in the squad room, with all the dumb Irish jokes and the sexist stuff. Like being called Sergeant Dowling's crack investigator. Saying they'd like to get my slant on a problem."

"Sam, you can't—"

"I wash the blood off my hands every day now. But I was on the edge when I got back from Christine Muir, and they *joked* about her. They have no feelings. No values."

"Sam, try to hear this. These guys have been washing blood off their hands for years, not for days. Chronic stress numbs their sensitivity. They stop feeling so that they can survive. They get so numb to their own suffering, they forget that other cops still feel. It works for them most of the time."

She was making tiny circles on the table with her finger, and Dowling added, "Cops don't rag on anybody they don't like, Sam."

"They must like me a whole lot then."

Dowling thought it was over and got up to leave the room but Sam didn't move. " 'Twas the note. 'Twas the note. It said—" She had trouble getting the words out, so handed it to Dowling, who read silently. "Scott. We had a deal. Wait for me."

* * *

The following morning, when Sam entered the huge
squad room, a computer printout banner covered much of
the far wall. It read: WE *LOVE* SAM MULCAHY.

Each detective was going about his business, a bright
green party hat on his head. On her desk were a dozen
red roses.

"'Tis a strange place you have here," she said, laughing and shaking her head. "A strange place."

Dowling left the station and drove twenty blocks to the
waterfront. When he dead-ended at Harbor Drive, he
made a left, and a minute later swung onto the G Street
pier. It was another place he liked to think. It wasn't a
typical pier anymore. It was a street really, jutting out into
the water like a finger. Except for the long, one-story restaurant on the end, no buildings blocked the splendid view
of the downtown skyline and the blue, curving, dipping
bridge spanning the bay and separating San Diego from
the city of Coronado.

He got out of the car, fed a meter and walked to a
concrete bench affording the best view of the giant aircraft
carriers docked in the distance.

A young woman in orange running shorts jogged by,
reminding Dowling of Holly Novikoff, forcing him to turn
his attention to the rape series. Hell, two cases hardly
qualified as a series. He had come to the pier to think and
not be interrupted by ringing phones and people wanting
something. It was possible, though he hated to think about
it, possible that their rapist was a cop. And the *only* reason
it was knocking at a corner of his mind was because of
the hold the suspect applied. It was a classic San Diego
P.D. lift-them-off-their-feet-they-never-knew-what-hit-
them hold, taught in the defensive tactics course for train-
ees. A lot of cop wives told tales of being put to sleep in
the living room because their recruit husbands were admonished to practice at home.

The department taught it because, in their eyes anyway,

it was humane. It was a lot more desirable than thumping some half-drunk troublemaker with your baton or getting into a fistfight in front of the Greyhound depot. Dowling had probably used the hold a hundred times, mostly when he graduated to a downtown patrol beat where you could expect at least a fight a night, especially on navy and marine paydays. Or when big carriers, like the *Ticonderoga* or *Bon Homme Richard* lumbered into port after being at sea for the better part of a year.

The sleeper hold was simple to apply once you got the hang of it. From the rear, the forearm slips under the chin, the crook of the elbow lined up with the Adam's apple. Then the free hand grips the hand of the arm under the chin, squeezing inward, catching the neck in a vise and applying pressure on the carotid artery. If the suspect was taller, you leaned over sideways while you were applying the hold, hoisting the guy up so he was arched backward. If it was done right, the person would be out in about five or ten seconds. Then you could put them on the ground, and they'd be coming to just as you put the handcuffs on. Other than maybe a sore neck, there were no aftereffects. Oh, it looked awful if you came in on the end of it, when the feet were dangling and the arms hung still and limp.

"The son of a bitch started to take a swing at me, so my partner made him do the chicken," is what you heard in the locker room.

Dowling never knew of anyone injured from the hold in the old days, when there were fewer crackheads running around. But in the past several years, a couple of prisoners had died several hours after arrest and the chief had all but banned the hold, limiting it to emergency circumstances. Whatever the hell those were. Stun guns and the rest of the new restraint stuff worked great on normal people, but normal people weren't strung out and playing Superman, heaving startled cops and helpless citizens through plate glass windows.

Dowling and the team had carefully reenacted the hold with Annabelle Dominguez and questioned Holly Novi-

koff about the technique. There was no doubt it was the
"sleeper," and Dowling had never known anyone but
cops to use it. Annabelle described it "like a steel bar
across my neck."

Bones had spoken with her yesterday, asking a few
questions, inquiring about her well-being. "At work,
whenever someone comes up behind me and taps me on
the shoulder, I go through the ceiling. I never used to do
that," she told him.

A man on a bench near Dowling lit a cigarette, and he
watched with envy when the man inhaled.

When he considered the emotional trauma rape victims
suffered, he felt a sense of urgency and helplessness. The
guy had to be caught, but so far the pattern did not lend
itself to stakeouts. The eastern portion of San Diego was
bigger than a lot of cities, and even as many as fifty detectives hiding behind trees and bushes would be a mere
sprinkling. And with manpower problems, he wouldn't be
able to come close to fifty anyway. Ten would be more
likely.

For a lot of reasons, he was not close to considering an
artist's composite sketch of their suspect. For one thing,
Holly Novikoff was the only one who really felt she
would know the guy again. His looks just had not registered with Annabelle, and that was understandable given
the darkness and the trauma.

A composite sitting on their desktops would not help
them yet. Flashing it around the neighborhood or putting
it in the hands of the media would result in a thousand
leads they were ill equipped to check out. As far as they
knew, this rapist had no distinctive features to help the
artist, and calls would come in with sightings from Pacific
Beach to Valencia Park.

And you could get stung from time to time messing
with composites. Sometimes, the victims swore the sketch
was accurate, but when the suspect landed in jail, wrapped
up with physical evidence and a confession, the dissimi-
larity left everybody shaking their heads. That created de-

fense attorney delights and big puffs of smoke that got blown around the courtroom on cross-examination.

No, a composite didn't figure. They would stay on the streets, keep knocking on doors and work the cases whenever they weren't handling a murder.

Dowling sucked in a deep breath of sea air. Clean-cut and attractive. That only covered about 90 percent of the Patrol Division.

Traffic was heavy when he turned back onto Harbor Drive. He headed north, passing Anthony's famous Star of the Sea restaurant and the *Star of India* schooner as George Strait, from the car radio next to him at the stoplight, asked if Fort Worth ever crossed his mind. Dowling punched in the same station, then caught another red light at Hawthorne Street, where a real pier, narrow and wooden, stretched into the bay next to Portuguese fishermen mending their nets on the large tuna seiners. When the light turned green, he gunned his engine and banged the steering wheel with the heel of his hand. Jesus, he hoped it wasn't a cop.

His daughter, tall and slender, brown-haired and pretty like her mother, was home when he arrived. Curled up in a chair reading, she reminded him of Helene.

Jenny had blamed herself for Helene's alcoholism, thinking it stemmed from her own shortcomings, typical teenaged girl shortcomings of untidy rooms and homework not being done on schedule. It had broken Dowling's heart. In the month following Helene's death, Jenny had gone on to assume her mother's habits, like sleeping without a pillow or reading the newspaper while standing on the front porch.

"All natural behavior under the circumstances," a psychiatrist explained to Dowling, as Jenny further and further developed a woman-of-the-house role.

Dowling had finally broken down and admitted to her and Matt that Helene had become a drunk because solving murders was more important to him than being a husband and a father. He still ached when thinking about it, and

all of the group therapy in creation wasn't going to erase
it.

Since then, he had watched Jenny closely, and she
seemed to be on a good track. She admitted the group
sessions were helpful, and she and Dowling spent long
hours talking about it. They also spent a lot of time together, having become a twosome when Matt left for college. They became obsessive about a miniature golf
course near the house, and he competed for time with her
first real boyfriend. He smiled when he recalled the first
time she mentioned him.

"Who's Oliver?"

"A friend, Daddy."

"What kind of friend?"

"Oh, Daddy. Does everything have to fit into a nice
neat package? A category? He's a friend from school."

"Then he's a boyfriend."

"There you go again, Daddy. But isn't Oliver a wonderful name? A *strong* name?"

"That's just what I was about to say, Jenny. A strong
name."

When Oliver's father was transferred to the Philippines,
their miniature golf time increased to a ridiculous fifteen
hours a week. That was also also about the time Jenny
quit calling him Daddy.

"I've got all the fixings for your favorite salad," he
told her as he took off his jacket, handcuffs and gun.
"Including Romaine *and* red-leaf lettuce, mandarin or-
anges, bermuda onions and, you got it, *walnuts*."

"Oh, Pop." She looked pained. "Jason's taking me to
Guns N' Roses tonight. We're going to grab something
there."

"Jason? What happened to Max?"

"Max, silly boy, fell for Linda Cauley. But it doesn't
matter. Jason is the real thing."

"Look, I've got all this stuff. Couldn't you and . . .
what's his name, Jason, have dinner here?"

"Sorry, Pop. Big crowd. We've got to get there early.

Besides, Matt eats enough for three people.''

Then it hit him. "Wait a minute. You're not going to the Sports Arena, are you?"

"If we want to see Guns N' Roses, that's where we have to go."

"Jesus, Jenny. Patrol is setting up a command post for that thing. Last concert they held there seventy-five people went to jail."

"Speaking of jail, Pop, how's the rapist thing going?"

"It's been thirty-six days. We're nowhere."

"You'll catch him. You always do."

"I hope you're right."

She kissed him good-bye and upon reaching the door called back, "When you get him, cut off his balls."

"JENNY! Young ladies don't talk like that."

"I'm not young anymore. Cut off his *cojones* then."

"JENNY."

"I'm not a lady either. Cut off his *huevos.*"

"Get out of here," he yelled, throwing a dish towel at her.

Whenever he was alone, he believed the house fell especially silent. He opened the fridge, started to grab a beer, then settled for a Diet Pepsi. If he changed clothes, then threw the salad together, it would be good and cold when they sat down. Matt *could* eat for three, and he spotted a package of french rolls he could smear with butter and parmesan cheese, then stick under the broiler.

Theirs was an older three-bedroom house, and when he wandered into the bedroom it happened again. He was certain he picked up the scent of Helene's powder. Standing at the doorway connecting the hall, he looked on the wall, then straightened the small frame holding the paper napkin from Angelo's, the tiny restaurant in Little Italy where they'd first laid eyes on each other. On the huge oak dresser were a grouping of large and small photos that Jenny had selected and framed. Dowling and Helene on the harbor tour boat when they were dating; then a goofy pose in front of the zoo's orangutan cage; a very

young Tom and Irene Stacy at a police picnic in the late
sixties; family shots at De Anza Cove and Balboa Park;
and Dowling's favorite: Helene, alone next to the hibiscus
bush in the yard, looking soft and dreamy. That was a
long time ago, he thought. Before Jenny was born. Before
he went to Homicide. Before Helene learned to drink.

He changed into a polo shirt and wash pants between
sips of the Pepsi, then sat in the brown leather easy chair
he refused to get rid of. They had picked it up cheap at
a furniture auction when they moved into the house, and
Helene would read in that chair, waiting for him to come
home when he worked the swing shift in patrol. After
listening to much advice, he had gotten rid of their bed,
which he had found her on. Found her on with the note
on light blue stationery between her fingers. The note he'd
torn to pieces and flushed down the toilet. But he remembered every word. Every word. It still pained him.

*Thanks for letting me play the fool. It was some sleigh
ride. Make Matt and Jenny understand somehow—if you
have the guts. You were the love of my life, Vincent. I
wish it could have been different.*

She had signed off, "Till death us do part."

He got up when he heard Matt slam the back door.
Dowling found him searching the refrigerator, wearing a
white T-shirt with "Shit Happens" neatly printed across
the front in large green letters.

At six five, his son towered over Dowling. He had been
tall for the last few years, but since graduating from high
school his chest and shoulders had filled in, and his hands
were huge. Like the other Redlands basketball players, he
sported a crew cut, and unlike his father and sister, he had
no freckles. Matt was smart and industrious, putting in
long hours at a service station over the summer and picking up decent spending money.

He had long been somber over his mother's death. In-
ternalized everything, had felt more a sense of betrayal
than Jenny when Dowling finally got around to telling
them the truth. Dowling regretted not submitting to group

therapy sooner because Matt admitted from the start how helpful the family sessions were. Now, grateful for the second chance, he watched his son carefully and was generally satisfied with what he saw.

"Hi, how are you doing and don't eat too much. I'm fixing dinner in a minute," he told him.

"Gonna eat at the ball game, Dad. Phillies are in. Tommie Green. Dykstra. Daulton. Kruk. Super cool."

"Jeez, am I the only one that eats at home anymore?" he groaned.

"Come on with us."

"Naww."

"When's the last time you went to a Padres game, Dad? Before Mom died, huh?"

"I suppose, yeah. Who's going?"

"Me and Clay. Maybe Richie."

"That's no good. You guys will sit so far away I won't be able to see."

"Not tonight. Plaza. Section Twenty-three. Extra ducat, too."

"Yeah?" The salad stuff would keep and he liked Richie and Clay. "I'd have to drive alone, though."

"You're up, huh?"

"Not for a murder. In case one of my rapes go down."

"You'll get the guy, Dad. You always do."

They sat at the kitchen table and talked. About Matt's job. About regular and pressure basketball zones, and Larry Bird's technique of "fronting." About two prospects coming in from Long Beach and Las Vegas. About a girl from Santa Monica whom Matt had been dating at school and whom he talked to on the phone almost every night.

"The thing is, her folks don't think I'm too cool."

"Because?"

"Because of . . . how Mom died and all."

"What the hell do they know about your mother?" Dowling asked, wishing he had a cigarette.

"Well, see, JoAnne and I talk a lot. About everything. Like they say in group, Dad, 'Feelings. Honesty.' So, her folks, especially her father I think, he's giving her big lectures on marital stability and responsibility, you know.''

"What does he do?'' Dowling asked.

"Corporate law.''

"Figures. And what does JoAnne think about all this?''

"She says her parents were born fifty years too late and keeps encouraging me to talk to her about our family and says I have a really good outlook about it and about a lot of things. Says I'm more focused than other guys in our class.''

Dowling drained his Pepsi. "JoAnne sounds to me like a girl you'd want to spend some time with.''

They were locking up the house when Dowling asked, "Hey, where did you get the T-shirt?''

"It's your shirt, Dad. Somebody in group gave it to you. Why? You want to wear it?'' Matt was grinning.

"No, I don't want to wear it. Put a jacket on so the neighbors don't see it. You're a cop's kid.''

In the fifth inning, Dowling had let his mind wander and was enjoying the ballpark sounds when his pager went off.

"You got one, Dowling,'' the watch commander told him over the telephone in the stadium foyer. "Your victim this time does it for a living.''

Five

Choice McGraw. Dowling couldn't help smiling at the name. She had slept in cramped jail cells from San Diego to Phoenix, with occasional stops in Long Beach and Los Angeles according to the rap sheet in his hand. Mostly prostitution charges, with a few petty thefts and scattered forgeries. She had never been to prison, which did not surprise him, though Phoenix had held her for 180 days.

"I'm through in Arizona," she told them. "Those fuckers *live* in air-conditioning."

Dowling expected her to look harder and older than her twenty-seven years, and had been surprised. There was an attractive softness about her dimpled face and light brown hair. The lower teeth needed work and an ugly four-inch scar crossed her forehead, then curved downward to the corner of one of the very blue eyes. Annabelle Dominguez and Holly Novikoff would evoke a lot of sympathy with a jury. It was his hope, but not his confidence, that Choice McGraw would make them like her, too.

She had been attacked in another residential neighborhood, on Louisiana Street, between the intersections of Howard and Polk, a few minutes after nine. About the time Tony Gwynn had doubled home two Padre runners. They were dealing with a span of eleven blocks east-west and seven blocks north-south.

Choice McGraw had been walking to a customer's

apartment when it occurred. "I took the bus up. Was going to use a cab going home," she told them.

Her high heels cut through the grass when she was dragged beneath a poplar tree in a front yard, and the residents had seen her later, wandering dizzily, carrying her panties, groping for her purse. "I wasn't going to call. If those fuckers hadn't seen me, we wouldn't even be talking. Who was going to believe me? And who cares about me anyway?"

The M.O. had been identical, but Dowling's hopes for identification were dashed as they spoke.

"I wouldn't know the fucker if he bought me breakfast."

To coordinate the hospital investigation, Dowling had arranged for a detective from Sex Crimes to help them. San Diego P.D.'s unit was a model for area law enforcement agencies. He listened carefully as the detective introduced herself to Choice McGraw; told her about herself and her police background and training; explained why and exactly how a physician would examine her, and why vaginal swabs would be requested; how she and the district attorney would protect her from unfair invasion by defense investigators and defense attorneys into her personal life; to forget what she'd seen on television. She was in San Diego now.

"You know, you're the first cops I've met in this town that isn't a Vice." Her hospital gown was cut away at the neck, but she pulled it up so her breasts were not exposed, touching her throat gingerly as she talked. "That roly-poly guy, what's his name, Shea? You fuckers are all right."

Dowling mentally lined up his cases while they talked. June 15, Wednesday. July 4, Monday (a nineteen day span). And now August 9, Tuesday (a thirty-six day span).

If there was a pattern, he couldn't read it. A helpless feeling began to chip away at him. He had planned some investigative steps in advance but didn't feel optimistic about any of them.

Bones was arranging transportation for Choice to the Buckner Hotel at Tenth and F Street, an old, old structure six blocks from the police station. Dowling was glad he didn't live there.

"This serves me right for leaving downtown," she said.

He looked at her for a long time. "We're going to give you a phone number, Choice. For some counseling." He saw the look of surprise. "This is a terrible thing you went through."

"Those fuckers aren't interested in counseling me."

He talked to her some more, trying to convince her, feeling frustrated and ineffective. His mind kept jumping to the investigative plans, and he couldn't discuss them with her. He made another move to leave.

"Hey, Sarge. Why'd the fucker have to do it that way?"

"There's a hundred theories, Choice. It may be he wanted to humiliate you." She looked puzzled. "Make you feel like dirt."

"He got the job done then." Dowling was on his feet when she added, "Can't you stay and talk some more?"

"Nah. We fuckers have a lot of work to do."

She laughed for the first time. "How long have you been doing this?"

"Twenty-nine years."

"God, what a way to make a living."

It was after midnight when they assembled in the critique room. Dowling, at his customary spot standing next to the blackboard, tossed chalk up and down. The others sat with notebooks in front of them. They all looked tired.

"We can't buy a break on the neighborhood check," Dowling moaned. "Somebody *has* to have seen that son of a bitch coming or going."

"When I worked a robbery murder with Team Two, the sergeant went to Vice and Narcotics asking the lads to put the word out among their informants," Sam said.

"Yeah. He probably plugged Fencing and Criminal Intelligence too," Shea said. "Stick-up men and burglars talk to the other shitheads on the street about their work. But sex crimes suspects are a different breed, Sam. Half the time they won't admit to themselves what they do."

"Sam," said Dowling, "you're going to be on the phone for a couple of days. I want you to call the sex crimes units in all these cities and see if you can't get a hit on the M.O. We can't do the whole country but we can cover the West. Write these down." The list was long: Seattle, Portland, Oakland, San Francisco, San Jose, Sacramento, Los Angeles, Phoenix, Tucson, Albuquerque, Santa Fe, Las Cruces, Denver, Salt Lake City, Boise, Las Vegas, Reno. "Research and Analysis is compiling a list of cities with navy and marine bases. When we get it, call the P.D.'s in those cities and run it by them, too. Maybe our boy just got transferred to San Diego."

"Talk English to them, Sam," Bones said, "so they have a fifty-fifty chance of understanding you."

"Yeah. Gaelic doesn't get it," Shea joined in.

Samantha Mulcahy didn't bother to look up. "When I want a bit of shit from you lads, I'll squeeze your wee heads."

"Jesus," Dowling said, "you were so sweet when you arrived here, Sam. What have we gone and done?"

He detailed more assignments. They would talk to every resident on Louisiana Street for a three-block stretch, as well as an equal distance on Polk and Howard Streets. "Somebody had to see something," he preached again. His other plan was concocted more out of frustration than a belief it would be productive. Sam, Shea and Bones would sit, one to a car, on the street at each crime scene between the hours of 7:00 P.M. and 10:00 P.M. Over a period of four nights, using binoculars when necessary, they would record the license number of every car that passed. "I guess computers have some damn use," Dowling growled, explaining how all of the numbers would be entered and matched. "And I don't care what the driver looks like. Take every number. He had a reason for driving in those neighborhoods.'' At least, he told himself, they were doing something.

The final job he assigned to himself: identifying the patrol officers who worked the beats where the crimes had occurred. He wasn't sure what he would do when he obtained the names, but it was a start. The team had been sworn to secrecy, and Dowling would work discreetly through a friend in patrol administration. The whole idea of a cop suspect bothered him. Booze was what usually got cops into trouble. Booze and the stupid things that followed when the brain got soaked. Women cops weren't immune to getting into the grease either. Though when they did mess up, it wasn't usually as dumb a thing as men were able to fashion.

Instances of sexual deviance were rare among cops, he told himself as he thought back over the years. The most shocking case in the department's history involved an off-duty patrolman raping women on the beach at gunpoint. But that case had been solved by the department and vigorously prosecuted. He hoped it would turn out he was just going through the motions on the internal investigation. That they wouldn't have to put handcuffs on a cop.

Dowling took Bones aside as they left the critique room. He had been smiling and in a lighthearted mood of late.

''How are things going?'' Dowling asked.

''Couldn't be better, Sarge.''

''Really?''

''Thaddaeus.''

''That's good, Bones. That's real good.''

Bones smiled. ''In fact, I'm planning a trip home pretty soon.''

''Damn, that's what I wanted to hear. You let me know when you want time off and I'll work it in.'' He slapped Bones on the back. ''We'll clean up this series first. Do you have a time frame?''

''You'll know pretty soon, Sarge.''

* * *

The kitchen was fairly small, so a number of his baking utensils hung from overhead beams. Dowling sat at the table that evening, the paper spread out before him, and rotated his attention between the news of the day and his pastry scrapers, suspended between the two wire whisks and his nine-inch tart tin with the removable bottom. His handwritten recipe book leaned against the coffeemaker. If he threw together a batch of tarts or croissants, he could run away from crime for a little while.

"The Choke-Out Rape Series" the columnist dubbed it, as always, protecting the identity of the victims. "The third vicious assault in thirty-six days occurred in the quiet Louisiana Street neighborhood, and as in the two prior crimes, police are without a suspect."

The last time he baked, his pastry had not been flaky enough to suit him, though others deemed it the best they had ever eaten. He had carefully dried his hands before combining the ingredients, so he knew it was not a case of damp fingers dissolving the flour and preventing the butter and shortening from incorporating. Perhaps he had not allowed the dough to rest and chill long enough between rollings. The gluten may have overdeveloped.

"Police have provided few details, but a source close to the investigation relates that the suspect uses a police-type sleeper hold on his victims and . . ."

Maybe he would run the problem by his longtime friend Rudolph Petrasovic, pastry chef at the U.S. Grant Hotel. If he could just keep Rudolph from wasting time pestering him with questions about contact wounds, liver temperature and postmortem lividity.

In the early days of their marriage, when he was concentrating on an important measurement for a cream filling, Helene would sneak up and towel-snap him on the rear end, usually causing him to lurch and make a mess. It always irritated him for a moment, because she did it every time, and he, always so engrossed, failed to be on guard. But he could never stay angry for more than a moment because she would double over and laugh until tears ran down her cheeks. He would end up kissing her, and sometimes the genoise for peach shortcake would be forced to wait on the sideboard while they made love. Glancing around the kitchen, he would have given anything to be towel snapped again.

The following morning in Stacy's office, Dowling received unwelcome news. A Rape Crisis Center group had made a request of the chief's office that the detective in charge of the series attend their meeting that evening. The request had been quickly approved, and Stacy was directing him to go.

"Get someone from Crime Suppression," Dowling pleaded.

"Nope. It's you."

"Assign that hotshot from Community Relations, Tom. He eats up that public appearance stuff."

"You weren't listening, Dowling. The '*detective in charge.*' The honor of *his* presence is requested." Stacy reached for a stack of reports, indicating the conversation was nearing an end. "It's important you change with the times. I keep telling you that, Dowling. We have different responsibilities now. With community-oriented policing, citizens look for us to keep the lines of communication open. It's the least we can do."

Hoping the speech was over, Dowling edged toward the door, but Stacy wasn't finished. "Take your daughter to the meeting with you; it'll ease the pain."

"Oh, sure. You can see me taking Jenny to that—"

"Not Jenny. Your redheaded daughter."

"With all due respect, Captain Stacy, you can be an annoying son of a bitch."

Dowling and Sam, easily the two most formally dressed in the room, arrived at the appointed time of 8:00 P.M. to find the meeting already under way. Comments were halted while they were introduced to the five other attendees, all women, seated around the table with a scarred Masonite top. Everyone seemed pleasant, telling the detectives how they appreciated their coming. It was explained that when the presentation in progress ended, Dowling and Sam would be asked to take part in a discussion about the series.

The speaker, using a flip chart, outlined the three theories of rape that had been advanced since the 1970s: the feminist theory, the social learning theory, the evolutionary theory.

Using a pointer, she explained that acquaintance rapists were more likely to be extroverts, while stranger rapists had been found to be introverted.

The woman sitting across from him looked a little familiar. In her early forties, brown hair at shoulder length, she wore a short-sleeved T-shirt with "Bryn Mawr" written over a crest. Twice they smiled politely at one another.

"We will focus now on the feminist theory," said the speaker, who turned out to be a registered nurse. "Rape being the result of long and deep-rooted social traditions wherein males have dominated all important political and economic activities." Dowling made a sincere effort to focus. "Because of the fear of rape, women tend to limit themselves to safe activities and protective conditions . . . difficult therefore to succeed occupationally . . . males wanting to act in a possessive, domineering and demeaning manner."

Sam kicked him under the table when he tried to stifle a yawn.

"Thus, sexual gratification is not a prime motive but merely a vehicle to establish and maintain dominance and control over women."

Dowling applauded with the others when the woman finished.

A general discussion about the presentation took place for the next half hour, and Dowling realized he was in the company of sharp, intelligent, service-oriented women who truly cared about the women who had been victimized. The comments were pointed and concise. Compassionate. When he was asked to speak, he rose and gave a general briefing about the series, including the times, dates, locations and M.O.

"Which of the theories we discussed do you believe attach to the perpetrator?" one of the women asked.

"Quite honestly," he answered, "until a few minutes ago I had never heard of any of the three.

"This disturbs me," the questioner said. "How do you propose to be sensitive to the needs of the victims without understanding basic principles?"

He took a deep breath and was thinking of an ugly response when the woman in the Bryn Mawr T-shirt spoke. "The sergeant is a guest of ours. So far, he has said nothing to indicate he is in any way insensitive to the needs of anyone. I think your characterization of him is unfair."

A few more questions followed. The woman who made the presentation said she had heard the latest victim was a prostitute.

"I won't answer that," Dowling said.

"Your nonanswer is an answer," the woman said.

"If she were a prostitute, would it make a difference in how her case is treated?" someone asked.

"Why should it?" he answered. Nobody said anything, and Sam spoke for the first time.

"Had you been there, you'd know she was treated gently and respectfully. Like the others."

Somehow, the subject shifted to irresponsible language in newspaper coverage, and a long discussion followed that Dowling did not participate in. He was grateful for the digression.

"In the New Bedford, Massachusetts, gang rape, they even described how 'pretty' the female detective was."

"That's nothing. In the Central Park jogger case, a gang rape, too, the damn coverage said the victim was 'fondled.' One magazine said those animals 'had sex with her.' "

Dowling felt himself getting angry. They kept all news

clippings in their work file, and he would look at them first thing in the morning. "Fondling" and "having sex?" Annabelle and Holly and Choice McGraw sure as hell were not being fondled. They were being grabbed and pawed and tugged at by some creep who was raping the shit out of them, not having sex.

"We have a meeting scheduled with an editor of the Copley Press, to make sure the *Union-Tribune* remains more sensitive than their counterparts in the East," the chairperson announced.

Dowling thought he was off the hook, but as the meeting was about to break, he was asked about physical evidence, specifically seminal fluid. "I'm sorry, but that's one of the things I don't talk about," he said. Choice McGraw's vaginal swabs had examined negative for semen.

"Don't you trust us?" asked the woman who had raised the sensitivity issue.

"It's not a question of trust. It's just how I do business." He hoped no one had gotten wind of the tennis shoe impression they had picked up on the last case.

"A pessimist?" someone teased.

He smiled. "You know what they say about the advantage of being a pessimist. 'Most of the time you're right and the rest of the time you're pleasantly surprised.' "

They had said their good-byes when the woman in the Bryn Mawr shirt approached them. "You don't remember me, Sergeant, but we've met before and I owe you an apology."

He must have looked surprised because she smiled and went on. "Angela Lord. I was the physician on duty the night you were in the emergency department inquiring about Holly Novikoff."

My God, Dowling thought, of course. The surly one. Nurse Ratched in doctor's clothing. At the hospital her hair had been up in a bun. Tonight she looked soft and smiled easily.

"I was out of sorts that evening and treated you badly and I'm sorry," she said.

"As I recall, I wasn't on my best behavior either, Doctor. So we get to start over."

"And another thing. I can't tell you how much I admire you for volunteering your time tonight. A lot of police officers would have considered this a nuisance."

He buttoned his sport coat and squared his shoulders. "It's important that we police officers change with the times. We have different responsibilities now. With community-oriented policing citizens look for us to keep the lines of communication open. It's the least we can do."

"That's a terrific attitude," Angela Lord said.

"How *could* you?" Sam asked as soon as they were in the car. "All the way over here you were complaining about . . . how *could* you?" When he smiled but didn't answer she said, "And you have no shame."

They were southbound where the freeway ended and Tenth Avenue began when Sam added, "She liked *you* a wee bit, too."

"Who?"

"That lady doctor."

"Naww."

"Trust me. She liked you."

Two days later, Dowling received what turned out to be more unwelcome news. The woman who had chaired the meeting at the Rape Crisis Center called with information, third hand, about a possible additional victim. "All this person really heard is that the woman's name is Rene and she lives somewhere on Howard." Rene was said to be mentally underdeveloped. "Normally we would call sex crimes, but supposedly she was choked. So . . ."

It took them four hours of door-knocking on the seventeen blocks of Howard Avenue to locate Rene Scheffield. At first, she wouldn't talk, but Sam gently persuaded her to confide.

The rape had indeed occurred. On July 20, a Wednesday. Sixteen days after Holly Novikoff and twenty days before Choice McGraw. It was difficult to get a read on how Rene had been affected. Her reasons for not reporting it were many. Embarrassment to begin with. What could be done anyway? She'd been in the middle of her menstrual period. *Embarrassment again.* And . . . the reason that seemed to most upset her: her father would be angry.

When they brought Rene home from headquarters, a man answered the door with a can of beer in his hand and a cigarette dangling from his lips. His T-shirt said, "When Daddy's Unhappy—Everybody's Unhappy."

"I got one question," he told Dowling. "One goddamn question. What was she wearing when it happened?"

"Shorts and a blouse."

"Real *short* shorts, or regular ones."

"Regular ones."

"Okay. Maybe she didn't ask for it then." He gulped on his beer. "I always told her, if it's gonna happen, may as well lay back and enjoy it."

"Is all the advice you give her that good?" Dowling asked, his teeth clenched.

"You bet your ass it is."

That night the team canvassed Wightman, an east-west street off Twenty-eighth where Rene had led them. The other three cases had occurred on north-south streets, Dowling remembered, at the same time cautioning himself against placing much importance on it. The location mattered, though, conveniently lumped into the cluster of other streets the team had spent so much time doorknocking on.

They turned up nothing. Walking between houses, growing more frustrated, Dowling allowed himself to think of Dr. Angela Lord. She had certainly gone out of her way to make peace, defended him at a sticky moment during the meeting, then was gracious afterward. There was something about her looks he liked as well.

Two nights later, speaking softly on the telephone at

home, lest he be overheard, Dowling reached Angela Lord at the UCSD Medical Center and asked her to dinner.

"Not exactly a date. We could meet somewhere. Of course, I'm buying dinner," he said.

"If it's not a date, then what is it?"

"Well, it's a—a date I guess." He was sorry he'd called.

She was not available for two more nights.

"Okay. Friday. You live—where?" he asked.

"Old Town."

"How about Tom Ham's Lighthouse then, on Harbor Island? At seven-thirty?"

"Seven-thirty it is."

"I'm not married, you know."

"Oh?"

"That is, a lot of cops—they—anyway, I'm not married."

"What a relief. I'll see you Friday."

He felt good the next day, nervous but good. The team caught an uncomplicated boyfriend-murdered-girlfriend case just after reporting to work and had wrapped it up by dinnertime. The evening he spent at the dining room table, working on his to-do list and thinking about Angela Lord. He wondered what would motivate a physician to accept a date with a homicide cop. He was still wondering when Tom Stacy telephoned him. Stacy, normally so direct, fumbled for a moment after Dowling said hello.

"I'm sorry, Vince. Bones killed himself tonight."

Six

It was an hour before midnight when Dowling parked his car across from the large apartment complex. He had put the phone down and hurried out of the house, not bothering to grab a jacket to ward off the chill of an evening turned cool. Two patrol cars sat dark and silent at the curb. A coroner's attendant smoked a cigarette next to a van with the County of San Diego's seal plastered on the side. This isn't happening, he kept telling himself, this can't be happening.

He walked slowly around a corner of the building, bringing the courtyard and pool into view. Stacy had assigned Jack Cassidy's team, and Cassidy was talking quietly with a detective at the foot of an outside stairway. A patrol sergeant made his way toward Dowling, throwing his arms around him.

"It was a 'shots fired' call," Speedy Montoya said softly. "The neighbor who heard it said the guy lived alone, he didn't know anything about him. Said the guy'd only been here about a month." Speedy paused for a long time. "Sarge, I thought Bones was still living in Mission Village. I get in there and . . ."

Dowling patted the back of Speedy's head, still holding him close.

"I loved Bones," Speedy said. "He was so good to me when I came over to the team. He ragged me about

78

going full speed all the time, but he taught me so much. About all kinds of stuff." Speedy cried into Dowling's shoulder. "Why, Sarge? Why didn't he come to us?"

"He didn't know how to," Dowling said after a moment.

"When you've done the scene, I'd like to go in alone," Dowling told Cassidy a few minutes later.

"Sure." Cassidy shook his head. "Vince, there's a note."

The one-bedroom unit was clean and uncluttered. Bones was seated in an easy chair, his badge pinned to the lapel of his sport jacket. At the collar of his white dress shirt, a Windsor knot had been neatly fashioned. Bones slumped slightly to his left, a blood-stained pillow propped between his head and the wing of the chair. The .357 Magnum had fallen to his lap. Blood trickled from a jagged entrance wound in the right temple.

A pillow. Considerate old Bones, Dowling thought. Make it easier on the cleanup crew. An oblong coffee table in front of the chair held a number of things. A nearly empty half-pint of vodka, an empty can of Rainier Ale, several photographs. A smiling Bones and his wife at their wedding, Bones and his daughter when she was an infant, a recent picture of Bones with a small boy. Beneath that photo, on a sealed white mailing envelope was written, "To my grandson—to be opened on his eighteenth birthday."

Dowling's hands were in his pockets and he read a note on the edge of the table without picking it up.

Sarge. All my interview notes are dictated so Shea won't have to read my horseshit handwriting. The gun from the Winfield case is in court—the D.A. entered it at prelim. That clears everything up. See that I get home, will you, Sarge? Maybe I'll find some peace there.

A stack of commendations was at the other edge of the table, and Dowling picked them up. The first bunch recognized Patrol Officer D. G. Boswell: 1975—for alertness and observation skills. 1976—for bravery. 1980—exceptional knowledge of beat and suspects residing therein. The others had later dates, some originating from Dowling. To Detective Delbert G. Boswell: investigative ability—interrogative ability—family of deceased expressing appreciation for empathy shown.

Dowling took a last look around the room, then kneeled in front of the chair. He curled his hand around the lifeless one resting near the gun. ''I'll take you home myself, Bones.'' His voice broke. ''I'll take you home myself.''

%% Seven

He walked circles around the living room, too on edge to sit. Transfer denied. No doubt from having to report to a bitch boss. She was probably saving it for a woman. Opportunities for promotion would have come faster in the other division, he was certain of that. He had been there, what, three years now and had done everything asked of him. Community involvement was almost as stressful as work itself—stupid talks and handshakes with a bunch of boring Kiwanis Club people and the like. His wife was getting on his nerves and had jumped on him again this morning.

"When we bought this house, you said it was just what you wanted. 'A little fixer-upper. We'll make some money on it,' you said. Lately you haven't raised a finger. With the house or the baby. When's the last time you changed her?" He refused to argue back but she wouldn't let it alone. "Why do you look at me like that? You scare me." Last week, when she kept harping about the garbage disposal he asked if she was going to leave him. "No, I'm not your mother and I'm not leaving and how many times do I have to tell you that?"

Well, his mother had left. Twice. Had run off with some city guy for a bunch of years, then came back for a few months when he was fourteen. Between times his father would sit on the porch at night, looking out over the wheat

81

*field with a prayer book in his gnarled hands, telling any-
one who'd listen that he'd married a virgin who'd turned
into a whore and no woman alive could be trusted.*

Later, when he was sixteen, he understood what his
father was talking about. He'd taken a line drive on his
left shinbone pitching batting practice, and the thing had
swollen up so bad it got infected because he hadn't stayed
off it. And when old Doc Raddison got him on the table
and drained it, the stuff he squeezed out was like black
tar. And the doc stitched it, then ran off to the hospital
for something and told his nurse, who was also his wife,
to dress it. She'd dressed it, all right. Kept rubbing her
elbow in his crotch while she was wrapping the leg, and
he thought it was an accident at first. But when he got
hard she kept rubbing against it and looked at him and
smiled. She wasn't all that bad looking. Forty-five years
old maybe, real firm under the clean, white uniform. But
the doctor's wife! The next thing he knew she was un-
buttoning her top and taking out her tits and she grabbed
his hand and rubbed it against one of them and he wondered what would happen next, but all she did then was
button herself up and smile, so he slid off the table and
never went back there again.

He thought about it a lot, though. Thought about it
every day but never told anyone. When he was seventeen
he did it for the first time, with a girl at school who knew
what she was doing and had to put it in for him. It didn't
feel all that good either. He never went back to her.

When he was eighteen he hitchhiked the 170 miles to
Wichita and took a room at the YMCA. Wichita was twice
as big as any other city in Kansas so he figured he could
find work.

On his third night in town, near McKinley Park he saw
a lady bending over putting something into her car and
then it just happened. He pushed her inside and pretended
he had a gun and she kept pleading with him not to hurt
her and he made her drive outside of town—on Central
Avenue near the Beech Aircraft Corporation plant. But he

*couldn't get it hard and made the slut put it in her mouth
and held his finger against her head and yelled at her to
suck it harder. It finally got almost hard enough and he
tried to jack off in her mouth, then kicked her out of the
car and dumped the car off back in town.*

*By the time he realized his wallet had fallen out of his
pocket, he was in his room, so he made his way back to
where he did it to her. He stooped down and was combing
the brush on the side of the road. Searching, hoping and
sweating all at the same time. Two tough-looking cops
came out of their hiding place, handled him real rough
and told him he was going to prison and get fucked in
the ass for twenty-five years. But a bunch of things happened, all in his favor, and he ended up in a youth authority camp for a few months. The lady's old man was
getting transferred to another air force base somewhere
and the last thing she wanted to do was come back to
Kansas for any reason, much less testify in court about
what went on in the front seat of her station wagon. He
and his father kept it hushed up back in Finney County;
then the whole thing got chased off his record when he
turned twenty-one and had stayed out of trouble.*

*Getting away from his self-pitying father and eventually
out of Kansas was his goal. His ancestors had pissed off
the cattlemen by plowing up the buffalo grass and plant-
ing corn. Turned out the cow people were right, because
after one good crop, a horrible drought took hold and it
wasn't until good irrigation systems sprung up that things
turned out right. Now the whole region was known for
bumper crops of corn and alfalfa, among others, and if
your idea of a good time was to get the red winter wheat
planted in the fall and hope the summer rains came at the
right time, then western Kansas was the place for you.*

*Unlike his father, he'd never gotten himself a virgin,
except maybe the bitch on Arizona Street. He'd felt resistance down there getting into her and later discovered
she'd bled. He walked to the window and looked at a
small flower bed in need of weeding. If this harassment*

*from his boss and his old lady kept up, somebody was
going to pay for it.*

Dowling should have been exhausted, but he wasn't.
The pilot announced they were on final approach to the
Roanoke airport, and he wondered if things would go
smoothly when they touched down. There had been long
delays in Los Angeles and Pittsburgh due, he was told, to
the logistics of transferring the casket.

"We can send the deceased air cargo," the funeral director in San Diego told him. "You can fly commercial
and connect much more conveniently."

"Where he goes, I go," Dowling insisted. He had almost forgotten to leave word for Angela Lord that their
date was canceled.

He silently thanked the flight attendant in Pittsburgh for
making him smile. "The Carol Burnett of the aircraft industry," his seat companion muttered, hunched over a
laptop computer and a gin martini with two olives.

"In the event of an air emergency, complimentary ox-
ygen will drop . . .

"This is, by federal regulation, a nonsmoking flight. If
you should be caught smoking in the rest room you will
be invited to step onto the wing for our feature movie,
Gone with the Wind."

The past four days had been a whirlwind. At a memorial service in San Diego, Bones's ex-wife decided
against a trip to Virginia. She softened when she saw
Dowling, draped her arms around him.

"Bones told me recently he'd looked his whole life
over and he hadn't made a difference," she said. "But I
never expected this."

Dowling hadn't either. Bones seemed happier recently.
Dowling knew from investigating a ton of suicides that it
wasn't uncommon for victims to take a cheerful turn in
the final days because their decision had been made.

And that part about not having made a difference. My
God, the entire life of Bones Boswell had been justified

by his devotion to the citizens of San Diego. He'd had a desire to make San Diego a little better place, and he did something about it. That was more than most people could say. Why hadn't he *told* Bones that? Why hadn't he taken the time to—then he answered himself, feeling the head-ache coming on. One of the troubles of the job. Always chasing a print or fucking with some pawn ticket or prep-ping for some interrogation when the cop sitting across the table really needed you but wouldn't let on.

To his surprise, everything clicked when they landed. His rental car was ready, and he followed Bones and the mortuary's hearse for fifty-five miles, northeast to Lynch-burg on Interstate 460. It was dark when he checked into his motel. In the morning he would go eleven miles far-ther, to Bones's hometown of Rustburg. A long, hot shower relaxed him a bit, and he threw down two ounces of bourbon from the flask in his suitcase before getting under the covers. Tomorrow he would see about getting Bones into the ground.

At midnight he awoke in a sweat. Bones had only been gone a week and already he'd had the dream. The god-damn marching dream again. It was always the same but always different. Cops. Dead cops. Marching down some avenue in a parade of some type. In perfect formation. And crowds lining the curb and the crowd always well dressed. No shorts or tank tops or go-aheads or bare-chested assholes drinking beer. Respectful people, quiet and solemn, but the thing was, the cops were the ones doing the smiling. *Smiling.* Dead cops smiling and their heads pivoting from one side to the other, hamming it up for the crowd on the curbs, cocky like, as if they knew something nobody else did. Some secret of the dead. And the music. Always one of two marches. Some military quickstep or that bouncy theme from *Bridge on the River Kwai.* Last night it had been a quickstep and Bones's face was in there somewhere. Most of the faces he didn't know—or they were too blurred to recognize anyway. But Bones was there. And a couple of young patrol cops

they'd buried and an LAPD robbery detective named
Gene Sloan. The faces changed from time to time, but
Gene Sloan and the young patrol cops were always
marching and waving. Sometimes pointing at somebody
and winking and tossing in some exaggerated body English at just the right beat of the music. Sometimes there
was a voice-over introducing the cops as they marched.
He wondered if the dream would ever go away.

The morning rose hot and humid, hotter than usual for
the end of August, the desk clerk told him. Over toast,
coffee and a poached egg he thought of what he had
learned of Bones's family in the past few days. The
Lynchburg police and Campbell County sheriff, contacted
by phone from San Diego, had been more than helpful.
Bones's mother and father were buried side by side in a
graveyard next to the Rustburg Baptist Church and, yes,
a site was available quite close to them. Dowling knew
there was one sibling. A sister whose whereabouts were
unknown.

They were getting down to it, he told himself as he
drove into Rustburg, population 550, with lovely green,
tree-filled hills. He made a wrong turn at the post office
but was immediately glad when he saw magnolia trees
with full white blossoms on a row of lawns. A sign pointing east read APPOMATTOX—18 MILES. Turning around, he
realized how un-Southern-California-like the whole land-
scape was. He returned to the post office and drove west
for less than a mile on Highway 24, a narrow roadway
running through the heart of town. He passed the Rustburg Hardware and Farm Supply on his right, then the
Central Fidelity Bank, then the old courthouse. Jeremiah
Rust founded the town in 1780, a sign informed him.

When he reached the school, home of The Devils, he
recalled Bones at the 153 Club, telling stories to the table
about a championship basketball game lost in the final
second. Dowling made a left onto State 655, an even narrower blacktop road with homes sprinkled on either side,
set well back, with large green lawns and shade trees. The

church he sought, redbrick with a sloping red shingle roof and a glass front prow, was on the left. The simple beauty of the cemetery surprised him. It was on the roadway, right next to the church, unfenced, near a grove of trees. The headstones were mostly low and unpretentious.

He chatted with the pastor, agreed on a time the following morning, then found a phone booth. The editor of the small newspaper politely explained that they did not run obituaries for people who had been so long removed from town. Dowling said he understood, then mentioned Appomattox.

"You're not a Civil War buff by chance?" Dowling asked.

"I most certainly am. Are you?"

"Well, lately I've become interested," Dowling lied. "Could I buy you lunch and pick your brain about the surrender?"

When he arrived at the restaurant, he pulled a pack of unopened Camels from the glove compartment and stared at them. He'd bought them in the hotel lobby that morning. He tossed them up and down, finally stripped off the wrapper, lit one and inhaled deeply. It tasted good, better than he remembered. He took another drag, then stuffed the stack of Bones's commendations in his jacket pocket. He was ready to meet the editor.

That evening he met with Lynchburg detectives, drank far too much and swapped sea stories into the early morning hours. He was delighted to learn Bones would have a motorcycle escort on Highway 501 from Lynchburg to the cemetery.

The next morning was as beautiful as the one before. At the grave site a police honor guard took their place beside the casket, and scores of on- and off-duty cops and sheriffs paid their respects.

On the plane going home, Dowling read the eloquent newspaper obituary that would find its way to the memorabilia box of Bones's grandson. He thought about the effect the death would have on Larry Shea and Sam. Gus

Denver would be reporting to him in the morning, and Dowling decided they would dedicate the solving of this rape series to Delbert G. Boswell.

He needed to control his emotions, so he decided against having drinks. Focusing on the blinking red light on the end of the wing, he thought about the rainy day he had driven himself along Interstate 8, crossing into Imperial County and stopping his car on the shoulder of the desert roadway, near the railroad tracks, between the tiny towns of Ocotillo and Coyote Wells. His guilt wouldn't allow him to keep on living. The pain would stop, finally, and photos of his body wouldn't have to be scattered around the squad room at the San Diego P.D. The Imperial County sheriff could figure out why some sad-sack homicide sergeant blew his brains out. He fingered the barrel of his service revolver, wondering if he would hear the explosion or if sudden death would precede the noise like an echo in a canyon. Helene's photograph was in his hand. She had been dead for fourteen days. His finger was on the trigger when his thoughts turned to Matt and Jenny. They would always remember how their old man had handled his crisis. Would maybe do the same when their lives turned upside down some day. A few minutes later, he had stuffed the gun back in its holster and returned to San Diego.

Dowling was startled when the flight attendant admonished him to fasten his seat belt for landing. Bones was gone, and he had another hole in his life to fill. He wished he could have convinced his friend he didn't have to die to get better.

# Eight

In Dowling's mind, the eyes were the most prominent physical feature. They didn't exactly bore into you when Gus Denver looked your way, but you noticed them immediately. They were large and round, and it occurred to Dowling that if the ebony circles in the black face fascinated *him*, they would surely be intimidating to a whacked-out smokehead explaining away a stolen gun and a sack full of money.

The face surrounding the eyes was expressionless most of the time. A vintage 1940s salt-and-pepper razor-thin moustache matched the color of the wavy hair on top of the head. He was built like Dowling, but three inches taller and six years older.

If pressed, Dowling would have been unable to come up with any one reason why he handpicked the twenty-year veteran of the armed robbery squad as Bones's replacement. He had teamed up with Denver on a handful of robbery-murder cases that Stacy had thrown his way over the years, gaining respect for the man's ability to do police work. But there were a lot of detectives who did good police work. Denver had a lot of informants. Not paid informants, not informants trading information to work off charges they had accrued, but informants who talked to Gus Denver because they liked and trusted him. To Dowling, there was a lot to like.

He remembered the first case they worked together. A poker player with marked cards and his pockets turned out was dead in a vacant lot. One small, neat bullet hole under his armpit had put him there. Gus Denver took to the streets and the shooter was theirs within a day. Dowling and Gus made the collar in the parking lot of the high school where the old man swept floors.

"Lord, you is making one big mistake here," the man said.

"Otis. Have you ever known me to put my hand on a man's shoulder and it not be him?"

"Why no, Mr. Gus. I guess I haven't."

The rest was easy.

"7-Eleven Gus" his partners sometimes called him. When Gus roused a witness out of bed at three in the morning, he stood at the door with steaming cups of coffee and an apologetic look on his own tired face.

Dowling smiled when he recreated Gus's spiel to mothers of young crooks they held warrants on.

"What worries me most, ma'am, is all these young patrol cops out there with Isaiah's mugshot tacked up on the visors of their cars. Those young lions all got itchy trigger fingers just *thinkin'* of seeing your baby and drillin' holes in his black ass. They know your boy's done some bad things and they ain't gonna fuss with him for one minute, they see him jiving on the set. Now if you could talk that youngster into phoning me, I'd see to it he'd get in the lockup without harm coming his way." Gus received a lot of phone calls over the years.

The morning Gus reported to Dowling's team, the morning after Dowling returned from Virginia, they stood on the terrace in front of the station smoking cigarettes. Dowling flicked ashes into the dirt of three-foot-high stone pots containing latticework supporting bright red bougainvillea. No clouds diminished the summer sky, and the warmth of the day made Dowling wish he'd shed his jacket.

"I've only been in Homicide for twenty minutes. Am I allowed to ask any questions yet?"

"Fire away."

"Am I gonna work *all* the homicides, or just the ones in Southeast?"

"Huh?" Dowling exhaled smoke through his nose.

"Seems in the last nine or ten years, all the stick-ups I catch are in Southeast. You know. Black suspects, black detective to catch them."

"Let me see your badge, Gus?"

"What for?"

"Let me see your damn badge."

The big detective fished a leather holder from his pocket, opened it and handed it to Dowling.

"Yep," Dowling grunted. "Just what I thought. It says 'San Diego' on it. Doesn't say 'Southeast San Diego.' Yeah, Gus, you work them all."

They chatted under the trees for a few minutes with two burglary detectives. Then when they were alone again Dowling said, "Tell me about yourself, Gus. Personal shit. I know what kind of cop I'm getting."

"Like what, Sarge."

"Like your name. I was looking at your folder on the plane. August Denver. That's a helluva handle."

"You really want to know about my name?"

Dowling nodded.

"Dowling, I've been on this man's police department for a lot of years and you're the first person ever asked me that."

"Well?"

"First person *ever* asked me that. Well, okay. Light up another of them horseshit Camels and I'll lay it on you." They strolled to a concrete wall and sat next to the grass.

"It shakes out this way. Colorado's where it happened. Somebody finds me all swaddled up, on a damn sidewalk in the middle of the night. I'm about three, four hours old is all. Cops get called. Hell, this is 1938. No social services eight hundred numbers to call. So the cops take me to an orphanage and the people there want a name, so the cops tag me August for the month it is and Denver for the city I'm in. I guess they didn't have time for no middle name."

"Crissakes, Gus."

"Glad it wasn't April in Albuquerque."

"Then what?"

"Then I kick around in that orphanage and get stuck in a badass trade school and when I'm twelve years old I chucked it and left on out of there and rode the rails and end up in a little burg called Waynesville, North Carolina. It's at the foot of the Smokies, Sarge, and the most beautiful place in the springtime you ever seen with all that new green. And white flowering dogwood, and pink flowering dogwood, and anyway I'm in this railroad yard and this old man working there finds me. He was supposed to call the railroad bulls, but he asked me what was going on." Gus paused. "You sure you want to hear all this shit?"

Dowling nodded.

"He was a kind old man. Dark-skin man, not brown skin like me. I told him. Then I started crying. Tears running down my motherfuckin' cheeks. You know, Dowling, I'd never in my life cried before. Never in my life. And this old man—he had eight children—he took me on home."

Gus stopped talking until a noisy city bus roared by. "This old man says, 'I'm gonna make you part of my family.' And he did. Sweet old wife, which figures, someone who deserved a sweet old man like him. And hell, Dowling, I had a good life. They sent me on to school and them other kids were good ones, too, and the teachers respected me because I was from the family. And we were never poor people. We were broke sometimes, but we were never poor because we had family. And then the old man cut his hand off switching a damn train and they put him on a pension, kind of a reduced one had to be, looking back, and he took to drinking a tad. Old man hardly never touched anything before that 'cept maybe at Christmas or on his birthday. Yeah, he started taking a taste and anyway, he steered me into the navy and I ended up here. Next thing I know I'm a cop.''

"You ran into good luck with that old man, Gus.''

"I did, I did. That old man always told me, 'Be nice to people.' Used to say, 'You start out ugly and want to get sweet, it's very hard. Like backing up a steam engine.' ''

"Is he gone?'' Dowling asked.

"Oh, sure. Gone a long time.''

"You took after him, Gus.''

"Well, I try to.''

"Did the old man sport one of those Don Ameche, Sugar Ray Robinson moustaches like you've got?''

"He did,'' Gus said, smiling.

"You're nice to everybody, and that's one of the reasons you do your job so well. It's why you've been cleaning up so many robberies over the years.''

"You know my M.O. I try and get these scumbag stickup men to like me and tell me all about it; then I put 'em in the slammer.''

"That's why I wanted to get you over to Homicide, Gus. Come on, let's walk around the block. I've got some preaching I have to do, and I can do it out here in the smog as well as in the office.'' Dowling looked up. At a pale, beige layer of haze, filtering the blue sky. "When I first hit this town you couldn't see the air.'' He paused near the monument in front of the station, looking at the names of officers killed in the line of duty.

"In Robbery, Gus, you're always in a hurry. Come in to work, check your in-basket and find half a dozen cases piled up. Patrol has a couple of in-custodies for you sitting in the jailhouse and you got about ten minutes to decide if they can be charged, and not much longer than that to get paper work to the D.A. so they don't have to cut them loose. Then you get a call from one of your overnight victims. What time are you coming out and interview

them? Then you get another call—some bad actor you
really want is on his way over to his old girlfriend's
house.'' They started walking toward Fourteenth Street.
''That's why I see you pounding down those half-pints of
milk, Gus. Trying to soothe those stomach juices. First
the milk, then popping bicarbs for that stomach gas.''
They both lit up again.

''The thing is, you'll be popping 'em working with us,
too, but at least you won't be in such a hurry *all* the time.
See, you make a mistake working Robbery, maybe you'll
get another chance. But us, hell, we mess up, we can blow
the whole case forever. You have to remember your victim's going to be dead for a long time, so what we do at
a crime scene we do in slow motion. Crime scenes are
like going to a baseball game, Gus. People are always
complaining how slow the game is. Hell, I've never in
my life gone to the ballpark and been in a hurry to leave.
So you'll never have me landing on your ass for taking
too much time at a crime scene. Am I putting you to sleep
yet?''

Gus laughed, then, without slowing, handed a dollar to
a lady with baggy stockings in front of the Salvation
Army building. ''You got me all fired up with your
locker-room speech.''

''I'm almost done. An old medical examiner from
Michigan named LeMoyne Snyder said, 'A homicide detective stands in the shoes of the dead man, protecting his
interests against the world.' A cop messes up a case with
a burglary victim, hell, his life goes on. He can take care
of business. But some poor son of a bitch laying next to
the cash register at the Safeway full of holes, well . . .''

They entered the building and were approaching the
elevators, nodding to people, when Dowling asked,
''What about your wife, Gus? What's she think of this
move and all the bad working hours?''

''This is wife number two and we're still on the honeymoon, Sarge.''

''Shea's the only murder cop I've had who's a lifer. I
hope it holds for him.'' Dowling shook his head. ''She's

a good woman. Shea passed the same sergeant's test Speedy passed, but he ended up way down on the list. They won't reach him before the list runs out.''

"I know," Gus said. "I saw him moping the other day.''

"Shea's wife told him, 'God intended for you to be low on that list, Larry. He put you there so you'd stay in homicide another year and catch that rapist.' ''

"My, my. No wonder he's a lifer.''

"Wives get pretty tired of me," Dowling said. "Calling you out to work at three in the morning. Or on Sunday just when you're putting dinner on the table for company.''

"Shea says you can be grouchier than a bear with a sore ass, Sarge, but I'll make sure she don't blame the messenger.''

"Something else. I had this detective once. Used to use the job for cover when he was all over town wearing out his Johnson. His wife would call and light me up real good. 'I haven't seen him in *three* days. Don't you believe in giving a man *any* rest? *Ever?*' ''

Dowling punched the button for the fifth floor and looked at his wristwatch. "I'm glad you're on your honeymoon. Let's go to work.''

An hour later, at his desk, Dowling readied himself for the critique. It would be the first time they had been together as a team since Bones's death, and Dowling had asked Speedy Montoya if he wanted to attend.

"Bless you, Sarge. I *need* to be there, with my old team.''

A telephone call tied him up for a few minutes, and when he hung up it occurred to him he had to do *something* about Angela Lord. True, he'd been back in town just over a day, but he had canceled their date. His mind was racing. On the plane he had tried to read over literature on the goddamn rape theories because he was feeling an allegiance of sorts to that women's group. They had given him the Rene Sheffield case, and God knows it might never have been reported otherwise.

He'd just started to evaluate the confidential data on the patrol officers when Bones ended it all. So he had to get back on that, and it was work better done in the privacy of home. Jesus, he hoped it wasn't a cop.

The coffee in the cup in front of him tasted bitter. Like unstirred machine coffee. Nothing else was tasting good lately either. He pushed it aside and went into the critique room.

"Bones got his laps in," Shea declared, after Dowling had passed the suicide note around. It had been read silently.

Shea stretched. "Some of the secretaries ask me how old Bones was and when I tell 'em forty, they get upset. But then I tell 'em, 'Don't cry. Forty was Bones's chronological age. Event-wise, he was a hundred and three.' "

"I know somebody who's not crying over him," Speedy said. "His ex-brother-in-law."

"Tell Sam," Shea said.

"Well, we get off work one afternoon and instead of heading for the 153 Club, Bones hotfoots it to the airport. Jumps on a plane to Virginia. Rents a car there. Drives to his sister's house, leaves the motor running and rings the bell. The brother-in-law answers. Bones knocks him silly, gets back in the car. Straight to the airport. Catches the red-eye to San Diego and he's at his desk at seven A.M."

Sam looked bewildered. Shea took it from there. "He'd warned the guy. Said, 'I ever hear of you hitting my sister again, I'm gonna come punch your lights out.' "

Speedy fidgeted with his car keys. "It's the job, man. Patrol's worse than it was last time I worked it. Fuckin' gang-bangers driving around with AR-15s sticking out of the window. More dope out there than you can fit in a moving van. Calls never stop till you drive in the lot and cut the radio off."

"At the university the studies showed it was the most stressful occupation in the world," Sam said. "Even worse than air traffic controllers. The researchers used three key indexes. Suicide, divorce and alcoholism.''

"Hooray for the researchers," Speedy said.

"And the single most important factor leading to police suicide was marital discord," Sam continued.

"Then I should of been dead a long time ago," Shea said.

Sam put her arm around him. "The devil takes his time with those he's sure of, Larry." She rubbed his shiny pate and winked at the others.

Dowling stood next to the blackboard, then began pacing. "If we're going to solve this caper for Old Bones, we better get our asses in gear." He pointed at them. "The answer is on the street. Not in some computer. Not in some goddamn FBI profile that Administration has been trying to sic on me. It's on the street. And that's where we're going back to. That guy may have pulled up next to one of us at a stop sign. He's out there."

Things were not going well. Sam Mulcahy had turned up zero in her scores of telephone calls throughout the West. A few M.O.'s had aroused their curiosity enough to make follow-up calls for details, but in the end, they were on their own. Their suspect's method of operation was alarmingly unique. Of course, that fact cut two ways. They would get no help from other jurisdictions, but . . . if they could catch their boy in the act, the peculiar M.O. could work in their favor. It would help to convince district attorneys and judges and jurors that the man they snared was indeed the man who had so calculatedly attacked and raped Annabelle Dominguez, Holly Novikoff, Rene Sheffield and Choice McGraw.

Sam, Gus and Shea had recorded five hundred license numbers of cars driving past the crime scenes during their sit-ins.

"So, what are you going to do with them?" Stacy demanded.

"Tom! I'm surprised at that question. They're all going

into the computer, of course. I'm changing with the
times.''

There were worse ways to have spent twenty-seven
hours. They were doing *something*. The analysts had
found no one car at all three sites, and Dowling wasn't
ready to run registrations on all five hundred. As always,
he was thinking a few innings ahead. If they got onto a
suspect who didn't live in those areas, and if his license
number popped up when they went back to the computer,
that would be important.

He paused, looked at the plot map on the wall and
continued. ''Tomorrow, we go to the sidewalks and reen-
act every job. We've got to make something happen.''

*He pressed against the tree, then thought better of it
and stepped onto the sidewalk, walking as nonchalantly
as he could. Every headlight wasn't going to belong to a
patrol car, and what if it did? How would it look? Making
love to some tree instead of just being Mr. Casual out for
a stroll on a fine summer night like all the other fools.
Until a couple of months ago, he hadn't realized how
many people were out there.*

*Of course, a couple of months ago patrol cars wouldn't
have had any interest in him either.*

*Until tonight, he'd stayed close enough to home to
make whatever story he'd pitch to them seem believable.
Being stopped on foot for a routine contact was a possibility, and being stopped in the car for a taillight shorting
out could happen any time. He had tossed that scenario
around in his mind a lot lately. A whole lot. By staying
inside of his circle, he could tell them he was going to or
from the gas station. Or the market. Or KFC to get a
bucket of cajun-style buffalo wings. No law against that,
right? Still a free country. No curfew yet for a person
walking off the stresses of an honest day's work.*

*The fear of a stakeout had driven his decision to be
where he was now on Van Dyke Avenue, a full twenty
blocks east of his circle. But he was still wary, intense,*

and that is why he jumped when the deep-throated roar of the boom box startled him. He heard the heavy rock music long before he saw the car conveying it.

The day had started crappy enough at work, evened out some, then turned to shit again when he walked into his kitchen. All he'd wanted was a cold bottle of apple juice and to be left alone, but it hadn't worked that way. Not even close. She'd started with a lecture about the garbage disposal—how he had promised for a week to look at it and how tired she was of wrapping scraps in newspaper—and he'd been dumb enough to counter with a litany about how people survived not long ago without mechanical kitchens. Then everything went downhill.

Pushing the red button on the bottom of the disposal hadn't helped dislodge whatever the hell was jamming it, and the Allen wrench wouldn't budge it, so he couldn't move the mechanism and that was when he inadvertently loosened the hose running from the dishwasher. Brown water flooded the bottom of the cabinet.

"Call the fucking plumber in the morning," he had shouted.

"You said you wouldn't say that word around the baby."

"She's only six months old."

"You said you wouldn't say it."

A few minutes later he had taken his turn at the changing table and gotten the baby wiped and powdered and was reaching for the diaper when she peed all over the place. She had cried when he pounded three times on the table.

His attention was drawn back to the street when he saw the woman. She had turned from a side street onto Van Dyke and was traveling at a relaxed pace. He had become a student of women's walking habits of late, and this one wouldn't be looking over her shoulder. Not that it mattered if she did, because he was already jogging out of sight, cutting over to the first street that parallelled Van Dyke, and if she was still on the block when he cut back *over, he would get her. He'd get her good. Jam it in hard. Hard enough to hurt if she was awake and looking up at him, but of course she wouldn't be.*

It was funny how his legs didn't tire as he ran. How his breathing never seemed to get strained. How he could see everything in sight and still have a vivid picture of the nice round ass. He had only seen her from the rear, and she wore dark slacks that tapered up to a tucked-in blouse of some sort. Her shoulders were squared and her hair was dark, and a cat ran in front of him as he neared the cross street. Goddamn he loved this.

He slowed to a walk as he reached Van Dyke again and looked to his right, moving toward her. She was right where he wanted her, about two houses away. Heading toward her, he made a show of drifting as far as he could to the left edge of the sidewalk. *Make this bitch relax. Show her a real gentleman was heading her way, giving her a lot of room to navigate the pass.*

She looked good from the front, too. A smooth, pretty face with nice tits pushing out from the blouse. *About seven to eight feet away would be just right, not too close now. Slow the walk just a little, and a smile, and . . .* "Excuse me, do you know what time it is?"

She wasn't slowing, was looking right at him, kind of cheerfully, and said it without glancing at her wrist. Said it right away. "Just after nine."

He nodded his thanks, smiled again and kept walking until he was one full step behind her. His breath was racing now and he pivoted, reaching for her with his right arm almost at the same time. She'd lowered her chin, though, and it was kind of pressing against the bottom of her throat, causing his forearm to squeeze against her face, preventing him from getting her around the neck. The rest happened too fast for him to recall later. Not only hadn't he gotten her around the neck, she had slipped his hold altogether. Had kind of eased herself down, almost to a crouch, then fired back up to a standing position, and now the dumb bitch was squaring off against

him. Wasn't screaming for Chrissake, was doubling up
her fist and taking a swing at him. Like she did this every
goddamn night. Policewoman decoy jumped into his
mind, but there wasn't any sound and nobody was rushing
at him from the bushes in front of the house. He swung
as hard as he could, just as she finally screamed. He
heard a crack when his right fist drove into her cheek-
bone, sending her down in a heap. He wanted this bitch's
pants off and he wanted her bad because she had ugly
manners and—then he heard the voice from across the
street.

He didn't look, forced himself not to. Just started walking slowly in the direction he'd come until he heard her
voice, strong and getting stronger, and then the other
voice, a man's voice he thought, getting stronger, too.
Then he started to run. Ran fast, reaching the corner in
a few steps, allowing himself a sneak look back. Saw the
guy was coming after him. Coming fast.

He turned it on. Legs churning, racing over streets and
curbs. Christ, he'd planned for things like this, but it was
really happening. He took another glance back. The son
of a bitch was staying right with him, maybe gaining. He
could only see one pursuer, but even a quick turn of the
head cost him time. Now the guy was shouting. An old
fuck walking a dog was approaching. A car slowed next
to him. Christ, that was all he needed, a posse forming
up, attracting members as they ran.

He had gone five blocks, staying in the residential areas, avoiding Fairmount or University Avenues where
traffic was heavy. He felt no fatigue. Now, though, for the
first time, he could hear the guy's steps closing in. He
darted into the street again, unable now to orient himself
as to where he had parked his car. Only it didn't matter,
because he couldn't take the chance of going to it. If he
did leap behind the wheel, this crazy mother would probably end up in the seat next to him, or at least catching
his license number. Goddammit, he couldn't have covered
his fucking plates. Leave in a hurry, tool down the boul-

evard with a pillowcase over them—jailbait for the first cop who saw him. No, it was lose this guy or be caught, and if he chose to stop and fight there'd be no telling how badly that might turn out.

When he thought the steps had gotten even closer, he turned it on again, straining badly now, feeling some lightness in his head, some fatigue in his legs, and when he could no longer hear the steps behind him, he looked again and he was alone.

It had been a long day, and the digital time and temperature reading on the savings and loan marquee read 11:00 P.M., seventy-one degrees. A little warm, even for August. Dowling absently clicked his heel against the twelve-pack of beer on the floorboard as Larry Shea, behind the wheel, passed the bag of tortilla chips to Gus Denver and Sam in the backseat. They were the only car parked in the Union Bank lot on Forty-fourth Street. A steady hum of East San Diego traffic noise drifted in through the open windows.

In midmorning, they had painstakingly questioned Adrienne Roe about her encounter on Van Dyke Avenue. Dowling and Gus had spent three hours with her, while Sam and Shea, in another room, interviewed the passerby who had intervened. All of the information had been exchanged during a critique.

"Adrienne Roe is a twenty-five-year-old elementary school teacher. Caucasian like all of the other victims except Annabelle Dominguez," Dowling told Sam and Shea. "She'd taken an apartment on Van Dyke so she could walk to school. Was coming home from a faculty meeting. Prepping for school opening in a couple of weeks. For now, I'm ready to call it part of our series. Gus'll tell you how it went down."

Gus Denver, shirtsleeves rolled up, took his place by the blackboard and diagrammed the scene. Then he told of the suspect's approach. "She can't say an *arm* went around her neck. Can only say something was squeezing her hard on the face. This woman's a triathlete, was a medalist in the Finest City event at the bay last week. She worked her way out of the hold and came up swinging. She takes the hit that fractures her jaw. That's when your witness heard her yelling and gave chase." Gus flipped the pages of his small notebook. "She puts the guy mid-to-late twenties. Fuzzy on the height. Nice build. An athlete she says. Clean looking. Pretty attractive. Dark, short hair. Too rattled to remember his clothing. Is pretty sure she *cannot* ID him."

"The guy who chased him is a black male, nineteen years old," Shea said when it was his turn. "Didn't see the attack. Came out of his house across the street, heard Adrienne yell, saw her lying there and took off after the guy."

"Did he know the victim?" Dowling asked.

"No," Sam answered.

"Why'd he give chase?"

"Just a good citizen, Sarge. You didn't think there were any left out there," Shea said. "Never saw the suspect except from the rear. 'Ass and heels,' he says. Puts him wearing a light-colored T-shirt, dark pants. Can't say about footwear. Dark hair. And *fast*." Shea paused. "Our hero was a free safety at Hoover High last year. Said, and I quote, 'He had moves, man. One time I was close enough and thinking about tackling him when the dude zigged and zagged like a damn running back. Fast for a white man.' " Shea laughed. "I had to explain that one to Sam."

"The 'what time is it?', the residential neighborhood, the suspect's physical and him grabbing her from the rear makes me list it as our suspect. With an asterisk next to it," Dowling had said as the critique ended. "It *was* twenty blocks out of the pattern, and there are a lot of guys who look like him running around in a big city."

Now, in the car, Dowling took a swallow of beer and fished a piece of paper from his pocket. "Got to remember to give this witness a commendation," he said as he scribbled. Absently turning the paper over, he looked at his list.

June 15	Annabelle Dominguez	24 years
July 4	Holly Novikoff	19 years
July 20	Rene Sheffield	30 years
August 9	Choice McGraw	27 years
* August 23	Adrienne Roe	25 years

White male
Twenties
5' 9" to 6'
Medium build
Dark, short hair
T-shirts
Nice looking
Nice smile???
NO SEMEN
RUNS FAST

"There has to be something we've missed," Dowling mused.

From early evening until just before buying the beer, they had visited each crime scene and reenacted the event. With each victim present except Rene Sheffield. Dowling had opted to pass on her, vividly remembering Rene's pain when she took them through the paces on Wightman Street. It occurred to him that when they caught their suspect, he would suggest to the D.A. they file one less count. He knew it wouldn't make any difference in the actual prison time served, and Rene would be spared the ordeal of courtrooms and photographers.

Adrienne Roe's rescuer took them through the exact chase route. Citizens being crimebusters wasn't something Dowling liked to think about, but thanks to another Good Samaritan, they had gained a potful of good intelligence information about their choke-out rapist in the past twenty-four hours.

"This homicide duty makes me thirsty," Gus said, reaching over the seat and exchanging an empty can for a full one.

"Aren't you lads afraid of getting caught with booze in a police car? On duty?" Sam's question was really directed at Dowling.

"First they have to catch us," Larry Shea said, belching. "The only time they ever did, the Sarge told some chickenshit patrol lieutenant we were on a surveillance and were using empty beer cans for props so we wouldn't look like the heat."

"Didn't he want to check the cans?" Sam asked.

"He kind of wanted to," Dowling said, smiling. "But he thought better of it."

"How do you three stand the smoke in this car?" she asked, sticking her head out the window.

Gus laughed. "You should of had my training officer when I came on. *Big* guy, smoked long, nasty old black cigars one after another. Windows had to all the time be rolled up tight, 'cause he was always cold. This great big guy with a booming voice, stompin' ass all over the street when there was trouble, and he was always cold."

"I know who that was," Dowling said. "Milo Crabtree. They partnered me with him, too. When he wasn't smoking those nasty cigars or stompin' ass, he was sleeping."

"That's him, that's him," Gus said, raising his voice. "Always made the rookie do the driving."

"Yep. And he'd be riding shotgun, sound asleep, facing the front, with his hat pulled down over his eyes, but he'd turn his hat *sideways*. So if the sergeant saw him from a distance, he'd think Milo was looking out the window."

"Another thing," Gus added, "he'd be snoring loud enough to wake the preacher, but let that radio sing out our car number and old Milo would be writing that mes-

sage on the clipboard and ten-fouring it before I could
even get my hand on the mike.''

They traded a few more stories, then talked about the
reenactments.

Watching the women relive the torment pained Dowling. He had been trying to get a fix on where the suspect
may have been when he first saw the victims. By having
the women walk their identical routes, the team went
through the motions, in vain, of trying to determine their
suspect's M.O. Did he see his victims from the car, then
park it and go after them? Or park, then prowl around on
foot until he spotted them? Considering, of course, that
they were dealing with random sightings and not women
who had been targeted on previous days.

Nothing pointed to the latter, even though Annabelle
Dominguez habitually left classes at San Diego State University, then took a bus to within four blocks of the attack.
Even though Holly Novikoff patronized daily the small
market she had been walking from when assaulted. Poor
Rene Sheffield, struggling through life with the mental
capacity of a nine-year-old, allowed Dowling to call his
shot. Rene had picked up food at a McDonald's. *But,* she
had never been to that restaurant before, and only a lapse
by her older sister allowed her to be out alone that night.

Before Rene had traveled two blocks, she got grabbed
on the sidewalk in front of an equipment rental store
closed for the night, leaving french fries and hamburger
wrappings scattered in the gutter. She was choked unconscious, then dragged behind the building and raped. The
only victim thus far taken out of view of the sidewalk.
An old drunk living alone in a dilapidated motor home
next to the building found her when he went outside to
urinate. He shepherded her into his coach, provided blan-
kets, and Rene Sheffield dozed fitfully until daylight. The
drunk had slept on the floor and was cleared of any
wrongdoing.

Choice McGraw had walked four blocks from a bus
stop, then got dragged under a poplar tree before she

could deliver favors to a first-time trick. Then Adrienne Roe.

"The jobs are random," Dowling told the team. "Which means he has a better chance of screwing up and getting nailed." A rapist who targeted his victims, knew their schedule and studied their habits reduced the odds of capture by happenstance.

"We can say for sure, Shea, that Roe's attacker was not a marine," Gus said, winking at Dowling. "If he'd been a jarhead, Adrienne would have whipped his ass and dragged him off to jail."

Shea yawned. "Nothing worse than being around two broken-down old sailors. Reminiscing about how they hated to go on liberty and leave their buddy's behind."

"He has to have a car, given the distances, but nobody's ever seen one," Dowling said.

"Nobody's ever seen shit, except for last night," Shea said.

"He broke my heart when he stretched out to Van Dyke Avenue. I was afraid he'd broaden his area, but I was hoping he'd stay in tight. Our chances of scoring on a stakeout just went from poor to terrible." Dowling watched a man and woman arguing on the corner, in front of a Vietnamese restaurant with barred windows.

"Roundtable time, boss?" Shea asked.

"I guess," Dowling answered wearily.

"What's a roundtable?" Sam asked.

"We'll get our five victims together. I want Rene Sheffield, too. Sit them down all together for a couple of hours. Look for a common denominator. Grocery stores, hairdressers, gas stations, organizations they've belonged to, that kind of stuff. Another long shot, but we've got to do it."

The beer was warming him and Dowling leaned back in his seat. "You know, there was a pitcher for Cleveland back in the twenties. Named Stanley Coveleski. Died in my home town, South Bend, a few years ago." Dowling took another long swallow. "This guy won two hundred and fifteen games and he had an ERA under three. Coveleski said once, 'The pressure never lets up. Don't matter what you did yesterday. That's history. It's tomorrow that counts. So you worry all the time. It never ends. Lord, baseball is a worrying thing.' '' He fingered his beer can. ''Coveleski fretting like he did, and he's in the Hall Of Fame.'' Dowling looked at his team. ''Lord, this homicide work is a worrying thing, too.''

Joy Larson had been doing her share of worrying lately. Most, but certainly not all of it, revolved around her widowed mother. She had seen the symptoms before anyone else, or at least anyone else who would admit it. Not the forgetfulness. Her mother was what, seventy-two years old, exactly twice her own age. Some forgetfulness was to be expected.

Rather, it was her mother's inappropriate use of words and the inability to remember significant events from the past—like her wedding date, her late husband's middle name. Joy had arranged for the neurological examination, and the doctor would only say ''too soon to tell'' when Joy pressed him about Alzheimer's disease.

Her husband's ship would be in port over the weekend, and she needed him home and their two children needed a full-time father. In six short months—she hoped they'd go quickly—he would have his twenty years in. With a navy retirement and the job he had lined up, life would be better.

She pulled the car into the alley off Madison Avenue and wished for the hundredth time they'd been able to afford a remote garage door opener. Leaving the engine running and the driver's door open, she moved into the headlight beams and hoisted the heavy door upward until it banged to a halt. She had taken to reading a slew of self-help books lately and she was seeing things more clearly. What she did not see as she drove the nine-year-old Toyota into the garage was the man standing next to her neighbor's garage, wearing a white T-shirt.

 # Nine

The woman shepherding two children down the hallway near Forgery reminded Dowling a little of Angela Lord, whom he had not spoken to since breaking their dinner date for the second time. She seemed to understand when he explained his murder-rape case was barely twenty-four hours old. They had no suspect. He couldn't just walk away from it. Not yet. And unless you believed in the hereafter, he told her, Joy Larson would never shepherd her two children around again.

On his way to Tom Stacy's office, Dowling wondered how many times he had briefed the captain of Homicide in the past fifteen years. Probably thousands. It wasn't Stacy's style to slam his detectives against the wall, but Dowling sometimes felt less than adequate going in. His mind scrambled, searching for answers, hammering out possibilities. Just what Stacy wanted.

"That was the executive director of WOW, a woman named Rachel Tiffany," Stacy said when he hung up the phone. "She wonders how seriously Sergeant Dowling is taking this series. Says according to her sources you're not breaking a sweat."

"Well fuck Rachel Tiffany and fuck WOW, whoever they are."

"WOW stands for 'Women of Will.' They want you to appear on Channel Two's Town Meeting with her."

"This case already has me talking to myself. You make me get on stage with some crackpot feminist and I'm pulling the pin."

Stacy smiled slightly. "I think I can get you out of it."

Dowling collapsed into a chair and draped his arms toward the floor. "Tom. The fact is, I got a load of trouble."

"You're certain the lady in the garage is part of the series?"

"Yep."

"Because?"

"Because her bra and T-shirt were pushed up around her neck. Because her pants and panties were down around one ankle. Because she was on her back with her legs apart. Because the cartilage of the larynx was fractured. Because there were fingernail marks on her throat and the sides of her neck from when he throttled her. Because it was in the general area he's been hitting. It's him, Tom."

"Tell me this. The reports say it's her habit to get out of the car, open the garage door, drive in, then close the garage door from the inside and go into the kitchen. Then how—"

"Then how is that compatible with him stalking the other five victims? Having the time to set up on them? How does he have the time to see Joy Larson and move in on her?"

"Very good anticipation of my question, Sergeant."

"I can't explain it."

"But you're sure it's your boy?"

"I'm sure."

"That's good enough for me. I'll tell the seventh floor. I'll let the Old Man know we're going to make this case, that you're busting your ass."

"That's just it, Tom." Dowling slumped deeper in his chair. "When I don't get results it makes me feel like I *haven't* been busting my ass. I'm running out of gas."

"Dowling, I'm not half as hard on you as you are on yourself."

"I feel helpless."

"Occupational hazard."

"Joy Larson wouldn't be on that slab with her lungs and kidneys being weighed on a butcher's scale if I had done it right or caught a break."

Stacy leaned back in his swivel chair, ran fingers through wavy white hair and let Dowling ramble.

"Holly Novikoff's the only one who can ID him. She *says* she can ID him. But so what if they all could. They can't ID him if I haven't caught him. I'm missing something. I have to be missing *something*."

Dowling got up and started pacing. "I got one break. I got a palm print. An identifiable palm print from the electrical box on the inside garage wall. Right next to the body. No fingerprints, just the palm. He could have lost his balance as they were going down and . . . It's not Joy Larson's print. Not her kids'. Not her old man's. We printed the electrician yesterday. Not *his* palm. I might have my suspect's palm, and I can't do shit about it until I get a suspect."

Stacy interrupted. "Because the county jail doesn't take palm prints when they book people. Because they only put fingers in the ink."

"Because it's too costly. Too time-consuming," Dowling moaned. "The most reliable, most undisputed item of physical evidence known to man. I wonder how those bean counters would have liked wandering out to that garage with Joy Larson's thirteen-year-old. That's who discovered the body, Tom. The thirteen-year-old watching over her younger brother, and getting worried because it's getting late and Joy was only going to be about an hour— over to her mother's. The kid phoned Grandma and Joy had left, and that bean counter should have been standing next to that little girl when she looked on the floor next to the car and found her mother lying there." Dowling sat down again. "You've heard all this before."

"Tell me the chronology again," Stacy said.

"Wednesday, Monday, Wednesday, Tuesday, Tuesday, Thursday. That's the order. Try making something of that."

"What's the spread of days between jobs, Vince?"

"Nineteen, sixteen, twenty, fourteen, two. Two-day gap between missing on Adrienne Roe and getting Joy Larson." He stood up again. "We did a roundtable the other day. Zero."

"You haven't hit me up for stakeout manpower," Stacy said.

"Would you have given it to me?"

"Given the pattern. Given the geographic spread. Given the fiscal dilemma. Probably not."

It was Stacy's turn to pace. "Naw, even if we'd have staked out, we wouldn't have caught him. Can't have a cop on every corner. What I feel a little guilty about is throwing those other two cases at you last week. Maybe if you'd had more time."

Dowling waved off the suggestion. "I wouldn't be any closer."

There had been no physical mystery to the other two cases. In the first, a street mugger used an umbrella to menace a man out of his money. The victim drew a gun and dispensed the death penalty on the sidewalk.

The squad room had a good time with that one. "Give me your money, or I'll open my umbrella and give you seven years of bad luck."

Nobody found anything to laugh about in the second case. Tom Mallory, a twenty-nine-year old cop and father of four, responded to a radio call about a family disturbance on the outside walkway of a second-story apartment. Neighbors said a man was acting crazy. As it turned out, the man wasn't crazy at all. He knew exactly what he wanted and how to get it.

Standing bare-chested and fondling a butcher knife, he advanced, ever so slowly, on Tom Mallory, who, gun drawn, cautiously backed up, step by step, using his free hand to guide himself along the railing.

"The cop kept yelling at the guy to put his knife down, that he didn't want to shoot him," two witnesses told Dowling.

When they reached a point where Mallory could back up no further—had to shoot or be in greater peril—the man dropped the knife, and as it clanged on the concrete he drew a handgun from the waistband in the small of his back. He and Tom Mallory killed each other on the balcony, and another face had been added to the ranks of Dowling's nocturnal parade.

"Who can say why he didn't shoot sooner?" Gus had answered Sam in the critique. "He had every right to."

"He'd shot a guy five years ago," Shea said. "Maybe he was thinking of the headlines. COP KILLS FOR SECOND TIME. Thinking of all the motherfuckers writing letters about how he should have wrestled the knife away from the guy. Or shot him in the kneecap." Shea drove his fist into the tabletop. "Any patrol cop will tell you it's their most dangerous call, Sam. SDPD handled over eleven thousand cases of domestic violence last year."

"He was a good street cop. Helped me a lot when I was in robbery," Gus said. "He must have had his personal reasons."

"Maybe we'll get a chance to ask Tom some day," Dowling said.

The squad room revived the old saw. "Better to be tried by twelve than carried by six."

Out-of-town requests had cut into Dowling's schedule in the past week as well. Tucson P.D. Homicide was chasing a suspect whose girlfriend lived on Island Court in Pacific Beach. Could Dowling check it out? Portland had a warrant for a guy they wanted real bad, and a source told them he drank wine coolers at The Golden Lantern on Pacific Highway. Could Dowling check it out? San Antonio homicide and a D.A. were coming in to interview a witness. Could Dowling line it up and meet them at the airport? The answer had been yes because that is how he worked. It kept alive his sense of fraternity.

"Semen?" Stacy asked, shaking Dowling out of his reverie.

"None."

"How can that be?"

"Retarded ejaculation."

"Bullshit."

"Remember that Crisis Center meeting you made me go to? I learned some stuff. It isn't that rare on predatory rapes."

"If you say so. We all know rape isn't about sex. But they were all definitely raped? Except Roe?"

"The vaginal area contusions make it definite."

"I'm almost through picking on you," Stacy said, reaching for his note pad. "The media's asking about a composite."

"It's none of their business whether I did or didn't do a composite."

"It's my business."

"I haven't."

"But you will." It was not a question.

"Compromise?"

"Go."

"For our eyes only. Yours and mine. Let me get a sense of how I think it looks. No releasing it without my okay."

Stacy hesitated. "Deal. Now, last thing. The choke hold. You were looking at cops who work the area."

"I'm still looking."

"If you sandbag me on this, it's your ass."

"I'm still looking."

"Jesus, that'd be all we need." Stacy stretched. End of business talk. "How are things at home?"

"I haven't been there a lot lately. But good. Things are good."

"You're still going to your group therapy?"

"When I'm not looking at dead bodies."

"Watch yourself. So you don't get ulcers like me."

"Ulcers come from conscience. Not giving your all for the company."

"Well, you skate then. No conscience. Since you go to group I guess you don't see Boudreaux anymore, huh?"

"My friendly neighborhood shrink? No," Dowling said, opening the door, "but I will be."

He sat at his desk a few hours later, struggling with literature forwarded to him from the moderator at the Rape Crisis Center meeting he and Sam had attended. What he did mostly, thumbing through pages describing the theories of rape, was try to keep an open mind.

"Would you be minding if I took another go at Rene Sheffield?" Sam asked as she approached.

"Why?"

"We didn't spend the time with her we spent with the others."

Dowling put his booklet down. "You think we missed something?"

"What I've got is a gut feeling she can tell us more."

"Sam, we spent less time with her because she's thirty years old with a lot of misfortune. Misfortune to be about age nine mentally. Misfortune to have been raped. Misfortune to be saddled with a father I'd like to toss off the Laurel Street Bridge."

"I've thought about all of that, Sergeant. And how the poor thing, after she's choked out and raped, spends the night in that shanty of a trailer coach."

Dowling looked into the soft Irish eyes. "Then go for it."

Going back to his notes, he wrote, "acquaintance rapists = extroverts; stranger rapists = introverts." He mused about what percentage of San Diego County's two and a half million people were introverts. Under "The Feminist Theory" he scribbled, "man wants to possess, dominate and demean: i.e., sex = gratification not prime motive." He had no trouble—never had—with the idea that rape was a vehicle for certain suspects to maintain dominance. To control women.

The trouble for him came with the social learning theory. Maybe repeated exposure to almost any type of stimulus did tend to promote positive feelings toward it, and maybe aggression *was* learned primarily through imitation. But, Jesus, who could say that the models for aggression came from three sources: primary association with family members and peers, a person's culture and subculture, and the mass media.

He read that aggressive behavior toward women was learned by imitating rape scenes depicted in the media: from horror films, from myths like "women want to be raped." That viewers were desensitized to the pain and fear of sexual aggression.

Well, maybe. Hardly anybody would argue that movies and television were more violent than ever. But how did it help him and Shea and Sam and Gus nail the animal that caused Joy Larson's husband to be a single parent? Maybe Boudreaux would know.

He got all bogged down in the evolutionary theory, asserting that males, expressing assertiveness, want numerous sexual partners and women want control over those they choose to mate with. It interested him that "the reason predatory rape seldom results in pregnancy is because only half of predatory rapists actually ejaculate." When he was partway through a 1986 orangutan study, declaring that in half of the forced sexual experiments there was no sign of male ejaculation, he shook his head. What if his old training officer, McNamara M. McNamara could see him now. Chasing a rapist-murderer and considering how often orangutans unload.

It didn't surprise him that studies asserted convicted rapists showed poor social skills in interacting with women. But something else he saw made him glad he had not brought Larry Shea to the meeting he and Sam had attended. Evolutionary theorists had proved, through primate studies, that species females tended to copulate with males, especially for the first time, after "nuptial" feedings. Where food offerings had been made. Also known as "courtship" feedings. Larry Shea would have told the attendees there was still plenty of that going on after dinners in a lot of San Diego restaurants.

There was a lot to decipher, and he tried to decide if he could put it to investigative use when the phone rang and he heard Matt's voice.

"Dad. Could you be in Las Vegas in six hours? I need you to be there. I'm getting married."

Ten

"Okay. What's the joke?" Dowling said. "Fraternity pledge trick, huh?"

"Dad, this is for real. JoAnne and I are getting married."

Dowling unconsciously put a cigarette between his lips, fumbled for the Zippo lighter he refused to discard and lit up. A secretary passing his desk stopped and stared, looking astonished that anyone would so overtly violate the building's strictly enforced smoking ban. Dowling looked through her.

"You're getting married because?"

"We're getting married because we're in love. We don't *have* to, if that's what you're thinking."

"I wasn't thinking that at all." He tried to sound convincing. "This is just . . . sudden. Isn't it?"

"How long had you and Mom been dating when you got married?"

"I don't remember."

"Jenny remembers. About six months. Like JoAnne and I."

"What does your sister have to do with this?"

"She's picking up plane tickets for both of you. You'll be here, won't you?"

Dowling didn't answer right away. He did remember. Remembered it vividly. It had been closer to five months,

118

actually, and he had proposed to Helene in the car. Parked
in a turnoff on the Sunrise Highway while the Laguna
Mountains flirted with autumn colors.

"How about her folks, Matt?"

"I went to them, Dad. Had this big speech rehearsed,
but her father cut me off pretty quick. Said when JoAnne
and I thought more about this we'd reconsider. *Then* he
starts talking about career choices. I'm trying to marry his
daughter and he's . . . anyway, he turns his nose up at any
law school except Stanford. Then when I told him all law
was boring except criminal law and I wouldn't want to
be a defense attorney and was going to be a prosecutor
that torqued him and anyway . . . I've got a chapel lined
up for nine P.M. You'll be here, right?"

Dowling thought about Joy Larson. He'd been on the
way to a critique at Thirty-second and Adams when the
phone had rung. "Why not wait . . . have a San Diego
wedding? All your friends are here."

"We thought about it. But I thought it would be dis-
respectful to her folks. Her father wants no part in it, so
we thought rather than being formal we'd just go to Vegas. In case you're wondering about money, we're fine.
One of JoAnne's health science profs is going on a sab-
batical and we're house-sitting her place. For just the cost
of utilities. And we both lined up part-time jobs. So you'll
be there, Dad?"

Digging his fingernails into his scalp, Dowling stared
at a crime scene photo of Joy Larson. Goddammit! Didn't
anyone understand the significance of the first seventy-
two hours of a mystery murder? How people's memories
get foggy, often on purpose. How perishable evidence
gets washed away and guns and knives and clothing end
up at the city-fucking-dump because some homicide sergeant would rather be flipping hamburgers at a family
reunion than pounding the bricks or putting the hurt on
some lying-sack-of-shit witness. A leader is supposed to
lead, and that meant standing in Joy Larson's shoes, not—

"So you will be there, Dad," his son repeated.

"Of course I will, Matt."

Two short phone calls followed. Gus Denver and Shea delivered unpromising updates as his daughter bounded across the squad room floor with a smile that covered her whole face. She waved a packet of airline tickets at him.

"I'm so proud of you," she said, hugging him.

"Because?"

"Because you kept your promise. The one you made in the kitchen almost a year ago. You promised if you went back to Homicide it would never get in the way of family again." She hugged him a second time, harder. "I know you caught a murder yesterday. But I know how important Matt and JoAnne are to you."

In the dry heat of the Las Vegas night, Dowling thought about a lot of things as he stood up for his son in the small chapel just off The Strip. About Helene and how he wished she were there. About how much Jenny, the maid of honor, looked like her mother. About how radiant and gracious his son's bride looked in a navy blue suit with a white lapel corsage. And like Tevye, he wondered where the years had flown. Most of all, he wondered who besides himself would remember or even care about all of the cases that had drawn him like a magnet from his home. And how or if he could balance his two worlds. He had sworn he would never hurt his children again, yet he had come close. Had almost blurted out to Matt he had no right to drop a wedding on him with six hours notice when he had three detectives going full speed and . . .

And then it was over and he stood in a sea of tears and rice and laughter as traffic hurried past Caesar's Palace and the MGM Grand Hotel.

Mr. and Mrs. Matthew Dowling had been wed for three days when Sam Mulcahy told the team about her walk in the park with Rene Sheffield.

"A lovely day it was, so warm and all for September,

and we ended up at the zoo. A sweet girl she is.''

''Anything new?'' Gus wanted to know.

''Rene thinks our suspect said something to her when he was on top. The poor thing went unconscious first, right after she told him what time it was. As she and I sat and talked about it, she recalled opening her eyes for an instant, seeing a red-and-white sign flashing somewhere. That's when she heard it; then she lost consciousness again.''

''None of the other victims heard anything. What did he say?'' Dowling asked.

''She can't recall. Started asking me about whether America was what I expected. 'Twas hard to keep her on track, you know.''

''Stay with it, Sam,'' Dowling said.

''I will at that. We're going to have a bit of lunch together on Friday. So we'll work on it. I went back to the crime scene. When I lay down on the dirt, where the old-timer said he found her, I could see, just over the fence, a big sign from a petrol station one hundred meters away. I checked with the manager there, and his sign lights up red and white at night.''

They were breaking up the meeting when Larry Shea asked, ''What did you tell her when she questioned you about Ireland and America?''

''That everything was bigger than I imagined. The cars. The buildings. The highways. Even the sandwiches, for goodness' sakes. And so many cars.''

''The cars?'' Gus said.

''Yes. *Everybody's* got a car. Nobody walks anywhere like at home.''

They were disbanding again when she added, ''Speaking of cars, Sergeant. I had a wee accident driving back from Rene's.''

''In the detective car?'' Dowling looked pained.

''Just a dinger it was. Nobody hurt.''

''You called it in?'' Dowling asked quickly.

''I did. A fine lad in uniform did the workup. I'd had

a knicker fit and he was most understanding.''

"A knicker fit?''

"That means I was annoyed,'' she said, seeming to become annoyed again.

"I'm afraid to ask who was at fault,'' Dowling said, shaking his head.

"I was 'vehicle number one' according to officer Harper. Damon Harper it is. Is that good or bad?''

"That's bad. Vehicle number one is the vehicle responsible for the accident.''

"It was a busy intersection where at home they'd have a roundabout instead of four corners. I pulled out a bit too soon I suppose.''

"Sarge, let's get the girl equipped with a car with right-hand drive. So she'll think she's in County Cork,'' Gus suggested.

"'Tisn't the car. 'Tis the pace of things here,'' Sam said, clutching her purse and notebook and getting up. "The heart beats slower in Ireland.''

"Do you always keep your callers waiting so long?''

It was a man's voice Dowling didn't recognize. "Sorry, busy place today. How can I help you?'' he asked.

"You're probably not tracing the call. I've given you no reason to. Yet.''

"Who is this?'' Dowling said, showing some annoyance.

"You *are* the sergeant in charge of the little rape cases?''

"You haven't told me who you are yet.''

"And maybe I never will.'' In a kind of singsong this time.

Dowling sketched a crude sailboat on his notepad and said nothing. A detective leaving the squad room had hollered that a phone call was waiting while Dowling spoke to the coroner's office on another line. He was in no mood for pranks.

"What do you want? Last chance," Dowling growled, his finger on the disconnect button.

"Oh, my. Aren't we impatient?"

He had decided to hang up when the caller said, "Don't you want to talk about poor Mrs. Larson over on Madison Avenue?"

"Sure, I'd like to talk about her." Sketching kinder-garten-looking sails on the boat now. "Tell me who you are, then let's talk."

"If I told you who I am, you'd come arrest me."

"Because?"

"Because I'm the one you're looking for."

"You killed Joy Larson?"

"With the very hands I'm holding this phone with. I suppose you'll try to trace it."

"No, I won't." Dowling said honestly. No matter what Hollywood showed the world, he had never gotten an im-promptu trace in less than half an hour, and it usually took much longer. "Why did you kill Joy Larson?"

"Let's just say it's my nature."

"Is it your nature to make this up and mess with my tired old mind?"

"You think I'm kidding, don't you, Sergeant?"

"The answer is *E*. Insufficient data to tell. Help me out by telling me more."

"I did the other ones, too. Just didn't kill them."

"Um-humm."

"Just gave them a good fuck is all."

"Why are you telling me about it?"

"That's a hell of a question. I'm telling you because you're in charge. And I'm down to a minute of phone time left."

Dowling fumbled in drawers, trying to find his record-ing device. "You've got me in a tough spot. I don't know if you're really the one who's been messing over those poor women on the sidewalks, or whether you're a gilt-edged, blue-chip fucking fruitcake who missed an appointment with your shrink this afternoon and decided to phone me while you're jacking off.'' He couldn't find the recorder.

"Trying to make me angry, aren't you?"

"Do this, please. Call me again tomorrow. If you're a phony, I don't mind a little telephone time. If you're our suspect, you need some help. Maybe you're reaching out right now. Call me again."

"Good-bye, Sergeant Dowling." The line went dead.

Dowling cursed to himself and started making notes. In charge of "the little rape cases," huh? A few killers had telephoned him before. But they called to fence with him, to play "what if." What if I came down and talked to you? What if I was acting in self-defense? What if I gave up the people who were on the job with me?

As far as he could remember, all of them had eventually stumbled down to headquarters and sat down with him. He'd never had a cutesy call like this one. This guy hadn't told him anything that wasn't in the newspapers. The voice sounded like it could be Caucasian. No regional accent. Age was sometimes difficult to judge over the phone, and this was one of those times. No foreign noises in the background, just strict silence during pauses.

But he'd gamble some time on it if this character gave him a chance, rather than brush it off like a lint ball on the lapel. It wasn't as if he had a bunch of things going for him. No, if he called again, and Dowling suspected he would, he'd try to string it out long enough to get some significant answers. Record the call. Murder was a funny business, and the longer he was in it the more apt he was to look at the far-out side of things. He picked up the phone and dialed. Maybe the phone company's technical division had developed a magic wand since he last checked.

The lights of San Diego's skyline were just beginning to glow as the setting sun caused the water in the boat basin to shimmer. Tom Ham's Lighthouse was at the north end of Harbor Island, two miles from downtown.

Dowling made sure he arrived first, passing up a seat in the lounge, choosing instead to linger near the front door. When he saw Angela Lord in the distance, he quickly extinguished his cigarette, ducked back inside and fired two squirts of breath freshener into his mouth. Straightening his tie for the third or fourth time, he still managed to look casual as she entered the foyer. They smiled politely at one another, exchanged pleasantries and were seated, by mutual agreement, at a no-smoking table next to a wide window overlooking the marina. The vantage point allowed them to see the affluent from La Jolla and Point Loma clinking convivial glasses aboard the sloops and motor yachts anchored nearby.

Dowling wore his best charcoal brown suit, normally reserved for testimony in celebrated murder cases. As nervous as he usually felt prior to swearing in, it was nothing compared to the anxiety he experienced as the waiter softly inquired about cocktails. She ordered iced tea and Dowling opted for a bourbon and water. He wanted a double, or at least a short water, and wished he had thrown down a couple beforehand. This was, he kept reminding himself, his first real date in twenty-eight years. Perhaps it had been a bad idea. He had slipped the maître d' a ten-dollar bill earlier, not so much for a table with a view as for a quiet table where his hearing loss would not be conspicuous. With background music and other noise, he had difficulty with high-pitched sounds and voices. He had slipped into a place called Miracle Ear once, asked a few awkward questions and slipped back out, telling the receptionist the cure was worse than the disease.

Dr. Lord wore brown slacks with matching brown pumps and a lightweight, handknit sweater with beige and cocoa tones. Small white earrings and a gold pin sufficed for jewelry. Dowling was the interviewee early on, and he explained how his family had been forced to San Diego from Indiana, how his mother, an asthma sufferer needing the Southern California climate, died when he was young.

How his bus driver father had raised him and his brother.
Of his four-year navy hitch and joining the department in
1965.

"So now you're up-to-date on me," he said, trying to
catch the waiter's eye for a refill. "How did you end up
here, or has this always been home?"

Dr. Angela Lord's face was rather oval, more studious
than attractive, Dowling thought. Her eyes were very
brown and very clear. He saw nothing else prominent
about her features.

"I'm a Philadelphian. Was."

He finished his first drink and waited for her to continue.

"I'm not drinking because I'm going in at midnight to
administer some training. Which makes me subject to
E.R. work if certain types of traumas come in." She said
it as if she thought an explanation was necessary. "You
must not be on call." It was more of a statement than a
question.

"I started the night second up." He watched the waiter
place the fresh bourbon in front of him.

"Meaning?"

"Meaning it would take two murders to disturb my
sleep. The truth is, I've been known to have a couple
when I'm first up."

"No corpse has ever complained about booze on your
breath, I take it."

"Most of them had enough on their own, but the important thing is no commanding officer ever complained
about booze on my breath."

She smiled without showing her teeth, a habit he had
noticed. He also noticed they were very nice white teeth.

"I'm waiting for more," he said after a silence.

"More?"

"Yes. My investigation so far has only gleaned the fact
you're from Philly. I still don't know how you landed in
San Diego."

So she told him about an upbringing on Philadelphia's

Main Line, of undergraduate days at the exclusive women's college at Bryn Mawr, of Harvard medical school.

"My future had been well mapped out, input from me considered highly unnecessary. I was to move, after internship, into a lucrative family radiology practice, which I did, in fact. All the time being groomed—I think that *is* the proper word—groomed to replace my father on the faculty at Penn." She rimmed the top of the glass with long fingers. "He was a lovable old fellow. Just never understood me, though he tried very hard."

"Gone now?" Dowling asked.

"Um-humm. Stomach cancer which he diagnosed himself."

"Before or after you left?"

"After. My father said I was kind of a dichotomy. Marching around with banners protesting Kent State. Then being a *M.A.S.H.* fan, which my father said meant approving of the Korean war. I loved to go to the Philadelphia Ballet. But what I really liked was going to the Vet. Drinking a beer and watching Steve Carlton pitch to Johnny Bench." She sampled a deep-fried mozzarella stick. "Do you get all of your subjects talking so much, Sergeant?"

"I'll make a deal with you. I won't call you doctor if you won't call me sergeant."

This time the smile exposed her teeth. "I don't even know your first name. Do you have one?"

He laughed, wondering if the bourbon or her company was warming him. "Vincent. I know your name is Angela."

"Because I told you at the Rape Crisis Center."

"Because you told me the first night we met at the hospital. Though it was hard to hear because you were growling."

She feigned being indignant. "And just when I thought I was beginning to like you."

"And . . . I looked you up in the County Medical Society directory."

"Then you already knew about Bryn Mawr and Harvard Med."

"But it didn't tell me how you got to San Diego. I still don't know." He munched on a cheese stick. "Did *M.A.S.H.* inspire you to chuck radiology for emergency med services?"

"My, how perceptive. You must catch all of your murderers."

"I wish," he said, also wishing he were inhaling a Camel.

"But you're right. Quite an idealist, wasn't I? I thought emergency room work would be exciting. Challenging. Emotionally rewarding."

"And?"

"It wasn't like I was naive, because I had worked the E.R. during internship. But I could use some of that old idealism now."

"You get tired of shootings and cuttings and beatings and wonder sometimes if normality *ever* comes through your doors?"

"Oh, yes. And especially when the patients are elderly or youngsters."

"Because you've learned by now that those in between brought it on themselves half of the time."

"Spoken Sergeant—excuse me, Vincent—like a true and cynical campaigner of a big city hospital trauma room."

"But there's one significant difference," Dowling said, taking a big drink. "You lose a patient today, and maybe it rips you up some. But tomorrow you save a life. You bring somebody back. See, there's balance in your world."

"But not in yours?"

"How can there be? Scrape up dead bodies. Slam jailhouse doors. All negative stuff."

"But people appreciate your efforts."

"People appreciate firemen. Firefighters, I mean. Everybody loves them. Nobody 'loves' cops. Except other cops. Jeez, how did I get going on this? I *still* don't know how you got to San Diego.''

Angela looked out of the window for a long time before she answered.

"When I walked out on that radiology practice, I decided I'd just as well keep walking. News travels fast in medical communities. Gossip. Distortions. It would have been distracting.''

"So you walked to 'America's Finest City' and right on into UCSD Medical Center?''

"With a short stop in Los Angeles first. But nobody took me seriously there. You know, Main Line rich kid wanting to handle blood and guts in the emergency room.'' She looked at the strings of lights ringing the yachts against the darkness. "I don't have . . . good looks. Which opens some doors. So I tried San Diego, which is still less sophisticated than Tinseltown, and I've not been sorry. End of chapter.''

Dowling was hungry when broiled halibut was placed in front of them. The rolls were doughy, inexcusable to his baker's way of thinking. Soft music from *Phantom of the Opera* streamed into the dining room from a grand piano played by a young black man in formal wear. Fresh flowers were on the table between them, and he wondered if other diners were spreading tales of death and destruction.

"Why would you accept a date with a cop?'' he asked.

"Because the 'cop' was nice enough to ask me, and, as I believe I also told you at the Crisis Center, I admired the cop for taking the time to attend and address the group.

"Is there something scurrilous about dating a police officer?'' she added.

"Can be,'' he answered, savoring the thick, meaty white fish.

"The halibut is wonderful,'' she said. "Where is it from?''

"San Diego. My brother and I used to catch them in

the bays and inlets.'' It was as good a time as any to tell her.

"I'm a widower. My wife committed suicide a year ago.'' He watched her carefully and would not forget the kindness in her eyes when she looked at him.

"You are a very nice person, Vincent. A compassionate person, I think. I hope you're doing well. You seem to be.''

"We have two children. A son at the University of Redlands, very recently married, and a daughter in her senior year of high school. Jenny and I live together. She used to be quite fond of her father, but that was before she met a fellow known to me only as Jason, and I don't see much of her anymore.''

Angela laughed loudly. "She still loves her dear old dad.''

When they finished dinner, he excused himself, went to the men's room and quickly violated the NO SMOKING sign on the wall. He took only three drags, then listened to the rest of it sizzle as he plunked it into the toilet. Then he doused his mouth with spray and hurried back to the table.

"I've never been married,'' she told him. "I was— what's the term?—'engaged to be engaged' to a chap who was astounded that I wanted to leave Philadelphia. He feared there really wasn't much civilization that far west of the Hudson. Or the Alleghenies, I should say. I doubt it would have worked well anyway. Doctors can be about as boring as I imagine cops can be interesting.''

"This is my first real date,'' Dowling said. "A few months ago some well-meaning friends played matchmaker and I ended up going out with this woman. A very nice person. But it wasn't working, and partway through the evening we looked at each other and started laughing and that was that and I never saw her again.''

Angela nodded knowingly.

They sipped coffee and chatted about problems facing the health care industry, the advantages of living in San

Diego, and the difference between East and West Coast lifestyles.

"Did you know the center put us onto another series victim?" he asked, needlessly stirring his coffee.

"I know. Are you making progress?"

When he finished briefing her, she tried to be encouraging. "You'll catch him, Vincent."

"Oh, we'll catch him all right. I wake up every morning at three A.M. and start plotting ways to do it. Never have any trouble *getting* to sleep. I'm out when I hit the pillow. Just can't get past three." He looked out the window at a couple kissing on the landing. "The trouble is, how many is he going to kill before I get my act together and catch him?"

They shook hands and said good-bye in the parking lot next to her red Mercedes.

"How would you like to see Andy Benes pitch to Barry Bonds at the stadium some night?" he asked. "Still about a month left in the season."

"That I would like very much."

 **Eleven**

Next morning, briefing his team about the anonymous phone call, Dowling found his mind drifting to the dining room at Tom Ham's Lighthouse. He'd taken his morning coffee on the front porch, passing up the newspaper to think about the evening. If only he hadn't talked so much. Iced tea wouldn't have loosened his tongue like the bourbon. Of course, Angela Lord had been pretty chatty also, he reminded himself. Talked a lot about her personal life and even volunteered the broken off engagement stuff. He was glad she had agreed to a second date.

A secretary interrupted the briefing, shrugging as she delivered the message. "Some guy who says he's your telephone friend just called. Said, 'Tell Sergeant Dowling I'll call him in ten minutes, at the third telephone from the left, Second and C Street.'"

Dowling made it to the bank of public phones in just under nine minutes, running the last signal light to do so. He hooked his recorder to the earpiece while a woman at the next phone frowned at him. He smiled at her, causing her to frown more. When the phone rang, the same voice spoke to him.

"Would you like to see the pictures I took, Sergeant?"

"Tell me about them." There was still no background noise from the other end.

"I have a real good one of the Mexican girl taken on

132

the campus just a week before the little rape.''

"I'd like to see it. Will you send it to me?"

"And another nice one of the late Mrs. Larson. She looks so . . . alive."

"I've got a question. Aren't you afraid of HIV? Not using a condom and doing this to strangers.'' It sounded feeble and Dowling knew it.

"Oh, my. Are you the clever one. Trying to get me to tell you insider information. You're standing there trying to decide whether I got all of my information from the news, or am I really the psychotic little turd you're after. You've got to do better than that.''

"You're right. How about this one. Did someone ever interrupt you and chase you away when you were trying to do one of the little rapes?'' The news media had not been told of the attempt on Adrienne Roe on Van Dkye Avenue.

"Like Ronald Reagan used to say, 'There you go again.' Sorry, no comment.''

"Are you going to mail me the pictures?''

"I don't know. Can I tell you something in great confidence?'' The voice got lower.

"Go," Dowling grunted, straining to hear and silently cursing two motorcyclists revving their engines at a red light.

"I can't hold out much longer. Tonight it may happen again.''

"Why don't you—'' The line went dead.

Dowling disconnected the recorder, massaged his temple with thumb and index finger and wished he hadn't left his cigarettes in the squad room. The answer was still *E*, and there was nothing to do but wait.

Later, Dowling stared at the face looking up at him. The composite on his desk wasn't a composite in the true sense because Holly Novikoff, at Dowling's insistence, had been the only victim providing input.

"You're relying too much on her," Tom Stacy argued.

"I either have confidence in her or I don't. The others can't ID him. They could gum it all up."

"Risky."

"Life is eight-to-five against, Tom."

Stacy agreed not to release the drawing to the media and reluctantly agreed with Dowling to hold off showing it to Dominguez, McGraw, Sheffield and Roe. Dowling knew he would be unable to handle the thousands of "sightings" that would flow in if the news did get hold of it. He always considered a composite an investigative tool at best. A tool best used to eliminate rather than apprehend.

The face Dowling studied was a very undistinguished one. Attractive. Not in a movie idol way, but certainly appealing. Dark short hair, not parted. Holly hadn't remembered it being parted. She had no recall of how the hair was worn. Only of the face itself.

"I told you. I'll know him when I see him. I'll never forget him. Not ever." Her fists were clenched when she said it.

Dowling spent the next few days attending around-the-clock patrol lineups of East San Diego units. He hoped they would be motivated by a homicide sergeant caring enough to meet with them at the odd hours. He loved patrol lineups. Always had. Standing with his jacket off and sleeves rolled up, looking at the attentive faces of men and women officers in neat tan uniforms. Healthy and eager. Leather gun belts clean and polished. Patrol was where things happened.

"I'm Sergeant Dowling from Homicide and we need your help," he always began. He charted the cases for them on the map, though by their comments it was evident they had been studying the crime reports and following the series. He pinned the drawing to the wall behind him.

"I'm not handing these out right now. Just take a good look at this one. Fix it in your mind. Hell, you're cops. You can rattle off license numbers, addresses and birth dates of half the shitheads on your beat without opening your notebooks." He pleaded for them to be out there digging with their traffic stops and field interrogations. To not alert a potential suspect. Merely forward the information to him on a confidential memorandum.

"Who in hell do you think solves crimes in the police department?" He pounded on the lectern. "It sure isn't the Detective Division. We're over there sitting on our asses while this guy's working. Chrissakes, you people hand detectives most of their crooks on a platter with an apple in their mouth." He gave them a couple of recent examples.

"Our suspect is out there driving around on your beats. He figures he can fart in your face because he's Mister Cool." Dowling loosened his tie. "He figures if he's careful, doesn't run into you somehow, that he's home free. Let me tell you something, if you people are gonna catch him for us, it won't be while he's committing a rape. If you nail him, it's gonna be because you're out there *looking* for him. Watching the faces of all those drivers. Looking at people coming out of stores and movies and—this bastard has to eat, you know. He brushes his teeth so he has to buy toothpaste. You give us all the names or license numbers you can. We'll check out every goddamn one. You'll catch him for us."

"You want to know my definition of 'introvert' as it would pertain to a rapist, huh, Dowling? I'd say a guy who's only interested in himself. Doesn't give a rat's ass about family or people he works around. Only has time for his own problems."

"That's why I love coming to you, Doc. Getting this clinical, textbook-type help."

Leonard Boudreaux, M.D., psychiatry, laughed and coughed a smoker's cough. An overweight man in his middle fifties with a red face, bulbous nose and half-glasses, he had long examined in-custody homicide suspects at the request of the district attorney's office. He would later testify as to their ability, or inability as the case may be, to form the intent to commit a crime. Would form an opinion as to their ability to have confessed voluntarily to homicide detectives. Would make life tougher for defense attorneys claiming diminished capacity or insanity defenses. At Stacy's coercive urging, Dowling had allowed Boudreaux to counsel him, months after Helene Dowling's burial in El Camino Memorial Cemetery, as Dowling had plummeted to the bottom.

"You're not looking for a profile, hey, Sarge?"

"Not now, Doc. A profile won't help me catch him. Maybe it could help after I get looking at somebody. I hope it doesn't come to that, though. Hope I can nail him nice and clean."

"You're looking for a little investigative dope, huh?"

"Kind of. I'm thinking about needing a confession some day. Sitting down face-to-face with this guy. I'll need some ammo. I don't have to tell you sex crimes suspects are hard to cop out."

"Even for you? That is something."

Dowling briefed Boudreaux about the series; then they talked for an hour about sexual offenders.

"The two patterns I see most often are the anger rape and the power rape," Boudreaux said. "Anger rapists want their victims to feel like a piece of crap. Strip 'em of their self-worth. These guys usually have screwed-up relationships with the important people in their lives." He used a tissue to wipe his glasses. "A power rapist wants to possess her sexually. He's feeling inadequate. Has to show himself he can master somebody. These guys may tell you they do this for sexual gratification, but that's bullshit. Capture, conquer and control. That's what it's about with him. I examined some deadhead the other day, a sheriff's case. The guy says to me, 'I always thought sex was something you did *to* a woman, not something you did *with* a woman.' So how do you get inside of a head like that?"

"Where do you fit my suspect, then?" Dowling asked.

"That's just it. You line up all the experts, read all

those books''—Boudreaux pointed to the shelves behind
him—''you may never be able to get a consensus on
where your boy belongs. See, there's a third pattern. Sadistic rape. Where anger and power become eroticized.
Now on Van Dyke Avenue, your guy broke that poor
girl's face up. And you say the pathology on Joy Larson
makes it look like he meant to choke her to death, didn't
just hold on a little too long. Maybe your guy doesn't fit
anywhere. That's a bad fellow you're chasing, Sergeant.''

''Right now he's a ghost.''

''And as far as your telephone caller, I wish I had some
nifty stuff that would tell you if he's the real thing. But
all you can do is continue to draw him out. Too close to
call right now.''

Boudreaux leaned back in his chair and played rat-a-tat
on his belly with both hands. ''Tell me about yourself.
And Matt and Jenny.''

After Dowling brought him up to date, he added,
''We're doing okay.''

''The first sit-down I had with you last year you told
me you were doing okay,'' Boudreaux said. ''You were
full of shit then. I hope you're not now.''

''That was then. I was a mess, wasn't I?''

''I'd seen worse. In some dark ages mental facility
when I was in med school.'' Boudreaux opened a desk
drawer. ''Hell, it's after five. You want a drink?''

They sipped whiskey from paper cups and competed
blowing smoke rings. ''You're still going to group, I
hope?'' Boudreaux said.

''You sound like Stacy. Sure, I'm going.''

''And?''

''I'm careful who I say this to. But I love all those poor
old sickos and they love me and I love the group leaders
and hell, Doc, the other night we're in our circle singing
our good-bye song and I'm looking at the faces. Looking
at these cokeheads and burglars and recovering alkies and
shoplifters and whatever. Thinking, *my God*. All my life
I've been hauling them in or picking up the pieces when

they overdosed and now I get so jazzed up at these meetings I'm baring *my* soul to *them* and hugging them. Life's funny. At group, we're all getting to believe we're the normal ones and people on the outside are the ones who need help."

Boudreaux nodded approvingly. "Don't stop going." He filled their cups. "And don't be falling in love with any of those lady counselors either. Some of them are pretty susceptible. Most of them had a crisis of their own before ending up as a facilitator. Start playing footsie with them and it doesn't work out good for anybody." He blew ashes off his sleeve. "I was sorry to hear about Bones Boswell. I liked that guy."

Dowling said nothing.

"I'll admit," Boudreaux said, "I wondered how you handled it. There's a fine line between normal grief and pathological mourning."

"What's the difference?"

"The first one doesn't require therapy. But pathological mourning can make a wreck out of a person. In the case of your wife, you crossed the line because of psychological reasons, given the way Helene died and the things you did."

"I've had my share of death, personal death to handle lately. I'm doing okay," Dowling said.

"Yeah, but you had time to anticipate and prepare for your father's death. Helene and Bones were sledgehammer blows. You were pretty destructive for a while. Now you're doing better but we want to keep you on track. This thing with Bones can slip you off to a side railing."

"Are you seeing signs you don't like, Doc?"

"No, I'm just a cautious old fart. Want to tell you a couple of things that might happen. You might find yourself dreaming about Bones for a while."

Dowling nodded.

"You may get depressed, Sergeant. May get angry at Bones. May feel guilty that you could have done something to prevent it. Now nothing that *I* say is going to keep those things from happening, but it helps a bit if you anticipate them.''

Dowling rose and was leaving when Boudreaux got up from behind the desk. ''About this interrogation you hope takes place some day. There's a lot of would-be experts out there, professors, shrinks, writers. The journals are full of them. But be cautious. Follow your instincts.''

''Thanks, Doc. I'll remember that.''

It was important to Dowling that Samantha Mulcahy not get off lightly, that she recognize the importance of driving a police car safely. Closing the yellow pages of the phone book, he wrote the telephone number on the ''while you were out'' message slip. Would Sam call a ''Mr. Jones.'' When she dialed she would hear a voice say, ''National Driving School.''

He called across his desk to Gus Denver. ''Call that woman in personnel who thinks you're so sweet. Find out what you can about patrol officer Damon Harper.''

''That's the guy who investigated Sam's accident, isn't it?''

''Yeah, Sam said he called her, full of concern, wanted to know if she was all right. Looks like he's getting ready to make a run on her.''

Gus reached for the phone. ''Yeah, we've got to look out for that girl.''

When Dowling finished meeting with his team the following morning, a Patrol Division officer in coat and tie was waiting to see him.

''Officer Sean Garrett, huh?'' Dowling said as they shook hands and the young officer introduced himself. He was shorter than Dowling, who, looking him over, decided the well-built cop spent considerable time in the weight room on the third floor. ''Must be going to court or a funeral.''

''DWI and a ticket,'' Garrett said, holding up two fingers. ''The dirtbag drunk driver has to fight it—it's his third. And the other dude blew the light at Thirtieth and El Cajon like it wasn't there. Ran it *so* bad the court will probably think I'm making it up. The driver will say I'm trying to get my quota.''

"Sounds like it might be your day off."

"Seems like I only go to court on my day off, Sarge. My wife says I got a girlfriend.''

They took seats near Dowling's desk. "I was at second shift lineup the other day when you showed the composite. Been thinking a lot about it and I remembered an F.I. I made on some asshole a while back. He looked like the composite. So I researched it and started to write you a memo and figured, hell, I was coming down to court anyway. I'd drop in.''

"I appreciate that. What have you got?" Dowling asked.

Garrett pulled a photocopy of an index card from his inside coat pocket. "This card is a form I made up. I keep my own set of files at home. On tickets, field interrogations, arrests. Everything.''

"And your wife says you spend more time with your card file than you do with her?''

"You've got my house bugged, Sarge." He handed Dowling the paper. "See, I contacted this guy on June thirtieth. You'd only had one case then, fifteen days earlier. I didn't have any reason to try and connect him to Annabelle Dominguez.''

Dowling scanned the document. "You stopped him on Florida Street. Why?''

"We'd had a two-eleven strong-arm from in front of the TraveLodge at Mississippi and El Cajon. Two suspects muscled a guy for his wallet. This guy was on foot a couple of blocks away and I figured, you know, the suspects could have split up.''

"He checked okay though?" Dowling asked.

"Sure. I'd never have connected him to your series if you hadn't come to lineup. I stopped in Records on my way over to see you. Thought there could be a mug shot, but the guy's never been busted.''

"Curtis Forman, huh? What did Curtis have to say for himself?''

"That's just it. I didn't spend much time with him, so I don't know what he was doing there. While I'm talking to him, unit three-sixteen John was asking for cover on a car with possible suspects he was stopping at Thirtieth and Adams, so I zipped over there. They checked out okay, too.'' Garrett looked sheepish. "I didn't make out an F.I. card for records.''

Dowling read the data carefully. "He gave you a California driver's license for ID. Gave an address in La Mesa.'' La Mesa. The bedroom community of fifty-three thousand people on San Diego's eastern border. "Clothing: white T-shirt, Levi's, tennies. How did he come across to you?''

"Well-spoken, confident type. But see, the physical is good. This asshole's twenty-seven years old, five eleven, one-eighty, dark brown-blue. Seems in good shape. Wore his hair short. Pretty good-looking guy.''

"You've got a line drawn through the box labeled 'jewelry.' ''

"There again, being in a hurry, I can't say about rings, wristwatch, so forth. Usually I get all of that, Sarge.''

"On foot though? And Florida Street is all residences on that block?''

"Right.''

"How much time did you spend with him?''

"Five minutes tops.''

"Good job, officer,'' Dowling said. "We'll get on him. And we'll get back to you.''

Setting the stage, they had stopped teasing Sam Mulcahy about the traffic accident, but she took Dowling's bogus telephone message slips in good spirit. A bicycle shop answered when she made the second call, and the third was to the Superior Optical Company. As it turned

out, patrol officer Damon Harper was single and Sam
Mulcahy went on a date with him.

*He loved thinking about it. Had thought about it every
day, reliving it, savoring it.*

*After a last look at the body, he had stood for a moment
in the darkness by the still-opened garage door. He carefully looked both ways in the alley, saw nothing, then
walked the short distance to the sidewalk on Madison Avenue.*

*His car was two blocks away and he moved toward it
casually, seeing no one on foot and only two or three cars.
Pausing one hundred feet from where he'd parked, he
looked in all directions. He thought he saw movement in
a driveway several houses down the block. Opening the
door quietly, he slid behind the wheel. The keys were still
in the ignition. Jesus, would that be something? Have
some low-life criminal clout your car at a time like this?
But he'd weighed the odds, and they favored leaving the
keys in the car as a time saver in case he was being
chased.*

*He drove carefully onto the boulevard. Not fast enough
to get stopped for speeding but slow enough to not attract
attention. Past the Taco Bell and the ARCO station until
he neared home. The calm within him soothed. It had been
hectic earlier, the emotional rush better than orgasm. Better than any orgasm he had ever experienced. But now
. . . just the calm. How many men were out there, he wondered, wishing they could pull off what he'd just accomplished.*

*When he'd arrived home, the sound of the television
told him his wife was in the front room, and he put the
small bag of groceries on the kitchen table. "Who's home
and who loves you?" he called out.*

"My love," he heard her answer.

"I'm going to take a shower."

*He closed the bathroom door tightly and removed his
clothing. Sitting naked on the toilet top, he carefully ex-*

amined each item of clothing. The Nikes looked all right. But to be sure, he blotted the soles and sides with toilet paper, checking for grease stains. The white sweat socks were still clean. He got up and held the white T-shirt close to the light over the sink, turning it slowly. Finally, the Levi's. The knees were what worried him, but he could see no evidence of where they had pressed the floor of the garage when he mounted her. He put them, with the other clothing, into the hamper and stepped under the showerhead.

The steam from the hot water—almost too hot to take— reminded him he had failed to turn on the ceiling exhaust fan. When he had scrubbed twice and washed his hair, he washed his penis and pubic area again. After drying, he used the baby powder to sprinkle himself, then put on his robe and sat again on the toilet top. Now he could reflect and relish the moment.

It had been a wonderful moment. As her car entered the alley, he had instinctively ducked into the shadows next to the garage. When she'd gotten out of the car and hoisted the garage door, he'd known it was meant to be. Just meant to be.

It had looked like the house could be entered from the garage. He'd gambled she would drive inside, cut the engine, then walk back and close the door from the inside.

He'd crouched and almost duck-walked to her right rear fender while her car was still slowly moving along the wall. He could sense her probing for the proper spot to stop so the garage door would clear the rear of the car. The dome light was the only illumination when she switched off the headlights. She'd stayed in the car for a long time with the door open. Still crouched, he could not see her. He'd heard a loud snap—maybe the glove compartment being closed. Smelled her light, floral fragrance. If she'd turned on an overhead light he would have run.

She didn't, though. Just walked through the darkness to the rear of the car. As she reached up for the door cord, he'd put the hold on her. No "what time is it" nec-

essary. Her purse had dropped to the floor with a thud. He'd kicked it under the car at the same time he was choking her. He'd used his left hand to jerk her head up by the hair and squeezed hard with his right forearm.

He'd dragged her into the shadows next to the driver's door and put her down. She'd moaned softly as he jerked her T-shirt up around her neck. Not bothering to unfasten the brassiere, he'd pulled it up roughly. Enough light had spilled in from the alley to allow him to see her breasts. Not big, but well shaped. Maybe the best shaped yet. He hadn't touched them.

Water had begun running. Perhaps from a kitchen sink on the common wall. He'd choked her with both hands until she was silent, then pulled the pants and panties down, roughly yanking her right leg and freeing it. He'd used his knee to spread her legs, undid the buttons on his Levi's and pulled them down to a point just above his knees.

He'd had trouble entering her for a moment, choking her again with both hands, and when he did break through he plunged into her, thrusting hard, choking harder, trying to see her face in the shadows. He had smiled because he knew he wasn't going to stop choking this one. It had been quite a night.

He stood up, raised the toilet top, brushed his hair and admired himself in the mirror. Then he went to the kitchen, pulled a loaf of nut grain berry bread from the fridge and organized his sandwich makings. He lathered one piece of bread with mustard, the other with mayonnaise. Then he placed slices of cheese, chunks of avocado, bits of onion and a large pile of lettuce between the pieces of bread. He took a huge bite, put the sandwich down and went into the nursery. His daughter was asleep on her back, a rose-colored sleeper her only cover. He hadn't touched her, just stared, then walked back into the kitchen.

 **Twelve**

Dowling draped himself over a table in the critique room and wished he had the answers. He closed his eyes as he thought.

Curtis Blaine Forman, huh? Who are you anyway? Do you work? And if you draw a paycheck, what do you do to earn it? Sort nuts and bolts? Put up drywall? Chase down deadbeats? Teach Renaissance literature? Sell jewelry or furniture or used cars or computer products or men's clothing or real estate?

And when, Curtis? What *time* do you work? When you break for lunch do you hit a nice place like Zolezzi's with fine silverware and linen napkins or do you hustle over for a Taco Bell with extra green sauce? Or maybe you brown bag it because you're pinching pennies. What are you usually doing between darkness and ten o'clock at night, and *what in the fuck were you doing on Florida Street on June thirtieth*?

If you don't work, Curtis, how do you pay the mortgage or the rent on 1653 Maple Avenue in La Mesa? Or does somebody else worry about that? By the way, is that a bum address or a good address? Is that a used-to-be address, Curtis, or do you still hang your hat there?

Just because you're not in our Records Division doesn't mean you've never been arrested. Where have you had your fingers in the ink, Curtis? Los Angeles? El Paso?

145

New York? Eaton, Ohio? If we knew, we could shuck the trouble of the drawn-out FBI query.

What do you like to do in your spare time? Is golf your game, Curtis? Tennis? Pumping iron? Outsmarting blue-gills at Lake Henshaw? Or maybe a little nine-ball up on the boulevard?

Are you the spectator type? Is your idea of a good time watching hang gliders soaring out over the beach at Tor-rey Pines? Or climbing down the cliffs above Black's Beach—pretending you're a nudie—catching a peek of tittie and nookie and a whole assortment of sunburned buns.

Light beer or the real stuff? Martinis straight up or rocks? Regular or decaf? If we had a crystal ball, it'd save us the trouble of following your ass all over town to find out.

You cheating on your wife, Curtis? Or girlfriend? Or both? Maybe you like the boys better? Is that it? Spend a lot of time in Hillcrest, do you? Or hanging around the shithouse in Presidio Park?

You didn't think we'd forgotten about you and a police record, did you? What were you in the can for anyway? Swiping hubcaps? Clouting cars? Shoplifting rubbers from the corner drugstore? Low-grade smack peddling? How about a little burglary? Rolling sailors?

Or—hush—sexual offenses? Wagging your weinie through the chain-link fence at the elementary school? Selling porno flicks? Putting it in some girl after she told you a hundred times she didn't want to? And what in the fuck were you doing on Florida Street on June thirtieth?

Four hours ago he hadn't known Curtis Forman existed. All of a sudden there was a lot of work to do. He relished having someone to look at. Someone who might, after ten minutes or ten months of investigation, earn the title of suspect. That was the thing. In this series, he'd had no one to talk to except his traumatized victims.

In most of his murders there were people to sit down with. People willing to cough up information or people to be soft-soaped or badgered or threatened who could at least get him pointed in some direction. Not eyewitnesses maybe, but people *somehow* connected. People connected to the body cooling on the floor or connected to the bad boy with the butcher knife.

And talking to his victims had become depressing. Holly Novikoff's mother called twice weekly begging to hear news of a fresh arrest.

"My daughter is a basket case, goddammit. Are you doing *anything*?"

Larry Shea could not forget the last time he spoke with Annabelle Dominguez. "I'm afraid when I go anywhere. To the store. To school. Daytime or night time. It doesn't matter. I'm always afraid."

After the Choice McGraw case, a clinical counselor from a women's center had sought him out. "This suspect of yours is an anger rapist. He doesn't want to murder anyone. He wants his victims to always remember this crime. He wants them to live in fear of another attack." Explain that, once again and slowly please, to Joy Larson's family.

And physical evidence was almost laughable. For every time some English chief constable on PBS showed off a dirt sample from Birminghamshire that nailed their killer, Dowling had scores of cases with nothing. He could count on two hands the number of murders that had been made on prints. Positive makes could be made on firearms—sometimes. But normally it was just slugging it out; talking to people and people and people. Hell, he could even forget about the shoe impression he'd held high hopes for on the Choice McGraw case. Gus and Sam had cleared that up. The shoes were on the feet of a guy from across the street who'd been trying to rescue a kitten stranded on a tree limb.

No, it came down to interrogations and interviews. The system informally defined the former as talking to a suspect; the latter, to anyone else. To Dowling there was little difference. Some were easy. Some were tough. Most everybody lied about something. Even when the truth would help. You were usually asking someone to bare their soul. He'd cured the veteran criminal lawyers in town of trying to screw him over on the stand when it came to interrogations. Once in a while he'd have to break in a fresh-faced type from the University of San Diego or Cal Western Law School who would hammer away during a motion to suppress the voluntariness of a statement.

"When you took my client into the interrogation room, you wanted a confession, didn't you, Sergeant Dowling?"

"I wanted the truth."

"But you hoped to get a confession. That was your goal?"

"My goal was to learn the truth. If it turned out he'd shot Lottie Carmichael, fine. If he was innocent, that was fine, too."

But to get to that point, to be able to lead some flesh-and-bones into the eight-foot-by-eight-foot interrogation rooms, it still came down to shoe leather and scut work. It was why he had again gathered the team in the critique room. He hadn't been smoking long enough this time to totally annul his sense of smell, and the odor from his coat sleeve reminded him he was closing in on two packs a day.

"I asked Stacy to leave us alone for a couple of days so we could work up this Curtis Forman. See if he shows us anything. As of now, we're off call," he told them. "Our goal is like always on these kind of deals. Work to eliminate the guy as a suspect. The faster we do it the better. So we can either get him or get on to the right guy."

"If we can't eliminate him early," Shea said, "the shit that points to him keeps piling up. If it turns out he is our suspect, we've been building our case the cheap way."

Sam looked up from her notebook. "A couple of things look good. It could be him."

"Could be," Dowling said, picking up white chalk and turning to the blackboard, which stood on scarred wooden legs. He had personally transported the blackboard from the old police station on Market Street when the moving vans came. To no avail, Planning Division and Stacy harped on him that the contractor was installing wall-connected multipurpose boards in the new building. Anymore, the other homicide teams pushed it out of their way when using the room, and once it cost Dowling a round of drinks at the 153 Club to discover where they'd hidden it. He'd solved his first murder using that board.

"What points to him," Dowling said while scribbling, "are his age, his physique, his clothing, his good looks, according to the officer, and the location." He stepped back from the board. "Anything else?"

After a long pause, Sam said, "You said the officer described Forman as well-spoken. A confident type."

After hesitating, Dowling moved to the board again. "Okay. I'll buy that. I don't think we're dealing with a brain-dead suspect on this series. Not the way he carries out the jobs."

"Patrol shakes him down on a Thursday. A weeknight. All our jobs been on weeknights," Gus said. "They get Foreman on June thirtieth on Florida Street. That's fifteen days after case one, Annabelle, and seven blocks away from Anabelle." Gus raised three big fingers in the air. "And this many blocks from case number four, Choice McGraw."

"If it's him, he got spooked," Shea said. "Waited four days, then moved twelve blocks east to Kansas Street for case number two, Holly."

"I wish I knew the streets like you lads know them," Sam said, consulting a Thomas Brothers map book.

Dowling took his seat, folded back a few pages of his yellow sheets and ran his hand over his face. "Too risky to question this guy's neighbors. Word always makes its way back to him."

"Remember the old days, Sarge? We pick up the phone, call the phone company or gas and electric and ten minutes later they're reading off his application info to us.''

"I remember, Gus." Dowling smiled. "Now it's subpoena all the way. No wonder we're losing the goddamn war. We gotta earn it the old-fashioned way."

"The Smith Barney surveillance team," Shea said. "Pair me up with Sam, Sarge. I can sniff her River Shannon cologne instead of the tobacco factory you and Gus smell like."

The next morning, a Tuesday, they took their positions. Dowling had driven past 1653 Maple Avenue a few hours after the critique ended. In the dusk, he got a good enough look at the wooden two-story house in midblock of an old residential neighborhood that had seen better days. The small front yard needed some care, though no more than the homes on either side. A Westfalia was parked in the narrow driveway and a baby buggy sat on the small porch near the front door.

He had decided, even in undercover cars, they would be too conspicuous parking on Curtis Forman's block.

"We'll try it using two cars at first," he told them at the five A.M. briefing. "See how he drives. If we can't stay with him, we'll add a car. I hope we won't need four cars because that means Crash Mulcahy will get behind the wheel."

Larry Shea and Gus Denver parked on a side street, half a block from the house with a view of the driveway. Dowling and Sam parked a block and a half in the other direction, next to a small shopping mall, Dowling's concession to the urinary tract of his partner.

"You lads get the call and only have to seek out a fire hydrant. Unfair it is," Sam had muttered.

Both cars were littered with bags of sandwiches and munchies, coolers with water and soda, walkie-talkie radios, map books, notebooks, handheld tape recorders, camera equipment, sweaters and jackets, and in Shea and Denver's car, two empty quart fruit juice bottles. Neces-

sary, Shea told Sam, when fire hydrants were not convenient.

Gus Denver, in Levi's and a Dallas Cowboys T-shirt
slouched on the passenger side of the front seat, a ball
cap pulled low over his eyes. "Black man sittin' in a car
all morning in La Mesa can draw cop cars like flies," he
said looking around, wondering which resident might be
dialing the police at that moment. "Used to be there
wasn't anything but white faces out here. Now the Crips
and Pirus swing on up from Southeast, do their shit and
bye-bye blackbird. Fly on back to San Diego and split up
the take."

"Anybody gets nosy, Gus, I'll tell them I own you.
That you can go anywhere I go. Even La Mesa."

"Even La Jolla?"

"Well, *almost* anywhere I go." Shea looked at his wrist
watch. "Six-thirty. If he's a day worker he'll be coming
out soon."

They watched sparse traffic roll by as the neighborhood
came awake. "I get fidgety after a while on surveillance,"
Shea said, blotting a coffee spill on his blue denim wash
pants. "Now Bones, Bones liked surveillance. He could
sit sixteen, twenty hours if he had to. Never complain.
Never lose the eyeball on the target."

"And Bones wasn't a lazy man, was he?"

"Oh, hell no. Bones was a workhorse. He just had the
tolerance for it. Used to say, 'When a good surveillance
pans out, Larry, I get the warm feeling all over. Like
pissing in your pants.' "

"Well, I'm more like Bones. 'Cept I quit pissing in my
pants about fifteen years ago when I quit drinking gin,"
Gus said, reaching for his empty bottle.

"Gin ought to be in the twelve-oh-twenty section, right
next to dirks and daggers and billy clubs and sawed-off
shotguns. Grace won't let me drink gin unless I'm hand-
cuffed to the coffee table. Says I'm an asshole when I
drink gin."

"Everybody's an asshole when they drink gin. Gin

gets you there in a hurry and fucks over what little brains cops have.''

A yellow Christian school bus with bald tires and foul exhaust fumes roared around the corner in front of them. ''Look at that son of a bitch, Gus. First rain in November he'll end up on Curtis Forman's front lawn and all those kiddies'll be pissing *their* pants.''

Gus screwed the cap tightly on his urine bottle and started laughing.

''Surveillance must be getting to you, Gus. Laughing at my stuff.''

''I just remembered something happened to me the first surveillance I was ever on. That's what I'm laughing about.'' He watched a middle-aged woman pass the car, clutching a small white plastic bag, guiding a schnauzer on the end of a long leash. ''Tickles my ass how much these people love their dogs, Shea. Look at that old tax-payer. Gonna bend down and stuff that dogshit in that little bag and cart it on home.''

''Your first surveillance?''

''Yeah. I was working patrol. Only been on about a year. Vice was working this old man running a dice game out of his house down in Southeast. Right off Escuela and Guymon. They were pretty short of black cops in those days, so they yank me out of Patrol to help on their surveillance. They weren't going to bust him that night. Just needed to get a line on the players and all. Had this old beat-up panel van with curtains on it they used for stake-outs. Shit, all the self-respecting burglars and stick-up men in Southeast knew that van, but these were just old gentleman crapshooters. Anyway, the only place to get a good look is next to this fire hydrant across the street, 'cause all the other parking places are taken.''

The lady and the schnauzer passed again, eyes straight ahead.

''Now remember, Shea. This is 1962. We didn't have walkie-talkies except in the armory for emergencies. So

I'm in that van with zero communication. What do you think happens?''

''Patrol writes a ticket for the fire hydrant violation and finds you.''

''Patrol tows the fucking van away.''

Shea laughed, spewing bits of glazed buttermilk bar on the dashboard.

''I can't pound on the windows for patrol's attention, 'cause a couple of players is watching the driver hook up. Jacks it up on a forty-five degree angle, my black ass rolling all over the floor and we hit every pothole on Imperial and Euclid. Can't do nothing till I get to the tow yard.''

The police radio secreted in the glove box crackled, and Gus turned the volume lower.

''That dog lady reminds me,'' Shea said. ''Me and the sarge were interviewing this motorcycle mama. Sweet-talking her. Bunch of Axemen at a party had shot up a Hell's Angel and stuffed him in the trunk of a car and— Anyway, we're trying to get this girl, her name was Venus, to turn her boyfriend because she was there when it happened and we could jam her up some. And she says, 'I can't say anything bad about him because I *love* him.' And the Sarge is trying all his tricks and nothing's working and finally he reminds her again of how much trouble she's in and he says, 'Venus. Do you love Pig Pen or do you just lust him?' She looks at him funny. Sarge says, 'Do you know the difference between love and lust, Venus?' She says, 'I'm not sure.' Sarge says, 'Next time you look out your window and you see two dogs humping on the front lawn, take a look at that dog on top. He doesn't love that dog on the bottom, Venus. He *lusts* for that puppy.' She thinks it over and gives old Pig Pen up. Tells us where he stashed the gun.''

Shea ate, Gus smoked and for two hours they traded stories. It was warm, with the feel of a day that would be in the mid-eighties by noon.

"You got fifteen years on, Shea. How long you going to do?"

"I'm going to do forever. Got five kids to finish raising. Never going to make sergeant."

"You're just one of these assholes loves being a cop. That's why you don't ever want to retire."

"Like you, huh, Gus?"

"Like me, yeah. How long you been a murder police now?

"Five years."

"And you don't want to work nothing else?"

"What else is there after Homicide?" Larry Shea stretched and belched. "I fucked up my first case though. A double-header. Thought I was through."

"Now you got my attention."

"Lady comes home drunk. Found out her nine-year-old had stabbed her six-year-old. She thought he stabbed the four-year-old too. Thought both kids were dead. Figured she better cover it up so she sets fire to the house and she and the nine-year-old boogie. Turns out the six-year-old had been stabbed superficially and the four-year-old hadn't been cut at all. The two kids looked like burnt toast by the time the fire department cleared out and we were able to get in there and do a crime scene."

Gus shook his head. "What did you do wrong?"

"We get her downtown. She says, 'I'm gonna lose six hundred bucks welfare a month on those two babies.' I threw her across the room. In front of a neighbor lady and two secretaries." Shea turned and looked at his partner. "There was no doubt in my mind I was going to be back in Burglary detail in the morning. But Dowling took care of it. Then he sat me down and said—well, he said a lot of things. Said 'em for about an hour. But he kept me."

There had been no movement at the house, so at 1:00 P.M. Dowling sent Sam, wearing a snug fitting T-shirt, sun hat and designer jeans for a walk down Maple Avenue.

Surveillance gave him idle time to think and he had done a lot of it during the morning. Not about his series.

About his wife. His "late" wife he had to keep reminding himself. It still sounded strange—awkward—when he said it out loud. Perhaps it was eight consecutive hours in the company of Sam Mulcahy. Perhaps it was a woman he had seen walking across the parking lot who from a distance could have been Helene's sister. It could have been when he was picking out a necktie the day before and remembered a silly little joke they used to share.

He wondered if his thoughts were guilt driven for daring to have a pleasant evening with Angela Lord. He told himself he was a shit for choosing Tom Ham's Lighthouse for their dinner. After the date had been made, he recalled Helene's desire to dine there. On an evening walk, holding hands, the skyline sparkling across the harbor, they had seen the construction site and he promised to take her there. Another broken promise.

He wondered how to describe those early times. Carefree days? Tranquil days? Leisure days? They were all of that, and more. Trips to the zoo and the park and the white sands on the shore behind the Hilton Hotel. Swims and cookouts with their pals at De Anza Cove. Confiding and touching and holding and loving. Before Helene grew fond of booze.

"You say it's *her* drinking problem, Sergeant? I'm not in the business of chiding people," Helene's counselor had told him, when red blotches and lines were appearing in his wife's smooth face. "But either you get real and start sharing and caring, or it's not going to end up well for anybody."

He was startled when Sam opened the car door and shouted, "I saw him. I saw him." Her bright blue eyes fixed on him and she talked with her hands. "I walked past the first time on the far side of the street and saw not a thing. But I came back on his side, and there he was. They were." She talked so fast, her brogue grew thicker and he slowed her down. "Him and a woman and a baby in the driveway. Talking. Near their porch steps. About fifteen meters from the sidewalk. But I got a good look at him.''

''And?'' Dowling asked.

''He's perfect. He was facing me. A pair of shorts he wore, no shirt, nice body. A good-looking devil he is.''

''The Westfalia's still in the driveway?''

''Aye.''

''The woman and baby?''

''I only saw the woman from the rear. The babe was looking over her shoulder. Less than a year old, I'd say.''

''So we wait,'' Dowling said, pleased for the first time in several hours.

They waited only a few more minutes, when Gus Denver announced the Westfalia was heading in Dowling's direction. ''Can't tell who's in it from here.''

''Remain where you are until we can see,'' Dowling ordered. Less than a minute later they picked it up at a stop sign one hundred feet from them. As Sam logged the time at 1:30 P.M., Dowling radioed, ''Just a woman in it. We'll see if we can do it alone. You stay there in case he leaves in another car. The garage door was closed.''

It was an easy tail, over in less than thirty minutes. A stop at a bank, then a dry cleaner's.

''I can get out and go get a closer look,'' Sam offered.

''No. We don't need a closer look yet. You've been by the house once. On surveillance, save showing yourself until you really need it.''

The registration query on the car came back to Lauren L. Forman at the Maple Avenue address. Dowling kept them on post until 10:00 P.M., trading locations to combat boredom. Sam carted pizza from the mall, and they took turns stretching their legs in the darkness of the September night.

''We'll make it six A.M. tomorrow morning,'' Dowling told them finally, when they rendezvoused a mile away. ''He's got to leave the nest sometime.''

* * *

He was glad he hadn't made it later, because at 6:27 A.M. the Westfalia drove past Gus and Shea. Their target was the only occupant, and within minutes it was evident to Dowling it was a four-car job. The Westfalia drove steadily at ten miles an hour over the posted speeds and Dowling and Sam fell out of the running early. Gus and Shea stayed with him for several blocks, lost him, then picked him up by accident at a signal light moments later. At that point Dowling lost radio contact momentarily. When he next heard Gus Denver's voice he was requesting a meeting in front of Sears at the Fletcher Parkway shopping center.

Sam spotted them and they pulled in, driver's window next to driver's window.

"Did you lose him?" Dowling asked quickly.

"We did and we didn't," Larry Shea answered. "We got lucky and followed him to work."

"Where?"

"La Mesa P.D., Sarge. La Mesa fucking Police Department."

 # Thirteen

"Jesus," Tom Stacy said, "a La Mesa cop. I hope it turns out he's not your suspect." They sat in Stacy's office with the door closed. "You'll have *me* smoking again."

Dowling wore his casual surveillance clothing. "This was just an hour ago we saw him go into the P.D., so nobody knows except you and my team."

"But we have to tell La Mesa."

"The chief only, right? Highest confidence?"

"Yeah, and I have to tell the Old Man."

"Then they'll want to do chief talk."

"Here's a break for you, old Sergeant. I went through the academy with their chief, Toddy Claiborne. He's a pal."

"How long was he on our department?"

"For two years. Good cop." Stacy pulled himself out of his swivel chair. "Went over there and did very well for himself. I'll give him a call on his private line. Ask him to meet you and me away from the station."

"Ask him to bring Curtis Forman's service jacket, Tom."

By midmorning, the three men sat drinking coffee in a quiet, leather-padded booth of a steak house in East San Diego. The bar, close by their table, was closed, and a stale boozy odor drifted their way. They spoke low

158

enough so a busboy stacking glasses and refilling ice bins couldn't hear.

"I didn't need this news when I walked in this morning," Toddy Claiborne said. He was a huge man. Big all over. Dowling couldn't tell if his head was shaved or totally void of hair. "I picked his file out of personnel myself, so nobody knows. Chief in a department your size can't get away with that." He tossed a thin manila folder on the table. "Help yourself, Sergeant. You'll notice he works Patrol. Day shift. Mondays and Tuesdays off."

Dowling sipped coffee and noticed more than that. Curtis Blaine Forman's sister lived on Cherokee Avenue in East San Diego, four blocks west of where Adrienne Roe had almost been numbered as a rape victim; that Forman, a three-year cop, had outstanding performance evaluations.

" 'Hard worker . . . Dedicated . . . Good public relations . . . Street savvy . . . ' "

"What's your plan?" the chief asked.

"Surveillance," Dowling answered. "We can't approach him. We have nothing." He explained the identification problems.

"DNA?" asked Toddy Claiborne.

"No semen," Stacy said.

"Crissake. He's using a condom?"

"I'm more inclined to think he's not getting his gun," Dowling said.

"Come on."

"It's not that uncommon on stranger rape—predatory rape. All I know is we don't have any physical."

Toddy Claiborne wiped his mouth with a napkin and, with some difficulty, pushed himself away from the table. "I can't let this go too long. We've got to know. This guy is a cop out there. If I pull him off the beat and put him behind a desk, and if he is your suspect, I may as well have sent him a telegram."

"We appreciate that, Toddy," Stacy said.

"I know your reputation, Sergeant Dowling. Seems like

my man will get a fair shake.'' He was on his feet. ''If you decide you want to talk to Forman's sergeant, I'll give her a call and arrange it.''

Had the critique been held in the squad room, instead of the parking lot of the mall near Curtis Forman's house, Dowling would have written on his blackboard: cop, so knows choke out–hold, *knows* territory; i.e., sister's house.

Instead, he added those things in his notebook under the ''what points to Forman'' category.

''Not only does he know the territory,'' Gus said, ''he's got a big-ass excuse to be hanging around over there if he gets pressed. 'Just going to visit my sister, Officer.' ''

''Time. That's our enemy both ways,'' Dowling said. ''La Mesa can't keep this guy on the beat much longer. He's going into women's houses on radio calls every day.'' He put out one Camel and lit another. ''It's been sixteen days since the murder, and he's gone as long as twenty. Between Rene Sheffield and Choice McGraw.''

''The murder could cool him down,'' Sam said. ''Or hasten the dirty bastard.''

A large family loaded themselves into a station wagon next to them. ''That little boy gets that Baby Ruth bar too close to Shea, it's a goner,'' Gus said.

''The other way around it is,'' Sam said, ducking away from Shea's side. ''Larry offers the candy. Tries to get the wee lad to reach into his pocket for it.''

''So sweet,'' Dowling said, shaking his head. ''So sweet and so *ladylike* when she got off the boat.'' He checked his wristwatch and wrote in his book ''4 p.m. Sept 12 begin surv.''

''Our boy's getting off work. Go get set up, but move your vehicles around some. He's a cop. He notices things,'' Dowling said.

When Dowling felt confident the other three cars were in a good position, he pulled to a far corner of the parking lot and shut his engine off. He had assigned himself the radio code one hundred and dubbed the others according to the first letter of their last names: Dogbite (Denver), Marathon (Mulcahy) and St. Louis (Shea). He winced when he thought of surveillances past with "Bismarck" Bones Boswell, now under the grass in Virginia. It was difficult sometimes, convincing death to stop toying with his head.

The team watched Forman arrive home. Two hours later, they easily tailed the family to a nearby Dairy Queen where they ate dinner. Their suspect, wearing shorts and a T-shirt, drove a bit slower with his wife and daughter in the car.

When it got dark, Dowling hoped Forman would come out alone, was afraid he wouldn't, then got energized when he did.

Dogbite: "He's heading toward Spring Street. Who's got him?"

St. Louis: "I've got him. He's signaling right. To a gas station. The Exxon."

One hundred: "Give him room and set up. Who's getting the eyeball?"

Dogbite: "I've got it. I'm only good if he comes out the north driveway though."

Marathon: "I have the other exit. He's taking petrol."

The Westfalia left the pumps, drove back out onto Spring Street, then headed for Interstate 8, a quarter of a mile away. "Take Eight West," Dowling whispered. "Eight West to San Diego."

St. Louis: "Westbound it is."

They had no trouble staying with him in the medium traffic. Continuing west, past the College Avenue off-ramp and San Diego State University on the hill to their left, the Westfalia drove at a steady seventy. Dowling grew more hopeful.

"Take Fairmount or Texas Street, you son of a bitch," he growled. But the Westfalia sped past Fairmount and for a moment seemed to be ignoring Texas as well.

Dogbite: "He's . . . he's . . . taking Texas. Southbound on Texas."

Dowling recognized the enthusiasm in Gus Denver's voice. *Where in hell is he going?* Dowling asked himself again. *Could it be this easy?* A long ascent and they were slowing, passing the intersection of Meade Avenue, two short blocks from where Choice McGraw tried to call on a customer, four blocks from where Holly Novikoff's life got turned upside down. *Only the second night out and this son of a bitch is* taking us there, Dowling thought.

Ninety seconds later, the degree of difficulty increased tenfold. The Westfalia made a slow right-hand turn onto El Cajon Boulevard, went three blocks and made a slower turn onto Georgia Street. A residential street, a street so like the crime scene streets that Dowling felt his blood pulsing. Tailing anyone in residential neighborhoods without being spotted was challenging. Tailing a cop ... But, he reminded himself, Curtis Forman was driven. Maybe, just maybe, the excitement and danger of the mission would fog his brain. Dowling needed all the help he could get.

St. Louis: "He's going slow. Shit. I got to pass him, he's going so slow." A moment later. "He's looking around, I got a glimpse as I went by."

Dowling's mind was racing. They couldn't stick close enough and not be made. As he was scheming, they lost Forman.

Dogbite: "He either flat-ass drove away on us, or ... or he's out on foot."

"Everybody but Marathon hit the bricks. Split up. Keep the ear plugs in the radios and keep them hidden. *Marathon*, find that goddamn car," Dowling ordered, trying to keep his voice flat.

Marathon: "I can get out and be a decoy. Maybe he'll go for me."

Dowling was standing at a dimly lit intersection, searching the sidewalk in both directions when he heard her transmission. "*Marathon*. STAY IN YOUR CAR." Perspiration ran down his cheeks. He couldn't decoy her now. There was no time to set up. To cover her. *Lord, don't let Forman find a victim.*

Five minutes later, while Dowling imagined the worst, Sam's voice penetrated.

Marathon: "I've got the car. Alabama and Monroe. He's not in it."

Dowling was starting to order Shea to station himself within eyesight of the Westfalia when Sam's voice covered him. "I see him. He's on foot. I think the street is Meade and . . . Dear Mother of God, he's not wearing a wristwatch. I saw him in good light."

"Clothing?" Dowling demanded. "Clothing?"

Marathon: "The T-shirt and blue jeans."

What happened next happened quickly. Curtis Forman climbed back into the Westfalia, drove slowly back to El Cajon Boulevard, headed east to Texas Street, then pulled to the curb. Pulled to a curb with a plain view of a McDonald's restaurant. And sat. Facing the parking lot where customers, alone and in pairs, with and without cars, straggled inside, under the bright lights of the take-out counter.

Dowling lit the first cigarette he had been able to manipulate in half an hour. Rene Sheffield, he told himself. Rene Sheffield had been walking home from a McDonald's twenty blocks to the east.

He wondered if he could cope. His confidence was waning. Sure, if Forman tried to pick off a woman walking from the restaurant, they could cover it. Catch him in the act as he was choking her. Save her at least from being raped. But sweet Jesus. If he didn't choose a victim now, and he hit the side streets again? If they lost him again? What the hell was their priority here?

Options: Storm his car and tell him it's over. "We're on to you, boy. Get your ass out of Dodge City." Or grab him now? Take him downtown and try to cop him out. Make Curtis Forman think they had more than they had. Make him think they had *something*. He remembered Joy Larson's dark pubic patch staring at him from the dirty garage floor. Remembered her grotesque face and twisted throat and—

The Westfalia started up, swept across a service station parking lot and headed for La Mesa. Retracing the route in reverse. It was 10:00 P.M. when they watched Forman enter his driveway. At midnight, when the lights in the house went out, Dowling hurried to the liquor store in the mall where the little boy, six hours before, had munched his Baby Ruth.

He walked quickly back to where the four cars were parked in the shadows of large trash Dumpsters, ripped the bag containing the twelve-pack and tore a can free. Swallowing half of the beer without stopping, he lowered the can and looked around. "Let's get the hell out of La Mesa. Get on our side of Seventh Street. I don't want to be explaining to any La Mesa cops what we're doing here."

Perspiration still clung to him though the night had cooled to a comfortable sixty degrees. Leading them behind a darkened building off University Avenue, he lectured himself. He was too old for this stuff anymore, and that was all there was to it. You live too long, you see too much. His nervous system kept reminding him it was a younger man's game. Reminded him that five, ten, fifteen years ago he thrived on the thrill of the hunt. Walking on the edge. Matching wits with these motherfuckers and knowing, just *knowing* who would win. Curtis Forman would have been another notch on his belt in those days. He would talk to Stacy about getting out as soon as they wrapped up the paperwork on this one. After Forman's arraignment.

"I can see it in your eyes, Sam." He was drawing on his second beer. "You wanted to get on the sidewalk and be the bait, and you're mad because I didn't let you."

"All I want is to catch him," she said as Shea and Gus turned away, pretending to busy themselves with traffic humming by.

"We all want to catch him. But there's a right and a

wrong way. A wrong way would be to have you jump out of your car, the three of us scrambling like a shithouse mouse trying to coordinate it, and Curtis Forman sneaking up on you from behind instead of his 'what time is it' routine.'' Inhaling deeply, he went on. ''If we put you, or any lady cop out there, it will be with a definite two- or three-block parameter. With twenty officers covering you so you don't ... oh hell, your heart's in the right place, Sam. Now drink your Guinness and let's critique this thing.''

''I like it,'' Gus said. ''He knows M.O. Old Curtis is thinking like a cop. The last two cases, he had us moving east. Now he's gone back west. He knows we can't stake out all of East San Diego.''

''And he knows he can't score every time out.'' Shea strolled away, looking for a place to relieve himself.

''I'll have the film in the lab when they open their door in the morning,'' Sam said. She had shot half a roll with a telephoto lens at the Dairy Queen. ''Will you be showing pictures to Holly Novikoff now, Sergeant?''

''I've thought a lot about that. No, no photos for Holly. If she says it's him, I won't arrest him. If she say it's not him, I won't get off the guy. So there's no use confusing things now. Photo IDs have a way of putting the screws to you.''

The team lounged in the lot for another hour, finished the beer and were ordered in at 7:30 A.M. ''No matter what he shows us tomorrow night, we've got to take him down. Can't let it go any longer,'' Dowling said. ''We've got a lot of prep work to do.''

''Do you think he'll come out tomorrow night?'' someone asked.

''You can count on it.''

Late the following afternoon, when Dowling's team took their surveillance position again, eight additional undercover cars, carrying two officers each, were waiting in East San Diego. Sam Mulcahy and three other women officers had been outfitted with on-body recorders. All the participants had attended a briefing at noon, after Dowling's team spent three hours in the area Curtis Forman had taken them to the night before. All carried carefully sketched diagrams, describing which sidewalks each decoy officer would walk and where each cover officer would lurk on foot.

When they headed for the police station with Forman in custody, Tom Stacy would be notified. "I've got to be down there, Dowling. This is heavy stuff. I was hoping he was running over to Florida Street to see a girlfriend." They'd granted Chief Toddy Claiborne's request to have Forman's sergeant, Hillary Baker, called at home. "She'll stay offstage when you bring him in, but I gotta have an ongoing update," the La Mesa chief had said.

At 9:15 P.M. they watched the Westfalia, carrying only Curtis Forman, turn onto Interstate 8 toward San Diego. By the time he drove the Texas Street hill and eased onto El Cajon Boulevard, Dowling's players were in position. The Westfalia turned onto Georgia Street, as it had the night before.

Then it happened. And neither Sergeant Vincent Dowling or any surveillance cop alive could prevent it.

"We've got an eleven-eighty, eleven-forty-one, Alabama and Madison."

Dowling didn't recognize the voice, but it hardly mattered. The broadcast came from one of the cops on foot duty and he knew it was over. "Eleven-eighty." Police radio code for a serious injury traffic accident. "Eleven-forty-one." Ambulance needed.

Curiosity seekers streamed from their homes, even before the black-and-white patrol units, emergency lights flashing, peppered Alabama and the surrounding streets, laying flares to divert traffic. Dowling was three blocks away, his head in his hands, when a surveillance unit reported that Curtis Forman had circled a two-block residential area, drove slowly past McDonald's, then headed north on Texas Street. Toward Interstate 8, Dowling knew. Toward La Mesa. Toward the comfort and security of home.

"One hundred to Station A," Dowling said into his microphone, "have a patrol unit make a stop on the Westfalia on Interstate 8 at College. Tell the unit I'll be backing him up in a cool car."

Dowling wanted to let Forman get some distance from the crime scenes. He had little going for him—another important case that hinged on a confession—but he could control arrest conditions, could try to relax Forman just a little. Not make it quite so obvious from square one what he was being pulled over for.

As planned, Larry Shea abandoned his undercover car at a service station a block away, puffing as he ran and jumped into Dowling's car. He had decided to use Shea rather than Gus or Sam in the interrogation. They had teamed up many times and were facing horrendous odds on this one. If Curtis Forman refused to waive Miranda, or waived and denied everything, it was over. He might be finished as a cop, but he'd sleep in his bed on Maple Street, convincing his wife that overzealous San Diego detectives had made a horrible mistake, had needed a scapegoat who fit his description and decided an out-of-town police officer was fair game. In Dowling's experience, Mrs. Forman would buy the story in a heartbeat.

"We won't say we're from Homicide, Larry. We'll ease him down to the station. See what his reaction is." He pulled in behind the patrol car that had stopped the Westfalia.

Curtis Forman, wearing a white T-shirt, Levi's and tennis shoes, shrugged his shoulders as he stood on the edge of the highway talking to the uniformed officer. The officer, flashlight tucked between chest and bicep, was facing oncoming traffic and nodded when Dowling approached. The detectives turned to Forman.

"Hi, my name's Dowling," he said easily. "This is Shea. How you doing tonight?"

"Doing okay. Trying to find out why I got stopped."

"We need a little help from you. You can give us some time, huh?" He didn't wait for an answer but turned to the patrol officer. "Thanks for stopping Officer Forman." When he said that he looked at his suspect's face for a reaction.

"You know my name?"

The surprised expression looked real to Dowling. "There's not much we don't know about you, Curtis."

"You guys been tailing me?"

Dowling hesitated. "Yeah, we have."

"How bad is this thing?" A poker face now.

"We'll go downtown and talk about it. You don't have a problem with that, do you?"

Shrugging again. "I don't have much choice."

"The officer here is going to transport you. We'll see you in a few minutes. We appreciate your cooperation, Curtis."

Dowling quietly pulled the San Diego officer aside. "You don't know what this is about, do you?"

"No idea. Radio told me to make the stop."

"It's better if we keep it that way. Just be a listener on the way downtown. And take him up the back way to Homicide so he doesn't see the signs on the door. Make notes right away on everything he said. But take your time. Let me and Shea get there first."

"What do you think?" Shea asked as Dowling sped south on Highway 163.

"Can't tell. The voice is similar. At first I thought my telephone friend's was a little higher pitch, but now I don't know."

"I think old Curtis Forman may be easy pickings," Shea said.

Twenty minutes later, with their suspect waiting for them in an interrogation room, Dowling shook hands with Hillary Baker, sergeant, La Mesa Police Department. She was off duty but smartly dressed in navy blue slacks and a pale blue blouse, combining the pretty looks and hardened visage he had grown used to on the faces of lady cops. Above all, the streets were democratic.

"You never quit getting surprised on this job, do you?" she said. "I feel like I've been kicked in the guts."

"Tell me about him," Dowling said.

"Good cop. Wish I had more like him."

"Anything you think will help us before Shea and I take him on?"

She thought for a moment. Dark brown eyes looked right at Dowling's. "He doesn't think much of me. When he swore in a few years ago, all fresh and eager, I don't think he figured he'd have a woman boss."

"You've given him good evaluation scores."

"He's earned them. He doesn't have to like me as long as he keeps my sector clean. Keeps throwing those dickheads in jail."

"How long have you been a cop, Hillary?"

"Eight years, Sergeant."

"Call me Vincent." He pointed to another room. "You can listen in with Sam Mulcahy and Gus Denver if you'd like."

To Dowling, Curtis Forman was the prototype of a young patrol officer. Clean, freshly showered look. Well-groomed hair. Attractive features. Sharp, alert eyes. A rugged yet not imposing physical specimen. His own eyes strayed to the folded hands that had vetoed the remainder of Joy Larson's life. Hands that rocketed the spiritual essence of Holly Novikoff and his other victims to an emotional hell.

"Let's get through Miranda first." Dowling smiled. "You have the right to remain silent during questioning, now or at any time. Anything you do say can be used . . ."

When he finished the entire warning, he paused, clearing his throat. "Do you understand each of the rights I have explained to you?"

"Who ever thought I'd be on this end of Miranda?"

"Do you understand the rights?" Dowling repeated.

"Of course I understand. I'm a cop." Forman was looking down.

"Having in mind and understanding your rights, are you willing to talk to Larry and me?" He held his breath on this one. He'd seen so many suspects come this far and suddenly apply the brakes.

Curtis Forman grunted, let out a sort of muffled snicker. "What's the difference? I'm screwed either way."

"Will you talk to us, Curtis?" Shea said gently.

"Sure. Sure, I'll talk to you. But I got a question first. How did you guys get on to me?"

"Investigation," Dowling said, determined not to relinquish control of the interrogation.

"It was that patrol cop who F.I.'d me on Florida Street last month, wasn't it?"

"That was part of it. What we want to do is—"

"Does my department know yet?"

"Your chief knows."

Curtis Forman tried to pinch his eyes together with his right hand, then ran it deliberately down his face. "There goes my job, huh?"

Unreal, Dowling thought. He'd seen it before though. Dumb sons of bitches, like his old nemesis Cliff Edwards a year or so ago, sitting there looking prison in the eye and worrying about losing their badge.

"How long have you been following me around?"

"We'll get to all of that. Why don't you start by telling us about it. Clear some things up," Shea said.

"It was all so dumb, wasn't it?" Forman looked at Shea for an answer.

"When did it start?" Dowling asked.

"A couple of months ago."

"Who have you told about it?"

"My wife. We don't have any secrets."

The answer startled Dowling. Weird. He was glad he worked Homicide and not Sex Crimes. Didn't have to deal with these crazy motherfuckers on a daily basis. He'd take his whacked-out shooters and stabbers and . . .

He drew tiny circles on his legal pad. "Let's start with the girl wearing the orange-and-white striped workout shorts. We can go forward and backward from there.''

"What girl?''

"The girl on Kansas Street.''

Forman looked up and said nothing.

"If you'd rather,'' Shea said, "we can start with the Mexican girl on Arizona Street. The one carrying an armload of books.''

"I'm not following you guys.''

"Come on, Curtis. You've been very cooperative so far. But either start cleaning this thing up or we just quit messing around and book you.''

"I don't know about any Mexican girl. Or Arizona Street. Or any orange-and-white shorts.''

"How many women were there, Curtis?'' Shea asked.

"Just the one, honest.''

Dowling leaned forward, placing both fists on the table. "You're twenty-seven years old, Curtis. I was pounding a beat when you were eating pablum and shitting your pants. By the time you went through the police academy, Shea and I had worked more cases than—''

Forman put both hands in the air. "I'm not trying to give you guys a hard time. How about if I just lay it out as it went down? Okay?''

"Go,'' Dowling said, trying to disguise his frustration.

"My wife and I are having financial problems. I stop this lady for speeding. She's from La Jolla. I'm writing her up and she asks do I know any private investigators. She's sure her husband's got a girlfriend. Wants to know who the girlfriend is, that sort of stuff. I figure she's just giving me bullshit, trying to get out of the ticket.'' He ran his fingers through the short hair. "But she keeps going on. Says money's no object. She has to know who this woman is. I just shine her on but then I get thinking about it and a day or two later I pull my copy of the ticket and phone her. Next thing I know, I'm working for her.''

"Go on,'' Dowling said when Forman paused.

"All she can tell me is the girlfriend lives on a street named after a state. She'd seen something her old man had written down once. Gives me the description of her old man's car—a silver Chrysler New Yorker 788 KHM. Well, I don't want to try a one-car tail from La Jolla so I figure if the old girl is right about the street, I'll eventually find the car. Find it parked, and go from there.''

Dowling and Shea exchanged looks.

"That's what I was doing when your officer nailed me on Florida Street that night a few months ago.''

"You were doing what exactly?'' Dowling said.

"Looking for the right house. I'd found the car but didn't know what house he was in. And I couldn't tell your cop I was a cop. Shit, I was really sweating it. I mean, I'm doing *two* things wrong. I'm moonlighting on a job that's a conflict of interest because I'm a cop, and I'm practicing P.I. work without a license.''

"Tell me exactly how you were looking for 'the right house,' '' Dowling said again.

"Like I said, one night I found the car. But I didn't know if she lived in the house he was parked in front of or what. Turns out she didn't. I had to stake out the car, see what direction he came from, then the next time move closer to where he came from. You know, do it piecemeal. I ended up finding the house, 4439 Georgia, next block over.''

"Keep going,'' Dowling said.

"So every night I'd drive over there from home. My client wanted to know every night he was there. I guess she was building a case on him. Anyway, this guy had to park a couple of blocks away sometimes, so it would take me a few minutes to find the car. *If* it was a night he was there.'' Forman paused. "That's the story.''

"Let's talk about last night, Curtis,'' Dowling said. "When you were parked, all by your lonesome, watching the McDonald's lot.''

"I wasn't watching the McDonald's lot.''

"BULLSHIT,'' Shea yelled. "We were right with you.''

"I wasn't even thinking of McDonald's. The parking

lot for The Green Lantern borders the McDonald's lot. They go there for drinks pretty often. I log the times. I was looking at the Chrysler in the Green Lantern lot last night. Tonight, he was parked on Madison so I knew he was at her house. So I headed on home.''

Dowling said nothing, trying to clear his mind.

"I wrote reports about The Green Lantern."

"Where are the reports?" Shea asked.

"The client's got 'em. I've got copies at home."

"What's your client's name?" Dowling asked wearily.

"Aww, hell. I can't tell you that. It's con—"

"*Goddammit*," Dowling shouted. He was beginning to believe he was listening to the truth. A truth he didn't want to hear. He was a hypocrite. "You cough up that client's name, and knock off this confidential info bullshit. You with me, Curtis?"

"What detail do you guys work? What have you got me down here for?"

"We work homicide. H-O-M-I-C-I-D-E."

"H-homicide?" Forman's face lost color.

"We are working rapes and a murder and we want the total truth from you," Shea said.

"Aww, Christ. I don't believe this. Man, I'm telling you the truth. I'm no rapist. I'll . . . I'll give you DNA. Give you blood, saliva, anything. You can DNA me."

Curtis Forman stayed in the interrogation room for the next hour while Gus and Sam drove to La Mesa, then telephoned the office from the Forman living room. Curtis Forman ordered his wife to hand over the client reports, and his entire statement was corroborated. Mrs. Forman verified everything. To clinch it, Dowling listened on an extension phone while Curtis Forman called the La Jolla woman. Her husband was not home yet; of course she could talk. The traffic ticket? She had told no one about it. She appreciated the good work Officer Forman was doing.

When they finished, Sergeant Hillary Baker relieved Forman of his badge and suspended him "pending an investigation.'' They were arranging transportation back to his car when he asked to speak with Dowling and Shea again. He doesn't look like a cop any more, Dowling reminded himself to tell Shea later. Forman's shoulders slumped and he sat with head bowed, moving his hands slowly, in tiny arcs, on the interrogation room table.

''When I walk out of this squad room it's all over. You guys know this 'suspended pending investigation' means I'm gone. Fired. And I just need to sit a minute.'' He twisted his gold wedding band in circles. ''I don't want it to end.'' Nobody spoke for a minute. ''I was so proud when I made it through the academy. Wanted to do something important. Wanted to take care of my wife and daughter.'' He looked at the ceiling. ''We were putting college money away for my daughter. I messed up the finances, but we never stopped putting the college money away.'' He rubbed his eyes. ''I was proud to be a La Mesa cop. My sergeant thought I didn't like her. Hell, she was a good sergeant. Taught me a lot. I was just insecure, you know. Kept thinking I had to prove too much. Put a lot of pressure on myself. But that's why I made good pinches. Gave it everything I had.''

He got to his feet, then sat down again. ''You know what I wanted to be? I wanted to be like you guys. Wanted to learn everything there was to know on the streets, then be a detective and maybe make sergeant some day. End up with a good retirement.'' He wiped his eyes again. ''Lord, my wife. She believed in me and I pissed it all away.'' He got up, reaching for the doorknob. ''In a way, I'm still a cop though. You know why? Because you take some citizen down here for four hours and sweat 'em and end up finding out they're clean, they're going to raise holy hell and yell police state and—'' He gave them a wave. ''But I know you were doing what's right. What you had to do.''

He opened the door, took a step and turned around. ''At least I can say one thing. I can say that for three years, *three* years, I was as good a cop as there ever was. No one can take that away from me.''

After he watched Curtis Forman leave, Dowling grabbed his windbreaker and walked out of the office. Tom Stacy, alone on the elevator, held the door for him.

''I'm buying, Vince.''

''Not tonight, Tom. Tonight, I embarrassed everybody. Embarrassed my department, La Mesa P.D., myself.''

''It couldn't be helped. These things happen.''

''Not to me, they don't.''

''Come on. Let's have a drink.''

''I don't have time, Tom. I gotta get home and slit my wrists.''

When he did get home, he found his daughter sitting in the living room. It took him a moment to realize what was odd. The quiet. A blank television screen and an amplifier with the power off.

''It's after midnight. What are you doing up?''

''I need to talk to you.''

He tossed his jacket on a wingback chair. ''Is there something wrong?''

''It depends on how you look at things.''

''Trouble at school?''

''No.''

''About Jason?''

''Kind of.''

''Jenny, are you getting married, too?''

She didn't answer and he took a seat next to her. ''What is it?''

''I'm pregnant, Pop.''

🌿 Fourteen

Dowling smiled, patted her knee and focused on the brass candlesticks lining the oak mantelpiece behind her.

"This is a bad time to kid. Tonight's been awful."

"I'm not kidding though."

"We had a guy bought and paid for. The captain even had a press conference lined up. Turns out we had the wrong guy."

Jennifer Dowling fidgeted with a tiny sapphire ring her mother had given her in the sixth grade. "I have been sitting on this sofa for three hours waiting for you to come home." She brushed her hair back. "I wouldn't make jokes about something like this."

He looked into her eyes but couldn't get a read. There was a weariness perhaps. Or maybe, just the soft lighting.

"Every time I heard a car I hoped it wasn't you."

"Jenny, what the hell is going on here?" He was on his feet. "If you're not kidding, it means . . . it means you're pregnant."

She said nothing as Dowling walked to the bay window and pretended to examine the large magnolia tree in the darkness.

"*Jesus Christ. Pregnant!* How did you—when did you find this out?"

"Two weeks ago."

"*Two weeks ago?* Then how come I'm just being

told?'' He turned toward her. ''And don't give me crap about my not being around. Except for the last couple of nights I've been home—''

''Pop. Can we just talk about this calmly?''

''We *are* talking about it calmly. I am.''

''No you're not. You're upset.''

''Well, I beg your pardon. I come home and my seventeen-year-old daughter, my seventeen-year-old daughter who's in high school tells me she's going to have a baby. My *unmarried* seventeen year old daughter. Excuse me for being upset.''

''I knew this was going to happen,'' she said getting up.

''*Date rape!* My daughter's the victim of a date rape.''

She shook her head.

''Did you get drunk? You got drunk, didn't you, Jenny?'' He continued pacing and shook his head. ''Old Jason boy picked up a six-pack or a bottle of gin and the next thing—''

''*Please.* Please sit down next to me and talk.''

''We are talking.''

''We're talking, but we're not saying anything.'' She began to cry.

''Christ almighty. Here I am, up to my neck in a vicious street series, getting nowhere—I come home and—''

Jenny buried her head in a pillow, her screams muffled. ''You're always a cop. You . . .'' She threw the pillow against the wall, knocking down a picture. ''You don't even know who I am.''

Everything was moving too fast for him. The room should have been spinning, but it wasn't. The coffee table, the music stand by the piano, Helene's books. It all looked the same as when he'd left early that morning. He walked to the mantle, rubbed his fingers over the dark oak and straightened a candlestick holder.

''This is my fault, not yours,'' he said. ''We never talked about that. When your mother . . . died, I should have known it was up to me to give you guidance. About drinking and boys and all.'' He put his hands in his pockets and his shoulders slouched. ''I thought you and I were doing pretty well here alone, though. Not perfect, of course, but pretty good.''

''Pop, we're living in a different world. This isn't the fifties. We're growing up faster.''

She coaxed him to sit beside her again and wiped her eyes. ''I wasn't drunk. Does that mean you hate me now?'' When he didn't answer she said, ''I love Jason.'' For the second time in forty-five minutes, someone told him, ''These things happen.'' Suddenly, Curtis Forman and press conferences, homicide squad rooms and visiting Irish cops, sociopathic rapists and battered women were not important.

''Are you sure?'' he said.

''Yes, I love him.''

''I don't mean Jason. Are you sure you're pregnant?'' She nodded.

''How do you know?''

''I went to Planned Parenthood.''

He was on his feet again. ''What in hell does Planned Parenthood have to do with this?''

''Do you even know what Planned Parenthood is?''

''Some agency George Bush got into arguments with. What does it have to do with you?''

A short time later, after she explained about the counseling, the affirmative testing, the due date in May, the recounseling, he asked her to go out onto the large cobblestone porch so he could smoke.

''You mean you might have an abortion?''

''I have that choice. And I'm still thinking about things.''

''But you might have an abortion?''

''I might.''

''What does Jason think of all this? Crissake, I haven't even asked you about him.''

Jenny walked to the eighteen-inch-wide flower bed, tucked between cobblestones at waist level, and gently pushed the rich dirt against the stems of red and white pansies.

"Are you going to get married?" Dowling asked.

"Jason doesn't think there's any rush to do that."

"He doesn't, huh? Just what *does* Jason think?"

She started to cry again. "He says we can make it all go away."

"With an abortion?"

"His parents agree with him that we shouldn't get married. Matt said I shouldn't let his parents influence—"

"Jason's parents? Matt? Am I the only one who doesn't know, or haven't you told the newspaper boy?"

"I have a lot of thinking to do," she said when she turned around. "A lot of thinking." She came closer to him. "I was hoping you'd be a part of whatever I'm going to do, Daddy."

Dowling blew smoke into the September night and didn't answer.

"I guess you just told me where you stand," she said.

He walked to the edge of the porch and leaned against a column. "It's only been a few minutes since I walked in the door. This is like a kick in the stomach." He put his arm around her and hugged. "Somehow, we'll have to make it be okay."

"Another round for my friends," Gus Denver yelled above the din in the 153 Club.

Sergeant Jack Cassidy of homicide Team Four quickly polished off his fifth vodka rocks. "The honeymoon must be over for Gus. New bride allowing him to slosh around with his degenerate teammates. You guys ever gonna solve one, by the way?"

"My new bride don't care when this man comes home. That sweet woman married me because I know how to *love* her."

"We'd cancel our cases, too, if Stacy gave us the slam dunks he saves for Team Four," Shea said, reaching in front of Sam for another handful of chips.

"Slam dunks, shit," Dowling said. "Even Michael Jordan's got to expend a *little* energy on a slam dunk. Cassidy just walks in and has the suspect fill out the arrest report."

One Beer Babcock from Forgery occupied the sixth chair at the table, whose top had not seen a bar rag since they sat down.

"Caught a complicated one today I hear, Sergeant Cassidy," Sam said. A glass of Jameson Irish whiskey and water, minus ice, was in front of her.

Cassidy nodded thanks to the waitress and grabbed his drink. "My dead guy's talking to his girlfriend on the kitchen phone. Doesn't know his wife is listening on the upstairs extension. He's telling Sally Lu how fond he is of her and what he's going to do to prove it when he sees her tomorrow night." Cassidy sucked in the two large green olives. "Anyway, his wife walks into the kitchen, so our boy changes his tune. '*Yes*, boss. Most certainly, boss.' Doesn't see her opening the knife drawer. 'Of course, boss. I'll bring the papers on the Barnett matter with me tomorrow night.' " Cassidy drank half of the glass and jiggled ice. "She was sitting on the curb waiting for patrol."

Everybody laughed except One Beer Babcock, who only smiled.

It had been a horrendous day for Dowling. He had awakened with a headache, having hated going to sleep after saying goodnight to Jenny because he knew how gloomy the morning would be. "We're back in the rotation," he had told the team glumly. "Second up after Jack Cassidy."

Larry Shea filled glasses for himself and Gus, then turned the pitcher toward One Beer Babcock. "Just once, One Beer, I'd like to see you take a second one. Even for a sailor, you're a fuckin' disgrace."

"Moderation is a word few patrons of this sleaze hole know the meaning of," Babcock said, hand covering the top of his glass.

"They don't serve One Beer's drink here: Chivas Regal and Dr Pepper," Cassidy said.

"One Beer's a social drinker. Like the culchies in the public houses," Sam said.

"What's a culchie?" Gus asked.

"A country fella."

"Speaking of the old sod, Irish," Dowling said, "how come you're not drinking Old Bushmills?"

Sam lowered her voice and looked around slowly, "'Tis made in the North and I'm partial to whiskey from the Republic."

"Why are you whispering?" Jack Cassidy wanted to know, signaling for another round.

"Habit, is what. People often whisper when referring to The Troubles."

"I notice you're not having any trouble with that Jameson," Shea said.

Sam laughed. "Aye. Reminds me, it does. My poor mom posted me a letter. She's lost half a stone worrying. She says, 'Hardly eating, I am.' "

"What kind of stone," Cassidy asked, dripping salsa on his sleeve.

"It's a measure of weight. There are fourteen pounds to a stone," One Beer Babcock said. "But who would expect a homicide detective to know that?"

"Mom worried about her little girl?" Dowling said. The bourbon tasted good, and he had no intention of slowing down.

Sam finished her drink and reached for the fresh one stacked behind it. "Worried about my being run over on the freeways. Worried I'm not eating properly. Mostly worried I'm consorting with a slew of jackeens, as indeed I am."

"What's a 'jackeen,' One Beer?" Cassidy asked.

Babcock shrugged and Sam answered, "Jackeens are city fellas."

"Old Mom doesn't have to worry about these old shits you're hanging around with," Cassidy said. "But she ought to worry about that good-looking patrol cop who's been squiring you around.''

"Ah, yes. Officer Damon Harper,'' Gus said.

They all looked up when a red-faced burglary detective stumbled by the table on his way to the men's room. "Hey, Dowling. What's the matter? Superman and the super team can't solve a little old rape-murder series?''

"No, we can't,'' Dowling said. "Got any ideas?''

"Yeah. Hit the bricks like real detectives and quit hanging around gin mills.''

Jack Cassidy jerked his thumb toward him. "Hit the road and go catch a shoplifter, Dobson.''

"How many cases now, Dowling?'' Dobson asked.

"Six.'' Dowling looked into his glass.

"Five really, huh? You ain't counting the whore from downtown as a victim, are you?'' Dobson said.

Had he not been standing just to Dowling's left when he said it, Dowling's punch, delivered as he got to his feet, might not have knocked him down.

Jerking him by the necktie to a sitting position, Dowling growled at him. "Fuck with me and fuck with my team all you want, Dobson. Just don't fuck with my rape victims.''

"Call a cop,'' an off-duty patrol officer yelled from a corner of the bar. "Got a guy impersonating a fighter over there.''

Dobson's two drinking partners hurried over, still clutching glasses. Everyone got to their feet and Dowling told them, "Take your ill-mannered friend back over there and have a round on me.''

When things settled down, Dowling tuned out the chatter at the table. He didn't even know the woman his son had married. His daughter was pregnant and a rape-murderer was outsmarting him. And . . . he looked at his team. "Yesterday, I ruined the career of a young cop. A good young cop.''

"Curtis Forman did it to himself,'' Shea counseled.

"But I helped,'' Dowling said. He read eight o'clock

on the dial of his wristwatch. Jenny's closest girlfriend was sleeping over and they wouldn't miss him. "Another round over here," he called.

"Seeing Dobson there on the floor reminded me, he did, of Fergus O'Laughlin," Sam said, "a Garda who went through the training center with me, a fine broth of a lad." She took a swallow. "Got into a ruckus with some ne'er-do-wells. Caught the fat end of a bottle of poteen, he did, and had to have his head stitched. They were patching him up and a townie said, 'This may not be the job for O'Laughlin. His skull is entirely too thin for a constable.' "

"Gardas, huh?" Cassidy said, laughing.

"Aye. The Garda Siochana, civic guard. Sometimes affectionately called 'Gardies' or 'coppers' or 'blue bottles,' because of the uniforms. Not tan like your lads wear."

"Do you get homesick, Sam?" Dowling asked.

"A wee bit. Then someone from my family rings me up and tries to make it well."

"How come," Shea said between belches, "when you ask an Irishman a question he always answers with one?"

"Who told you that?" Sam said.

"I don't know, I just—"

"She got you good, Shea, got you good," Gus said, punching his fist in the air, and they all laughed.

One Beer Babcock studied the last ounce remaining in his glass. "The Troubles? Religion still gets in the way of everything, doesn't it?"

Sam finished another Irish whiskey. "My uncle Liam always says, 'Sure, I'd rather die than be buried in a Protestant cemetery.' "

"*No more!*" they all yelled.

"Then," she went on, "''tis the one about Patrick and Kathleen on their wedding night. Kathleen was a virtuous young thing and that evening Patrick performed quite well indeed and come the morn, Kathleen said, 'Patrick, you're a San Diego policeman. You're very smart. You know everything there is to know. Tell me now, the Protestants,

when they get married. Do they do what we just did?'
Patrick looked at his bride and said, 'And sure they do;
now, why do you ask?' And Kathleen said, 'I was just
thinking. It's too good for the likes of them.' "

They had all run from the table by the time she finished.

A few minutes later, Dowling was waiting his turn at
the pay phone near the jukebox. He wanted to give Jenny
a quick hello. Sam Mulcahy stopped on her way to the
ladies' room.

"You drink like a cop," he said. "Won't even put your
glass down to go to the can."

"What's the matter, Sergeant? You look sad."

"I'm not sad."

"Then tell your face," she said, hurrying off.

When Dowling returned to the table, Gus Denver was
describing for Sam the twenty-foot-high statue of El Cid
on horseback in Balboa Park.

"Sits in the middle of the damn Prado area. I'm a
rookie. A few of us are sitting in the park in our beat cars
and they gonna give me a dollar can I sit up with old El
Cid on that horse. So I grab a ladder from the maintenance
shed and I'm up there whooping and hollering and they
grab the ladder, drive my car away, and radio the sergeant
to come meet me at the statue. Got my ass chewed."

"You can't get down without the ladder?" Sam asked.

"You can if you got wings," Cassidy said.

"When I worked Sex Crimes," Shea said, "we got
paper work on a guy who climbed up there and played
with the horse's balls."

More drinks came, two rounds actually, compliments
of narcotics detectives at the next table who had been
smiling at Sam Mulcahy.

"Tell Sam about your blind man caper, Cassidy. That
was another slam dunk," Dowling said.

Cassidy stuffed chips into his mouth. "Old blind guy
walking his dog shoots a guy he thought was gonna rob
him. Turns out the stiff is an old wino hitting him up for

a drink. Team Four was up to the challenge. Copped him right out.''

''Cassidy told the shooter if he didn't confess, Team Four would sneak in and rearrange his furniture every three days,'' Shea said.

''If that'd been my case, the blind man and the dog would have been the witnesses,'' Dowling said.

One Beer Babcock had left and Jack Cassidy was checking the time when Sam, who had bought another round, put both elbows on the table. She pretended to bang a gavel.

''The judge says, 'Thirty pounds or thirty days, Slattery.' Slattery says, 'I'll take the thirty pounds.' ''

''Jeez, Sarge. Next time we do an exchange program, get a cop who doesn't know corny Pat and Mike jokes,'' Gus pleaded.

Sam ignored them. ''Two years ago you swallowed a ten-shilling piece, Finnegan. Why in heaven, man, didn't you come to me then? Finnegan says, 'Sure, Doctor, I didn't need the money until now.' ''

''This is a good time for me to be taking my leave.'' Cassidy drained his glass as he said it. ''And you guys have to work with her.''

''If your sainted mother could see you now, she'd lose the other half of the stone,'' Dowling said.

''If God had intended the Irish to rule the world, he wouldn't have invented alcohol. Don't get her started again, Sarge,'' Gus cautioned.

There was no stopping her. ''Killian dropped from the scaffold and fell two stories. 'Did the fall hurt you, Eamonn?' the foreman asked. 'Wasn't the fall hurt me, boss. 'Twas the sudden stop.' ''

''That does it,'' Shea shouted. ''Innkeeper. Eighty-six the Rose of Tralee over here.''

At midnight the waiter, an aspiring Shakespearean actor, surveyed the wreckage. ''Our noble minions of justice,'' he said, shaking his head.

''Just lay the drinks on us, Brute,'' Shea told him.

The crowd was thinning when Dowling said, "How are we going to catch this son of a bitch? When's he going to hit again? How come everything I think of to do is a 'been there, done that'?"

"That's three questions," Gus said, "and I don't know the answer to any of them."

"He'll fuck up," Shea said. "We'll catch a break."

Dowling grunted. "Heavy cost though. How many more dead women are we going to have to look at? We can't wait; we have to make something happen."

Sam fingered her glass. "I feel so helpless."

Dowling emptied an overflowing ashtray into a wet napkin. "Enough work bullshit. Have you heard of 'road bowling' Sam?"

"Have you heard of baseball?" she answered. "Of course I know road bowling. Most common in Cork and Armaugh. Why might you be asking, Sergeant O'Dowling?"

Homicide Team One had the table to themselves. They leaned forward, the easier to understand each other's slurring.

"I saw a documentary." Dowling said the word deliberately. "A bunch of guys were rolling this damn ball down the road. Yelling and clapping, money changing hands and . . . ?"

"Aye. They pick a distance, maybe one and a half kilometers. The bowler reaching the spot first wins a bob or two. Takes many rolls. Sure and you saw clips of Mick Perry."

"Who is Mick Perry? I demand to know," Gus said.

"Asking an Irishman who Mick Perry is?" Sam shook her head. "Like asking one of you who Mickey Mantle is."

"Aww, come on," Shea said. He and Gus had switched from beer to gin after they became a foursome. "You can't compare hitting a curveball to heaving some bowling ball down a country road." He giggled.

Sam examined her glass of whiskey. "Not a bowling

ball. 'Tis about the size of your curveball, a tad bigger, and it takes a great deal of skill to get a good roll and keep it straight.''

They all laughed.

''How far does this champion of yours roll his little ball?'' Dowling said, still smiling.

''Well now, a good bowler may strike it two, three hundred meters at a whack.''

''And I suppose, you being such a tough, athletic lad, you know how it's done?'' Dowling said.

''I've bowled a bit, I have,'' she answered.

''Well, some day, we'll go out and show you how easy it is to roll a ball a couple of hundred yards on a hard surface,'' Shea said.

Sam licked the last drop from her glass. ''Sure and why don't we do it right now? I have a ball in the trunk of my car.''

''You-have-a-ball-in-the-trunk-of-your-car?'' Dowling said.

''I do. Damon Harper and I were taking a dander through Balboa Park, and at the International House, a lovely old man from Ballycotton gave it to me as a reminder of home.''

''Well, we sure as hell can't do it now,'' Gus said, steadying himself on the edge of the table.

''And,'' Shea added, ''you're drunk, Sam.''

She lifted her chin. ''Now, who would have to be sober to show up a bunch of Yanks? Not a word of a lie in that.''

''Even if you could get your Irish ass out of that chair, we don't have any place to do it,'' Gus announced.

''*We do,*'' Dowling shouted, pounding the table. ''We do have a place. Harbor Drive. Harbor goddamn Drive from Market to Eighth Avenue. That's about a mile,'' he said proudly.

Sam's eyes got bigger. ''You could do that?''

''I am a San Diego police homicide sergeant. Of course I can.'' Dowling removed the leather badge holder from his pocket, flipped it open, breathed on the gold shield, then buffed it on his coat sleeve, paying particular attention to the eagle perched on top.

Shea shook his head. "It can't fly. We'd need flares, traffic control. Patrol will never go for it."

"If Melancholy Johnson was working we could pull it off," Gus volunteered, "but he's still on swing shift."

Dowling ignored them. "Here's the assignments. Shea, get a box of flares from traffic. Get *two* boxes. Sam, you get the damn bowling ball. Gus, you get a detective car out of the lot; I'll get a second one. Hurry up and finish your drinks. We're going bowling."

"Sergeant Dowling, what in hell is going on here?" the young patrol lieutenant asked forty-five minutes later. Columns of honking cars were at a standstill, blocked by rows of orange flares and two detective cars at Eighth Avenue and Harbor Drive. Arriving patrol cars had emergency lights flashing. The array formed a psychedelic backdrop against the skyline.

"We're on an evidence search, Lieutenant," Dowling said, chewing on five sticks of peppermint gum.

"Evidence search?"

"Yeah. We caught a break in an old unsolved murder. Informant told us the shooter thought we were getting close. Today he hauled ass down Harbor Drive and threw the gun and ammo out a car window." Dowling straightened his tie. "We sure didn't want to tie up daytime traffic. You guys were supposed to be here to lay out the flares. We called the patrol office this afternoon."

"Somebody screwed up, then. It wasn't in the daybook." The lieutenant looked Dowling over carefully. "Are you about done searching?"

"We just got started."

"*What?* You got the Convention Center, the Marriott Hotel and the Hyatt Hotel sealed off. There's no way to divert these goddamn cars. The only access to these places is this stretch of Harbor Drive."

"Sorry, we'll make it as quick as we can."

When the team had moved safely out of sight from the black-and-white patrol cars staffing the roadblocks, Sam Mulcahy began the lesson. She held the hard ball in her right hand, ignoring a couple in evening clothes on the sidewalk in front of Exhibit Hall B.

"Some lads put a side spin on it, and it's vital you gauge where the ball will first meet pavement. When it hits the curbing you lose a wee bit of speed and distance."

She demonstrated, and Dowling told himself it was the finest exhibition of athletic ability he had ever witnessed outside of Jack Murphy Stadium. Sam Mulcahy took a forty-five foot run, at surprising speed, left arm straight down at her side. Her ball-carrying right arm made rapid, full circles as she ran. Then, an instant before release, she threw her comely body up and forward, skirt hems flying, propelling the sphere with tremendous force. It struck the asphalt roadway with an ominous crack, then darted rather than rolled northwest, past the Convention Center parking entrance and on into the darkness, toward the Marriott's brightly lit half-circle driveway.

Larry Shea fell not once, but twice on his four attempts. Gus Denver's best efforts skidded to a stop less than one hundred feet from the start line, after ricocheting from curb to curb. Dowling, trying vainly to imitate Sam's hop-skip-and-jump release, had difficulty preventing the ball from jumping the curb itself. He pivoted and crashed to the ground.

"None of you are of a condition to get behind the wheel," Sam told them, loading all three into the backseat of her leased car. Gus was asleep before she started the engine while Shea lamented his torn shirt. Sam slowed and smiled sweetly at the patrol officer removing flares at the Market Street blockade. Snores rose behind her. When she looked back, it was difficult to determine which arms and legs belonged where. She tapped on the steering wheel as she drove, speaking out loud.

"Sleep nicely, for tomorrow me fine lads, we crank it up again. He's out there somewhere just waiting for us."

 **Fifteen**

"Are you too proud to toss freight around a warehouse?" Dowling asked. Even the act of speaking softly made his head ache, but since he had grudgingly decided against calling in sick, and since Curtis Forman had returned his call from the day before, he found himself on the telephone at 8:00 A.M.

"No sir, Sarge. Getting a sixty-day suspension without pay, I have to put beans on the table somehow."

"That's what I figured. Call OMS Trucking in Kearny Mesa. A friend of mine runs it. I told him who you are and why you need work." He thought about looking up the phone number, but the thick directory looked ponderous.

"I can't thank you enough," Curtis Forman said. "I learned a lesson."

"I've done some dumb things myself." Dowling cradled the phone gently and looked across the desk at Larry Shea. "At least you changed your shirt," he told him.

Shea rubbed watery eyes. "At least I came home with police breath. The day I don't, Grace will figure I'm screwing around on her."

"You got Gus home okay?"

"Sam propped him up, rang the doorbell and ran. I think he may have fallen into the flower bed before the door opened," Shea said.

"Where is he now?."

"Either in the morgue or still trying to hold a cup of coffee without dropping it. Jack Cassidy was trying to talk him out of admitting himself to the hospital."

They looked at each other. "Irish must have been pouring her drinks in a potted plant," Shea said.

"Youth, that's what it is. She buzzed in here a while ago when you were still trying to zip your fly, picked up her stuff and headed for Rene Sheffield's."

Shea shook his head, then cursed himself for doing so. "Anybody in the squad room know she had to drive us home?"

"Our little secret," Dowling whispered. "To take to the grave with us. Which may occur before quitting time."

They limped through the morning, hardly cheered when Sam brought them news.

"Ciao, baby," she told them. "That's what our suspect said to Rene, *'Ciao, baby.'* Italian for good-bye."

"Those were his words?" Dowling asked.

"They were."

"His exact words?" Dowling shook his head. "How in hell would Rene Sheffield be in tune with that term?"

Sam made a complete circle in her swivel chair as she interrupted. "To Rene it sounded like 'chow.' Her father uses that word when he wants her to cook his supper. She's never heard the avant-garde term, 'ciao.' But that's what our suspect said. 'Ciao, baby.' "

"He did, huh?" Dowling rubbed his forehead. "Pretty high tone for a street rapist."

"Indeed it is. But he said it. Spoken when he was on top of her."

Dowling almost forgot the storm raging in his head. "If he really said it, if Rene's not trying too hard to help, it could mean a lot some day. Good job, Detective Mulcahy."

"By the way," she said, "I'll be on another patrol ride-along on second shift today. Part of my orientation."

"Don't forget to put a dab of *eau* de Killarney behind your ears," Shea said. "I imagine Damon Harper will be in the left-hand seat."

Sam merely winked.

"When the day shift gets Code Seven from a Roberto's, I can smell taquitos and frijoles for the whole ten hours," Damon Harper said. He grunted while dislodging the backseat of the Ford Crown Victoria, pulled it clear of the floor for a moment, then jammed it back into place.

"What are you looking for?" Sam asked, taking in the buzz of shift change activity in the police garage.

"Guns or knives. Sometimes in an emergency you have to throw somebody in the backseat without handcuffs."

"Maybe someone from the last shift got put in without a frisk and stashed them there then?"

"You got it. Pleasant way to start a work day, huh?" He grabbed paper towels and helped her finish cleaning windows.

Sam looked through the rear window at the stout metal grill forming a barrier between the front and rear seats, noticing the lack of inside door handles on the rear doors, then focused on the Remington 12-gauge shotgun stored in the dashboard bracket. A blue steel spire of death between driver and partner. Damon Harper's Swiss-made 9mm SIG-Sauer clung to his right hip, and she pondered what kind of situation would require using all fifteen rounds of ammunition stored in its clip. Uniformed cops carrying guns still struck her as strange, even given the sorrowful aftermath of violence she had been exposed to in such a short time.

"When I came on," Gus Denver had told her, "we carried six-shot revolvers. Hell, the way things are going they'll need rocket launchers pretty soon."

She knew Gus was in no condition today to look at a shotgun, much less pick one up and fire it. It had been an effort for her to maintain and function last night, and she still didn't know how she managed. Before putting her head on the pillow, she remembered praying they did not get a call-out, and when her alarm buzzed next to her head four hours later, it was evident only one thing would enable her to face the day.

After taking twice as long as usual in the shower, she made her way to the kitchen and put a saucepan of milk on the burner at low heat. A scattering of family pictures relieved the sparseness of her one-bedroom furnished apartment. She had arrived in San Diego lugging two suitcases, and it didn't seem practical to put too many home touches in a place she would leave in January. That made her think of the holidays, and she wondered what Christmas would be like away from her family. She knew that at home her father would demand potato stuffing in the turkey, though she and her brothers secretly preferred a cornmeal filling. After mass, relatives and neighbors would drift in for short hellos; then she and her mother would transform the cozy kitchen into a den of pleasant aromas.

She scurried between the kitchen and the bedroom, dressing hurriedly, constantly checking the time on the travel clock next to the bed.

By the time the milk properly boiled, she had lined the bottom of a bowl with clumps of white bread torn from an unsliced loaf. It was her first attempt at making "goody" alone, but her mind's eye easily pictured her mother and grandmother carefully layering bread and sugar until the pile rose above the rim of the bowl. When she gently poured the steaming milk over it in a circular motion, the concoction plopped heavily and she mashed it around with a spoon. It would be ready to eat by the time she finished dressing. Already she felt soothed and less hungover. Not that goody was used much in Ireland to remedy the curse of drink, but it helped most ailments, real and imagined.

"You're a little bleary-eyed today. That homicide sergeant's working you too hard," Damon Harper said as

Sam watched him put finishing touches on the inside of the windshield.

He looked like a recruiting poster in his uniform. Tall, sandy haired and square shouldered. It occurred to her he would be even more striking in the navy blue of the Garda Siochana. When he spoke she thought he'd read her mind.

"It's not that I'm such a neat-nik, but the more you can see, the better police work you do," he said, standing back to look through his windshield from several angles.

She had pinned her hair close because she remembered from the other shift she had worked with him—a partial shift actually—that he drove with both front windows down.

"Even in the colder months?" she asked.

"In the colder months you wear a warmer jacket. You can't get a *feel* of your beat with windows up," he told her. "This is my office." He smiled when he said that.

At 2:45 P.M. they left the police lot and turned almost immediately onto Broadway. She was surprised when he turned east instead of west. The easy path to unit 511's beat, the streets adjacent Balboa Park, was north on Eleventh Street, which melded into the south end of the Cabrillo Freeway, or west from the station and north on Fifth Avenue. "Taking a different route to your beat, are you, Damon?"

"Got a different beat today."

"Oh?"

"When we rode last week you said you were researching a graduate paper on gangs, so I asked the watch commander if I could orient you tonight on my old beat in Southeast. We won't be taking calls. Just cruising. Showing you gang-banger territory."

"I don't know much about the Asian gangs or the Latino ones. But Crips and Pirus, I'll talk your ear off about them." Damon made an easy right-hand turn onto Thirtieth Street from Broadway and reduced his speed to fifteen miles per hour.

Since her arrival, patrol officers were the only people

Sam had witnessed driving slowly. The rest of the population, some in such huge cars, were forever rushing to and fro. "As if the hounds of hell were after them," she wrote her family.

"We're close to the set of the West Coast Crips," Damon said. "You probably already know, a set is like a ... oh, a territory a gang claims."

She watched small groups of black men standing on a parking lot next to a liquor store on the corner of Thirtieth Street and Imperial Avenue. Some were drinking out of bottles, only the necks of which protruded from small brown paper bags. "Are all of them Crips?"

"Nope."

"How do you tell one?"

"Crips have a look. Blue is their color, so you look for that. But see those guys with their hair wrapped in little twigs. That's Crip. And the chin whiskers to make 'em look bad. Hell, after a while you just know." He pulled to the curb and put the car in neutral. "They've only been out of bed a few hours. Just hanging out with their homeboys now. We'll be hearing from them tonight."

"How come you no longer work this beat?" It seemed like every car she saw had smoked windows, and she considered the uncertainty of night traffic stops.

"I got burned out. When I started working it, I thought only half the people were dirtbags. Then it got to eighty-twenty. After five years it became ninety-nine to one and it was time to go."

Rap music blared from a car stopped next to them. Two occupants, in their twenties, made peculiar faces at Sam as they gyrated to the rhythm of Public Enemy. "The people down here didn't change. I changed."

"Would you like to be a detective?"

"Sure, I'm ready. Maybe there's something in the wind. A friend of mine in personnel said some detective was asking if I'm married, asked other personal questions, too, so maybe they're looking at me."

He waved to someone on the corner. "You know what

cracks me up? Citizens I meet. They say, 'I'd like to be a detective. I think I'd be a good one.' They can't believe everybody starts in Patrol. Paying dues for a bunch of years learning the soul of this damn city. What makes it breathe and where it takes long easy breaths and where it's always huffing and puffing. When someone names a section of town, La Jolla, Kensington, Mission Beach, Paradise Hills, cops get a picture in their mind based on what the streets have taught them.''

As they cruised east on Market Street, under Interstate 15, past small businesses and intersecting residential streets, under the inland freeway, Interstate 805, Damon explained more about gangs.

At Forty-seventh Street he told her, ''Now you're in the heart of the Neighborhood Crips set. Big rivals of the West Coast Crips.'' He put both hands on top of the steering wheel and extended his arms. ''At night, the West Coast Crips may drive onto a Neighborhood Crips set, guns blazing, and shoot down any black kid on the sidewalk. If they hit a Crip, good. If a non–gang member gets it, well, the WC's say they should have known better than to be on the set after dark.'' Another patrol car cruised by slowly, and the man and woman cop nodded.

''They shoot up the sidewalks in your country, too, huh?'' Damon said.

''In the North, yes. When I was seven, there were thirty pub bombings in Ulster.''

''So what's the difference?''

''Wolfe Tone and Padraic Pearse died for a cause at least, and though I despise the ruthlessness of the IRA, the sorry souls at least believed in something.''

''There's no difference to me. Crips, Irish Republican Army, all a bunch of lawless assholes.''

Near Forty-third Street and Boston, a middle-aged black woman pulled weeds from a neatly tended garden on an otherwise run-down street. ''Your flowers are pretty, ma'am,'' Damon Harper yelled as they stopped in front of her house.

"Why, thank you, Officer."

"It takes some work, doesn't it?"

"Indeed it do." She came to the low-slung chain-link fence, and they chatted for a while.

"That's who I work for," he said as they drove away. "Not those fuckhead gang-bangers. That lady can't come out of her house at night, has to plan her life in daylight hours. Nothing I do out here is going to change that, and pardon my language."

"You don't have to worry about cussing. It's okay."

"It's not okay with me. Two years ago I cleaned up my mouth. Well, kind of cleaned it up. It happened real suddenly. I was in this cocktail lounge, and not a cop hangout, standing at the bar talking to a guy and this waitress taps me on the shoulder, says, 'Sir, please keep your language down. We've had complaints.' And I look over her shoulder and there's this white-haired old guy and his wife sitting at a table looking at me. I thought, who am I any more? That old couple could have been my mother and father. I left without finishing my drink, I was so embarrassed." He braked for a red light. "Sam Mulcahy, I'm telling you things I've never told anyone else."

"I'm complimented, Damon."

"See that kid there?" he said when they had driven again to the north side of the sector. Sam looked out at a much younger boy in a blue sweatshirt and black pants shuffling along the sidewalk. "He's a thirteen-year-old wannabe. Wants to be a Neighborhood Crip."

"How do you know that?"

"I just know. He idolizes the older guys, and they cuff him around and taunt him. 'Hey, Pee Wee. You ain't shit. What you ever done?' I'll tell you what he's gonna do one of these nights, Sam. He'll get his hands on a gun, clout a car and drive onto a Piru set and blast the first thing he sees on the sidewalk."

She shook her head in disbelief as Damon Harper checked his wristwatch. "Let me show you something else," he said. Making a series of turns, he pointed out a city bus slowing at a passenger bench. "You're going to see a man in his fifties wearing a brown ball cap get off that bus." A moment later the man stepped gingerly off the bus and limped toward Forty-fifth Street.

"That's Buster Morris. He's the daddy of that wannabe. Every day Mr. Morris rides the bus up to Naval Hospital and stands on his feet washing pots and pans. He lets his wife take the car. Mrs. Morris scrubs floors and cleans other people's toilets all day long."

"Lord in Heaven, you lasted five years here."

"That little shit is gonna break that old man's heart pretty soon."

At dark, they picked up barbecue and collard greens from Sister Lillian's, and Damon Harper selected a dark spot behind a row of warehouses to eat. "I caught a burglar this way once. We get to do police work while we eat." They spread the feast on the hood of the car and piled on extra napkins. "The engine block keeps dinner warm."

Sam was trying to decide what the collards tasted like when he said, "I've done all the talking. Now I'd like to hear about home. All about Garda S. C. Mulcahy."

"And just what would you want to be knowing?"

"Everything. About where you live. Why you're a cop."

"Oh my. Well, I was raised where my mother and father still live, in County Sligo. In a rural area called Templeboy. Sligo is in the west of the Republic, and quite backwards compared to most of the eastern coast. Good backwards. We were milk farmers, still are, and it was a wonderful, peaceful place to grow up."

"Near the ocean?"

"On our land, a stroll of two hundred meters would take you to the top of a bluff looking down upon the Atlantic. Quite turbulent it is there. And the house—it had a thatched roof when I was a child—has been in our family for over a hundred and fifty years." She closed her eyes. "Rows of blackthorn hedges, and we'd try not to scratch up our legs when we'd pick blackberries and mushrooms. Then salt the mushrooms and grill them on the fire. With eggs so fresh the hens had hardly missed them."

"Are you describing Ireland or paradise?" Damon Harper asked, watching her closely.

"There was a great deal of work to do. My father, God bless him, is a wonderful man but a bit of a backward one at that. A fine, wry sense of humor he has. I wouldn't say he could hold his own in the squad room, but with a bit of practice . . ." She smiled at the thought. "He's given in somewhat to the machine age, but once in a while he'll still hook the pony to the cart and let the cars on the road be damned while he carries milk cans to the creamery."

"Carts and ponies on the road. What a lifestyle. The Irish mystique."

"The question is, can it last?" Sam looked at the row of dark loading docks. "Where one group reveres leisure and neighborliness, the other favors advancing the economy. Which dents the old way. But I've gone on quite enough," she said, wiping sauce from her fingers.

"Almost," Damon said, gathering up food wrappers and bags. "Why the police? And what did your folks think about that?"

"When I was at TCD, that's Trinity College, Dublin—don't laugh now—as a sociology major, I did research and met many Gardas. And was keenly impressed by their professionalism. 'Tis a very respected job in Ireland. And very pensionable. When my mother and father learned there was to be a Ban Gardai in the family they were shocked at first, then proud."

" 'Ban Gardai' is Gaelic for . . . ?"

"Lady police. The old language will never be entirely forsaken, I hope. All street signs in the Republic are still written in both Gaelic and English." She opened the door to the passenger's side. "Actually, they did away with the term 'Ban Gardai' just last year, and now 'Garda' is used for both sexes.''

"What didn't you like about patrol work in Ireland?''

"Breaking up fights when drinkers get pissed up and make fools of themselves. Family disturbances and seeing the wee children who'll be the real sufferers of it all. And arresting intoxicated drivers was not enjoyable either. Did you know there is a heavier penalty for it in the evening than in daytime? The government's incentive for them to get on home. But you know, Damon, even being a Garda did not prepare me for the amount of violence and drugs I've seen here. I can't get over that lad you pointed out a bit ago, the one running up to a car at a signal light to make a dope sale. Didn't care that the world knew what he was doing.''

He started the engine and said, "Have you always been single?''

"Yes,'' she said, pleased that he asked. "I haven't had much time for relationships either. There was a lad went through the Garda college with me I cared a great deal for. But he was sent to County Mayo and I to Kerry. So that was that.''

She wondered whether Damon Harper would continue to ask her out. What if she were staying in America? Or he lived in Ireland? It was a pleasant thought.

"Is there no way out for these children?'' she asked as they passed a housing project with groups of teenagers scattered about. Some talked in hushed tones, others were animated, yelling over loud music. Several wore Chicago Bull jackets. Bloodred Piru colors she had learned.

"Unlikely. Take that wannabe I showed you. He sees his mother and father work their butts off for near minimum wage, then he looks at all those cool gang-bangers wearing two hundred dollar workout suits they ripped off when they drove a car through the window of a shop last night. Flashing big money from stick-ups or burglaries or dope deals. Fine Criplette girls hanging on their arm, wanting to smoke crack and lay down with them. Some kids get groomed. For prep schools, Dartmouth and Wall Street, but these kids—'' He interrupted himself when the radio crackled.

''National City's bringing drive-by victims to Paradise Valley Hospital,'' he translated for her. ''Let's go snoop.''

A few minutes later, when they crossed the border from San Diego into National City, radio advised the shooting had occurred in San Diego.

''So they drove their wounded twenty blocks and National City P.D. scooped them up,'' he said.

She heard the next transmission clearly. ''All units. Be advised additional victims en route Mercy.''

''But Mercy's a San Diego hospital. In Hillcrest,'' Sam said.

''That means a lot of caps got popped. We don't like to overload one emergency room.''

He turned into the emergency parking lot of Paradise Valley Hospital. She saw several other police cars, some with lights flashing.

''These two hospitals are like M.A.S.H. units,'' he said.

''Sure, and I may see Hawkeye and Trapper themselves then.''

She saw a National City officer hurrying to the parking lot entrance carrying a shotgun at port arms. ''We seal off the hospital, limit access,'' Damon Harper said. ''In case anybody wants to carry the fight here. We want to make the hospital staff feel better.''

''What have you got, Barry?'' Damon Harper asked a National City officer when they entered the E.R.

''Haven't put it together yet. The answers are up on San Diego's end. We've got two Bloods here. One in bad shape and one superficial. I stopped them for speed. Two bailed and these two were laying on the floorboard bleeding.''

''DOASTW,'' a young black nurse with blood stains on her smock told Damon Harper. ''DOASTW, and the other one has a hole through his hand. Too bad it's not his head," she whispered.

"Dead-On-Arrival-Stayed-That-Way," he explained to Sam as they greeted a San Diego uniformed sergeant coming in. "Can't keep crime down since I left, huh, Sarge?"

"Shit, only thing's changed since you went up to Wussytown is nobody sells as much coffee and doughnuts. Your partner was dead weight," the sergeant told Sam after they had been introduced.

"What happened on Duval Street?" Damon Harper asked.

"Neighborhood Crips sitting around kickin' it on the steps. Grand Am with just a driver showing cruises by. Couple minutes later it comes back full of 5/9 Brim Piru and they open up. But the N.C.'s were ready for them. Three wounded Crips went to Twenty-five and K. Those Pirus sure killed the front door of the house though."

After a bathroom call they walked across the lot toward their car. Sam heard footsteps and shouting behind them.

"Stop that motherfucker, Damon!"

A stocky black man wearing a red bandanna was racing from the building. A National City officer struggled with another man. Damon Harper lunged and collided with the fleeing figure, which only slowed him as Harper stumbled to the pavement.

Sam was already gaining on the black man when Damon Harper yelled, "Let him go, Sam." A minute later Sam and the Piru dodged traffic on Euclid Avenue and started running west on Ninth Street. She brought him down in the middle of the street with a perfectly timed tackle, then she hung on as the momentum rolled them to the far curb. Her face scraped the asphalt, and she feared the car with screeching tires would hit her as they grappled. The man was strong but his breathing told her he was fatigued, and when a uniformed officer crashed a nightstick over his head Sam felt him go limp, blood from his wound squirting onto her face.

She heard handcuffs clicking and saw the man thrown

roughly across the hood of the police car. From down the block she watched Damon Harper half run, half limp to her as a second police unit arrived.

"I don't believe you did that," he yelled. "Jesus, look at your face."

"What did he do?" she wanted to know, catching her breath.

"Was just being an asshole," the National City officer said. "Just wanted to bust in and see his dead asshole friend. We'll book him for interfering."

When Sam came out of the bathroom near the emergency room, Damon Harper examined her face. "I still think you should have it looked at. We're right here."

"It was mostly his blood and my lip doesn't need stitches, so let's get out of here."

"I *still* don't believe you did that," he said when they were back in southeast San Diego. "You can partner with me any time."

When two young men on a corner saw the patrol car, they shook their fists, then formed the letter *C* for Crip with their thumb and forefinger.

"Tell me something," Damon Harper said. "How did a boy from Akron and a girl from the land of blackthorn hedges ever end up in this shithole?" He didn't wait for an answer. "How about a drink after work?"

"You're on," she answered softly, using a Kleenex to blot blood from her lip. "You're on."

Sixteen

"Times like this, I bet you wish Mom was here," Jenny said. She was on the sofa, legs curled under, with a copy of *Newsweek* next to her. Dowling thought she looked like a child, lost in the ankle-length lavender robe. He'd seen the magazine cover when she'd brought it home, a kaleidoscope of art work with large red block print spelling TEENAGERS IN TROUBLE. "Withdrawn" was the word he would have used to describe her in the four days since she had told him she was pregnant.

"It's funny," he said, "I look at you sitting there and I don't think of you as a teenager in trouble. I'll read that article, and I'll expect to see wandering, forlorn kids who . . . this will sound crazy now but, you're my daughter. You're not a kid in that magazine. This is our *home*. It's a nice, warm place to live. We're safe here." He sat next to her. "I told you this would sound crazy, it's just, things running through my head all the time. See, we're going to handle this. You said this morning we'd talk again when you'd thought more. And this isn't pressure about talking. I just want you to know I'm here."

Jenny took his hand and looked at it. "Thanks, Pop." He thought she was going to cry. "I've been thinking about Mom a lot. Wondering what she'd think. What she'd do."

"The first thing she'd do is say, 'I love you, Jenny.'

Then she'd come up with those magical solutions only she could come up with. I could never anticipate her. She just always got it done.'' He put both arms on the back of the sofa. "When I became the problem, she ran out of magic.''

"Do you miss her just awful?''

He nodded. "There's this old guy in group. Older than me anyway, and his wife committed suicide. And he said, 'My wife didn't die when she jumped off the bridge. Everything I loved about her—her laugh, her love of people, her humor—all of that died long before that day.' '' Dowling got up and started pacing. "I chewed on that for a long time, and I can't say the same about Helene. I was still in love with her right to the end, I was just too dumb to know it.''

He sat down next to her again. "Jeez, I'm a master of timing. I've got a . . .'' He took a deep breath. "I've got a date tonight. In about an hour. And I've been trying to tell you about it. Isn't that something? We're having a discussion about a very serious subject, and I can't even get up the nerve to tell you about a little old date.'' He watched her carefully.

"Who is this 'date' with?'' she asked without looking at him.

"With a doctor.''

"Is he cute?''

"Oh, come on Jenny.'' He was pacing again. "How can you be joking when your father's going out with someone other than your mother?''

"Looking at your face, somebody'd think you were going to the dentist, not on a date. It's okay. Tell me about it.''

So he did.

"Actually then, this is the *third* date,'' Jenny said. "A dinner at Tom Ham's, then the ballgame and now she's having you over for dinner.'' She smiled at him and squeezed his hand. "I wondered if you'd ever see anyone.

In a way I wanted you to and in another way I didn't. It
seems strange. But I'm glad.''

"You amaze me, Jenny. Just like your mother always
amazed me.''

Dowling had no difficulty finding Angela Lord's house,
though it was out of the way, a small redwood bungalow
tucked among a half dozen unpretentious others, secluded
among layers of green leaves and red bougainvillea vines
behind the tiny state historical park in Old Town. Dowling
loved Old Town, had worked it as a young patrol officer
in the sixties, then watched the city carefully develop the
area. But not into the trendy array of tourist shops and
made-over buildings that were so popular across the country. As a concession to visitor's demands for Mexican
food, the Bazaar del Mundo, with a few stores sprinkled
between restaurants, had sprung up. But Old Town, where
San Diego began in the middle 1800s, before the railroad
replaced the overland stage, before no-nonsense Joseph
Coyne gave up gold mining to become San Diego's first
chief of police, was still an interesting place to Dowling,
nestled out of sight but across the highway from the Marine Recruit Depot and directly beneath prestigious Mission Hills, with its luxury homes and the grassy sloped
hills of Presidio Park. There were still relatively few
homes in Old Town, and the majority were lower income.
No prosperous plaintiff lawyers or captains of industry
hosted junior league costume balls or political fund-raisers
in the heart of Dowling's old beat.

The rustic interior of Angela's small, two-bedroom cot-
tage was furnished colonial style.

"I lived at Crown Point Shores first, then got that out
of my system and found this old place by accident. Being
five minutes from the hospital is a huge plus.'' Angela
wore a navy blue dress with a string of pearls around the
high neckline. Dowling thought she sounded apologetic
when she told him she had spent "a little money'' on the
interior.

"There's the bar, such as it is." She pointed to a round, Ethan Allen maple end table. A bottle of gin, a bottle of bourbon and Noilly Prat vermouth were on a tray next to glasses and an ice bucket. "Shows what a social butterfly I am."

"Are you on call tonight?" Dowling asked.

"No. A dry martini, please, if you know how to make them." She disappeared into the kitchen before finishing the sentence.

"Do I ever," he answered.

She was at the doorway quickly. "*Not* dry like flash the cork over it. Just dry."

He picked up the bottle of Beefeater. No chic new label like Bombay Sapphire for Angela Kingsbury Lord of the Philadelphia Main Line. Old reliable Beefeater that old Vincent Dowling had indeed acquired a taste for. He and gin had helped each other get into trouble a few times, and after some hesitation he opted for the bourbon.

"Wild Turkey," he said, admiring the bottle. "Say, you go first class when you do entertain."

"You'll notice it's unopened," she called. "I bought that because you drank bourbon at Tom Ham's. You remember. You were having an awful time trying to drink slowly like a gentleman."

"What a diagnostician you must be, Doctor."

"Were you wearing, carrying—what's the word—a gun at dinner that night?" She was still talking from the kitchen.

He was in the process of sniffing the Beefeaters and the question caught him by surprise. Helene had asked him the same question on their second or third date.

"Yes."

"I just wondered. I didn't think of it at the restaurant. How about when you met me at the hospital and we went to the Padres game?"

"Yep."

"How about tonight?"

"It's in the trunk of the car."

"Why carry it those nights and put it in the car to-night?"

"I didn't figure anybody was going to pull a stick-up in your house. I can go out and get it."

"You can be an ass. Have you had your best foot forward, is that it?"

He carried the drinks to the kitchen door. "Am I allowed in here?"

"Sure, all you'll find is some Price Club lasagna heating up and Safeway salad in those cartons on the bottom shelf of the fridge." She was slicing thick pieces of sourdough bread. When he handed her the martini they clinked glasses.

"Why did you ask about the gun, Angela?"

"I don't even know. Is carrying it required?"

"It was when I came on. Now it's optional."

"But you're a dinosaur?"

"I'm a cop." He sipped his bourbon. "Is your drink okay?"

She gave him a thumbs-up, sprinkled parmesan cheese onto the bread from a container, then placed plastic wrap over it. The kitchen was too small to do anything but cook in. Three blue and white Delft china plates were hung in a vertical row on one wall and an oversize garden window, a *huge* garden window, looked out on a small flood-lit garden of chrysanthemums, gladiolus and agapanthus.

"That's my vice," Angela said when she saw him at the window.

"They're beautiful. Do you forget about work when you're out there?"

"I forget about everything when I'm out there."

The aroma of the Italian food took him back twenty-eight years. To Angelo's. Where he had posed as a waiter in a silly but successful attempt to meet his wife-to-be. Helene and he had frequented the little restaurant until Angelo became infirm and returned to Sicily to die.

"Earth to Sergeant Dowling," he heard Angela say. "Were you at work?"

"No, I just drifted into another world for a minute," he said as they walked into the living room. A circular plate of cheese and crackers, sliced carrots, celery, broccoli, radishes and a vegetable dip covered half of the table between their chairs. Soft classical piano flowed from speakers suspended in nets from diagonal corners of the room. He wondered if she noticed how slowly he was drinking his bourbon. They talked for a while, then he blurted it out.

"I smoke. Just started again. Could I excuse myself for a minute and go out on the front deck?"

She just looked at him.

"You don't have to give me a doctor lecture. Hell, I've seen lungs at autopsies looking like footballs from Harvard-Yale in the 1890s."

When he returned she had made them a second drink. She swirled her olive and rested her chin on the knuckles of her other hand. "The first night we went out, you talked about 'balance' in my profession. Losing a life, saving a life and so forth."

Dowling nodded.

"Then when we were leaving the ballpark you asked me about the life flight trauma from the construction accident, and I said, 'Oh, he jumped in the box.' "

"Meaning the casket. I remember," he said.

"My God, Vincent. If I had dreamed when I was interning that I would have said that to you, my idealistic little psyche would have been fractured."

"You've said things like that before. You've been in the business a while."

"Only to physicians have I said them before. *That's* the difference."

"I'm complimented you loosened up with me, then." He patted her hand, aware it was the first time they had ever touched. "I'll get more ice."

As Rudolf Serkin made the transition from the "Moonlight'' Sonata to the ''Pathétique,'' Dowling stood in the kitchen doorway and mimicked an overhead page. ''Doctor Lord. Calling Doctor Lord.'' When she looked up, he was displaying a package of Benson & Hedges filter tip cigarettes. ''You've had a break-in. The burglar left these stashed behind your toaster.''

He watched her sigh. ''In the morning I'll have the lab boys dust them for prints,'' he said.

''I was *going* to tell you.''

''Oh. The old 'I was going to tell you' trick.''

They stood on the deck and smoked, listening to crickets and faint traffic noise in the September night. He told her about his daughter's pregnancy and their discussions, then felt a twinge of guilt for betraying Jenny's confidence.

''It's natural that she's being very protective of Jason. She still thinks he's wonderful,'' she said.

''The girl is seventeen years old. She has her life before her.''

''How profound.''

''What?'' Dowling said.

''What exactly do you mean 'her life before her?' And please remember, whatever is being said to you now is uttered by a childless woman who has never been married or pregnant.''

''I don't know what I meant by that. Verbiage. I'm so goddamned upset and confused. This abortion versus prolife has never been an issue with me. I've never let it. I work murders and I'm too busy to listen to a bunch of extremists on both sides yelling into microphones and marching in the street. But a part of me is bothered by abortion as birth control, and it's not a religious thing with me. But if that's what she wants, I'll drive her to the doctor. It'll break my heart, Angela, but . . . .''

''Stop right there,'' she said. ''Why will it break your heart?''

Dowling hesitated. ''I guess . . . because this life is inside *my* daughter. Not some stranger who's a test case for the courts.''

''Vincent, does Jenny have to spend the rest of her life paying for one mistake she made when she was seventeen?''

Dowling looked at her for a long time. ''Whatever call she makes, the decision will be with her the rest of her life.''

They smoked in silence for a few minutes.

''I'm so out of touch,'' Dowling said, after they'd gone inside. ''A couple of months ago I find a video in her room. 'Buns of Steel' it's labeled. I figure it's a porno flick and I'm getting ready to land on her. You know what it was?''

Angela pointed to the entertainment center. ''A copy is on the second shelf with my other aerobic tapes.'' She leaned forward in her chair. ''If the decision turns out to be an abortion, give me a call. I'd want to refer you to the most competent physician. By the way, may I ask what your son's take is?''

Dowling got up and walked to the window. ''He said it's okay to give her guidance. Okay to tell her what I think. But he admonished me about forcing my will on her. He said, 'Jenny's bright. To help her make the call that's going to have the best odds of being right for her, she needs input and love and support.' ''

''It sounds like you have *two* bright children, Vincent. It's so difficult either way. Let's paint the ideal picture with her keeping the baby. Presuming Jason's out of it. Jenny lives at home, goes to UCSD and the two of you manage quite well. There will be rough spots socially with men on the campus. 'Oh, there's that Jennifer Dowling. She's really nice. Oh yeah. She's got the two-year-old, huh?' And some of those meatheads will say she must be an easy score. A hell-with-it-all woman. But say things go well, commencement time rolls around and Jenny's holding a degree and a four-year-old child and the key to her own condo and a job.'' Angela took a sip. ''Then what? Would she like a father for her child? What percentage of the good men out there want to take on a kid? How lucky does Jenny have to be, given all the losers out there? No recommendations here, Vincent. I'm saying these things so you hear another voice."

"You're a good friend, Angela Lord."

"A hungry friend. Let's eat."

Everything tasted good, and after they had eaten for a while she asked about the rape series and he brought her up to date. He told her how demoralized they'd been after the Curtis Forman investigation and how two other suspects had been cleared.

"One guy, a parolee for rape out of Modesto, works for an auto parts house right in the crime area. He was a perfect physical. I mean *perfect* physical. But he took a header on a motorcycle three months ago and his right foot doesn't work any more. It's can't be him because our rapist runs like a gazelle."

Dowling reached for more cheese bread. "Another guy looked almost as good. And wouldn't talk to us, which always makes you get more interested. Turns out he was job hunting up in Coeur d'Alene late afternoon of the night Choice McGraw gets it. Larry Shea spent two days on the alibi. Even with an hour time difference there was no way he pulled that job.

"What do you know about WOW?" he asked as they cleared dishes.

"Women of Will? A splinter group of an extremist's organization that disbanded. Real hardheads. Usually loud and wrong. Why?"

"They've been poking around my investigation. I'm just curious about them." He stacked plates next to the sink. "Remember how upset you were? Saying 'jumped in the box' to an outsider? Now I'm going to surprise myself and tell you something. After we pour some 7-Eleven coffee, which will taste just fine with me by the way," Dowling said, causing her to shake a fist at him.

On the deck, they smoked and drank from pewter cups.

"Having to consider the possibility that my suspect is a cop, I've been doing some highly confidential, low-profile snoopy poop investigation. The people working Internal Affairs may get used to it, but I never will." He stopped talking and watched a cat spring from the ivy onto a rail of the deck.

"You have to do it because of the 'choke' hold and . . . ?" Angela said.

"And the physical. Well-built—handsome—athletic."

"My, my. Aren't we modest?"

This time *he* shook his fist. "You ought to go to Patrol lineup sometime. See what I mean."

"I'm not sure my feminine heart could take it."

"Why are you being a butthead? Because I made fun of your coffee?"

"Because you need loosening up," she said, taking a deep drag on the cigarette. "Are you still waking up at three A.M?"

Dowling nodded. "I used to keep a pencil and pad and a little penlight on the nightstand. Now I use a microcassette recorder."

"Finish telling me about your police officer investigation. How do you do it?"

He butted his Camel. "Make a list of all male cops that live or work in the crime scene area. Go from there and eliminate. I can't tell you how many hours I've spent listening to communications tapes. Verifying they were in fact where their daily journal says they were when our crimes occurred."

"Because the journal is filled out by the officer himself?"

"Yeah. To look department wide isn't reasonable given what we *don't* have. There's a few more to check out. After that . . . I don't know what to do. Stacy should have given this series to someone else. Probably would have it solved by now."

"Am I actually hearing this from the Sherlock Holmes of the San Diego Police Department?"

"You really are being a butthead."

"I don't usually drink three martinis. It's getting chilly."

Dowling left her in the living room, went to the refrigerator and removed the large paper sack he had brought with him. Ten minutes later, he put a plate of chocolate cake for each of them on the table. Individual cakes actually, rounded at the top and about the size and shape of an upside-down coffee cup. A puddle of chocolate sauce, not visible, was under each cake, which was surrounded by glazed syrup. A dollop of whipped cream with a bay leaf protruding hugged one side of the cake.

"Thank you for bringing the desert, kind sir." She broke into it with her fork. "And such a lovely looking one at that."

"My humble pleasure, madam."

"This is *really* good, Vincent. It has chocolate liquid oozing around in the center."

He wiped his mouth with a napkin. "That's ganache. A frozen plug of it goes into the cake batter, then when the cake bakes the ganache melts."

"Where is it from?"

"The ganache?" he said.

"The desert. Where did you buy it?"

"When someone is kind enough to invite you for dinner, you make the desert."

She looked up quickly, believing and disbelieving at the same time. "*You* baked *this*?"

"I did, and I'm glad you like it."

Angela poured more coffee. "I taste almonds."

"Some of the flour is almond flour."

"Now *that* you buy at a specialty shop," she said.

"You can. I made this almond flour, though."

"You made the almond flour." It was a statement. "Hmmm, the ganache is sinful."

Dowling had made the ganache using heavy cream and semisweet chocolate. When he made the cake batter, he refrigerated it in pastry bags, eventually pouring it into ramekins, using one of the ovenproof porcelain molds for each of the cakes. He believed the proper placement of the collar of parchment paper into the mold was as important as the careful mixing of the batter.

"The chocolate has an exceptionally good taste," she said.

"Valrhona chocolate."

"You *buy* that?"

"I did this time."

She looked at him for a long moment. "So you make chocolate, too?"

"Uh-huh, sometimes. I'm very particular when I do."

"Why doesn't that surprise me?"

When they finished and returned to the easy chairs, she said, "I'd like to risk one more question. That lovely little sauce on the plate around the bottom of the cake?"

"That's the easy part. Water, sugar, a vanilla bean and bay leaves."

Dowling had considered Angela Lord less than attractive at first, and found it interesting that his view had shifted so quickly in a few short weeks. Perhaps it had something to do with the way she carried herself. Or her smile. Or the ease with which they talked and shared their thoughts, comfortable and amusing give-and-take. A few hours ago he was nervous, but now he was totally relaxed. The evening had been wonderful, and he felt sorry it was ending.

He stood at the door, navy blue jacket slung over his shoulder when they kissed. Not a long kiss, he said to himself during the drive to Point Loma. A sweet kiss though, and the memory of her lips on his made him giddy. This Angela Lord was an exceptional woman, and he wished there were plans to see her again tomorrow. It was too early to be thinking long range he said twice as he tapped his fingers on the steering wheel, but still . . .

The next evening he hurried home from work and was glad to find Jenny playing a Scott Joplin rag on the old upright grand piano. Most of the way along Harbor Drive he had rehearsed what he was going to say. When she finished playing he began his serious pacing from the front door end of the living room to the fireplace end.

"You told me you weren't 'wishing' to get pregnant, therefore you have this decision to make. Does your getting caught by . . . surprise make your choice detached? Or dispassionate? I don't think so.

"You have your baby or you have an abortion. Whichever you decide, I'm with you." He leaned on the mantle. "People make decisions early in their life and sometimes it haunts them forever. They're never exactly the same people again." He avoided looking at her. "I tucked you in when I got home last night and you had this wonderful, peaceful look on your face. I want to make sure you realize that your brother and I and everyone who truly loves you will help you hold on to that look."

He loosened his tie. "Two years ago, if you'd asked me what my goal in life was, I'd of said, 'to be the best homicide detective ever.' I wish my answer would have been, 'to be the best husband and father I can be.' The trouble is, for me, it's too late for either. So you take your time deciding. A life of second-guessing is hell, Jenny."

She got up and walked to him. "I've thought a lot about this. My decision will impact the rest of my life, I know that, and I'll have more hard choices in the future. But . . . I've decided to keep my baby."

⚉ Seventeen

Dowling wanted to hurl the can of Diet Pepsi through his television screen. He shouted obscenities and was glad Jenny had gone to bed. Rachel Tiffany seemed to be looking right at him, and the goddamn reporters were tossing lollipop questions at her. The banner behind her was almost as big as she was, WOMEN OF WILL emblazoned across it, and her entourage in the audience wore blue and gold WOW pins and carried gaudy placards.

"Have you met with the chief investigator, Ms. Tiffany?"

"If you could call it a meeting. Sergeant Vincent Dowling was as disinterested in talking to me as he appears to be in solving these brutal attacks on woman who dare to walk the streets of 'America's Finest City.' " Long blond hair swayed as she turned to face a camera zooming in from her left side.

It sure hadn't been a scheduled meeting. The skinny little shit had raised such a ruckus at the lobby reception desk that administration flat ordered him to sit down with her. She was a hard-looking forty, Dowling thought as they studied each other across his desk. He suspected there was no Mr. Tiffany. Only flashes of their conversation stuck in his mind.

"*I* have *liaisoned with women's organizations. The Rape Crisis Center.*"

"Well-intended group. Nonaggressive. You probably got along quite well with them. . . . If men were being victimized, more than four detectives would be assigned to the case. . . ."

Stacy had walked by the desk once and raised eyebrows when Dowling's voice got loud.

"Whether I have a wife or daughter is none of your business. . . ."

Watching Tiffany's eyes scan his desk, he was glad he had turned all of the reports upside down before she was admitted to the fourth floor. He almost welcomed the break when Stacy motioned him away from the desk for a few minutes to calm him down. Returning to Rachel Tiffany, he'd felt his neck getting red.

"I don't know when we'll solve the case. We're doing everything I know how to do, lady. And I don't know what good the case number assigned to the investigation will do you, but you can have it: 94-6387."

Now he felt himself getting even angrier as Rachel Tiffany told the reporters, "I invited Sergeant Dowling to attend the press conference. He apparently doesn't work at night."

What happened next stunned him. Rachel Tiffany held up the artist's conception of the man Holly Novikoff had described for him. One of the drawings that had been on Dowling's desk that afternoon. The drawings that had been unlabeled, save for "94-6387" scrawled in his writing on the lower left hand corner.

"We implore the citizens of this community to call Sergeant Dowling at 531-2284 if they have seen this man. In the morning I am meeting with the mayor, and she has promised full cooperation in establishing the formation of a county-wide task force to solve these heinous crimes."

"It doesn't look at all like me," Dowling's telephone friend told him the next morning. "Oh, maybe a little bit around the eyes. But the hair and the mouth . . . no way."

"I'm through talking to you," Dowling said, having

decided on the new tactic. "You're a lulu bird. Fly away and bother someone else." There was silence; then he thought he heard muffled sobs.

"What can I do to prove I'm your killer?"

"Answer my questions. You remember them."

"Okay, okay. I'm not afraid of getting AIDS. I don't wear condoms because I want those women to procreate with my seed. Genetically I believe—"

"Good-bye, my friend. You just flunked the acid test."

"Put it behind you," Stacy counseled Dowling later. "You've handled bigger crises than Rachel Tiffany. The chief says, for now, he can hold the mayor off on a task force. He says, 'Tell Dowling to solve the case. I can't ride much more heat.'"

"Here's three shoe boxes," Dowling told Sam later. "Calls are going to start pouring in on the blasted composite. Mark the boxes 'hot leads,' 'medium leads' and 'cold leads.' The chief set up a special phone number as a concession to city hall." He picked up one of the boxes. "The important thing is *no* lead gets trashed. No matter how far-out it looks."

"I understand. Shea told me about the lady in the bay," Sam said.

The lady, what was left of her, was in a green plastic trash bag. Arms and legs never were recovered. The homicide team working the case had been told by the coroner the unidentified lady was between twenty and thirty years old. So they scrapped all phone-ins on missing women over forty-five. A reexamination three weeks later put the age closer to fifty, the trashed leads were not retrievable and the case had gone unsolved.

"Shea will work with you on sorting leads," Dowling told her. "Larry's been through this and you've got good instincts. But I want to see *every* one that goes in the hot box."

Gus Denver had been assigned from the start to keep in contact with the victims and be a liaison with the department's Crisis Intervention Team, formed to assist victims and witnesses of traumatic incidents. Annabelle Dominguez and Adrienne Roe bawled him out for not having been shown the suspect sketch before it appeared on television. Neither could say it was or wasn't him when they looked at it closely. Holly Novikoff and Rene Sheffield were keeping to themselves, and Choice McGraw was not easy to keep track of.

"You fuckers pay a lot of attention to a girl. I appreciate that," she'd told Gus.

Suspect sightings were reported from Oceanside, the home of the marine base at Camp Pendleton thirty miles to the north, to Carrizo Gorge Road, sixty miles east near the San Diego–Imperial County border where a shifty-eyed hitchhiker was seen urinating on the side of the road.

The team paid close attention to call-ins involving men in the area of the crimes, but surprisingly few East San Diego leads came in. In fifteen years, Dowling could remember few cases actually solved by publicizing a composite photograph.

He prayed something would pop for them. If so, he could relax about the specter of a county-wide task force screwing over his investigation. He had the best homicide team he could ask for. They needed to catch a break.

A few nights later, while Dowling half concentrated on a PBS feature about national parks, a group of young women in an apartment building at First and Walnut kept looking at the clock. The guest of honor was late, and her friends kept telling each other, "Annie Richards is always on time. *Always*."

◈ Eighteen

God's little gift to homicide detectives, Dowling thought to himself as he felt the stiffness settling in the musculature of Annie Richard's jaw. The process of death had already affected the muscle protoplasm, alkaline being hustled out and replaced by lactic acid. Rigor mortis had started where Dowling's fingers probed the face and within hours would work its way downward to the lower extremities. The wonder, the gift, was that it disappeared in the same order. Were it otherwise, if rigor left the body starting in the *feet*, and they found a corpse half enveloped, who would know for certain if they were dealing with the onset or disappearance of the phenomenon? It was one of the tools so helpful in establishing an approximate time of death.

Not that this little piece of medical detective work even mattered tonight. Plenty of other evidence convinced Dowling that the blond-haired, blue-eyed, twenty-three-year-old had taken her final breath in his world at about eight P.M. on September's twenty-eighth day.

He remained crouched, casting his eyes over every inch of the body. The red sweater and bra were around her neck, half covering the face and concealing fingernail marks on the throat, marks they would later closely examine and photograph on an impersonal stainless steel table at the morgue.

Peculiarly, he imagined her romping in warm, white sand at Mission Beach, playing volleyball, because a golden California tan was defined by bathing suit outlines over her breasts and pubic area. In the early years of homicide work Dowling had not allowed himself such musings. It was becoming harder and harder to be clinical.

One white tennis shoe lay several feet from the body, at the base of a tall yellow hibiscus bush. Her blue jeans had been pulled entirely free of her left leg, and he surmised the shoe must have been forced off in haste, allowing the legs to be spread. The waistband of the jeans rested on the smooth calf of the right leg. Larry Shea's crime scene description would record the heels as being twenty-one inches apart.

Joy Larson had met death in her garage. Annie Richards lay on damp earth, her head a foot away from the foundation of a house, only partly secluded from the sidewalk by a row of flowering bushes. Dowling carefully studied her again before getting up. Photographs could never duplicate the calamity before him. If he was going to catch this sadistic motherfucker, rally himself and his team, work this case at the expense of his increasingly complicated personal life, he needed to burn deeply into the recesses of his brain the image of life's final cunning on Annie Richards.

In the living room of the apartment, Dowling thanked the shock factor for the ability of family and friends to function between sobs, to piece together for him the events that had led his victim to the front yard on Walnut Avenue when she should have been kicking off her bachelorette party.

"She was due here at eight," one of the bridesmaids explained. "On Wednesdays, she volunteers at the Community Center for two hours. Tutors adults who can't read. We didn't start making phone calls until nine." The woman stopped to wipe her eyes. "The two limos got here at nine. We had dinner reservations at El Torito and . . . then, you know . . . barhopping." She put her head in her hands. "Tell me this didn't really happen, Sergeant."

"While they were calling hospitals, I checked the Community Center," Annie Richard's fiancé told Gus Denver. "Then I traced the route here a couple of times. I never thought to look down the block for her car. Who would ever think she'd parked and—?" He looked to Gus for an answer. "When I found the car I started running down the sidewalk calling her name. That's when the neighbor came out of his house."

The short round man mopped his brow and kept shaking his head as he talked to Sam Mulcahy. "It has to have been around eight. I took the dog out and saw the clothes bag and the shopping bag on the sidewalk in front of the house. Asked myself who in hell would drop that and leave it laying. I knocked on my neighbor's door. They didn't know anything. So I took it inside."

Sam lightly touched the clear hanging bag with the red silk dress. She opened the shopping bag and found a strapless bra, a silver chain and matching earrings, makeup, hair brush and hair spray.

"Then at eleven—I know it was eleven because I go to bed at eleven every work night—at eleven, I hear this fellow outside yelling somebody's name. I go out and . . . this is awful, I go out and I show him the bags. Then we start looking. The fellow found her there on the ground. Right under my bedroom window. If we hadn't found her, I'd have slept all night and that girl . . . My God," he said, "they were getting married Saturday."

"I don't care that it's one-thirty in the morning," Dowling told them as they stood under a streetlight. "Start banging on doors. You tell 'em there's been a murder in the neighborhood, they'll shake the sleep out of their eyes." He assigned Gus and Sam to team up. "Patrol is handling north of Walnut. You two go south. Hit Upas and Thorn. Go all the way to Third Avenue. We can't keep striking out. *Somebody has to have seen something.*"

Dowling walked the block and a half back to the scene. The coroner had left with Annie Richards, but Larry Shea and lab personnel were working under floodlights. The area would be cordoned off and guarded until Shea and the lab returned for a daylight examination.

Dowling crushed his cigarette out on the street, then put the butt in a piece of notebook paper, which he folded tightly and put in his pocket. He walked the perimeter with his hands in his pockets. Seven cases and nothing at the scene to positively connect to their suspect. He had stopped hoping for semen from the vaginal swabs.

"We can't even buy a shoe impression," Shea moaned. "There are drag marks from her heels through the grass, but you saw how only her upper body was on the dirt. Our suspect only stepped on grass."

"Pure bad luck," Dowling said. "The son of a bitch didn't plan it that way. It just happened." He looked around. All but one or two of the curious had returned to their homes. "By the time they perfect this fingerprint on skin stuff you and I will be long retired."

An hour later he hurried to meet Gus and Sam, who had radioed for a meet. When they piled into Dowling's car at Third and Thorn, Gus was rubbing his hands together.

"Sarge, we might have caught our break this time. That alley right there," Gus said pointing. "Mr. Van Cleave's garage is right on the alley, two houses up from Walnut. He was up on top of the garage with a mechanic's light, worked from dinner to darkness trimming the damn hedges that had grown higher than his garage."

"Tell me something good," Dowling pleaded.

"Mr. Van Cleave noticed a car come down the alley," Sam said. "Just glanced at it, he did. But then, a few minutes later the same car comes back around with its lights out."

"Going the same direction?" Dowling asked.

"Aye. And *parks* in the alley twenty-four feet from the sidewalk of Walnut.

"So this time, Mr. Van Cleave moves over to that side of his roof to take a better look. He looked at the car a couple of times in the next five or ten minutes. Trim some hedge. Look at the car. Trim some hedge. Look at the car. He can't say anybody did or didn't get in or out. The angle wouldn't let him see somebody sitting in it," Gus explained.

"But," Sam added, "fifteen, twenty minutes later the car was gone."

"How solid is his time element?" Dowling asked.

"You'll like this." Gus said. "Eight o'clock. He knows because he was going in the house to see *Unsolved Mysteries* on TV. Never misses that show."

"Tell me he got a license number," Dowling said, closing his eyes.

Sam waved smoke from their cigarettes out of her eyes. "He used his mechanic's light to try and get a license number, but there was no plate. Mind you now, he only saw the rear of the car."

"Tell me something good," Dowling said again.

"There was an advertising placard where the rear plate would be. Like when you've bought a new car and you're waiting for the new plates from DMV," Gus said quickly. "It said 'Mission Bell Honda—San Diego.' "

"Physical?" Dowling asked.

Gus shook his head. "Smooth dry alley. No way to pick up tire impressions. We cordoned it off, though."

Dowling half turned in his seat. "And does Mr. Van Cleave tell us what kind of car it is? Independent of what the placard said."

"Says it's a light-colored Honda sedan. Looked new. Can't say if it's a two-door or a four-door," Sam said. "But definitely not a hatchback."

"This guy's reliable, Sarge," Gus added. "Seems he lived up in Shasta County years ago. Became a town hero for taking down a suspicious license plate that let the sheriff cancel a bunch of burglaries. Got his picture in the local paper and all. Says 'I've copied down a lot of plate numbers since but never hit again.' I think the guy saw what he says he saw."

Dowling raised his hand. "Don't say anything. Let me think." He got out and walked around the car several times, feeling good. If the Honda hadn't been there for a legitimate reason, this was their suspect. The alley was only two hundred feet from where Annie Richards had dropped her red silk dress.

"Everybody goes home and gets three hours of sleep," Dowling said when he'd gathered the team together. "In the morning, Shea takes the crime scene again. I'm going to Mission Bell Honda, and the two of you are going to flat kill that neighborhood. Every house. Does that Honda belong there? Did some kid drop in for a quick hello to his folks? Somebody run in and pick up a package? Are we talking about a guy visiting a married girlfriend and he's afraid to park on the street?"

"You got it," Gus said excitedly.

"It will depress the shit out of me if that car belongs there," Dowling said. "But we have to know."

It was hard for him to think of anything that tasted better than corn tortillas from El Indio. Worth the wait in the long take-out line and worth jockeying for a space in the undersized parking lot bordering Kettner Boulevard. The thin tortillas were still warm, and he had eaten three on the short drive home. His appetite hadn't been dulled because at dinner he put away two cheese enchiladas, a chile relleno and more frijoles and rice than he needed to. His wife just picked at her food, all the while holding the fussy kid over her shoulder with one arm. At least it gave him an excuse not to carry on a dumb conversation while he was enjoying his dinner. It boggled his mind how they could have such good sex together, then watch everything fall apart the first step out of the bedroom. She didn't appreciate him any more than his bitch boss did. No wonder he was half angry all of the time.

Working in the yard relaxed him a little, but he looked down and was disgusted when he saw how much of the redwood stain had flicked off the brush onto his bare foot.

The contractor had skinned him on the price of the twelve-foot-by-twelve-foot deck outside their bedroom, then compounded it by sending out a blond whore with a sassy mouth to be in charge of the other two carpenters. That had taken him by surprise, and he hoped he could forget her so it wouldn't tarnish any small joy he might someday experience sitting out on the goddamn deck. If he ever got the promotion he deserved, they could afford a fancy hot tub with those eggbeater jets and maybe he could take a soak before bedtime and mellow out once in a while.

He sure hadn't relaxed when he'd picked up the Union-Tribune *a few days ago and seen his face staring up at him from page one of the local news section. It never occurred to him this artist's sketch or whatever it was would be in his living room. The hair line was a little too low and the nose a little flatter, but it was him all right, and he wondered how many people who knew him would pick up on it. It had been tempting to dump the newspaper before his wife looked at it, but he was curious to see what her reaction would be. Curious and nervous.*

He'd watched as she shuffled between the local news and currents sections. She'd taken a long time reading, then said casually, "There's been some rapes in our part of town. Let's be sure we keep the doors locked."

"What do you think of the picture?" he'd asked.

She'd picked up the paper and looked at it again. "I don't know. These things never look like anybody to me." She'd shrugged. "I hope they catch him."

Well, they weren't going to catch him as long as he didn't do something stupid. This morning's paper only had a paragraph about it. An unidentified body on Walnut Avenue—no details. They must have found her just before press time, he reasoned. It hadn't been convenient to catch a radio report at work, but he'd picked up the afternoon edition and it was all there. So she was only three days away from walking up the aisle and making some unsuspecting son of a bitch miserable for the rest of his life. He wondered how she'd liked their little honeymoon

in the flower bed. He liked not coming, staying in control
and not surrendering himself. Made him feel good to vi-
olate them and not reward them the dignity of receiving
his seed. Passion? Sure, but not the lustful variety. The
passion that came with wanting to show somebody who
was in charge.

Annie something or other according to the paper. He'd
forgotten her last name already. Once, when she'd started
to come to, her eyes opened and she just seemed to stare
at him. The dumb cunt didn't know she had about five
minutes more to live. It made him smile.

Even with only two hours sleep, the day had gone
quickly for Dowling. He stood in the darkness of his front
porch, guided by a light near the front door, and ripped
open a bag of potting soil. A dozen mums, in four-inch
plastic containers, sat ready to be stuck in the brick planter
box. He wiped one hand on his pants, then fine-tuned the
radio station that would have carried the Padres-Dodgers
game from Los Angeles. He vowed to boycott next year.
Pay them back for striking a season with Gwynn hitting
.394, poised to add six points and reach the magic number. As he listened to music and worked, he reflected on
the day's events, good and not so good.

Jenny had served up an array of sliced fruit and whole
milk for their breakfast.

"It's so hard sometimes, Pop. I want to eat right for
the baby. But I'll order a salad and Jason gets a big
cheeseburger and fries. He knows it makes it harder for
me."

"Umm-humm."

"And he smokes in the car. Today I made him stop
and I got out. He thinks secondhand smoke is a joke. Says
'that's bull' about the baby ingesting it."

Dowling knew she was fragile. A few moments before
she had pressed him about details of the murder, then ran
off crying when he told her. She had never reacted quite
like that over one of his cases.

Dowling put the trowel down and leaned closer to the radio, hoping to hear the name of a composition that was ending.

Gus Denver and Sam were convinced the new Honda was not connected to residents of homes near the alley.

"I'll tell you how slick the Irish cop is," Gus said. "One married lady cops out to Sam that she sleeps with a guy who parks his *Toyota* truck around the corner and sneaks in the back door."

"You did a good job," Dowling told them. "But after I talk to Mr. Van Cleave, we'll tell him we appreciate his help, but the car checked out okay."

"Ten-dash-four. Keep him from running off at the mouth to the media. Your girlfriend Rachel Tiffany would be down at that Honda dealer sitting next to you, Sarge," Gus said.

"If that Honda turns out to be our suspect's, I'll see to it Mr. Van Cleave gets his picture on the front page," Dowling said. "Hell, I'll trim his hedges for him every year."

The Department of Motor Vehicles investigators advised Dowling that the average new car buyer received license plates within six to eight weeks. The sales manager at Mission Bell Honda, citing privacy, was reluctant to provide information on the 144 customers who had purchased sedans in the past two months. When Dowling inferred that the hit-and-run victim was a toddler, he weakened a bit. When a description followed, of pink and blue bunnies painted on the walls of the rehab unit at Children's Hospital, he relented. Dowling had picked the package up at quitting time and spread it out on his dining room table.

On his yellow sheets, he had written:

1. Run criminal record checks on new owner names.
2. Check new owner names against computer list of license numbers taken during surveillances.

   3. Check new owner names against people identi-
      fied by callers responding to composite photo
      hotline.
   4. Check names against SDPD employee roster.

Between trips to the Honda dealer, Dowling walked
the alley behind Mr. Van Cleave's house. Stood where
the car had been parked. Timing would have been tight
for the killer to see Annie Richards get out of her car,
race his Honda around the corner, then down the alley
and park in time to intercept her where he did. He'd have
had to jump out of his car as soon as the wheels stopped
turning.
   Dowling felt all right about that. He sought out Mr.
Van Cleave. Found him sitting at the work bench in his
garage, smoking a White Owl cigar and having a noon-
time sip of sherry.
   "She won't let me smoke these in the house, Sergeant.
Says they look like something a Doberman would drop
on the lawn."
   He was in his late sixties, Dowling guessed, a gaunt
man with wispy white hair, a plaid work shirt tucked into
denim pants held up by two-inch-wide cloth suspenders.
   "No, I didn't go right over and look at the car. I kept
clipping away for a bit. About five minutes later, I wondered if it ever turned out onto the street. That's when I
put the clippers down, went over and took a look and saw
it settin' there. About ten minutes later I took another look
and it was gone."
   Dowling had broken the car sales down into categories:

Joint owner	95
Men	31
Women	18
Reside in crime scene area	12
Medium distance from crime scene	48
Far distance from crime scene	84

Light-colored car	70
Medium color	30
Dark color	44

He used color sample strips and formed subjective opinions about the last category. Most of the cars were Civics and Accords. Of the twelve cars sold to people living in his circle of interest, seven were light colored, eight were jointly registered and two each were sold to men or women as sole owners.

Maybe Mr. Van Cleave knew a light- from a dark-colored car and maybe he didn't. Maybe the car in the alley was in fact a new Honda, or maybe it was one of many used cars sold by the agency. They would end up making contact with all one hundred forty-four, unless one of the first twelve knocked their socks off.

There was no doubt in Dowling's mind the hit-and-run ruse was the way to play it. They would carry phony portfolios with them to the homes, with photographs the interviewee could just catch a quick glimpse of as they fished the bogus report from the folder. They would specify there was extensive front-end damage to the car, to relax those thinking a spouse or sibling may have been involved and were keeping it a secret. It had to be a good ploy—a real good ploy—because if they were sitting across the coffee table from the suspect, he'd almost have to feel little rivulets of paranoia swimming around in his demented brain. By going solo instead of teaming up, it would look less ominous, and he planned to borrow business cards from the traffic division.

Dowling walked to the end of the porch, picked up the watering can and watered the newly planted flowers. Then he pulled a piece of paper from his pocket. Holding it under the light, he read the twelve names again, wondering what the people looked like. Tomorrow they'd start to find out.

 Nineteen

The explosion took place the next morning, not as violent as last January's earthquake, but intense enough to register on the Richter, Dowling told himself.

"And you, Gus Denver, supposed to be my friend, are you?" Sam snatched Gus's briefcase and slammed it against the critique room wall. "I was searching your case folder for a victim phone number and what do I find? A wee note you'd written to yourself. *'Damon Harper—married??? Call personnel—find out.'* Prying into my business like a swarm of meddling relatives." Her face reddened as she shouted.

Dowling tried to say something and was cut off immediately.

"Oh, I know how you work. Like cops everywhere. You, Sergeant—though you're not acting like a sergeant now are you?—want to take the blame. Going to tell me you ordered Gus to make the phone call. Well, so what if you did?"

Larry Shea, who knew nothing, made the mistake of saying something in a stage whisper, causing Sam Mulcahy's jugular veins to dance up and down.

"I should have expected that from the likes of you, Shea. Blame the ills of the world on PMS will you now?" She banged her fist on the blackboard, and two pieces of chalk fell at her feet. "Doing ride-alongs with Damon

Harper does not in the least impede my work on our series, and as far as my off-duty time, I have a right to date who in hell's name I wish.''

Shea joined the other two in looking sheepish, and as Dowling fumbled with his yellow sheets, it was obvious she was not finished.

''A sorry lot the three of you are. Products of a town where they worry more about whether the surf is up than about their sewer lines pumping shit into the waters off Point Loma.'' She scooped up her folder, her Thomas Brothers map book and her purse. ''I'll be off now, to the tulies, where it's nice and safe, checking out car owners while the three of you divide up the twelve stops in the 'dangerous' area.'' She held her hand up when Dowling started again. ''You explained it once, didn't you?'' She did her best to imitate Dowling. '' 'Tis a rapist we're after and I'm a lone woman knocking up the residents so you're reducing the odds of a conflict.''

She'd reached the door and Dowling thought they were in the clear. Sam opened her folder with a flourish. ''Escondido. Rancho Bernardo. Poway! Wherever in God's holy name that is. But I'll do a quality job for you because my work ethic is intact. For now, you can all of you . . . *stuff it*.''

After the door slammed, and he was sure she wasn't coming back, Dowling said, ''What did we do that was so bad?''

Gus shrugged. ''Damned if I know, but I'd hate to have that woman mad at me if I really messed up.''

Dowling had briefed Stacy on the phone in the early morning hours, weathered the storm that was Sam Mulcahy, then set out to hunt down the four names he had assigned himself. They had not gotten a match on any of the names when Planning and Research rushed them through the computer network with the category list Dowling had submitted.

He wanted to avoid Stacy for a while at least, fearful

that the task force issue would surface. If they could just generate something on their own, he would be in a good position to hold the task force advocates at bay. The reality was, he could avoid Stacy forever, but if the task force was going to happen it was going to happen.

He had purposely not told Stacy about Mr. Van Cleave and his trusty mechanic's light. That was a tiny nugget he liked carrying around in his pocket until there was really something to talk about.

The first address Dowling selected was on Oregon Street. Strangely enough, he calculated, almost the exact geographical center of the series. In the living room, he drank coffee with a middle-aged widow who easily convinced him she was the sole driver of the shiny new car in her garage. A forty-five-year-old dentist on Thirtieth Street was cooperative in what turned out to be a very short stop.

The final two stops were uninteresting, and it reinforced his belief that jobs like this were best performed by homicide detectives, not task force assignees or special unit officers. He and Shea and Gus and Sam *knew* this suspect. They had lived with and lost sleep over this series for almost three months, had knelt beside the bodies, had looked into the deadpan eyes of those who'd been allowed to live.

"I'm not saying I know what he *does* look like," Dowling had told Jenny. "But I have a feel for what he doesn't look like. Does that make any sense?"

"Nothing," Gus Denver reported at the 6:00 P.M. critique. "I had three nice people and one guy who's going to write his congressman. Says the free world is crumbling when the gestapo can bang on a taxpayer's door and accuse a man of committing a felony while he was attending a motivational seminar at the University of Illinois." Gus arranged his paper work. "He's the only driver of the car. And as far as the physical, he could play center for the Celtics."

Sam Mulcahy was businesslike, speaking in clipped

tones reserved for strangers. She had made nine stops, found nothing promising, and met people more interested in asking her about Ireland than discussing hit-and-runs. One man's car had been totaled in an accident two blocks from the showroom floor the day he'd picked it up at Mission Bell Honda. Sam flipped the accident case from Records Division across the table to Dowling.

"Shea is running late," Dowling said. "Take the company cars home with you, go straight to the field in the morning and find this guy. Then we'll regroup here at the same time." It occurred to him he had lost track of days and it was Friday.

"Avoid the game traffic when you come in tomorrow night. Chargers have a six P.M. exhibition game with Miami," he told them.

"Take Shula's team and give the points," Gus said. "It's a Thaddaeus. By the way, Sarge, they call them 'preseason' games now."

Dowling watched the team leave, stood by his desk for a moment and thought about dinner. Picking up a pizza was convenient, but counterproductive for his daughter. He'd slap some white fish between folds of hardware cloth and grill it in the backyard.

Moments later he was driving out of the police lot when Larry Shea was driving in, so Dowling backed up and they talked to each other through open car windows as the sun went down.

"Too chickenshit to face Mulcahy, huh?" Dowling said.

Shea rolled his eyes. "Monday, there's a guy I want you to look at, Sarge."

"Why?"

"Because he's thirty-four years old, works in a bank and his Honda has license plates on it. Not the advertising placard, so it's not a Code-Two deal. Let's work up those that are left and see what we find. But I still want you to look at him."

"Okay," Dowling said slowly, studying the man he

had worked with for so long. He'd long ago learned to trust Shea's instincts. "Monday it is."

They put in long hours over the weekend, each polishing off about ten stops a day, and when Dowling did his count Sunday night, only forty-three owners remained to be contacted. He thought of Shea's discovery several times but resisted the temptation to query him. It helped him focus on his weekend mission, and perhaps he was afraid if he learned much more about the banker before Monday, he would mentally eliminate him, too.

The banker part didn't scare him off, but he didn't care much for the guy being thirty-four years old. Witnesses could be mistaken, but four of had them placed their suspect in the mid-twenties range. Nine years was quite a leap. And the goddamn plates were on the car. So if it was Shea's guy in Mr. Van Cleave's alley, the license plates had been put on within two days. Had coincidentally arrived from Sacramento, or had arrived before that, and their suspect, being cautious, had put them on the day after the murder, knowing the car could have been seen? More likely, the plates had been on for some time, and while Annie Richards was being throttled, Shea's guy was sitting in his recliner looking at the *Wall Street Journal* or *U.S. News and World Report* or whatever in hell bankers read for pleasure.

Dowling took the time to think about Angela Lord's sweet kiss as he crisscrossed San Diego. Jenny had questioned him about her, and he'd mumbled something evasive. Evasive because the truth was, he didn't know what to say or think, or especially, what to feel. Everything seemed so upside down. A fifty-year-old widowed homicide cop with a pregnant high school daughter keeping company with a *doctor* for Chrissake. It was a hoaxed-up version of *The Dating Game*, he told himself.

Before he fell asleep Sunday night, he thought about Angela Lord again, then ended up dozing off to Larry Shea's banker.

At ten the next morning, Shea and Dowling stood on the corner of Fifth Avenue and B Street in the heart of the financial center. The bright red German-built Tijuana Trolley whizzed by a block to the south, and an old rag-picker with scabs on her face competed for space on the sidewalk with bevies of navy blue suits.

Three Hell's Angels yelped and high-fived in front of the twenty-four-story building they had exited, then drummed their fists atop the row of newspaper racks. "Look at those assholes," Shea said.

"Probably just came from their lawyer's office and got good news," Dowling said.

"Yeah. The judge suppressed a search warrant for their fucking meth lab."

"Or the only witness to their triple homicide just got run over by a beer truck."

A black-and-white stopped a Porsche for a traffic ticket right in front of Dowling and Shea, so they moved down the block.

"You haven't told me a damn thing," Dowling said. "What do you want me to do, just go in and look around?"

"Go in and try not to look like a cop. Which is like telling Toscanini not to look like a conductor. See if you spot anybody you like."

"Western Bank of San Diego, huh?" Dowling buttoned his jacket and strolled to the corner of Sixth Avenue and B Street. At times like this he was sure he had "police" written all over him.

"Holy shit!" he said less than ten minutes later, rejoining Shea.

"I was wondering if it was just me. You know, you get an image in your mind . . ." Shea smiled.

"Let's walk," Dowling said, and they headed west. "The guy in the Commercial Department, first desk to the right of the teller's windows?"

"That's him. James Danko."

"He doesn't look his age. And with a T-shirt and

Levi's . . . jeez, the physical is just right. He got up and walked over to another desk while I was horsing around at the writing table.''

"Let's get hot dogs," Shea said, so they crossed Fifth Avenue. "The La Mesa cop's face was so-so. I figured maybe another case of a composite not looking like the crook. But *this* face."

They turned left on Fourth Avenue, heading for the long New York–style lunch counter next to the old California theater. Another Santa Ana had blown in and it was already in the mid-seventies.

"Goddammit, Larry. I wish the plates hadn't been on his car forty-eight hours after our job."

"Nothing's easy," Shea answered as they ordered two each to go, with kraut and mustard. After stuffing extra napkins in their pockets, they turned right on C Street, still walking in the direction of the bay.

"What did Danko tell you on Friday?" Dowling asked.

"That's just it," Shea said between bites. "I never hit him up. He was my last stop. I was downtown anyway, deposited my paycheck in Union Bank and figured I'd just step across the street, interview our friend Mr. Danko, then hustle back for the critique."

"If I wasn't holding on to these franks so tight I'd hug you, Shea. I take back every shitty thing I ever said about you." Dowling sniffed the sauerkraut before taking the next bite.

"I was just about to ask for him, Sarge, and I look over and see this guy sitting there and I say to myself, 'Could it be that the nameplate on that desk is going to say "Danko"'? Then someone called his name, he got up, so I just did an about-face and hauled ass. Why even take the chance of spooking him if he is our guy?" They stopped for a red light. "We should have got three dogs. This sleuthing makes me hungry."

They passed the fenced, judge's parking lot, a few feet from the enclosed courthouse walkway that formed a bridge over C Street.

"So you saw the car?" Dowling said.

"I saw it, but not at the bank. I walked the parking garage and couldn't find it, so I drove up to his house. It was in the driveway."

"Then he didn't drive it to work. I don't like that."

"But you are going to like where he lives," Shea said. He made Dowling wait a moment. "On Maryland Street, just north of the Uptown Mall."

Dowling calculated. Before Annie Richards, their crime sector had been three miles wide. Choice McGraw's case on Louisiana Street had formed the western boundary. Poor Annie had gotten it at First and Walnut, a full mile and a half farther west. And Maryland Street, where James Danko parked his Honda, was just a five-minute drive from there.

In front of the Greyhound package store, Dowling abruptly turned around. "Come on, Shea, old pal. You just found us a bone to chew on. I'm going to buy you another hot dog on the way back to the car. We've got some *real* sleuthing to do."

≋ Twenty

It was important, Dowling told himself, not to get skittish because of what happened with Curtis Forman of La Mesa P.D. Not let their enthusiasm for working up James Danko be tempered by that experience. It wasn't as if the Curtis Forman fiasco was that unique. Like all detectives who pay attention, Dowling had learned how easily coincidence can jam up the works of an important investigation. Coincidence was something to be wary of but not feared. Coincidence plus fact sometimes made a good mix.

Maybe Sherlock Holmes and Angela Lansbury solved *their* cases without a boost from Lady Luck, used extraordinary powers of deduction to pick out the killer in a crowded room, but humble working cops like himself needed all the help they could get. And the Honda in the alley was the first serving of help in three long months.

He looked at his yellow sheets:

JAMES DANKO

PRO	CON
Face is good	34 years old
Physical descrip = good	Rear plate on car
Lives in area of crimes	
Owns new light-green Honda	

Dowling remembered something Holly Novikoff had told him when he interviewed her in the hospital. "He had a nice smile, if that helps." It seemed too trite to add to his list, but he'd noticed in the bank that James Danko smiled often.

If the car in the alley *did not* belong to the rapist, they were going to be spending a lot of time, losing a lot of sleep, investigating a man whose only crime was buying a Honda instead of a Toyota. But for now, as far as Dowling was concerned, they'd caught a break. And what separated the good teams from the mediocre ones was what you did after you caught it. His mind raced as he started his to-do list on the second yellow sheet.

complete crim record ck.
drivers license ck.
get a feel of 4652 Maryland St.
surveillance?????

"A banker, huh?" Dr. Leonard Boudreaux said over the telephone the next day. "Thirty-four years old and no criminal record. That would be unusual for a serial rapist."

"Ted Bundy?" Dowling said.

"And you can't approach this guy right now, correct?"

"Correct."

"If this is your suspect," Boudreaux said, "and you get deep enough into his background, you'll find some stuff that may key you."

"Like what, Doc?"

"This guy needs to be forcefully dominant over women. Any breach of this . . . masterly authority of his usually leads to violence. Is he married?"

"Don't know yet."

"Well, it doesn't matter. Sexual sadists do marry and at times quite successfully. If he can find a woman who can satisfy his sexual appetite and be patiently submissive and loyal to his authority, then he can accept and marry this woman." Boudreaux paused and Dowling knew he was lighting a cigar. "He's got to be able to bully this woman most of the time. Then, when he thinks life is screwing him over, he can go on these nocturnal missions and violate and shame and defile some poor girl walking down the street."

They were about to hang up when Boudreaux said, "Remember Dowling, the sexual sadist is a psychopath, but he's not insane. He's very clever. Makes fewer mistakes than the average fuckhead you guys deal with. Most of his life he's taught himself to strictly hide his abnormal sexual habits."

Dowling took the phone from his ear until Boudreaux finished a coughing spell. "And one more thing, my sergeant friend. If your banker *is* doing those crimes of yours, he's an angry son of a bitch, no matter how he comes across publicly. Some little thing, some encounter that would only irritate or frustrate most people may make this guy lose it. I don't know how you can use that, but it's something to remember."

Ironically, pulling into the driveway of his home, Dowling had congratulated himself on how smoothly he and Jenny were handling things. Day-to-day decisions were being made about her pregnancy, and he assured himself that teamwork and understanding would carry them through. Then he opened the door and found her in tears, throwing a book on prenatal guidance across the room.

"He's gone," she screamed. "He's gone *and I want him gone.*"

"Who for God's sake?"

She picked up the book and threw it again. "JASON. You remember him? The father of my child."

"Where did he go?" Dowling asked, unsure what to do.

"He didn't *go* anywhere. He's gone from my life."

When he was able to settle her down a bit, she told

him it had been her decision. Told him many things. In the past month she had come to despise Jason's parents for their cavalier attitude, lost all respect for Jason and his unwillingness to accept responsibility for the life within her.

"And I'm anemic, Pop. I have to go on iron."

"Well, we'll just get some iron then and—"

"I have no support system," she sobbed. "Matt said . . ." She cried violently. "Matt said he'll be my support."

Dowling went to her and threw his arms around her neck, drawing her close.

"Matt is your long-distance support system. I'm your local one."

Then they'd jumped in the car, headed down the hill and found the greasiest cheeseburger on Rosecrans Street for dinner. With fries.

James Danko graduated from Kansas State University with an M.A. in business administration according to a copy of his employment application form in the possession of Homicide Team One. The security director of Western Bank, a retired auto-theft detective, had provided it after receiving assurances from Gus Denver he would not be burned.

They learned that Danko had been employed for three years and, as an account officer in his department, was responsible for overseeing auto loans and credit card accounts. The file informed them he had been married to Karen Danko for two years and had a six-month-old dependent. An emergency contact on his date of hire was a father in Kalvesta, Kansas. Interestingly to Dowling, a Myrna Pulaski had been listed as the local emergency contact on the same date.

The next afternoon at 5:00 P.M., Dowling and Sam Mulcahy secreted themselves in the rear of a police undercover van, peeking between curtains through smoked windows. They were parked across the aisle from James

Danko's pale green Honda in the parking garage at the bank.

A half hour later Danko walked toward his car carrying a tan attaché case, wearing a dark gray suit, white shirt and flowered necktie. As he put his key in the door, a well-dressed woman approached and spoke to him from the aisle.

"Excuse me. *Sir.*"

Danko looked up and said nothing.

"Your car," the woman said, pointing at the tires. "You didn't park your car in the center of the lines. People like you have no consideration for others parked next to them."

"Are you for real?" Danko said. His voice was loud.

"Oh, very much for real. My silk dress has to go to the cleaners because I couldn't get past your car. Will you try harder next time, or are you just another self-centered man who only worries about his car door being scratched?"

"What I'm going to do," Danko said, putting down his attaché case and advancing toward her, "is try and forget that I worked hard all day, then ran into a dumb bitch like you in the parking lot." He bared his teeth. "Fuck you and fuck your painted lines." He opened his door, threw his briefcase into the car, backed out hurriedly and burned rubber making the curve at the end of the aisle.

When he was out of sight, the woman walked to the van, opened the passenger door and got in.

"Ellen Crane, meet police officer Sam Mulcahy," Dowling said. "Sam, meet Police Officer Ellen Crane, Northern Division. Thank you, Ellen. A job well done."

Ellen Crane saluted. "My pleasure. Does this get me an A in your class?"

"It gets you a pitcher of beer at the 153 Club," he said.

"What was this all about?" Ellen Crane asked.

"I just had to find out something," Dowling said.

░ Twenty-one

Captain Tom Stacy looked over Dowling's shoulder at the road atlas spread out on his desk.

"They tell me Kansas is lovely this time of the year," he said. "Your mood got better the past twenty-four hours. You got something going?"

"Not really," Dowling said.

"What's with the Rand McNally and the World Almanac then?"

Dowling pushed them both aside. "Just checking out some stuff. I have to go to Records." He got up quickly and took several steps before Stacy summoned him back.

"Sit your ass down here and talk to me, Dowling. You got something going, don't you?"

"I told you we—"

"If you sandbag me on this one, you'll be walking Balboa Park on the night shift, swear to God. The Old Man's phone has been ringing. That Rachel Tiffany is driving him crazy about a task force. By the way, she just announced for the city council vacancy." Stacy snapped his suspenders. "Now what have you got?"

Dowling loosened his tie and sat down. "Look, Tom, I told you there was a car seen in the alley on the Annie Richards case. We're checking out over a hundred owners. That's a lot of taxpayers. Tell the chief I got stung on that La Mesa cop and we're being especially thorough.

Tell him to hold Tiffany off on the task force. Ask him to trust me."

Stacy said nothing, nodded to a Team Three detective, looked at Dowling again, then got up and walked away.

Dowling put the two books in front of him again. Kalvesta, Kansas, was hard near the intersection of state highways 156 and 23; ten miles south of the Pawnee River. It wasn't included in the population count of either book, though towns of similar sized lettering were, like Cimarron and Jetmore, with sixteen hundred and eight hundred people, respectively. It pleased him that geographically Finney County was the second largest of Kansas's 105 counties, because he would be dealing with a larger sheriff's department if he needed the help. For now, he was leery of gossip that a call from San Diego could stir up in western Kansas and was far from ready to let anyone outside of there learn of his interest in James Leon Danko.

"Kalvesta? That's a farm town," the lady from the Kansas Travel and Tourism Division told Dowling on the telephone. "If you visit in the spring, you'll see the corn and wheat and alfalfa growing."

"Alfalfa? I call it a cross between grass and clover," she answered in response to his questions. "Terrain? Wide open prairie. Essentially flat and rolling."

"That's the sergeant's way," Shea told Sam later. "He has to get a 'feel' of everything. Doesn't know if it'll help him, but he sticks it in his bag. When he doesn't say much, that's when he's getting interested in a guy."

"We'll be putting in some hours, then," Sam said.

"That's a Thaddaeus, Irish. That's a Thaddaeus."

Very much at the front of Dowling's mind was the time element. Seven days had passed since the Annie Richards murder. He had memorized the span of days between cases: 19-16-20-14-2-34.

The two-day period between Adrienne Roe and Joy Larson's death he attributed to the bungled attempt on Roe. The thirty-four-day spread between the two homicides relaxed him a little, but not much. If James Danko was indeed their boy, they were messing with a time bomb. It was the only thing that ever made him yearn for an assignment in Burglary. How much importance could anyone put on the life of a TV set?

He had added another fact on the plus side of Danko's ledger: works day job—could be on streets at night.

They still couldn't pin down the loose end about Danko's license plates. It had not surprised him that, in a state with twenty-two million registered vehicles, DMV was unable to provide the mailing date.

Maryland Street was sandwiched between the Cabrillo Freeway on the west and Louisiana Street to the east. Louisiana Street . . . where Choice McGraw had been victimized. Maryland dead-ended on the north, against a dry, scrubby hillside that, in summer months, haunted firefighters and nearby home owners. The hillside sloped drastically downward, toward the Radisson Hotel and Mission Valley Shopping Center off Interstate 8.

Dowling had cruised by 4652 Maryland the day before and glanced at the small home with the narrow driveway leading to a detached one-car garage. Most of the homes sat close to the sidewalk and were early California–style stucco with red Spanish tile roofs.

On this morning, Dowling had borrowed a three-quarter-ton stake-body truck owned by the San Diego Gas & Electric company. A G&E supervisor, a high school classmate, had weekdays off but was authorized to take the equipment home.

"Hell, I'm fireproof," his friend said. "I got my time in. And this is for a good cause."

Dowling wasn't looking for anything in particular when they parked the truck at the curb next door to Danko's house. In ten hours of feigning work, he figured to learn *something*.

"If anybody asks, tell them you're 'potting,'" his friend had instructed. They would dig potholes in the grass between the sidewalk and curb, then fill them up again. "If Maryland Street is scheduled to be repaved, you have to see how deep the gas or electric lines are. You'll look just right walking around with your hard hat and clipboard, Vince. Police sergeants don't work anyway."

The team had borrowed two trucks actually, the second a "locator" van. Dowling had wanted the second truck as a backup, for quick transportation to an undercover car parked around the corner.

"Walk around with this thing that looks like a metal detector and put the headphones on. You're locating underground electrical wires," they'd been told. "And by the way. The second truck is going to cost you *two* pitchers of beer at that sleaze ball cop hangout of yours."

They got into position at 7:00 A.M. on a Thursday, and thirty minutes later watched Danko, dressed for work, leave in a 1985 Nissan sedan. Two hours later, a woman with a baby in a car seat backed the Honda out of the garage and drove south on Maryland. Gus and Shea made it to the undercover car in time to follow.

"An easy tail," Gus said an hour and a half later, moving the metal detector over a patch of grass. "Drives like Grandma Moses. Took the kid, a little girl by the way, to a day care in Mission Hills, then went to work at a stationery store in Fashion Valley." Gus took a swig of cola from his thermos. "We phoned the house like you said. Got the answering machine. Guess it's just the three of 'em living there."

"And . . . we learned they split up the cars," Dowling said. "A good day so far."

At 5:30 P.M. the woman returned, parked the car in the driveway, then made two trips to carry the baby and groceries inside. A few minutes later Danko drove up, got out without looking around and entered the house. Thirty minutes later Dowling dismissed one vehicle. He and Sam were loading picks and shovels in the stake truck when Danko came out wearing running shoes, shorts and a plain white T-shirt, did some calisthenics on the front lawn, then took off at a fast jog toward Monroe Avenue.

"A hard body," Sam said as they started the engine.

Dowling noted the time on his clipboard next to the license number of the Nissan. "I like it Sam, I like it."

The next morning Dowling received his return call from the security office of Kansas State University in Manhattan, 250 miles northeast of Kalvesta.

"It's been eleven years since your fella was here, Sarge, so it took a while to check, but we have nothing on him. He never came to our attention in his four years here."

"Thanks for checking," Dowling said. "Are your Wildcats going to kick the Jayhawks' butts tomorrow?"

"You can count on it. For our sake, I'm glad they're playing it over in Lawrence. Civil War football is a big day for security." They chatted for a few more minutes before he added, "By the way, Sergeant Dowling, I decided to pull the 1981 annual. Your fella ran varsity track. The low hurdles."

Instead of classical music, Wynton Marsalis trumpeted "Hot House Flowers" from the speakers in Angela Lord's living room. The idea was to drink as many martinis as she and Dowling wished, then walk the few blocks for Mexican food at the Casa de Bandini.

They had spent the first hour commiserating about their stressful work lives. Dowling felt very comfortable, very warm, sitting in the cozy room with hardwood floors and braided throw rugs. Even before his first Beefeater and vermouth, he thought there was something very right about it. It was how people were supposed to live, wasn't it? Perhaps fifteen years of homicide work were enough. He figured on working another ten years if he lived that long, but cops were old at fifty and he was old. Tom Stacy would get him a job by the fireplace. All he had to do was say the word. Juvenile Division? That would work. Forgery would work, too. Hell, sergeants there only left the station if they wanted to. He could hit the third floor every day—pump a little iron, learn how to use those fancy strength and aerobics machines—and lose some pounds. When they wrapped up the series, maybe that's the way he'd go. Who knew? Angela Kingsbury Lord, M.D., might want to spend more time with a man keeping regular hours.

"Tell me more about your Mr. Danko," she said. She wore a classic shirtwaist dress. He thought she looked wonderful.

"We surveilled him for three nights after Kansas State University filled us in. He didn't show us anything, though. Never left the house alone. One night they piled in the car, went to one of those health food places and were back in forty-five minutes." He finished his drink. "Chrissakes, you battle the world. Yesterday morning I'm driving around. See this Honda with the right advertising placard. Just on a whim, I radio for patrol to make a stop."

"Why? If it had been sold before Annie Richards's murder, it would have been on your list. Right?"

"Oh yeah. That's where you battle the world. Turns out it *was* bought before September thirtieth. I raised hell with Mission Bell Honda. Are you ready for this?"

"I'd better make you another while you're telling me," she said, picking up his goblet.

He smelled her cologne or perfume or powder and lost his thought for a moment. "Anyway, I raise hell. Seems the woman who put the list together for me knows the family of the car I had patrol make the stop on. 'They're wonderful people. Couldn't possibly be mixed up in anything the police would be interested in.' So she left them off the list." He sighed. "I ought to get out of this murder business."

"Do you think Danko is the guy?"

"I don't know, Helene. He's a helluva good suspect, but it's a helluva big city." He looked at his wristwatch. "It'll be dark in an hour. He could be getting ready to go do somebody, and I'm sitting here drinking gin."

"Was your wife's name Helene?"

The question startled him. "Yes."

"You just called me that." He couldn't read the expression. "It's all right," she emphasized quickly.

"Could we go out for a cigarette? I got wrapped up in my case." He thought it sounded lame.

They smoked on the deck and listened to distant tones from a mariachi band. She stood closer than the night he'd been over for dinner.

"Did you talk to Helene about your cases?"

"Not enough. I didn't talk to her about how the cases made me *feel*. Figured she didn't need to have that dumped on her. So I just drank my booze and worked my murders."

"Was she a lovely person?"

He'd felt uncomfortable a moment ago. Was better now. "Yes, in every way." He looked at Angela Lord. "I cheated her out of being a part of my whole life."

Dowling put out one cigarette and lit another. "When I was here for dinner, we talked about my daughter. You were making a point and mentioned how many losers there were out there." He took a deep breath. "Am I a loser, Angela?"

He didn't look at her when she answered. "Oh, you're not a loser, Vincent Dowling. You're a keeper. You just need a little repair work. Like all of us."

The mariachi band had stopped. "I'm no catch, you know. I'm middle-aged. I have a paunch. More chin than I need. I smoke. Sometimes I drink more than I should. No money. Sometimes I think I'll always have enough to eat but never enough to retire." He wished he had another martini. "I used to drink too much routinely. Now I go a bunch of days without one when I feel like it. I suppose by the *Reader's Digest* standards I'm an alcoholic. You know those quizzes you see floating around. Ten questions. Answer any one 'yes' and you're a lush. I always qualify."

Angela laughed. "I understand."

"I drink sometimes when I'm insecure," he added.

"Like our first date?"

"Yes."

"How about tonight?"

"Yeah," he said. "I'm a little insecure tonight."

"Me, too."

"If you make me another martini . . . you make good ones . . . I'll make a confession to you."

When they were seated again with fresh drinks, he told her, "That night at the Rape Crisis Center meeting. You sang my praises about volunteering my time to attend. Dedication and all that stuff?"

"Yes. . . ."

"My captain held a gun to my head to make me go. I hate going to those things."

"You lied to me!" He couldn't tell if she was faking being indignant. "Why didn't you tell me that then? You *lied* to me."

"I can't be held responsible. I was starting to tell you the truth; then when I looked into your beautiful eyes the words wouldn't come out."

"You are so full of shit. And you *lie*."

"Wait one small minute, madam. Speaking of lying, how about the cigarettes you hid behind your toaster the other night?"

"So we're even," she said. They sipped in silence to Mariah Carey's "Vision of Love" until Angela said, "Name me ten things that you like."

"What?"

"Just play this game with me. Rattle off ten things you like. And none can have anything to do with work. Or with a person."

Dowling made a face, took a drink of Beefeaters and started counting on his fingers.

"The smell of new leather, campfires, the San Diego skyline from the Coronado Bridge, my daughter's eyes." He caught himself. "Oops, that's a person. Uh . . . hamburgers cooking on the grill, sunsets over the ocean, pretty girls like you wearing pastel-colored dresses on spring days. How many is that?''

''Just keep going.''

''Extra-inning ball games, seeing an elderly person eating an ice-cream cone, walking in the rain, the death penalty.''

''Nothing to do with work,'' she admonished.

''And Beefeater martinis. That's ten.'' He sank back in his chair. ''What's this all about?''

''I had to go to a one-day retreat last week. Kind of like you getting forced to go to the Crisis Center. Chiefs of staff of the various disciplines along with hospital administrator types. Very plush meeting room.''

She put her hands together, prayerlike, the fingertips touching her chin. ''Breakfast was eggs Benedict and exotic juices. They started it out with some ridiculous get-acquainted game where everybody had to name ten things that they like. And I couldn't think of *any*. I mean, I wasn't even the first one to go. I had time to think and I still couldn't come up with anything. Is that pathetic? What does that say about me?''

''It says,'' he counseled, ''that you're not very fond of get-acquainted games with a bunch of people you don't feel close to. Or,'' he raised one finger, ''eggs Benedict destroys your thinking process.''

''I just want to be a doctor,'' she said. She leaned forward and put her hand on his knee. ''And all you want to do is be a cop. We're a hell of a pair.''

''Good thing you're driving, Shea. I get lost out here,'' Gus Denver said. They climbed the Narragansett Avenue hill at Chatsworth Boulevard, the point where residents begin to argue about the mythical boundaries separating haughty Point Loma from Ocean Beach. Shea and Denver were driving toward the heart of Ocean Beach, separated from Mission Beach by the San Diego River floodway and Mission Bay Channel.

No one answered when Shea knocked on the door of

the bungalow on the 5000 block of Cape May Avenue, but a voice without a face from next door told them why. "She's at the store. Walks down every morning when they open."

They got back in the car and cruised for fifteen minutes. "That's gotta be Mrs. P," Gus declared. "Beat-up old housecoat's almost dragging on the sidewalk."

Myrna Pulaski was the name of the local emergency contact James Danko had listed when he accepted work at the bank. A year, Dowling calculated, before marrying Karen Danko. "Go bullshit Myrna's mother," Dowling told them after some snooping around. "Figure something out. Back off if you think it's risky."

The lady answering their knock was about fifty. "You're from the Fugitive Detail, huh? Well, come on in boys. Lock me up where somebody'll fix me three squares a day.

"Instant coffee and these damn generic cigarettes is all I can offer you," she said, flicking on the heat under a kettle. They sat around a small table in a small kitchen, near a sideboard where a carton from last night's TV dinner lay under a dirty plate.

"Instant coffee and generic cigarettes. Sounds like home," Gus said. "We appreciate it, Mrs. Pulaski."

"So who's this character you're trying to find, boys?"

"Herman Pulaski. He's wanted out of Cleveland for armored car holdups," Shea told her. "This is pretty routine. We're talking to all the Pulaskis in San Diego. Looking for a family connection."

"Hell, he's probably part of my ex-old man's family. Let me get that coffee."

They talked for a while before Mrs. Pulaski walked them to the door. "Thanks for all the family info. You've been very kind," Shea said.

"This daughter of yours, Myrna, you said she works at Mrs. Field's. I hope she slips a couple oatmeal cookies over to you now and again," Gus said smiling.

"God love her, she slips them home to her husband now. Finally got the girl married off."

"Hope it's working out for her," Shea said.

"We'll know soon enough," Mrs. Pulaski said, clutching the throat of her housecoat. "He works down at National Steel. Pretty nice fellow. Stops for beers on paydays, but hell, they make enough money now he can't swallow the whole check like my old man used to down at the Red Garter."

"I got a daughter about Myrna's age," Gus said. "Don't know if she'll ever decide to get married. She just broke up with some guy I didn't much care for. He works in a damn bank."

"Hah! No wonder you don't like him. Myrna fooled around with some jerk who worked in a bank. Moody SOB. Acted like he was way too good for us."

"He's out of the picture now, I guess?" Shea said.

"Thank God, yes," she said. "I asked her about him a short time back. Myrna said she's lost all track of him. She never would admit it, but I think he bounced her around a couple of times. One time she told me a dog jumped up and scratched her face. Another time she said she bumped into the medicine cabinet door. But I don't think so."

When they reached the car she called to them. "You boys drop in for coffee any time."

Two hours later, on her lunch break, Gus and Shea interviewed Myrna Pulaski Holmes over tuna sandwiches at an outdoor table in the mall, across from Mrs. Field's. Ironic, Shea thought; they were sitting less than five hundred feet from the store where Karen Danko sells pens and pencils.

They talked for a while; then Gus leaned forward, smiling at the attractive twenty-five-year-old. "Myrna. We haven't been entirely straight with you. But we badly need your help in a very important, very confidential investigation." Gus waited for a reaction.

"It's not about some wanted guy named Pulaski then?" she said.

"No. It's about something you can't even tell your mother about right now. We think we can trust you. Can we?"

She pushed the rest of her sandwich aside. "If it's not about my mother or my husband, then I'll help you."

"The thing is," Shea said, "it's about somebody you used to know. And we still can't be totally up front with you about the type of case. It'll be kind of a one-way street because we'll be doing all the asking and none of the telling. Can you live with that?"

She nodded. "It's about James Danko, isn't it?"

"Yes," Gus said.

"I'll help you, then."

At 6:00 P.M., after Dowling and Sam Mulcahy had finished contacting the last of the new car owners, Gus and Shea briefed them in a 7-Eleven parking lot in East San Diego.

"We were hoping she'd tell us he used to choke her out and do the number with her clothes before he climbed on," Shea said laughing, "but here's how it went."

He put his notebook away and spoke from memory. "First time Myrna laid eyes on him, she was walking home in the middle of the afternoon and Danko pulls up next to her on a bicycle, tells her she's beautiful and rides along next to her, telling how he's going to date her. She thought he was squirrely but cute and gives him her phone number.

"Two weeks later they were dating. He had an apartment in O.B., was working at a sporting goods store and trying to get hired with a bank. They went together for about six months. After they'd been having sex a while, he quit kissing her. Would just be sitting around the apartment and he'd say, 'Come on,' and they'd go into the bedroom and do it without any touching or kissing. Dogs-on-the-lawn stuff.

"She agrees with her mother. He was very moody. Generally hostile toward women. Spoke in derogatory terms about his mother and resented the fact that Myrna was not a virgin.

"She was getting tired of him anyway when he started hitting her. Actually, it happened on three occasions, she believes. The first two were open handed, but the last time they were visiting friends of his, having a cookout, and he whacked her and she ran crying to the bathroom. He followed her and knocked her around pretty good. Kicked her when she was folded up on the floor. That did it for old Myrna. She showed him the door. Talked to him a few times, but when he found out she really wouldn't see him, he gave her hell over the phone. Called her a whore and a cunt and she hasn't talked to him since. Doesn't know if he's married or where he's working. And we didn't tell her."

Shea took a deep breath. "This briefing crap makes me thirsty. Are we working tonight or can we drink?"

"We're surveilling him tonight," Dowling said.

"When we said good-bye to her," Gus said, "she looked us right in the eye and she says, 'Whatever it is you're investigating him for, I bet he did it.' "

℀ Twenty-two

It was bad luck for Dowling that the telephone call had not been taken by a secretary, who would merely have placed the message slip into his folder without comment. But the phone had been answered by a detective from Team Five and there'd been no opportunity to defend against the barrage.

"*What* are you signed up for, Sergeant Dowling?" A Team Four detective got it rolling.

"Lamaze classes," Dowling muttered, hoping it would be over quickly.

"We can't hear you!"

"Don't you comedians have any work to do? Why don't you try solving a murder sometime?" Dowling said, reaching for a report, just to have something in his hands.

"He's going to *Lamaze* classes when the eighth month gets here," Sergeant Jack Cassidy announced.

They had waited until Dowling's team was fully assembled.

"Probably the whole team is going," another yelled. "They do everything together."

"Probably their Irish chauffeur will have to drive them."

"If she's kissed and made up with them."

"When it happens in the delivery room, I hope the kid sees the doctor first," Team Six called out.

"Amen," said Team Two. "Imagine coming into the world and the first thing you see is Dowling."

"It'd be the first baby in history to turn around and go back."

"What's all the noise in the background? I can hardly hear you," Dowling said. He was on the phone with his son.

"Bunch of Harleys just blew out of a gas station."

"When are you and JoAnne going to get your own phone?"

"Payday maybe," Matt said. "Phones aren't a big priority anymore, Dad."

"You guys are doing okay, though?"

"We guys are primo. This married life is good. School's good. Work's good. And we're kicking ass in City League. I mailed you scores, right? How's Angela?"

"How do you know about Angela? Oh, yeah. Your pregnant pipeline. I was waiting for a good time to tell you about her."

They talked about the three women in their lives, and as they were getting ready to hang up, Matt said, "How's the surveillance coming?"

"He's still not showing us anything. Maybe we can make something happen."

"Are you using the old icepick trick?"

It caught Dowling by surprise. "I never told you about that."

"You didn't have to. One night years ago when you had a few beers you were talking to Bones Boswell about it. I've got a steeltrap memory. Talk to you soon, Dad."

The fact was, they *had* punched tiny holes in the red taillight lenses on both of Danko's cars. The little glimmer of white light they created was helpful when they momentarily lost him in traffic. Danko was seldom out alone, and when he was they were for short, direct trips to the market. Twice they tailed the family to restaurants; a pancake house and an Italian place.

"Follow them in and get me details, Sam. You know the kind of stuff I need," he instructed.

The phone-in leads on the composites had predictably dwindled, and with the extra time, he decided to surveil Danko from home to work once or twice. Sometimes in the Honda, sometimes in the Nissan, Danko made a routine of stopping at a coffee shop in Mission Hills, avoiding the freeway en route to the bank. They watched him sitting at the uncrowded counter, reading the morning paper over coffee.

Dowling had not seen Angela Lord but phoned her most days when he could connect.

"Why on earth are you surveilling Mrs. Danko?" she wanted to know.

"Just to see what there is to see. Suppose she has a boyfriend. That would give us a hell of a twist on her that could be useful to us down the line."

"Does she?"

"Nope. Works about three, four days a week. Sam went in and bought a little notebook from her. Very pleasant person. Quite attractive."

"Aren't you violating her rights? Following her?"

"I'm a homicide cop, Doctor. Not a constitutional lawyer."

Maybe they were and maybe they weren't trampling on rights. All Dowling was certain of was twenty appellate court judges, lined up like ducks in a row and presented the issue, would eventually divide about ten-ten on their opinions. Or, more accurately, their law clerk's opinions. After three months of research and deliberation.

He reflected on his talks with Jenny, Matt and Angela. This was all a first for him, sharing the details of his investigation with others. So far it felt pretty good. What would life be like today, he wondered, had he done that from the start?

He didn't allow himself to wonder for long. Fourteen days had passed since the Annie Richards case, and he was feeling the strain. After much thought, he had decided against telling Stacy about Danko. For Stacy's protection, he falsely rationalized. At morning meetings with assistant chiefs, Stacy would be pressured for details. If he didn't have them, he couldn't provide them. In Dowling's mind, cops didn't maliciously leak information that would hurt a case. Tidbits here and there for political gain, sure. They were people first and cops second. But everybody had friends, and with people like Rachel Tiffany on the prowl, casual conversation could be devastating. He'd been on the short end of the fallout. Stacy would be irritated for a while, but the satisfaction of an arrest would soothe that. Dowling wished that were his most serious problem.

The small offices of the SDPD Air Support Unit are in a hangar next to Runway 27 at Montgomery Field, a general aviation airport ten miles north of downtown. Sam Mulcahy sat with Dowling in the small office of Lieutenant George Cardas, commanding officer of the unit and an academy classmate of Dowling's. Coming through the hangar, the homicide detectives had paused to look at two fixed-wing police surveillance aircraft and several police Bell Jet Rangers.

Cardas was tall for a pilot, over six three, and almost as slender as the long cigars he favored.

"Well, you must want something, Dowling. Been a long time since you cared enough to drop in on an old pal. And you brought your persuasion along." He smiled at Sam who smiled back. A police radio chattered from the edge of the desk.

"As a matter of fact, George, we could use some air support. Some surveillance. We're looking at a bad actor."

"For you, anything. You got the paper work?" He reached out a large hand.

"Well, that's just it. See, the seventh floor doesn't know the details of what we're doing, and I want to keep it that way. I figured you could just—"

"Jeez, Vince. I'd love to help you, but I can't put units up without approval. The demand on our time is overwhelming. And there's liability insurance factors. It's just a formality. Send the request up the line, I'll see it gets first-class attention."

Dowling looked at the framed photographs and newspaper stories on the wall. "So you're going to be a horseshit company man, huh?" He looked at Sam. "Times sure change, Sam. I remember when Lieutenant Cardas was pounding a beat. Believe me, he was quite a different guy then."

Cardas leaned back in the chair and clasped both hands behind his head, puffing on the cigar without taking it from his mouth. "I see it coming, Dowling. You're going to make up some horse hockey story from the old days." He spoke to Sam. "This is your sergeant's M.O. Tries to muscle his friends."

"That's not my style, George." Dowling got to his feet and signaled Sam they were leaving.

When they got to the door he stopped. "If you think I'd stoop so low as to snitch you off about stealing the Cessna from Jim's Air Service that Sunday afternoon . . . then buzzing the nudist colony in El Cajon. That's an unsolved case, George."

"That was a long time ago, Dowling."

"Flying upside down."

"I'd been drinking."

"San Quentin is full of guys who told the judge they'd been drinking."

Cardas smiled. "But I got a safety valve. Vincent Dowling is no snitch. You know, I'd almost blocked that uh . . . incident out."

Dowling walked over to the wall and studied an old photo of Cardas in the cockpit of a navy helicopter. "I'll bet those two cocktail waitress passengers haven't blocked it out. One wet all over the seat when you made the second pass thirty feet above the ground."

Cardas got up and put his arm around Dowling. "Boy,

we had some good times before this fucking department got professional, didn't we?'' He slapped Dowling on the shoulder. ''Don't worry about a leak. Get that approval signed and fire it up here.''

They shook hands and Dowling started for the door again, stopped and returned to the edge of the desk. He fumbled around the inside pocket of his sport coat, then removed a colored photograph and put it on the glass top in front of Cardas. A smiling young woman, surrounded by other smiling women of all ages, sat in a big armchair opening gifts.

''Is that your daughter, Dowling? Chrissakes, she was carrying her lunch pail to school last time I saw her.''

''No, that's not Jenny. This kid's name was Annie. Annie Richards. At one of the bridal showers they threw for her.'' He laid a second photo next to it. ''This is kind of a before-and-after, George.'' The photo was of a head. One eye was open, the other closed, and the tongue was protruding. ''Actually, she posed for this one just before they made the Y incision in her chest. Cute kid, huh?''

Dowling pivoted. ''Come on, Sam,'' he said. ''We're out of here. Guess it's just my bad luck to run into someone who follows policy and procedure.'' He had his hand on the doorknob. ''Let's go find somebody who has a heart.'' He closed the door behind him.

They had reached one of the helicopters when Cardas shouted at them from the doorway. ''All right, Dowling. Meet me at the Ninety-fourth Aero Squadron after work. We'll have a cold one and talk about it. Maybe I can bend the rules a little.''

They waved and were almost out of the hangar when he called to them again, directing everything to Sam this time.

''Hey, Red. Want to see San Diego from the heavens some starlit night? I'll let you fly the plane.''

It was time, Dowling reasoned, for Holly Novikoff to take a look at James Danko. His views remained unchanged. If Holly identified him, there still wasn't enough to move on. If she said it wasn't Danko, they still couldn't get off him. A solid identification was improbable, given the conditions. Hell, a solid identification could be improbable given any conditions. More than once he had shown lineups to victims who, during the crime, had seen suspects in good light for extended periods of time. Sometimes Dowling had the gun, the money and the confession *before* the lineup was even held.

"Number three is the one, Sergeant," a victim once told him. "That's a face I'll never forget." Except that number three, standing next to the real crook, had been doing time for traffic warrants when the stickup went down.

Under an old Warren Court ruling, the suspect had the right to have an attorney present at a live lineup. If Earl Warren had his way, they'd be present at photo lineups too, but Earl Warren was toes up, a painful thorn long removed from Dowling's paw. Besides, live lineups were for arrested suspects, and they were a long way from arresting James Danko.

At this point, he was maybe 90 percent sure they had the right guy in their sights. For Vincent Dowling, ten more percentage points were needed. There were things left to do, so he would talk to Holly Novikoff in the morning.

"No way. I don't ever want to see that animal again."

"He wouldn't be seeing you, Holly. You'd be in a van, with smoked windows. We're just asking that you watch people pass by on the sidewalk. If you see the man, tell us. That's all."

"You're not listening, Sergeant." She was yelling into the phone. "I want nothing to do with any of this. EVER."

"Holly. I know—"

"No you don't. You don't know anything. Because you're not the one who's afraid to go out of the house any more. You're not the one who's afraid to answer the door. You're not the one who goes to therapy. So you don't know anything, do you?''

Before he could answer, she said, "Besides, Rachel Tiffany says I don't have to do anything I don't want to. She said if you were doing your job you'd have the man in jail already. I have a lot more faith in Women Of Will than I have in the San Diego Police Department.''

Just after dark the next evening, at a market they had followed Danko to, a police officer with tan shapely legs, wearing white shorts and a T-shirt, carrying a small overnight kit questioned an employee at the checkout counter. She had timed her approach to coincide with Danko's arrival in the line, where he juggled bread, milk and bags of vegetables. The officer didn't look his way but spoke loud enough for him to hear.

"How long will it take me to walk to Utah and"—she looked at a piece of paper in her hand—"Utah and Adams Avenue? And how do I get there?''

"You're at Cleveland and Meade," a teenager at the next checkstand told her. "Ten blocks over and three blocks up.''

"Shithouse luck," Gus Denver said fifteen minutes later. "Why did Danko have to drive straight home? Even if he'd just gone out of his way to take a look at her. Show us a *little* something.''

"I'm getting desperate," Dowling told them. "Nothing's clicking. Maybe he's not our boy.''

"Did you decide against the stiff call to his wife?'' Shea asked. "Try to snooker him back onto the sidewalks?''

Dowling would have a woman telephone the house when Danko was at work. The caller would ask for him, then act surprised to find a woman at the house; be evasive when Karen Danko queried her.

"I decided against it," Dowling said. "If he is our guy, the hell his wife would raise may set him off. May make him hit the streets and walk right into our setup.'' He lit a Camel. "But if we're wrong, if it's not Danko, then it's a shitty thing to do."

Lieutenant George Cardas had been more than willing to help with surveillance.

"We'd have to use a fixed wing. He'd hear a chopper, and besides, we don't have to get that low," he said.

Sketching the streets as Dowling briefed him, they saw the problem at the same time.

"We put the little infrared device on his bumper, he could drive to San Francisco and our I.R. binoculars won't let us lose him," Cardas said. "But let's say he's on a dark residential street. We can tell you he put his headlights out, which means he pulled to the curb and stopped, or, like on your last case, he's snarking in an alley. At that point though, we can't tell you if he's still in the car or out on foot."

Dowling nodded, fingering his bottle of beer.

"Try this one on, Vince. You're on the ground two blocks back. We're in the sky. Your boy sees a target real close to him, pulls to the curb and jumps out and grabs her. He's got her in the bushes while we're pulling our pud."

The picture was all too vivid for Dowling. "You're right," he said, head down. "Air surveillance won't work. I'll have to come up with something else. I'm running out of gas, George."

He liked the small coffee shop that had recently opened for business. It suited his sense of order to stop on Mondays, Wednesdays and Fridays for coffee. There was nothing not to like about it. Easy parking in the lot next door, hot coffee, an uncrowded counter and polite help.

He felt somewhat relieved because it appeared two good things were going to happen at once. A transfer to the Trust Department and promotion to assistant vice president. People could kid all they wish about the way banks throw titles around, but that was the system. He had earned it, and the money would be helpful. Prestige

*was important to him, and it would be nice not to deal
with credit cards and auto loans anymore. It also meant
he would be reporting to a man instead of a woman, and
for that he was grateful. Women didn't understand him
and he could not recall one who had ever made an effort
to try.*

*With his world improving, he was not motivated to take
to the streets. His wife was leaving him alone for the most
part. Perhaps she felt a sense of contributing, producing
revenue now instead of babies.*

*"I see your Kansas team won again," the old man next
to him said. He hadn't noticed him sit down at his elbow
and order.*

"Yes. You follow Kansas State?"

*"Like I told you last week, I follow college football,"
the man said. "Everything from the Big Ten to Shippens-
burg versus Clairon." He nudged Danko's elbow.
"Course it's the Big Eleven now that Penn State slipped
in there."*

*"Do you come here every day? It seems you're here
every time I am." He didn't feel like talking this morning,
so he began hurrying with his toast and sliced fruit.*

*"Every day," the man said. "My cardiologist told me
to take long walks. That's how I discovered this place. He
didn't say anything about these big cinnamon rolls,
though." The man smiled when he said that.*

*"Not good for you, old-timer. Especially if you have a
heart condition. I told you last week. Fruit. That's what
you should have. And decaffeinated instead of regular."*

The old man picked up the Union-Tribune *and turned
to the local news.* "Haven't seen anything lately about
these rapes and murders out in the east end of town," *he
said, picking up a large forkful of bun. Some of the glaze
dripped on his chin, and he wiped it with his hand.*

He ate the last orange wedge in his dish. "I've heard
a little about them," *he said.*

"If you can keep a secret," the old man said, lowering

his voice and looking around, "they're going to get the guy pretty soon."

"Really. How do you know?"

"They know who it is."

"They do?" He wiped his fork with a napkin. "How do you know? You're not a policeman, are you?"

The man ordered more coffee, and when the waiter had left he poured a lot of cream into the cup. "My sister-in-law's neighbor is a secretary down there." He lowered his voice again. "She types reports. Says they're following the guy around."

"Really?"

"Just at night, though. The guy works in the daytime."

"Where does he work?"

"I don't know. But they don't have any trouble finding him. They stick this little device under his rear bumper. This gal tells my sister-in-law it's about the size of the palm of your hand." He sipped some coffee. "Then, with this thing they carry in the police car, they hone in on him. The gal always has trouble remembering the name of it. A 'transponder' or something like that." The old man wiped his mouth with a napkin this time and got up slowly. "I hope when they arrest him, they cut his nuts off. Well, I'm out of here. See you tomorrow."

He waited until the old man had crossed the street and headed in the opposite direction. Then he paid his check and walked to the parking lot. He opened the door of the Honda, removed his attaché case and took out a legal pad. With the pad in his hand, he went to the rear of the car and stood for a moment, looking around slowly. Then he took a quarter from his pocket and dropped it on the ground. Putting the pad under his knee, he pretended to search for the money, at the same time running his hand under the entire length of the bumper. He found nothing, got to his feet, repocketed the quarter and drove off.

From the second floor of an office building across the street, Sam Mulcahy turned away from the window, pulled the walkie-talkie from her purse and raised it to her mouth.

"Marathon to one hundred, come in. Marathon to one hundred. The son of a bitch went for it."

※ Twenty-three

"He finally made a mistake," Dowling said. He had been smiling for an hour. "I was beginning to think he was a machine." They were all smiling.

"While you guys were watching Danko look for the bumper device, Gus and I were going through his trash. You did good and we didn't," Larry Shea said.

They had arranged with the trash truck crew to set aside the bags from Danko's curb until the detectives met them around the corner.

"Sanitation employees don't get paid enough," Shea said. He sniffed his hands. "I've washed three times and I still feel cruddy."

"Nothing?" Dowling asked. He had hoped for anything. Notes. Newspaper clippings. A desperate measure by a desperate detective.

"Nothing," Gus said.

"We can tell you they're big corn flakes eaters. Shave with throwaway razors. Use lemon oil to polish furniture. Her Aunt Carla in Seattle is having a hysterectomy. That's about it," Shea said. "Oh, one more thing. We can tell you with absolute certainty—absolute certainty—Mrs. Danko is *not* pregnant."

"You're disgusting, Shea," Sam said. "You're both pigs."

Gus raised his hands in protest. "What did I do?"

"You're his partner."

"We stick to him like glue if he goes out after they get home," Dowling said. It was just after dark of the same day, and they were bunched together in Dowling's undercover car. They had tailed the Dankos from home to a Chinese restaurant on Midway Drive, gotten the eyeball on the Honda, then Sam, Gus and Shea parked their cars and piled into Dowling's for final instructions. From the used car lot they parked in, exit could hurriedly be accomplished in any direction. Dowling's Oldsmobile was at the end of a row of vehicles with price tags on the windshields.

He had opted against the transponder-assisted tracking device for the same reason air surveillance was too risky. A close tail was necessary, and that meant visual contact. Sam Mulcahy had been wired with an on-body recorder, and if Danko left the house alone, Dowling would see if they could jockey her into position to be a temptress. There was nothing left for them to do, he moaned, except catch Danko in the act.

An hour had elapsed when Sam announced she had to go. "To the wee deli on the corner. I'll not be but a minute."

"Too far. They could come out any minute. Go potty in between the trucks," Dowling urged.

She examined the long row of trucks in the darkness, all facing perpendicular to the sidewalk. "No harm, I suppose. The lot is closed." She took just a few steps and returned. "Don't be getting out and spying on me, now. I'm deadly serious."

"We promise," Dowling said.

Sam walked one hundred feet away, then disappeared, leaving the three sitting in the car.

"When we see her head raise up and she starts back, slam the car door hard. She'll think we've been out of the car peeking," Shea said.

Gus shook his head. "She'll go ape shit."

"She just got over being mad," Dowling said. "Count me out."

They thought they had talked him out of it, but a moment later Shea reached over, opened the door wide, then slammed it shut.

"Lord, Shea. That was loud enough for Danko to hear," Gus said, slouching down in his seat.

Sam Mulcahy started trotting as soon as the door slammed. "Who got out of the car?" she demanded when she reached the window.

"Nobody," Dowling said. "Trust us."

"I heard the door close. You peeked at me, didn't you, now?"

"The sergeant was standing next to the car flipping a coin. He dropped it and Gus and I got out to help him look for it. That was all," Shea said.

"We had to get down on our hands and knees and look under the trucks," Gus said innocently.

"You promised you'd not," she yelled.

"We were down there looking for the quarter and saw the moon," Shea said. "I've never seen the moon set that low before."

"Me neither," Dowling added. "Only about a foot above the asphalt."

"The moon's diameter is supposed to be two thousand one hundred-sixty miles according to the Jeopardy Game."

"This moon wasn't *that* wide. Not quite."

"I've seen harvest moons and Indian moons."

"Silvery moons and new moons."

"This is the first time I've ever seen an Irish moon."

"I got a moon shot."

"I was moonstruck."

"I got moon-eyed."

Sam tried not to laugh. "Little boys stay little boys," she sighed, slapping Gus Denver on the side of the head. "That's for being the ringleader."

Dowling logged the time at 8:17 P.M. when the Dankos arrived home. He had resigned himself to another three hours of idle sitting just before Danko left Maryland Street in the Nissan. At 9:07 they watched him carry a small bag from the store at Cleveland and Meade.

"Dogbite to all units. He's not going home this time. Staying east on Meade. That's east on Meade," Gus reported.

He's in Annabelle Dominguez–Holly Novikoff country, Dowling told himself.

"St. Louis reporting North on Hamilton, crossing Monroe. Now east on Monroe," Shea added.

"Keep a tight group," Dowling told them. This was a first. Danko had never traveled quiet residential streets for them. He felt excitement wash over him. If he made a quick decision to use Sam as a decoy, he would hurry her into his car, then decide where to drop her off. Danko would dictate that. It meant dumping her car, making a tough surveillance tougher yet.

"Dogbite: he is north on Oregon, crossing Madison. Driving *slow*."

Oregon and Madison. One fucking block from where he murdered Joy Larson. Dowling hammered the steering wheel, then picked up his microphone to have Sam meet him. It was time. He was just depressing the key when Larry Shea cut in.

"St. Louis advises still on Oregon, north of Adams . . . he crossed Collier, heading toward Copley now. Holy shit! There's some kind of event breaking at Our Lady Of Peace. Girls all over the place."

Dowling banged the steering wheel again. He couldn't have concocted a worse nightmare. OLP was the Catholic girl's academy. Danko wouldn't be intimidated by the flurry of sidewalk activity. Could use it to his advantage, in fact.

Dowling cruised in front of the school. Scores of girls scurried out of the two-story white stucco building. There were some in pairs or triplets, but he spotted several walking alone, branching off into the dark streets.

"Who's got him?" Dowling said. There was no response. "I said, *who has the eyeball?*" He drove beside a girl walking alone in midblock, wanting to grab her, shield her with the safety of his car, drive her to yet another single girl and do the same.

"Does ANYBODY have the damn eyeball?" he said again, afraid of the answer.

"We've lost him, one hundred," Gus announced.

Dowling felt the sweat on his hands. He had blown it. Right now, right this goddamn minute, Danko could be tugging at a brassiere. Could be hidden behind an oak tree, a victim ten steps away. *Could be asking what time it was.*

"St. Louis: the car's not on Oregon."

"Marathon: Not on Copley either."

If Danko was still cruising, and he called Patrol in Code Three, they might find him. Make the stop and . . . but Danko would know then. Would know he was the one the cops were watching. Then they'd never get him. Danko was clever. He'd find another way. Change his M.O. But if he didn't call Patrol . . .

"Dogbite to all units. Our boy's sitting at the Texaco, Thirtieth and El Cajon. Been here a while 'cause he's just putting the lid on his tank."

Dowling had trouble believing it. Danko had never slowed at the high school. Had headed east, then south.

"I thought I saw his damn Nissan going east, but it was a long way off," Gus told them after they had escorted Danko home. "I took a flyer and it was him. Didn't want to put it out on the air till I was sure, 'cause you were all needed around OLP."

"Close call, boss," Shea said, opening a can of beer.

Dowling didn't answer. Just sat and watched cars streaming by on Washington Street. Wishing he were in one of them. Wishing he weren't in a police car. Wishing he weren't a police officer. They were standing in a dark corner of a parking lot, and after he sent them home, he sat in his car for a long time before strolling to the phone booth.

"Hello." She sounded sleepy.

"It's me. I needed to call you," Dowling said.

"Where are you?" Angela asked.

"At a pay phone on Washington."

He told her what had happened. "If we moved too quickly, and he got on to us, and we never arrest him, I thought about all the women he could murder in his lifetime." Cigarette smoke got in his eyes. "All I had to do was call Patrol in right away, or start honking our horns and . . . the hell of it is, I still hadn't made up my mind when Gus located him." He clenched his fist. "What does that say about me?"

"Come on over," she said softly.

"It's midnight."

"Come on over. I'll put the key under the mat."

≋ Twenty-four

"So how late did you work last night, Pop?" She was putting things back in the fridge as Dowling rinsed breakfast dishes and wiped the kitchen table. He had told her about the incident at Our Lady of Peace.

"Late-late. Do I need to pick up more vitamins for you?"

"I woke up at three and you weren't home."

Dowling rinsed two dishes he had already rinsed.

"How serious are you and Angela Lord?"

"What do you mean, how serious?"

"Are you sleeping with her?"

"Jennifer Dowling, you're talking to your *father*." He turned his back, rolled down his cuffs and buttoned them. "I'm going to forget you even said that." He patted his pockets for car keys. "I'm meeting the D.A. for coffee before I go to the office. Tell Matt so long for me."

She smiled. "Matt lives in Redlands. He got married a couple of months ago."

They sat at a corner table in the coffee shop across the street from the courthouse, which housed the district attorney's offices.

"So you want to kidnap me for three hours this morning. What's this big mystery all about?" Arland Hayes asked, buttering toast.

He was thirty-five years old and bald. He wore black-rimmed glasses. He had a smooth face with pale blue eyes that did the smiling for him. He was the best trial lawyer Dowling had ever seen, and he had watched Belli and Bailey and Jerry Spence work their magic on a jury. Race-horse Haines he had not seen, but it was inconceivable the Texan could be better than Arland Hayes.

Hayes's parents had worked at a General Motors plant for forty years, their feet moving sideways at a snail's pace, hands furiously bolting the seats of lumbering Pontiacs crawling down the assembly line. He had gone to the University of Michigan on academic scholarship, then stayed in Ann Arbor to take a degree at the prestigious law school. Arland Hayes was an exception, he told Dowling when they'd teamed up several years prior.

"There's an old saying. The A students become professors, B students become judges and C students are the trial lawyers. I never wanted to be a damn academemician. I'd miss having characters like you, Dowling, make my life miserable by bringing me trumped-up cases with witnesses who have trouble giving their name under oath."

Hayes turned down lucrative offers from megabuck legal firms in Detroit, New York and San Francisco, instead hanging out a shingle in lawyer-saturated San Diego, where his grandparents lived.

"I starved. Figured I was a hell of a trial lawyer though. Signed on with the D.A.'s office just to get a little experience before going back out on my own and setting the world afire."

"Then it was too late," Dowling said. "It was in your blood."

"Yeah. Real lawyers are able to argue everything both ways. I wanted to stay on the side of the angels."

Hayes had risen to chief deputy, two rungs on the ladder below the district attorney himself. Law enforcement's good luck, Dowling had long believed.

He had also long believed it was prudent not to give the D.A. piecemeal information on circumstantial evidence cases where a suspect was not in custody. By their nature, the cases looked weak until the full impact of events were laid out on a table and studied by the D.A. He would make an exception this time.

Not that he had expectations of getting a warrant issued for Danko. They were short a full deck. But he needed to bounce this one off Hayes, needed to stimulate the prosecutor. Make an investment in tomorrow.

"I'm going to take you on a trip around East San Diego," Dowling told him when they took the Washington Street ramp off the Cabrillo Freeway. "Don't bother taking notes or anything; just let me be a tour guide. You'll find stuff out just as it came to me."

For the next several hours, they covered the cases by order of occurrence, getting out at each location. Hayes stood in Holly Novikoff's flower bed, traveled the route Adrienne Roe's protector had chased the suspect, ran his fingers gently along the interior garage wall where Joy Larson perished. Dowling was careful in his narration, smoothing the details, not jumping ahead.

They used a ladder to climb to the roof of Mr. Van Cleave's garage, and half an hour later Dowling provided Danko's name for the first time. He showed Hayes the house at 4652 Maryland, the Chinese restaurant on Midway Drive and the Academy of Our Lady of Peace.

Then they went to Hayes's office. A giant poster in black and white, frayed at the corners, was pinned to the wall behind his chair. W. C. Fields faced the viewer, shuffling cards on a green felt poker table. The strip above the poster, in large print, said HAYES DOESN'T MAKE DEALS.

"I hate that damn poster," a chain-smoking defense attorney told Dowling once. "It hits me right in the face when I come in to plea bargain."

"Frustrating is an understatement," Hayes said, taking a big swallow of black coffee turned lukewarm. "You have nobody who can . . . who will ID him. No fingerprints. No shoe impressions. No blood or semen. You can't even isolate a suspect pubic hair." The prosecutor doodled on a yellow pad. "That retired cop you put next to Danko in the coffee shop, did he ever hear Danko say, '*Ciao*, baby?' That is what he said to the Sheffield victim, isn't it?"

"Yes, he said it to Sheffield and no, he didn't repeat it in the coffee shop."

"So, to summarize. You have a description of a Honda, but no license number. A guy who lives in the area of the crimes. Who fits the physical description. Who can run fast. Who wears T-shirts and, arguably, looks somewhat like the composite sketch." Hayes got up and walked around his office. "Oh yeah, I almost forgot. He has a nice smile. Big fucking deal."

They sat in silence for a while. When Hayes started talking again Dowling noted he used "we" instead of "you."

"We have a banker with no criminal record, who has a pretty wife and a little poop-ass kid with pink bonnets who could make a corporate raider smile." Hayes sat down, then sprung up again. "An ex-girlfriend who says he whacked her a couple of times and an Irish police-woman who saw him drop a quarter in a parking lot." He took a deep breath. "Why didn't I stay in Michigan?"

Dowling went outside for a cigarette and watched a hooker collar a young sailor on West Broadway. Smelled hamburgers frying from a café and salt air, thanks to a southwest wind.

Tomorrow he'd be talking to Danko.

"You're going to pull him in?" Arland Hayes said when Dowling returned.

"I have to. If he beats us he beats us, but I've got an obligation to all those potential victims."

"You know I can't give you a criminal complaint? It's just not there."

"I know, Arland."

Dowling's pager beeped and he dialed a number he didn't recognize.

"Dr. Lord told us Holly Novikoff was traumatized and

wouldn't talk to you, Sergeant," the coordinator of the Rape Crisis Center said. "We just had a little meeting with her. Why don't you give her a call?"

"Cripes," Hayes said after Dowling hung up. "If Holly Novikoff can pick Danko out of a photo lineup, even if she can say 'similar,' I'll give you a complaint for two counts. Rape on Novikoff because she ID'd him, and murder on Annie Richards because that's where the Honda was seen. Would it make you feel better having a warrant in your pocket for leverage when you interrogate him?"

"Yeah. But the warrant would just be based on probable cause, huh? Won't stand on its own?"

"Right, Vince. It would come down to a confession. You get a confession, or short of that, damaging statements, and we take him to trial. If he won't talk to you, or denies it, we release him the next morning and dismiss. That's the best I can do."

"The Rape Crisis Center people straightened me out a little. I owe you an apology about the things I said," Holly Novikoff told Dowling in the squad room three hours after he left the District Attorney's office.

"Holly, none of us can even imagine what it's like in your shoes. You don't owe us an apology about anything. Not ever."

The envelope in his hand contained five photographs, one of Danko and the others of police officers Dowling had recruited. A crime lab photographer had taken them the week before. Using a telephoto lens, he had captured a good head shot of Danko in a shopping mall. A few days later, with the same shoe store in the background, they staged the scene with plainclothes cops. Danko's photo had been labeled number 4.

"In a minute, Holly, I'm going to have you turn around, and I'm going to lay five pictures out on my desk. Then I'm going to ask you to look at them. The men in the pictures are about the same age, same general appearance." Dowling saw her hands trembling. "I'm not

saying the man who . . . attacked you is one of the pictures. He may or may not be.''

"Let's do it,'' she said, pivoting to face the wall.

When he turned her back around, she looked at the
photos a long time, not a good sign in Dowling's experience. Her expression never changed.

"I don't think so,'' she said finally. Dowling had noticed she looked at number 4 longer than the others.

"Do you see anyone similar?'' he asked.

"Well, number four looks more like him than any of
the others.''

"There's a difference, Holly, between looking more
like him than any of the others, and being 'similar.' Do
you see a photo there that is similar to the man who attacked you?''

She didn't hesitate. "Number four is very similar. He
may even be the one.''

At 5:35 P.M. the next day, a patrol unit flashed its lights
and stopped Danko's Nissan on First Avenue, a few
blocks short of the on-ramp to Interstate 5.

Dowling pulled his detective's car behind the black-
and-white, getting out a moment after the uniformed officer had Danko's driver's license in his hand. Danko
wore a medium-gray pinstriped suit and a white shirt that
still looked crisp. Dowling extended his hand.

"I'm Sergeant Dowling, Mister Danko. We're investigating a series of crimes out in East San Diego, and we
need your help. Would you come down to the station and
talk with me?''

"Am I under arrest?'' Danko asked, smoothing his tie.
His eyes shifted from Dowling to the taller patrol officer
for the answer.

"Not unless you want to be,'' Dowling said. "Come
on, we'll park your car here and go down in mine.''

✂ Twenty-five

"You have the right to remain silent during questioning now or at any time," Dowling said. He pretended to read from the card he held in his hand, but he was accurately reciting from memory. Defense attorneys liked to pick on cops who didn't use their card, arguing that a lost word here or there changed the context of their client's understanding of his Miranda rights.

"Anything you do say will be used against you in court.

"You have the right to have an attorney present during this or any conversation, either an attorney of your own choosing, or if you can't afford an attorney, one will be appointed for you prior to questioning, if you so desire."

Danko nodded.

"Do you understand each of your rights as I have explained them to you?" Dowling asked.

Danko nodded again.

"I need an audible answer," Dowling said. He had learned just before picking up Danko that the video equipment wired into the seven-by-ten-foot interrogation room was defective, not operative. The audiotape's mechanism was fine and he had checked it moments before the arrest.

"Yes, I understand my rights. This is quite an experience," Danko said.

"Having in mind and understanding your rights, are

you willing to speak with me?'' Dowling concluded. Then he held his breath. Danko had come willingly as Dowling suspected he would. So it figured he would waive his rights, volunteer to talk. Still, he had seen suspects change their minds at the last minute. If Danko refused to waive, it was all over. A night in jail, oatmeal and scrambled eggs on the county, then the ID bracelet snipped off his wrist and the fresh air of the streets.

"Sure, I'll talk to you," Danko said. "I have nothing to hide."

We're here, Dowling told himself, feeling the pressure. The ghosts of Joy Larson and Annie Richards would taunt him if he failed, and he'd wonder the rest of his life what he might have done differently, said differently. He wasn't good at putting things behind him when it came to murder.

He wanted a cigarette badly but knew it would agitate the health addict sitting across from him. Shea had been sent home following emergency oral surgery, and Gus and Sam were parked around the corner from Danko's home. They would move in and question his wife when Dowling signaled, but that would be after the interrogation. A phone call now to a lawyer from Karen Danko would end it. That was what got all the interrogation hoopla started in the first place. Dowling knew the history.

In the early sixties, Danny Escobedo's shyster playing tag with cops all over an Illinois police station, trying to find his client, while Danny boy was frying himself in an interview room. Cops hadn't been saddled with giving rights before that, just sat a crook down and started talking. Then, about the time Dowling was pinning on a badge in 1965, the courts required suspects be given their Escobedo Rights. They could remain silent, statements could be used against them, they could have a lawyer. And just as cops all over the country were memorizing Escobedo, Ernesto Miranda was telling the Phoenix P.D. how he pulled a kidnap-rape. And everybody in the system thought Phoenix had done a fine job of making sure old Ernie understood his rights. Well, almost everybody.

In a 5–4 split, Chief Justice Warren and four of his brethren on the big court changed the rules. They reversed Miranda's conviction, then added a word here and there to the rights form until it looked like the one in Dowling's hand.

Well, Dowling told himself, pushing his yellow pad aside. He couldn't put it off any longer. It was time to go to work.

"I appreciate your coming down here, Mr. Danko."

"Sergeant Dowler, is it?"

"Dowling. D-o-w-l-i-n-g."

"Sorry. Sergeant Dowling. You said it was about crimes in East San Diego. May I ask what exactly?"

Dowling reminded himself to soften the wording. No rape or murder talk yet.

"A man is harming girls walking the streets. Having sex with them. A couple lost their life. We're talking to a lot of people who live in your area. We need help."

Danko shook his head and sighed. "That's terrible." He paused and looked thoughtful. "Is that the stuff I read about where there was a . . . what do you call it, a picture in the newspaper?"

"A composite photo," Dowling said.

"That's it, a composite. No wonder you dragged me down here. I do look like him, don't I?"

"You sure do, Mr. Danko."

"Me and a lot of others, I bet."

"Why do you think a guy would do that kind of thing?" Dowling asked.

"God only knows, Sergeant. Maybe he doesn't get enough at home. Says '*Ciao*, baby' to the Mrs. and ducks out."

Ciao, baby. Dowling hoped Danko didn't see him stiffen. God bless Rene Sheffield. He *had* said it to her.

"Do you think those crimes are about sex, Mr. Danko?"

"I don't know; I'm not an expert like you, Sergeant. What do you think they're about?"

Dowling leaned back in his chair. It was going all right. He felt himself relaxing a little.

"Damned if I know," Dowling said. "I'm an old cop that the world is moving too fast for. Robberies and burglaries I understand, but I'm out of my element here." He rubbed his nose. "Would you like coffee or soda, Mr. Danko?"

"No thanks." He looked at his wristwatch. "How long will this take, Sergeant? I don't want my wife to worry."

"Let me speed it along," Dowling said. "There's some specific questions I need to ask you. These aren't accusatory, you understand. A matter of routine."

Danko waved him on. He had chosen to keep his suit coat on, his top shirt collar still buttoned. The bastard was a fashion statement.

"Were you home last night?" Dowling asked.

"As a matter of fact, my wife and I . . . and daughter of course, went to dinner at a Chinese place over on Midway Drive last night."

"Anywhere else?"

"No."

"Didn't leave the house again?"

"No."

"Do you know where First and Walnut Avenue is, Mr. Danko?"

"Afraid not. I'm not much on street names. That's pretty bad because I work in the commercial department and have customers all over town."

Dowling carefully spread a map on the table and circled the intersection of First and Walnut. "Did you ever pull your Honda into an alley right . . . here?" Dowling said, drawing a line approximately through the garage of Mr. Van Cleave.

"Now, that I *am* sure of. Absolutely not."

"Did you ever walk up to a woman on the street, at night, on Kansas or Louisiana, Arizona, Van Dyke or

Wightman Street, Mr. Danko?'' Dowling drew circles around all of the locations.

"Absolutely not."

"We're almost done," Dowling said. "Did you ever throw a choke hold on a woman at those locations, drag her off and rape her, murder her perhaps."

"I know these questions are necessary, Sergeant, but . . . this is a terrible thing to have to go through. No. The answer is no to everything."

Dowling leaned forward and clasped his hands on the table. Innocent people would come unhinged if you suggested they'd murdered someone. Danko was responding like any good sociopath. Clicking off answers as if he were taking questions from a census taker. Dowling made a show of taking a deep breath.

"I'm not going to waste any more of your time or mine. We've been sitting here playing chess with each other, and I don't need to play any more. The reason I've horsed around with you is because I *wanted* you to make the denials you've been making."

"Why did you want me to make denials?" Danko's confidence had eroded a bit, Dowling believed.

"It's a point of criminal law," Dowling said. "Let me give you a for instance. Last year we had a guy, an investment broker up in the Golden Triangle, he wanted this woman killed because she wouldn't go out with him any more. We could prove he did certain things. Withdrew sums of money from the bank. Met a would-be hit man in Presidio Park. Provided a map of the woman's house. That sort of stuff." Dowling stopped for a moment. "We knew it was him when we sat him down in this room, and even though he didn't confess, his denials were all admissible in court, and since we proved he lied they convicted him."

"How does that . . . I don't get it. What are you telling me?"

Dowling stood and stretched. "Here's how it shakes out, Danko. In my office I keep a chart of all my murders.

And when we solve one, I pick up my marking pencil and draw a big, fat line through it. This afternoon, I drew a big fat line through my Madison Avenue murder and my Walnut Avenue murder. It was right after the district attorney handed me the warrant for your arrest.'' He reached in his pocket and laid the warrant in front of Danko, running his finger over the critical wording, then put it back in his pocket.

"When we break up our little tête-á-tête you're going to jail.''

Danko loosened his tie. ''You're making a horrible mistake. Just because I look like that picture in the paper. I'll take a lie detector test.''

"We only use the polygraph when we have doubt about a person's statement. There's no doubt here. I *know* you're lying, so there's no use hooking you up to the machine.''

Dowling sat back down. He was in a fragile area and had to move quickly. What he didn't want was to jar Danko into saying the ''L'' word. He looked at his wristwatch.

"Look, James. I have tickets for a show at the Civic Theater that starts in exactly forty-five minutes, and I'm going to be there when the curtain goes up. I'm not allowed to tell you everything we have on you, but I can run a few things by you. What the hell, we don't have as many secrets now.''

Dowling got up again and pretended to yawn. ''We have these cases starting out in the area you live, so we start looking at men who look like our composite photo. We take a picture of you coming out of Mansfield's in Fashion Valley where you bought that pair of cordovan wing tips, and we show it to those women and they say, 'Yep, that's positively the guy.'

Dowling saw no reaction and continued. ''Now prosecutors love it when victims ID defendants, and juries love it because it makes their job easier. But this homicide sergeant,'' Dowling pointed to himself, ''I never in my career built a case on eyewitness identification and I wasn't about to start now. Victims make honest mistakes sometimes. I couldn't live with myself if I put the wrong man in the gas chamber, so I told the D.A., 'Don't arrest this Danko guy yet. Christ, he works in a *bank*. Let me work on it some more. I want to be sure.' "

Dowling noted him paying strict attention. "So we started following you around. Recorded what days Mrs. Danko works at Whitecroft Stationer's. Watched you do your jogging routine a few minutes after you'd get home from work."

"You actually followed me around?"

"Mr. Danko. We know that when you go to The Breakfast Factory you're partial to sour cream on your blueberry pancakes. It looked so good to my detective in the next booth, *he* ordered some too. And believe me, he doesn't need that any more than I do." Dowling patted his paunch.

"It was interesting to learn how much of Kansas's corn is raised around your town of Kalvesta. By the way, Jetmore, down the highway a bit, is Jetmore the county seat of Hodgeman County?" Dowling said.

"Ah . . . yes, it is." Danko's eyes were fixed on Dowling.

"Where was I?" Dowling said, checking his wristwatch again. "Oh, yeah. So this suspect is grabbing these women off the sidewalk and having sex with them." Dowling lowered his voice. "I'm not so sure a couple of them didn't mind all that much. Anyway, this guy, when he's on top of them says, '*Ciao*, baby.' Just like you said it a few minutes ago.

"I'm running out of time, Mr. Danko, so I'm going to be talking faster and you'll just have to listen faster." Dowling shook his head. "Then I messed up pretty bad one night. We had followed you right into that alley there off Walnut Avenue. The one you said you'd positively never been in. Followed you in there, saw you put the Honda's headlights out and park right next to that garage.

Then—and this is where I messed up—a patrol officer puts out a call for assistance a few blocks away and we leave to cover a fellow cop who's fighting some guy and when we come back you're gone. Course if we'd known when we came back that girl was laying under those bushes against that house, we'd have flat-ass come over to Maryland Street and arrested you. But since we didn't find her for a while, I said, 'Let's play with Danko a little more.' ''

Dowling knew a con-wise guy wouldn't go for that horseshit story. Would know cops wouldn't back off a target on a murder surveillance.

''Of course that's a powerful piece of evidence, James. You in that alley. That was about enough to send you away. But the D.A. who's going to handle your case likes to hoist up these big display boards in court for the jury. You know, red pins and green pins and yellow pins and cripes, he's display happy. The D.A. will have that black guy testify . . . the black guy who's a defensive back and couldn't run you down over on Van Dyke Avenue . . . then right after the black guy steps down from the witness stand, the D.A. will show the jury videos of you taking the silver medal in the Big Eight Relays in 1980.'' Dowling put a bewildered look on his face. ''How in hell a human being can clear hurdles at that speed is beyond my comprehension, James.''

He put his hand on Danko's forearm. ''There's just one thing left. In the morning the D.A. is going to ask me, 'What did this Danko fellow have to say?' And there's essentially two things I can say. I can say, 'Well, Mister District Attorney, Mr. Danko said he was real sorry for doing these things. A lot of pressure had been building in his head, probably went all the way back to childhood days in Kansas. He fought the urge real hard, but it got the best of him. He knows he has a serious problem. He has a lovely wife and a cute infant daughter and a little house they're fixing up. He has a responsible job. He'd like a chance to make all of this right, take his place as a useful member of society again.' ''

Dowling got up once again. ''Or, we have to say, 'Well, Mister D.A., James Leon Danko, account officer, oops, excuse me, you got promoted, Assistant Vice President Danko denies it all and is saying, ''Fuck you, prove it, Cop.'' ' ''

Dowling neared the door. ''At which time the D.A. will say, 'Well, *fuck him, too*. Let's airmail him up to San Quentin. Those cons up there don't like rapists. They've all got mothers and wives and daughters. We'll provide Mr. Vice President Danko a needle and thread so he can sew up his poop chute.'

''Hell, James. Guys I've sent up there tell me after the first few times they won't have to beat you up any more. You'll see them coming and start taking your drawers down.''

Dowling put a hand on the doorknob. ''I feel a little sorry for you, Mr. Danko. I think you've got a good heart.'' He opened the door and started out.

''*Wait*. Wait, please, Sergeant. Can we talk some more?''

''Not if all I'm going to hear is more bullshit.''

Danko lowered his head. ''It won't be bullshit this time.''

''These are some *fine* ribs,'' Dowling said, looking for another napkin to wipe his hands on. Sam had picked up orders at the Kansas City Bar-B-Que after leaving Karen Danko's. They were in the critique room, taking a short break from listening to the Dowling-Danko tape. Dowling had carefully punched out the tiny tabs to prevent accidental erasure. Gus was in the squad room sorting reports, compiling a case notebook for Arland Hayes.

''Danko's wife was in a state,'' Sam said. ''The poor lass sat on the sofa, hugging the wee one and crying her heart out.'' Sam munched on a pork sandwich. ''She didn't know anything, Sergeant. Total shock. Just couldn't believe it. You know what, happy as I was to hear you copped him out, it broke my heart telling it to that lady. When Gus and I left, she actually thanked us for coming. As if we were company.''

Dowling flipped the recorder on. ''Okay. Here's where he talks about Joy Larson. Remember, we wondered how he'd spotted her so fast. Listen up.''

I'd been watching a girl and was about to make my move when a friend stopped and picked her up. So I headed back to my car, through this alley. A car pulled in off Madison and I ducked back. Then the driver got out, opened the garage door. The next thing I knew I was . . . I was on her. When she stopped breathing, I tried to revive her. I remember kneeling next to her crying. I'm so sorry. So sorry. Jail is not the place for me.

''Listen to this, Sam,'' Dowling said.

. . . The bitch with no tits, that was number three, on Wightman Street. I don't mean ''bitch,'' that's not nice. I'm really upset now, dredging all this stuff up. . . . Some of this is my wife's fault. I could never talk to her. . . .

. . . I only parked in an alley once, the one with the girl with the hanging bag. . . .

. . . Does the bank have to find out about this? . . .

. . . The thing is, it was like . . . all the stresses. I felt like they were going to destroy me . . . like I was losing control. I was maybe going insane. Does any of this make any sense, Sergeant Dowling? . . . Can somebody help me? . . .

Dowling put the cassette tape in a small cashbox, locked the box and put it in his desk drawer, which he also locked. ''Tomorrow, Sam, you can take the cassette down to the audio department, have them make copies, then log the original in the property room.''

''I don't know how you did it, Sergeant.'' She looked at the clock. ''It's half ten. Sure and get some sleep now.''

It hit Dowling suddenly. He had forgotten to notify Tom Stacy, and he hurried to the phone.

''Dowling, I *knew* you were holding back.'' When he

finished briefing him, Stacy said, "You're also the second one to wake me up in the last thirty minutes. Channel Thirty-nine just called me. Your friend and aspiring city councilperson, Rachel Tiffany, is holding a press conference at nine A.M. right in front of the goddamn police station. We're invited. How the hell did she find out about the Danko arrest so fast?"

"I don't think it's about Danko, Tom," Dowling said. "How about if we just follow her onstage with our news."

When she turned to her right, the morning sun caught her in the eyes, so she faced the camera crew next to the flagpole. Her entourage was much larger than at her previous press conference, made considerably more noise.

"I invited Sergeant Dowling and apparently he accepted. I see him in the audience," Rachel Tiffany said into the microphone. "He will probably make an attempt to explain away an announcement I am going to make. The police department had the East San Diego murder-rapist in their grasp and let him get away."

When the "Oh's" and "Ah's" had quieted down, she swept the hair from her face and continued. "A well-placed, confidential source has identified the killer as Steven Anthony Petrillo, the former employee of a local trucking company." She repeated the name at the request of several reporters.

"My action team contacted OMS trucking and they verified, reluctantly I might add, that an employee named Petrillo left their employ last week."

Tom Stacy looked at Dowling, who shrugged.

"The rapist is on the loose. If I am elected . . . *when* I am elected to the city council, I will fight for a strong and caring police department, responsive to women's issues—sensitive to women's needs." She halted for the applause and waving of WOW placards.

"Sergeant Dowling has mercilessly badgered one of the victims of these horrible assaults. For privacy purposes, I shall call her 'H.' 'H' was understandably traumatized by the experience and is receiving much-needed therapy. Sergeant Dowling, against the advice of her counselors, tried to get 'H' to confront Petrillo to identify him. Our sources also advise that Petrillo is a convicted rapist from Florence, Italy. My action team is in the process of verifying this as we speak."

A red-faced man in the back of the crowd buttoned his jacket to conceal the badge on his belt and called out, "What are the suspect's initials?" Then he winked at Dowling.

"I couldn't hear the question," Rachel Tiffany said.

"Someone asked for Petrillo's initials," a reporter told her.

Rachel Tiffany looked perplexed. "For whatever significance it may be, the initials are S-A-P." She waved to the crowd and stepped down.

When the cheering stopped, Dowling and Stacy stepped to the microphone. The captain of Homicide looked over the crowd, waiting for some of the booing to subside before he spoke.

"We have a short announcement. At nine P.M. last night San Diego Police Department homicide detectives, after an extensive investigation, booked James Leon Danko of San Diego for murder and rape in connection with the series in East San Diego. Danko is thirty-four years old, lives in the area of the crimes, is employed by a local bank, and when arrested, made statements about the crimes. We expect to arraign him within two days and expect additional charges to be filed by the district attorney, whom we have kept apprised of our investigation."

Stacy refused to take questions, citing legal issues, and Dowling had to wait for the bedlam to die down before he answered the Channel 10 reporter's question.

"This exclusive of Ms. Tiffany's is news to me," Dowling said. "I do know a *Joe* Petrillo, a longtime friend who just retired from OMS trucking after more than thirty years on the job. A very fine, law-abiding family man. If

Joe's been to Florence, that's news to me also. Florence, Colorado, maybe. Joe Petrillo, nor anyone named Petrillo was ever a part of our investigation.''

Dowling stepped away, then returned to the microphone. ''What were those initials again of Ms. Tiffany's suspect?''

''You son of a bitch, you set me up.''

''I don't know what you're talking about,'' Dowling said.

''She's not acting like a lady, Sergeant,'' Shea said through a swollen jaw. They stood in the lobby of police headquarters.

Rachel Tiffany raised her fist. ''I was called by a woman claiming to be a secretary at the police department,'' she screamed. ''She even gave me her name after I promised I wouldn't use it. Those two goons at the desk over there deny there's a Regina Carmichael on the department roster.''

''I'm not interested in your make-believe tactics and I'm not going to throw you in jail for disorderly conduct because I hear gutter language every day and besides, you'd swear I was just being vengeful. But those two goons''—Dowling pointed to the uniformed officers at the reception desk—''they may put your ass in the slammer if you don't get out of here.''

''You wouldn't want your opponent to flash your booking photo around on election night, would you?'' Shea said.

''If you're still a candidate by then,'' Dowling said. ''Good day, Ms. Tiffany. We have to go be responsive and sensitive.''

✺ Twenty-six

"Tell me again how you lost it," Dowling said softly. He closed his eyes, tapping his forehead with his fingers. "Tell us very slowly this time, and we'll spread out and find it."

"You lost the confession tape?" Shea said.

Sam Mulcahy was close to tears. Her brogue thickened and Gus leaned in to hear.

"I was on my way to the audio department to make the copy, but needed to stop in the loo . . . then, when I washed my hands I put it on top of the paper towel dispenser and—"

"Not in your purse?" Dowling said, not looking up.

"I don't carry my purse around the station." She bit her knuckles. "Screaming and yelling and like thunder off the walls it was. I ran to the door. Two patrol officers were in a donnybrook with a man in the hall. And a very pregnant lass on the floor, kind of scooched partway up against the wall. To her aid, I went. Kept the fighters from stepping all over her."

Sam made pushing motions with her arms. "Detectives came pouring out of the offices and the fight was over quickly, but the poor woman was having difficulty breathing. Somebody called for paramedics. But as soon as I could get somebody to comfort her I went back in the loo. It was *gone*. I'd left it alone for but a minute."

"It may have seemed like a minute, Sam, but it was a lot longer than that and *it was the goddamn confession tape*." Dowling banged his fist on the desktop. "The only copy of a goddamn confession that I don't have any *witnesses* to."

Arland Hayes looked pained a few hours later.

"You're positive it's gone, Vince?"

"We looked everywhere. Property room. Audio department. We emptied trash cans. Raised hell in every office on the floor and on floors above and below. It's gone."

"We arraign him tomorrow," Hayes said. "They don't get discovery for a while, so Danko and his lawyer won't have to be told until we put the reports in their hands. Maybe the tape will turn up by then."

Dowling focused on W. C. Fields's green visor. "Not many years ago we didn't tape everything. It wasn't a problem. Used to be my word against a crook's."

"More often it was *two* cops' word against a crook. And the system wasn't spoiled by the electronic age. The worst they can do is file a motion to suppress the statement."

Dowling could see the prosecutorial wheels spinning.

"I'll put the contractor on the stand," Hayes said. "Have him produce his work order for the video repair—prove *it* was on the fritz. Then I'll put Shea on, tell about his oral surgery—why he wasn't in the interrogation room with you. Then I'll put you on. Then Mulcahy testifies she heard the tape with you in the critique room right afterward. We'll be all right. The judge will rule for us, they'll see they're doomed, and the bastard will cry his eyes out wanting us to take a plea."

Maybe it would be that easy, Dowling thought. Danko begging for a life term to keep from getting gassed. Well, that would be Harland Hayes's decision, and he was welcome to it.

*   *   *

The next month went quickly. Bail for Danko was denied, and Dowling's team intensified their investigation, interviewing friends, neighbors and coworkers. It didn't surprise Dowling or Arland Hayes that nothing of evidentiary value was produced. Danko was a sexual psychopath, a deviant among deviants, and the predictable response of shock and disbelief was received from those who knew him.

Stacy had put them back in the rotation, so they'd worked a couple of murders. The confession tape had not turned up, and a motion to suppress Danko's statement was scheduled for November twenty-second, two days before Thanksgiving.

"I'm going to miss these ride-alongs," Sam told Damon Harper from the passenger's seat of the patrol car.

"Don't say that. It reminds me that you're leaving in five or six weeks." He slowed and studied a group of Crips in front of a 7-Eleven. "Can't you extend?"

"Why?"

Harper turned to look at her. "Because I can't imagine your not being here. Hell, you jump into my life and then . . . you're gone."

"The old 'what might have been?' " Sam said softly.

"Yeah, two different worlds and all that."

They rode in silence for a few blocks.

"Talk is you're doing real good work in Homicide," he said.

Sam lowered her head. "I wish that were true."

"What? You got your suspect in the jailhouse, right?"

"I'll tell you about it over dinner tomorrow night."

"Why not tell me—"

The radio interrupted.

"Units four-twenty-five John and four-twenty-six John. Four-fifteen family. Number thirty-two Rand Way."

Harper grabbed the mike. "Four-thirty King. Have the John units disregard. We're two-person and can handle." He made a U-turn and checked his wristwatch. "Jot down

3:02 P.M. will you, Sam.'' He drove several blocks, then made a right turn. ''Another family disturbance. I'd rather roll on a stickup in progress 'cause at least you know what you're getting into.''

Dowling, Gus and Shea were sorting paper work on a murder-suicide when a uniformed lieutenant from the watch commander's office opened the critique room door. He was younger than any of the three detectives, but his shoulders sagged when he put his hand on Dowling's arm.

''This is a shit business, and I've got bad news,'' he said.

''What?'' Dowling looked up. Jenny was driving to Redlands. Spending the weekend with Matt and her sister-in-law. Should have arrived by now. He pictured a traffic accident.

''Your Irish cop is eleven–forty-four, Sarge. Took a head shot at a family disturbance call in Paradise Hills. Off Reo and Potomac. I'm real sorry.''

''Sam is *dead*?'' Gus Denver grabbed the lieutenant's arm.

''Time element?'' Dowling snapped.

''Twenty minutes ago. I don't have details yet.''

''Suspect in custody?'' Dowling said without moving.

''In custody eleven–forty-four. Shot himself after he ran into the bushes trying to hide.''

''She was on a ride-along.'' Larry Shea's eyes looked like they weren't seeing anything.

''Dead at the scene, or did they roll with her?'' Dowling asked.

''At the scene. Sergeant Cassidy's team is handling,'' the lieutenant said. ''I didn't know officer Mulcahy. I'm sure sorry.'' He stood in place for a moment, turned and left quietly.

Gus was the first to speak when they were alone. ''That girl's not gone. Something crazy's just going on. Sam's not dead.''

"Yeah, she's dead," Dowling said. "Got killed by some asshole at a four-fifteen call and the asshole's dead, too." He looked at his detectives. "I don't need to go see her. We'll talk to Cassidy when he's had time to sort it out. Get filled in."

He picked up the folders in front of him. "It's almost midnight in Ireland. I'll call the chief superintendent in charge of her division. They have to notify her family. Someone'll go out to the farmhouse. Sit with her mother and father. She's got five brothers, you know.

"Gus, you return her rental car. Shea, you go tell her apartment manager. Secure the place. We'll work with her family on what has to be done."

Dowling got up, walked deliberately to the side of the room and punched his fist through his blackboard. He hurled it to the floor and watched it splinter. "It's all over," he said. "Sam Mulcahy is gone."

An hour later, on the phone, Sergeant Jack Cassidy raised his voice. "I don't want to hear that, Dowling. The husband stepped out of the bushes with his gun pointed and cranked off five shots rapid-fire. Two hit the police car, two didn't hit anything and one got Sam between the eyes. The guy was back in the bushes before the patrol officer could get his gun out of the holster, for Chrissake."

"I shouldn't have let her go on ride-alongs," Dowling said.

"Don't 'should' on yourself, either," Cassidy scolded. "I want you to listen to this, Vincent Dowling, Tom Stacy, Jack Cassidy, the Lord Himself, any son of a bitch stepping out of the passenger side of that police car was going to be dead. *It just happened.*"

"Then why do I feel guilty?"

"Guilty? You want to talk guilty? That patrol officer she was with, Damon Harper. He wants to turn in his resignation."

*   *   *

Dowling moped through what was left of the late afternoon. He reached Jenny and Matt in Redlands to tell them. Jenny wanted to drive back to San Diego but he talked her out of it. Tom Stacy, on a desert vacation in Borrego Springs, had been notified by the department.

A little after five, he reached Angela Lord in her room at the Los Angeles Hilton.

"My God. 3:07 P.M. I was giving a paper at USC. Standing at a lectern while Sam was . . . I'll come home tonight."

"No. Present your other paper tomorrow. I'm okay."

He walked to the elevator with Gus and Shea.

"The 153 Club, boss?" Shea asked.

"I'm buying the first round," Gus said.

Dowling shook his head. "I need a quieter place tonight, and if you don't mind, I think I'd like to be alone. Go on home to your wives."

The Sunsets American Bar & Grill was on the fifteenth floor of the circular Holiday Inn at First Avenue and Cedar Street. Tourists and conventioneers, mostly software salespeople, were scattered around the lounge and Dowling took a seat at the end of the bar, pleased several stools next to him were unoccupied.

"Irish whiskey and water. *Jameson* Irish whiskey," he instructed the bartender.

It wasn't as though he hadn't gone through this before, Dowling thought to himself. Burying a cop wasn't exactly a phenomenon in homicide work. He'd only worked for Stacy a short time when he examined Benny Hogue's body on the coroner's slab, and Benny had been a pal, too.

There'd been others since, of course, not that it made things easier, but people got used to almost anything, didn't they? Still, it was that indescribable twisting of the gut that occurred the *very instant* you got the news.

Two hours later he switched to a small table by the window on the First Avenue side. From right to left, he watched airliners landing, watched them drop below the horizon, their lights blending with miniature lights on the hills forming a backdrop.

The harbor was calm, and dark clouds at sea had a purplish tinge at the top, looking like rugged mountains he had seen once in Las Cruces, New Mexico.

Looking at the sky, he hoisted his glass and said softly, "There's a new star up there tonight, folks."

The hell of it was, and he had thought a lot about this, it was different when cops died. Soldiers were killed in battle by other soldiers. Burning roofs collapsed on fire fighters. But cops were killed by assholes. Where was the nobility in being killed by an asshole?

Dowling started drinking doubles, and when the waitress left at ten o'clock, he padded to the bar for refills. The bowls of popcorn hadn't looked good earlier, but he wished he had some now.

Fewer planes were landing and traffic below had diminished when he walked unsteadily to the men's room, his glass in his hand. Zipping his fly one-handed, he almost caught himself. Time. Time was what he was running out of, he told himself when he looked in the mirror. Once he had believed the department would be there forever. He'd never listened to the people who warned him he loved the job too much. He wanted to believe there was more time. The thought of retirement terrified him.

His ashtray was overflowing, so he took another from the empty table next to him. She was wearing kelly green slacks and a beige blouse when she waved good-bye to them after lunch. He closed his eyes when he imagined the autopsy report.

"Stomach contents consistent with beans and rice. . . ."

Of course they'd be consistent with beans and rice. They'd had lunch together, the entire team. Not everyone was lucky enough to have their final meal at Chuey's, who only served up the finest cheese enchiladas in a town full of fine cheese enchiladas.

When he got up and put his drink on the pay phone's

ledge, he became confused. L.A. Hilton or L.A. Marriott? He tried them both.

"It's midnight," Angela Lord said.

"It is also the very first day of my retirement."

"Where are you, Vincent?"

"I am coming to get you and take you to Idaho."

"Idaho?"

"A little town in Idaho where there is no crime."

"Go to bed, Vincent."

"Pack your bag. I'll pick you up in front of the hotel in exactly two hours."

"Please tell me where you are. Are you alone?"

"S'matter of fact, you don't have to pack your bag. I'll buy you a new bag in Idaho. We're going to start all over."

"Umm-humm. And your daughter?"

He cursed himself for not thinking about Jenny.

"She's coming, too," he said.

"We'll all make a fresh start?"

"Good. You've been thinking about it, too."

"Please tell me where you are. Are you driving?"

"You can be a country doctor. The most beautifulist country doctor in Idaho. In all of the world."

"Is Gus or Shea with you?"

"I'll buy you a buckboard 'cause I love you."

"You love me?"

"That's why I'm taking you to Idaho."

Later, he was slouched over the table when the bartender picked up the empty glasses.

"Sir, it's closing time. Just you and me. I've locked the door. Vice squad gets upset if I go extra innings. Are you staying in the hotel? You shouldn't be driving."

"I was going to drive. I was going to go to Idaho." He got up and sat down again. "I'll finish off this drink and get out of here so you don't get in the grease."

Dowling tossed the whiskey down quickly, then found enough change to buy another pack of Camels and fed the machine.

"Sir, is your name Dowling?"

"That's me, innkeeper."

"There's a guy pounding on the door calling for you."

"Describe him, innkeeper."

"He's an old guy with white hair and a polo shirt."

"Are you okay?" Tom Stacy asked when Dowling made his way to the glass door that separated the bar from the foyer and elevator.

"Of course I'm okay. I'm getting a little drunk."

"I called the house, then the 153 Club. I was running out of guesses when I found you," Stacy said as they got into his car.

"You're supposed to be in the desert."

Stacy pulled onto First Avenue, made a couple of turns, then cruised east. "CHP stopped me for speed near Alpine. Nice young Chip. I think he may have smelled a little booze on my breath. Says, 'Slow it down, Captain.'" Stacy smiled. "So I cut it to seventy the rest of the way."

"I can't buy you a drink because it's after two o'clock in this squeaky-clean goddamn town you and I created." Dowling belched. "You can buy pussy or rock cocaine after two o'clock, or hire somebody to knock off your uncle Melvin, but you can't buy a fuckin' drink. That's why I'm going to Idaho."

Stacy pointed to the back seat. To a twelve-pack of beer and a bottle of Jack Daniels.

"We can drink at my house or your house or we can go to the tracks," Stacy said.

"The *tracks*. Hot damn." They high-fived as Stacy floored it for downtown.

Dowling leaned back in the seat. He and Stacy had worked the vice squad ten years apart, but traditions dying hard was one of the things he loved about police work. Quitting time was four in the morning, but for years vice squads would gather at the railroad tracks, the whole squad, sixteen strong, and drink the beer they had stashed, swapping tales of the evening's wins and losses until the sun came up.

"Seems like yesterday," Stacy said, as he skidded the car to a halt at the corner of Union and Island. "Except," he got out and looked around, "except all the warehouses are gone." He popped a can of beer.

"And somebody took the ice house," Dowling said.

"Worse yet, somebody took the tracks, old Sergeant."

They shuffled around the deserted intersection, amazed to find a patch of grass and trees near a three-foot-high chain-link fence.

"There are the tracks," Dowling announced proudly, pointing into the darkness. "We just have to navigate this fence."

"Be careful with the supplies," Stacy cautioned, handing him the paper bags.

When they finally cleared the obstacle, Dowling sat on a rail and put both feet on the ties. "So how come you came in from the desert, my captain, my captain?"

"Because I was worried about my sergeant. I've been around longer than you. Learned to take these things in stride."

"I'm handling it just fine, thank you."

"You're not handling it fine or you wouldn't be going to Idaho." Stacy slurred when he said it.

Dowling looked indignant. "I'm going to Idaho because I'm pulling the pin. Giving you my official notification of resignation right this very minute."

"That's an impulsive decision. You haven't thought this out."

"I've thought it out all evening and it's final." Dowling got up and urinated. "Sam was so sweet, Tom. She was so, so sweet. The job killed her."

"The job killed her," Stacy agreed.

"Like it killed Bones. And it killed Tom Mallory."

"The young cop on the balcony who got shot?" Stacy said.

"You remembered! That's why you're a captain. Tom Mallory let that motherfucker live five minutes too long, or he'd be here with us drinking Jack Daniels.''

"It's a good thing I came in from the desert,'' Stacy said.

"It's my fault Sam is in the morgue. I should be up there so she's not alone.'' Dowling wiped his eyes. "In the morning, Tom, in the morning they're going to carve her up and take pieces of her insides out. Like making melon balls for a goddamn fruit salad. I should go there now.'' He tried to get up.

"In the first place,'' Stacy said, handing Dowling a beer, "it is *my* fault. When she got here, you wanted to shitcan her to Juvenile Division and I wouldn't let you. If I'd let you have your way, she wouldn't have worked homicide and wouldn't have gone out and interviewed that Rene Sheffield and wouldn't have got in that police equipment accident on the way back and met that good-looking young patrol cop and she wouldn't have gone on ride-a-fucking-long and got killed. It is all my fault.'' Stacy wiped his eyes.

"I'm a failure,'' Dowling said, looking at his beer in one hand and whiskey bottle in the other. "I failed with Helene and failed with my daughter and they loan me an Irish girl for six months and I can't even take care of her.''

"You and I fuck everything up,'' Stacy said. "I let my partner die in that gun battle in 1955.''

"You weren't even there. You were on a day off.''

"It doesn't matter. I let him down.''

Dowling got up to urinate again. "Don't you ever have to take a leak, Captain?''

"I'm too old to take leaks anymore.''

"What time does the train come?'' Dowling asked, looking at the two sets of tracks.

"At exactly 4:30 A.M. It always comes at 4:30 A.M.''

Dowling took a glug of whiskey. "I am not going to Idaho.''

"Good.''

"I am going to lay down in front of the train. This is the end, Tom."

"That is an impulsive decision, too." Stacy tried to throw an empty across the tracks.

"If I'd done my job right and caught Danko in time, Joy Larson would not be dead and that girl who was going to be a bride would not be dead. I am a fuckup."

"We are both fuckups."

"When the train is running over me I wish you to stand aside and sing 'The Mountains of Mourne,' " Dowling said.

"I can't do that because I am going to lay down next to you."

"Because you're too old to take leaks?"

"Because Irene is going to outlive me anyway, so what's the difference of a few years? I won't have to have ulcers and bury cops. I want to die with you, Sergeant."

Dowling put his arm around Stacy. "I would rather get squished by a steam engine with my pal then be retired and have the mailman come to find me dead in my rocker on the porch."

"That would be terrible," Stacy agreed.

"Probably I'll a' been there two days and be stinking it up for the neighbors."

"After they find us, they'll go to our motel room at Casa del Zorro in Borrego where I left Irene tonight. I hope she cries when they tell her."

"If they can ID us after we are squished." Dowling took another drink. "I have nobody to cry for me."

"Your kids will cry."

"What for? Jenny has her baby. Matt has his wife. Nobody needs me."

"What about the lady doctor? The lady doctor will cry for you."

"She's too busy going to meetings. She's too busy to go to Idaho with me. So she doesn't have time to cry."

Dowling burned his finger trying to light a last cigarette.

"I'll be able to see Helene. God, I love her, Tom."

"You can't see Helene because Helene is in heaven and we are going where cops and lawyers go."

"I'll get a forty-eight hour pass and go to heaven and take her to a movie in heaven. Our first date was at a movie. We saw *The Sound of Music* at the Spreckles Theater and she wore a light blue dress and we bought popcorn and I put my arm around her near the end of the movie when the captain tried to sing 'Edelweiss' and got all choked up and Julie Andrews had to take over for him.'' Dowling sighed. "I didn't exactly put my arm around *her*. But I put it around the seat behind her."

"They'll tear the Spreckles down like they tear everything old and beautiful down," Stacy moaned.

"I want you to have me buried in El Camino Memorial so I can be next to Helene."

"How can I do that? I'm going to be dead, too. You're not thinking clear, Sergeant."

"If I don't lay down in front of the train and if I don't go to Idaho you'll give me another case tomorrow. Some old pensioner will be stumbling down the street with his food stamps on his way to the corner market to buy beans and coffee and some Iranian is gonna shortchange him and on the way home somebody's gonna kill him for his beans."

Stacy nodded. "Or some working stiff with five kids will come home and find a burglar and the burglar will kill him."

"Worse of yet," Dowling said, "he will kill the burglar and the D.A. will charge him with murder."

"And he'll have to go into his savings to get a lawyer and the five kids won't have anything to eat."

"I must lay in front of the train because I either have to do that or go to Idaho and I can get dead faster."

Dowling took a last drink. "Which track does the train come on?"

"The one closest to us."

"Are you sure?"

"Of course I'm sure. I'm a captain."

They faced each other and shook hands.

"Good-bye, Tom."

"Good-bye, old Sergeant. You were the best."

They lay down on the tracks and Dowling instantly passed out. Immediately, and with great difficulty, Stacy staggered to his feet. He hovered over Dowling, and by Stacy's estimate, over thirty minutes passed before Dowling moved and spoke again.

"*Tom!* I see it. The tunnel of light they talk about."

"It is Melancholy Johnson's flashlight you are seeing, Dowling. He is going to take us home."

"What happened to the train, Tom?"

"It came and went. We were on the wrong track."

Cigar ashes dropped on Dowling's chest. Melancholy Johnson, gravy stains on his uniform shirt, stood over him and belched. He looped both hands over his gun belt.

"I'm going to take you two beauties home. And if you promise not to shit your pants, I won't put you in the trunk."

The next day, when he was able, Dowling pulled himself out of bed and rattled around the empty house in his underwear. A hot shower was tempting, but it required a degree of steadiness, a measure of physical balance. He looked at the shower stall and decided to wait.

It was not a good day to take phone calls, so he listened to messages as they came in.

"When I went back to get my car this morning, two homeless guys were sleeping in it," Tom Stacy reported.

"Thinking of you, Pop. I love you," from Jenny.

"Please, please call me, Vincent," from Angela Lord.

By midafternoon he felt better, having chanced the shower and eaten a large bowl of cold cereal. The crib Jenny had selected arrived while he was eating, and he surprised himself by getting it assembled. The nursery, Matt's old room, was taking shape. An outlandish purple and white clown Dowling had taken a liking to at Bullock's sat on a window ledge—a windup device that played a happy melody—and he listened to it several times working on the crib as the voice of Sam Mulcahy danced in and out of his mind.

As his confidence grew, he went to a nearby market and bought heavy cream for a truffle mix and two bags of chopped pecans. The second cigarette of the day tasted no better than the first, so he flipped it into the flower bed next to the garage. By dark, when he was satisfied with his caramel turtle truffle tarts, he packaged all but two in Saran Wrap and passed them out to neighbors, knocking on their doors, then making lame excuses why he couldn't linger.

On Monday morning, the team met Colum Mulcahy at the airport. The family had designated Sam's oldest brother to take her home. The following morning, as the casket was being boarded, Colum Mulcahy hugged Damon Harper, then handed Dowling an envelope.

" 'Tis the last letter we received from Sam." Colum turned away from them and faced the downtown skyline. "Received it the day she went to heaven. We thought you'd like to share it with your lads."

Dowling read it, alone, in the Union Street parking lot across the street from the court house. His stomach knotted when he saw her handwriting.

> . . . *the team is a sweet bunch, thinking of themselves as my protectors, they do. I threw a knicker fit when they did something about a lad I'm dating, but more about that when I get home.*
>
> *This lad I'm dating is a Garda, a fine sort, and if I was staying here or he was in Ireland, maybe something would come of it . . .*
>
> *. . . I'll not go into details by mail, but we are working cases where young women have been murdered. My sergeant said it was a terrible waste of young life. Not so, I argued, and when he gave me that look of his, I told him it was never a waste if*

someone provided love and was a decent sort during their stay. That people die but memories live.
"*You have your sociologist's hat on,*" *he muttered.*

Perhaps he is right. I try not to dwell on these matters, as it may blur my vision for the task before us.

A colorful lot these San Diego officers are. The other day I was telling how Yeats is buried in a churchyard near our home in Sligo. A detective passing by looked puzzled. "William Butler Yeats, the poet," said I. He looked relieved. Said, "I thought she was talking about Tom Yeats from burglary. I knew he was at Mount Hope. I saw him get planted."

Gus Denver is a fine, compassionate man. I've learned much from him about police work and life. And the streets of Ireland are full of the likes of Larry Shea. Wonderful detectives, the both of them. They try to take care of me, then tease me mercilessly.

Sergeant Dowling . . . well he is special. Going through a lot now, however. Getting to know him makes the whole trip to America worthwhile. But more about him when we are together, having tea in the kitchen.

Despite the wickedness of these cases I mentioned, my life is full and happy, thanks to my new friends. I love them all. I hope they love me back.

⚅ Twenty-seven

The 1538.5 Penal Code motion, to suppress Danko's statement, was heard before a full courtroom. "I figured out why he switched attorneys," Arland Hayes told Dowling. "He's going to testify. He must have confessed to his first attorney about the confession. Then, when they found out the tape was lost, Danko wanted to get on the stand and deny he copped out to you."

"And the first attorney had an ethics problem, couldn't put him on, knowing it was perjury?" Dowling said.

"Exactly. So he changes lawyers and gets a fresh start. Probably instructed the first lawyer not to discuss the case with the second lawyer, so the second one can stay pure." Hayes picked up his case file. "Stand the fuck by, Vince. This is going to be a three-ring circus."

Dowling seated himself, adjusted the microphone, and felt the nervousness he always felt the first few moments of testifying. The empty jury box was to his left, Judge Homer Bicklow to his right. He had been before Bicklow several times, a competent judge from a family of legal scholars.

Danko's new attorney, Lee Straus, was not a stranger either. They had traded punches two or three times in motions or preliminary hearings. Straus was a no-nonsense, go-for-the-jugular advocate with a good reputation. Danko was coming up with money.

311

Dowling looked at Danko, who tried to stare him down before looking away. He believed defendants came up with that tired tactic on their own, doubted the Lee Strauses prompted them. Danko wore a navy blue suit, not the jail denims Dowling had seen him in at arraignment.

The clerk swore Dowling in, he furnished his name and occupation, then Straus rose and stood in front of counsel table. After he laid a foundation with some preliminaries, he asked, "So you were forced to interview the defendant alone, because Detectives Denver and Mulcahy were outside of Mrs. Danko's house and Detective Shea was ailing?"

"Correct."

"Tell me, Sergeant, why didn't you have Denver and Mulcahy contact Mrs. Danko *while* you were interrogating the defendant? Why did they have to wait for your signal to go in?"

"Because that is the way I prefer to do it."

"You were afraid Mrs. Danko might call an attorney, weren't you? Gum up the whole works. Call a halt to your interrogation."

"That's true," Dowling said. "If a suspect is going to get a lawyer, I like it to be his idea. Nothing wrong with that."

"Normally not. But isn't it true, contradictory to what your reports say, you in fact never gave Mr. Danko his Miranda rights?"

"That's not true. I gave him his rights very clearly, as soon as we sat down, and he made an intelligent waiver."

Lee Straus sat down. He had Dowling repeat, word for word, the warning he had issued. "Surely you have some notes you took about exactly what he said when he waived his rights. Where are they?"

"I didn't take notes. I knew we were on tape."

"But notes are excellent backup, aren't they, Sergeant? Notes show legitimacy."

"Notes make some interview subjects freeze up. I relied on the tapes."

The attorney took Dowling through more details, then asked, "Tell us please, what you told Mr. Danko about your personal life."

Dowling looked at Danko who was half smiling. "My personal life was never discussed."

"Never?"

Dowling thought for a moment. "I told him I didn't like cases built on victim or witness identification. That was a personal view."

"But your testimony is, you never discussed your family, your personal background?"

"That's correct. I did not."

Straus picked up a stack of Dowling's reports. He appeared to read them for a few minutes.

"Sergeant, you told Mr. Danko the victims had positively identified his photograph, didn't you?"

"Yes."

"Was that the truth?"

"No. One victim said his photo was similar. The other victims, those who lived, were not shown his photo."

"So you lied to Mr. Danko?"

"Yes."

Straus looked at another report, or pretended to.

"Sergeant, you told Mr. Danko you and your detectives followed him to an alley near First Avenue and Walnut Avenue. Watched him drive in the alley. Did you tell him that?"

"Yes."

"Was that a lie, too?"

"Yes."

With a flourish, Straus moved laterally in front of the table. "Did you really have tickets to a concert the evening you grilled Mr. Danko?"

"Objection. Argumentative as to 'grilled,'" Hayes shouted.

"Sustained," Homer Bicklow said without looking up.

"The evening you 'interrogated' Mister Danko. Did you have concert tickets, Sergeant Dowling?"

"No."

"Did you *ever* tell my client the truth?"

"OBJECTION!" Hayes was on his feet.

"Withdrawn," Straus said calmly. Pastoral-like, he folded his hands in front of him.

"Lying to a suspect. That's an interrogation technique, isn't it, Sergeant? Make the person you're interrogating believe the evidence against him is overwhelming. That it's futile to deny the crimes?"

"It's something I do sometimes, if I think it will ultimately result in the suspect telling what is 'in fact' the truth."

"Let me get this straight. You *lie*, then expect truth?"

"I think I already answered that."

Straus whispered something to Danko, straightened up and smoothed his necktie. "I only have a few more questions, your honor." He approached Dowling.

"A confession was very important to you, wasn't it?"

"The truth was important."

"Sergeant Dowling, if you had not obtained a 'confession' from Mr. Danko, would he have been charged with the crimes?"

"That's a district attorney's decision to make."

"Well, you'd discussed the case with Mr. Hayes, hadn't you? Discussed it before you interrogated the defendant?"

"Yes."

"Did Mr. Hayes tell you a confession was necessary for prosecution? That the complaint would be dismissed if Mr. Danko denied the charges? That Mr. Danko would be released from jail within a day or two after you arrested him?"

"Yes, he told me that."

"I have no further questions. Sergeant Dowling's subject to recall, if it please the court. Thank you, Sergeant."

Hayes and Dowling stood at the end of the corridor sipping machine coffee during the recess.

"He was guessing about my telling you that," Hayes said. "He guessed right because he's a good lawyer, knew it was a weak case . . . hell, knew it was *no* case without the confession."

"Can't wait to hear what Danko's going to say," Dowling said.

Hayes slapped him on the shoulder. "We'll be okay."

"I was shocked. Absolutely shocked," James Danko said from the witness stand. "When he showed me the warrant, I thought maybe some of my friends were playing a joke on me."

He recounted his version of the traffic stop, the intimidating presence of the interrogation room. "Most of the time Sergeant Dowler—I mean Dowling—hovered over me. He's bigger than I am, you know." Danko related he had heard Miranda warnings on television, had been shown them by his attorney.

"But from Sergeant Dowling, definitely not. Never. As soon as we sat down, he wanted to give me coffee or a soft drink. Told me he had to get to a concert or something at the Civic Theater. Then, he started kind of a . . . I don't know . . . kind of a 'this is your life' story."

Danko picked up the glass of water the bailiff had provided.

"He said he was glad to be back in Homicide. Had been kicked out a couple of years ago because he wasn't doing a good job. Was trying to get over his wife's death. He told me her name but I forgot it. She committed suicide, he said. I really felt sorry for him."

Dowling gripped the arms of his chair and looked at the judge, who was looking at Danko.

"The sergeant told me he liked my neighborhood in University Heights, that he preferred older homes to tract models. He said he lived out on Warner Street in Point Loma. Told me he'd lived there for twenty years or so. I wondered what was going on. I mean, he was just . . . rambling on about himself. He'd said he wanted me at police headquarters because he needed my help about some crimes."

Danko looked at the judge. "He told me his son was going to college at either Redlands or Pomona, I forget which. That he was in kind of a fix at home. His daughter was pregnant, going to high school, and wasn't married."

Dowling wrote "HE'S LYING" on note paper and pushed it in front of Hayes.

"When I realized he was serious about thinking I'd committed these crimes, I was terrified. I mean, I thought, well, like the sergeant said, maybe people did mistakenly identify me. I knew I looked like the picture in the paper." Danko drank more water. "And I lived kind of in the right area. But when he said he followed me to some alley near Walnut Avenue, that's when I knew it was all a lie. Because I had *never* been to any alley anywhere near there. I didn't even know where Walnut Avenue was. That's when I told him I wanted a lawyer. He told me a lawyer wasn't going to help me. That I was going to the gas chamber if I didn't confess. It was like, all he could think of was getting me to say I'd done something I hadn't done."

Danko wrung his hands. "He told me if I'd confess he'd see that I got help. That the district attorney would go easy on me."

"Did you ever tell Sergeant Dowling you had committed a crime, sexually assaulted or murdered any women? *At any time,* did you tell him that?" Straus shouted the last sentence.

Danko looked at Judge Bicklow. "Never. I kept swearing I hadn't done anything. That he had the wrong man. Then Sergeant Dowling said, pardon my language, Your Honor, he said 'Fuck you. You're going to jail.' The next think I knew I was locked up."

Hayes couldn't shake Danko on cross-examination and Dowling only half listened to Lee Straus's summation.

". . . clear and convincing there was no Miranda warning . . . overzealous detective . . . circumventing defendant's wife from notifying counsel . . . the tape is conveniently lost. The only person other than Sergeant Dowling who allegedly heard the tape is dead . . . how could Mr. Danko know these things about the family if Sergeant Dowling had not told him . . . the sergeant testified that without a confession, the defendant walks. Your Honor . . . a bank vice president, a member of good standing in the community . . . member of various civic organizations . . ."

Dowling tried to be calm. Tried to look unaffected. Character assassination in court was to be expected, but he had never been belted like this before. Been lied about before, but never so convincingly, never so outlandishly.

"I'll rule Monday morning," Homer Bicklow said, stepping down from the bench. "Happy Thanksgiving to all of you."

℘ Twenty-eight

"This was not an easy call," Judge Bicklow began. "If the only issue had been the content of the confession, I would have ruled immediately after the hearing. I would have allowed the statement and let a jury decide who was telling the truth, Sergeant Dowling or the defendant."

He read from his notes. "But there is a voluntariness issue here. Did the defendant receive and waive Miranda, or did he not? It is a unique situation. The sergeant *admits* telling the defendant things that are lies—about witness identification, about surveilling him to an alley.

"But the sergeant *denies* telling the defendant things that are true. History on the sergeant's late wife, son and daughter. Even when he purchased his home."

Judge Bicklow looked at Dowling. "I have a fear there may have been a confession. That the defendant admitted to Sergeant Dowling that he committed these horrible crimes. But I cannot rule on my fears, I must rule by the law. My interpretation of the law requires I grant the motion to suppress the defendant's statement."

Hayes's head slumped.

"Mr. Hayes?" Judge Bicklow said.

Hayes got to his feet slowly. "In light of the court's ruling, we have no choice but to dismiss, Your Honor. Subject to refiling."

Homer Bicklow gathered up his papers.

"We're adjourned. You're a free man, Mister Danko."

Dowling drove home from court too numbed to be bothered by the late afternoon traffic. Though he could not have remembered, he traveled Reynard Way through Mission Hills to Pacific Highway, Barnett Avenue past the Marine and Naval Training Center, then finally up the Talbot Street hill toward home.

He had allowed himself a glance toward the defense table as the judge ruled. Danko had been smiling at him. Smiling at everyone.

Here he was, driving home to his children, taking his turn being tortured by a depraved individual who thought of himself as a victim of other people's flaws; an individual whose rape and murder victims were beneath his respect; who somehow managed to exist anyway on the margin of society.

"You two believe my testimony, don't you?" They were eating turkey sandwiches, Matt having stayed over an extra two days after his wife returned to Redlands.

"Of course we do," they said, almost at the same time.

"When I first heard Danko lay out my personal life stuff to the judge, my mind was mush. But here's the thing." Dowling wiped his mouth with a napkin. "He could have hired someone to go to Public Records—the assessor's office—and get the info on our house. And Helene committing suicide and my getting kicked out of Homicide is common knowledge around the courthouse and the defense bar."

"How about Jenny's pregnancy?" Matt asked.

"I've been thinking about that. You know our mail doesn't go in a slot in the front door because we have the box next to the porch. Jenny got some stuff addressed to her from Planned Parenthood."

"Some sleazeball could have rifled our mailbox," Jenny said.

"I've lost cases before a jury. Not very damn many

but . . .'' Dowling pushed away a side dish of cranberries. ''The way that judge looked at me. And wondering whether Arland Hayes may think—''

''Dad. Let me see the photos,'' Matt said.

''One of them is grim.''

''I want to see them.''

Dowling reached toward his jacket on the empty chair and removed the two pictures he had shown Lieutenant George Cardas at the airport. He flipped them on the table and Matt and Jenny looked them over. They had seen his crime scene evidence over the years, whispered to classmates about it in their younger days.

''I told JoAnne how you always carry your victim's picture in your pocket on mysteries, to motivate you when you're down. You'll get this guy, Dad. You'll find a way.''

''Maybe,'' Dowling said. ''There's no statute of limitation on murder. I'm going to be a cop for a while yet, so I'll be around in case he messes up.''

They wrapped leftovers and stuck plates in the dishwasher.

''While you were in court, Jason signed the papers at our lawyer's, Pop.''

''Do you still feel good about it?'' Matt asked. Jason had relinquished all claim as the biological father.

''I feel real good. We bought him off. Who needs him or his money.'' She folded a dish towel and put her arm around Dowling and her brother. ''I've picked out a name if it's a girl.''

They turned to her.

''Helene Samantha.''

Dowling felt the tears coming but didn't care about fighting them back. ''Your mother would be honored. But you didn't know Samantha Mulcahy.''

''I knew her through you, Pop.''

''What is Danko feeling now?'' Boudreaux said over the telephone. ''Well, he used to go out on the streets when the stresses built up on him. He can't do that now. In his mind, you're watching him every night. He has to find another way to satisfy his aggressions.''

Boudreaux coughed his smoker's cough. ''On top of that, he's on paid administrative leave while the company lawyers decide what to do with their little problem boy. Bank lawyers move just a little faster than those statues in the park, so Danko knows his fate at work won't be resolved for a while.

''His wife probably wants to believe in him, but he has to know she must have doubts.

''The whole thing got tremendous media coverage, so in Danko's mind, anyone who ever knew him figures he's guilty. He never was a rational thinker, so he's in a fine state now.''

Boudreaux put Dowling on hold and came back in a moment. ''He kind of outsmarted himself. Now he's in his private hell. In a macabre sort of way, Sergeant, he's put himself in prison.''

''Do you have to put sauerkraut on everything, Shea? This critique rooms stinks,'' Gus complained.

Larry Shea bit into one of the sandwiches. ''We gonna surveil Danko tonight, Sarge?''

''We're through surveilling him. I don't know what he's going to do, but it won't be the same M.O. That's Hollywood stuff for us to go out and catch him in the act now,'' Dowling said. ''I got to think this out for a while, and we've got other cases to work.''

''While you're thinking, let me have a forkful of that damn kraut,'' Gus said, leaning toward the carton.

When they finished, they cleaned off the table and gathered their paper work.

''Who are you picking to come on our team?'' Gus asked, sliding a pickle out of the bag.

''I have to think about that, too. Did you go by the trophy shop?''

''I did, I did,'' Gus said. He left the room and returned

carrying a small package. He pulled the paper off and handed the plaque to Dowling.

"Good job," Dowling murmured. "Good job."

It was high-quality walnut, eight inches by five inches. A smiling Sam Mulcahy's photo on her Garda identification card, mounted just above her San Diego P.D. badge. The inscription on a plate near the bottom read:

Garda/Detective Samantha Caitland Mulcahy
Killed in the line of duty November 17, 1994

Dowling got up and the others followed him out of the critique room. He hung the plaque on the wall behind his desk. They saluted in unison.

They worked shorthanded the next two and a half weeks, rolled on two murders plus an officer-involved shooting, trying their best to separate the specter of death from the Christmas lights and carols that washed over San Diego.

Danko had quit looking at the presents under the tree. He wished the three days would pass quickly, get the stupid decorations down and try to establish some degree of normality. The kid was seven months old for Chrissake and would no more remember her first Christmas than he remembered most of his.

He was confident Dowling would hound him Christmas Eve as well, though letting him alone in the daytime. Except for the cop disguised as a roofer messing around on the house two doors down. Yesterday, a delivery van had supposedly broken down and spent the night on the corner. At midnight he'd thought about getting up, walking down there and making faces at whoever was hiding in it.

He'd wanted to change phone numbers, expecting harassing calls from the fucking public because he was listed in the directory. His wife talked him into holding off, and she was right for once. None of the calls had been ugly.

In fact, two or three were supportive. One guy from Citizens Against Police Suppression or something like that had sympathized with him for being persecuted. Another wished him luck and offered moral support. He probably talked to them longer than he should have but had been careful not to discuss the case in any way.

Ironically, a headhunter from Cleveland telephoned, and it was obvious he knew nothing about what was going on in San Diego.

"I called you at home instead of at work for confidentiality purposes. You came highly recommended and I have a valuable position available. In Buffalo."

He chatted with the man for a while, more out of boredom than any perverse desire to return to cold weather country. Besides, it would look bad if he skipped town.

He had barked at one caller, an obvious prankster pretending a van full of new furniture was scheduled to be delivered.

His wife was mad at him again. He refused to watch the baby, insisting she drop their daughter at day care on her way to work. That was all he needed. He was picturing forty hours of screwing with diapers, bottles and pacifiers when the phone rang just before noon.

"I got that tape recording I heard about on the TV. How much is it worth to you?"

A woman's voice with loud music in the background. He stiffened, having wondered if Dowling would try something like this. Also wondered if some fuckhead acting on their own, who had read about the testimony, would fake having the tape. At least he was ready. The important thing was to measure every word. Pretend the call was being tape recorded. Picture Dowling standing next to the caller.

"How interesting," he said. "And just where did you get this tape?"

"From my jacket pocket where I jus' now found it where I put it that day I picked it up and forgot about it till just now when I put that coat on to wear." She stopped and shouted, but not into the phone. "Timothy, you turn that damn music down. I can't hear nothin'. You hear me?" A kid's voice wailed something Danko could not make out.

"And just where did you . . . get this tape?" he said.

"In the crapper at the police department. I was down there trying to get one of my kids out of a jam. Twenty-one years old. I'm still getting him out of jams."

She told him she had not turned it in because she'd been raised to "pick up everything that wasn't nailed down."

"I think you should take the tape down to Sergeant Dowling right now," he told her.

"Oh, I don't think you want me to do that, mister. I don't—TIMOTHY, I'm gonna kick your butt all over this house you don't get out of here."

"Did you play the tape?" he asked.

"Yeah, course I played it. This morning. That's when I figured out what it was."

Danko sat down with the portable phone. "And tell me, madam, what did you think when you listened to this tape?"

"I thought you're an asshole."

His stomach was knotting. The second lawyer, Lee Straus, had debriefed him in Straus's office a few minutes after the judge cut him loose. "If you're telling the truth, Mr. Danko, and if Sergeant Dowling is lying, you have nothing to worry about." Straus explained "jeopardy" to him. "A defendant is placed in jeopardy when the first witness has been sworn in at a *trial*. Then, if the charges are dismissed or you're found not guilty, they can't have another crack at you. But ours was a hearing, not a trial. You've not been in jeopardy. You can still be charged."

"Put Sergeant Dowling on the phone," Danko said.

"What are you talking about?"

He was tempted to hang up but couldn't. "Why don't you play the tape for me. Right now, lady."

"*Timothy*. Bring me that damn thing on the table. *Now*."

He heard her fumbling with something. "I ain't got one of them fancy entertainment centers in my living room like you probably got," she said. "In fact, I ain't hardly got a real living room. That's why I'm putting the bite on you." There was a pause before she said, "Are you ready, buddy? I ain't gonna play all of it either."

He almost vomited after he heard her push the on button. It was a spot in midtape. He heard his voice, "I don't know what you're talking about . . ." Then Dowling's: "Here's how it all shakes out, Danko. In my office I keep a chart of all the murders . . ." Then he couldn't hear anything because the background music blared again.

"*Timothy*. This time I will kick your damn butt." She talked over the music onto the phone. "I gotta hang up and kill this kid. I'll call you right back." She ended the conversation and he kept the phone in his ear, hearing nothing.

It had to be a setup. They'd found the goddamn tape somehow and were . . . But if they'd found it, they wouldn't be playing games with him. They'd be on his front steps with a pair of fucking handcuffs. The phone rang again and he picked it up quickly.

"Sorry about that," the same woman said. "Try to raise 'em right and look what happens."

"So tell me this, lady. Let's suppose you've really got this uh . . . tape you say you found. You listened to it all?"

"Sure."

"And what does it say?"

"It says you killed them two girls and did dirty things to some others."

"Really?"

"Really," she said. "You're gonna ask me how I feel about them two girls. How I can be siding with you, huh?"

"That's you talking, not me," he said carefully.

"I feel like they're in a better place. Wish I had the guts to put myself there with 'em."

"Why don't you just take this tape you say you found to the police?" he asked.

"What good would it do the police? You already *been* to court. They can't try a man twice for the same crime. Everybody knows that. What would the police want it for?"

He waited a long time before speaking again. Thought deeply.

"Then if I can't be tried again, why should I pay you money for the tape? Not that I've done anything, but just playing hypothetically?"

"What's that mean?"

"It means kind of pretending."

"Let me light this cigarette," she said. A pause. "I figure you care about what people think of you, I guess. Hell, I don't know. Anyway, I'm tired of talking. I'm not much good at this. I want five thousand bucks." She waited a bit. "There's a Denny's in Linda Vista and I go there every day for coffee. That's life's big treat for me. There's a bench outside. You ought to be there at seven tonight."

Danko put his hand to his forehead. "Not at night. To-morrow morning maybe. At nine. I may show up, just out of curiosity. What do you look like?"

"I know what you look like, mister. I'll find you. Hell, there's only one bench."

"And if I don't show up, you'll go to the police?"

"I don't know. Maybe I will and maybe I won't. What would they want it for? A souvenir?"

✺ Twenty-nine

They sat in Angela Lord's Mercedes at La Jolla shores, the only car in the parking lot.

"I thought we'd watch the sunset," she said, "then slip up to Del Mar for Mexican food."

"Sounds good to me," Dowling said. The sun was still a few feet above the horizon. They sat in silence for a while.

"You've got something on your mind," he said

Angela pursed her lips. "Ever the detective." She started to light a cigarette but put it back. "I've had a job offer. A very good job offer."

"Where?"

"I'm considering it and I wanted to talk to you about it."

"Where?"

"In Boston. At Mass General. Chief of Emergency Services and regional director."

"Is it a done deal?"

"I *said* I'm considering it."

A couple holding hands stood at the water line, their backs to the parking lot, watching the ball of orange sink lower.

"Looks to me like you got me up here to give me bad news."

"Would it be bad news if I went, Vincent?"

He folded his arms. "You do have a career to think about."

"You haven't answered my question."

"Hell yes, it would be bad news. What do you think?"

"I don't really know what to think," she said. "The only time you ever said I meant anything special to you was on the phone . . . when you wanted to drive to Los Angeles and take me to Idaho."

Dowling winced. "Jeez, I was going to invite you for Christmas Eve dinner at the house. Meet Jenny and Matt."

"But you can't ask me now, of course. Since I've had a job offer."

"It wouldn't be the same now. I thought maybe we had something. I was wrong," he said.

"Do you want me to stay, Vincent?"

He got out of the passenger's side and walked around the car to her window. "What do you think?" he answered.

"Goddammit, *tell me*."

"Goddammit, I think I love you." He opened the driver's door.

"Then goddammit, I'm staying." She started to laugh.

They were kissing when the sun sank and the sky turned crimson.

Danko looked through powerful sports binoculars at the woman on the bench drinking from a styrofoam cup. Her hair was unkempt and the clothing, a plain gray hooded sweatshirt and jeans, were sloppy. Too big for her. There were huge stains on the sweatshirt near the pockets, and it didn't look like she wore makeup. Late thirties he guessed, maybe forty. She lit another cigarette with the one that had been hanging from her lips.

He felt lucky to have found the spot on the hillside, in a cluster of overgrown shrubbery where even residents a hundred feet away couldn't see him over their fences. It put him almost level with the top of the oversize Denny's sign. A lot of old fucks had pulled into the parking lot, taking forever to get out of their cars, hobbling toward the door, past the gaudy banner advertising discount breakfast for senior citizens.

His car was close by on a winding road that made its way down to the main street adjacent to the restaurant parking lot. He was chilled from squatting in one spot, so he pulled up the collar of his windbreaker.

The dumb cunt was lighting another cigarette, watching her empty cup blow off the bench. When she gave a half-hearted stab at leaning over and picking it up, it blew away.

She looked around constantly, seemed to be studying every car coming onto the lot. Figuring he'd be stupid enough to breeze on in and lay some money in her hand. That he'd be stupid enough to pocket the tape and think he'd never hear from her again. Stupid enough to think she wouldn't tell somebody who'd tell somebody who'd tell somebody else. The blackmailing whore needed to be taught a lesson.

An hour passed, and about the time he began wondering how long she'd wait, he watched her get up slowly, stretch, and walk to an older car. He couldn't see her when she climbed behind the wheel, but when her car rolled forward, he ran to his car and drove quickly down the hill.

He'd never tried to follow anyone in a car, and she drove fast. Twice he lost sight of her, afraid to get too close. A car leaving a service station cut him off, and he gave the finger to the driver. When he was sure he'd lost her again, he spotted her in another lane several cars ahead at a red light.

Traffic thinned when she left the boulevard and turned down a residential street. There were no cars between them, so he laid back a bit, beginning to feel stimulated. Perspiring under the arms a little, too.

She pulled abruptly to the curb so he did the same. Next to a fire hydrant, because cars lined both curbs. He didn't like being next to the hydrant, thought about pulling out again, but she got out of her car and headed for the two-story apartment complex on the opposite side of the street. An older building, tan stucco, with a small ROYAL ARMS APARTMENTS sign off the sidewalk.

Turning off the ignition, he pulled a white, floppy tennis hat over his head, grabbed sunglasses from over the visor and trotted to the narrow exterior entryway where he'd lost sight of her. He spied a small swimming pool in the middle of the courtyard before he caught sight of the apartment doors. Seeing no one, hearing nothing, he feared she'd entered a ground floor unit near the entry. Then he saw her back, on the second deck near the rear, fumbling with her purse. Reaching for a key maybe. Unlocking the door. Entering. Good, maybe that meant loudmouth Timothy wasn't home.

He really hadn't planned much beyond this point. No specifics anyway. It probably would come down to a knock on the door and then . . . A gardener pulling a wheelbarrow loaded with equipment—rakes, shovels, pruners, bags of mulch—nodded to him. A man left a downstairs apartment and walked to the manager's office near the entryway. Then it happened and he couldn't believe his good luck.

The door opened to her apartment and she came out, carrying a full laundry basket, one arm over the top of the dark blue plastic container, pressing it against her chest while reaching for the doorknob with the other hand. She was a good hundred feet from him, navigating the outside stairs, a jug of detergent almost slipping off the top of the pile; then she disappeared down a narrow sidewalk leading to the rear of the complex.

He climbed the stairway next to him, then followed the walkway past doors until he made the left turn, walking down the long side now, hearing music from one of the units, seeing no one. When he was a few steps from her door, he took a look around, turned the knob and entered, closing the door tentatively. Quiet greeted him, and standing in place, he quickly decided he was in a one-bedroom unit. Three feet of hallway separated the bathroom, door just partially open, and the bedroom. The kitchen was on the far side of the living room, a tiny, two-person dinette table next to a counter.

"Delivery, anybody home?" He said it loud enough, still heard nothing, then moved quickly, making a room-by-room inspection. The tape could be in her purse, which he spotted on a mahogany dresser next to the unmade bed. He was starting for it when he heard a commotion at the door, so he backed off, then ducked into the bathroom, leaving the door slightly ajar, and held his breath.

He heard her come in, heard the door close. If she came into the bathroom, he'd have to jump her. Crissakes, at least on the sidewalks he was in control of things. This was close quarters. There were apartments on both sides, people could hear things and . . . she was walking past the bathroom, had to have gone into the bedroom. The bathroom door opening was on the wrong side, dammit. When he tried to peek, he couldn't see into the bedroom, could only see the hallway wall with a religious painting on it, could see part of the living room.

He could hear her bustling around in the bedroom. Pulling his hat lower, pulling his collar higher, he touched the doorknob and paused. If she screamed, he'd run like hell. Down the same stairs she took with the laundry, out the back way and from there it would really be a crapshoot. Perspiration was fogging the top of his sunglasses. Bothersome, but not affecting his vision. He opened the door slowly.

She was across the bedroom, back to him, fidgeting with something on the dresser. In bra and panties. Rose-colored bra and panties, and though because of the bed he could only see her legs from the knees up, they were good-looking tan legs. This bitch spent time on those recliners by the pool, lazing around smoking cigarettes, soaked in sun lotion. Reading fuck stories and never getting that shapely body wet. Never swimming laps.

He stood in the doorway, not moving. Really perspiring now. When she did turn around, she didn't see him an for instant. Started making the bed, tugging on a green comforter and must have seen him out of the corner of an eye because she shot up straight, looked at him crazily and put a hand over her mouth. He saw what he thought was surprise in her eyes instead of fear. She looked toward a telephone on the nightstand, six feet away from her, then back at him. It was hard to read the bitch. He decided to wait, let her speak first.

When she did her voice was measured, low-pitched. Both hands at her sides now.

"Who are you?"

He didn't answer, just smiled.

"How did you get in here?" Neither of them moved.

"Goddammit. This is my house. Get out of here." She moved toward the phone and he raised his right fist, moved a step or two toward her, then stopped.

"Don't do that," he said sharply.

"What do you want?"

"I decided to make a house call. Pick up my tape." He said it softly, casually.

"Jesus, it's *you*. Get out of my house."

"After I get the tape. Where is it?"

She pointed to the sweatshirt, in a heap on a small chair in the corner. "In the pocket of the sweatshirt. Take it and get out of here."

The chair was between them and he moved toward it slowly, looking at her. He kept looking at her while he picked up the sweatshirt. No tape in the first pocket. In the other he felt it. Glanced hurriedly at it, then focused on her again. He was less than six feet from her now. She still hadn't moved.

Holding the tape at chest level, he could examine it and still see her. A gummed label on it. Penned on the label, "Dowling-Danko 10-30-94." There were two sets of initials he couldn't read. The bitch was probably too dumb to have made copies. He had it in his hand. He could walk away. Could.

"I could only come up with five hundred," he said.

"Never mind the money. Just take it and leave."

"But I owe you something. It wouldn't be right to just leave. Would it?"

Her voice raised an octave. "You don't owe me anything. Please. You've got what you want. Please go."

He put the tape in his pants pocket. "Do you like to wear panties?"

"Jesus, what kind of a question is that?" turning sideways slightly as she said it. "Just go."

"You have very nice breasts. I don't think you need to wear a brassiere. They'd stand right up there without any help."

"Look, Danko. Right now, you've got what you came for. I don't give a shit about the money. I don't know anything, okay? This never happened."

"It never happened?"

"You know what I mean."

He felt himself getting hard. "Why don't you take your panties off?"

"Please leave."

"Do you want me to take them off? Is that it? I know how to take panties off."

He heard someone bouncing a basketball in the alley under the window, passing by, faint voices getting fainter.

She was kind of pretty, though a little hard looking. Kind of a strawberry blond he thought. For a smoker, she took pretty good care of herself after all. No flab over the panty waist. He put his hand on his crotch, rubbed his erection through the pants.

"Take your brassiere off and then I'll leave," he said.

"Why should I believe that?"

"You just have to trust me."

"What would happen after I took my bra off?"

"What would you want to happen?"

"I'd want you to leave."

"Then I'll leave. Go ahead. Take it off OR I'LL TAKE THE FUCKING THING OFF." He moved to within a step of her.

"I'm a cop, Danko. So this isn't going anywhere, see." She backed against the dresser. "This is a setup."

"Oh, you're a cop. And the place is surrounded. Sergeant Dowling, Sergeant Fuckface Dowling is outside at this very moment. He's waiting for you to take your panties off before he comes busting in because he wants to see your pussy, too." He put his hand on her shoulder. "Or has he already seen it? Is that it?"

"Look, I—"

"Where's your police badge, police lady? Under your panties?"

She hesitated. "I . . . I'm not a police officer. I said it to scare you. Because I'm scared. I'm a waitress who just lost her job and tried to make a buck at your expense and I'm sorry."

He smiled. Rubbed the back of her neck with the hand that had been on her shoulder. Then he felt her tense again, more than before.

"Who did you tell about finding the tape, waitress friend?"

"Nobody."

"Did you tell loudmouth Timothy?"

"No, I swear."

He lowered his hand to her right breast and felt through the weave of the fabric. A handful of firmness.

"You told Tillie the waitress or some dumb-ass short-order cook, didn't you?"

"No."

"You told somebody. Who are you fucking?"

"Nobody. Please, if you—"

"You're not fucking loudmouth Timothy, are you? You're not an incestuous little cunt, are you? Shit, I don't even know your name. What's your name?"

She put her hand over his forearm, the one still touching her breast. "My name is Velda."

"Take your hand off my arm, Velda. Take your hand off my arm and reach back and unhook your brassiere because I want to see your nipples. I don't want to touch them, Velda. I just want to look at them. I don't touch bare breasts. Not even my wife's."

She looked down. "If I do that will you leave?"

"I will. I promise."

Slowly, she put both hands behind her, raised them, grimaced. "I'm having trouble getting it unhooked. I'm scared. Just give me a minute to—"

In midsentence, her knee came up sharply, heavily, toward his groin. Toward his groin, but not into it, not a direct hit on his testicles because somehow—his hand had felt her body twitch perhaps—he moved slightly to the side, deflected the kick so that she caught him in the thigh.

Blood spurted from her nose when he crashed his fist into it, but she didn't crumble. Kicked him again instead, hit him in the side of the head twice with a fist, tried to push him backward onto the bed, moving to her left at the same time, groping for something on the nightstand. The blows didn't hurt him and when he hit her in the face again, she sank to her knees, still reaching out, still trying to hit him. The dirty bitch was bleeding all over the place and half of her brassiere was off, so he punched her in the face again and when she kept fighting he smashed her in the bare breast. Felt his fist mush into it. Grabbed her hair with his left hand, jerked her head up and smashed her in the face again with his right fist. Looked into her eyes, which were fiery, cocked his right fist again and held it there.

"Do you want more, *bitch*?" He said it smiling, leaning down.

She tried to answer, gurgled blood instead, then spit in his face. Sprayed his face with blood and sputum so he kicked her in the stomach, not as hard as he wanted because his foot nicked the bed rail, and he held her hair and hit her three more times in the face. This time she went limp, and when he released his hold, she fell backward to the floor, her arm knocking her purse and an alarm clock from the nightstand.

He kneeled and started throttling her before he saw her left hand pulling something from her purse. A gun! Her fingers gripped the barrel, and she was trying to work it loose from the purse. The bitch had a fucking gun and wanted to shoot him and she *really* needed to be taught a lesson. And while he was saying it to himself he easily broke her hold on the semiautomatic pistol with his right hand and it thunked to the floor. He grabbed it with his right hand, put his finger on the trigger, then smashed her in the face again with his left hand.

He was choking her, trying to mount her, holding the gun against her face, wondering how he'd get his pants undone, feeling his wetness all at the same time when he heard "DANKO" shouted from behind and turned to see Dowling in the doorway.

Dowling in the goddamn bedroom doorway. He couldn't see past him, sensed Dowling was alone.

Still clutching her hair with his left hand, he spun, pointed the pistol at Dowling, who was standing still, arms at his sides but extended a little, like a hokey gunfighter on the streets of Dodge City waiting for somebody to slap leather.

But *he'd* already slapped leather and was surprised how steady the gun felt in his hand. He wasn't looking through the sights, just had it leveled at Dowling's chest, feeling the bitch come to life a little under his grip. Dowling didn't look scared, was even eye-fucking him for Chrissake, sneering when he spoke. Didn't even yell it.

"It's all over, Danko. Put it down."

He still saw nothing behind Dowling. Just saw the brown eyes staring him down. Heard a diesel engine car driving by in the alley. Using the sights now, he closed his left eye and drew a bead in the center of Dowling's necktie.

"You're not gonna shoot me, Danko. Put the goddamn

gun down or I'll pull mine and shoot you. Do it the easy way. It's all over."

"Fuck you, Dowling. I'll kill you and kill the bitch, too."

"You're gonna get your chance then, because I'm going for my gun now. I'm going for my gun real slowly, so why don't you just put yours down. You may get me, but I got two thousand friends in this town and they always get cop killers. So put it down."

Dowling's right hand was moving deliberately, under his sport coat, under the left armpit. The crazy redheaded motherfucker was really going for his gun, taking it carefully from the holster, leveling his own right arm and pointing it at him. He'd never had a gun pointed at him before. Dowling's gun was different than the bitch's gun: it had a round cylinder and he could actually see some of the bullets. He swung his gun hand around and held it against the bitch's face again. His own voice sounded loud to him.

"I'll kill her, Dowling. Put your gun down or I'll kill her."

"Fuck you, Danko."

"I'll kill this bitch, I swear it." Keeping his eyes on Dowling, he moved the end of the gun to her lips. Felt the steel barrel clank against her teeth. Tightened his grip on her hair.

"I'm telling you, Danko. It's all over. One way or another, it's all over. Shoot me, shoot her. You're still a dead man and I don't think you want to be a dead man. Do you, Danko?"

He tried to shield himself with her, jerked her head roughly, moved his own head closer to hers, both of them facing Dowling now, she still on her ass, bare tit still hanging out, leaning slightly back. He was on one knee, still sighted on Dowling's necktie.

"Open your mouth, bitch." When she didn't obey he shouted it and her lips parted and he jammed the gun in her mouth, as far as he could. "Put your gun on the bed,

Dowling.'' Using his shoulder, he tried to get his sunglasses off because he was sweating badly now, and after a couple of attempts they fell to the floor. "I'm counting to three, Dowling, and if your gun isn't on the bed I'll shoot the bitch.''

"You're a minor leaguer, Danko, and I play in the majors.''

He saw Dowling kneel, get a two-handed grip on his gun and use the bedpost as a platform. "See, Danko. I'm nice and steady now. Can't miss. But you got it wrong— I'm the one who's going to count to three. So put the gun down.''

"If you shoot me, I'll shoot her. She'll die, too.''

"*One,*'' Dowling said.

"You're bluffing.''

"*Two,*'' he heard Dowling say.

He felt his gun hand tremble, wondered if Dowling would finish the count. Thought about putting his gun down.

"*Ciao, baby,*'' he heard Dowling say, but never heard the roar from Dowling's gun, never felt the bullet slam against his forehead and penetrate his brain. Never felt her lurch to her left, never saw her throw herself across the bed and crawl across it. Didn't see her look back at his corpse, didn't see her hug Dowling's right leg while she still sprawled across the green comforter. Didn't feel blood seeping into his eyes, flowing from the entry wound above the brows.

 **Thirty**

They were in the squad room three hours later, briefing Shea and Denver, when Sergeant Jack Cassidy walked in and waved to the woman with the bandaged face sitting next to Dowling.

"Hey, Sinner, good-looking sweatshirt. You don't have to cover your face: I don't want to kiss you today."

"Ease off, Cassidy, or I'll kick your butt. Hey, I put a quarter on your desk."

"What for?"

"I had a dream about you last night."

Dowling had picked detective Velda "Sinner" Lockwood to be the fourth member of his team.

"You did a first-class job, Sinner," Dowling said.

She tried to adjust a wrapping across her nose, winced and put her hand in the pocket of the sweatshirt. "My first assignment over here with the big boys, and you kill some son of a bitch in my bedroom. I probably won't sleep more than twelve hours tonight."

They continued with the briefing and she said, "When I looked up and saw Danko, I didn't scream. Not a cop's nature to scream, huh? Maybe I should have. Maybe he'd have split."

"You were saying, about the cop thing?" Shea said.

"Yeah, I told him I was a cop. I mean, I'm standing there in my skivvies. This psycho's glaring at me, rubbing his weinie. So I'm desperate. I tell him I'm a cop, but he wants to see the badge and I can't tell him the badge is in the purse because the damn *gun's* in the purse so I shift gears and tell him I'm not really a cop.'' She gingerly touched her face again. ''Is that girlfriend of yours I met in the E.R. going to give me a discount, Sarge?''

''The nose job might be an improvement, Sinner,'' Gus said.

''What I want to know is''—she said it looking at Dowling—''could you really see that the lever on my gun was in the 'safety on' position, or were you just guessing?''

''Naww, I couldn't see it. Figured Danko may not know his way around guns. Wouldn't know that a nine millimeter has a safety and a revolver doesn't. I figured I had a fifty-fifty chance.''

''Come on, I gotta have a straight answer,'' Sinner protested. ''Gimme a straight answer and I'll forget to put on the report that you said '*Ciao, baby*' instead of counting three just before you dusted him.''

Dowling smiled, winking at Gus and Shea. ''Yeah, I could see the safety was on. It was a Thaddaeus.''

''Going to the 153 Club?'' they asked Dowling as they walked out of the office.

''Nope, I'm going home.''

Dowling had his car door opened when he remembered something, then hurried back to the empty squad room. When he got to his desk, he removed the case folder, took the two photos of Annie Richards from his pocket and placed them with the reports. He found a lighter in his pocket also, but since he'd quit smoking the day before, he chucked the lighter in the waste basket.

Tom Stacy walked in. ''Dowling, you drive me crazy. Are you ever going to learn to color between the lines? Learn to start giving me updates so I know what's going down *before* you shoot up the neighborhood?'' Stacy didn't try for an answer, just sighed.

''Let me see if I have the sequence straight so I can

tell the Old Man. You had bogus phone calls made to Danko. From the headhunter, the furniture people and other people pretending to support him. You taped those conversations, then had the audio department record your voice and splice up a phony confession tape.''

Dowling nodded. ''Like Danko told the furniture guy, 'I don't know what you're talking about.' That line fit right in with a part of the actual interrogation and I banked on Danko's remembering it. Reminds me, I owe that guy in audio a pitcher of beer.''

Stacy sighed. ''If Danko had showed up at Denny's to buy the tape from Sinner Lockwood, you would have busted him on the spot?''

''Right. Arland Hayes said it would have been a slam dunk after that. The D.A. would tell the appeals court that Judge Bicklow relied on Danko's credibility as a witness when he ruled. Danko buying the tape would have shot his credibility to hell. The DCA would have reversed Bicklow, my testimony about the interrogation would have gotten in at trial and Danko would have been cooked.''

''I like him better in the morgue,'' Stacy said. ''What in hell happened between the time Danko was a no-show at Denny's and when you shot him?''

''Jeez, I wish I was smoking again.'' Dowling patted an empty pocket. ''Sinner was wired and we were monitoring. When Danko stood her up, she got in the car, briefed us, so I told her to wrap it up. To go on home. We were on a side street in three cars. Shea drove Hayes back to Hayes's office, Gus headed for an interview on another case and I headed for the squad room.''

''And?'' Stacy asked.

''And, I got halfway to the station and got thinking, what if Danko was being cute. Had a plan to get Sinner *and* the tape. So I stopped and phoned her—no answer. Turns out she'd taken a load of wash downstairs. Well, the no-answer rattled me, so I decided to head for her place. Just to be on the safe side. You know the rest.''

"I wonder if the real tape ever will show up?" inquired Stacy.

"Who knows?"

"Goodnight, Vince. Merry Christmas," Stacy said. They shook hands.

"Goodnight, Tom. Merry Christmas to you and Irene."

When Stacy left, Dowling went to his desk again. An unsolved case from last year nagged at him: an elderly lady had been murdered during a daylight burglary. He'd felt all along that a witness three doors down, a dance instructor, had been holding back on him.

He put the folder under his arm, blew a kiss to Sam Mulcahy and walked out the door. When he got home, he would devise a new to-do list. Gus and Sinner Lockwood would have a go at the dance instructor—a fresh look. They were missing *something*.

Edgar Award-winning Author

LAWRENCE BLOCK

THE MATTHEW SCUDDER MYSTERIES

A LONG LINE OF DEAD MEN
72024-8/ $5.99 US/ $7.99 Can

THE DEVIL KNOWS YOU'RE DEAD
72023-X/ $5.99 US/ $7.99 Can

A DANCE AT THE SLAUGHTERHOUSE
71374-8/ $5.99 US/ $7.99 Can

A TICKET TO THE BONEYARD
70994-5/ $5.99 US/ $7.99 Can

OUT ON THE CUTTING EDGE
70993-7/ $5.99 US/ $7.99 Can

THE SINS OF THE FATHERS
76363-X/ $4.99 US/ $5.99 Can

TIME TO MURDER AND CREATE
76365-6/ $5.99 US/ $7.99 Can

A STAB IN THE DARK
71574-0/ $4.99 US/ $6.99 Can

IN THE MIDST OF DEATH
76362-1/ $5.99 US/ $7.99 Can

EIGHT MILLION WAYS TO DIE
71573-2/ $5.99 US/ $7.99 Can

A WALK AMONG THE TOMBSTONES
71375-6/ $5.99 US/ $7.99 Can

Nationally Bestselling Author
of the Peter Decker and Rina Lazarus Novels

Faye Kellerman

"Faye Kellerman is a master of mystery."
Cleveland Plain Dealer

JUSTICE
72498-7/$6.99 US/$8.99 Can

L.A.P.D. Homicide Detective Peter Decker and his wife and confidante Rina Lazarus have a daughter of their own. So the savage murder of a popular high school girl on prom night strikes home . . . very hard.

SANCTUARY
72497-9/$5.99 US/$7.99 Can

A diamond dealer and his family have disappeared, but their sprawling L.A. estate is undisturbed and their valuables untouched. When a second dealer is found murdered, Detective Peter Decker and his wife Rina are catapulted into a heartstopping maze of murder and intrigue.

And coming soon in hardcover from
William Morrow and Company,
the new Peter Decker and Rina Lazarus novel
PRAYERS FOR THE DEAD

SENSATIONAL
87TH PRECINCT NOVELS
FROM THE GRAND MASTER

KISS	71382-9/$5.99 US/$7.99 Can
LULLABY	70384-X/$5.99 US/$7.99 Can
POISON	70030-1/$4.99 US/$5.99 Can
LIGHTNING	69974-5/$4.95 US/$5.95 Can
ICE	67108-5/$5.99 US/$6.99 Can
VESPERS	70385-8/$5.99 US/$7.99 Can
WIDOWS	71383-7/$5.99 US/$6.99 Can
CALYPSO	70591-5/$4.99 US/$6.99 Can
DOLL	70082-4/$4.50 US/$5.50 Can
MISCHIEF	71384-5/$5.99 US/$6.99 Can

FAST-PACED MYSTERIES
BY J.A. JANCE

Featuring J.P. Beaumont

UNTIL PROVEN GUILTY 89638-9/$5.99 US/$7.99 CAN

INJUSTICE FOR ALL 89641-9/$5.99 US/$7.99 CAN

TRIAL BY FURY 75138-0/$5.99 US/$7.99 CAN

TAKING THE FIFTH 75139-9/$5.99 US/$7.99 CAN

IMPROBABLE CAUSE 75412-6/$5.99 US/$7.99 CAN

A MORE PERFECT UNION 75413-4/$5.99 US/$7.99 CAN

DISMISSED WITH PREJUDICE

75547-5/$5.99 US/$7.99 CAN

MINOR IN POSSESSION 75546-7/$5.99 US/$7.99 CAN

PAYMENT IN KIND 75836-9/$5.99 US/$7.99 CAN

WITHOUT DUE PROCESS 75837-7/$5.99 US/$7.99 CAN

FAILURE TO APPEAR 75839-3/$5.50 US/$6.50 CAN

LYING IN WAIT 71841-3/$5.99 US/$7.99 CAN

Featuring Joanna Brady

DESERT HEAT 76545-4/$5.99 US/$7.99 CAN

TOMBSTONE COURAGE 76546-2/$5.99 US/$6.99 CAN